Also by L. J. Hutton

Power & Empire series:
The Darkening Storm
Fleeting Victories
Summoning Spectres
Unleashing the Power

Menaced by Magic series:
Menaced by Magic
No Human Hunter
Shards of Sorcery
The Rite to Rule

ISBN 13: 9781791850425

eBook first published 2012
Paperback first published 2013
This edition: 2021

Copyright

Chasing Sorcery

L. J. Hutton

Wylfheort
Magical Mystery
Fantasy - History
Books

Acknowledgements

My thanks go to the following people who helped make this all possible.

Firstly to Karen Murray who has been the best first reader any new author could wish for. Always encouraging, she has been the essential outside view looking in, spotting things I was too engrossed in my world to see.

Dr Philippa Semper has also been a catalyst in this process, both for introducing me to the joys of Old English, and for some very perceptive comments when the book was in its first incarnation. Alongside Philippa I should thank the other students on the Medieval Studies course – Gemma Sturtridge, Verity Stokes and Lucy Allenby – who enthused over all things medieval with me on many occasions, and to Sianne Shepherd and Mary Ward who did likewise at the post-grad' stage. I don't think any of them suspected where those conversations would lead me!

I also need to thank my husband John for putting up with me disappearing into the spare room to write for long periods of time, especially as there was no guarantee as to the outcome in the first few months.

And in particular I would like to dedicate this to my lovely lurchers past and present. The current three who rule our roost are Minnie, Blue and Raffles, who snoozed their way through this book as furry presences beside me but kept me sane in the process. Boris and Speedie saw the start of the project but not the end, and are greatly missed.

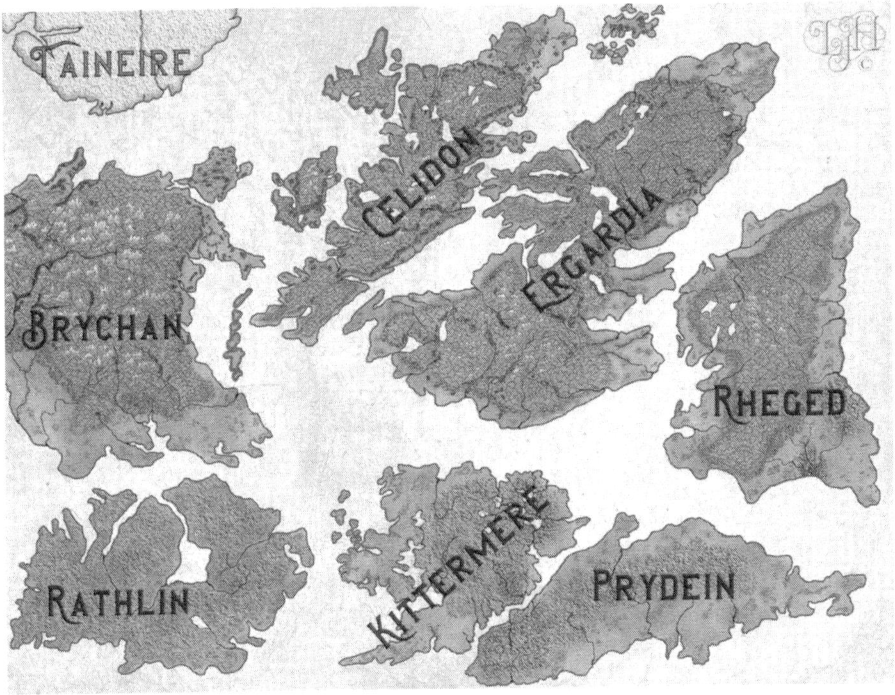
TAINEIRE
CELIDON
ERGARDIA
BRYCHAN
RHEGED
KITTERMERE
PRYDEIN
RATHLIN

Western Islands

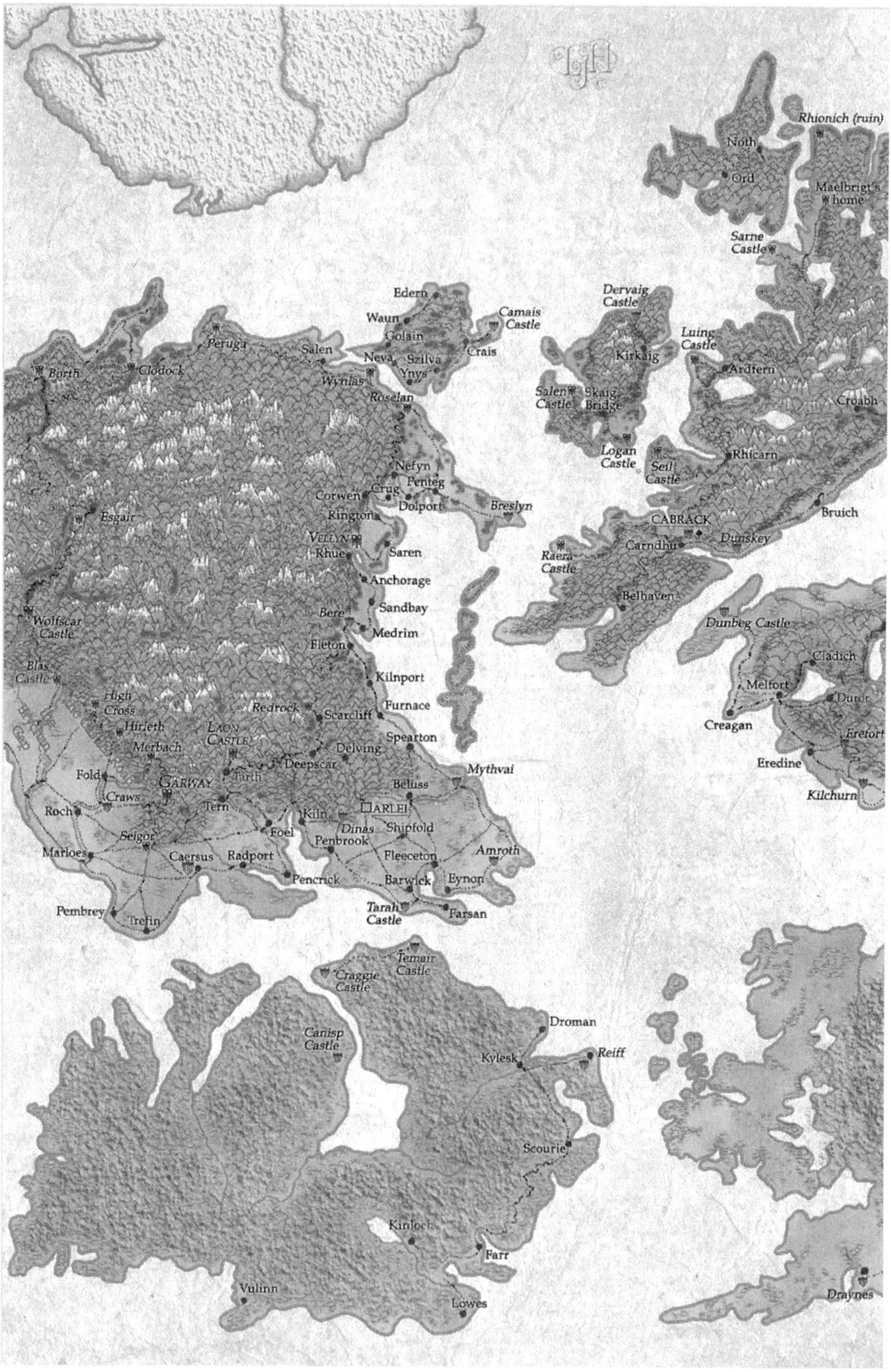

Eastern Islands

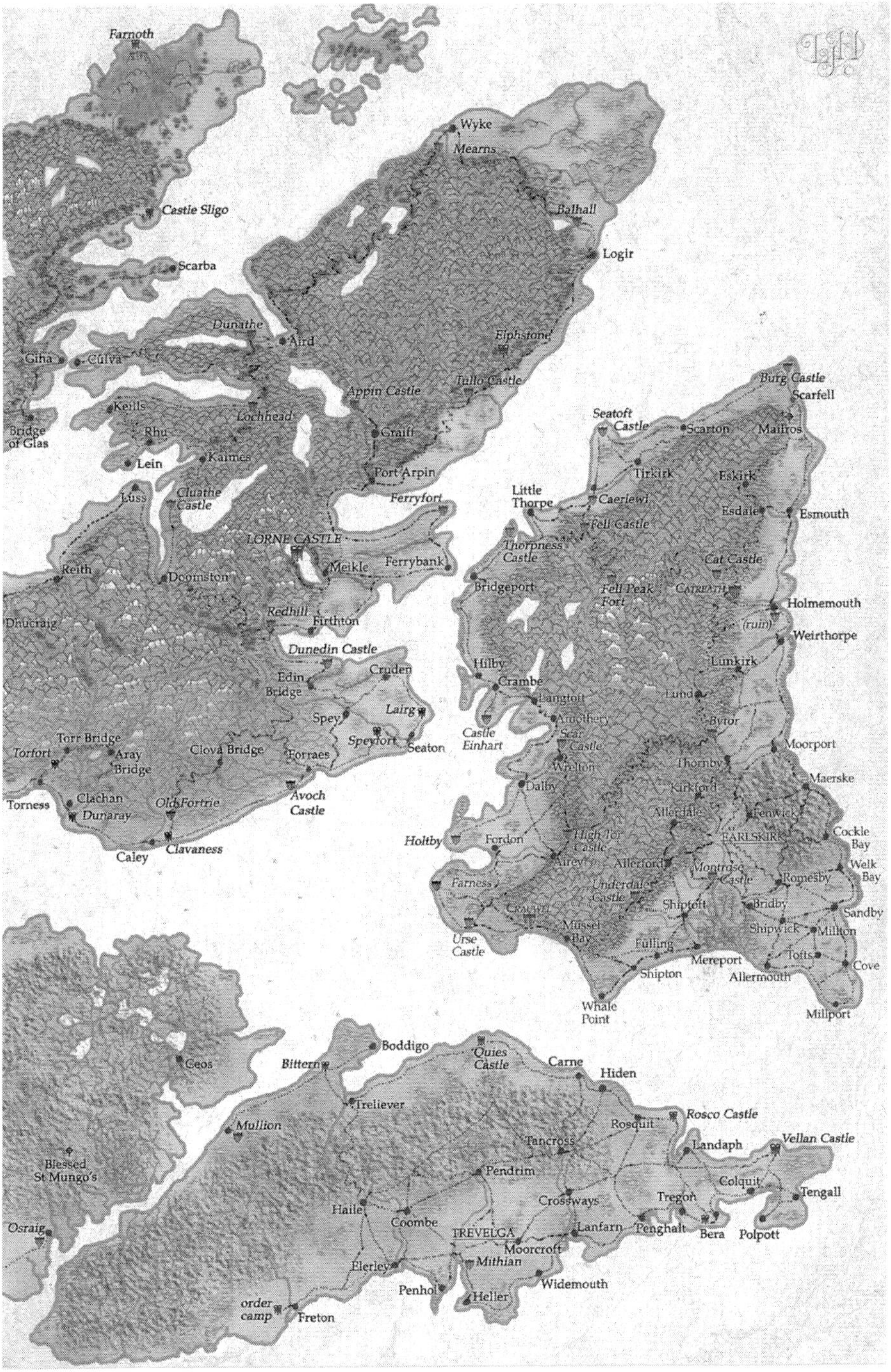

RHEGED

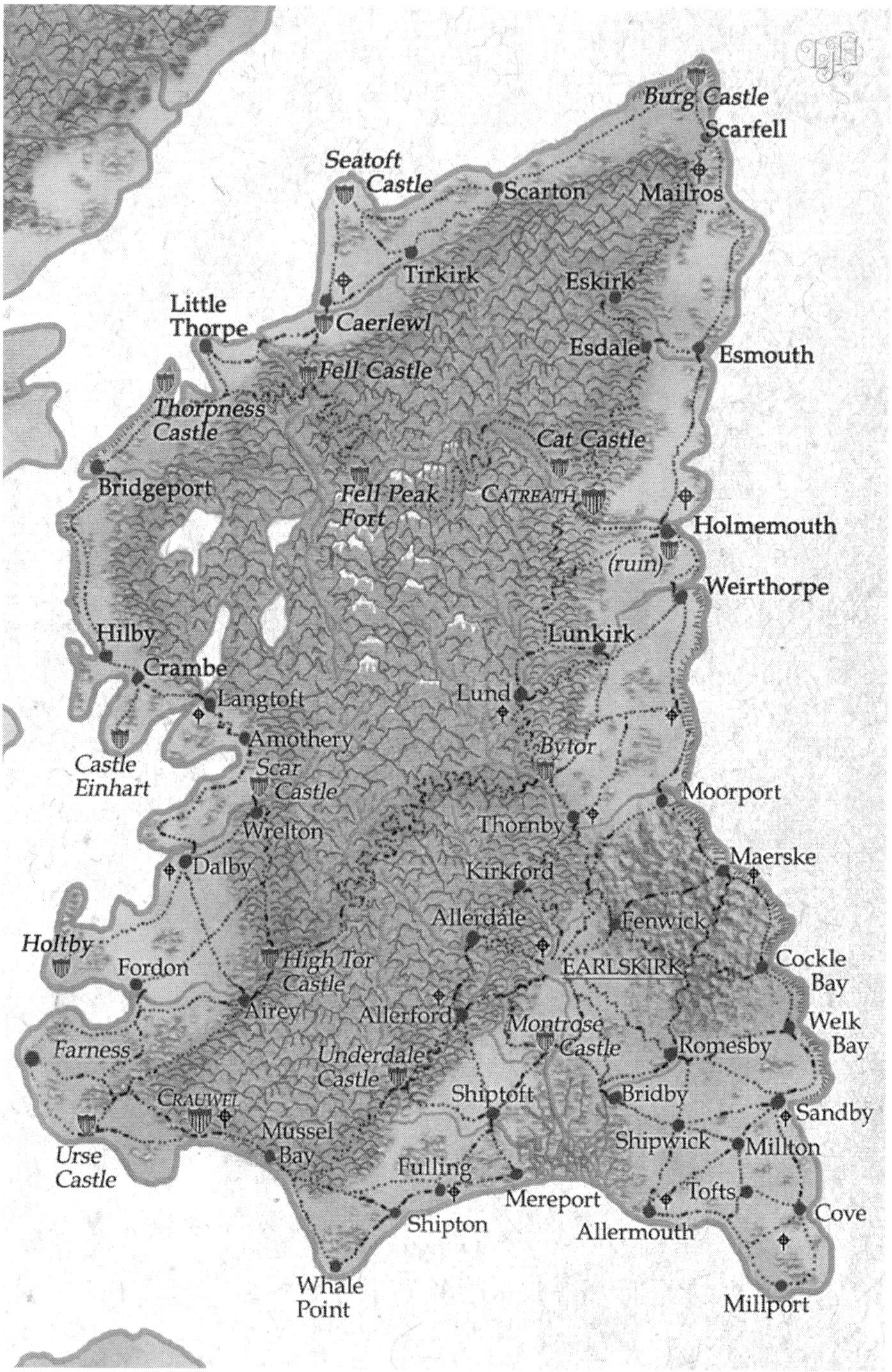
Burg Castle
Scarfell
Seatoft Castle
Scarton
Mailros
Tirkirk
Eskirk
Little Thorpe
Caerlewl
Esdale
Esmouth
Fell Castle
Thorpness Castle
Cat Castle
Bridgeport
Fell Peak Fort
CATREATH
Holmemouth
(ruin)
Weirthorpe
Hilby
Lunkirk
Crambe
Langtoft
Lund
Amothery
Bytor
Castle Einhart
Scar Castle
Moorport
Wrelton
Thornby
Dalby
Maerske
Kirkford
Allerdale
Fenwick
Holtby
Fordon
High Tor Castle
EARLSKIRK
Cockle Bay
Airey
Allerford
Montrose Castle
Welk Bay
Farness
Underdale Castle
Romesby
Shiptoft
Bridby
CRAUWEL
Sandby
Mussel Bay
Shipwick
Millton
Urse Castle
Fulling
Tofts
Mereport
Shipton
Cove
Allermouth
Whale Point
Millport

Chapter 1

A Surprise Return

Rheged: late Harvest-moon

The wind tore at the clouds as they scudded across in front of the full moon. By its light a small fishing vessel raced before the storm that chased hard on its heels. As the opening to Maerske harbour appeared from between the towering cliffs, the fishermen fought to get the sails down before the craft was dashed to pieces at their foot. With a skill born of years of practice the wet canvas was wrestled down and tied to the stays, while the first mate and a hand strained against the tiller to negotiate the tide.

"A rough night to be coming home," one of them said to the man standing in the bows. The moonlight silhouetted his hawk-like profile against the darkness of the approaching coast. He smiled, but said nothing and continued his watch as a small town came into view, nestled on either side of the river mouth which formed the harbour. Huge stones had been heaved into the water on the approach to form breakwaters on either side of the immediate entrance, making a funnel which broke the pounding waves before they reached the channel. Within the shadow of their bulk a couple of other small craft had already reached safety, and were heading into the quays which projected out in regular ranks down both sides. The larger vessels were closest to the entrance, while the smaller boats lowered their masts and made their way under the spans of the huge timber and stone bridge that connected the two sides together.

What distinguished this from any of a number of other ports along this coast was the huge monastery which loomed on the south cliff above the town. In moonlight near as bright as day, vast, spired towers rose at the crossing and the west end of the church, and it shone off the three tiers of traceried windows which connected them. With its magnificent north-end window facing out over the sea, the abbey seemed to be defying the elements to do their worst to break such an airy blend of stone and glass. Behind it the massed ranks of the cloisters and other buildings of the complex stood in silent support of its defiance. As if on cue a bell began to toll, calling the monks to prayer, and, as candles were lit within the church, the light shone out of the windows making it a beacon on the headland.

"We normally tie up on the south side," the captain said. He came to stand by his passenger's side, trying not to show his curiosity. He had been well paid to bring this man across. Enough to make a difference to a simple man like him with winter coming on, but the condition had been the continued anonymity of the man. "Do you have somewhere to stay tonight?"

"Not yet," the stranger replied, "but I was thinking of trying *The Mermaid*."

The fisherman laughed. "You've been here before, haven't you! Who are you?" his curiosity getting the better of him

The other man turned piercing blue eyes to face him and tried to keep his tone of voice easy going, not wishing to cause offence.

"It's best if you don't know. What I said when you took me on still holds. I promise you I'm doing nothing illegal. I'm not smuggling anything and I'm not a criminal, I'm just a soldier, and I'm not a deserter. I've got a message to deliver and it's not good news, so I don't want word of my arrival to get out until I've found the person I need to speak to. .... And yes, I know this place! So I've got no intention of sleeping at *The Ferry Boat Inn.* I want to wake up with my saddle bags intact and minus bed bugs!"

The men around him laughed in good humour. *The Ferry Boat*, sitting at the end of the coast road to the town, was notorious for cramming travellers into any corner they could find, and fleecing them blind for bad food, bad beer, and cold, lousy bedding. It was also owned by the bishop and paid a large cut of what they acquired to his priests, who never seemed to have a problem over the conflict between such practices and their beliefs. The locals never set foot in the place, preferring the humbler inns closer to the fish markets, each of which had its own specialty fish dish and ales, and a warm welcome for those returning home.

The boat nudged the quayside, and while the crew tied it up and began offloading their catch, the stranger hoisted his saddled bags onto his shoulders and walked past drying nets and salt barrels to the road. Further along to his right he could see the lights of *The Mermaid Inn*, but he turned left first and walked towards the harbour mouth. Between the houses a gap appeared, and a long flight of steps rose straight up the headland towards the abbey. For a moment he paused and looked upwards. Tonight he had no intention of going that way, but tomorrow he had to make the decision of whether to approach the monks for information. That would depend on who was in charge up there now, and he needed to find out beforehand. In a four year absence much could have changed, and despite what he had told the captain, he was not entirely sure of his reception. It was also another reason not to stay at *The Ferry Boat.* The townsfolk had little to do with the monks on a day to day basis and minded their own business, except for the taxes sent up the hill. But a stranger arriving at night from across the sea would have had a messenger running straight from *The Ferry* to the priest, and him to the abbey.

Turning back, he walked along the wharf to *The Mermaid* and ducked inside. Immediately he was accosted by a blast of warm air, tempting smells and a deafening mixture of voices from the packed bar. *The Mermaid* was not a sophisticated inn. One long open room was served by a bar along the back wall, with a fireplace at each end. In between, rough partitions had been made from old boat timbers with equally rough tables and benches in the cubicles, but most of the room stood open with shelves for beer mugs around the thick timber posts which supported the upper floors.

Shouldering his way to the bar, the man finally managed to catch the eye of the wizened little man organizing the barmaids, although most of them didn't seem to need it. So far, so good, the passenger thought. *The Mermaid* was still in the same hands. The little barman scuttled over, wiping his hands on his grubby apron.

"Yes sir? What can I do for you?" Then the little man stopped and looked again and a broad smile appeared. "By the Spirits! Ru…"

"No! No names! Not yet! Have you got a room I can have for tonight?"

"For you? Of course! Come on round." The barman looked puzzled, but beckoned his guest to the side of the bar where a gap led through to the back rooms and the stairs. Rushing into the kitchen he called,

"Sal! Sal, look who's here!"

A huge woman with arms like a butcher turned round with an equally huge cauldron of something aromatic in her hands. She too broke into a grin and, dumping the cauldron onto the table as though it was a mere saucer, walked over and clasped the stranger to her more than ample bosom.

"You young bugger!" she scolded. "What were you thinking of disappearing like that and not a word for years!"

Managing to get her to arms' length, the stranger smiled back.

"Fighting with the Jarl, Sal! They don't let you home for feast days, you know! But I'll tell you more in a moment. Have you got a room where we can talk without being overheard?"

"Ooh, being mysterious now are you?" she laughed. "Alright. Go upstairs and the room at the end is free. We haven't got many staying at the moment, so the rooms at either side are empty too. I'll send this out to that starving rabble in the bar, and then Ron and me are coming up! We want to know what's got you scuttling around in the night like a stranger!"

He gave her a hug back, and then turned and went up a narrow flight of stairs which was sandwiched between the kitchen and the bar. On the first floor, a long passage ran down the centre of the building with rooms running off on either side. There were not many – the place was not that big – just three small ones to either side and a long narrow one at the far end. Another flight of stairs running up to the family's rooms under the eaves continued the flight he had just come up. In the dim light of a small lamp the doorways loomed darkly, and he padded silently towards the end, pausing at each of them to listen for signs of habitation.

Satisfied that he was the sole occupant on this floor for now, he entered the far room and put his bags on the oak chest. The sight of the deep filled mattress and thick quilt was enough to tempt him to just flop on the bed and sleep. Until now he had paid no heed to the amount of time he had been travelling and the lack of sleep. Yet suddenly, being back here, in a place he had known as a boy, and the sense of comfort and security that brought with it, almost overwhelmed him. With great difficulty he forced himself to move away from the bed, and sit on the stool by the window which looked out on the back street. He did not even trust himself with the large chair piled with cushions placed at the opposite one looking to the quays.

Luckily, he did not have long to wait. The protesting of the floor boards and the delicious aroma that wafted along before her announced Sally's arrival. She entered the room bearing a tray with a large bowl of the smoked fish dish she had been cooking, a hunk of warm crusty bread, and a tankard. Behind her, her husband came in and pulled a small table up to the big chair.

"Come on, you look like you need some proper food in you," she said. "And while you're eating you can tell us what's got you all furtive, Ruari MacBeth."

Hearing his name spoken in his home dialect was almost painfully welcome, especially as he knew that he would have to leave again as quickly as he had come back. He had never thought that his homecoming would be quite this way. Taking a spoonful of the aromatic fish stew he almost burnt his mouth, and so took a swig of the dark, malty ale before starting his story.

"By the Trees, I hardly know where to start for the best," he said, taking another swallow of ale, "but you know it was decided that the raids that were burning villages up this coast had to be stopped?"

"Aye," the little man, Ron, piped up. "Jarl Michael, your half-brother, took some of his army out of this very port!"

Ruari nodded, and began to tell his tale. The ruler of the Island, the Jarl, had responded swiftly to the sudden raids from the east which had left fishing villages along the east coast deserted and in flames. The army had been called up and he had personally led them in a fleet, scraped together from all the vessels he could commandeer, across the narrow sea that separated them from their neighbours. For centuries the two peoples had traded peacefully to their mutual benefit, and it had been obvious from the outset that whoever these raiders were, they were not from the low lying lands on the opposite coast.

"They found folk living on a whole network of little islands, and those weren't much more than sea-marshes," Ruari explained, knowing that Sal had never seen further than a day's travel from here. "They're small communities hanging on on the western edge of the sea that divides us from them. Yes, the islands get more substantial the further inland you go, and between the huge rivers they have drainage channels to make the most of the fertile soil. But they were never more than extended families of fishermen and farmers – there was no way that they were the ones who torched our coastline."

Ruari shook his head wearily. "But that made for problems almost as soon as Michael and his men landed, because most folk had retreated to hideouts only they could find, taking their stores with them. And further inland the raiders had beaten them to it – not a loaf of bread or a chicken to be had for miles! So that meant short rations before they'd even drawn a sword." He grimaced. "It wasn't going to be a quick campaign like my brother thought. Michael believed it would be a couple of set battles and it would all be over – not a chance! Instead the raiders swooped on them in the night, cut them to pieces, and then vanished into that maze of waterways before we could fight back."

"Cowards!" muttered Sal darkly, affronted that such men would not face her heroes.

"Maybe," Ruari sighed. "But is it cowardice to fight the way you know you'll win? No, Sal, my grievances lie elsewhere. They sent back urgent demands for supplies, but by the time winter came on all they'd done was halt the raiders' advances."

At this point Michael had returned during the winter and pleaded for help from the Grand Master of the Knights of the Order of the Cross, professional soldiers to a man, who took vows much like monks to the Church, and lived the non-military side of their lives in almost monastic conditions. Ruari, as the illegitimate older son of Michael's father, had been sent to the Order as he approached adulthood, in order to prevent the political complications of having a Jarl's son older than the official heir around at court. As it turned out, the soldier's life had appealed to him far more than that of the courtier, and he had risen swiftly to become the second-in-command of the Order in the Island.

"You know how fond I was of Michael, even though we were so different, even as boys," Ruari continued, "and so although me and my men had only just got back from the far north, dealing with a different set of raiders up there, I was the one who begged Grand Master Robert to help. I told them both, 'you need to conscript some more proper troops', as well as offering to go myself. The regular army has always needed the Order's help for anything other than protecting our coast.

"So my men and I brought a lot of much-needed expertise as well as weight of numbers, and we trained what men Michael had hard that winter. That meant that the second summer of fighting was more successful. We actually got to the solid farmlands of Margen and took the town of the same name." He gave a bitter laugh. "They welcomed us as their saviours. If only they'd known what was to come!

"The first blow was that severe winter. By the Trees, it's cold out there! Nothing stops the wind ripping across those lands. We were cold and we were wet, and that meant when the sickness struck, it hit us hard. Men coughed and coughed until they brought up blood, and most were too weak to move, much less forage or march. The only consolation was that while our men for the greater part recovered, even if it was slowly, those raiders – whoever they were – died like flies. Before too long we started to see corpses floating in the channels, and it just got worse and worse.

"As soon as the winter gales died down enough, we were sending men home to recover, and we'd had to pull back our positions to those limited places where the water supplies hadn't been contaminated by the dead. So

Michael sent home for yet more men. …Seemed the obvious thing to do. But what came out, well, they weren't troops or my name's not Ruari – the sweepings of the town gaols, more like, and anyone else who the local lords wanted shot of. Trouble-makers, thieves and murderers, that's what we got. Time and again I went to Michael to plead for caution before committing those dregs …those pathetic excuses for soldiers, to any sort of fight. But there were always the new commanders – the sons of men who had hung around our father's court to no great effect – who kept telling Michael what he wanted to hear."

Ruari stopped and rubbed the several days of stubble on his jaw as he looked away out of the window.

"Go on!" Ron said, sitting spellbound on the edge of the bed, but Sally's eyes narrowed as she watched Ruari.

"Was that when Michael died?" she asked. Ruari looked back, his blue eyes sad, and nodded.

"Aye…. that was when it happened." His voice choked as he struggled to find the right words to explain. "We argued. Michael and me. I can't ever remember him talking to me like that before … he said I didn't want to fight … he called me a coward."

Sally gasped in shock. "He called you what? Michael? But you two were so close! He knew you!"

He ran his hands through his ragged blond hair, and had to clear his voice before he could continue.

"The battle plan got drawn up without even consulting me – I'd *never* known him do that before if I was with him. …And even more unbelievably, the enemy looked as though they were going to take the ridiculous bait they were dangling for them! Not that I could do anything about it. I was consigned to guarding the rear, while all those idiots just kept egging Michael on."

He swallowed hard, remembering it all too vividly now. "Then the battle began. It was like it all slowed down into some horrible dream, and one I can't forget. Spurred on by the illusion that the enemy was falling back, Michael led the way forwards. Poor deluded fool! He just kept going deeper and deeper into the enemy lines. I can only think he thought it was going to be a rout.

"I disregard his orders, you know. I got my knights drawn up into our fighting phalanx, and with our swords drawn we started cutting our way towards him. But we'd barely got hooves on the ground before those supposedly 'wounded' enemy soldiers got back up on their feet and closed ranks behind Michael. …And that's when the worst of it happened. Those new 'recruits'? They just folded! Turned on their heels and ran like hares with the Hounds of the Wild Hunt chasing them."

Ruari took a deep swig of the ale, and then another to fortify himself. "I was furious and heartbroken all at the same time. They betrayed their Jarl. They betrayed my brother! …All I remember is swinging that sword of mine like a scythe at everyone of the treacherous scum who came near me, regardless of whether they were raiders attacking or the gutless bastards running, and we nearly got to him. Nearly. I saw the last of his household faithful go down under the knives and swords of men not fit to lick their boots."

With tears unashamedly in his eyes, Ruari said to Sally and Ron,

"Do you know what the last thing he said was? … He caught my eye and I saw him mouth, 'I'm sorry, Ruari,' and then he was gone." It had then been all Ruari and the Knights could do to cut themselves out of the fray.

"I'd have done anything to bring him back." Ruari half whispered, cuffing at his eyes. "But we spent months running and hiding ourselves… Well …all year really. The loyal men from Michael's army all died that day. I don't know what happened to the rest….."

"They came back in the ships." Ron told him.

"What ships?"

"Sacred Trees! They must have been waiting for them!" Ron looked sickened as the truth sunk in. "The Spirits damn them for cowards! They never were going to fight were they?"

"Aye, … proves it, doesn't it!" Ruari spat back bitterly. "Michael was murdered! Now do you see why I can't let anyone know I'm back? I have to get to the Grand Master and we have to figure out how to tell Oswine. He should know how his father died."

"Oh Ruari!" Sally exclaimed. "You don't know? Grand Master Robert died two winters ago! And then the men coming back said you and the Knights were dead! Officially the Order doesn't exist anymore!"

Ruari looked back at her, stunned. His plans had suddenly collapsed. He had been relying on Robert being able to take over the organization of a means to send boats back to retrieve the troops, while he continued to court to tell his half-nephew the dreadful news. Worse than this was the news that the armed support he had hoped for, to help him retrieve the men he had left encamped on the far shore, was apparently no longer in existence.

"What did they do with the granges, the recruitment camp, the old soldiers?" he asked in numb bemusement.

"Oh, they're still all there!" Sally said emphatically. "At least they are for now! But without a leader they're nominally under the control of the church. I'd bet that Archbishop Fulchere's been taking a nice cut out of their produce. Let's face it, if they could make enough to keep the Knights in the field, the crafty old sod will have wanted a finger in that pie!"

Ruari exhaled deeply, although not entirely relieved. The problem now would be to let those men in the granges know that he was still in the land of the living, and get his forces back to Rheged unnoticed. If he could arrange that, then he would have a force to back him up when the time came to confront Michael's betrayers. Temporarily, however, until elections could be held to nominate a new Grand Master, he realized he was the leader of the Order, and that complicated things no end. He was now responsible for the extraction of the entire dispersed companies of Knights he had left hidden in the coastal villages across the sea. His personal quest might have to wait, but should it?

"Is Abbot Jaenberht still up the road at the Abbey?" he asked his friends.

Sally and Ron shook their heads, which deepened his misery.

"No," Sally told him, "he got moved on up to Mailros when the abbot up there died, oh …over two years ago. The new abbot here's a real crook! He's raised rents and chased some of the Abbey's old tenants off their homes when they couldn't pay the new rents!" She was full of indignation at this, which was of more importance in the upset of her small, personal world than Ruari's news. However, as an old soldier, Ron saw the wider consequences.

"You were expecting Jaenberht's help, weren't you?" he said, frowning in concentration at Ruari's predicament.

Ruari nodded. He had not anticipated Abbot Jaenberht's total absence. The abbot was now elderly, but the last time Ruari had seen him he was sprightly, and had had an energy that would have shamed many a younger man. Standing a good six feet tall, with a mane of white hair and patrician features, Jaenberht was not only physically commanding but was possessed of a formidable personality. Utterly incorruptible, he had taken an uncompromising stance against any form of moral deviance, but could be moved to equally vigorous acts of generosity on behalf of the genuinely needy, or the impassioned defence of the victims of those whom he regarded as the ungodly. Ruari had been terrified of him as a mischievous boy caught in various tight spots (such as scrumping apples from the Abbey orchards), but as an adult he had developed a huge respect for this one-man ecclesiastical whirlwind. If anyone could have advised him on who would have betrayed Michael, Ruari would have bet it was Jaenberht, who kept a close eye on the political comings and goings as the best way to defend his flock.

"Mailros, you say?" he queried, pushing the tray away and going to look out at the now silent quays. Their nods confirmed this and complicated his life beyond his ability to sort out in one night. Mailros was a monastery a long way north of where he was, lying outside of Scarfell and in the opposite direction to the capital of Earlskirk, where the court and the headquarters of his Order lay. Ron came and reached up to put a hand on his shoulder comfortingly.

"Sleep on it, Ruari," he said. "You're too tired to think straight tonight. Don't worry, Sal and me'll throw the last few drunks out, and shut up the inn for the night. Our other guests are regulars who'll keep quiet. Nobody need know you're here at all. You'll be safe."

Awakening to the full impact of Ruari's predicament, Sally backed her husband up. "Whatever you do now, me dear, it won't bring Michael back," she sympathized. "So what you don't want to do is go rushing into something until you know what's been going on. Ron's right, sleep here and decide in the morning. Better to think with a clear head."

Ruari nodded and thanked them. When they had left him, he sank into the softness of the bed, but sleep was slow to come. Finally, close to dawn, he sank into a deep, exhausted sleep, only awakening to a loud hammering on the door of the inn down below.

Sitting up with a jolt Ruari was temporarily at a loss to know where he was. He had his dagger in his hand, and was on his feet before he realized he could hear Ron's good-natured banter with someone delivering something into the kitchens. His pulse still racing, he forced himself to walk casually to the front window and gaze out, as if an innocent traveller watching the sights. Everything seemed utterly normal down below, and a couple of seconds later he saw a heavy wagon pull out from the side of the inn and carry on along the quay to its next delivery. His disorientation was not helped by the realization that it must be approaching midmorning. It had been many years since he had slept so late, and just for a moment he wondered whether he had been slipped a sedative in his food. That was ridiculous, of course, and common sense told him that it was actually because he trusted these people that he had relaxed so thoroughly. Even so, he was conscious of the lost time, and headed for his bags to see if he had something that resembled a clean shirt.

To his horror he found all his small clothing and shirts gone, but, before he could fathom out why that should be, Sal barrelled her way into the room.

"Ah! There you are! I didn't think you'd sleep through that!" she exclaimed cheerily. "Here's some breakfast for you, and since when, young Ruari, have you taken to sleeping in a civilized bed fully clothed? Your mother taught you better than that!"

Ruari was nonplussed at this chastisement. It had been so long since he had had the luxury of sleeping safely in a proper bedroom, it had never occurred to him to sleep in any other way than he had for the last few years in camp. Luckily, he was saved from having to answer by Ron appearing, clutching a basin and pitcher of steaming water.

"Hush, Sal!" Ron said, shaking his head in mock exasperation. He turned to Ruari, "She doesn't understand!"

"What?" Sal demanded, glaring at them suspiciously for this implied male conspiracy in case it was insulting.

"He hasn't had time to sleep in a bed, woman! And if he got undressed and someone attacked the camp, he could be dead before he got his boots on! A soldier has to do that."

Sal gave Ron a black look and disappeared back downstairs, muttering darkly under her breath about men. Meanwhile Ron, totally ignoring her departure, poured the hot water into the basin and produced soap and a razor from one of his capacious pockets.

"Now then," he turned to Ruari, "I've taken all your stuff downstairs and given it a good scrub." Ruari's face dropped at the thought of how long it was now going to take to leave, but before he could say anything Ron had carried on. "It's one of Sal's baking days, so I had all the washing ready for when she finished and it's drying on a pallet in the bread-oven. By the time you're washed and fed it'll be nearly dry."

Ruari smiled ruefully at Ron, who was bustling around tidying the room, his bobbing walk making him look like a chirpy little bird. He had totally forgotten that, after retiring from active duty, Ron had been an excellent servant to the Order before his brother's death had resulted in him coming here to care for the bereaved family. If Sal was one of the best cooks in the shire, for everything else there was Ron, and it was his skills as a host and organizer which kept travellers returning time after time to the *Mermaid*. Ruari admired Ron, and not only for his organization – he had often thought if his brother's widow had been Sally, he would not have had the courage to marry her himself in order to keep her and her girls safe, he would have to have found another way!

"Come on! Hurry up and shave while that water's hot," Ron chirped at Ruari, disturbing his reverie. "You'll have to be respectable to come up to see Father Walter."

"Father Walter?" Ruari spluttered through the soap suds.

"Well, you need information, don't you? You can't go all the way to Mailros and back, and you can't go to Abbot Alsige. Now, when Jaenberht left he wanted to take Walter with him, but Walter said he was too old to uproot and go so far away, so he stayed. He didn't want to remain prior under Alsige, so he took over the old hermitage just down the road. I go up there every week and take him one of Sal's pies, to make sure he's alright and the monks haven't forgotten him. He's got rheumatism in his legs badly, so he doesn't get about much, but lots of people come to him, and they tell him stuff because they think he never sees anyone to tell it on to. He knows more of what's going on than anyone else round here. So get a move on and I'll take you up there while Sal cooks dinner. No-one will question me going up there, and if they ask I'll just say you're a traveller who had news from Mailros."

Ruari looked at Ron in amazement, who gave a gratified little chuckle before scurrying off on some other task. In one fell swoop Ron had sorted the first problem for him, and it suddenly occurred to him that Ron might be the ideal person to get a message out to the granges too. What had seemed set to become a list of increasingly impossible jobs had been reduced once more to the possible.

It was hard to resist the temptation to revel in the luxury of plenty of hot water and soap to wash in, and Ruari justified to himself taking longer than he might have on the basis of making himself presentable, so that he would not stand out now he was back in civilization. Just looking out of the window again, and watching the ordinary people of Maerske going about their daily business, made him realize how long it had been since he had seen such normality. If some of the clothes he saw were old, they were always clean and mended, and nobody looked as though they had spent the night sleeping rough. This was partly due to vagabonds being rounded up on a regular basis by the local magisters, and if they would not work they got conscripted into the Jarl's army. Of course, this led to the kind of men Ruari had seen running from the last battle, but it also meant that he had to give the appearance of being a man going about legitimate business. Nothing would attract attention to him quicker than wandering around looking like a mercenary or an outlaw, and he could not afford for that to happen.

Ron reappeared as he was towelling himself dry, and handed him a shirt that was several shades lighter than when it had arrived. A stiff bristled brush then appeared out of another of Ron's pockets, with which he proceeded to pound the dried mud off Ruari's coat on the ledge of the back window. Ruari also realized that his boots had somehow disappeared and returned mud-less and buffed up during the night, so that once Ron handed his coat back to him, he was now more respectable, if a little worn at the edges. Standing back to check his handiwork, Ron gave a little bob of approval and then scurried out of the door.

"Come on!" his voice sounded from the other end of the corridor, and Ruari had to hurry to catch up with him.

As they emerged from the back door of the *Mermaid* a brisk breeze was coming in off the sea, playing cat's paws with the waves, and there was a chill in the air despite the bright sunshine. They took the long flight of steps up to the headland which, to Ruari's chagrin, left him puffing behind Ron, who was far more used to the climb.

At the top they came out on the small town's graveyard, which adjoined the monastery's, and had its own little chapel sitting very humbly in the lee of its mighty neighbour. Under the pretext of pausing to look at the view, Ruari caught his breath. Over in the far corner was his mother's grave, but he did not dare go across in case they were being observed from the monastery, and someone came out to see which name the stranger had been paying his respects to. Intuitively Ron waited quietly by his side, until Ruari turned back to the path. They struck out on a well-worn path that took them out of the other end of the graveyard, past the great imposing gatehouse to the monastery on its land-ward side, and onto an exposed track that led south. It followed the coast, but well away from the edge and the long drop down the cliffs. On this coast strong winds were common, and nobody with any sense walked too close to the edge for fear of unexpected gusts, which had been known to sweep the unwary off onto the rocks below.

Under other circumstance the walk would have been pure pleasure for Ruari. The coming autumn had already started to turn the leaves, and the open moors lying to their west were bathed in warm browns and golds, with intermittent hazy patches of purple from the heather. It was perfect walking weather, and he drank in the clean air. He had forgotten how much the marshy conditions he had spent the last years living in gave an all pervading dank, slightly rotting edge to the air, as seaweed and other plants disappeared into the soggy mixture. Here even the sea air smelt of nothing more than the brine, and the moors had a wonderful array of subtle fragrances depending on the varieties of plants that were in any given spot.

In a dip in the way, sheltered from the sea, they came to a small stone hut. Around it a neat little garden contained what Ruari assumed to be herbs, although he had never got round to learning any but the most common ones. On a bench by the door, basking in the warmth, sat an elderly monk, his habit supplemented by a woollen blanket wrapped around his legs.

"Father Walter!" Ron called out and gave a cheery wave which was returned, and the monk reached for a stout stick and began to lever himself up onto his feet. He stood very slowly and then took a few tentative steps towards them, by which time they had reached the dry-stone wall of the garden. The older man grinned and said,

"The knees are playing up again! I'll be alright once I get moving. I just stick when I stay in one position too long. Is that a pie?" He looked hopefully at the canvas bag over Ron's shoulder.

"Would I come without one?" Ron answered jokingly. "It'd be more than me life's worth! ...But I'd have thought you'd be more interested in who it is I've brought to see you."

"I know I'm getting on," Walter said, feigning to be in a huff, "but I'm not that far gone that I don't recognize that young rascal, MacBeth!"

Ruari was not sure whether to be offended either. It was the second time in two days someone had called him young, which was something he had not been in quite a while. He now had a niggling worry that these people were not taking him all that seriously, which for their sakes as much as his was something he would have to change. He was therefore somewhat relieved when Father Walter became serious as he said,

"I'm so sorry about Michael, Ruari. As Jarl he was too impulsive, but he could have been a lot worse, and I know how fond you were of him."

Ruari nodded, and as they returned to sit in the sun he once more went over his story. When he came to the end, Walter drew a deep breath.

"Well, that's news indeed!" he said, rubbing his bald tonsure. "I don't know what use I can be to you, unfortunately. You're right, Jaenberht's the one you really need to speak to if you want to find out about what's going on at court. I'm afraid I don't move in such illustrious company, although I'm flattered by Ron's confidence in my ability. But of course you're also right – Mailros is a long way in the wrong direction, and if this helps you, I'll tell you in confidence that I think the reason Jaenberht got moved so far was exactly that.

"Oh, he always had a soft spot for the old monastery. It's where he joined as a novice, after all. But he didn't return willingly. Archbishop Fulchere really pushed him into a corner over moving, which must be about the only time he's won an argument with Jaenberht, but it came to a point where it was down to hunches. Jaenberht couldn't prove that Fulchere was manoeuvring him out of the way, and I know he was sure that someone brighter than Fulchere was pulling the strings, but couldn't prove that, either. We were pretty sure it was someone at court, because Fulchere was always a political appointment, so if as you say, there's a traitor in their midst, I'd say you're looking for one and the same person. There's a clever and nasty mind at work here, and the two things smell too much alike for it to be a coincidence of more than one person acting the same.

"I don't know about you, but I find it too convenient that Jaenberht got separated from the court just before those reinforcements you just told me about got sent out. And the more I think about it, the less I like the fact that your Grand Master Robert died in his prime not so long after they left. It's all too convenient. If Jaenberht had been nearby it would have been our Order that would have taken temporary control of the Knights, and you can be sure that Jaenberht would have had a new master elected. Somehow word of Robert's death never made it out of the capital for months. The excuse was, with you abroad, it was a temporary measure 'til you got back. Then when you were reported killed, nothing happened and a year had passed, so it was difficult to persuade people that there was any urgency to act." He shook his head in exasperation. "What I don't understand is why someone closer to the heart of things hasn't tried to take action to stop all of this?"

"You don't know, maybe they have." Ron tried to be optimistic. "Like you said, we're a bit out of it over here. Perhaps they have and it's all sorted but the news hasn't reached us yet."

"I don't know," Ruari sighed. "Oh, I wish it would turn out like that – but I've a nasty feeling it won't. If it was sorted, someone should surely have been sent out to see what had really happened to us? It would be the first action of anyone with the best interests of the Order at heart. And if they believed we were dead, why not elect a new Grand Master, even if it was someone less politically 'awkward' than Robert? They could have put a figurehead in place. Father Walter's right, this sounds like some long-term scheme being put into place, and I don't like the sound of it."

Suddenly it felt much colder despite the drop in the breeze. They mulled it over for more than an hour longer, but to no avail. The best plan of action they could come up with was that Ron would go to Thornby, where the nearest grange lay just outside of, with word of Ruari's return. As someone who had been merely a lay servant he would not need to be taken directly to whoever was in charge, so if a puppet now controlled the grange, he could circumvent him and talk to the ordinary soldiers without comment.

Ruari, on the other hand, would have been unable to enter inconspicuously, and they decided that such an appearance might be too dangerous in the circumstances. If Robert could die mysteriously, then it behoved them to be cautious. However, Ron would wait a week. By then, the fishermen would be out en masse, taking advantage of the calmer weather after the equinox, when gales had driven them into port. *The Mermaid* would be quiet and it would arouse no comment for him to be absent.

Ruari, on the other hand was going to make directly for the capital, Earlskirk. Whichever way they looked at it, they found they could make no sensible decision when they had no idea of what had happened at the heart of the country. They were operating blindly and the only solution was for someone to go and observe – which had to be Ruari. Walter's health prevented him, despite great willingness to be of use and a deep reluctance to send Ruari into danger, and Ron didn't have the contacts to get close enough to find out.

Ron got up and decided to go straight back to the inn. He wanted to investigate the store of abandoned property left at the inn to create a suitable disguise for Ruari. Anything that would make him look less like a soldier, which might trigger people's memories, had to be a good thing, they felt. Wishing Walter farewell, Ron trotted off and Ruari lingered on the pretext that an abbey messenger might have business to discuss, and so it made sense for him to return later. It also saved him from having to either hide in his room or sit in the bar, either of which might be cause for comment.

Once Ron had disappeared, Ruari turned back to Walter.

"You know what I have to ask you, don't you," was more of a statement than a question.

Walter gave a knowing smile.

"Yes, of course, and he's safe. Jaenberht took him with him under the pretext of being his personal assistant. He'd never have left that to chance!"

"Thank the Spirits! You know I couldn't ask, even in front of Ron."

A growing dread had been growing in Ruari as they'd spoken. His family had a close kept secret which only a few outsiders, and not all of the family, knew about. Ruari's father had had an older son by his first wife. The son had grown up into a healthy and strong boy until tragedy had struck. In an age where violence was common, it was normal for any youth from a good family to undertake weapons training, if only as self-defence. Such weapons included swords, quarter-staffs, maces and morning-stars – a lethal spiked ball of steel on a chain, wielded on a bar – which if mastered was devastating, but which was fiendishly difficult to control. Few men used it as a weapon of choice for that reason, but it had had its moment of fashion until the number of casualties from practicing grew too great.

One of those had been Hubert, the Jarl's son. One minute he was the heir most men aspired to have and then, one blow to his helmet later, an idiot who could barely string a sentence together. His father had been devastated. Hubert's mother had only died weeks before, and as an adult Ruari had later wondered whether that had been the cause of Hubert's lapse of attention.

The Jarl had called in every physician in the land, and a few more from outside, but to no avail. Hubert remained mentally and physically crippled, and had been sent to the quiet of a manor in the hills with a carefully chosen group of servants, while the Jarl consoled himself with Ruari's mother. Ruari's birth had done much to ease his father's pain, and then, when the political necessity of producing a new heir had forced him to remarry, Michael's birth had filled that gap.

Now Ruari sighed at this small relief. "Few people knew that Hubert had fathered a son, Spirit be praised, and with the boy's mother being just one of the serving women it was hardly as though any great family was involved. But my father was furious when it happened, knowing that the lad would always be a potential pawn for others to use. We were also so grateful when Jaenberht offered the solution of taking my half-nephew into his care. And little Kenelm was always much more suited to the quiet life. He'd never have survived at court."

Whenever Ruari had visited he had found Kenelm to be a child of a sunny disposition, never happier than when he was helping out in the abbey gardens, where he seemed to have a natural talent. Although they were so unalike, Ruari had felt a protective attachment to his half-nephew, not least because their bastardy made them both politically sensitive pawns in the games of jostling for favour and power around the Jarl.

"I know my father became Jarl by hereditary, but the history of it once being an appointed title, back in the era when there was a high king over all of the Islands, is something many of the other noble families haven't forgotten. Father always felt we'd only have to put one foot wrong for everything to change. He only ever had limited power to force his wishes onto the council of earls, so I understood why it was so vital to have a clear line of succession. But that meant that in a way I was the one person who *could* take an interest in Kenelm, because neither my father nor Michael dared in case they drew the wrong kind of attention to him."

Now he had become increasingly worried over Kenelm's fate. He doubted whether the child he had known had undergone a sudden change of personality, and he could only imagine the fear and confusion Kenelm would feel if he fell into the hands of political schemers. As far as Ruari knew no-one had ever told the child who his father was, but that would be no protection against those who might see him as a useful tool and a puppet to put on the council, to control and to rule from behind. His relief was visible, then, as he realized that if whoever was behind the current chaos thought Mailros was far enough away to neutralize Jaenberht, its distance also meant that Kenelm was probably safe for now.

Walter had obviously come to the same conclusion. "As far as anyone at Mailros will know, Kenelm was found on our gate steps and taken in. I know you haven't seen him of late since he's begun to grow up, but certainly the last time I saw him there was nothing in his appearance that would suggest who he's related to. He's still fair-haired like you, but unless he grows extraordinarily fast there's no sign of him being tall like you and Michael, and he's more round-faced, but not like Michael's Oswine. He's quite angelic, actually, which I suppose makes him ideally suited to fit most people's idea of a monk, and that can't be a bad thing under the circumstances."

Ruari gave him his heartfelt thanks and reluctantly made his way back down to *The Mermaid*. By now the nights were beginning to draw in, and by the time he was descending the steps from the abbey, the occasional lamp was being lit in the houses he passed, giving him glimpses of the family lives going on inside them. Part of him felt a sadness that the option to lead such a normal life had been taken away from him without him ever having the choice.

He walked to the harbour wall and silently vowed that if ever he got out of this mess he would make sure that Kenelm got that choice. As far as he knew Kenelm had not taken vows that could not be undone, and Ruari would not let that happen unless it was by an active choice by his nephew. There had to be a better way of protecting his life.

Not that Ruari had anything against someone becoming a monk if that was what they truly wanted. He had seen enough of the world to know that there were many worse options. Watching the waves roll in, he knew that his bleak mood was brought on by his own sense of being swept along by forces beyond his control. All his life he had been trained to protect and serve, to take control of dangerous situations, and now his every move was being predetermined by the actions of people he had no knowledge of. If the first rule of engagement was to get to know your enemy, then he had failed spectacularly so far.

Slipping in through the back door of the inn he crept past the kitchen and went up to his room. In a while he would go down for food, but first he had to pack. Tomorrow he had to leave for the capital and find out what was happening. Blundering around like this was getting him nowhere and he was sick of it.

Chapter 2

Adrift in the Fog

Rheged: late Harvest-moon

The next morning dawned in total contrast to the previous day. A damp sea mist had wrapped itself around Maerske, muffling sounds and soaking everything. Ron had talked to a wool-trading guest who had come into town on business, and now had an empty pack horse he was returning with to his hamlet high on the moors, so Ruari could ride part of the way. Once well away from the coast, he could take the chance of hiring a horse without too many questions being asked, but he had to get there first. It was a large, broad, placid beast who stood patiently by while Ruari said his good-byes to Ron and Sal. The scene was made awkward by the hovering farmer and their wariness of saying anything compromising in public, and all three had a hard time making it seem normal when they knew Ruari was riding into danger.

Keeping it brief, Ruari mounted up and turned the horse to follow the sheep farmer, who had already started across the bridge. He turned out to be a taciturn man who spoke little, which suited Ruari. It saved him the trouble of making up explanations and he was in no mood to make the effort for small talk.

If their progress was not fast it was steady, as they climbed along well-used roads up onto the moors. Ruari had hoped that the mist might lift once they got out of the river valley, but it was widespread and showed no sign of ending, even higher up. Luckily, they took a broad highway which ran parallel to the coast for a short way and then turned west on an equally broad, metalled way that cut inland, so there was little chance of going astray.

As the morning wore on, the mist seemed to get even thicker, and it bothered him that it muffled all sounds. All he could hear was the steady clip-clop of the horses' hooves. There was no sound of the birds who lived up here, which in itself was not abnormal for the weather, but they could provide good advance warning of anyone approaching off the road when they were up and about foraging. The only consolation was that the fog was so thick you could have been within yards of the road and not seen it, or who was on it. Ruari could only hope that any outlaws had had the sense to stay in camp, rather than risk getting hopelessly lost in the vague hope of finding someone worth robbing on a day like this.

The morning passed and they finally came on a wayside hut, little more than walls and a roof, which was there as a refuge for travellers, especially in winter when sudden snow storms could drift and leave people trapped. The farmer dismounted and led his horse to the stone trough by the side of the hut and Ruari joined him.

"I don't like this," the farmer muttered worriedly. "This is full-blown fog not just mist."

"Aye, it's early in the year for this, isn't it?" Ruari asked, his instincts aroused to full alert by his companion's anxiety. "This isn't normal, is it?"

"No!" the farmer said emphatically, his fear now giving him voice. "And this isn't the first of the year either, it's been happening off and on for the last three months."

"Three months? So it happened in the summer too?"

"Oh, yes! But there's something worse."

"What?"

"I don't know."

"What do you mean, you don't know?" Ruari could see the man was truly scared. Whatever it was it was real to him, even if it turned out to be nothing more than fireside stories which had got out of hand.

"Sometimes there's something in the fog… I know that sounds daft, and I don't know what it is. But after the first couple of these fogs, word started to go round that stock was disappearing. And you needn't look at me sideways, I'm no fool. Yes, I thought it was just tall tales, at first. But then the one night the folks in the next farm to me heard a racket outside. The sheepdog was howling, not growling like he does when there's a fox in the sheep pen or anything, whining like he was scared to death. Well, Ted goes out to see what it was … and, well … that was the last anyone saw of Ted."

"What? He fell? Drowned?"

The farmer shrugged and raised his hands. It turned out that no body was ever found, and in that area there were no deep pools or steep drops. The whole hamlet and surrounding farms had turned out to search without success.

"The weirdest thing was it looked like his footsteps just stopped. Well, that shook everyone. Him and his wife were real close, so it wasn't like he took off with some other woman – poor soul, she's not been right since. Then last month we had another one of these fogs, and afterwards I went out to check my flock. Three were missing but we found the body of a fourth." He stopped and shuddered. "The head and shoulders were there, but behind that it was stripped to the bone to where its back legs would have been, but they'd gone completely."

"You saw this yourself?" Ruari questioned. The man nodded. So, there was no chance that this was just whispered stories that had got bigger with the telling. Nor did he need telling that this didn't sound like any normal predator.

"You said stripped to the bone?"

"Aye," the man confirmed, "and when I say stripped, I mean stripped! There wasn't a scrap of flesh on the ribs, and where it started it was like a clean cut. I tell you what else, as well – there was no blood! Nowhere. Not on the ground, or on the bones, or coming out of the front bit. Horrible it was!"

Ruari could begin to feel his skin creep. No wonder the wildlife was keeping quiet.

"But it, whatever 'it' is, isn't all through the fog? It just appears in spots?" he asked.

The farmer confirmed it. Sometimes nothing happened in their area at all, but the word had spread that other parts of the moors had had similar experiences, and whenever such things took place it was always in the fog. To Ruari it seemed that something was using it as cover to hunt in, but he had no idea what that might be. That made him suddenly realize why the farmer had been so eager to have a travelling companion, and he could not blame him for that. When he asked, it turned out that the man had been storing up his yarn until he had as much as his horses could carry. He had set out with both fully laden and him leading them, on the day Ruari had landed, knowing that the gales would keep the fog at bay, and had walked into the night to reach Maerske to get in early before the other autumn traders arrived. The horses had needed a rest, so he had waited the day. He was now wishing he had walked back, so leaving them unladen, but which would have meant he could have returned the same day.

Ruari clapped him reassuringly on the shoulder and gestured him to mount up.

"Come on, at least there's two of us. How far do you think we have to go?"

The farmer thought about it, and then said he thought that they probably only had an hour to go before they reached a small hamlet on the crossroads between the road they were on, and the one that ran from Moorport to Romsby. It turned out that the farmer's name was Martin, and now he was quite happy for Ruari to ride alongside him. Ruari had been introduced to him as Rob, but it was hard to keep his identity concealed.

He was glad that he had taken the precaution of putting his mail shirt on under his borrowed clothing, thinking then more of an assassin's knife. His sword lay strapped farther back than usual so that the fall of his heavy, felted boat-cloak covered it, but as they rode he hitched it back to its normal spot. Surreptitiously he tucked his leather gloves into his pockets and slid his hand into the saddle bag to retrieve the mail backed ones he was used to fighting in. The feeling of frustration was back again. He knew that Martin would probably feel much safer if he knew he was travelling with a trained Knight, but Ruari did not dare tell him in case he let it slip when he was retelling the tale back at home.

It was a little over the hour, in the mid afternoon, when they smelt wood smoke in the air and guessed they were almost at the crossroads. Martin kneed his horse forward so that Ruari was lagging back by a horse's length when he suddenly felt something behind him. Without thinking the training took over. In one fluid movement he had kicked his feet out of the stirrups and vaulted to the ground drawing his sword as he spun to face back the way they had come. Behind them a block of the fog suddenly seemed more solid.

Ruari stepped and then fléched at it. Whatever it was, it was totally unprepared for the explosion of movement towards it, and even less for the driving force behind Ruari's outstretched arm and sword. As the fine pattern-welded, Trees-blessed steel blade seared its way into the fog, there was an unearthly shriek and an acrid sulphurous smell. Before Ruari could reprise, there was a crack like distant thunder and a rush of wind as though something had been sucked away, as the thick patch of fog disappeared into thin air.

Almost instantly around them the rest of the fog began to lift to little more than a mist. Ruari swung around, questing to either side, sword at the ready, but there seemed no sign of anything else. He spun back to the horse, which stood shivering alongside Martin who had caught its reins, and then caught sight of Martin's shocked face.

For a moment Ruari thought it was the understandable shock of what had just happened that had turned Martin white. Then, as he strode forward to take the horse's reins for himself, he realized that Martin was staring at him wide eyed.

"By the Spirits! You're a Knight!" Martin gasped weakly.

Ruari suddenly remembered that their distinctive dragon-headed cross was emblazoned in the weave on the back of his gloves, and that he was still brandishing a sword that had an equally distinctive guard in the shape of the same cross. It was one thing he had not had to guard against showing in the east, where his enemies were a known quantity.

"Ahh…." he muttered ruefully, wondering what to say.

"You saved my life! …That thing, it was behind us wasn't it?"

"Aye. 'Thing' is about the right description. I don't know if I killed it or what. It didn't feel like I hit anything or connected with it, it just went."

Martin shook his head. "I don't care what it is as long as it doesn't come back. But you? Who are you?"

Ruari groaned inwardly. Why did his life have to be so complicated? Before he could answer though, Martin went on,

"Why would a Knight protect someone like me? They said you were all just out to get rich. That you were corrupt, and say prayers to the old gods and raise up demons and stuff, when you're not too drunk or having orgies."

"Where in the Tree's name did you get that crap from?" Ruari asked in astonishment.

Martin had the grace to look shamefaced, and admitted that it was the word that had been going round the markets for the last couple of years. "That's why the Church took you over. They said you lot needed bringing back to the ways of civilized decent people, not lording it about and preying on innocent folks."

Ruari groaned and leant his arms on his saddle, looking up at Martin. "Look, I promise you, I've never preyed on anyone, and I've certainly never seen an orgy at any place associated with my Order – a few amongst conscripts when they've won battles, but never Knights, alright? I'm going to have to trust you not to tell anyone what you've just seen, so let's get to that inn and get some food, and I'll try to explain why I'm here. But please, please don't say what just happened. Tell them we just made it here when we heard that thing kill something else and go, alright?"

Martin nodded thoughtfully. "Alright. Whether it's true or not, I owe you my life, so yes, I'll keep your secret in there, but I want to know what's going on."

By now the mist was lifting, and they could see they were almost at the highest point on the moor. Out of the gloom it was another bright autumn afternoon, with the lowering sun bathing everything in shades of rich golds and reds. The inn stood right on the crossroads and was full of travellers, all obviously unwilling to risk moving on in the fog. Ruari and Martin managed to arrange for a hot pie and a beer each, and then found that their news that the fog was lifting resulted in a mass exodus, as travellers rushed to retrieve packs and horses and move on before the fog could return. And luck was with them. The thing had obviously been lurking around for some time and several other travellers had had narrow escapes, so they only stood out in being the last to see it. By the time the pie arrived they were the only ones in the room, and were able to take the seat in the window, away from the bar. The landlord and his wife were tired out from having had a full house all night and for most of the day, and retreated to the kitchen to recover, so Ruari and Martin had the place to themselves.

"Right," Martin munched round a mouthful of pie, "come on, let's hear it then."

Ruari gave him an edited version of the events of the last few years, carefully avoiding mentioning his rank within the Knights, or the conclusions Ron, Walter and he had come to regarding Michael's murder.

"So you see, don't you, I have to find out what's going on. But I promise you, I've been in the Order since I was a lad of sixteen, and the granges were respectable places, where men like me got training, and older men retired to. Not everyone was an angel, I grant you, but then most were like me from the wrong side of some nobleman's blanket. Or their much younger sons, sent to the Order to save them the trouble of providing for them, or splitting the family land's up. Some were better suited to the life than others. I knew a few who would have done better in the Church, but there was always a place for them, because we needed someone to keep the books and take vows to be able to take the services for the rest of us, and the Church trained them for us! So it's rich to say we weren't making the proper observances!

"Others, I'll grant you, were a blood thirsty bunch, but amongst us they were forced to toe the line, and believe me, the punishments were severe for anyone bringing the Order into disrepute. Going back a fair few years, I remember one lad who came to us who was a complete monster. Nothing we did made much of an impression on him. Then one night he got out, went to a local farm and raped and murdered the younger daughter there. Rolled back up to the grange drunk as a lord, he did. Thought we'd just stick him in the prison for another spell. Well, we did, until Grand Master Robert could get there. Then we marched him into town, and in front of her family and every person the Order could round up, the Knights were drawn up in rank and he was executed in front of them. There was no messing about. He'd proved himself to be no better than a wild animal and he was put down like one."

Martin was wide-eyed at this.

"Executed? You mean hanged?"

"Oh no. Hanging wasn't thought to be a public enough sign of our disapproval. The two he'd been closest to had to hold his arms while he was pulled over a block, two others held his legs, and a giant of a knight with a sharp axe took his head off."

"Bugger me!" Martin said in amazement. "What do you lot do with a traitor then?"

Ruari chuckled. "Don't know. We've never had one of them! They don't last that long if they're dodgy. They're first on the boat to the nearest war, which usually sorts their priorities out. It clears the mind something shocking having screaming hoards of raiders, Attacotti or DeÁine coming at you."

"I bet it does!" Martin's voice was filled with awe. "Have you seen many wars?"

"Aye, a few. The really big one was when I was still a novice, twenty-five years ago. That was when we all went with the Jarl's army to join the massed armies from the other island states in Brychan to stop the DeÁine."

"Why did you go, I mean the Knights?" Martin asked.

Ruari could not believe how uninformed he could be of the biggest event of their lifetimes – and Martin travelled, so he was probably better than most for knowing what was going on. No wonder it had been so easy to blacken the Order's name. Had they done this to themselves in some way, by not communicating with the ordinary people, or was this further evidence of the ability of their unknown adversary?

"Don't you know the Order's history?" he asked.

Martin shook his head. "Not really. Bits and pieces, but I never understood why there was an Order, or for that matter why there's the Church and then the different orders of monks."

Checking the view out of the window Ruari could see that they were headed for a clear night.

"Look, I tell you what. Let's get going. It'll be safe to ride all the way to your farm now, if you can give me a bed for the night, and I'll explain on the way."

Martin was only too pleased to have an armed escort to his door, and so they paid the weary and incurious landlord, and mounted up once more. This time a pleasant breeze greeted them, and to Ruari's relief the air was filled with bird-song as the wildlife resumed their usual habits – the best sign, as far as he was concerned, that everything was returning to normal. As their horses walked on, Ruari restarted his history lesson.

In the long gone past the high-king of all the Islands had been faced with fighting to secure his people's right to live on the Islands. A race they'd known little of, the DeÁine, had claimed overlordship and vicious battles had been fought. Their enemy's almost supernatural strength had intimidated the normal conscripted armies, and so the high-king had ordered the formation of a military order. The initial prohibition on marriage and families had been to ensure they would have no ties to hold them back, and the religious training had been included to provide them with the moral and spiritual strength to cope with whatever came their way in the battles to come. It had not been made public why the DeÁine had retreated back then, but after five hundred years they had returned to claim their right over the Islands.

Ruari remembered the call to arms. For many veterans it had been the chance to prove that they were as good as the soldiers of legend whose names were still revered. As he explained to Martin, the difference this time was that they were the only force that operated on all of the Islands. With the high-king by now long gone, it had been the respective Grand Masters who had coordinated the response, and pressured the separate chancellors to respond to the threat. It had been more good fortune than anything else that the men in charge had been of a temperament to see cooperation as being to everyone's benefit. Choosing his words carefully Ruari went on.

"Here in Rheged we were lucky. The Jarl of the time – that's Jarl Michael's grandfather – was too old to fight himself, so he sent my…" He checked himself just before he said 'father', "*ehhm*, his son, and he was prepared to work alongside the Knights. We shipped out to Brychan, and found that their leaders had spent the last decades fighting amongst themselves. Over there it was the monks who were holding things together.

"Originally, I discovered, there was only one church, but then some amongst them decided that it was becoming too corrupt and worldly. So they approached the high-king to be allowed to form a separate group who would live their lives away from the world. The idea was that they'd spend their time in prayer while the church's main function would be to minister to the spiritual needs of the people. Well time went on, and the world changed. The church on each of the Islands developed its own character. So did the monastic groups, and us Knights too. In the western-most Island of Brychan, the monks became rich and powerful, holding vast amounts of land." He snorted in disgust. "By the time we reached Brychan the church was a rival to the leader of their earls – silly bugger was even calling himself the 'king' – and they'd both undermined the strength of the Knights.

"Apparently, the chancellor of Brychan decided to call himself a king because that was where the old high-kings had their seat, but he was still powerless unless he had the backing of his nobility. Our monks don't have much time for the Brychan lot – they think they lost their way a long time ago – but nevertheless, when they sent the initial messages asking for our help, the abbots here met up and decided to petition the Jarl."

"Why?" Martin asked, feeling very much the simple countryman in the face of such a wide sweep of events.

"Well, they had the old scrolls that recorded what happened the last time the DeÁine fought us. The monasteries are now the only places where anyone studies the past much, but that meant they saw the danger as not just something threatening Brychan. Over on its eastern border is a huge mountain range, which is about the best natural barrier besides the sea. They knew if the DeÁine got across that in numbers, Brychan would fall; and then Prydein, in the south, and even we in the east would've had little chance. There's less of a strait between any of us and Brychan within our inner seas, than from us to the lowlands across the sea in the east where I've just been. Even Celidon and Ergardia, with their mountain strongholds, would've had small chance of holding out on their own, and they knew it."

When the Grand Master of the Order in Brychan sent out a call for help to all members of the Order, the other Grand Masters each went to their own rulers with the monks, and together they had pushed and persuaded until the force was brought together. For three years, Ruari told Martin, the combined army fought the DeÁine until they secured the mountain passes, and then won a great battle at Moytirra allowing a truce. In that time, the Knights of Brychan regained lost prestige. Also, the ruler of Brychan had been fatally wounded leading his troops, and the Grand Master of the Prydein sept, Hugh de Burh had taken over command of their whole forces.

Then eight years ago the flower of a whole generation from Celidon, which was always a sparsely populated island, had been virtually wiped out when their Knights and their supporting soldiers had fought a heroic stand against a surprise attack by vastly superior numbers of DeÁine in the north of Brychan. Their near neighbours, Ergardia, now undertook to send Knights for their defence from their sept should the need arise.

"So you see," Ruari explained, "that's why *we* had to respond to the eastern threat. The sept in Brychan still guards the mountain passes. In Prydein they've always held the line against the Attacotti, and although they're not a fraction of the threat the DeÁine are, because they're within the inner seas of the Islands, if they get out of control they can cut us off from one another. Ergardia is next closest to the Attacotti, and they still have responsibility for Celidon. Therefore we couldn't afford to let the eastern raiders get beyond us in case they joined with the Attacotti. This is what we do. We protect. The individual Islands might argue with one another, but we Knights don't get involved in that. The Order doesn't get dragged into territorial disputes. We're here to protect everyone. That means you and your family, and people like you in all the Islands."

Martin rode on in silence for a while thinking about that before asking, "Then why did the Church say they needed to take you over?"

Ruari scratched his jaw thoughtfully.

"I don't really know. That's one of the things I need to find out about. My best guess at the moment is that as the current archbishop was always a political appointment – he belongs to one of the great families who'd love to have one of their own become chancellor – it's political. On the other hand, our Order has a lot of resources, like granges and houses in the main towns, and while the Church might be concerned with the hereafter, it's also never turned down the opportunity to line its pockets in the here and now."

Martin muttered scathingly about the local churchmen he knew who, as far as he was concerned, were good for little besides fleecing the very people they were supposed to help. By this time the moon had risen and they were descending the western shoulder of the moors. They now took a small track off to their right, and Martin led them down to a group of small farmsteads nestled in the valley of a stream. His house was closest to the road. Stabling the horses, they went into the house where an anxious woman and a teenage boy sat waiting expectantly.

The relief at Martin's return was overwhelming and, as his wife pressed food and hot herb tea on them, they had to tell their tale. To Ruari's relief, Martin made no mention of who he was, brushing over Ruari's encounter as a warning which had given them time to reach the inn. A truckle bed was wheeled out from beneath the settle, and Ruari was left to sleep for what was left of the night.

In the morning it was overcast, but with high clouds which showed no sign of turning misty again. After breakfast Martin offered to ride a little further with him to a large manor in the next valley, where he was sure Ruari would be able to buy a horse. The story would be that it had been Ruari's horse that the thing had preyed on, which was why he was now riding Martin's horse. By turning up with a neighbour, Martin felt there would be a better chance of them helping Ruari, especially as, having sold his yarn, he could now pay his rent for the next few months to them. Had he died they would have been one less tenant, and they were already in the position of having to leave Ted's widow in her farm, even though she was struggling to pay, because nobody could be persuaded to take up tenancies on the moors at the moment.

Martin obviously knew his neighbours well, and they responded exactly as he had predicted. Ruari handed over his money and received a solid, healthy moorland pony. If it was unlike the sleek, highly-trained war-horses he normally rode, it was also much livelier and nimble than Martin's stolid packhorse. Back on the main road, Martin was going to turn for home while Ruari was continuing east, and they bade each other farewell.

"Look, I believe you." Martin said. "I hadn't ever thought of things beyond the moors before, to be honest, but it sounds like round here we might have to before long. So don't worry, I'll keep your secret, and if you're passing again and there's anything I can do to help you, just come and find me, alright?"

Gratefully Ruari thanked him, and then a thought occurred to him. "Actually there is something you could do for me," he said. "In a week's time Ron is going to try to reach Thornby's grange for me. Normally he'd come over the moors, but after yesterday I don't want him travelling alone up here, and I don't think they know much in Maerske of what's happening round here. Could you get a message up to that inn at the crossroads to be taken on to *The Mermaid*? Let them know what's going on, and tell Ron to catch a boat up the coast and then go to Thornby up the river. It's a bit longer but it's safer now."

"Of course," Martin said willingly. "I know Ron and Sal well, we all stop there when we go to Maerske to trade. I'll have no trouble letting them know, and there should be several wagons coming through within the next week to get to the boats before the winter storms start, so there'll be plenty of chances to get a letter down there."

Thanking him once more, Ruari turned and kneed the sprightly pony into a brisk trot. At the top of the steep scarp which led down off the moors, he turned and looked back and saw Martin in the far distance give a final wave before he disappeared as Ruari descended.

The road snaked tightly down the nearly sheer, white limestone escarpment, and at the bottom Ruari found himself in softer countryside. On the moors most folk farmed sheep, but down in the valley on the better soil all manner of crops were grown, giving the countryside a patchwork quilt effect. As the day wore on, the land he was travelling through became more populated, and by the time he stopped for the night, the land was crisscrossed with lesser roads and lanes, and he had plenty of choice of stopping places. Almost every crossroads of any size had some sort of inn, ranging from small places that were little bigger than the normal village house, to great establishments catering to the high and mighty who might be travelling to the capital.

He chose a medium sized place, big enough to have plenty of travellers where he would not stand out, but not one of the more prestigious ones that he may have stayed in on official business in the past. Ruari sat in the corner of the bar and ate alone, trying to listen to the conversations going on around him which might provide a clue as to what he could expect to find. Unfortunately, being on the direct route up to the moors, the strange goings on up there were of more current concern. Many of the bar's customers were either heading for the east coast ports or knew someone who was, and this time of year was one of the busiest trading periods. Wool which had been sheared in the spring had now been woven into cloth, and was waiting to be shipped round the coast or further afield for dying and then to be returned, or for garment making at the other end.

Coming back were loads of grain from the fields in the south and west to help supplement their own crops over the winter. Normally these came by boat as being quicker and easier to move in larger quantities, but Ruari gathered that many merchants had chosen to hire teams of horses and wagons to come around the mountains rather than risk the moorland roads running inland from the eastern ports. Of course the price of such stock was going up, as bringing goods the slow way round by road took longer and was more costly. A general air of gloom pervaded the room as the travelling merchants speculated on the knock-on effect to their respective trades, not least an increase in the cost of stopping in inns if the price of food went up.

Feeling unwilling to join in, Ruari made the excuse of an early departure and returned to his room. He had learned little of any use to him, and spent most of the night tossing fretfully on the rock-hard bed as his mind played out random scenarios and refused to turn off. By the morning he was feeling tetchy and tired. As soon as he heard people up and about, he took his bags and went downstairs. After a quick breakfast, he paid and left, anxious to be on his way. The pony had obviously had a better night of it and was fully rested and bouncing with energy, so Ruari let her set her own brisk pace, and they were soon clipping along the main road into Earlskirk.

The capital sat on a knoll and was visible from many miles away except on the murkiest of days. The roofs of the royal complex rose above the town, accompanied by the towers of the great cathedral which sat alongside it, and Ruari halted as they came into sight to scrutinize the scene. As far as he could tell it all looked very normal. Flags flew where they ought to have, there was a steady stream of traffic going in and out of the great gate he could see from this angle, and there seemed every indication that the same was happening on the other main roads in. So far so good, but then he had not expected anything else at this stage. If there had been anything drastically interfering with the daily life of such a large number of people it would have been noticed far and wide. Whatever he was looking for would only become apparent closer to the court itself.

It took the rest of the morning and part of the afternoon to get close to the town gate. In many ways the gate was symbolic rather than defensive. Like the others leading into the town, it stood with two massive towers flanking the opening, and a pair of iron-studded oak gates. However, you only had to look to the side of the towers to realize that the walls were much less imposing. They rose to only half the height of the gateway and were of rough cast stone, trimmed only as far as necessary by the masons to make them sit on one another with the aid of some equally rough mortar. Their main purpose was to ensure that traders passed through the gates to pay their tolls, and to stop opportunistic raiders riding in and catching the town unawares.

They were not designed to withstand a siege. If it came to that, the defensive position was up the hill at the castellated court. What bothered Ruari was that normally the walls were kept in decent repair, whereas he could see as he rode along the road that they were now festooned with weeds. Even the odd small bush had been allowed to root itself in the mortar, providing handholds for anyone of reasonable agility.

A wide deep ditch lay in front of each gate, forcing the traffic to either side of it and channelling it into a single file by the time it reached the gate. One side had wagons and people going in, the other, similar traffic going out. It seemed to be a purely logistical solution, but Ruari knew that it also stopped the heavy wagons getting up speed and ploughing straight into the town while the toll keepers were busy with another. He dismounted and joined the in-going queue. The only people who rode through the gates were people of consequence, and while his position entitled him to ride, it would single him out straight away. So he would blend in with the ordinary travellers and traders by leading his pony in. In front of him the woman driving a wagon laden with turnips kept up a constant harrying of the poor man walking beside it, who was obviously her husband. She had a shrill voice that set Ruari's teeth on edge and he hung back slightly, feeling embarrassed for the man having such a public humiliation.

The wagoner behind him chuckled. "She don't give up, do she?" he commented to Ruari.

"Poor bugger! Fancy being married to that!" Ruari replied, thinking that this was a good opening to engage someone in conversation. Traders were usually the best informed about goings on in any town, because their livelihood could depend on knowing if trouble was coming. The man seemed willing to have someone to while away the wait with, and as they made their slow progress towards the gate he regaled Ruari with tales of the city. It made it easy for Ruari to act the part of a returning trader and passed himself off as the journeyman to an armourer, so that it was natural to ask of the court in the guise of seeking arms commissions. The man sucked in through his teeth and shook his head.

"Doubt if you'll have much luck here then, mate," he told Ruari. "These days the king don't seem worried about the army much anymore."

"King?" Ruari queried in astonishment. "What king? Rheged has only ever had a chancellor!"

"By the Spirits, you have been away a long time, haven't you! When the news came that Jarl Michael died, oh ages ago, his son declared it was time for a change."

"Oh did he now!"

"Aye. Said we'd not seen hide nor hair of anyone from the other Islands for so long, we should forget about them and start looking after ourselves. Said it was ridiculous losing his father to some daft war overseas just to satisfy some ancient idea of obligation. From now on he was going to take full control of Rheged for its own people and look to them first. Very popular that was! People lined the streets so deep even the pickpockets couldn't work when he went to the cathedral to be crowned."

"Crowned? With what?" Ruari was almost speechless in shock at this news. Rheged had no traditional regalia except for the chancellor's chain of office, which was to remind the incumbent that he was chained to the obligations of the needs of the people.

"A crown you twit!" the trader said good-naturedly. "They found an old one deep in the treasury, or so it's said. It looked pretty old anyway, as far as any of us could see when he rode back to the castle with it on."

Ruari scoured his memory for what might have been buried in the strong room at the castle. He had not been down there for years, and then only rarely, but there were not that many such items in it that it would have been possible to overlook one. In sudden horror he turned to the trader again and asked,

"Did it look like it was made of iron, not gold or silver? No jewels, and more like a fancily worked helmet?"

"Aye, that's the one," the man answered cheerfully, oblivious to Ruari's shocked appearance.

Luckily they reached the porter at that moment and so Ruari was not required to explain. He handed over his silver penny and left his new companion to sort out tariffs on his load of barley, evidently heading to the town brewers and subject to increased charges.

Ruari, meanwhile, was feeling physically queasy at the thought of what Oswine had done. The 'crown' was nothing to do with Rheged itself. It had been brought to the safe keeping of the castle after the DeÁine had left the first time, and was one of a number of pieces which it was believed harnessed their power. He found an open inn, but ordered a mug of caff – piping hot and invigorating – rather than beer and sat on the bench outside, desperately racking his memory for what he had been told of the piece.

He had a memory of his father taking Michael and himself down to the strong-room one wet afternoon, and telling them of how the great alliance had first driven the DeÁine back, but he also had vague memories of being told that this had only been possible because the DeÁine had been too presumptuous. Thinking that the Islands' people would provide little resistance, the DeÁine had brought objects of power to give them strength to overrule the people, and had distributed them among their number on the different Islands. The people had fought a hit and run war and had managed to take one of these objects, a gorget – a deep collar of fine mail designed to protect the throat. Afterwards they had noticed that their enemy was weaker without it, and had sent messages to the other resistance fighters for the need to try to acquire the others. The helmet had been discovered in another Island, Prydein, Ruari thought, but as they also hid another piece – a scabbard – it had been decided that the Helm should be separated from its fellow power-holder and it had been brought to Rheged, where it had remained buried for centuries.

The one thing Ruari remembered clearly though, was that they had been told under no circumstance to ever put the Helm on, not even in play. His father had known the lure of old armour and crowns to a pair of mischievous, imaginative boys, and had seen them playing out the stories of the old kings of legend in the practice yard with their wooden swords. So he had gone to great lengths to impress upon them that this was no small matter. He was well aware that while they should not normally be allowed in the room, there was nothing like inquisitive boys for finding their way into places they should not be. The pieces of power corrupt, he had told them.

"They weren't meant for normal people like us to wear, and we aren't strong enough to wield them. If you were stupid enough to put it on it would creep into your soul and start to control you. The DeÁine are pulled to the pieces and the pieces are pulled to them, so without knowing it you would start to do things to help it make its way back. It will head for the nearest DeÁine like iron filings to a magnet," he had warned them, "and if you're with it, who knows where you might end up."

The Scabbard was still in Prydein, as far as Ruari knew, and the fourth piece, the Gauntlet should still be in Celidon. The Gorget had been in Brychan until the return of the DeÁine and the battles Ruari had fought in. Then it had been decided that it was too dangerous for such a piece to be so close to the frontier, and so it had been removed under the protection of the Knights, to a safe place in Ergardia – the only Island not already hiding another piece. Ruari had seen evidence of its power himself. Because of his family connections he had been selected as part of the guard drawn from the Knights of each of the Islands to escort the Gorget to Ergardia.

No sooner had they left the fortress of Breslyn where it had been hidden deep in a dungeon, than they had run into trouble. It attracted like flies those who were already twisted or corrupt in some way. They had been constantly harried by footpads, vagabonds and thieves, slowing their progress down, to their growing concern. A boat had been waiting off the northern tip of the island of Camais which lay in the northeast of Brychan, to make the short crossing to Celidon, but the tides there were treacherous and the times of sailing were limited. This route had been deliberately chosen to keep them away from inhabited areas as much as possible, and given how much it pulled at the weak-minded, the Knights had been grateful they had not had to try to take it by a more populated route. The problem had been that the weather had led them to an enforced wait of a week on the coast, waiting for the vicious whirlpools off-shore to subside in strength again, and by then the DeÁine had appeared.

Ruari still did not know how they had made it through the army lines and gone unnoticed that far. He had later guessed that they had gone north and followed the difficult northern coastline around the mountains – in itself a remarkable feat as there was little except goat tracks, even when the towering range lowered at the coast with its chain of Knights' castles. There had only been six DeÁine Hunters, but that had been enough to inflict heavy casualties on the Knights, even though they were all experienced warriors themselves. Out of a party of thirty Knights, there had only been nine left to continue the journey when they had finally killed the last of the DeÁine.

Rather than bury the bodies, they had taken them out in the boat with them and fed them into the current to take them down into the whirlpools. There were stories that the DeÁine could raise their dead, and while it seemed unlikely, nobody felt like taking the chance of having to fight them all over again. In the close proximity of the boat, one of the Knights had succumbed and tried to kill his fellows, and they had been forced to tie him up in the bows, where he had gone completely mad. Even after they had delivered the cursed thing and it had been buried again in a lead casket in another dungeon, the poor man had not recovered, and had been left to the mercies of a monastery as far away from the Gorget as Ruari and his friends could find.

Now, though, Ruari wondered if Oswine had gone rummaging in Michael's absence. It would explain so much of the peculiar goings on if Oswine, never the brightest of young men, had been tempted to try the thing on. He had always been somewhat easily led, and Ruari could see that having once put it on he would have been drawn back to it time and again, with its hold on him getting stronger all the time. However, it still did not explain the cunning mind behind the events of the last few years. From what Ruari knew of the pieces, they drove the person's emotions, and he was fairly sure that they had no intelligence of their own. So it could not possibly be the piece that had contrived to create the situation that had led to Michael's death, since it could not give Oswine intelligence that he did not have to start with.

He was also pretty sure that its influence only lasted while someone was in relatively close proximity to the thing unless they had actually touched it, so it had not been what was driving the men who had come over to join the army. That smelt of much more worldly offers of rewards. The more he thought about it, the more he was convinced that he was still looking for something of flesh and blood, even if it had been corrupted beyond its normal bounds.

He drained the dregs of the caff and set the mug on the window ledge where it would not get smashed. Unhitching the pony's reins from the hook in the wall, he was just about to mount up when he heard horses trotting briskly towards him. That meant they were being ridden not led and that meant someone who might recognize him. He averted his face and pretended to be adjusting the girth on the saddle, glancing up as they drew level to see who it might be.

To his delight it was the three men he would most have wished to find here. There was no mistaking them. Gerard was a huge man, deeply tanned and with an unruly mop of black curly hair, who even when dismounted towered over others. Built like a castle keep, he required the services of a massive horse, which under other circumstances might have looked more at home pulling one of the brewers' drays which could be seen within the city walls. Osbern was nearly as tall and dark, and although Ruari was a little over average height they were both bigger than him, but whereas Gerard was bulky, Osbern was of medium build. Gerard usually had the appearance of an unmade bed on the move but Osbern was always meticulously turned out, his collar-length dark hair neatly combed down and the simple, almost severe, clothes he favoured were always freshly laundered except under the most desperate of circumstances.

In total contrast, Edmund was a little shorter than Ruari and of the same lean build, although again dark like the other two. Quick-witted, amusing and lively, he could jolly the sometimes morose Osbern, and moderated Gerard's occasional overbearing ebullience. Long ago they had all been on campaign together and the friendship had lasted, despite the complete contrast in personalities, or perhaps because of it.

Dropping the saddle flap, Ruari turned and called out.

"Edmund! Gerard! Osbern!"

The three men halted and turned his way in astonishment, but to his surprise they quickly crowded round him as if to hide him.

"By the Spirits! It's you!" Gerard exclaimed.

"Quick, get on that shaggy thing and ride between us!" Osbern commanded.

"Gerard, your house is closest, we'll go there," Edmund said. "Not a word, you," he directed at Ruari, "I'll explain later, now move!"

Ruari found himself hustled along for the half-dozen streets it took to reach the rambling town house which Gerard's family had owned for generations. Massive oak timbers in-filled with wattle and daub rose four floors from the street, each one leaning out over the others, so that with its neighbours it seemed to be trying to join with the similar houses on the opposite side. The street was consequently always in shadow, and the three scoured the darker corners for loiterers as they trotted into the yard behind the house, through an arched gateway at its side.

The yard was more private but was still overlooked by the houses in the street behind, so they barely allowed Ruari time to dismount before they hustled him inside. He was dismayed and alarmed. He would have sworn that these three were incorruptible, but their actions now were inexplicable and worrying. Had they been close enough to the Helm to be twisted by it? He hoped not, but suddenly he found he could not be sure.

Chapter 3

Old Friends, New Enemies

Rheged: late Harvest-moon

Ruari stared glumly into the fire in the confines of the small room. The tiny attic room at the top of Gerard's house just had room for a bed, a chest, and a rickety stand for a wash-basin and pitcher. Sitting on a three-legged stool, he was wedged in so close to the fire he felt as though his shins were singeing, even though the grate was barely bigger than a pudding bowl. This was not the reception he had envisaged in any of the possible scenarios which had run through his mind on the way back, either. Things were not looking good.

A tap on the door announced the presence of Gerard with Edmund and Osbern. They slid in and settled on the side of the camp bed in front of him, which was no mean feat, given its limited proportions and Gerard's girth. It creaked miserably under the strain and Edmund shifted nervously to the bottom end, over the legs, as if he expected any minute for the whole thing to fold up and catapult him into the other two. Osbern shoved the makeshift pillow out of the way and edged to the other end, but even so the bed sagged like a swaybacked nag.

"How bad is it around here really?" Ruari asked tentatively, hoping to break the tension.

"Bloody awful." Edmund replied. "I'm sorry we had to bundle you in here like that, but the Spirits only know what would have happened if it was known that you'd survived and were back here."

With a wry grin, Gerard said. "We kept saying you were too bloody awkward to die, but nobody listened to us."

"And a damned good thing that was!" Osbern cut in. "If they had, you'd have had every paid cutthroat in the kingdom sailing out to find you and bring your head back."

"Why?" asked Ruari, somewhat taken aback.

He was still trying to figure out who to approach at court to discover who had betrayed Michael. It had never occurred to him that he might be a target for any other reason than that he knew what had happened on the battlefield so far away. And as far as he was aware, nobody else had come back before him who would have let that slip. The thought that he could have been a hunted man before he had set foot back in the country, utterly wrong-footed him – as did the realization that he might have to radically revise his plans *again*.

"Because you're someone who could be a focus for resistance to the throne, you fool," Edmund said, slapping him on the shoulder to rouse him from his daze.

"Resistance?" He was now utterly lost. "What on earth are you talking about, Edmund?"

"Wake up, Ruari! You're not out in the wilds on campaign now. Everything's changed. These days around here it's hard enough knowing who're your enemies, or who's ratting on you, when you're one of the crowd like us. If there's one thing your half-nephew doesn't want it's anyone asking questions about how he's ruling. At the moment he's got everyone forgetting that there's been a war, and that there's a member of his own family who's a real leader, proven in battle. He's riding high for now, but that could change in an instant if ever we came under an actual threat. He couldn't fight his way out of a pillow fight, and, while he'd never admit it, deep down he knows it. In peacetime he's got it made, because most people have short memories as long as things are going well in the here and now. But how long can that last? "

The wind whistled mournfully through the shutters as if in sympathy with the grim news. Osbern nodded.

"You have to understand, Ruari, those troops you fought with took a lot of paying for back here. …I know, I know," he raised his hands in a placatory gesture as Ruari went to interrupt, "it was to defend us that you went. But the only people who ever saw an enemy raid were the fishing villages on the east coast, nobody else saw a whisper of anything. They've forgotten that Michael's leadership and fast response saved them from anything worse. All they remember now is the swingeing taxes. So they don't ask what's going on in the castle. They don't ask what the taxes which are being collected *now* are funding, they're just glad they aren't any worse."

Ruari told them about the barley trader he had spoken to, and they agreed with what he had been told. Without a threat to remind them, the ordinary people were swallowing the stories fed to them from the castle hook, line and sinker.

Gerard sighed deeply. "You should see what it's like up there Ruari. You wouldn't recognize the place. It's full of silly boys decked out in daft costumes saying 'yes, my lord king' and 'whatever you say, your highness' to anything Oswine says, even if he's pissed out of his brain and talking rubbish."

"And he's pissed or stoned most of the time," Edmund added. "It's been a long time since he listened to anyone who was saying something he didn't want to hear. The Maker forbid that he should hear the truth. That the country's going to the Underworld in a basket, that the army *here* hasn't been paid in who knows how long – let alone you lot abroad that he's *really* forgotten about. If you open your mouth and try to burst the pretty bubble he's created, you can end up in prison or dead."

"Dead!" Ruari exclaimed. "Here? No, you're joking!"

He looked across at his friends in disbelief, desperately hoping it would become obvious that they were wrong, or playing one of their extended pranks on him. When he had left this had been a civilized country. There had always been the odd one or two hotheads at court who had thought themselves beyond restraint, but they had had the error of their ways shown to them, and for the most part had confined their worst habits to their own estates. So if life was not perfect, then it was not as bad as most of the other places Ruari had seen in his long years of campaigning.

What shook him most was that under his half-brother, and their father before him, the last course of appeal for a fair hearing had been to come to the capital and request an audience with the Jarl. Ruari remembered as if it were yesterday asking why this took so much of his father's time, and being told it was a privilege to be the Jarl, the first earl amongst equals, not a right. And with that privilege came responsibilities to see that justice was done for those who did not have the power to change events. Now that world seemed to have been turned upside down, and his friends were shaking their heads at this depressing truth.

"Oh, it's no joke," Gerard said resignedly. "People disappear these days. Do you remember that old sergeant who used to wander around the practice yards shouting, and waving his sword about, after he'd had half his brains knocked out in battle? Well, Oswine's sycophants had a lot of sport tormenting him to death in a 'tournament'. It didn't go down well with most of the court. Several people protested, and loudly at that. Others, strong-minded, decent men tried to stop their 'fun', including some very respected members of the nobility. Then the next thing we know, Oswine's personal guard are dragging them away, and the next day they're swinging from the battlements with Earl Harvar, his steward, his brother, and two of his knights, and Earl Brusi's nephew keeping him company – and you know how Brusi idolized that lad after his son died"

"So that was one of the old generals down, and one tamed," continued Edmund. "Then Earl Einar was all set to weigh in to the fight, but he got the message that his daughters were being held in the royal dungeons here, and at Catraeth, and Crauwel. You should see him now, Ruari, the poor old sod looks every one of his years. That twisted bastard, Oswine, has threatened to let them 'entertain' the troops if he lifts a finger to free one of them or acts against the throne. Einar's looking over his shoulder at every turn, and scared witless to sneeze in case someone rats on him and the next thing he knows he gets a bloody rag doll returned to him for burial, instead of a living daughter."

Osbern nodded in sad agreement with Edmund, while Gerard had the expression of someone who had swallowed something very bitter.

"Sacred Trees, that's sick!" Ruari gasped.

A damp twig in the grate exploded with a hiss and bang that made them all jump. Edmund, nearest to the door, had his dagger out and was halfway to the latch before he realized what it was. Gerard smacked his head on the sloping ceiling as he jumped up, and Osbern was tipped unceremoniously into the middle, nearly getting sat on as Gerard subsided, rubbing his head and swearing with great feeling. Propelling himself off Gerard, Osbern wriggled back to the head of the bed, while Edmund cautiously resumed his seat at the other end. Ruari was torn between laughing hysterically at the ridiculous spectacle, and horror at the thought of the circumstances that had reduced three of the bravest men he had known to jumping at fire sparks.

Almost dreading the answer Ruari asked, "What about Will?"

Turning to face him once more, Edmund replied, "I'm coming to that."

He ran his hands through his hair, and drew them over his face as if they held cold water, to clear his head and his thoughts. He drew a deep breath and plunged on.

"I think at first Will was prepared to turn a blind eye to some of Oswine's peculiar tastes. I suspect he thought that once the initial shine wore off, that the little monster would settle down to the job. Better the devil you know and all that."

"Yes," Gerard chipped in, "after all it seemed better to have someone of the old royal family – anyone – than have the kind of power struggle we've seen Brychan suffer from. We'd no more of a single outstanding contender for the throne amongst our nobles than they had. You two saw that mess first hand, like we did. Civil war is war of the worst kind. It wasn't hard to see Oswine as preferable to that at first. So as a result Oswine assumed that Will was tame." He sighed. "But then there came the problem of what to do with little Wistan."

"What do you mean, *problem*?" Ruari asked, aghast, suddenly aware of the sounds of children chasing one another in play in the street far below. "He's a child of what, nine years old? He can't be capable of doing anything worse than those kids playing down there. How on earth could he be a problem?"

"He's eleven, and he's the late king's son, even if like you he's from the wrong side of the blanket," Edmund pointed out. He shook his head in exasperation, "And that daft woman of a mother of his didn't have the sense to get out while there was a chance. She kept turning up at court mouthing off about what her son was due. Didn't take long for Oswine to figure out how much trouble she could cause with the right allies. So he shipped the two of them off to Will for safe keeping. Will was happy to have them, because by then he'd begun to have second thoughts. He thought they'd be better off with him, and the boy would be safe from the sick, twisted sadists at the court."

The other two nodded sagely in agreement, and Osbern added wryly,

"I thought the world of Michael as a leader and a man, but flaming Underworlds, he had lousy taste in women! At least Oswine's mother had the decency to die once she found out what a monster she produced, and she was as much your father's choice as Michael's. But what in the Spirit's name attracted him to Eleanor? She was always a shrew and she could hardly be described as decorative! The only sensible thing he did with her was *not* marry her."

Ruari could only shrug his shoulders.

"I don't know. The only thing was, I suppose, that he wasn't around much to find out what his women were like. He was always being trained up to take over when father died. ….But what about Matti?"

Gerard grinned "Still carrying that torch, Ruari?"

Ruari scowled at him.

"She's my close friend's wife! Of course I'm concerned! Why wouldn't I be worried? You know what Will's like. There's no-one I'd want watching my back more in a fight. But thinking about consequences isn't his strong point."

Gerard's grin faded, and Osbern sighed, "Oh yes, that's Will, alright. If you don't like it thump it 'til it stops, and then ask questions afterwards!"

"You're right," Edmund agreed, "and that's sort of what happened."

Ruari looked quizzically at him as Edmund continued.

"We don't know what happened exactly, but the transfer of Wistan and his mother went off just fine. Things went quiet for a month or two. Then the next thing we know, Will was being sent off on some wild goose chase down into the southwest. Some tale about pirates or raiders having landed at a village. Afterwards we realized how crafty Oswine had been. It was just enough. Enough to need to send someone like Will, with experience *and* authority, to deal with the situation. Not enough to warrant sending anyone else, or more than one company with him. Not enough to get the people thinking too hard, and just enough to appear like he was taking care of everything that came our way to keep them sweet. Before you could sneeze, the message came back from Montrose Castle that Eleanor was now the *late* mistress of the late king, Wistan was dead too, and Matti was wanted for their murder."

"Bollocks!" Ruari exploded. "Matti? Commit murder? Never!"

"Bloody right! That's what we said" Gerard growled. "But before we could go there and find out what in the Underworld really happened, there was a proclamation. Will was outlawed and there's a warrant out for his arrest. There's supposed to be 'evidence' – the Trees only know what kind – that proves he was involved in some wild plot to remove all the members of the royal family and claim the throne for himself! Well, we all know how utterly daft that is! But it didn't take long for us to realize who was really plotting."

Ruari sat open-mouthed, shaking his head in disbelief.

"And did *anyone* believe such a *stupid* idea?"

"Oh yes! I hate the little shit," Edmund said, "but it was cleverly done. Let's face it, we know Will, but to most people he's just another general. Just another member of the nobility. If your own lord is a corrupt, swivel-eyed moron, who robs you blind, what would you think of a noble you'd never laid eyes on? Most of the gutless bastards have been so busy preserving their own hides they've just gone with the flow. If the royal family can get away with murder, then they won't rock the boat. With Will discredited the last of the threats to Oswine was eliminated, and, while nobody would have cried much if it had been Oswine dead, murdering an innocent child was something else. It was enough to provoke the required reaction and get rid of the remaining focus for insurgence in one fell swoop."

Osbern nodded. "And discrediting Will was far easier than fighting him. Personally I think it's too clever for Oswine to come up with. Let's be honest, he's as thick as a brick. This was way too subtle for him to work out, there has to be someone feeding him ideas like that. The trouble is we can't work out who."

"Which is the problem," Edmund continued. "After that we all realized we had to be a lot more careful. These days the three of us trust each other and nobody else. We're reduced to skulking around and meeting in private, and that not very often! Outside, in public we act as though we're not sure of each other, either. That we're no longer the friends we used to be. We've even thrown the odd idea out that we're doubting Will, and that we're not sure if one of us knew what he was up to.

"It's worked so far. Oswine can't be too heavy-handed or there'll be nobody left to do the work while he and his mates party all day. So as long as we all look like we're at one another's throats he thinks he's pretty safe. The only way we'll worry him is if he thinks we're ganging up on him."

Ruari got up, opened the window shutter and breathed in the cold air to clear his head. Turning back to his friends, he told them about his suspicions of Michael's murder. By their stunned expressions they had had no inkling of what had gone on. Osbern had taken an arrow in the chest some years previously and was no longer expected to serve in the army, while Gerard's family had an obligation to guard the far northern seaboard, which had fallen to him to organize after his father's death eight years ago. Only Edmund had gone out with Michael, and he had been the one charged with escorting the sick and wounded back, so he had never seen the replacement recruits. Ruari hardly needed to spell out the implications to three veterans of other bloody battles, and they all nodded sagely when he said he agreed with them that someone must be pulling Oswine's strings.

He had been wondering if he dared use Will to find out what was going on, given that subtlety was not Will's forte at the best of times, but that option was now totally closed off. As was any hope of asking the three in front of him to get into the inner circle of the court. It was evidently far too dangerous for them to suddenly start ingratiating themselves with anyone on the inside. It was all such a mess and so much worse than he had expected.

"Has anyone heard from Will himself?" he asked them, in the hope that Will had found a hiding place and made contact, although they had really known Will through him, rather than Will being one of their group.

They shook their heads.

"If he's got any sense, though, he'll be keeping well away from this town." Osbern said, stretching his legs in the space Ruari had vacated.

"Let's face it Will's not daft that way. If he's gone anywhere it will be to the garrison at Catraeth. They know the real man there, he'll be believed. I can't believe he'll go anywhere near any of his estates, either, especially Montrose Castle. That's just where Oswine, or whoever organized this, would like him to go."

"I think it's actually good news that we haven't heard a squeak about him after the outlawing." Edmund carried on. "If they'd had even the faintest whiff of his scent they'd have broadcast it. Nothing would fit in better with what we've seen of this plan than to have him lynched by a mob of common folk, enraged by his 'anti-royal' murders."

Osbern chuckled. "In which case they've played Will for a fool and lost, because he's way too much of a survivor to fall for that!"

"But Matti isn't," Ruari said sombrely.

"No," Edmund agreed, "and that's been much more worrying. We've heard nothing of her either, which is bad in one way, in that she hasn't Will's experience of surviving in enemy territory. But look at it another way. Wouldn't Oswine have made the same song and dance if he'd caught her as he would have over Will?"

Ruari reluctantly conceded him the point. "I suppose so. And she's a smart girl. If wits alone can get her through she'll be alright. I was just thinking that if Einar's daughters can be fed to the rabble just to keep one old man quiet, what would they do to Matti to use her as bait for Will?"

"Sacred Trees, that's a gloomy thought!" Gerard exclaimed. "I bet they wouldn't bother wondering if he'd rise to it, given that they can't stand one another. She could be a lost cause before they've even caught her."

"Hang on," Ruari countered. "I know those two better than any of you. They don't really hate each other, they just don't have anything in common. Will might have humped his way through every whorehouse in town while Matti stays with her books at Montrose Castle, but he'd kill anyone who hurt her. Whatever else happens she's part of his family, and above all things, Will's loyal. What goes on between them would go out of the window if he was faced with a defenceless woman being harmed on his account."

"And I wouldn't go too far with the 'defenceless' bit either." Edmund said with a half smile. "This is the Matti who grew up whacking the living daylights out of us cousins! Brute strength she may not have, but she's a better swordswoman than most soldiers I know, and she learnt tactics at her father's knee with her brothers."

Feeling a touch relieved, Ruari clapped Edmund on the shoulder.

"You're right!" He had to smile at the memory. "That was always as much the problem as anything between Will and Matti. He does like his women to worship him just a bit."

"And he was shit out of luck if he thought Matti would ever do that!" Edmund replied.

Gerard coughed pointedly.

"I hate to disrupt this sudden rush of optimism, you lot, but isn't that rather besides the point seeing as it's Ruari who's here in the lion's den, so to speak? We can worry about what to do to help Will and Matti when we know where they are. But at the moment we need to come up with a plan for how to get Ruari out of here before anyone realizes he's been and gone. No-one in this house will talk, but I can't keep him penned up like a songbird for long. Sooner or later something's going to give the game away. And what then? We won't be able to fight a way out, and we're no good to anyone else if we're corpses."

"And you accused us of being gloomy!" Osbern muttered.

Ruari gazed out at the ragged skyline of roofs and the rising motte of the castle beyond them.

"Don't worry Gerard. I'm not thinking of staying. It's not that I'm not glad to see you three – I am. And I'm glad to have such willing friends, but you're right, four of us alone won't make any difference to things the way they are now."

"You're not going to give up, are you?" Gerard asked in astonishment.

"Don't be daft!" Edmund snorted "Ruari give up a fight? Never!"

"Thanks for the vote of confidence," Ruari said in sardonic amusement. "And no, of course I'm not going to give in. For a start off, two of my best friends are in mortal danger, and you three aren't exactly out of the woods yet, are you? No. I think the best thing we can do is for you three to carry on as you have been. At least that way someone is keeping an eye on what's happening up there." He nodded his head over his shoulder at the motte. "If Will's gone to Catraeth – and I think you're right, it's the place he would go – then he'll have others to help him. At the worst they'll hide him. He'll be one more soldier amongst hundreds, and harder to spot. But there's just the remote chance he might get them to back him, and if he comes here he'll need intelligence. So I want you to start thinking along those lines and taking notice of patterns of movements – troops and who leads them and to where.

"The other thing is, I don't want you three to end up being outlawed with Will. If I can find them, we're going to have to hide them somewhere. Osbern, does your family still have that old manor house out on the southern marshes?"

"What? That damp, smelly old barn of a place that gets infested with midges every summer?"

"Yes, that one."

"Why?"

"Can you get it habitable?"

"Yes. But who'd want to go there? Oh … I see!" Osbern grinned wolfishly. "No problem! I can't vouch for the roof, but those walls were so thick they'll never fall down of their own accord. I'll cook up some story and go down there. There's a couple of old boys who harvest reeds who can be trusted to keep quiet. I'll get them to sort some new thatch out if it's needed. Other than that you could hide a whole troop down there and nobody would see them. It's a road to nowhere."

"Aye, but that's its weakness as well as its strength," Ruari cautioned. "So can you make sure there's a boat tied up somewhere safe nearby, too? If things go base-up, our best bet to escape will be to go deep into the marsh. Some place where only shallow-draft craft can go so they can't ship in men to trap us – so nowhere on the main channels. Can you see if there's an old boathouse out there we could use as a bolt-hole if someone comes snooping round?"

"I should think so. It won't be much on comfort, but I reckon there should be at least one of the old huts where I can hide supplies and blankets, although you'd have to be fireless. Smoke stands out for miles down there with it being so flat."

"Better cold there than in a dungeon," Edmund said philosophically.

Ruari nodded. "Too right. Now that could take the longest to sort out, so if Osbern goes off first and gets things moving, then comes back, I've other things in mind."

"Great Maker it's good to have you back!" Gerard growled, enveloping Ruari in one of his bear hugs. "This dithering around's been driving me nuts!"

"Yes, well don't forget it's got to be covert," Ruari cautioned, trying to extract himself from the rib-crushing embrace and breathe. "Now, Gerard, your peel tower up north. When Osbern gets back, can you go and get that in order too?"

" 'Course I can!"

"In fact I don't think it will do any harm if you go immediately Osbern gets back," Edmund said thoughtfully. "We could put it around that you two have had a disagreement and aren't on speaking terms. The less time we spend in each other's company, the less it will look as though we're collaborating."

"Good thinking," Ruari agreed. "So if you go tomorrow, Osbern. Edmund, can you hide me out at the grange for a few days while we get supplies together? That would get you out of town too. Gerard could call in there on his way to the tower, and Osbern on his way back, which would be less conspicuous."

Edmund nodded.

"Mmm, I think that would work, but I'll keep going backwards and forwards between here and the grange. It's only a couple of hours ride after all, and that way it won't look like we're all disappearing off all of a sudden."

"Even better."

"Right, well I'd better go and get packing." Osbern came and clasped Ruari to him. "Gerard's right. It's bloody good to have you back. I just wish we didn't have to split up again so soon, we should've been celebrating tonight, not hiding in attics."

"I know," Ruari said sadly. "I wasn't expecting things to be like this, either. Out in the Flat Lands no-one's heard neither hide nor hair of what's been going on here. We didn't have a clue. But the sooner we act, the sooner we can try to get things back to sanity, although it's looking like more of a tall order by the hour. With that in mind, before you go you should know something else."

"Oh bugger, I'm not going to like this am I?" Gerard moaned.

Ruari looked apologetically at him and the others. "No I'm afraid not. Did you lot see Oswine during this coronation ceremony I was told about?"

Osbern and Gerard had, but Edmund had barely landed at the time and had not found transport for all the wounded, so had not been in the capital.

"That crown, the one like a mail helmet …it's a problem."

"The crown itself?" Gerard asked, perplexed. "How can the crown be a problem? The twit underneath it yes, but it's just a bit of old iron mail."

"Oh it's more than that," Ruari told them. "It's the DeÁine Helm!"

"By the Cross of Swords!" Osbern exclaimed in horror making the sign of a cross over his heart. Gerard swore vehemently and also crossed himself, while Edmund sank, pale-faced, back onto the bed. Ruari told them how he knew what it was and, although none of them had been with him at the time he had escorted the Gorget to Ergardia, they had heard him talk in horror of it enough to understand the true depth of the problem the Helm's reappearance would cause.

"So you see why I want you all to be careful," he told them. "I'm not just being fussy. That thing corrupts absolutely – so no heroics – and keep well away from Oswine if he's wearing the cursed thing. I still think there's someone human plotting behind this, though, and that's who I want you to try and find, but on no account tackle them at the moment. When we do that it's got to be well away from the Helm, because I've a nasty feeling that whoever it is knows more about how that thing works, and how to use it, than we do at the moment. Where we've got the edge is that we now know what it is and that it's being used, so we'll be on our guard from now on."

Osbern grimaced, squared his shoulders and edged his way to the door, although he was still leaving in a more optimistic mood than when he had arrived.

"I'll see you out," Gerard said, following him and ducking to avoid the low beams. Their footsteps receded down the creaky stairs, leaving Edmund and Ruari standing by the little window, from which they heard Osbern wishing his host an acrimonious farewell, and storming off in a deceptively convincing huff.

"So what did you have in mind for me?" Edmund asked, turning to face Ruari. "I hope you aren't leaving me to kick my heels while you go off sticking your head into the jaws of dragons. I've been as frustrated with being powerless as those two, I don't just want to be the quartermaster."

Ruari grinned at him, his blue eyes sparkling with energy now that he had more of the measure of things.

"We are going to find out what really happened. We're going to Montrose Castle!"

Chapter 4

A Narrow Escape

Rheged: early Harvest-moon

Matti was muttering darkly under her breath as she did the usual morning battle with her hair. It was the bane of her life. Some women were blessed with glorious tresses which fell into whatever the current fashion was, but Matti's was fine and straight, except for a few kinks which resolutely appeared in just the spots where she would never have wanted them. It was not even a decent colour, she thought. All her life she had longed for it to be a pale corn gold, but instead it was a rather uninteresting pale mousy blonde. Giving up on the clip she was attempting to insert, she fought the shoulder length pest into the usual short plait and tied it off with the tightest knot she could manage. With any luck it would hold for at least a morning's ride without coming adrift, and a quick fix when she stopped for a break would get her back to Montrose Castle without looking as though she had been dragged through a hedge backwards.

Pulling on the long riding cloak, she marched out to the stable and took Elven from the groom who had brought him out of his stall. She had given the smoky-gray gelding the name from a folk legend, which said that the hoof rot that sometimes afflicted animals was caused by the fairy-folk cursing them, and called it elven-hoof. He was certainly a horse that the grooms cursed frequently, since he was given to being more than a little free with his teeth and hooves, but Matti liked his contrary attitude. It suited her that few people would ride with her when she was on such a mount. That way she got to ride in peace without a gaggle of hangers-on, who otherwise might have thought to take the opportunity to force their acquaintance on the wife of one of the most important generals in the army.

Today, though, she was heading back after a visit to one of the Montrose family's more far-flung estates, and as she cantered along, letting the big horse set his own easy pace, she mentally cursed Will. Why in the Islands had he offered to give the late king's mistress lodging in their home? The woman was an utter pain in the neck, constantly demanding she be waited on hand and foot, and never missing the slightest opportunity to remind everyone that her son was the king's brother. Will was not the one having to deal with her. He had disappeared off on some military manoeuvre *again*, supposedly to deal with some pirate raids down in the south – although he himself had said he thought it likely that the rumours were greatly exaggerated in light of the east coast raids of a few years ago.

So now he was gone, like he always was when needed, and she had stood as much as she could until she had had to escape on the pretext of estate business. Even then the stupid woman had protested that she would not have anyone of the right rank to talk to, and asked Matti to send a servant instead. Matti had told her in no uncertain terms that if she had ever had to run a home of her own, instead of being accommodated in the royal apartments, she would not even consider such a thing. Making a fictitious excuse of light-fingered staff who needed disciplining, Matti had made her escape.

However, a week was about as long as she could string out her absence and now she had to go back – no doubt to a long list of complaints from her harassed staff. As she had told them, though, they could spread the load between them, but she was stuck with Eleanor for whole days at a time, which was enough to drive anyone insane.

At least the day was gray and dull for the ride. Had it been gloriously sunny she would have resented the return even more, since normally she could have got back as late as she liked and just have had something cold to eat. This time she had to be back in time to eat the main meal in the big dining hall, which was earlier than normal to accommodate Wistan, since Eleanor insisted he went to bed early. Poor boy, Matti thought, he never got the chance to go out and be a normal child, playing with the other youngsters who lived in the castle and its adjacent wooden houses.

She herself had grown up in a very relaxed household due her grandfather's folly. Having frittered away the family fortune, his son had been forced to marry a woman from the merchant classes, who came with a massive dowry from an extremely wealthy father who wanted to move in aristocratic circles. No amount of money, however, had fully opened the doors of the topmost members of the nobility to them, and as Matti's mother had never been fully instructed in the courtly proprieties, she had not seen anything amiss with letting her daughter play with whomever she wished.

A whole tribe of brothers and boy cousins had resulted in her becoming a first-class rider, and a fair swordswoman and archer. Even now, when Will and his men-at-arms were away, she would wait until mid afternoon, when all the household servants were below stairs doing the lesser tasks, and sneak into the armoury. In the ground floor hall which ran the length between two of the castle's towers, were archery butts and straw men for sword practice, which Matti made full use of. She knew it was no substitute for moving targets, but at least her aim was true with a bow, and she had kept enough muscle tone to be able to pull the compact hunting bow repeatedly.

She also still had enough strength in her sword arm to be able to fence for as long a bout as the soldiers practiced for. Although it had not done much for her marriage to Will over the years, she thought with a grimace. Scared half witless by the tales of horror from the older women before her wedding night, she had sneaked her sword into the bridal chamber. When Will had arrived roaring drunk to their wedding bed, she had threatened to slit him from stem to stern if he laid a hand on her. He had spent that night on the floor and had never approached her again.

Years later her dear friend Ruari had told her that Will was completely intimidated by such an assertive woman, although Matti could not see why a soldier who already had several years service in the Jarl's army, and was in his twenties, should have been so disconcerted by a slip of a sixteen-year-old girl. Yet intimidated he was, preferring the compliant girls of the village to Matti, and at the slightest excuse would leave the castle for anywhere she was not. It was a good thing, she thought, that she was not the maternal type, since the chances of her having a family were nil.

On the rare occasions when she reluctantly had to attend court she was always surprised to find that most of the men there also trod around her with great care. There she seemed to have some kind of reputation as a mental, if not physical, castrator of men. Only Ruari, her cousins, and their close few friends remained unbothered by her love of the outdoors, and her steady amassing of a formidable library at the castle – which seemed nearly as bad in the eyes of the court. A woman who read books, even military treatises! Whoever heard of such a thing!

Consequently, though, armed with the bow and sword she felt no qualms about travelling unaccompanied, which had horrified Eleanor. Eleanor would be even more shocked if she had realized that while she went for her afternoon lie down, Matti had taken young Wistan, in the company of the kindly monk who was his tutor, and begun to teach him the basics. As she had explained to the monk, Andra, in Wistan's position it was vital to be able to defend himself even if he had no intention of a military career. The quiet and peaceful monk's initial objections had faded when he realized that the first things Matti was teaching Wistan were as much about self-control, both in physical coordination and in maintaining mental calm and clarity of thought. Andra had only been Wistan's tutor for a few months before Jarl Michael had died, and Matti had come to realize that Andra had done more than anyone to console the little boy over his father's death, and to give him refuge away from his mother's hysterics.

Indeed she was quite surprised at finding herself looking forward to seeing those two again. Andra was the first person, other than the monks at the priory she had just visited, to whom she could talk about books; while Wistan reminded her of her younger brothers, one now under the thumb of a viperous wife who prevented him visiting, and the other who had died in the first year of Jarl Michael's expedition over the eastern sea.

Thinking of the priory, she returned to the conversation she had had with its newest member, a former Knight called Iago, who had been badly wounded in the same skirmish as her brother; and who had chosen to join the monks rather than retire to a grange when Archbishop Fulchere had seized control of the Order. Iago was convinced that despite what the court said, that Ruari was not dead, and while he believed that so would she. The other monks had been full of the appalling news of the archbishop's appointment of an unknown priest to be his prior at the cathedral monastery, and that the same man was now also the royal chaplain. They were angry at the passing over of other worthy candidates, but Iago thought there was something more sinister going on. Their own prior had returned from a visit to the capital while she was there, with reports of how Fulchere now seemed to defer to the strange man, which Iago thought highly significant given the archbishop's political leanings. In a lengthy conversation in the potting shed where Iago was cultivating an impressive array of herbs for the medicinal garden, they had been unable to fathom out what might be happening other than it was not good. Iago thought it probably had something to do with why Matti had had her house guests wished on her, too.

Deep in thought, as she was emerging from the woods behind the castle, she almost rode into the last of a band of armed men who tore past her on the crossing of their paths, galloping away from the castle as if the Wild Hunt itself was on their heels. The last man gave her a startled glance, but with no hint of recognition or break in his headlong flight. Reining in Elven, Matti remained in the shadow of the trees and watched the group until they had gone down the dip to the small river, which fed into the major one below the castle. She watched until they had appeared on the other side, to finally disappear as the road to Earlskirk crested the next rise and went into more woods. Puzzled, she heeled Elven into a brisk canter down to the drawbridge and into the castle courtyard.

Pandemonium reigned. People were rushing everywhere, and it took her riding Elven almost in front of one of the grooms before he realized who she was. As he called out her name, others suddenly saw her, and within seconds she was confronted with dozens of people all talking at once, crowding so close she could not even dismount.

"Silence!" she finally barked.

The chaos slowly subsided.

"You," she pointed to the most senior of the male house servants, "what's been going on?" Several others tried to join in but she silenced them with a wave of her arm.

The man gulped and then said,

"The king's men have been here to see Lady Eleanor and Prince Wistan. They just turned up last night unannounced and they've only just gone. …But they got drunk last night and some of them tried to force the girls to spend the night with them …and then they picked fights with those of us who tried to stop them. …Four of our men have broken limbs …the cook's had hysterics and shut herself in the kitchen with all her girls and won't come out …and the housemaids have barricaded themselves in the tower. …When they went, they loosed all the horses from the stable …and we've only just got them back in their stalls."

"The king will hear of this!" Matti growled furiously. "Your master will see to that! I'll not have some bunch of ruffians coming into my home and upsetting everyone. I don't care who their leader is, he doesn't have any authority here!"

Dismounting, she threw Elven's reins to someone and strode into the keep, and in her split riding skirt managed to take the steps to the tower-base two at a time. Having persuaded the housemaids to come out, she headed for the kitchen. Curse Will to the Underworld! Why could the man never be here when he was needed? It took talent to have such a knack of dropping her in the midden heap at every turn!

She had just gained access to her own kitchen when a young maid practically fell down the stairs into it, sobbing wildly. Through her sniffles and wild gestures, Matti gathered that there was something wrong with her guests. Pounding up three flights of stairs and blessing the fact that she was not struggling with formal attire and silly shoes, Matti skidded to a halt at Eleanor's suite of rooms from where the sounds of wailing were emerging.

Manners thrown to the wind, she shouldered her way through the servants blocking the way to get into the bedroom. To her horror she realized that half of the noise was coming from Eleanor, who lay on the bed having the most dreadful convulsions. She was obviously wracked with pain and in her agony was thrashing around on the bed, back arching and collapsing, and limbs being thrown in all directions. Little Wistan was being rocked by Andra on the floor in the corner of the room as he retched miserably. Going by the state of the rush-matting, he had already emptied his stomach, but was having a lesser version of the convulsions his mother was going through.

As Matti stepped up to the bed to take Eleanor's hand, she gave an agonized howl and then went still. Seizing a hand mirror off the bedside table Matti held it to Eleanor's face, but there was no sign of breathing. She was about to try doing the resuscitating manoeuvre she had been shown once as a girl when Andra called out,

"Stop! Don't put your mouth to hers! They've been poisoned, and you may pick up traces!"

Matti turned to him in horror.

"I've read about this one," he sighed miserably. "It's fatal. There's nothing you can do when it's been taken in anything but the smallest doses."

White-faced Matti asked him, "Will Wistan live?"

"I hope so," he whispered back. "I think it was in the cakes. Lady Eleanor could never resist them. As near as I can understand, she ate all but a little piece and wouldn't give him any but a mouthful, because she said it was too rich for a little boy. Her own greed's killed her."

"Great Maker! Do you know if this is one of those poisons where it's worse if you bring it up or not?" she asked.

Andra shook his head woefully. "I can't remember, I don't think the book I read said. I don't know much about that sort of thing."

"No, me neither."

Matti paused for a second and then turned to the servants.

"Right, one of you go down to the kitchen and get a large jug of milk and a leather tankard – not a pot mug, we don't want him having a convulsion while he's drinking and breaking it! Somebody else get mops and buckets. We'll need one to clean up in here and one to take with Wistan. Oh …and someone go to the church and fetch the priest to say the words and arrange for Eleanor to have the funeral rites. Whatever she was, I'll not deny her a proper burial. Come on," she turned to Andra. "Let's get him out of here and into his own room. He doesn't need to see any more of this, and let's see if he can get any milk down. I may know nothing of poisons, but I do know sickness is dreadfully painful on an empty stomach. We may be cleaning it up as fast as he drinks it, but hopefully enough will stay down to put a lining on his stomach. It's not much, but it's all I can think of to do for him for now."

With Matti and the servants' help, Andra got to his feet. Then he and Matti between them carried the pathetic figure of Wistan into the next room and put him on his bed. When the milk arrived he had to be persuaded to take little sips, and at first he was having to use the bucket, but slowly he managed to keep some down and the convulsions slowly reduced to him complaining of stomach cramps. Utterly exhausted, Wistan finally fell into a fitful sleep, at which point Matti persuaded Andra to come into her rooms in the next tower while one of the maids sat with Wistan in case he woke. In the sanctuary of her private chambers, she forced Andra to have something to eat, and then began to quiz him over what had happened. For the most part his story varied little from what the servants had said, but in one point he shocked her to the core.

"The men who came in to see Lady Eleanor kept their hoods up even inside the castle," he told her. "I was with her because I'd just brought Wistan in to her from his studies. Their leader told her to dismiss me, but as I was going some of them were already throwing back their hoods, and I'm sure the one next to the man who spoke was King Oswine."

"Oswine? Here? By the Cross of Swords," she swore, making Andra's eyebrows reach for his nonexistent hairline. "The bastard! He was trying to murder Wistan so there's no-one left for the court to use to depose him. Brother Iago was right! There's something nasty going on at court, and I bet it has something to do with that weird man Fulchere has made royal chaplain."

"No, no!" Andra protested. "He's the archbishop! He's a man of the faith, he wouldn't be a part of this. And Oswine's the king! He's been appointed by the Spirits to care for his people. It can't be him, it must have been one of the others after he left."

"Oh Brother Andra, don't be naive," Matti sighed. "Fulchere was a political appointment right from the start, and where does this rubbish come from about Oswine ruling in the name of the Spirits?"

"Well …Archbishop Fulchere used to preach it at court," Andra admitted ruefully.

"Right," Matti emphasized, waving an admonishing finger at Andra. "You mark my words, Fulchere's in this up to his ears. I know I criticize Will, but he and Ruari MacBeth always said Oswine was nothing like the honourable man his father was. …Actually they said he was a small-minded, greedy little rat. And they knew him well enough to know! So forget all this about Oswine being above anything dirty. He wants power, pure and simple, and he'll step on anyone who he thinks is getting in his way."

Andra gave a reluctant nod of agreement, but Matti was not finished.

"Under no circumstances must they know that Wistan is still alive. We must convince that priest in the village to perform the funeral as if Wistan is in the coffin with Eleanor, and you're going to have to be the one to do that."

Andra tried to shake his head and protest, but Matti overrode him.

"Listen Andra, if I ask him, he'll come up with all sorts of reasons why I shouldn't ask this of him, not least because it's a lay person interfering with the work of the Church. He can't make those objections to you, and you can push for him to do it in the name of mercy and charity to save Wistan's life. I'm sorry but you must do it."

Andra's shoulders sagged, and he looked even smaller and frailer than usual, yet Matti suddenly realized that he was also probably much younger than she had first thought. With his thinning hair and sober manner she had thought him approaching middle age, but he was possibly as young as his late twenties. His naivety was mostly due to him having been given to the Church as a child, and being still young enough now that he had rarely ventured out of the cloisters. He was not sufficiently senior to be given the kind of tasks that would require him to travel often to other monasteries, let alone the court.

That must have come as a severe shock to him, she realized. Poor Andra. He must have been hanging on for grim death to the idea that people were fundamentally good during his time there, and now she had just knocked the final nail in that coffin. She put a comforting hand on his arm.

"Cheer up," she smiled at him. "You don't have to do it yet. You've got time to rehearse what you'll say, and just keep remembering you're doing this to save Wistan's life. That can't be bad can it?"

Over the next few days between them they nursed Wistan slowly back into the land of the living. The hardest part was having to tell him that his mother had died. They had thought about not telling him until he was fully recovered, but Matti had decided that to get him well and then pull the rug out from under him again would be worse. By a week after the event he was well enough to take a walk in the walled garden next to the castle wall with Andra, while Matti tried to catch up on all the household duties which had been put off for days. It was a glorious late autumn day, warm and sunny and so tempting to be outside in, that Matti was contemplating taking her pile of papers out to the bower to work on, even though she knew she would be even more distracted than she was up in the library.

She was just starting to scoop the papers together, when a male servant was heard racing up the stairs towards her, obviously taking the steps two and three at a time. Without knocking he threw himself into the library.

"The king's men are coming back!" he puffed. "Thank the Spirits we were cleaning the rooms on the road side of the keep. Gareth saw them coming out of the trees on the far side of the river, but they won't be long getting here!"

"Holy Spirits protect us!" Matti gasped, flinging the papers back on the desk.

Dashing into her room she grabbed underclothes, a few shirts and her two riding skirts, and stuffed them into a large canvas bag. Running across to Wistan's room, she grabbed clothes for him too, before running down the stairs towards the garden. As she took the picket gate out of the bailey into the garden, she heard the sound of hooves on the drawbridge. Hitching her skirt up she dashed across the grass to where a startled Andra and Wistan stood.

"Quick!" she hissed. "The king's men are in the castle! Wistan come with me!" She grabbed Wistan's arm, spun him around, and began propelling him to one of the turret-like gazebos in the garden's far corners.

"What are you doing?" Andra cried in alarm.

"Getting Wistan out of here before they decide to finish the job they started," she snapped back. "For the Spirit's sake, Andra, come on, get a move on! We don't have time to argue about this!"

But Andra shook his head and hung back, as she chivvied Wistan up the stone steps of the little gazebo.

"No, they wouldn't do that!" he almost cried. "That was just some fool acting on his own. They wouldn't try again, the king wouldn't let them!"

"Flaming Underworld, Andra! Don't be a fool yourself! I thought we'd had this conversation. Did the king send anyone to find out what had happened? No! So he knew didn't he! You saw him! He knew because he did it with his own hands, while he was here in disguise."

From behind the picket gate there suddenly came the sound of scuffling, the chink of armour, and someone crying out in pain. Obviously the grooms and men of the castle were trying to give her time to get away, and Matti would not let their suffering be in vain. The gazebo window arches stood at the same level as the top of the garden wall, and while two gave an elevated view over the garden, the other two provided vistas out over the confluence of the two great rivers which met far below the rocky promontory. The castle had purposely been built on it to guard the important bridges which spanned the foaming torrents.

Lifting Wistan up onto the westerly ledge of these windows, Matti swung him round so that his feet dangled out over the edge, then took hold of his hands and lowered him as far as she could manage before loosing him. It was still a good eight foot drop, but thick broom bushes beneath broke his fall. Throwing the bag down to join him, Matti swung herself over the ledge and was trying to let herself down when she heard the crash of the garden gate being smashed open. Losing her grip, she fell with a crunch, narrowly missing Wistan but leaving a clear signal that someone had been this way by the broken branches of the bush. Cursing, she hauled Wistan and the bag out of the bushes, and then managed to prop the broken bits up enough that she hoped that they would not be obvious from above. In a day or two when they started to die off it would be blindingly obvious, but she could only hope that by then her pursuers would have moved on.

Taking Wistan's hand she gave him a reassuring smile, and led him down the tiny track that wound around the rock down to the River Aller on the west side. It was so narrow that they had to walk in single file, with Matti in front holding on to Wistan in case he lost his footing. Through all of this, to Matti's amazement, he had not said a word. After a few heart stopping slithers on loose pebbles, they reached the bottom and the footpath that still ran many feet above the main riverside road.

"Are you alright?" she now had time to ask him. He was very white-faced, but then he had not really been a healthy-looking lad when he had arrived, and although he had started to get some colour in his cheeks since he had been at the castle, his illness had returned him to his washed-out pallor. It struck Matti that he was so used to being dragged here, there and everywhere at his mother's whim that this was hardly new, and he had had any natural childish curiosity crushed long ago. She knew time was of the essence, but she still stopped and pulled him to her in a warm hug.

"Come on," she whispered encouragingly in his ear as she held him. "Let's get away from here before those men come looking for us."

"Will Brother Andra be alright?" he asked in a worried voice.

"Oh I think so, "Matti replied, mentally offering up a prayer that it would be so. "They're not looking for him, it's us they want, so if he's not with us he'll be safe."

This seemed to satisfy him and he trotted alongside Matti, although he was holding onto her hand tightly. She could not help but think how young he was for eleven. It was like she had a much younger child with her. At that age her brothers would have thought it a great adventure to climb down walls, and be given free license to run away and skip lessons from under their tutors' watchful gaze. She would have had to be constantly on to them to not go off investigating and making a noise, but Wistan did not chatter away to her like they had, although as the surprise wore off she did notice his gaze wandering more.

To her relief they saw no sign of riders coming after them on the road below, but as the sun lowered, the question of food began to worry Matti. She had grabbed a small purse on the way out of the library, but she knew that if she tried to approach someone in the nearby villages to buy something she would be recognized. She knew that she was well liked by the ordinary people and that they would be unlikely to give her away, but she did not want to put any of them in danger.

In the end they found a small hawthorn growing in a clump of bracken and made a small nest beneath it, close to one of the hamlets a little off the main road. When night fell, Matti told Wistan to stay still while she crept into the houses and found some cheese in a dairy shed. An open window allowed her to reach in to a table and lift half a loaf of bread, on both occasions leaving a coin to pay for her thefts behind her. She had worried that Wistan might have come after her and got lost, but he was so used to doing what he was told that he was still in the hideaway when she got back.

They spent a chilly but not unpleasant night deep in the bracken, and then set out again, still following the river Aller. This was not a major road and carried very little traffic. In the middle of the morning they crossed the river on a wooden foot-bridge, and then took the drover's track across the countryside, until they could see Allerford in the distance as the river looped back towards them. The priory which stood a mile on their side of the town was where Brother Iago was, and Matti was keeping everything crossed that he would be there and not at one of the granges, for he would surely know what to do.

Creeping through the orchard, Matti led Wistan around to the back of Iago's potting shed. The sound of the choir rising from the church indicated that the monks were at prayer, but they did not have long to wait before they heard the sound of Iago's uneven tread on the gravel path. As the monk limped into the shed and struck a flint to light his meagre candle, they flitted in behind him like shadows.

"Hello, I wondered how long it would take you to get here," Iago said, turning round.

Matti's surprised expression made him smile.

"I didn't live this long by letting strangers sneak up on me," he said knowingly. "But you can't stay here. The king's men are here."

Matti gasped in alarm and Wistan shrank towards her.

"Here?"

"Aye, it didn't take them long to find that you'd visited here only a week ago, and they came in here like a swarm of angry bees with their horses all in a lather about lunchtime."

Matti sank onto the stool and put her head in her hands. She had forgotten the large map of the family estates which hung on the library wall. It would not take long for her papers to reveal that the priory had been a family endowment many years ago, and the continued ties between them.

"Don't worry," Iago reassured them. "I was expecting you as soon as they said they were hunting you for the murderer of Lady Eleanor and Prince Wistan. I take it this still-very-alive young man is the miraculously risen prince?"

Iago's sardonic humour lifted Matti's spirit as she introduced them to one another.

"But are they really saying *I* killed them?" she asked in disbelief.

"Oh yes. Gives them a good excuse to be hunting you, doesn't it? Not that anyone who knows you would believe that, but many will. Now look, I can't disappear until they go, so you're going out to the sheep pens in the far fields. I went out this afternoon and took food and water and a couple of blankets. As soon as they've gone I'll come and join you, and we'll head for Abbot Jaenberht. It'll be a long journey with him being in Mailros now, but it'll be less obvious if we travel as a family. Thank the Spirits I'm half bald anyway so it doesn't look like I'm obviously tonsured. They'll be looking for a woman on her own, or one with a boy, not a family."

Matti hugged him in thanks and took Wistan on a route back through the orchards, taking the long way round to the sheep pens so they would not be spotted by anyone at the priory. Iago obviously had not told anyone of his plans, and so the monks would be unlikely to unwittingly betray them. Through small holes in the hedging they could just see the courtyard of the priory, but were well screened themselves.

It took until the following morning for the soldiers to look as though they were making a move. When they were fully mounted up they rode out to the edge of the orchard, where their leader gestured four men off across the way Matti and Wistan had come. For an awful moment Matti wondered whether they would see their footprints in the soft ground, but the four put their horses straight into a canter, and by the time the last of them had passed over the furthest field, Matti was sure their tracks would have disappeared under those of the horses' hooves. The other soldiers headed off towards the great stone-paved ford across the river and the road back to Earlskirk. In their arrogance they were obviously assuming the fugitives would soon be caught, and were not making any attempt to track them.

No sooner had they disappeared from sight than Iago came limping across the field, a stout stick in his hand and a well-worn, but serviceable, filled pack on his back. He had reached them where they had come out to join him when, from a clump of bushes, a weasely monk with a sly face came out with two soldiers.

"You see? I told you this one couldn't be trusted. He's not one of us. He's a treacherous Knight! Filthy, lying pervert!" he spat at Iago.

One of the soldiers seized Wistan around the waist while the other grabbed Matti's arm.

"I told you the prior knew nothing," the weasel bragged. "He's nothing without me guiding him. You remember that when you tell Prior Tancostyl how you caught them." Turning to Matti he chortled, "You're going to hang like the disgraceful whore you are. Look at you! You're not natural! You're more man than woman. You're an abomination in the Spirit's sight, like this son of a bitch whom you're hiding!"

"Abomination, am I?" Matti snarled.

She pivoted on one foot, swinging her other knee straight in the groin of the man holding her. As he doubled over, releasing his grip on her, she grabbed him by the ears and yanked his head further down as she brought her knee up again. A crunch of broken nose, much blood, and he was on the floor not knowing which bit of himself to hold first. Iago's tall stick became a quarter staff as he jabbed the monk in the middle, spun it and struck the soldier holding Wistan straight between the eyes. The man went down like a pole-axed cow. The staff spun again and caught the monk across the temple just as he was rising. Iago grabbed one of Wistan's arms and Matti the other and they fled across the fields leaving two unconscious and one blinded by tears of pain and unable to move.

Chapter 5

The Long Trek

Rheged: Harvest-moon

The three of them ran until they were gasping for breath. By this time they were beyond the orchards and in a dip in the land out of sight from the priory. Pausing to ease their aching sides, Matti and Iago quickly conferred over which way to go. Matti had thought to go up the road to Allerdale, then over the hills to the high road and up past Lund, Catraeth and Esdale, to Mailros. She had been thinking that Will had friends at the garrison at Catraeth who might help them, but Iago rejected that.

"Don't forget," he told her, "the king will have sent messages to obvious places like that. The commanding officer might shield his friend Will, but he doesn't know you, and he might think he's saving Will the embarrassment of having to hand over a treacherous wife and do it for him. You've said yourself that you two haven't presented an image of marital bliss. They might think he'd be glad to see the back of you."

"No! Will wouldn't do that! He knows me better than that. He'd never believe I'd kill Eleanor! If he did why would he send her to me?"

"I didn't say *Will* believed it, or would hand you over. But in barracks, when all the men are together, it's common for them to moan about their wives. You know, she can't cook, or she complains about his muddy boots, all little things. The trouble for you is that they're never going to have heard anything about a close marriage to counterbalance that stuff. In their minds you may seem very different to those of us who know you. Will probably wouldn't even have thought about what kind of picture he's painted of you, but your life may now depend on that."

Matti found the thought upsetting. After seventeen years of marriage, it was sad to think that Will might have had nothing to say about her but complaints. Even worse was the thought that he might actually be glad to see the back of her. The more she thought about it the worse it became. While she knew he had resigned himself to having her for a wife, it had never really occurred to her to wonder what he would do if the opportunity came up to get rid of her? But in the current situation there would be no blame attached to him if he chose not to shelter her. In a horrible flash of reality, it dawned on her that Will might not find it so hard to reconcile his conscience to do nothing, and that was all it would take. Without his position she was nobody. Certainly no-one who could stand up to the king. She could not say so in front of Wistan, but now she was not sure she could count on Will's help at all.

However, there was not time to dwell on that now. Iago was proposing a hard trek through the mountains for a couple of days, but by crossing them here, where the chain was narrowest and already starting to descend to the sea, it would be easier than waiting until they were further north. And cross the mountains they must, he insisted. Once on the western side of the range, the grip of the king was much looser, for apart from rich sheep grazing there was little to generate wealth from taxes. The towns were more widely spread, and most of the castles were held by stewards for their lords, who preferred to be closer to the heart of things at the capital. A steward was much more likely to be in the dark about political intrigues, and may not have heard they were supposed to detain them, or if they had, the description may not have been good enough to identify them by instantly.

Reluctantly Matti agreed, partly swayed by the thought that the horsemen could not pursue them on the narrow fell paths. But it was going to be a long walk. Mounted on a good horse, the journey north would have taken nearly three weeks by this route, and, although they would be nearly as fast on foot over the mountains and on the high passes – leading past the mountain lakes and Fell Peak Fort – on the level they would be slower. It seemed as though they were unlikely to make it to Mailros before the turn of the month, and as Harvest-moon changed to Winterfalling, so to would the weather.

With little to be gained by tarrying, they set off, and for the first couple of days made good time. By then they were climbing ever more steeply into the hills, and by the third day they had risen above the tree line at times and were walking on scrubby grass with odd straggly bushes. Iago was the saving of them, for he had trained over these hills, and picked his way surely over the maze of sheep tracks, finding them a shepherd's mountain refuge to sleep in that night, without which they would have suffered dreadfully. Protected within the walls of the castle they had not realized how chilled the nights were already becoming, and at such an altitude the wind cut like a knife.

By the fourth day, Wistan was wearing several of his clothes at once to keep warm and was very unhappy, partly because Iago was proving adept at snaring rabbits to eat. In a life where food had appeared on the table ready-cooked, and where he had never been allowed down to the kitchens, it came as a shock to realize where some of his food came from. Matti was not delighted at the sight of Iago cleaning his catches out, but when the alternative was starving it was not much of a choice. So she simply did her best to distract Wistan while it was being done. The plentiful springs and torrents gave them more than enough water, and Iago had packed a good sized leather water flask for each of them which they were able to fill regularly.

Mercifully the weather held for them on this stretch, and it was not until they were descending towards the walled market town of Airey on the rise of the western slope, that the rain came down. By this time they were able to gain some shelter in the wooded slopes of the mountains on this side. Once down to the valleys they were constantly walking into herds of sheep, and having spent a night at a very meagre inn outside of Airey, they found themselves on a wide, well-paved road with sheep in the fields on either side. The road was well-used, but almost exclusively by the ordinary people who lived in the area. For two whole days they saw no-one mounted, with the only horses pulling carts. Iago had been right, this route was safer.

Against the odds Wistan seemed to pick up the further on they went. Once they could risk eking out Matti's money on beds in the cheapest of inns, or the stables of the slightly more expensive ones – but where he didn't have to see his dinner being killed – he cheered up and actually seemed to be relishing his new found freedom. Iago was constantly pointing out interesting wildlife, or telling him the history of the places they were passing. Such as the legend of High Tor Castle, perched high on a rocky outcrop watching the River Airey valley and its neighbouring one, which was reputed to have been built on a dragon's nest.

They reached Amothery after two weeks, and, as they began to turn to climb into the hills again, were lucky enough to have a lift from a group of carters who had brought huge drays loaded with timber from the high forests, and were returning only partly laden despite the supplies they had bought. Each wagon was pulled by a team of eight massive horses, in four pairs. Without the weight of the logs, even going up the increasingly steep inclines, they trotted along briskly. Wistan fell in love with the gentle, fuzzy-fetlocked giants, and happily rode on the backs of one of their team, insisting on changing horse each day in order not to show favour to one over the others. Iago spun the tale that he and Matti were taking her orphaned nephew back to their home at Caerlewl, Iago being a retired soldier whose home was still by the garrison. As he truly knew the garrison and Matti knew enough of the soldier's life to talk convincingly, it was a story they were unlikely to be caught out on, and they explained Wistan's naivety as distraction following the quite true loss of his mother.

Consequently, the toil over the projecting ridge to Fell Castle was halved, and they reached the summit of their climb in a mere four days. Even better was their transfer to another convoy, taking half a dozen huge straight pine trunks down to Caerlewl to be made into ship masts at the docks there. Iago had not planned on going quite that way, but when they could ride for another three days it was worth it in the time they would save. They were able to leave the wagoners on the outskirts of town, saying that they lived off the north road, and left them to go on through to the western docks. Once again they were on good roads, but they had barely set off when the equinoctial gales came in with a fury. As Ruari was landing on the east coast, from the road they were watching fishing boats hurrying into the far distant harbours, as they climbed in sheeting rain from the coast to turn back towards the northeast.

By the end of the month, with another two short hitched lifts they had made the northernmost tip of Rheged, and saw Burh Castle sitting as a lonely sentinel watching the northern strait out on the headland. On the first of Winterfalling they came in sight of the great monastery of Mailros and presented themselves at the solid gatehouse, a remnant of times when the monks had had to retire behind the walls for their own protection. They requested shelter in the guest hall, a right open to all travellers and one they were not likely to be denied.

Iago was unwilling to ask for Jaenberht straight away in case he was away on important business, having already been betrayed by a lesser member of his own priory. As they made their way diagonally across the wide open enclosure towards the hall, though, Jaenberht himself appeared out of the cloister's rear door. Striding along, white-trimmed black robe flowing and white hair shining in the watery sun, he appeared like a stately crane followed by rotund ducklings, as two brothers struggled to keep up with his long strides without tripping over the hems of their brown habits. His gaze swept from side to side, missing nothing as he checked his domain over, and in one of those sweeps his gaze lighted on them. For a second his eyes moved on and then whipped back to settle on Matti. The bushy eyebrows rose even further when they spotted the little figure by her side.

Dismissing his assistants instantly he strode across to them.

"Praise the Spirits! You're a sight I never hoped to see again! Come, come, let's get you indoors, you must be weary. Who are you? Brother Iago. Are you really? Mmm, less of the monk and more of the Knight if I'm not mistaken! But that's nothing to be ashamed of, and if you've helped these two, then you shall have my dispensation from any reproof you might have incurred."

With great speed he ushered them into the imposing abbot's house, and set about ordering rooms and refreshments for them. When they were seated and had eaten and drunk their fill, he leaned forward and fixed them with his steely gaze. He had already gently probed Wistan for his story, and had just sent him off with a solicitous brother named Kenelm, with the promise of a bath and some fresh clothing. Shrewd as ever, he had guessed that much of what the others had to tell would be distressing for the boy to hear repeated, and Jaenberht was always a compassionate man.

"Now," he said, leaning back in his chair and steepling his fingers before him, "let me hear your story. The full one this time. Every detail."

For most of the rest of the evening, Matti and Iago went over not only their journey, but everything they could think of concerning the build up to their flight. By the end of it, Jaenberht's brow had creased into a worried frown that just got deeper and deeper. When they finished, he poured them another mug of mulled wine each before breaking his own news.

"I have to tell you, I too am under direct orders from the king to hand you over. From what you've said, on the day King Oswine found you weren't at the castle when he killed Lady Eleanor, he sent a messenger to me. At that point it was simply to say that you'd murdered her and Wistan, so he obviously thought he'd killed the boy too. It must have come as a shock to realize that they'd ridden straight past you, which was why they came tearing back. But that first message got to me probably on the same day the men reached you again, so they were taking no chances. What you won't know is that they've implicated General Montrose and the warrant is out for his arrest."

Matti and Iago gasped in shock at this.

"Fear not," Jaenberht continued, "they haven't caught him yet. I hear someone in the royal barracks got word out by carrier bird to the garrison at Crauwel, where he was returning with the troops after dealing with the raiders. As far as I can gather, he had a good week and a half's head start on the henchmen sent to arrest him, and they've heard nothing of him since. The army's in uproar in the more far flung garrisons where they've only seen the real generals. I pray it won't be so, but we could have civil war in Rheged yet. The west can see that something is desperately wrong with the government of the country, but in the southeast where the influence from Earlskirk is strongest, they're blind to what's happening. They think the discontent is simply the product of rabble-rousers and needs to be put down. We pray constantly for peace, here. I feared the Spirits may have despaired of us and were waiting for us to sort ourselves out, but the fact that you saved Wistan, an innocent in this, and managed to get him all the way here without discovery, gives me hope they've not abandoned us. But I'm afraid, my lady Matilda, you cannot stay here."

Matti and Iago frantically looked from one another and back at Jaenberht with a dreadful sinking feeling. Why would Jaenberht betray her? Was he being blackmailed?

Jaenberht made to explain.

"Since that first visit we've had more royal messengers visit than in the last ten years. While you were in the middle of your travels they even came and searched the abbey. I protested but my monks couldn't resist armed men without huge casualties, and, as I had nobody to hide then, I let them. I now realize that they thought you were somewhere on the eastern roads heading for me. By the last visit, just a week ago, they were obviously thinking you weren't heading here after all, for it was to inform me simply that they'll be coming back to keep an eye on me.

"Having searched once, I think they won't search again unless they've good reason to think they need to. So I can hide Prince Wistan among the boy novices, and Brother Iago amongst the other brothers, but you, my dear, can hardly pass for a monk! We must get you away before they return, and I think I have a plan!"

Ushering his two guests off to get a good night's rest, Jaenberht went into his study. One of the benefits of getting older, he found, was that he needed less sleep, and it was easier to work when there were no members of his Order coming in and out to distract him. With a large map of Rheged in front of him he pondered into the small hours, but by then had worked out his strategy to cunning perfection. When his guests had breakfasted, he summoned them to the inner sanctum of his office once more and outlined the plan.

The cunning old fox was not to be outsmarted by a bunch of courtiers young enough to be his children. Keeping Wistan well hidden and safe, he was going to send a bird to the court to say that the fugitives had turned up at the monastery, and that he was sending them with an escort of monks to meet the men of the king as soon as they could come. If they went by the coast road towards Esmouth, which truly had been hit by the raids from the eastern raiders, the monks would then tell of 'armed strangers' attacking their party. There was an outlying grange of Mailros' not far from Esdale, where some of them could hide to give the impression of heavy casualties.

Jaenberht was fairly sure that as the first bird carrying this news would get no further than Catraeth, and as the commander there seemed to be Oswine's man, he would want to impress his master by acting fast without waiting for orders to come back from the court. In fact he was counting on it. A military man was likely to underestimate Matti's resourcefulness, and see nothing odd in her being sent with only an escort of monks. The garrison's men would find frantic brothers milling around searching for Matti and Wistan, which would make it seem as though Jaenberht was complying with his king's orders, and hopefully draw the focus away from the monastery and Wistan and Iago.

Matti, meanwhile, really would travel with the company and flee the 'raiders', but would then travel over the mountains again to the town of Scarton and on to the little port of Seatoft. Jaenberht knew a trustworthy priest in the church at Scarton who would help her, and he would arrange for a boat from Seatoft to take her across the sound to Ergardia, far from Oswine's authority, where Knights of Jaenberht's acquaintance – especially two people called Brego and Talorcan – would protect her. Iago immediately insisted that if Matti were going to the Knights, then he would escort her. Quite apart from being unwilling to let her make the mountain journey alone, the grange of one sept of the Knights was very like another, and he would be able to reinforce Jaenberht's message with his own authority. Jaenberht had rather hoped this would be the case, since he could not see Iago fitting in well with some of his more saintly brothers.

With no time like the present, Jaenberht had already sent the bird to Catraeth and had their escort preparing to leave. Wistan was distraught at losing more people he had grown to rely on, and for once showed more feistiness than any of them had seen before. He had to be carried kicking and screaming back into the novices' quarters by two brothers, who surprisingly had real trouble keeping hold of him. The long walk had built up muscles he had not had before, and going by the winces of pain, some of the kicks he lashed out were connecting very painfully to his restrainers. Matti had no problem pretending to be upset at being sent away, although her tears were for Wistan, and not for her fate as Jaenberht proclaimed to the aghast monks who watched them go. If any of them were questioned, they would not need to lie about what they saw.

It was a miserable day all round. A dreary fine rain soaked them through all day, and by the time the group of ten monks and Matti and Iago, with a novice stand-in for Wistan, made it to the first grange that night, nobody was in the mood to talk. A second equally wet day drenched them physically and spiritually, and by the third day they were all desperate to get off the exposed road which had no shelter from the driving rain coming straight in off the sea. When they saw a short cut leading through a stunted belt of trees, they all headed that way without any need for consultation. It proved to run for farther than had first appeared, and the relief that they no longer had to fight the sea wind to draw their cloaks around them meant that they were off their guard.

Suddenly they were in the midst of a gang of rough men. The monks, thinking they were the king's men took in their drawn swords and panicked. A shove, a push and a dagger in the wrong place and all turned to chaos. The leader of the monastic party saw a monk go down with a knife in his back and another being run through, while the burly monastery gardener used his walking staff to beat one of their assailants about the ears before a blow to the head rendered him unconscious. Matti found herself grabbed from behind and dragged off into the trees. Wrestling furiously with her captor, she feared he intended to rape her and was reaching back to claw at his eyes when she felt his grip go limp. As he dropped her, she felt Iago seize her hand and vaulting her assailant's body, together they fled the scene.

Some hours later, the remnants of the monks were bandaging their wounds and were limping back to their last night's refuge. Which was why they were already gone when the armed guard from Catraeth arrived on the scene. Finding the bodies of a young boy and six monks, they were puzzled as to what had happened, but were not about to pursue it too far when they had the proof they needed. Their orders were to receive the prisoners from the monks, and when they'd left, to dispose of them and leave the bodies for the crows to be made unrecognizable. Equally as miserable as the monks had been in the wet, they too were in a hurry to get back to the warm inn they had left that morning. Their inspection was therefore cursory, accepting that a slender dark-haired boy must be the prince, and that the body of a fine-featured monk must be Lady Montrose in disguise, since they did not bother to remove the hood of the cloak to reveal his tonsure. Satisfied duty had been done with little effort on their behalf, they left.

When the tattered remnants of the monks limped into Mailros three days later, Jaenberht was apoplectic with rage. The king's men attack and *kill* innocent monks, how dare they! A day behind them the brothers from the grange arrived with a cart with the bodies in, which were laid in honour before the great altar, beneath the stone canopy of the five trees' branches in the church.

While the brothers knelt in serried ranks around them and prayed for the Spirits to lift their souls to join them, a seething Jaenberht worked furiously. Birds were sent out until the monastic dove cot was empty. Some to each of the Order's other monasteries around the Island with summons to meet Jaenberht at Lund, the town nearest the centre of the Island. But others went to Jaenberht's own men with messages to be relayed on to contacts of his on other Islands.

Chief among these were Grand Master Brego on Ergardia, to whom he had been sending Matti, and to whom he now sent an urgent warning, and Grand Master Hugh de Burh, in Prydein. Hugh may nominally have stepped down from leading his own sept in order to take over as leader of the Knight's information gatherers, the Covert Brethren, but was in reality still the force behind his successor in Prydein. To him Jaenberht sent a frantic request for Knights to be sent to provide an escort to take Wistan over the sea to safety.

Rheged is falling into madness, he wrote, *the king is beyond control and the Church backs him against my Order. I go to rally our people, but I need you to send word to the granges of our Knights to shake off the yoke of the Church and rise to protect the innocent. Archbishop Fulchere has fallen under the influence of a rogue priest of the abominable name of Tancostyl. Fear fills me, can this truly be the same whom we knew and fought, and what evil enabled him to come here? Do not fail me, my friend, or I fear Rheged may fall and the other Islands will not be safe!*

PRYDEIN, KITTERMERE & RATHLIN

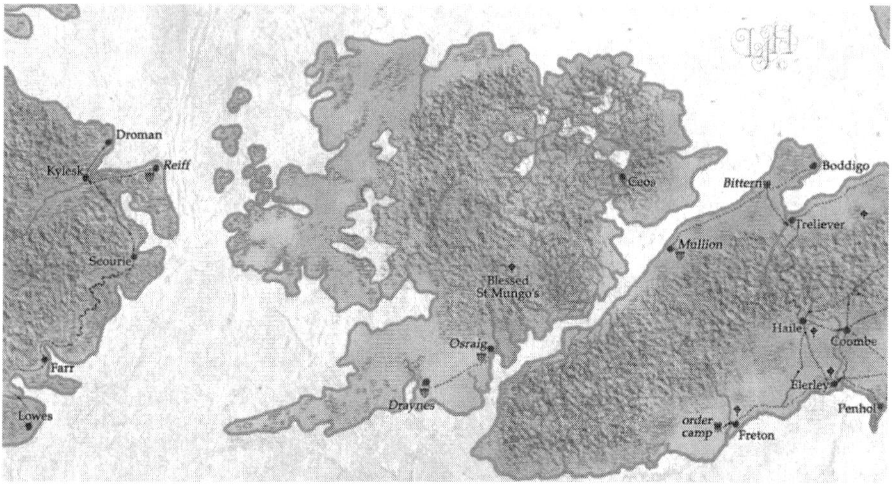

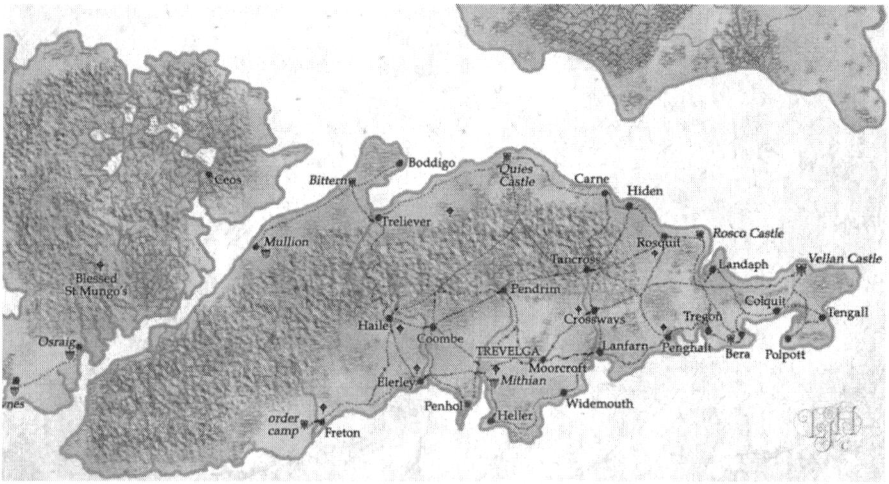

Chapter 6

Lost Loves

Prydein: early Harvest-moon

Alaiz carefully picked her way along the dock towards the waiting boat. Coils of rope lay everywhere, and it would not do to go flying over one of them when she was trying to maintain an air of dignity. It had been hard enough to summon the courage to go on this mission without having people question whether she could even control her own feet. She glanced to her side and saw that Gillies was being equally as cautious, which was a comforting sight since her companion always managed to seem so much more sophisticated than her. Yet even she was obviously not taking any chances with a whole contingent of courtiers at their heels, ready to report the slightest slip on either part.

A large ship loomed ahead, and part of their entourage now streamed in front of them to carry their luggage up the gangplank ahead of them to be stowed away in their cabins.

"This is a ridiculous amount of clothing to take," she muttered to Gillies, cringing as yet another trunk full of frippery went past them.

"Shhh!" Gillies whispered back with a sympathetic smile. "It's a diplomatic mission. We have to maintain the right image."

The only reason they were being allowed to undertake this negotiation was because the royal advisers had decided that it would be dignifying the proceedings too much if the king went, but that it equally had to be a member of the royal family. Since it was Alaiz's family who were the problem, she was the obvious choice, and Gillies had nobly volunteered to go with her, knowing Alaiz's lack of confidence when confronted with her arrogant older brothers. Before their feet had touched the gangplank, an unctuous captain was greeting them and ushering them aboard with assurances of his diligent preparation, although Alaiz could not see how he had had much time, given that the decision to go had only been made the day before. In a prolonged flurry of movements they were taken to their adjoining cabins, and were then obliged to stand with forced smiles on their faces as servants milled around them stowing endless trunks, which prevented them even having space to sit down.

When the door closed on the final servant, leaving Alaiz and Gillies in their respective cabins with only the connecting door open, they collapsed onto the bunks with sighs of relief. Too used to one another's company to feel the need for aimless conversation, they lay back and let the chaos above subside until they felt the ship begin to rock as it edged its way out from the harbour. What was left of the little girl in Alaiz wanted to dash up on deck and see the land slide away from them, but she had to make do with opening the window of her stern cabin and waiting for the ship to turn before the wind started to drift in. As they approached the headland that formed the natural harbour, she realized Gillies had leaned out of her own window, and was waving at a mounted figure who remained on the headland and was waving back. The sight made Alaiz feel horribly guilty. She felt she was a jumbled bag of mixed emotions that seemed to be pulling her ever downwards.

One part of her loved Gillies deeply. By the time Alaiz had been born, her father had been the only remaining member of the leading family of Kittermere, the island that lay off the northwest coast of Prydein and which was subject to it. Her mother had already been worn out with trying to supply heirs to ensure the family's survival, and with the next pregnancy had expired. Her father had struggled on for a handful of years, but then plague had come to the Island, decimating the population which had barely survived repeated Attacotti attacks.

"Six brothers," she sighed to herself. "Why did it have to be those two who survived? Why did father have to fall apart after mother died, and why did our family have to be so cursed significant?"

Even then, with two older brothers living, Alaiz would have been relatively unimportant. Yet fate had intervened.

Gillies, beautiful and vivacious, had been the centre of great court scandal when the heir of Prydein had married her for love, disregarding the demands of his imperious father and political necessities, and they had had two sons. Ivain, the younger of them was only a year older than Alaiz. At the time of the marriage, the old king of Prydein was hale and hearty and blessed with four adult sons, but the plague which had taken Alaiz's family then took the youngest of those sons too, and left Gillies' husband a shadow of his former self. When it had reappeared a year later he had died along with his older child. By now the old king was declining into senility, and within a year was buried alongside his sons and grandson.

Suddenly Prydein's royal family was also in crisis. Of the old king's remaining sons, the younger had turned into a near imbecilic, syphilitic, and childless drunk. The second of Gillies brother-in-laws, however, had one legitimate son and a whole brood by his long-term mistress, all itching for the chance to take their chance to rule. Something had to be done to prevent a civil war, and fast. So the seven year old Alaiz had been married to Gillies' eight year-old Ivain (unexpectedly now king by virtue of being the oldest son's son), to tie Kittermere's political alliance to Prydein, to stabilise the region, and Gillies became the nearest thing to a mother Alaiz had known.

That was sixteen years ago, though, and now Alaiz's elder brother, Turstin, was causing problems. There were dark rumours of his negotiating with Ivain's power-hungry legitimate cousin, Brion, and it had been decided that Alaiz must go and talk him out of whatever he was planning.

And so here we are, Alaiz thought miserably, *heading for Kittermere – like I'm going to be able to influence anybody!*

Gillies had become more of a friend over the last few years, and knew Alaiz's fear that there might be very little left of any family feeling to play on. She had therefore nobly volunteered to accompany Alaiz, but to her own detriment. The slim, dark-haired man on the headland was Amalric de Loges, current Grand Master of the Knights of Prydein, and as utterly besotted with Gillies as she was with him.

When Alaiz had first met Gillies, she had been in deep mourning for her prince, but time had softened even the loss of such a close relationship, and as Alaiz had grown into a young woman she had realized that Gillies was far from old. Yet while she was still of childbearing age there was no question of her being allowed to remarry for fear of further contenders for the throne.

That would have been regrettable under any circumstances, but from the moment Amalric had taken over as Grand Master from Hugh de Burh, and come to court to be introduced, the attraction between him and Gillies had been obvious. If her position was bad enough, his made it even worse. Most Grand Masters never married, and the few who had been were usually widowers by the time they took up office. The possibility of the Grand Master marrying the mother of the reigning sovereign was out of the question, and so the two snatched precious moments alone where they could. Now Gillies was leaving the court just as Amalric had returned, and Alaiz felt it was her fault that they were being deprived of the chance to be together even for a few minutes each day. So Gillies watched the headland hungrily as it slipped into the distance, and through tear-filled eyes Alaiz could see the tiny speck that was Amalric had not moved from his lonely vigil either.

Another part of her was also more than a little jealous, although she felt guilt-ridden that it should be so. At least Gillies had had a fulfilling relationship with Ivain's father, and now had someone who would miss her while she was gone. No matter how much she told herself not to be so feeble, Alaiz had become increasingly depressed over the last year or so. When they had been children, she and Ivain had been close playmates, all the more so because the little girl with all older brothers was quite happy to play boy's games rather than play with dolls. Then as they had come into their teens it had seemed very grown up that she was already married, when other girls her age were not even allowed unescorted in boys company.

But slowly she had begun to realize that she had missed out. For her there was no excited anticipation of social events, where prospective partners might be scrutinized and then discussed with friends – there was no point for her. Then the girls of the court began to get married, and there was all the excitement of the wedding to plan – but in her case it was over and done with when she was too small to remember anything, except being told to stop fidgeting, and that the cathedral had been cold and draughty.

To add insult to injury, Ivain had turned into a tall, well-built young man with sea-green eyes and dark brown hair, which, while not Gillies' dark rich auburn, still made him very handsome to most women's eyes. Alaiz, on the other hand, had been a skinny little girl who had turned into a willowy young woman, for whom the plunging necklines of the current court fashion did little. She too had green eyes, but of a paler hue and accompanied by dead-straight hair the colour of autumn beech leaves, only a few faded shades off her brothers' flaming ginger frizz. Where Gillies still turned heads wherever she went, Alaiz felt she could have disappeared into the wall-hangings and no one would have noticed, not even Ivain. And there lay the worst of her problems. While her feelings for him had warmed, his if anything had faded. He still seemed to think of her as his childhood companion, and their marriage was as chaste as the day they had met.

That was bad enough, but the court was now watching her like hawks for signs of a pregnancy. Nobody believed that nothing had happened between them and, for some strange reason, instead of thinking that he was not attracted to her, they blamed her for repulsing his affections. Alaiz was sure there were women he spent time with among the servants, and he had barely noticed when she had told him she was going away. Far from Amalric's romantic farewell, he had already gone hunting that morning before she had left, and so had not even said good-bye. Gazing at the waves below, Alaiz thought it was not possible to feel any more wretched than she already did.

She was so mesmerized by the water trailing beneath her she failed to notice that Gillies had turned from the window, and was now watching her in turn. Alaiz worried her. She was noticeably getting thinner and eating less, in part due to the frequent necessity of late of eating in public, when every mouthful was watched. Being more visible when there was a crisis might be good for public morale, but it was not helping Alaiz's at all. Gillies knew that there was a whole battery of old wives' tales about which food was good, or bad, for pregnancy, and Alaiz's every meal was inspected for signs she might be doing something wrong.

For all that Gillies loved her son dearly, at the moment she could have cheerfully strangled him. Her last attempt to persuade him to take notice of his wife had resulted in him not speaking to either of them in weeks, and she was at a complete loss to know what to do to help the girl she loved as her daughter. Even over food he had refused to consider not requesting the rich, heavily-spiced foods that he loved, for the more delicately flavoured dishes that Alaiz preferred, and unfortunately what he wanted was what everyone else ate in the great dining room.

If he was not careful, Gillies thought, come the winter Alaiz was likely to succumb to the first major sickness which came along and that might be the end of her, when no amount of being sorry would put things right. She felt sure that deep down he still cared about Alaiz, and that his indifference to her fate was partly because he too felt trapped by the lack of choice. Yet as a man he had the option of affairs as long as he kept them out of sight (not like his uncle). For the women there was no such release. Their behaviour had to be impeccable at all times, and if it was stressful for her at times, for Alaiz it was becoming obvious it had reached the point of being intolerable. What she needed was the chance to live her own life, regardless of Ivain.

It had been Amalric's idea to send Alaiz on this mission, and with Gillies' help the plan had been hatched to give Alaiz some breathing space away from the court. Not that either of the conspirators had any expectation that she would sway her brothers one hair's breadth from their chosen path, which was why Gillies had come along, so that no blame for failure would be attached to Alaiz. Secretly, she also hoped that with Alaiz gone, her son might either wake up to what he was losing, or that at least he would do something which might tarnish his golden image in the eyes of some of his senior advisers. The sycophantic admiration of some of the women was giving him delusions of his place in the grand scheme of things. Yet he had failed to see that some of the craftier schemers had found that dangling a pretty girl in front of him kept him out of their way while they took more and more control.

So from the capital of Trevelga they had travelled down to the port of Heller, which they had now recently left, and would make the trip south around the huge expanse of salt marshes which formed Prydein's southern region. Peat bogs gave way to salt marshes and then barely submerged mud banks which shifted treacherously with the tide, and many an unwary captain had found himself stranded for days. Yet with the right navigator it could be passed by swiftly. Once around the southern point, they would turn up the channel which separated Kittermere from Prydein and make their way to the port of Osraig. The urgency of their departure was the approaching equinox when the tide race between the two islands became treacherous. The southern route had been chosen, despite being more difficult to navigate, for with an experienced captain it was half the time the trip around Prydein would have taken, even if they had made the overland ride to the northern port of Treliever.

The captain proved to be as expert as he had claimed and they made good time in calm seas. Having spent her early childhood by the sea, Alaiz was at home on boats, and started to revive in the warm, sunny autumn weather, to Gillies' relief. Alaiz also began to eat the simple fish dishes the sailors served with a good deal more relish than Gillies had observed in a long time, and she was cautiously congratulating herself on the success of the first part of her plan.

Early on the third day they stood on the deck as the coast of Kittermere began to develop some definition on the horizon. But Gillies was looking westward in the direction of her own childhood home, the island of Rathlin, although Rathlin had fallen long ago under the control of rebels. The Attacotti were the native islanders of Rathlin and Kittermere, who had finally broken away from the control of the Island kingdom's more powerful members to regain control of Rathlin. Gillies herself was Attacotti, although her family had been one of those who had embraced Island culture so thoroughly they were indistinguishable from other Islanders, and as such had been driven from there by the rebels.

After all this time she was surprised at how much it still pulled at her, and she searched the horizon longingly for it while others only had eyes for Kittermere. That was why she was the one who suddenly realized that there were three galleys streaking across the waves towards them. There was no doubt they were Attacotti pirates. They were the only ones who still used the combination of a single massive sail and a great row of oars on either side, known as sweeps. Their use was limited in tricky conditions, but at a time like this, when they had the wind in the right direction and the tide with them, the speed they could produce was phenomenal.

Gillies yelled at the crew of their boat to alert them and the crew sprung to life. Every inch of sail was spread on the three masts, and sailors stood ready at the stays to trim the angle of them so that they could make the most of every breath of wind. Alaiz stood with her, gripping her hand as they watched the galleys gaining on them, despite the captain's best efforts.

"Trees preserve us!" Alaiz found herself praying softly over and over again. "I don't want to be a prisoner. I don't want to get raped!"

Within a couple of hours the vessels were close enough to hear the jeers of the Attacotti taunting their sailors as they tried to flee. The two women retreated below deck as the first mate began to hand round cutlasses to the crew, fearing that they would be more in the way than a help. Within moments, two thumps on either side announced the arrival of the pirates, and the noise rose to a deafening pitch as feet pounded across the deck above, coupled with shouts and the clash of cutlasses. In what seemed a frighteningly short time the noise subsided again, and they heard heavy boots on the steps down towards their cabin. The door burst open and the most villainous man either had ever seen seemed to fill the entire doorway.

"They'm down here!" he bellowed triumphantly back up to his companions, and turned to leer at the two petrified women. "Now my pretties, you're coming with us! Mad Magnus sent us 'specially to get you, and we don't want to disappoint him do we?"

Alaiz nearly passed out at this news. Magnus was the Attacotti leader, with a fearsome reputation. Mad as a hare for most of the time, he had flashes of lucidity when he was reputed to show a formidable intellect, and he had proven himself a talented raid leader, although some said he just had the luck of the Underworld. She could not imagine how he could have known about their specific movements, and thought that he must simply have sent out a raiding party when their sail had been spotted.

Gillies, however, felt her heart sinking. She had totally forgotten Magnus in her plans, but then she had never really expected him to carry a torch for her for all these years. Yet it looked suspiciously as though he might have had some informant send him a carrier bird when they left. Why else would the one boat carrying her, and no other valuable cargo which could be sold on, be stopped and boarded? And his men certainly seemed to know who they were looking for. The two of them were hustled up the stairs and hoisted unceremoniously over the side into a galley, where they were taken to the stern and sat on barrels under the guard of the villainous man they had first encountered. The pull back across the strait was taking a lot longer than it had for them to come out.

As night finally fell, they camped on a narrow beach on the far western tip of Kittermere. At first they had been too stunned to try to escape and after an hour in the biting wind, with no cover or cloak, they were too frozen to think of anything except huddling together for warmth. They were totally surrounded by the men, who did not even risk lighting a fire in case they were seen. Having rowed until nightfall made it treacherous to continue, the pirates only waited until the first glimpse of dawn before reloading their captives onto the boat again, and setting off to cross the current to reach Rathlin. Again night had fallen by the time they made it to the former fishing village Gillies had known as Farr, if anything even colder and more hungry than they had been the first night. It was all they could do to walk when they were prodded into getting off the boat, and they tottered numbly along the old quay towards a lit doorway.

It proved to be a former inn which had seen little change going by the number of drunken men it contained. The whistles and catcalls on their entry made both of them fear for their safety, but to their relief they were escorted up stairs to one of the bedrooms and the door locked after them. Within moments it was opened again, and a cowed elderly woman scuttled in with a rough tray containing two bowls of hot soup and some coarse bread, which she put on the only stool, before offloading the blankets she had draped over both arms onto the one bed. Without a single word she turned and scuttled back out, whereupon a grimy paw from a hidden guard reached out and slammed the door shut again. Gillies and Alaiz grabbed the blankets and wrapped them around their shivering shoulders, too cold to care whether they were lousy or not. They then got stuck in to the soup, which was surprisingly good and delightfully warming. By the time they had finished they were beginning to regain some feeling in their hands and feet, and had stopped shivering enough to be able to speak without their teeth chattering.

"Why would Magnus want us?" Alaiz asked tearfully.

"I don't think it's *us* he wants, I think it's me," Gillies replied ruefully.

"You? Why would Mad Magnus want you?" Alaiz countered in utter astonishment.

"Ah …well, you see …em, he used to be my sweetheart."

"Your *what*?" Alaiz realized she was beginning to sound like a cage-bird repeating her friend's words like this, but she was so stunned she couldn't think of anything else to say. "You *knew* him?"

"Oh, it was a long, long time ago. Way before I met Ivain's father. Back then Magnus was just the local bad boy on Rathlin … but he was very handsome …" Her voice trailed off wistfully, obviously lost in pleasant memories for a moment. "My parents disapproved of course, but we used to sneak off to the fishermen's huts where he lived. It seemed *so* romantic at sixteen and I was heartbroken when they finally put a stop to it. I thought I'd never recover until I met Ivain's father, which just goes to show how things change! After that I never gave Magnus a thought until the Attacotti started being much more successful, and word got out that they'd got a new leader.

"Oh, at first I didn't connect the two people, until word came to me at Trevelga that when Kylesk, my home village, was hit by a raid there was this man questioning everyone as to where I was. What surprised me more was that that seemed to be a turning point, because the local people were spared. Afterwards it was only ever non-Rathliners who were killed by the raiders, and the word the spies brought back to Trevelga said that this Magnus had united all the Rathlin rebels under one leader for the first time. But then Magnus always was charismatic! Of course the court was interested in him because the rebels united were far more dangerous than lots of splinter groups all off doing their own thing."

"I remember Grand Master Hugh saying it gave them an army to match ours." Alaiz said thoughtfully, also trying to bring the Knights into the conversation, even if it was by mentioning Amalric's revered predecessor. For no reason she could put her finger on she was deeply bothered by Gillies' reminiscences of this Magnus. She appeared to have a very different view of him from the one Alaiz had heard from Master Hugh, who had always seemed to have a very perceptive grip on what was going on in the world outside Prydein.

Alaiz desperately wished she could see the former Knights' leader at this moment. He had made it a personal task to instruct the young future queen once he had found her an intelligent and willing student, and for Alaiz he had become a surrogate father figure for the one she had lost. Now she would have given anything to have him walk in and take over. Gillies seemed suddenly to be more of a stranger than Alaiz would have thought possible, and it worried her that the faithful and devoted Amalric had been forgotten for the romantic image of some long past love, who now probably bore no resemblance to the person she once knew. Certainly all Alaiz's information led her to think that this Magnus was little more than a deranged thug, and that they might be in far more danger than Gillies seemed to want to believe.

Wrapping herself tightly in her blanket, Alaiz rolled onto the bed and tried to get some sleep, while Gillies went and peered out of the tiny window at the sea. Sheer exhaustion must have taken over, because the next thing Alaiz knew it was morning and the strange serving woman had returned with a breakfast of crusty bread and rather watery caff. She was quite relieved that they had hardly had time to eat before being bundled out of the inn and back on board the boat again, which meant they had no chance to speak in private, and even Gillies was not prepared to speak openly in front of the pirates. Mercifully they were allowed to keep the blankets, and as they were travelling close to the shore, in the warmth of the day they did not freeze this time.

Alaiz had expected it to be another slow pull, but the morning tide was with them, as was the wind. Before midday they shot along at a great rate, and even afterwards, when the tide turned, with the wind and the sweeps out they made good progress as they came gradually around from the eastern coast of Rathlin to the north. As the sky became filled with a blood-red sunset, she realized that they were in a wide bay with a castle on each headland. Gillies could no longer restrain her excitement.

"This was my home, Alaiz!" she exclaimed. "That castle you see on the southern headland with the village around it is Reiff, and the northern castle is Droman, but look, we're coming into Kylesk!"

Her outstretched hand pointed to a large cluster of buildings at the mouth of the river they could see winding down from the high rolling hills of the island. She had stood up and was now eagerly leaning over the side, which Alaiz was surprised to see their guard doing nothing to stop. With the wind ripping her makeshift blanket-cloak open and whipping her auburn hair into clouds of red, framing her face flushed with anticipation, Gillies looked stunningly beautiful. She almost ran to the prow of the ship and leaned out giving the galley a live figurehead as it raced into its home port.

A crowd had gathered at the quay, but as the sweeps backstroked to slow them and guide them in, the crowd parted like a wave for a figure dressed in swirling brown plaids. Tall and muscular with a mane of long jet black hair, and a cropped beard to match, he exuded a charisma that was almost visible.

"Gillies my love!" he roared as they docked, and reached out to sweep her off the prow and onto the quay. Personally, Alaiz thought this a bit over dramatic considering they had not seen one another in nearly thirty years, but Gillies was acting like she was sixteen, and disappeared into the crowd in his embrace.

"Come on, you!" one of the sailors prodded Alaiz into moving, and she was marched with much less ceremony in the wake of the crowd who had followed their leader. She was shoved into yet another poky bedroom and provided with another fishy stew like the previous night's, into which she miserably dunked her leaden bread. She had the feeling she might regret ever having wished for fish stew while faced with the spicy dishes at court. Too much of anything could make it pale with repetition. In a life of being tossed around by fate, she thought she had never felt quite so much the useless pawn as she did tonight. From the window she could see nothing, and so shut the shutters against the night chill which was seeping in. Curled up on the bed she waited for some sign of Gillies, but at some point drifted off to sleep feeling utterly worthless.

Come the morning there was still no sign of Gillies, and it dawned on her that if she was ever going to get out of here she was going to have to do it herself. Cautiously she tried the door, which to her amazement came open. She peered around the door jamb into the corridor, but could see nobody. From somewhere down below there was the sound of a riotous assembly. Creeping out, she tiptoed to the top of the staircase which seemed to turn several times on its way down. Glancing frequently upwards as well as down, she made her way to each landing in turn, only to find her way blocked when she got to the last but one bend and peered round the corner. The stairs came out half way along a wide open hall which was packed with men, women and children all dressed in endless variations on the Island's brown plaids. Realizing there was no way out here, she was about to retreat back up the stairs and try another route when, to her horror, she heard Gillies call her name. With a sinking heart she turned to see Gillies seated on the dais at the head of the room, next to the man she had disappeared with the previous night.

There was nothing she could do but go down now. Picking her way cautiously through the crowd, she found herself being directed to the dais, until she stood at its base. Steeling herself inwardly she looked upwards. Gillies was positively glowing, with a beaming smile which Alaiz could not find it in herself to return.

"Come here, girl!" Magnus had a resonant voice with a heavy local accent, but with a deep, lyrical lilt. Close to she could see that as a young man he must have been stunningly pretty, for, even with various battle scars and the lines which came with a life spent often at sea being chafed by the wind, he was still someone to turn heads. Together he and Gillies made a stunning couple – him all smouldering darkness and her shining like a fiery sunset. He sat with one leg nonchalantly draped over the arm of the great dragon-carved, wooden chair that dominated the dais, with an arm flung over the back with which he airily beckoned Alaiz forward. On trembling legs, Alaiz mounted the steps and went to stand before the two of them. This close to she realized Magnus had mismatched eyes, one blue and one brown, made even more disconcerting by the way they were darting everywhere and nowhere at once.

"My beloved Gillies tells me you're her companion," he purred. "Well she doesn't need a companion now! She has me!" He was suddenly all focused and alert in the way an animal could go from slumber to readiness to pounce in a heartbeat. In a fluid movement he was no longer reclining but leaning forward, with his hands on the chair arms as if to power off at the slightest provocation. Alaiz swallowed nervously.

"So what are we to do with you?" Magnus mused.

The eyes suddenly slid off her again and were darting across the crowd.

"What shall we do with her?" he bellowed out to them, causing Alaiz to jump in fright at the sudden switch.

He laughed uproariously, leapt to his feet and clasped her to him with one massive arm, while he held the other up to silence the torrent of ribald suggestions which were coming from the floor.

"Now, now, lads, don't all rush at once! This is a lady not some dockyard whore! Who will fight for her hand? We must show these ladies we can be as chivalrous as those peacocks on Prydein. I propose a tournament for my wedding feast, and you're all invited!" A roar rose from the floor again at this. "Tomorrow, on the beach, the best of my warriors will compete in a show of arms! First blood only! Can't have our girl's bridegroom missing his wedding tackle, eh?" Uproarious laughter from the crowd again. "How better to reward my best fighter, eh? My beloved's handmaiden for their own! So tomorrow you will show her what you're worth!"

Alaiz thought she might faint. Where on the Islands had he got the idea that she was Gillies' servant? And married? To one of those thugs? Had Gillies not told him she was already married, and to Gillies' son? Her head was spinning, not least because Magnus was so powerful she had been jerked around like a rag doll every time he made another expansive gesture, and she almost had her nose pressed into his armpit, smothering her in his odour. Suddenly he let her go and she sank to the floor gasping for breath. Gillies leant down from her seat beside the dragon throne and grasped her shoulder.

"Isn't he magnificent!" she breathed. "Now listen! Not a word of Ivain! If they find out who you are he'll be a lot less kind."

Alaiz could not imagine how marrying her off to some random barbarian constituted 'kind'!

"Now you'll find out what a real man's like!" Gillies whispered breathlessly. "Spirits but I'd forgotten what it's like! What a night Alaiz! You wait, you'll see things differently in a couple of days!"

Alaiz cringed miserably at the thought. What in the Islands was Gillies thinking of, spending the night with such a man? And 'forgotten'? This sounded as though there had been far more than a teenage crush in the past! As for a 'real man', whatever she had dreamed of for herself it was not that! She had to get away!

"But what about Amalric?" she whispered back in a desperate attempt to jolt Gillies back to reality.

Instead all she got was a derisive snort.

"Who do you think set us up? Magnus told me it was from someone very close to us that he got the news that we were setting out. Who else knew as much as Amalric? He was obviously just toying with me, pretending to court me, and anyway, how could that have come to anything? He must have known we could never marry."

All Alaiz could do was shake her head in denial. She could not believe – whoever else might have betrayed them – that it could be Amalric, if only because his honour was the touchstone of his life, and such duplicity would have been contrary to all he believed in. For her, Amalric's devotion was all the more deep because he could not marry, and had to settle for finding other ways to show how much he cared. In Prydein, Gillies had never been under any illusions that a wedding could have taken place, and it had not stopped her actively encouraging Amalric's attentions. He certainly had not had to force himself into her company or act his attachment.

"Oh and by the way," Gillies was continuing, "it's already too late to go to your brothers. Magnus also told me they've left Osraig to join with Duke Brion at his castle at Mullion. They're going to Trevelga in force to demand a role in governing Prydein."

"What about Ivain?" Alaiz asked frantically, "what about your son?"

"Oh, Magnus's spy says he won't be hurt." Gillies airily dismissed the problem. "Their argument is with the government, not him, and if he needs sanctuary, which he won't, Magnus says he can come here."

Alaiz's head was spinning again. How could Gillies be so naive? All this was coming simply from Magnus, and if ever a man had an ulterior motive it was him. If it kept Gillies sweet it was obvious he would lie through his teeth. Even if Magnus was right that the nobles of Kittermere were backing the other legitimate heir to Prydein, why would they leave Ivain alone when he would be a focus for resistance to them?

Master Hugh had told her long ago that Brion was a very different man from his late father, and was totally devoid of scruples. As far as Brion was concerned, he was the better man to rule. Ivain's love of culture and cooperation with the Church were just signs of fatal weakness, and lack of backbone to do whatever was necessary to take Prydein back to prominence among the Island politics. No, Ivain would never be allowed to leave unharmed, and if he did come here, she felt sure that he would disappear without Gillies ever knowing he had landed.

"I need air!" she gulped.

"Come on, then, let's walk by the sea." Gillies took her by the arm and led her out of the hall, Magnus having disappeared off somewhere in a haze of male pheromones. Outside the day was drizzly and dank, with the sea clouded in a heavy mist. In the less smoky light of day Alaiz thought Gillies' eyes were unnaturally bright with the pupils huge pools of darkness, and her steps were not as steady as normal. Gillies quickly decided that they should not linger in the chill, but it gave Alaiz an idea. Back in the hall she pleaded to be allowed to go and lie back down to help a headache, and as Magnus had reappeared, Gillies was content to let her go.

Back in her room Alaiz flung the shutters open and leaned as far out as she could. There had been an odd smell in the hall, and she was wondering whether some form of narcotic herbs were being burned, so maybe that was why Gillies was so befuddled? Perhaps it was just as well she had not been taken down there earlier. At least she could still think straight, and it was obvious that she had to find a way back at all costs. If only she could get to Amalric or Hugh they could advise her what to do, but they had to know what had happened. With a sinking heart she realized there was no hope of getting Gillies to come with her. Nor was there any way she could trick her into leaving, for a sure as night followed day she would find a way to get them noticed at the first opportunity. No, she was on her own now.

Watching the scene, below she realized the mist was getting worse not better, but down by the quay she spotted a fishing boat getting ready to sail. Turning back into the room she spotted a wooden chest and went to investigate the contents. Inside she found a well-worn, woollen knitted tunic and tightly-woven woollen pants, equally old but properly laundered before they had been packed away. She realized that they were probably made for an older boy, but that they would fit her well enough for her to pass as one too. Grabbing three of the heavy woollen blankets off the bed and making a bundle of the clothes in them she went to the door and listened. Nothing. Easing the door open she crept out and took the opposite way to the hall.

Sure enough there was another staircase that once upon a time must have been for the servants of the lord who had this manor built. Had this once even been Gilles' actual home? Was that another reason she was so keen to stay?

Taking each step carefully to avoid creaking noises, she slipped down to the bottom, where she could hear the noise of the midday meal being prepared on the other side of the kitchen partition. Peaking around it in little darting glances, she waited until everyone was facing away and then shot across the opening and eased the latch on the back door. Quickly slipping out, she closed the door again softly.

So far so good, she was outside and alone! Keeping her head down imitating a servant on an errand, she hurried down towards the lesser quays where the small working boats were tied up. Behind an upturned rowing boat, she pulled off her dress and donned her borrowed clothing, and tucked her long hair down the inside of the tunic to hide its length. She thought about leaving the dress behind, but then realized that once they started looking for her it would be quickly found and then would search for anyone in a possible disguise. So she bundled it up in the blankets.

Without any trouble she found the fishing boat, and noted with satisfaction that the men had left it unattended while they went for their meal. It was an easy matter to climb aboard and sneak along the deck. To her delight, she found the boat was stuffed with wooden crates of smoked fish which the Islanders had prepared, and were about to ship out to Kittermere and Prydein. Even the Rathliners needed money, and the smoked fish was their only export. For once being skinny paid off as she wormed her way into narrow gaps that a grown man would never have managed, until she was deep within the packing cases and far from view. A knife left on the deck came with her, and once she had buried herself away, she used it to hack her hair as short as a lad's. With the brown blankets over her she was near invisible in the dimly lit shadows of the crates.

Shortly afterwards the sound of feet on deck proclaimed the arrival of the crew, and the sounds of orders being issued and a rocking of the boat announced they were getting under way. Once or twice she saw a shadow fall across her hiding place as someone went by, but nobody came any closer. As night fell the movements of the crew became less and then ceased.

Risking a glance, she eased herself up until she could just see over the top of the crates and saw a lone lantern swinging at the wheel as the steersman kept his lonely vigil. As he was looking away from her, she risked moving a little along the gap, and realized that the bundles near to him were the other crew wrapped in their blankets asleep. She carefully worked her way back, and ever so gently let the dress with the locks of hair slip over the side of the boat into the inky waves of the boat's wake. Now all evidence was gone, and she could try to pass herself as a boy seeking adventure or escaping a miserable home life if she was caught. Tucking herself up in the blankets again, she allowed herself to doze through the night and wait for the morning.

As dawn broke, she saw the coast of Kittermere close by. They were evidently not risking the sound between the islands but were passing the northern coast. In her haste to leave Alaiz had had no chance to grab food or water, and also by now her bladder was bursting. She had been hoping for an early landfall on her home island, but that now looked unlikely. The only thing in her favour was that it seemed as though there were only four crew members, and the tricky currents were keeping them fully occupied with steering and navigating. As they fought the two sails during a particularly strong gust of wind, she managed to move to a gap between the crates further back in the stern where there was a hole in the side where the ropes to tie up to the quays could go. During the next flurry of activity she managed to relieve herself at this gully, which solved one problem but did nothing to ease her hunger and thirst.

It took until the coming night for her to seize a hunk of bread, put down by the youngest member of the crew, who was then teased mightily by the others for letting a seagull steal his food. On hands and knees she managed to edge forward and slide a water flask back towards her, and although it was only half full she drank its contents greedily. She toyed with holding on to it, but decided they would be more likely to think it misplaced than lost overboard, and the last thing she wanted was for them to start searching.

By the next morning they were rounding a rocky headland at the northern end of the dividing sound between Kittermere and Prydein. The isolated Knight's castle of Bittern was glimpsed on the top of the cliffs, and for a while Alaiz thought she might even be lucky enough for the boat to be heading into the busy port of Treliever. That hope was soon dashed, though, as she realized she had never seen an Attacotti boat there, and the boat began to change course, coming much too close into the coast to be able to clear the rocks which protruded out into the northeast end of Treliever Bay. Instead they were obviously heading round into the closer fishing port of Boddigo, and by the evening it lay just off the bows, where Alaiz could see a few boats were still tied up.

In an awful flash it came to her that having got onto this boat, she had no idea how she was going to get off. She had relied on the assumption that they would come into a busy dock where she could slip off and be lost in the crowd in seconds, even if she was spotted. Here, the quay was deserted and she would be apprehended in a second. The boat bumped up against the quay, and she shrank into the shadows as a sailor came to the bundle of rope by her hideaway. He looked huge this close to and her heart began racing. What was she to do?

Chapter 7

The Tolling Of Bells

Prydein: Harvest-moon

Alaiz shrank as far into the shadows as she could, and was sure the sailor would see her at any moment, but her luck held. As he bent to pick up the rope, someone called to him and so he faced away from her. She felt the boat bump against the quay, and saw his arm come up as he moved to the opposite side to her to throw the rope to someone on the quayside. The voice on the dock was calling urgently, and then to Alaiz's surprise she heard the men hurrying off the boat. All she could make out was something about the mist, which made no sense at all. Whatever it was, though, the sailors were gone and she risked a hesitant peak over the side of the boat. The men were being ushered across the quay by locals, going by their dress, who were making gestures to the hills where tendrils of thick fog were descending to the town. To Alaiz's astonishment there was not a soul around. At this time of the evening she would have expected the place to be a hive of activity, but not a thing stirred. There were not even any wagons hitched up and waiting to be loaded.

Totally mystified, she realized that whatever it was it had played into her hands. As the door to the large inn at the end of the quay closed on the group of men, she slipped like a ghost over the side of the boat and made a dash for the nearest pile of crates and drying nets. In little sprints from shadow to shadow, she made it to the end of the quay and then along the waterfront, until she spied a stable and heard the familiar snuffling and stamping of horses. She might not have had much experience of this sort of thing, but she did know that stables were normally warm places, and tonight she could not wait to bury herself in warm soft straw after two nights huddled amongst smelly fish crates. Flitting across the street, she found the side door and slipped into the stable, and then stood still, having closed the door, while she waited for her eyes to adjust to the deeper darkness inside.

Slowly she began to make out the outlines of the separate stalls and that there was a ladder in front of her heading up to the hay loft. That was what she wanted, but first she carefully walked the length of the stable keeping well back from the ends of the stalls. Partly this was out of experience of keeping well out of the way of any horse which happened to have a habit of kicking, but also because she was terrified of kicking something like a bucket and startling the horses into making a noise which might bring someone out. At the end she found what she had hoped for, a small table which had brushes and combs waiting for use on it, but also some rather withered apples and carrots as treats for the horses.

Mentally apologizing to the horses for stealing their food, she pocketed the eatable ones and then shuffled her way back to the ladder. Climbing up into the loft, she equally carefully edged her way over the few exposed boards and then crawled deep into the stacked hay. Even if someone came up for hay in the morning before she had had chance to get out, the likelihood of their needing to move that much hay down below was so remote it guaranteed her a refuge.

Between her blankets and the hay, within a few minutes she was warmer than she had been for days, and it was all she could do to keep her eyes open while she nibbled on her pocketed meal. It was far from substantial, but it stopped the dreadful growling from her stomach. Just as she was sliding into a deep and peaceful sleep there came an ear-piercing wail followed by a dreadful shriek. Then came the pounding of heavy hooves going at a full gallop, and a man's voice bellowing for help. Totally alert now, she strained her ears and realized that the sound of the horses was accompanied by the sound of wagon wheels. Someone was charging into the town as though the Wild Hunt was on his heels.

The wheels and hooves got closer, and then as they seemed almost on top of the stable, she heard the driver calling to the horses to stop, and the screeching of the wagon brake being thrown on hard. The man was calling for someone to help him, but nobody seemed to be answering him. Alaiz crawled to the edge of the loft and peered down through the trap door to try to make some sense of what she was hearing, which was how she got caught in the lantern light as the door got thrown open.

"Holy Spirits, help me someone, please!" the man begged calling into the stable, then looked up and saw her before she could pull back. "Please! You there, boy, please come and help me at least get my horses in here safe."

"What's going on?" Alaiz asked, as she reluctantly came down the ladder.

"There's something hunting in the fog," the man said, as he propped the door open and went to grab the head of the nearest horse. She realized he had not let go of the reins, and by the way the horse's eyes were rolling, if he had it would have bolted in a second. He went and stood in front of the team of two.

"If I hold their heads can you uncouple them from the wagon?" he asked Alaiz.

"What do I do?" she asked, totally ignorant of the workings of couplings.

The man gestured to where the chains from the horses' harness ended at a wide bar.

"You see that big loop? That's a pin. When I get them back can you pull it up? Then lift the bar so I can lead them straight into the stables. We'll undo the harnesses once we're inside."

She nodded and warily climbed onto the box of the wagon, letting herself down so that she could reach the coupling that connected it to the harness. For a second he just about got both animals to ease the tension off and she managed to pull the pin out, seeing that it lifted the two pieces apart. Without waiting to secure the wagon in any way, the man ran them into the stable and, as Alaiz scampered in behind him, slammed the door shut.

"Thank you, lad," he wheezed as he gasped for air. By the light of the lantern which he had put on a hook on the ladder, Alaiz could see that he was a middle-aged man, with receding hair and an expanding waist. He certainly did not look threatening. In fact he looked as scared as his horses. With shaking hands he was separating them out, and Alaiz took the first one he managed to uncouple and led it into the first stall, which was empty. She suddenly realized what was nagging at the back of her mind. Whenever she had travelled she rarely went into stables herself, but the stalls were normally filled from the door backwards to make for ease of getting the animals out. Here, though, the other horses were as far from the door as they could get, as if the doorway was unsafe.

"I'll pay your master in the morning as long as someone doesn't rob me as well," he said when the second horse was tied up.

Alaiz was torn between letting him think she was the stable boy here and admitting the truth. The latter won and she told him she too had come in out of the cold night, inventing a story about having been on her first fishing trip and being so sick she did not want to go back. The man was too distraught to question her hard and instead introduced himself as Bradley, a carter from Trevelga.

"I've been on the road for days now," he told her. "Nothing unusual in that – I do it several times a year. I come up here and drop off a wagon load of wool cloth, and pick up a load of fish to take back to the capital. Well it was alright up to Trenhaile. You know Trenhaile?"

Alaiz assured him she did indeed know the prosperous little town, which lay at the southern foot of the hills that formed a band across the northwest of Prydein.

"Well, I stopped for the night at the *Mucky Duck* like I always do, 'cause they have a decent-sized stable yard and I can get the wagon in there, see? I went into the taproom and there's this strange man sitting on his own at the table in the corner, but I didn't have much choice 'cause the place was packed, and so I had to join him. Right strange he was. Big tall man, bald as an egg, with this funny way of looking at folks. When the food came he gave the girl a right tongue lashing, said he didn't eat dead things. What a funny way of talking about meat? Wasn't her fault anyway, so I told him to stop it and he should have asked for what he wanted instead of taking it out on some poor lass doing her best. I wish now I'd said nothing. He gave me this filthy look and said I'd pay for my impudence. At the time I thought it was just hot air … you know, some of these folks get daft ideas they're really something they're not.

"Anyway he got up and left, but when my food came no sooner had I started eating it then all of a sudden it was crawling with maggots. I called the lass over and she nearly screamed the place down when she saw it. Luckily I know the landlord and his wife, and they cleared it away and I said I'd not say anything to harm their reputation. But then in the morning the stranger had left, and without paying his bill. Nothing I could do about that, I thought, so I paid up and carried on my way. It was as we got to the top of the first big hill, I'm sure I saw him striding out over the bracken, 'cause I saw the sun shining off his bald head. And he was wearing some strange sort of cloak that looked too flimsy to be of any use, but kept blending into the heather so you'd think he'd just disappeared for a second.

"I'd have thought it was my eyes playing tricks, but then I saw him stand and wait, and the next thing I knew there was this small army of riders coming up to meet him from over Mullion way. Well I don't normally use the whip on my two girls, but one sight of them and I was chivvying them along as fast as they could go on that hill. I was just going over the crest of the next rise when I looked back and saw him watching me! I tell you I kept them going as fast as we could until I was sure they weren't following me. Then when I got to Treliever they said he'd been there too, and since then there'd been some strange fogs about, and the shepherds were coming down complaining about something hunting their flocks in the fog. I'm not a fanciful man, but I'd been sure ever since the last sight of that stranger that I was being followed. Until Treliever I thought it was just some army scout making sure I didn't turn and tell someone what I'd seen, but when I saw that fog coming up tonight I was glad we were on the downhill run already."

"Is that why the people are all indoors here?" Alaiz asked.

"Expect so," Bradley said. "Normally they're real friendly here. I've never known it be like this before. I'm dreading the trip back as well."

Alaiz had a moment of inspiration.

"Can I come with you?" she asked. "If the fog's here, I haven't anywhere to hide except this stable, and they're sure to find me sooner or later, and I don't want to go back on that boat. At least you didn't hear of the fog until you were over this side of the hills."

Bradley agreed to pass her off as his apprentice, come the morning, as she had been the only one willing to come outside to help him save his horses, which he loved like his family. They took themselves up to the loft to wait out the night, but neither of them found they could sleep.

In the morning the townspeople were up and about once it was clear that there was no fog around. Nobody questioned whether Alaiz had arrived with Bradley, and the boat crew did not seem to have noticed her presence even when they began offloading the crates. The trader who took the cloth from the wagon gave a half-hearted apology for nobody coming to help the night before, but it was obvious that the whole town was terrified and that nothing would have persuaded them out of doors once the weather had closed in. However, the innkeeper did not charge Bradley for the night they had spent in the stables, not even for the horses' feed, and they were prevailed upon to spend a proper night at the inn so that they could set off at dawn the next day.

Although she was desperate to get back to the capital, Alaiz also knew that it would be safer travelling with someone, and quicker on the wagon than on foot. She also could not risk drawing attention to herself by being too eager to get away. The army Bradley had seen had to be Brion and his men, so it was too late to warn the capital now – they would be there. The best thing she could do would be to get into the city without being conspicuous, and try to reach the Knights; for if Brion got the slightest whiff that she was acting against him, it would be only too easy to make her disappear out here where nobody knew who she really was.

After a day hauling bales and boxes, she found herself ravenous for the evening meal, especially having not eaten much for days. To her joy and delight the platter which got brought out for her and Bradley to share had a huge hunk of pie but, best of all, loads of fresh vegetables piled high with just a knob of butter coating them. She happily let Bradley eat the spicy meat but devoured the vegetables until she thought she might burst. Washed down with a weak beer it was the best meal she could remember in years. Deeply contented, she went upstairs to the room they were sharing and collapsed on the little truckle bed, leaving the main one for Bradley when he came up from the bar. She was so exhausted she barely heard him come in before falling fast asleep again.

They were called early in the morning by the stable boy, but Alaiz felt better than she had in days and was willing to help him get the horses hitched. She was far from expert in the matter and had to be shown how to do everything, but managed to deflect the lad's curious questions. Luckily Bradley was soon out and helping, and they swigged mugs of steaming caff as they worked, taking hot bread rolls from the first bake of the day to eat on the way instead of waiting for breakfast in the inn. The day was chilly and dull, but the cloud was high and pale with no sign of possibly closing in, so they set off straight away.

The journey of the next three days was uneventful, and Bradley proved to be a cheerful companion who kept Alaiz amused with an endless string of tales about his family and friends, leaving no room for her to have to invent a past for herself. By the time they were leaving Coombe, for the final leg into Trevelga on the fourth day, Alaiz was becoming quite expert at hitching the horses, and had learnt the basics of how to drive the team as well. She was actually thinking that she would be very sorry to have to stop this pretend life – it was so much less complicated than her own. Despite mulling things over and over she still was not sure how she could change anything, and the news they had picked up in the inn the night before was not good.

The talk in the bar had said that Brion was in control of the capital and that he had Ivain prisoner. Alaiz wanted desperately to get to see Ivain and reassure him that she was working to help him, but she could not think of a way to get to him without giving herself away. If that happened she just knew she would end up imprisoned with him, so she was going to have to trust to the Knights to get him out once she had found them. That could be a problem, given that she had never really walked around the capital to find where things were in relation to one another. She had always been escorted out to places and then back, often doing more than one in a day. So all she knew were the ceremonial routes, which were the very things she thought she should avoid.

By midday they were outside the great walls of the city, and Alaiz could see that people were thronging in. The gates were always busy, but this seemed unusual even by market day standards, and that was not until tomorrow. As they joined the press to get in, Bradley called to another wagoner to find out what was going on.

"A summons by the new king, is all I know," the man said. "The criers were out all yesterday telling people to come to the main square today where there'd be a proclamation for all to hear. No idea what though."

Alaiz did not like the sound of that. Brion must be very sure of his position if he was calling himself king already.

When they got through the gate she thanked Bradley profusely for everything he had done to help her, but asked if he would mind if she went to try to find a friend who could give her a bed. He was very reluctant to let her go, but in the end agreed on the condition that she memorized his address, and promised to come and find him if she could not find her friend. To her amazement he told her he had realized she was a girl on the first day, but, because he had daughters of his own, thought it must have been something dreadful to have made her run away and so thought to keep her safe.

"My wife would never forgive me if I let any harm come to some poor girl in distress," he told her earnestly. "Now you be careful. There's some right villains in this place and they'll be out in force taking advantage of the crowd to lift purses, and anything else they think has value, so watch your back. Remember, we're the second house off Corn Market Lane, and there's a bed there if you need it."

Alaiz could not help but give him a hug for this, and felt very choked as she got down and took the main road away from him into the centre of the city. She had forgotten that there were real people like that in the world, away from all the political intrigues at court.

It seemed to take forever to walk the route up the wide main street she normally rode along, where the markets were held twice a week, and on to the huge square in front of the palace. The closer she got, the tighter the press of the crowd, until she was almost being carried along without her feet on the ground. Finally, there seemed to be no more movement, and she managed to wriggle sideways so that she had one of the great town houses to her back, and was not being squashed quite so hard. She had made it to the square just about, although she was as far back as it was possible to be.

Clutching at some of the ornate wood carvings on the house behind her, she managed to pull herself up and get a foothold so that she could see over the heads of the crowd in front. To her amazement, there seemed to have been some sort of wooden platform put up right at the palace door, obscuring the door itself but almost touching the first-floor balcony above it.

The bell of the cathedral on the eastern side of the square tolled three times, and then the door to the balcony opened and Brion stepped out onto it, flanked by Turstin and a weird pallid man who could only be Bradley's stranger. A scared hush fell over the crowd so that all that could be heard was the odd rustle of cloth and nervous cough. Brion stepped forward and began to speak in a voice that carried almost unnaturally across the space.

"My dear Islanders, I called you here so that you could witness justice being done. I can't tell you how much it pains me to have to do this. You've all heard by now that, along with some loyal, true nobles, I took control of the palace four days ago, but not *why*. It came to my notice that some within the palace had been negotiating with the Attacotti." He paused for effect. "Not for trade, which would still be a betrayal of those who have died at the hands of those vicious scum, but something even worse." A gasp ran through the crowd. "My weak and devious cousin was planning to allow them into the country because he couldn't be bothered to fight them!" The crowd howled in horror, and Alaiz too, but in disbelief at such lies.

"My friends," Brion continued, "we cannot allow such a thing to happen. *I* could not allow such a thing to happen, and so I acted. But to my horror, once we took over the palace we found things were worse. Much, much worse. The corrupt royal family have been running this great Island of ours into the ground for years. But I believe justice must be seen to be done. I'd not have you think that *I'd* held back from doing what must be done, because the worst perpetrator is my cousin. No! If the most humble man amongst you would have to pay the price for such treachery, then so must the greatest. Treason would cost any one of you his life, and treason has been done." He turned back and called into the palace. "Let the prisoner be brought out."

The palace door must have been opened, for suddenly there was movement at the base of the platform. Four guards came up holding a tall young man between them. Alaiz felt sick. There was no doubt whom they were escorting, even though his head had been shaved and he had several days' growth of beard. Ivain was led to the centre of the platform where there was a block of wood and was made to kneel behind it, then someone put a bag over his head. Another man came up onto the platform this time clutching a fearsome battle axe.

"King Ivain," Brion proclaimed, "you have been charged and found guilty of treason against your people. You have betrayed the trust placed in you. You have plotted with this Island's enemies to bring it down for your own profit. I therefore sentence you to the same punishment as a common criminal. Death!"

He gave a terse nod to the man with the axe, who had been watching him. Two of the guards took Ivain's arms and pulled him forward so that his head was on the block, while the other two held his legs. The executioner stepped up and swung the blade far above his head to bring it down straight onto Ivain's neck.

The crowd went berserk. Women screamed, men called out, others passed out, and suddenly everyone was trying to get out of the square as quickly as possible. The executioner picked up the head which was now free of the bag. Without the hair he had to dangle it by the ear, held aloft for all to see. Brion was saying more, but this time nobody was taking the slightest notice. As the crowd poured out of the square, he finished his speech and turned to retreat back into the palace. Turstin followed him, but for a moment the stranger stayed and watched the crowd, and through her tears Alaiz could have sworn she saw him throw back his head and laugh.

Only minutes later she was alone except for those who had fainted, or had been crushed and had not come around yet. She slid to the floor and sat with her head buried in her arms and sobbed as though she would never stop. Quite how long she had been there, rocking in almost catatonic shock she had no idea, but at some point the monks came out of the monastery attached to the cathedral, and began to tend to the shocked and crushed. Alaiz found herself being lifted up and taken into the infirmary, where a kindly brother wrapped a blanket around her shaking shoulders, and another pressed a hot, sweetened chamomile tea into her hands.

Time stood still for her for the rest of the day. She was too numb with shock to think about what had happened. All she kept seeing was the scene being played over and over in her mind. To think she had been so angry with him before she left. Now she would never have the chance to sit and play dice with him, or laugh over things they had done as children. How could this have been done to Ivain? Was there nobody in the court who spoke up for him? Where were the Knights? More to the point where was Amalric? What would Gillies do when she realized that her son was dead? Would she still be so besotted with Magnus then? It sounded as though it was not Ivain but Brion who had been negotiating with the Attacotti rebels.

It was dark when she became aware that the great bells were tolling again, but this time they went on and on and on. Moreover, she became aware that every one of the many churches in the city was tolling its bells in unison with the cathedral's. The monks were ushering all those who could manage it towards the internal door to the cathedral, and Alaiz let herself be taken along. When they got inside she could only gasp at the sight. Every possible candle holder had been filled and lit. Something she had never seen before, even for the few state services.

Equally unprecedented was the mass of people inside. The cathedral was huge and even on state occasions seemed to dwarf the people in it, but not tonight. Those monks not helping with the people, and all the novices and choristers, lined the clearstory balcony and were singing the mass for the dead, their voices amplified by the stone walls into waves of sound that filled the air. From the front doors, which stood wide open, came an endless procession of ordinary people who were coming in to pray. They were being directed to the side altars to each of the five Sacred Trees on the left, or those of the four Sacred Martyrs along the right hand aisle, before returning down the nave after praying at the main altar where the bishop, the abbot and the prior, with other office-holders of the church, were on their knees.

One name hit her at every turn.

"Spirits bless King Ivain."

"Sacred Trees protect King Ivain."

"Merciful Spirits hold King Ivain in your embrace."

The litanies went on and on, every person in their own way registering their shock and horror at what had been done that day. If Alaiz had wondered how such a thing could have been allowed to happen, this made her realize that the blame lay solely at Brion's feet. This was no act on behalf of the people. If one thing came across, it was that Ivain had been much more popular with the ordinary folk of his land than he had ever been at court. Whatever the truth of what had happened behind the palace doors, it was clear that the people would never have sanctioned the beheading, and Brion had acted with such speed because he knew he was on shaky ground.

As someone was overcome with emotion nearby, and her escort went to help, Alaiz made her way to the great doors. Standing on the steps, she could see the location of the other churches from the glow of candles through their upper windows shining out like lanterns into the night. The city was as busy as if it was day, but everyone was heading for one church or another. The two churches she could see also had orderly queues of people waiting to get in, all patiently waiting, with some already holding candles of their own. Overcome with emotion again, she sat and wept once more for this touching tribute to a young man that only she of all of them had known well enough to call her friend, but who seemed to have touched the lives of so many.

Chapter 8

Lovers and Brothers

Prydein: Harvest-moon

For Alaiz the next couple of days went by in a blur. Staying within the sanctuary of the monks' guest hall, where news was regularly brought in, she slowly realized that Brion must be frantically trying to rescue his position after such a dire miscalculation. The long queues of ordinary people expressing their shock and horror by congregating at the churches had shown no sign of diminishing by the morning after. By the afternoon, the crowd's mood was being fuelled by the appearance of the wandering preachers, who normally got little attention but now were sermonizing on street corners on the sin of regicide. The following day saw the crowds getting larger and uglier. Anyone who looked vaguely official coming out of the palace was being pelted with rotten vegetables, and was subjected to a constant stream of abuse as they attempted to get away as fast as possible.

At midday on the third day the word spread that another announcement was to be made, and by the appointed hour there was barely room to pass a piece of parchment between the people crammed into the main square. Along with others in the monks' care, Alaiz was taken up to a long corridor which ran behind the west front of the great cathedral. Small windows had been craftily let into the ornate carvings to allow the voices of the choir to be heard, so that the birds carved into the branches of the five Sacred Trees seemed to be 'singing'. These now gave those in the choir gallery an unrivalled view over the square.

The great bell tolled the hour and immediately Brion appeared on the balcony, again flanked by Turstin and the stranger. As Brion raised his hands for silence, against all expectations the crowd fell silent again, but up in her eyrie Alaiz felt something was wrong in the way it happened. It was as though someone or thing had laid a compulsion on the thousands in the crowd, which was forcing them against their will into stillness. Brion's voice carried eerily as he proclaimed that in response to his beloved people's grief there would be a state funeral for Ivain. Later today, he told them, the monks of the cathedral would come to collect the body, and it would lie there in state for two days for all to pay their respects, while a suitable tomb was prepared in that church which he had loved so much.

For a moment it was as though the whole crowd held its breath. Alaiz looked up hoping the Spirits above would strike Brion down. Instead, she saw a bunch of young street urchins scrambling across the roofs of the houses opposite her, armed with baskets. When they got within range, they began to pelt the royal balcony with the baskets' contents. Suddenly the spell was wavering and the catcalls began. Some semblance of dignity was maintained for a few seconds until one enterprising lad upgraded from rotten apples to rotten eggs. Then a well-aimed one caught the menacing tall, bald stranger straight between the eyes and he reeled back. He half saw, half smelt the rank shell and its even more disgusting contents dribbling down his cheeks, gave an ear-piercing shriek and turned a sickly green. Blinded by the reeking globules and his concentration shattered, he shot into the dark sanctuary of the doorway.

In that instant it was as though a cloud had lifted. The spell was broken and the crowd swelled and roiled, baying for blood once more. From the glimpse Alaiz got of her brother's face, he was utterly terrified as he almost trampled on Brion to follow him out of the way of the stream of projectiles which now assailed them.

That evening the monks closed the doors of the great nave for the first time to all but their own, and with great ceremony the casket carrying Ivain's body was brought across. Alaiz knew the monks who had gone to bring it across the square had feared for their lives, and had had the last rites said to them before their departure. Yet when they had emerged to go to the palace, a way had been made for them. And, as they had returned, eight brothers carrying the simple wooden box and another eight chanting prayers as they swung incense alongside it, the crowd had parted like waves around them. Brion had refused the abbot an armed escort, but in contrast to the events of the day, the respect that the monks were held in was enough to guarantee their safety; and to the body they carried, the reaction was one of near veneration, people falling to their knees as it passed.

She was not sure how she would stand up to the strain, but Alaiz was determined to be one of those who got into the nave to file past the body. Being already in the precinct it was easy for her to slip out and become part of the queue, but even so she was far from the front. One line was formed for each side of the bier, with each filing up the long nave and then being let back out by the small doors in the transepts of their respective sides. Even then, Alaiz could not see how everyone was going to get in. The people had begun queuing almost as soon as the announcement had been made, and as they had watched the numbers rise, the monks had changed their plans from opening the doors with the first office of the coming full day, to the first after midnight.

In the dark of night the candles were checked once more, and then the great copper-plated double doors once more swung in on their hinges, the first of a relay of choristers began their chants, and the procession of mourners began. Weary beyond words, Alaiz shuffled forward, too numb to focus on anything but the approaching doors, and blindly accepting the regular offerings of water and bread that the lay brothers brought along the line. The sun had risen on a cloudless morning by the time she moved once more into the relative gloom of the stone vaults, and still she shuffled on. It suddenly dawned on her that there was a buzzing of voices around her, and she woke from her daze to realize that Brion and Turstin had been led in by the abbot, who was wearing a very uncharacteristic scowl. He obviously disapproved of such men entering the sacred space, but by his own Order's rules was powerless to refuse them the right to pay their respects to the deceased.

What really jolted her was the realization that her fellow pilgrims were all asking,

"Where's the queen?"

"Where *is* his wife?"

"Why is his mother not *here*?"

And it was evident Brion and Turstin could hear this too, going by the frantic whispered discussions between the two of them. For the first time in days, Alaiz wanted to laugh. What a dreadful mistake to arrange for their kidnap! In his arrogance he had dismissed them, forgetting that they had appeared so often in public with all three of them together. While he had seen it as Ivain's weakness in relying on women, the people saw them as a family. The traitor could not know that the woman he most needed to appear and to show support for him was within his grasp, yet was slipping through it!

In her deep state of fatigue it was hard for Alaiz to remain alert, but she knew she must, for one slip might give her away, and she would not give them the satisfaction of dragging her off to be paraded at their will. The next queue had joined hers now they were in the nave, and she was walking alongside a tall young man, a handful of years older than herself she guessed. Strangely, he too looked as though he had been crying as hard as she had, beyond even that of most of the crowd. It struck her that if she seemed to be with him it would be less likely that she would be spotted, so she moved closer and gave his arm what she hoped would be read as a comforting pat.

"At least he's past them hurting him now," she said, her voice croaking after doing so little but sob for days now. The man whipped round and a pair of red-rimmed fierce eyes bore into her. For an awful second Alaiz thought she had made a dreadful mistake, and that he was about to make a scene. Instead, it seemed to take that moment for him to realize that she looked a grief-ravaged as himself, before he answered,

"You can't begin to know the truth."

What a strange reply, Alaiz thought.

"I think I can guess," she ventured back.

He shook his head, tears welling back up in his eyes.

"No you can't," he whispered emphatically.

Before they could continue any further they reached the bier, and Alaiz made the decision to slip across to his side as the two lines split once more. Her own queue was happy to move up one place quicker than they had expected, but surprisingly, the next few in line behind him must have been so put off by his manner that they said nothing as she came to move along with him.

As they came level with the huge carved candle stick which was at the foot of the bier, its light shone over the draped form, and by its light and those at the other three corners, Alaiz saw that a red silk cloth with the Cross of Swords was all that covered the corpse. Without thinking she edged a little closer, and then realized so had her companion. Giving rapid glances towards the group of monks nominally in charge of the pilgrims, and seeing that they were distracted with Brion, he suddenly moved. His hand darted out and under the cloth to touch the lifeless hand and Alaiz heard him sob,

"Good-bye, Lukas! May the Trees protect you now!"

He pulled his hand back, and was so overcome that he had the other hand wiping his eyes and nearly walked into the end candlestick. A monk stepped forward to help him, slowing the procession for a second, and as she paused by the corpse what she saw made Alaiz's blood freeze. The limp dead arm had slipped with the touch and hung below the shrouding silk, but, although it wore one of the royal rings, that hand could never have belonged to Ivain. Instead of slim artistic fingers which were inevitably stained with ink, this was muscular and calloused with chipped nails, and the kind of ingrained dirt that spoke of a life of hard work. It was not Ivain! Her heart skipped a beat. Was he dead though? If so why would they need to use another body? The harm had been done in announcing Ivain's death. They could not undo that, so why replace him with a stranger? But the man in front had called him by another name. He must know who it was!

Alaiz stepped quickly up to her companion and slipped her arm through his. Seeing her take charge of the still distraught man, the monk at his side stepped away and returned to watching the crowd for other signs of need. Most of the pilgrims were having to be chivvied away from the crossing where the corpse lay, but Alaiz guided her charge around them and they were outside in minutes. She pulled him around the end of the transept, so that they came to the wall that ran alongside the back of the monastery's domestic buildings. Periodically in the wall there were niches with narrow stone ledges to serve as temporary resting points for the elderly and infirm, and Alaiz guided him to a deserted one of these.

"Who was that in there?" she demanded, bending towards him as she forced him to sit.

"Lukas... My brother," he told her, beyond any pretence or deception. "He was my half-brother really, but my mother brought him up as well. He was so gentle. A simple man who worked in the village smithy, who wanted nothing more than to make sure the shoes he made for the horses fitted the best they could. ...That was until those bastards came along. ...I wasn't there and they never told my family why, they just clapped him in chains and took him. I got the message and went home. ...I rode like the Demon Horde was on my tail, but I got here too late. They'd taken him into the dungeons of that cursed place, and before I could find a way in, they brought him out and beheaded him for the king."

"You know that for sure?" Alaiz asked hopefully.

"Oh yes! I was right at the wall trying to find a way in when the soldiers cleared the way. I was stood close enough to see his eyes when he came out. Poor Lukas, he was terrified."

"Oh thank the Spirits!" Alaiz sobbed in relief.

The man sprang to his feet and Alaiz felt herself being shaken like a leaf.

"You miserable bitch," he snarled. "What was the king to you, eh? Nothing! I bet you'd never even set eyes on him! My brother was every bit as good a man as him, probably better! *He'd* never done anything to deserve to die! *He* wasn't some spoilt rich fool who never noticed the people he used! I wish it *was* the king who was dead!"

"No! No!" Alaiz wailed, trying to stop him hurting her. "Ivain wasn't like that! He cared about people! *You're* the one who didn't know him! I *did*!"

"Oh really!"

"Yes I *did*! He was kind, and he worried so much about what the other nobles were doing to the people. You wouldn't say that if you'd seen him sitting up 'til all hours of the night, trying to find a way to stop men acting in his name when he never knew about it 'til afterwards."

"Oh really? And how would *you* know this?"

"Because I was married to him!"

Silence descended as the stranger dropped her and stared at her, his mouth open in astonishment. For a second Alaiz thought he would laugh at her. After all it was ridiculous. Here she was, the queen, creeping around back alleys with hacked-off hair and in borrowed clothing like some thief. Even to herself she sounded like some mad woman.

But he did not laugh. His hand caught her under the chin and lifted her face up to what light filtered down between the walls. Then he took her hands and scrutinized them.

"Holy Spirits!" he whispered. "Are you really her?"

Alaiz nodded miserably, feeling the tears welling up again.

"We, that's Gillies, the dowager queen, and I got sent away. We thought we were going on a diplomatic mission to stop Turstin. He's the man who's been with Brion. He's my brother. We were off the coast of Kittermere and our boat got raided by pirates. I don't know what happened to our boat, but we got taken to Mad Magnus' camp on Rathlin. Gillies is still there. I got away on a fishing boat. I've been trying to get to the Knights ever since, but I'm so useless. I only ever saw Master Hugh or Amalric when they came to me. It never occurred to me to find out where all their granges were.

"So all I could think of to do was to get back here and then try to find them from here. I only got back the day they killed Ivain – I mean your brother. I'm so sorry. I didn't mean I was glad they killed him. They shouldn't have killed anyone. But I'm glad it wasn't Ivain because that must mean he's still alive somewhere. And they can't have him, or else they wouldn't have needed to kill someone in his place, would they?"

She looked up at the man and saw him watching her thoughtfully.

"Were you really trying to get to the Knights?" he asked, and Alaiz nodded again.

"Well then you won't mind being taken to them, will you?"

Her heart leapt, this was a turn of her fortunes.

"You know where they are?" she asked hopefully. "Who are you?"

He paused before answering. "You must either be her, or so mad you think you are, or you'd be frightened of being found out as a fraud. So …I'd better take you with me, then. My name's Hamelin and I'm a Knight. There's nothing I can do here now, so I'm returning to the sept at Quies. It's not the main one, that's at Vellan, but it's where Grand Master Hugh is. I don't know what's happened to Grand Master Amalric. Nobody's seen or heard of him since Brion took over, which isn't good."

"What, nothing?" Alaiz asked.

Hamelin shook his head. He admitted his ride to the capital had been as fast as he could change horses, with little time to speak to anyone, but he had heard nothing of the fate of the Grand Master. With a heavy heart they feared Amalric must be dead, which meant Hugh de Burh was effectively back in control. Alaiz agreed that they must get to him as soon as possible, and as she had no possessions to call her own to collect from the monks' guest hall, they set off.

Hamelin was much more used to finding his way around the streets of the capital than she was, and easily guided her around the back of the cloisters and service buildings, to a clear street leading back into the main square. They needed to get across to the eastern side of the city to reach the main road running north into the heart of the Island, and across the centre of the city was the quickest way.

They had passed quickly in front of the bespattered walls of the palace, and were almost out of the square when a commotion began behind them. For an awful second Alaiz thought it must be for them, but when they turned round she saw that the guards at the door were fighting furiously, not with someone trying to get in, but with someone coming out. Before reinforcements arrived for the guards, horses' hooves were heard at the gallop, and then half a dozen mounted young men pelted into the square leading three spare horses.

Swinging their mounts round so that they would pass the doorway where the fracas was happening, two moved in front and drew swords, with which they made killing lunges as they passed at the guards' backs. As the men went down, three figures appeared at the door, one limp in the gasp of another, and a tall, slim young man facing back the way they had come as he reversed out after them, watching their backs. The next pair of riders split and passed either side of the first two escapees, snatching the limp form up between them and dumping him across the pommel of the one saddle without trying to manhandle him on to the horse, which was obviously intended for him. The final pair manoeuvred the spare horses so that, as they passed the two remaining figures, they were able to vault nimbly into the saddles and were off.

Within seconds the small cavalcade had disappeared down the street next to the one that Alaiz and Hamelin were standing in.

"That was Amalric they dragged out!" Alaiz gasped, as Hamelin exclaimed in unison,

"That was Oliver!"

"Oliver?"

"My closest friend. Only he'd be so bold as to snatch a prisoner from out of the royal dungeons! ! The guard must have been relaxed after the execution. Quick! We must hurry. If we're lucky we can catch up with them."

Alaiz thought he must be mad to think they could catch up with mounted Knights when they were on foot. She was sure they would be far away by the time they had even reached the end of the street, but Hamelin assure her not. He thought they would have slowed down and split up as soon as they could. Nothing would attract attention more than a group of armed men riding like maniacs through the streets scattering people left, right and centre. Oliver would also have more sense, he told her, than to risk one of them being unhorsed by an unseen obstacle.

Although Alaiz was in no fit state to hurry, he almost dragged her along in a near run for what seemed like forever. She utterly lost all sense of direction as they wove through narrow streets to cut across to different main roads. By the time they reached the north gate she was almost dropping with exhaustion, but heard Hamelin exclaim softly,

"Got him!"

Still dragging her, he shouldered his way forward until they were behind a couple of seemingly drunken grooms leading four horses out of the gate. As the guard stepped forward to question them, Hamelin suddenly turned on her.

"I'll teach you to run off with that tinker, you whore!" he bellowed in her astonished face. "Think you'll make a fool of me, will you? Well you just wait 'til we get back and see what my mother has in store for you! You'll be sorry!"

This was just too much for Alaiz. She dissolved into hysterical sobs, as exhaustion, both physical and mental took over. Through the tears Alaiz realized the whole stream of people had turned to watch them, as he hauled her bodily through the gate and out on to the open road. She was past caring that he picked her up and threw her over his shoulder, as he marched off down the road. All she could do was try not to bit her lip in between gasps as she was bounced around. In a turn in the road as it reached some trees, he suddenly leapt down the small bank that the road was running on, and dived into a clump of coppiced hazel. With great care he now put her down as a cheerful voice beside her said,

"Hamelin! Glad you found us. Nice distraction at the gate, by the way! Bertrand and Friedl said you nicely deflected the guards away from them at the crucial moment. What in the Islands have you got there?"

Scrubbing her eyes free of tears, she looked up into the handsome face of a young man whom she realized must be the tall Knight from the rescue. "That was nicely done yourself!" Hamelin complimented him instead. "That was our lord and master I saw you hauling off across Bertrand's saddle? Where is he?"

In answer they were hailed from the road as a cart filled with turnips slowed down.

"In there," Oliver replied. "They were going to string him up at dawn tomorrow, so we had to go in today, but we hadn't anticipated Brion and his thugs would have had quite so much fun with him. We were hoping he was going to be able to ride so we could go across country. Is he conscious yet, Willem?" he called up to a man who was perched on the edge of the wagon. The man shook his head.

"No. A few moans but nothing else."

Oliver growled in frustration, but sent the driver and Willem to mount up with the others who were waiting amongst the trees. Apparently they too were heading as fast as they could to Quies, which was why they had been desperate to get their horses out of the city, and not leave them at the small preceptory the Knights had there. Alaiz hoped they would not expect her to ride just yet. The horses looked a long way off the placid jennets she had been allowed to ride at court, and she had visions of being endlessly hauled out of ditches.

Oliver gave orders to them to ride as escort on either side of the road, as far away as they could get to not be noticed, and then got up onto the wagon's seat and took up the reins.

"You'd better get up here with your friend." he said to Hamelin amiably. "It's not like you to come back with a girl on your arm, although that was more *over* your arm! Where did you get to anyway?"

"That was Lukas they executed instead of the king." Hamelin said grimly.

The other Knights were still within earshot of them and all turned in horror. A chorus of sympathy followed as they all came in closer to speak to their friend, and Alaiz realized Hamelin was a popular person amongst his fellow Knights, which at least boded well for her safety. She had seriously begun to think him as deranged as Magnus, and that she had jumped from the frying pan into the fire. Now she at least knew that Lukas truly was his brother, since all these other men knew of him as well, which was reassuring. And if they were rescuing Amalric they must really be Knights. There was hope yet.

Even better, Hamelin was being much kinder to her now they were out of the city. While he had been talking to the others he had been wrapping a spare blanket around her shoulders, and had picked her up in his arms, gently this time, and lifted her onto the wagon seat, before climbing up beside her and putting a supporting arm around her.

Oliver quirked an eyebrow at this, and cutting across the rest asked,

"But who is the girl? How's she involved in this?"

Suddenly a weak and wavering voice rose from immediately behind them in the cart.

"Hello, Alaiz," Amalric said, just as Hamelin replied, to the amazement of his friends,

"She's the queen."

BRYCHAN

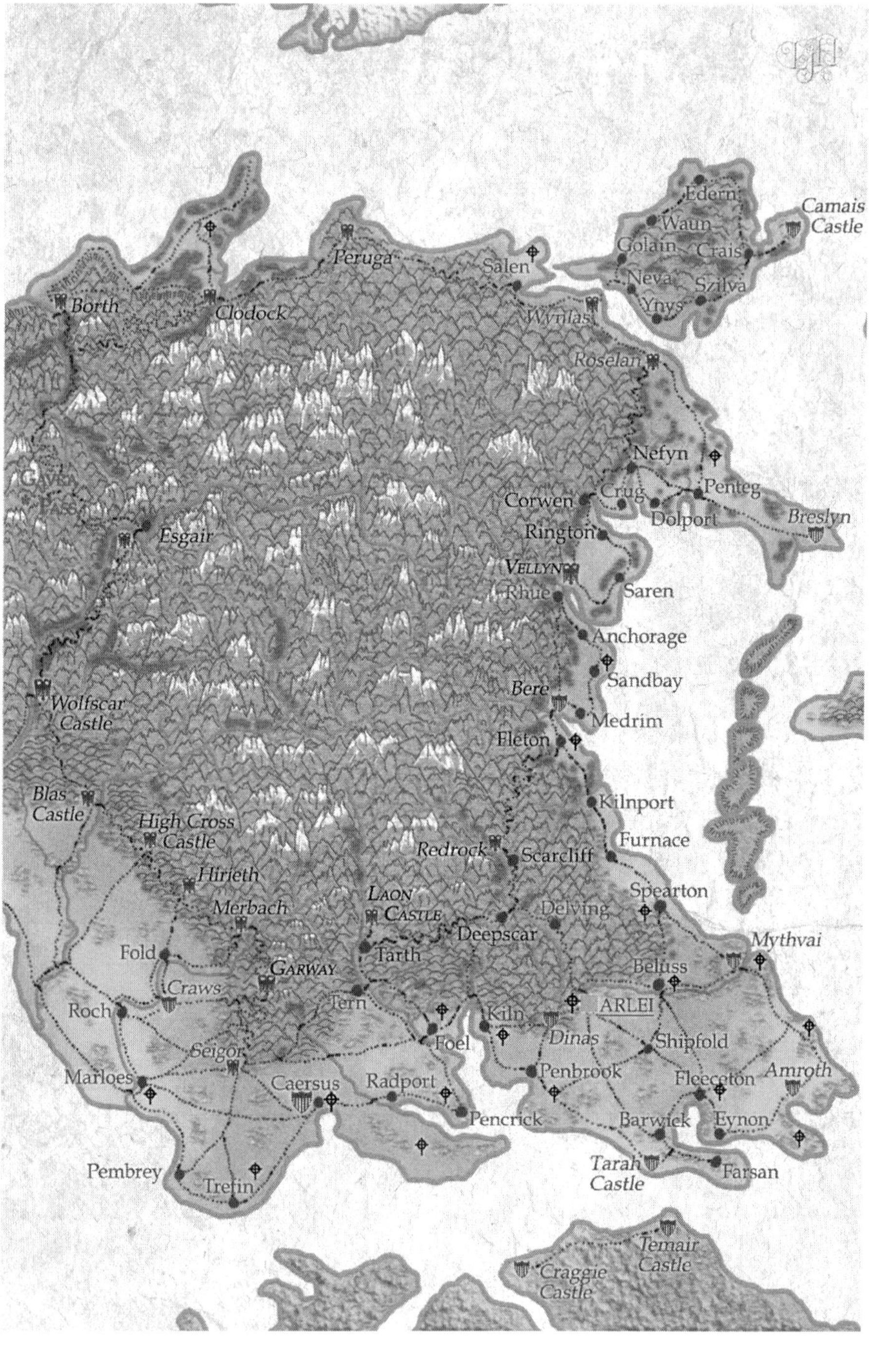

Camais Castle
Edern
Waun
Golain
Crais
Neva
Szilva
Ynys
Peruga
Salen
Borth
Clodock
Wynlas
Roselan
Nefyn
Penteg
Corwen
Crug
Dolport
Breslyn
Rington
Esgair
Vellyn
Rhue
Saren
Anchorage
Sandbay
Bere
Medrim
Wolfscar Castle
Fleton
Kilnport
Blas Castle
High Cross Castle
Furnace
Redrock
Scarcliff
Hirieth
Spearton
Merbach
Laon Castle
Delving
Deepscar
Mythvai
Fold
Tarth
Garway
Beluss
Craws
Tern
Arlei
Roch
Kiln
Dinas
Shipfold
Foel
Seigor
Penbrook
Fleeceton
Amroth
Marloes
Caersus
Radport
Pencrick
Barwick
Eynon
Pembrey
Tarah Castle
Farsan
Trefin
Temair Castle
Craggie Castle

Chapter 9

The Nightmare

Brychan: early Harvest-moon

Swein stood naked in front of the closet, practicing different poses as he tried to decide what to wear. It was a very special day today. Of all King Edward's favourite boys he had been chosen to play the part in the king's great plan, and he had to look right for the part. It was a great responsibility and he was determined to make sure he did everything right. Ever since the king had picked him out from amongst many other hopefuls to be another of his pages, Swein had worked hard to rise to this favoured position. The king had very specific tastes, and at times he had found it hard to pretend he liked what was being done to him. The bondage he found particularly scary, especially as Edward often got quite carried away once he had someone so fully subdued.

Swein had found the occasional trips to the dungeon, where he would be bound naked, facing the dungeon wall, while Edward 'played' with the torture instruments, particularly frightening. It had been so hard to whimper in just the right tone of voice and not scream as he wanted to. Edward hated screaming. He said it was defiant not submissive. So, as far as Swein was concerned, if Edward did not want it then there was no questioning him.

Now Swein felt he had paid his dues in pain and patience, and he was being rewarded for his loyalty. Tonight, a young actor who bore a striking resemblance to Edward was being smuggled into the castle for the king's little plan. Last night, here in Swein's room, after Edward had pleasured himself with him, he had told him the plot.

"I don't believe my heirs are mine," he'd told Swein with a sniff of disgust. "I'm so disappointed in them. They're nothing like me! Always running off to their mother when I try to play my games with them. Anyway, *you* know," he'd added with a sly wink to Swein, "that they *can't* be mine – me sleep with a woman? I don't think so! But what's my brother thinking of supporting her, hmm? What does the fool mean," and now his voice slid into a vicious parody of his brother Richert, "'you should be grateful for a queen like her.' *Hmfph*! 'She's been circumspect enough to provide you with heirs without any scandal, or revealing your lack of masculinity.' Me? Un-masculine? How dare he say that!"

Well now that was going to change tonight. The actor was going to take a sleeping draft and play dead. Then Swein was to go in and raise the alarm that the king had been killed. Under the cover of this, Edward was going to ride to the manor where the boys were being raised, and dispose of them and their mother. In disguise amongst his loyal men, Edward was then going to have Richert beheaded for murdering them, so getting rid of all his problems.

Then, he told Swein, he was going to return and find a proper little boy to be his heir and bring him here. No-one would blame him for adopting then, would they? He had lost his family, and he would play the part of being prostrate with grief to perfection in public, while here, in his private wing of the castle, life would finally be just how he wanted it. Which was nothing less than he deserved as king, was it not?

Swein had agreed readily, although somewhere buried deep in his soul his inner voice was protesting at the unnecessary death of two little boys. He had wanted to say, surely it would be possible to just send them away, or pretend they did not exist, as his own father had done to him, and that had turned out just fine – had it not? But he had kept quiet, because the way to make sure everything stayed alright for him, and never have to go crawling back home, was to keep the king happy. Even after all this time the thing which struck dread into Swein's heart was the thought that the king would tire of him and he would be left with nothing, which would force him back to his parents' scorn. So he would pick his clothing carefully, play his part and keep his mouth shut, which of course was exactly why Edward had chosen him.

He finally settled on a fetching midnight blue tunic with matching hose and boots, whose colour would allow him to make his way across the castle keep's yard unnoticed tonight, so that he could wait until he was required. When he was ready, he almost skipped down the stairs and slipped across to the next tower in the triangular keep. Most of the guards were over at the entrance to the keep, and so he went unchallenged into the royal apartments. Edward had been most specific in his instructions. Swein was to wait until the second change of guards that night, from those who had been on in the early evening to the later shift, when everyone was likely to be in their beds and the guards therefore fewer.

So Swein quietly made his way up to the second floor and waited near to the door for Edward to slip out, when he would wait for the king to get clear and then sound the alarm. However, once he actually got there it seemed awfully quiet inside. If Edward liked his partners to be subtle in their vocalization, he himself was never quiet in taking his pleasures. Swein waited a little longer and then slipped towards the door. On the one hand he did not want to get caught with his ear to the door just as the king made his exit – that would be sure to put Edward into one of his rages – but it was so very still in there. Even right by the door jamb he could hear nothing, and he was getting worried.

Had he taken too long getting ready and it was all over with? Surely he had understood exactly what was required of him? Edward had been so explicit he could not have been mistaken. Had Edward changed his mind at the last minute and decided to use someone else? That would be dreadful. He stepped forward and put his hand on the door, intending to press his ear to it, but it swung open into the room. And what he saw there made him scream… and scream… and scream.

The young actor was dead alright. Very permanently, in a way that owed nothing whatsoever to his performance skills. Swein had never seen so much blood. It was everywhere – dripping in puddles on the floor, sprayed up the walls, and some of it had solid bits in it. Somewhere in his stunned and dazed mind it registered that the young man had been torn limb from limb, at which point he turned and threw up his dinner before beginning screaming again. A bloody sword, which had obviously been used in the process, lay discarded on the floor somewhere on the periphery of Swein's vision. Something which could have been an arm lay near his feet, and a bare foot sticking out from the side of the bed and far too far away to be connected to the body, hinted at other limbs yet to be found. What he could not tear his eyes from, though, was the trunk, which lay with its half severed head hanging backwards over the footboard of the bed. Its empty eye-sockets fixed him with their vacant, bloody stare, but even worse was what was in its mouth. Someone had crudely castrated the man and stuffed the parts as far as they would go into the now silent screaming mouth.

If screams could really wake the dead then Swein's would have reanimated the bloody wreckage without any problem. Instead, they finally brought guards and servants who, in the latter cases, also screamed in horror. Someone slapped him hard and he slipped on something, collapsing into a heap on the floor. People rushed past him, then he got hauled to his feet by a terrifying soldier who shook him like a rat as he bawled questions in his face. Reduced to a quivering wreck, Swein could not even work out what the man was shouting at him, let alone force his mouth to come out with anything intelligible. At some point he was aware that he was dragged back to his room by two burly guards, tearing his fine woollen hose as they none too gently hauled him down and up the stairs, but he was beyond noticing that.

Dumped on his bed and left to himself, he shivered numbly through the rest of the night. He could not close his eyes for long, even though he was exhausted, without the nightmare scene returning to haunt him. At sometime just before dawn he realized that this time Edward had truly lost control, and at that point he had been unable to spend a moment longer in the bed he had shared with such a monster. Dragging the cushions off the chair and from the settle into the corner of the room, he had curled up in a foetal position and rocked back and forth, trying to find some comfort, but nothing worked.

By midmorning he was still alone. His stomach growled emptily, having lost his evening meal back in the other room and it was long past breakfast, but he could not face the thought of food. When the autumn sun began to fade he realized that no-one was coming, and nobody cared about what was happening to him. He slowly crept out of his corner, and on cramped legs tottered over to the wash stand. The person who stared back at him from the mirror above it was someone he did not recognize. The kohl he had used to accentuate his eyes the night before had run and formed streaks with the rouge on his cheeks, making him look like a demented clown. It was a state he had never let himself get into before. Far worse, however, was what lay beneath the paint. He was white-faced and haggard, with puffed-up eyes from the ravages of the night, but instead of dark hair above he was now completely white there too.

Feeling immeasurably dirty and used, he poured the now cold water into the basin and stripped off his clothes. He scrubbed and scrubbed, only stopping when he ran out of water in the pitcher, but at least, although he still felt dirty inside, on the outside he was now just white with pink patches where he had scrubbed so hard. Still shivering despite the lingering warmth of the day, he turned to the closet, and almost threw up again, if there had been anything left to lose. He could not believe that it was only a day ago that he had stood right here so full of excitement and hope. Now he felt like his entire life had been wiped away leaving a white, blank slate with absolutely nothing on it. The clothes which had been the focus of his world now repulsed him. Everything seemed tainted with the actor's blood, and there was not one of the multitudes of peacock-bright colours which he could have born to wear now.

His eye finally fell on a simple brown woollen tunic down on the bottom shelf. It was the tunic he had worn when he had arrived here, which he had kept to remind himself of how far he had come, and gloat at how far above his brute of a father he had risen. Now though it was the only thing which he felt he could call his own. He had paid for it himself out of the meagre wage his father had given him for stitching for hours on end. With shaking hands he drew it out, along with the hose and shirt that went with it, and put them on the chair. From sheer necessity he had to use the underclothes that he had worn on a daily basis in the castle, his old ones having long since disappeared, but once he had covered them with his old clothes he could at least forget they were on.

Picking up a standard issue rough cloak which was used for riding in bad weather, he turned and looked at himself once more in the mirror. Nothing remained of yesterday's Swein. In his place was a young man who could have been any age from twenty to forty. His appearance was made somewhat odd by the contrast between the white hair and eyebrows, and the dark eyes and lashes ringed with red, which seemed the only colours in his washed out face. Combined with the humble garments, he was virtually unrecognizable to anyone who had known him before, which suddenly suited him. He did not know what he was going to do, but staying here no longer seemed possible. If he saw Edward now he would be more likely to scream and run, or throw up on him.

Creeping downstairs, he passed through the hall where the remains of the evening meal were still lying. The events of last night had obviously suppressed even the heartiest of appetites, and there was far more food left than normal. It was a measure of the chaos within the castle that it had not been cleared away yet. Keeping his eyes off the long side trestle where the meat lay, Swein found the baskets of bread and stuffed as many large chunks into his cloak pockets as they would take. Not surprisingly all the beer and wine had gone as the household fortified its spirits. However, a pot of caff, the hot drink made from chicory and usually served at the end of meals or as refreshment for the ladies, stood still keeping warm on its oil burner. Finding the biggest flagon he could, Swein threw the dregs of its former contents into the hearth and then filled it to the brim with the caff. Slipping out of the side door, he made his way into the garden beneath the keep's walls where the king had held so many entertainments.

Long ago Swein had found a small bower in the one corner, which had become overgrown with its tangle of honeysuckle. Unlike the previous kings, who had had more mistresses than could be kept track of, Edward had had no use for the seductive powers of the garden's flowers on the court ladies, and so it had become Swein's private retreat. From it he had been able to listen to the gossip going on around him without being seen, but tonight the garden was deserted.

Sitting with his legs curled up on the bench, he nibbled unenthusiastically at the bread, and washed the morsels down with drafts of the heavily sweetened caff. The scent of the honeysuckle blooms filled the confined space, and for the first time he no longer imagined he could smell blood. Totally exhausted, he was in the half awake state just before sleep when he heard voices coming into the garden, jolting awake when he realized they were talking about him. To his horror he realized that these were some of his fellow companions to the king, but that somehow they had the idea that he was the one who had killed Edward. They had been completely taken in by the double of the king and were convinced he was dead. Even worse, they were talking about his own imminent arrest and trial for murder, and that he might be tortured to reveal his accomplices, for this evening the news had come of the death of the royal family at the manor, and a knife in the dark which had taken the life of lord Richert last night. It was all Swein could do to keep swallowing hard to avoid vomiting noisily again, and drawing attention to himself.

The gaggle of young catamites finally moved on, gossiping avidly, leaving Swein sweating and shaking again in his hiding place. It had been many years since he had had to make adult decisions for himself. Edward preferred his companions to show a childlike deference to him, and Swein had perfected a knack of showing naive innocence in his character to go with his youthful looks as the way to keep his position close to the king, when others who had shown signs of growing up had been dismissed. As a habit it had been seductive, as he had never been asked to accept responsibility for anything since he had got here, in such a marked contrast to his childhood where everything had been his fault. Even there he had been expected to do what his father commanded without question or show of initiative. Yet now the lack of practice threatened to get him killed as he sat paralyzed with fear, unable to think his way out of this mess.

It slowly dawned on him how perfectly he had been set up. Edward's insistence on secrecy meant that nobody else knew what had been planned, and in fact Swein was, as far as he knew, the only one who knew just how deeply the king was implicated in the death of all of his family. Others knew about different parts of the plan as necessity had dictated, but only he knew the whole, and he realized with growing horror just how much Edward now needed him to disappear quickly. It occurred to him that a swift trial after torturing, which left him swinging silently from the nearest gibbet, before Edward staged his miraculous return, would serve the king best. As a corpse he could not tell tales.

He suddenly realized that he needed to get out of the castle now, before the gates were closed for the night after the last of the courtiers returned from drowning their sorrows in the taverns in the town. If he left it any later someone might check his room, and raise the alarm when they found him gone. The only reason he had got this far was probably because they thought he was such a hopeless fool he would just sit up in the tower, waiting to be trussed up like a chicken, and fed to the mob which would surely be baying for his blood once the idea got out that he was to blame. Within the castle walls people were packed too close to afford any permanent hiding place, and once the gates sealed him in he would be found in no time.

Peering out of the foliage, he saw that the coast was clear and hastily retreated out of the garden. He was too scared to be subtle and took the direct route down to the gates. To his horror, he was just approaching the guards when the same group he had overheard in the garden came out of a side street and cut in front of him. He almost thought his heart would stop in fright, but they just carried on without even noticing who he was. Realizing that he could use them to shield him from the view of the sentry, he tagged onto the back of them, and was through the watch without anyone saying a word. As soon as the side streets appeared he dodged down one, relief flooding through him that the group were so absorbed in their speculation that they had just taken him for part of the press of normal people going in and out on everyday business. Out of sight of the guards, he now took to his heels and fled headlong through the maze of back streets.

He had no idea of where he was or where he was going, except that he kept looking back to make sure that the bulk of the castle walls were always behind him, so that he kept moving away from them. Which was how he failed to notice the steady decline in the buildings he was passing through until they were little more than lean-to shacks. As he glanced back one more time he careered into someone, and turning back found himself being surrounded by the roughest rabble he had ever seen without an armed escort around him.

"Well, well, what we got 'ere mates?" the one in front of him leered, showing missing teeth and blackened gums in a scarred face. Without any further incitement, Swein found himself being roughly manhandled as four others started to search him, pulling his cloak off in the process.

" 'E ain't got no money!" one of them exclaimed in annoyance, and the others growled menacingly.

"Get 'is clothes, then!" the leader told them, and a sharp knife sliced through the laces fastening the tunic. With a terrifying efficiency that Swein numbly realized meant that they were quite used to doing this, they stripped him of everything, but he had no time to protest. As soon as the clothes were off they began to beat him up and, as he collapsed, they disdained to stoop to hit him with their fists and just used their boots. If it was far more brutal than anything that Edward had dished out, it was also over far more quickly. There was no prolonging his misery for their pleasure, this was business pure and simple. He was being reduced to a state where he was incapable of raising the alarm against them, and here he was unlikely to be found if he could not make his own way out of the rat-infested maze of shacks. As fast as they had appeared they disappeared into the night, leaving Swein naked, battered and bruised in the gutter. To the side of a shack there was what could have been a log store, if it had had any logs in it, and Swein managed to crawl into it before collapsing insensible.

The next few days were a catalogue of misery of the kind he could not have imagined before. All he had found to cover himself with was an old sack, and he limped out of the city, surviving by scavenging from the back of inns and drinking from rain butts. Unused to such disgusting fare his stomach revolted and he was forced to find places to relieve himself so often that in the end he decided that it was less painful to simply not bother eating at all. Half delirious from lack of food and water, he staggered out into the countryside, finally taking refuge in a country chapel's graveyard behind some stones which were almost hidden by the boughs of a magnificent yew tree. Waking the following morning, he realized that there was a small spring by the chapel wall and, checking that there was nobody around, slunk like a kicked dog to the trough beneath it where he drank thirstily.

He spent three days hiding beneath the yew's branches and going to drink regularly at the spring. On the second evening he ventured out in the dusk, and managed to slip into a cottage and steal a loaf of bread before anyone noticed. In his hideaway he tore into it, relishing it more than he had many a feast. The next night he managed to acquire some cheese from another cottage and milk from a third house.

However, as he slowly came to his senses, he realized that in such a small hamlet he would soon be discovered. The only thing to do was to move on before his hiding place was revealed. Twice he had heard horsemen riding through in a hurry, and he was not taking any chances that they might be looking for him. So that night he hobbled to the end of the only street, and then managed to steal some ploughman's wooden clogs. They were far from comfortable, but they did mean he could walk without tearing his feet to shreds on the rough road surface.

He walked all that night, creeping like a ghost though more hamlets and picking up scraps of food where he could. After a week he had perfected the art of living rough. He walked at night and hid up by day, taking only small amounts of things which could be put down to a greedy child, or a dog or cat thieving, and most definitely nothing which would create more than a little irritation over its loss.

The summer was in its last stages and, as the moon came closer to full, he could see as he walked along that the harvesting had got under way. By now he thought he was probably well away from any place where he might be recognized from having been there before, and his appearance had changed so drastically he doubted whether he could be spotted just from a description of a wanted man read out in church, or called by a town crier. He decided to risk moving more by day, when he could travel faster because he could see what was underfoot. Several times a night he was falling over things and his legs were now covered in scabs and cuts which were becoming increasingly painful as he reopened them, or added another bruise on top of the old ones. He had acquired a tatty shirt and trousers, which had rubbed him sore where they touched, but he now longed for some semblance of normality, especially someone to talk to.

Over the next week he tried to get work, but the only sort that was going was rough labouring in the fields. To his ever growing sense of inadequacy, he found he was utterly inept at such menial work. The few farmers who were charitable enough to take him on for a day soon shook their heads in despair, and sent him on his way. He had no idea how to hold tools, and his life of sycophantic pandering had left him with no stamina. He was forced to realize that Edward's dislike of masculine muscle tone, and preference for boyish willowiness, had rendered him as physically inadequate as the behavioural preferences had destroyed his survival skills.

With the last vestiges of self-respect destroyed he was reduced to begging as he went along. There was no problem in looking needy. While he had always been slim and rather delicately featured, he now looked gaunt, and the lack of proper food had had its effect on his skin and hair as well as his size. If he had previously looked ten years younger than his real age, he now thought he looked ten older when he caught sight of himself in the ponds and streams he resorted to for washing in. Yet even at begging he was hopelessly inadequate. Either people seemed to think he was putting it on because he was too obsequious, or he could not bring himself to push himself forward enough and they ignored him.

In a life which had given him no chance to find a real personality of his own, he realized he was utterly lost without someone telling him what to do, what to think, and where to go. Fear turned into a feeling of complete worthlessness into which he sank more deeply at every passing day. It seemed now unavoidable that he would soon starve to death, but if by some miracle he kept going, then he was destined to freeze to death once the weather turned colder.

Already summer had given way to autumn, and once the sun went down it was much colder than when he had first run out of the castle. He had left Arlei, the capital, far behind and had finally reached the next big town more by default than planning. The broad river which ran from far above Arlei to the sea was already too wide to cross except by bridge or ferry, and he had not had the money to pay the two ferrymen he had seen along the way. Heading down river had been easiest as he had not the strength to start travelling up into the hills, and he had hoped that it would be warmer at the coast.

Yet he had never really travelled. The only long trip he had ever made was from his home town of Penbrook down to Arlei, and since then he had had no reason to go out of the town. So he had no idea of how long it would take to get anywhere on foot. When he had seen a large town appearing by the riverside, he had been sure that this must have been the start of the town by the sea, but when he had finally got to it he found it was not at all. A passing tradesman told him that this was Bettus, a name he had seen on the royal maps as just a humble town on the way to the coast.

In his mind he had thought that a provincial town like Bettus would be small, dingy and of little consequence, even meaner than Penbrook. The reality had come as a shock. Substantially built, with solid walls and a fortified bridge, the good burgesses of Bettus wanted no scruffy vagabonds in their neat streets, and the watch had dragged him by the scruff of his shirt away from the entrance to the bridge. That had been the nearest he had got to the town. All he could do was limp by on the side of the river he had started out on, and look at the disdainful walls on the opposite bank, listening to the shouts of the vendors in the market and other sounds of everyday life which he was shut out from. It dawned on him that he was not even on the main road, that lay on the opposite bank, and that was where most of the traffic was, explaining why he had not encountered that many people. Nobody saw him and no-one cared.

After the third week of dragging himself along every day, he reached the small town of Mythvai, with its massive castle towering on the sea cliffs above it. Yet far from being warmer on the coast, there was a biting wind coming in off the sea which cut him to the bone. During the last night a ferocious storm had drenched him and left him dithering in his thin rags, with the only shelter being the hollow of a dead tree. At one point he had heard a bone-chilling keening, which sounded utterly inhuman, and he had dug himself deeper under the tree and stuffed his fingers in his ears, too terrified to dare to look out. The storm had raged and thrown trees into the river, and as he limped down the slope towards the sea, he could see huge boulders had been thrown up by the wind and tide. People were busy tidying up, sweeping mud and water off streets and out of yards, and were far too busy to notice him.

There was no toll to pay on the great long bridge over the out-flowing river, as the majority of the inhabitants had boats which they could have used instead. Tottering weakly out onto the first span, Swein starred hopelessly out to sea. Having got here he had no idea of what to do. The whole focus of his mind had been on getting away to avoid being prosecuted for something he had never done, but now he could not avoid facing up to the future and it was bleak beyond belief. When he thought of living before it had always been of ways to acquire more comforts, but now he had to reckon with how he was ever to hope to obtain even the most basic of necessities. Despair flooded through him as he failed to see how he was going to live.

Resting his now almost skeletal arms on the rough stone parapet, he put his head down on them and sobbed. In the depths of his despair he thought that even going on one more day was more than he could hope to do. From there it was a small step to thinking that maybe it would be better to die here and now. What possible point was there in struggling on? His body hurt in places he had never known he had, and his mind felt shattered into pieces. All he wanted was for this to stop, to not hurt any more. The rhythmic swishing of the sea on the shingle beach was soothing, and suddenly the prospect of joining it became very appealing. It sounded soft and gentle, so without any effort the decision was made.

He walked out to the centre span where the water was deepest and the current strongest, as the mighty river flowed out to sea. Looking over the edge the water swirled invitingly. He threw his head back and gasped in a deep sobbing breath, then put his arms over the width of the parapet and tried to draw himself up. It took his last reserve of strength to get his body onto the wall. He had to pause, then managed to swing his leg up so that he was sitting astride it. With a last look at the sky he drew his other leg up and over, and leaned out into the void.

Chapter 10

Serve Revenge Cold

Brychan: early Harvest-moon

Cwen thought her world had ended that day. Lying on the curtained bed in the room she had shared with Richert, in the room overlooking the sea, she sobbed and sobbed until no more tears would come. The man around whom her world had revolved for the last five years was dead, and she had no idea how she would go on without him. The news had come from the groom who had brought his favourite horse back to the stables. Since then she had retreated to this room they had shared and for the last two weeks had been near insensible with grief. The servants had left her alone. They had no reason to disturb her since she would have no part to play in the arrangements for his funeral, or the disposal of his estate. That would fall to his wife, but she never came here.

The ancient castle of Amroth stood on the remote and wind-swept east coast of Brychan, far from the court at Arlei, and his wife hated it as much as Richert and Cwen had loved it. However, now there was a message that the wife was sending her steward to take stock of what was at the castle, and the servants knew they had to break the second piece of bad news to Cwen. She was much cared for by them all. A different woman would have used her position as the mistress of the king's brother to lord it over them, but Cwen had never forgotten her humble home, and treated them as her equals not her servants. They had also all been totally loyal to their lord first and foremost, and until they had good reason to act otherwise, his wishes would still be obeyed.

So they had drawn lots for who would have to go to the tower room, and the short straw had gone to the cook, Martha. Arming herself with a mug of caff and two of her newly baked spiced apple muffins on a tray, she puffed her way up the long spiral stairwell, gave a swift tap on the door, and entered without waiting for a reply. Cwen raised her head off the pillow to look at the door as she came in. Martha thought she looked dreadful. Richert had been attracted to her by her healthy rosy glow, sparkling blue eyes and ready laugh. Now her eyes were red and puffy from crying, she was white-faced, and had lost weight dramatically over the last weeks with the stress, and having eaten almost nothing at all.

Cwen looked at the tray.

"I'm so sorry, Martha, but I don't think I can face that, I really can't."

Martha put the tray on the chest at the foot of the bed and came to sit beside her.

"I'm so sorry, luvvie, but you must." Cwen started to shake her head but Martha did not give her chance to interrupt. "You don't understand, dearie, that woman's sending her steward. He'll be here tomorrow. We've got to get you out of here before he comes. You know how much she hated you, but while Earl Richert was alive she couldn't do anything to you or your family. But that's all changed now. You don't have the power to stand up to her, and if she catches you there's no telling what she'll do. We don't want you to end up forgotten in some dungeon."

"Oh Spirits!" Cwen groaned, burying her head in her hands. Martha stroked back her hair sympathetically.

"I know it's hard for you. You should have had the chance to grieve for him in peace, but it's not going to happen."

Cwen raised her head shakily.

"What am I going to do, Martha? Everything I hold dear is here. It's not the things, it's the people and the memories. I don't want to lose them. I can't stand the thought of her coming here and destroying everything he worked so hard to build. She could have had this years ago if she'd wanted it, but she didn't want him and she didn't want the castle or the estate. Why now?"

Martha grimaced.

"Because you had it and she didn't! It was one thing refusing or going against Earl Richert in all sorts of petty ways. It was her way of trying to get control. She was the new wife and her family weren't as important as he was, so she had to make a place for herself, or at least that's a charitable way of looking at it! But you're not in her class and now she means to make you pay for helping him, because without him here she thinks she can do what she wants to you."

"I suppose so. It just seems so unfair. She never seemed to understand that he wasn't free to do the things she asked. There was no way he could override his brother's decision not to promote her brother, or advance her cousin. Why couldn't she see him for what he was? Edward might have been king, but Richert was the better man."

"I know – we all know that down here! But this is the shire at the end of the country. Up in Arlei different things count."

"Well I'm glad I never had to go to court, then!" Cwen said bitterly. "I know I should be concerned that Edward's dead too, but I can't mourn for him after the way he treated Richert."

"Ah, that's a whole different kettle of fish," Martha sighed. "But for now we have to deal with this man who's coming tomorrow, so come on, eat up and then we'll get your things packed up. You don't have to go far for now. He can't cover the whole estate in a day, and at least you can deprive the bastard of the satisfaction of throwing you out, can't you!"

A weak smile appeared on Cwen's face.

"I suppose so. It's bad enough leaving Richert's things, but at least I don't have to have some pervert riffling through my underwear!"

"That's my girl!" Martha said encouragingly, putting the tray on her lap. "You eat up and I'll come back in a bit."

She eased herself up off the bed and went out of the door. When she got to the bottom of the stairs she found a reception committee waiting for her.

"Well?" asked Tom, the elderly manservant. "How did she take it?"

"Better than I thought she would," Martha replied, "although whether she'll ever get over losing him is another matter all together."

The five main household servants retreated to the sanctity of Martha's kitchen to discuss tactics. It was decided that Tom's grandson would go to the nearby farm his father kept and prepare them to take Cwen in the next day. The rambling old farmhouse housed much of Tom's extended family, in which the generations overlapped. It was difficult for newcomers to distinguish where one branch ended and the next one began, in a family where there was at least one aunt and uncle younger than their nephews. One more person would cause no comment or obvious disruption, and Cwen would be indistinguishable amongst them.

Meanwhile upstairs, Cwen had finished the muffins and for the first time actually began to think about what had happened. She walked over to the window and opened the shutters to look out at the sea. Amroth castle sat a little back from the headland, with a cluster of cottages at its feet, and scattered farmlands stretching out all along the fertile coastline. From her window she could watch cattle being brought in for milking, sheep grazing on the next headland, and the corn being harvested, while out to sea tiny distant fishing boats worked the sea. Richert had loved this view. He said it reminded him of who the really important people were, and he had often stood and looked out to remind himself of the real world when the court intrigues disgusted him.

Standing there now, Cwen could imagine the feel of his arms around her waist, and his breath on her cheek as he hugged her. Nobody could ever take that away from her whatever else happened. Now, though, she had to think about the future and it was not pleasant. Already she longed to go home to her father's comfortable inn on the south coast and to be cosseted by her mother. If ever in her life she had wanted the security of home it was now, and yet deep down she knew it would not happen that way. Twice in the last five years she had gone home for the weddings of her cousins and it had not gone well. Her own mother had never said a word of criticism about her choice to become the mistress of one of the most powerful men in the land, but her aunt had. Her mother had been endlessly bombarded with self-righteous sympathies from her older sister, who never missed an opportunity to point out the contrast with her own three girls. Cwen loathed her cousins. Perfect girls, with perfect figures, they had so far made very suitable marriages, if a dull wool merchant and a tax collector were your aspirations.

Until now it had amused Cwen and her mother that the daughter of a simple sheep farmer should look down on her sister for marrying an innkeeper, having caught the town's most eligible weaver. Even more so, later, when she aspired to climb higher in the small community, by shoving her daughters at men who were respectable only because they were too dull to be anything else. In the current circumstances, however, Cwen was forced to confront the fact that the oh-so-lawful taxman might just feel obliged to let Richert's wife know where Cwen was, if he thought the awful woman was in the right to want to punish Cwen.

Too used to their small world, he would have no idea of the trouble he would be bringing down on his own in-laws, as well as Cwen's family, once a powerful noble got it into their head to take revenge. Her aunt and her cousins might be small-minded and bitchy, but they did not deserve to end up in some dungeon, or being thrown out onto the road to scratch a living begging, any more than her parents did. Cwen brushed a tear from her cheek. No, there was no going home.

Yet she would have to go somewhere, but where? Richert had never given her property, for he knew that whatever he gave could be taken back by his wife as soon as he was dead. Most cottages were tied in some way to a lord, and were granted to someone who could provide a service – either directly, or by farming or being a craftsman. Nobody would just hand over a dwelling to a lone woman with no particular skill and no man around. They would probably think she was planning on opening a brothel if she asked! Cwen gave another sniff. Thinking such things brought back the huge void where Richert had been. But thinking of him also brought back a buried remembrance of something he had said.

She decided she would make for Mythvai first. That would take her well away from anywhere she would be expected to go, especially as her own home was deep in the southwest at Radport. Another reason for going to Mythvai, though, was that she had just remembered that Richert, ever thoughtful, had deposited some funds with a trusted merchant there. Maybe she would be able to buy her way into a craft guild or start trading in something? To the astonishment of the household she went downstairs and asked for a bath to be prepared, while she ate one of Martha's vegetable pies which had just come out of the oven. She readily agreed to go to Tom's son's home the next day, but insisted that it could not be for good. As she told them, sooner or later the steward would get around to visiting the farm, and the last thing she wanted was to risk them being thrown off the estate. However, there were many protests to the effect that they could handle the steward, which meant that Cwen had to agree that she would only go to Mythvai for a few days while the steward was around, and then come back.

A wary compliance was reached, and while the hot water was being drawn, Tom sent two girls to pack what Cwen would need for a journey with winter approaching, while she went to Richert's study. Carefully laid out in a large wooden chest were maps of all kinds. She knew she would need to take one to find her way by and it was simply a question of which one. She found a set of four small pocket-able maps on oiled cloth, which, by the state of them, had often been used. She was reassured by the threads of cloth that had attached themselves to the maps from Richert's riding cloak, from when they had obviously been stuffed in his pockets. If he had used them, then so would she. It looked as though the steward would come by the main road coming southeast from Arlei and so the Mythvai road, going northwards and away from the capital, would be safe.

When one of the girls popped her head round the door to tell her that the bath was ready, she carefully folded the maps and took them with her up to her room. There she took out her heaviest cloak and tucked them into the inside pocket. Saddle bags lay packed on the chest at the foot of the bed, for she would not be returning to this room even when she came back, and she laid out sensible clothes ready for an early start. She wanted to be out of here well before the steward arrived for the sake of the others as much as for herself. Their kindness did not deserve to be repaid with punishment for extending their loyalty to their lord to her as well. Finding a small leather satchel, she went to the chest and packed all the little things which had sentimental value. Richert had given her books and some lovely pieces of jewellery, which were small and delicate and nothing like the ostentatious jewels he said his wife wore. These were not being left behind for someone else to have. The final thing was to sink into the blissfully hot water.

After the best night's sleep she had had in over a fortnight, Cwen got up the next morning, put on her travelling clothes, and went down to breakfast. The household were eating theirs and she joined them, as had been her habit when Richert was not there. She felt sad and angry that this would be the last time for a long while, maybe even forever, when she would be able to sit here with them. They all had their own different ways of doing things, and sometimes there were arguments, but they were the family she had been part of for the last five years. This was as bad as when she had had to leave home, although at least then it had been joyful because she had been coming here with Richert. This was a new beginning of a very different sort.

Her pony was led round from the stables and her bags loaded up. She wished she could have taken Richert's horse too, but he was a valuable war-horse, and not the sort of thing a woman would ride around the countryside on. He would attract attention she did not want, and he was costly enough that someone might just come looking for him, even if they did not know he was with her. She said good-bye to him and fed him one of his favourite apples, praying that his new owner would be as good to him as Richert had.

Her own pony was a cheeky little brown cob of the kind that could be found anywhere. Richert had wanted to buy her a highbred ladies jennet and been surprised when Cwen had laughed at the idea. She had reminded him that such over-bred animals usually had all sorts of problems and very little stamina. What she wanted was a horse who would keep up with his on long trips and the sturdy cob could do that without any problems, even if it did not have the big horse's speed at the gallop. They had become a common sight all around here. The lord on his big fine destrier, dwarfing his lady on the rotund and fuzzy pony. The pony was looking round for his friend too, and Cwen felt the tears welling up as she saw him twist round to look at the stables.

She rubbed his muzzle. "No Twigglet, Shadow can't come with us this time."

"Don't you worry miss," Sam the groom said. "I left a message down in the inn, 'cos I heard the Knights are passing through soon. I'm going to take him out to the far fields, and then when I hears that them Knights have come, I'll take him down to 'em and take what they offers for 'im. He won't go to some silly peacock at court who don't know one end of an 'orse from t'other."

She had to smile at Sam. He would no more let his beloved charge go without a fight then she would. The big horse was battle-trained, and she knew the Knights were always on the lookout for good stud horses, and that they would be unlikely to turn down a stallion of such quality. It would mean a happy retirement for the old war-horse at the very least. She thanked Sam for putting her mind at rest, feeling she was not now abandoning another member of the family when she left. They all walked out to the castle gate where she said her good-byes, but just as she was about to turn and go someone shouted. One of the stable boys came pelting down the steps from the ramparts, waving his arms at the main road leading up to the castle.

"There's someone coming!" he panted excitedly. "Men on horses!"

They all looked at one another in horror. The steward was obviously earlier than they had expected.

"Quick! In the stables with you miss!" Sam said. "I'll make sure we stable their horses and they won't start their search there."

"Good thinking, Sam," Martha agreed. "We'll offer them caff and a meal, and while they're stuffing themselves on my pies you can slip away without them noticing. … Go on!"

Cwen led Twigglet into the back of the stables to the double stall used for mares and foals, and shut the half-door. She had barely got there when she heard the clatter of horses hooves on the cobbled yard and men's voices. Strangely, though, the horses did not get brought in. Barely an hour passed when she heard voices again and the sound of men riding out.

Sam appeared silhouetted at the stable door and called, "You can come out now, miss, they've gone."

Leading Twigglet back out, she saw the others gathered in the yard. "What was all that about?"

They all started to answer at once and she could only make out something about a search and the words "he's not dead." Her heart leapt in her chest.

"He's not dead? Richert's not dead?" She thought she might burst with joy.

"No, no, luvvie!" Martha rushed to her. "The king! King Edward's not dead." Cwen's face fell, and Martha put a consoling arm around her. "Those men were on the road looking for the murderer. They thought he might have gone south on a fast horse, so they were searching down there. Last night they got word, though, that King Edward has turned up at court. Something about a hunting trip and needing to visit a shrine!"

"Edward? At a shrine? Rubbish!" Cwen exploded angrily. "If he walked into a holy place the roof'd collapse round his perverted ears!"

"Aye, that it might!" Martha laughed. She was relieved that Cwen had not collapsed when she found out that it was not her beloved Richert who had risen so unexpectedly from the dead, and she was shrewd enough to see that Cwen's anger was significant. "The visitors we just had simply wanted food and drink, and water for their horses, so they could get back to the court. I don't know what's going on. They were as confused as we are. Their captain thought it a poor joke and pretty irresponsible of the king, 'cause as he said, where in the Underworld has King Edward been that he hasn't heard that he was supposed to be dead?"

Cwen's voice was ice cold. "Oh I think Edward knows exactly what's been going on. In fact, I think Edward probably set it all up, but who's going to question the king now Richert's gone?"

Horrified glances were exchanged as they realized what this implied.

"You think King Edward had him killed, don't you?" Ted the gardener asked her in a shocked voice.

"I think it was more than just Richert." Cwen answered grimly. "I think he planned to get them all out of the way. It's not one but four people's blood he's got on his hands, maybe more if their servants tried to defend them."

"Oh crap!" Sam sighed. "It's so obvious isn't it. 'E used the threat to the little ones to lure Earl Richert 'cos 'e knew 'e'd go to protect them. When 'e left me with the 'orses, I 'eard men riding by but I didn't think nothin' of it. Then when the girl from the 'ouse came a screamin' in, tellin' us they'd all been murdered, and we found Earl Richert in the road outside the gates, we was all too shook up to think straight. The bastard!"

"Yes, Sam, that he is!" Cwen said vehemently. "Well he might think he's got away with it, but he hasn't!"

"What are you going to do?" Tilly the maid asked, very confused. "What did *you* think had happened when you thought King Edward was dead?"

"I thought his past had caught up with him – maybe one of his favourites whom he'd dumped had decided on revenge – or that Richert had fought back and taken him down with him," she said. "But all this changes what I was going to do."

She looked off into the distance as a flood of memories washed over her.

It was high summer, and she and Richert had been walking on the beach of one of the small coves. He had come back from the court distraught at Edward's latest calumnies against Queen Nerys, and had wanted somewhere away from everyone where he could let vent his feelings. As he had fumed as he told Cwen what had happened, she had been moved to sympathetic rage,

"He's such a bastard! How is it that you two are brothers? You're nothing alike, nothing in common! Nothing at all!"

"He's not," Richert had said softly, so that his words were almost lost in the swish of the surf.

"What?" Cwen had exclaimed in astonishment.

She had turned to look at him, taking in his dark hair and his faced tanned a deep brown by the exposure to the sun. Until now she had not really thought much about it, having only ever seen Edward once and that from a distance. However, once Richert had said that, it had occurred to her just how different they were. It was not just in colouring, although Edward was as fair as Richert was dark, to the extent of having an almost sickly pallor despite his obvious health. In build too they were opposites. Richert was barely average height, but stockily built and strong. Only that morning, Cwen had taken great delight in watching him exercise with a great sword in the yard, stripped to the waist in the summer heat, and muscles rippling and flexing. Edward, on the other hand, was tall. Very tall, and lean with no spare flesh.

"Are you serious?" she had asked.

"Never more," he had said in a far off way.

Wrapping his arm around her waist, he had led her over to the great flat rocks which tumbled from the surrounding cliffs out into the sea, and there, perched above the waves with his arms wrapped around her tight, he had told her the truth.

"Back then our family was nothing special. We were just one of many noble lines. Father wasn't even heir to the family's lands until his older brother and some of the family died of a sickness. But the family still needed heirs, and so Father was married off to his very young sister-in-law to keep the alliance going. I suppose the alliance was the most important thing because his bride – later my mother – was only twelve even then, so there was no chance she was going to produce children for several years.

"Well, this was years before the Battle of Moytirra, but we were already suffering many DeÁine raids, and so father went with the army into the west. While he was there he came on some DeÁine hunters persecuting this young woman. He and his men ran them off, and it turned out that this woman was a young widow with a little boy. My father became absolutely besotted with her. Do you know, even on his death bed it was her name he called out?

"It didn't take long for her to become pregnant, but by the time Edward was born they were fighting like cat and dog. It seems to have been one of those incredibly passionate affairs between two equally headstrong people – they couldn't live with one another, yet they were lost without each other. The final straw was that he had to come back to the east, and there was no way he could bring her to court. My grandfather absolutely refused to allow her into the family homes, and there was no way she herself would settle for keeping quietly in the background. Grandfather sent armed men to separate them and bring father back."

"Good grief!" Cwen had exclaimed. "That was a bit brutal, wasn't it?"

Richert had shrugged, but pulled her closer and kissed her before continuing.

"Until I met you, I had no idea of what it must have cost him to let her go. He asked the Knights to escort her to safety. I gather she and her other son went north. Father let them go because he feared what grandfather would do, but he held onto Edward."

"And your grandfather let him?"

"Yes. Surprisingly enough he did. I've never understood, though, why she held onto her older son and let Edward go – perhaps she had some premonition of what he was going to turn out like! …Anyway, I gather Mother had turned out to be very slow developing, (by now she was in her mid-teens) and there was some concern that she might not ever be able to bear children. So they had Edward baptised in secret in the great cathedral at Caersus. Mother was brought there and kept out of sight for months so that she could reappear with a child without anyone commenting on the lack of signs of an advanced pregnancy. It took another eight years and two miscarriages before she had me, and she never had another child that lived beyond the first few hours, so I guess nobody asked many questions about the gap between us."

"Poor lady! I wish I'd known her," Cwen had cried sympathetically.

"You'd have got on well with her," Richert had murmured, kissing her hair again. "She put up with Edward, but despite her best efforts he was as contrary a child as he is as an adult. The real trouble came because of Moytirra. The king died. As you know, there was no clear line of succession and the major families dragged us into a civil war, while the Knights held the line against any new DeÁine threat and thought we'd gone mad. I think they weren't so far wrong, either! Perhaps it's a good thing that, between the skirmishes and the assassinations, the contenders from the three top families wiped one another out. If they couldn't make peace with the biggest threat the Island had seen in generations sitting on their doorstep, then the Spirits only know what mayhem would have erupted if one of them had got control.

"It was the Church who put father's cousin on the throne. I suspect because he was easily controllable. So against all the odds, cousin Lothar became king! I suppose in one way he wasn't such a bad choice. He let them make all the policy decisions and we've had over twenty years of relative peace. The people have carried a heavy burden of taxes, but the roads are well-kept, and we can get an army to the border far faster than ever we could before.

"Unfortunately Lothar turned out to be as randy as a rabbit and as sterile as a mule. He must have fucked his way through all his councillors' wives, and any willing woman who came to court, without even a hint of a bastard. Poor old sod was game to the end, but he hadn't got any arrows in his bow!"

Cwen had giggled helplessly at that. Richert smiled at her mirth, but shook his head.

"It would be funny, if it wasn't for the consequences. Lothar had no living siblings by the end, and that put Father next in line. I don't know what Father would have done if he'd lived to see the succession fall to Edward. Before his accident, I know he was talking about going to Caersus to find those baptismal records, and to the Knights to see if his old love still lived."

"Do you think he was trying to set things right?" Cwen had asked.

Richert had sighed,

"I can't be sure. The trouble was that Edward was a young man by this time. He'd been brought up to expect to inherit, and he'd already begun to make alliances of his own. My own guess is that Father was prepared to let Edward have the family lands, but that he wanted to show the proof of Edward's bastardy to Lothar, so that he would nominate another heir to the Island."

"Do you think Edward would ever have settled for that?" Cwen had asked in astonishment. "This is Edward we're talking about! He must surely have seen that he was in line for the throne!"

"I know! I think it would have been near to impossible without the Church or the Knights backing the action, and who knows what they would have done?"

"Is that why you're prepared to back Queen Nerys' children as the heirs, even though they can't be Edward's?" Cwen had quizzed him. "Because they can't be tainted with whatever's made Edward turn out the way he has?"

"It's not just that – although I'll grant you it's a serious consideration. No. It's about who else is there to inherit? That's what terrifies me. Edward has the right to nominate his own heir, and he proved right from the start he wouldn't be swayed by the bishops and abbots. He wouldn't choose me, and neither would they – but that's alright because I wouldn't want it. But who else is there? Our father's cousins have all died, and their only children who survive are those whom Edward can mould – which makes me suspicious. But I have no proof, and with one of them being a genuine accident it would be impossible to prove Edward had them disposed of the others. But that's the end of our branch of the family, because even if *we* had a child, I'd never let it within a mile of Edward! And my cursed wife's too busy fucking her dimwit cousin to produce an heir with me – and I'd disclaim any child she bore now with him.

"So the next lot in line are from grandfather's younger brother's line. Father's cousin Urwith had two sons, and his brother, Seebold, had several. Urwith's oldest, Uriah, is an obsequious, oily little youngster who follows Edward like a dog. The younger brother, Godber, is all muscle but with no brains. He'll do whatever his brother tells him, and he has no conscience, so he's a dangerous henchman but not a schemer. The ones who scare me witless, though, are Seebold's oldest who're twins. Lethi and Wicga are two of the nastiest pieces of work I've ever come across. They aren't even out of their teens yet, but I've feared for some time that the strange ends that have come to their younger brothers are down to them. Trees protect us, but I suspect them of murder when they were barely ten years old."

"Dear Spirits!" Cwen had gasped in horror.

"Oh they're evil through and through!" Richert had growled. "There must have been something wrong there to start with, but from little boys they've been around Edward and he's cultivated them to grow in his own form. So you see, at all costs those two little boys of Nerys' must grow into young men and succeed, because without them I fear Edward will nominate Lethi and Wicga as his heirs, with Uriah and Godber as their lords in the north – and Spirits help the Island then!"

"Miss! Miss, what are you going to do?" Tilly's anxious voice brought Cwen back to the present."

"I'm going to find some evidence Richert told me about which would bring Edward down if it became known. Edward is going to pay for this!"

"Good Spirits, miss! What are you going to do?"

"How on earth are you going to do that?"

"You're going to take on the king?" all came flooding at her as worried replies.

Quite calmly, Cwen faced them.

"If the proof is still there it's enough to bring him down," she told them. "It won't just be me when that comes to light. Richert would never use it because he thought it was in the country's best interest in order to keep it stable, even if Edward was useless as a king. He thought he would be able to stop Edward doing anything which would allow their cousins to inherit, and so keep the peace we've had for a generation. Now I know he'd think it was time things changed. Edward's changed and he's out of control. There's no telling what he'll do next."

"Well at least they didn't string some poor sod up for killing the king before he came back to life." Martha observed. "That really would have been injustice."

"I suspect that might be the one bit that failed," Sam commented observantly. "I bet 'e had 'is eye on some poor bugger 'e wanted to set up as the bait. Some poor sod who knew more than was good for 'im."

"Well I hope he or she has the sense to lie low until we can prove Edward's complicity, or they'll find themselves at the end of some other trumped up charge." Cwen observed.

Suddenly Tilly chipped in.

"How could he stay hidden for a whole week? The king I mean? Surely someone would see his crown and ask him who he was?"

The whole yard-full collapsed in laughter, breaking the tension. It had to be explained to Tilly, who was sweet but not over blessed with intelligence, that the king only wore his crown on special occasions, and that most people had no idea what the king looked like in real life.

However, Cwen realized that all this did not change the fact that the steward could be here at any time. Hugging her friends, she told them that she would now not stop at the farm. She could not explain why but she had a feeling of urgency about what she was going to do. This new news had brought it home to her the lengthy delay it took for even the most important messages to reach such a far flung castle as Amroth. Already Edward could have been back in his court for two, possibly even three, days. She could not afford to be so far behind him in reacting to his plotting. As it was, it would take her three days' steady riding to get to Mythvai if she used all the available daylight, and she blessed Twigglet's stamina as a lesser pony would have needed to be rested more.

Mounting up she waved good-bye and turned Twigglet across the lanes to connect with the coast road. Luckily it was a glorious day and they went at a brisk walk, with the cooling breeze ruffling Twigglet's mane and forcing Cwen to tie her long blond hair into a plait to be able to see. By the time the sun was going down she had made the main road and pulled off it to spend the night at a small homely inn, which reminded her very much of her father's.

Sitting in a corner of the only public room, she fretted about what would happen to her family. She had thought about sending them word that she had left Amroth, but then realized that if they were questioned by anyone from the court, it would tell them that she had been at the castle up until the previous day. That would narrow their search, if indeed they bothered searching for her, far too much. The household at the castle were much more used to playing dumb in the face of arrogant visiting nobility, and much less likely to be overawed into revealing anything. However, she knew her parents and brothers would be worried sick for her, given the state of affairs in the kingdom, and she still felt very guilty for not putting their minds to rest.

Despite being tired she found it hard to fall asleep, and got irritated with herself as the night drew on knowing that she would be even more weary the next day for lack of sleep. After finally nodding off in the small hours, she woke the next morning to a wet and windy day. Using the long cloak to shield Twigglet from the worst of the drizzle, they still had an unpleasant day's journey. The wind from the sea seemed to drive the fine droplets inside the oiled cloth whatever she did, and although the road was not on the edge of the cliffs, the hedges alongside the road had been kept trimmed short to prevent them from being used as cover by the felonious, and so afforded little protection. By late afternoon she was soaked to the skin and Twigglet had slowed to a dejected plod, shaking his head frequently to rid himself of the water that was now dripping in his ears. A village and inn appeared as they crested a small rise, and she decided to stop for the night. There was no point in making herself ill by getting thoroughly chilled only one day out.

This time she had no trouble sleeping and was up early and refreshed. As she drank the hot caff the landlady provided, she stared out of the window which faced the sea. After yesterday it was once again clear and bright, but on the far horizon storm clouds loomed. The landlady came and stood companionably by her with her own mug.

"Might take all day for that one to get here," she observed, "but when it does it's going to be a good 'un. It's the equinox tomorrow night and the tide'll be high enough without a storm coming in. You make sure you stop in time this evening. You don't want to be caught in that."

"Do you think I can make Mythvai today?" Cwen asked her.

"Probably best not to try to get all the way. There's a good little inn about four miles out this side – *The Bay Horse.* I'd make for that if I were you. In the town they'll likely be full up with travellers waiting for the storm to pass to catch boats, and you might end up not finding anywhere."

Cwen thanked her, knowing that such information had saved her from making a mistake that could have led to a very unpleasant night in the open if she had been really unlucky. Retrieving a dry and happy Twigglet from the stables, she continued down the road where today she encountered far more people, which was a good indicator of the proximity of the major port. The countryside was still much the same, but as the road swung slightly to the east to drop into the river valley, looking up it she could see a smudge on the far horizon which was the rising hills where Arlei lay. In the fields, farmers hurried to get the last of the grain stored away before the coming storm flattened and soaked it, rendering it useless, and far out to sea she could see little boats heading into shore.

The Bay Horse proved to be everything the landlady had promised when she got there in the early evening, and as she sat eating a delicious lamb stew, she heard the first of the rain pelting the shutters outside. By the time she was ready for bed, a gale was pounding the stone walls of the inn, driving the rain in sheets across the countryside. Late travellers arrived drenched and cold, with the last two scared half out of their wits, and telling of something hunting in the storm which had nearly caught them. It had taken a lone sheep that had got missed by its farmer instead, or at least they thought it was a sheep they heard being slaughtered. Cwen took her candle and made her way up to the cosy little room under the eaves, too tired to worry about what lay outside tonight, but in the small hours she heard an unworldly keening that woke her from her sleep and sent a shiver down her spine.

Chapter 11

A Strange Meeting

Brychan: Harvest-moon

On an altogether clearer morning Cwen made the short ride into Mythvai. The merchant turned out to be easy to find, and was everything Richert had said he would be. Consequently her business was easily completed, and within an hour her beloved possessions had been stored in a strong room. She had two purses of coins, one small with gold coins in it, which she hid inside her shirt, and a larger of smaller denominations of silver which was in the normal place on her belt. Even better, tucked in her saddle bags were three letters of credit from the merchant, which, he assured her, would be honoured almost everywhere in Brychan. So she had no fears of running short of money wherever her quest took her. But where to start?

Leading Twigglet out along the main street, she reached the main bridge across the river mouth and stood watching the tide while she thought. The obvious place to start was the cathedral at Caersus, but that would mean riding up the road into the hills and passing through Arlei. She could not say why, but all her instincts warned her about going too near the capital just yet. Edward had never met her, but there were enough of Richert's servants still there who might inadvertently give her away. If Edward's conscience was twitching hard enough, or if he still felt vulnerable, anyone connected with Richert might be seen as a threat. She also was not too sure about where the Church stood in all of this. After all, their records must have made it clear to them what Edward was, yet they had never shown any sign of reluctance in backing him as king. It was possible they were waiting for the right moment to step in and take control again. In which case they might be waiting for Edward to make a fatal mistake, but she could not be sure.

The other option was to ride north and try to find what had happened to Edward's mother. It would be the longer journey, but at least she would be dealing with the Knights. They had no real reason to back Edward, but then they had never shown any interest in Brychan's internal politics either, so they were unlikely to see her as a threat. It also had the advantage of being a straight road. All she had to do was to ask at every Knights' castle and preceptory along the way. Sooner or later she had to get lucky when there was no way she could miss one out. There were no scattered outposts going northwards because the bulk of the mountains cut the western side routes off, as the sea did east of the road.

Her mind made up, she turned to lead Twigglet back the way she had come when a movement at the other end of the bridge caught the corner of her eye. Looking back properly, she saw a painfully thin man struggle to haul himself onto the parapet of the bridge. For a second Cwen could not believe what she was seeing, but, by the time he had swung both legs out onto the seaward side, she had broken into a sprint. As he toppled outwards she made a frantic dive for him and seized a handful of shirt. Hauling backwards with all her strength she expected to struggle to hold his weight. Instead, she found herself falling back onto the road surface, with him landing in a heap beside her.

Disentangling themselves from one another, Cwen stood up and looked down at the sad specimen at her feet.

"What in the Islands do you think you're doing?" she asked in astonishment. "That water's freezing, and the currents around here are treacherous."

"Dying," the whispered reply came back.

Cwen blinked, and looked again. He really was in a dreadful state. Thin did not begin to describe him, haggard was closer to it, and the white hair with the pallor of his skin made him look like the living dead. Maybe he really was trying to kill himself! That really shocked Cwen. No matter how bad things had been over the last few weeks, and no matter how often she had wished she could join Richert, not once had she ever thought about actually killing herself to do it. Poor soul, she thought, to have reached that point, and all her better feelings came to the fore.

"Well you're not dying today," she said firmly. "Come on, I can't leave you here in this state. You'll have to come with me."

All she got was an uncomprehending blank stare, so she took him by the hands and tried to get him onto his feet. She immediately realized why she had catapulted him onto the road – there was nothing of him. When he finally stood up and she could see his face more clearly, she realized with a shock that he was not so very far from her own age. However, he swayed where he stood, and it was evident he was not going to be able to walk even a few steps. Pulling his arm over her shoulder, Cwen got a handful of the waist of the tattered old trousers he was wearing with the other hand and whistled Twigglet. The pony had been waiting where she had left him when she dropped his reins, but now walked obediently up to them. With some pushing and shoving, Cwen got the young man aboard Twigglet, who twitched his ears in disapproval. He was not used to such a clumsy rider, and obviously thought he was coming down in the world to be relegated to acting as a pack animal to such an ungainly burden.

"Where are you from?" she asked her new companion, as she led Twigglet off the bridge.

"Nowhere," the sad reply came back.

"Rubbish!" Cwen said, trying to keep a cheerful tone of firm practicality in her voice. "You must have come from somewhere to here. Where's your family? Aren't they worried about you? Surely someone is going to miss you?"

He shook his head.

"What, no-one?" Cwen asked again in amazement. "But where were you going?"

He shrugged. "Had to get away. …Can't go back. …Nowhere to go."

Even such a short reply seemed to exhaust him. Cwen led Twigglet onto the grass verge along the side of the road, now totally stuck as to know what to do with him. All she had thought in those first few brief moments since meeting him was that she would just be taking him back to some house outside of the town. Perhaps to where a frantic parent would harangue him for going on a drunken binge, and that would be the last she would see of him. However, that was not going to happen, was it? Her own common sense told her she should have realized that nobody got in that state after just a night or two on the town. Something in his voice said that whatever had happened was really serious, and the way he spoke made her think this was no country lad. On closer inspection, where the baggy sleeves had ridden up, she could see where the coarse cloth had chaffed his skin, which was far too smooth for someone who had spent their life outdoors. All of which made her think this was someone in an even more desperate state than she was.

One thing was for certain, she could not just leave him. As she had walked into the town this morning, the streets had been buzzing with the news that something had been out hunting in the storm last night. How he had survived that was a miracle, but she could not rely on him being that lucky again. The only thing she could think of was to return to the inn she had stayed at the previous night. The landlady had seemed a kindly soul, and at the very least Cwen could now afford to pay for him to have a bath, a meal and a change of clothes.

So she turned and led Twigglet back up the gentle slope of the road towards the headland again, with her passenger saying not a word. It was just approaching midday when they walked into the yard of *The Bay Horse Inn* once more, to the surprise of the landlady. Leaving the young man swaying on Twigglet's back, Cwen explained what had happened and asked for another bed for the coming night. At first the woman was sceptical, obviously thinking that Cwen had been taken in by some rogue of a professional beggar, however when she came out and saw him she relented. At first she was going to call two of the farmers out to help them get him inside, but when Cwen got her to help get him down off Twigglet, and she felt how starved he was, she was only too willing to help. Between them, the two women half carried him up to a bedroom larger than the one Cwen had had the previous night but which had a truckle bed as well as the main one, where they sat him in a wooden chair.

Luckily the inn was fairly quiet, so a tin bath appeared in short order, and was quickly filled with hot water, which Cwen took her turn at fetching from the cistern beside the kitchen range. Without thinking, when the last bucket had gone in, Cwen went to the semi-comatose figure and began to undo the knotted string holding up the trousers. With a squeak of embarrassment, he leapt to life and pulled away from her, promptly falling over as he stood up and the trousers slid round his ankles. Living in an inn, and with so many brothers, Cwen had long since got used to seeing men undressed and was not in the least disconcerted. So as he pitched forward onto his knees, she grabbed the hem of the shirt and pulled that over his head, completing the undressing.

Under other circumstances she would have laughed at his embarrassment, which reminded her so much of her younger, teenage brothers, but the sight of him stopped her in her tracks. Quite apart from endless sores, caused by the rough cloth without any underclothes to protect him, he was a mass of scars. Some looked like burns, others like small cuts, and Cwen felt the tears rising. He could never have inflicted such damage on himself, and she had never heard of any punishment inflicted by the law which spoke of such cruelty.

"Oh, you poor soul! Whoever did this to you?" she exclaimed, as he struggled to his feet and staggered against her. She caught him and held him steady and tried to make out whether there was anything she could do for the scars that were still fresh. He struggled out of her hold and cringed away against the chair like a whipped dog.

"No! Don't touch me!" he whimpered.

Cwen shook her head in horror. "Good Spirits, I'm not going to hurt you!" she exclaimed.

She stepped forward and pulled him to his feet again. "Come on, get in the bath. Let's get you and those sores clean, and then you can sleep in a proper bed for tonight. What's your name?"

She had asked this several times already on the way here, but this time, as he slid wincing into the hot water, she got a reply.

"I'm Swein," he said softly. "Why are you helping me?"

The only halfway sane reply Cwen could think of to that was, "Because you need helping."

It was not much of an answer, but it was better than trying to explain that she was running on instinct here. Quite why she felt she must help him was as much of a mystery to her as it was to him, but over the years she had come to realize that when all her impulses were pushing her so hard in one direction, it was prudent to heed them. While he lathered the soap up, she went in search of salves. Her hostess was horrified at what Cwen described, and they were so deep in conversation they did not notice an old man at the bar listening until he chipped in.

"He's been tortured," the old man lisped through missing teeth. "I was a soldier at Moytirra and I saw some of those the DeÁine left behind. They were covered in scars like that."

Both women jumped at the sound of his voice.

"Sacred Trees protect us," Cwen gasped, "There aren't any DeÁine left around here, are there? Why would anyone do that here and now?

The old boy shook his head knowingly. "Ah! Not round here they wouldn't, but my oldest is in the castle guard up at Arlei. He says you wouldn't believe what that king gets up to. Apparently there's a special dungeon that only he uses. My lad lost his promotion to sergeant because he wouldn't stand by and watch. He's transferring to become a lay brother with the Knights. Said it was more than any civilized body could be expected to look at and not be sick. If your laddie up there is scared witless, I'd put good money on it being the king or his men he's terrified of."

In Cwen's mind the puzzle suddenly clicked into place. That was what had been lurking in the depths of her memory. Now she remembered Richert telling her of a place that Edward would never let him see and what he feared it contained. It did not bother her how Swein had come to be in Edward's power. Whatever his tastes were he could never have anticipated what he would become embroiled in. He was as much of a victim of Edward's twisted personality as she was, probably more, and now she knew she had to take him with her.

Drawing Fran, the landlady, aside she asked her if there were spare clothes she could give Swein temporarily. Fran could not help with the clothes, but told her the farm next door had a pony their son had outgrown which they might be willing to sell. Clutching a pot of salve Cwen went back upstairs to the bedroom. Swein lay on the bed, rolled in the blankets deep in sleep which Cwen was reluctant to wake him from. Leaving the salve on the side table, she dragged the bath and damp towel to outside the bedroom door and then went down to Twigglet.

Mounting him once more, she rode to the farm and arranged to buy the pony, who was very like a pale version of Twigglet. The farmer's son turned out to be a huge ox of a boy, so it was no surprise that the pony could no longer carry him, but Swein would present it no problem. While they found the tack, Cwen rode back down into Mythvai and found clothing stalls, where she purchased the basics for Swein. It might not be what he was used to in the past, but at least they were good quality and serviceable and not likely to rub him raw. On the way back she picked up the pony, whom she christened Bracken, and got her stabled at *The Bay Horse* with Twigglet.

Even after all that time Swein still had not moved, and in a worried moment Cwen checked to see if he was still breathing. By the evening she felt obliged to wake him so that he would get a proper meal. His eyes opened wide at the new clothes, and to Cwen's embarrassment he burst into tears once he had got dressed. She was not sure how to take such a reaction and he seemed incapable of explaining. Once he had recovered enough to go downstairs, she found the next problem was that he had been so unused to proper meals, he could not manage the whole plateful Fran put in front of him. He bolted the first dozen spoonfuls of the chicken braised in cider with vegetables, but then got hiccups and could manage no more. In the end Fran let him take the plate away with him. The people around him seemed to make Swein nervous, and he was unwilling to linger in the public room. So Cwen got them a tankard of porter each, and, with Swein clutching his plate as though he would never let it go, they went upstairs.

In the sanctuary of their room, she carefully explained to him what she planned to do. Leaving aside her relationship with Richert, she simply told him that she knew of a story about Edward, which, if true, would be the undoing of him. Watching carefully to make sure he was taking it all in, she told him of the purchase of Bracken and that she planned to take him with her. The point when he really seemed to connect with what she was saying was when she told him they would be going away from Arlei into the far north. The visible relief on his face told her that the old man's guess was probably right. Swein suddenly seemed much more back in the real world once he realized he was going far away from the king.

Inside, Swein himself was feeling as though a cloud had suddenly lifted. Once upon a time he would have laughed at someone offering help to a stranger, seeing it as folly to leave yourself open to being taken advantage of. Now he was so weak and downtrodden he felt like a drowning man who had just found something to hang on to. Yet he did not know how to respond to Cwen's kindness. He was so used to cynical bitterness he felt sure whatever he said would come out wrong. Then again, he was so unused to women he was not sure how she would respond to anything anyway. What threw him most was her easy manner with him. He was not sure, but he was fairly convinced she was not flirting with him, and, never having had sisters or female cousins, he could not see that Cwen had simply gone into her big sister act without thinking.

That night Cwen took the truckle bed, on the firm understanding that from then on, if there was only one good bed, they would take it in turns. Swein found it strange beyond words to be sharing a bedroom with a woman, but when Cwen's breathing slowed into easy slumbers he relaxed and slowly drifted off himself. It was the early hours when Cwen was wrenched out of sleep by a broken howl. Jumping out of bed, she realized that Swein was thrashing around in the throes of a dreadful nightmare.

"No! No!" he screamed out. "Not you! You're not supposed to be dead! Get away from me!"

Lighting the oil lamp's wick from the hearth embers she sat beside him and softly called his name. It took at few attempts, but then suddenly his eyes shot open.

"Who are you? Where am I?" he gasped. His breath was coming in ragged gasps and sweat stood out on his brow, even though he was shivering.

"You're safe," Cwen reassured him. "This is *The Bay Horse Inn*."

She got no answer but he blinked and looked around, and slowly she could see what little muscle he had un-tensing. Suddenly his eyes shot back to her, as it dawned on him that a woman dressed only in her underwear was sitting on the bed beside him. From being white he transformed in seconds to scarlet embarrassment, as he realized that he was seeing more of her than he had of any other woman in his life. Giving an exasperated sigh, Cwen shook her head and got up to return to her own bed. As she settled down she tried to imagine what sort of life he must have led in the past. Would she only make things worse if she told him he was not her type? Or was his embarrassment just total naivety?

In the morning Swein hid himself under the blankets while Cwen washed and dressed, only emerging after she had closed the door to go and find breakfast for them. He came downstairs and joined her in only the shortest of times, and managed to eat a reasonable amount of Fran's newly baked bread, copiously spread with fresh butter and homemade raspberry jam. It was noticeable, though, that he avoided the bacon and sausages that the other guests were making short work of. Cwen wanted to ask why, but thought that was another question for later. For now, she was beginning to think it was best to let him build up some trust in her, and not to fear that she would be endlessly probing him about his past. So as he ate she told him that she intended to take the coast road north, outlining that she did not think they would be stopping for longer than the night at any one place until they got to the first of the chain of castles.

For his part Swein was still recovering from the shock of realizing he was not going to die. This strange young woman seemed to have a definite purpose in mind, but he could not begin to fathom why she would want to have him dragging along with her. It made no sense. He was no use as a bodyguard. He could not pay his way. And if she was hoping for payment in services rendered at night she was in for a surprise! Yet he could not believe that she meant him any harm either. Having gone to all the trouble to get him clothes and pay for his lodging, it seemed illogical to think she would then only wait until they were out of the next town and then do away with him. Taking another swig of the delicious sweet caff, Swein gave up on trying to untangle his thoughts. He would go along with whatever she told him for now and just hope it did not get him in another, even bigger mess than he was in before.

Having hardly ever ridden while he was at court, Swein was horribly aware that he had no idea what to do with the pony when Cwen presented it to him in the stables. However, she seemed to accept that it was another of his failings, without offering any criticism. Instead, she set about showing him how to put the bridle on and then the saddle. Luckily Bracken seemed to be a patient and quiet pony, who did nothing but twitch her ears at Swein's clumsy attempts to insert the bit in her mouth. When they were finally sorted out, with the bags secured behind each of their saddles, and Swein had mastered how, with more help from Cwen, to adjust the stirrups to the right length, they set off.

It was another chilly, gray morning, but it stayed dry. They kept the ponies at a steady walk and rode back down the hill to Mythvai. In the light of the new day, Swein felt queasy when they rode over the bridge and he saw the state of the river. Cwen had been right, the water looked freezing cold, and quite apart from the nasty jagged rocks sticking out in places, there were all sorts of flotsam where the river had washed things down, and the tide had thrown others in shore. Far from a quick end, he could see that he might have ended up being dragged and battered for ages, and shuddered at the thought. If nothing else she had saved him from a miserable end, and he decided there and then that he would try to do whatever he could to pay her back for her good act.

In the spirit of which he attempted to put on a good face as they carried on. Unfortunately, the rough clothing had left him with sores which even the soft wool underclothes that Cwen had bought could not fully cushion from a long ride. By midday he was feeling desperately uncomfortable, and could barely refrain from wincing whenever Bracken had to change her gait for a new incline in the road.

Seeing his grimaces of pain, Cwen took pity on him and they stopped for a prolonged lunch, sat on a soft grassy knoll in the lee of a small hill which cut off the stiff breeze. This rather set the pace for the next two weeks. Each morning they would set out from the small, homely inns they used, and would ride for the morning. They then made a good break if the weather was dry, remounting after a couple of hours and riding until early evening, when they would seek out an inn for the night. In the middle of the fortnight they had a prolonged spell of wet days, when even Swein did not want to linger, and so on those days they only paused briefly to eat during the day, but stopped earlier in the evening. For four nights they had to hang the clothes they had been riding in up to dry by the bedroom fire, where the wind had driven the rain under the waxed cloaks Cwen had purchased. She had her good felted-wool one, but was reluctant to subject it to such a constant soaking in the salty rain off the sea, and Swein had had no cloak at all until she found the small market stall. The cloaks may have smelt of the beeswax and goose grease that they had been treated with, but they did the job of keeping the worst of the rain off.

Each time they stopped, Cwen made a point of asking the landlord or lady for a recommendation for the next night. At first Swein had been dubious as to the quality of some of the inns, but without fail, even the ones which looked a little shabby on the outside turned out to be warm and comfortable once they got inside. Cwen explained that this had been quite normal practice when she had worked at her parents' inn, for it worked in their favour. Most inn keepers knew their counterparts in the neighbouring towns, and knew who the rogues were. By recommending reputable places they earned the gratitude of that inn keeper, who would recommend them in turn. In such a way they were guaranteed a regular trade from the commercial travellers who frequented Brychan's highways, to supplement their local trade.

Swein found the whole thing an eye-opener – almost as much as the towns and villages he saw. Bettus was by no means unusual it turned out. Spearton, Furnace and Kilnport were also prosperous places, although they were mining communities where the main industrial activities took place outside of the town walls. Cwen explained that almost any trade that involved fire, whether it was cooking, firing or smelting, was always on the opposite side of the town from the prevailing wind because of the danger of sparks carrying to the buildings and causing a major fire. While most of the houses along this rocky coast were built of stone and slate, the insides were still vulnerable to fire. Most people also kept stocks of wood for starting the locally mined coal in their home fires, which could catch fire.

Being the capital, Arlei had been more of a trading centre rather than producing anything, and Swein was surprised to see that, even if the humblest of people looked bent and gnarled by their hard work, they were also well fed and dressed in substantial clothes and shoes. He had always thought of the lesser folk of the provinces in the light of the scruffy beggars he had seen on the streets of Arlei. But now the nasty realization came to him that he had become one of those beggars, who would have died if not for this provincial woman riding beside him.

His recovery from his ordeal was slowed by these revelations, for even as he was able to start coming to terms with the fact that he had left his old life well and truly behind, it was constantly brought home to him how ill prepared he was to face this new world. Cwen did her best to be patient with him, but at times it was hard. His confusion was blindingly obvious, and yet whenever he did venture to comment on anything he unwittingly showed himself to have a very prejudiced and arrogant view of the world. At times the only way she could bit her lip, and not give vent to her feelings when confronted with some of his more ridiculous statements, was to hold on to the thought that these were not really his own thoughts, but those which had been planted in him at an early age and had obviously never been seriously challenged.

By the time they were riding over the headland and down into Fleton, she had drawn it out of him that his father had been a domineering character, who was the leader of the local weavers' guild. She had seen the type before: a man who was a very big fish in his local, very small pond and something of a bully. But to keep that position in the face of outside influences, he would resort to denigrating anything outside of his control. Cwen had little time for such men. Inevitably they wilted when someone faced up to them outside of their tightly controlled circle. It seemed such a shame that Swein had not discovered that for himself.

Swein on the other hand was increasingly in awe of Cwen's worldliness. His own mother had been a ghostly little woman totally under the thumb of his father, who had never dared to stand up for herself or her youngest son. Both of Swein's older brothers had been just like his father – heavily built, bombastic characters, whose sole purpose in life was to ensure that they came out on top in any situation. In such a family there were only winners or losers. There were endless rows between his father and brothers, but the old man was proud of his oldest sons' grasping natures, even if he had to fight ever harder to remain pack leader as they grew up.

For his artistic, delicately built youngest son he had had nothing but contempt from the start. Their mother might have found an ally in Swein, but instead she found he was the one person she could dominate. So he had spent his formative years believing competent meant overbearing. Cwen's quiet assertiveness was an alien thing to him. On the one hand she led him, but on the other, never tried to make him feel stupid for not knowing, and her gentle reproofs for repeating some of his father's fast held truths were done without any malice. She also insisted on making him think about this new world he was seeing, and that was the biggest challenge of all to someone who had perfected unquestioning obedience as his only survival trait.

The Rising Sun in Fleton stood on the far side of the town, and was another of the small, cosy inns recommended from their previous stop. Over plates of locally produced, delicately smoked fish, Cwen studied the relevant page of her map. By her reckoning they were barely a day's ride from the first of the Knights' northerly castles at Bere. When the serving girl came for their plates Cwen asked her if they had much contact with the castle, but the girl shook her head.

"Not really," she told them. "But then there aren't that many Knights up at the castle. I think it's only manned by a contingent from Vellyn. Most of the Knights don't travel along this coast any more, they go into the mountains. I hardly see them more than a handful of times a year, although my mother tells me there was a time when they were always riding up and down here."

Cwen's heart sank. That sounded as though the place could be almost deserted, which was the one thing she had not counted on. If Edward's mother had been brought through here, any records could have been locked away long ago with no way of getting to them now. Or worse they might have been transferred to another preceptory, which might be anywhere. The records she so desperately needed might be somewhere with no obvious connection to the people they concerned. How then could she hope to find them? Swein picked up her gloomy mood, but was unable to think of anything to say that would help.

"Are we still going to this castle, then?" he finally plucked up the courage to ask. On the one hand it all seemed rather pointless to him. How could some piece of paper be effective against someone as powerful as Edward? Yet he was scared of what would happen if Cwen decided that this strange mission was no longer possible. What would happen to him then? Cwen was sitting with her head cupped in her hands, elbows resting on the table as she stared blankly into the fire, and he could not read her expression.

Finally she sat up and took a long drink from her tankard.

"Yes," she said positively, "we're going to the castle. Even if there's only a skeleton guard there, they'll surely know what the Orders' land holdings were around here. Wherever that woman got taken to, it would have to be somewhere where she could be kept under guard, so it wouldn't just be some random house out in the countryside."

Swein leant closer to her to whisper, "Are you sure this story is right? I mean, this woman, she really was Edward's mother?"

He glanced nervously around as if fearing that even uttering such words, if they were heard, would constitute treason.

"Oh yes," Cwen said emphatically. "She was his mother alright."

"But how do *you* know about this?" Swein persisted. "I never heard such a thing."

"And *you* were close enough to the court to think you would?" Cwen countered.

Swein cringed. "Oh yes, closer than you would ever dream!" he said in a voice weighted with fear and misery.

"Well I was close in different way, and my source had *very* good reason to know all about it." Cwen insisted.

Swein still wanted to say he thought it was not possible, but to do that he would have to reveal just how he knew Edward, and he was becoming increasingly uncomfortable with the memories of his past life. Quite how Cwen might react to such news he was unsure, given that he was beginning to see just how abnormal that life had been. A part of him was growing to want her approval, and he did not think he could cope just at the moment with her outright disgust.

Cwen herself was toying with the idea of telling Swein of her relationship with Richert. The one thing which held her back was the thought that he might see it in the light of his relationship with Edward. She felt fairly sure that Swein had had no experience of a really loving bond. Having nothing else to compare it with, he might well see it as one of her being subservient to Richert, in the same kind of predatory, sexual liaison that Richert had told her Edward shared with his young men. How then could she explain the depth of companionship she had known? And her own emotional scars were still too fresh for her to feel up to laying them open to scrutiny so soon. She sighed. He would just have to trust her, if he could.

Having established that there was another small inn right at the foot of the castle, they moved on, and spent the night there so as to approach the gates first thing in the morning. Their host for that night had even less encouraging news. At this time of year, normally the gates were kept locked and barred, with the drawbridge pulled up. The gate keeper and his family lived a solitary existence in the great stone edifice and Knight's rarely stayed for more than a few days until winter came. So it was with heavy hearts that they rode up the small slope out of the cluster of houses, and around to the front of the massive stone walls, which rose on the other side of the steep defensive ditch which ran in a complete circuit.

To their astonishment the drawbridge was down and the gate on one side propped open. Dismounting, Cwen looped Twigglet's reins over one of the supports for the bridge rest and cautiously crossed on foot. Just as she came into the shadow of the great gate house an elderly man came out. For all that his rather scarred face appeared frightening, he spoke courteously.

"What can I do for you?"

Cwen cleared her throat nervously.

"I've come to seek assistance from the Knights," she began, and then thought that sounded a bit too damsel in distress, so she hurried on. "I'm trying to find someone. Someone who I know was taken into the protection of the Knights many years ago. I doubt if she's still alive but I want …need …to know what happened to her. …We have a message to deliver, if we can."

The gate-keeper's eyebrows rose at this, but before he could reply footsteps rang out from inside the entrance way. From out of the gloomy shadows of the defensive gateway strode the most physically perfect man Cwen had ever seen. Swein obviously thought so too going by his appreciative 'oh my!' as he stepped up behind her.

The newcomer stood well over six feet tall, with broad shoulders tapering to a narrow waist and hips. The almost sculpted muscles of his upper arms were shown off by the sleeveless shirt he wore under the classic Knight's black leather jerkin, and his dark brown skin almost glowed in the early morning sun. The close fitting black pants, and the Knights' standard calf-hugging, knee-high black boots, also did nothing but emphasize the perfect muscle tone which probably ran all the way down to his toes. His crinkly black hair had twisted into thick, long locks which hung to his shoulders, and were tied back with a simple black cord.

For several seconds Cwen was sure she just stood there gawping at this apparition, until he spoke.

"What do you want?" he demanded

Trying not to be so overawed, Cwen explained again.

The strange Knight was by now towering over her, and looked down his nose at her as he answered.

"We do not keep track of every waif and stray that passes through our guest quarters," he said imperiously. "I suggest you make inquiries elsewhere."

With that he turned on his heels and began to stride back into the castle, pausing only to command the gate-keeper to get rid of them.

"Yes, Jacinto …sir," the man replied, but with something less than respect in his voice.

Cwen was stunned. The few Knights she had met through Richert had all been kind and civilized, and had spoken of the Order's fundamental remit to help those who needed it. Yet here, at their first attempt they had been sharply rebuffed. With tears in her eyes, she began to shoo Swein back to where the two ponies stood placidly cropping the grass, when she heard footsteps behind them. Turning she realized the gate-keeper had come after them, although he was glancing over his shoulder to make sure Jacinto had not reappeared.

Motioning them to one side, out of direct line of view from the gate, he spoke softly.

"I'm sorry about that. He's one of the newer Knights. Well he's not really a Knight yet, even though he's been a squire for years. If he's as arrogant at Vellyn as he's been here, that's probably why." He checked the gate again before carrying on. "Look, there was a woman, I don't know if it was the right one. Not here, though. I only heard about her from one of the other sergeants. We trained together, but then later on he went to Breslyn – that's the fort right out on the edge of the open sea, facing Celidon across the sound. He said there was a woman they kept out in a house by the sea cliffs. Said they were guarding her for her own safety because she'd fallen foul of someone high at court. She died before I came here, though, so that's over eight years ago. I don't know how that's going to affect you, but if I were you I'd carry on up to Vellyn. The commander's a fair man, and if you can give him a good reason why you need to know, he'll probably help."

Cwen gave the man her heartfelt thanks.

"I promise you," she said, "there's a very good reason for us wanting to know. She had at two sons in the south – maybe more up here, we don't know – but the older one certainly came up here with her. The younger one we know of down there has gone mad and murdered his half-brother from his father's side, but if there are others still living then their lives may be in real danger, because he's now a powerful man."

"Then I'm sure they'll help you," the gate-keeper assured her, and giving them a casual salute he turned and disappeared back into the gateway. As they retrieved the ponies and mounted up, Swein kept giving Cwen sideways glances.

"What did you mean about another son?" he finally asked when they were on their way.

"Think about it," Cwen said. "If you were Edward, would you let your *older* bastard half-brother roam around the countryside? Up until now there's always been someone else from the royal family around to keep a restraining hand on things. And the Knights don't take orders from the king. But if Edward can arrange for his wife and his younger half-brother, Richert," her voice choked on his name, "to be killed, how hard would it be to get rid of someone nobody knows about except for a few Knights who've probably forgotten, if they ever knew, why he's important enough to guard."

Remembering the actor, Swein suddenly felt very sick again.

CELIDON

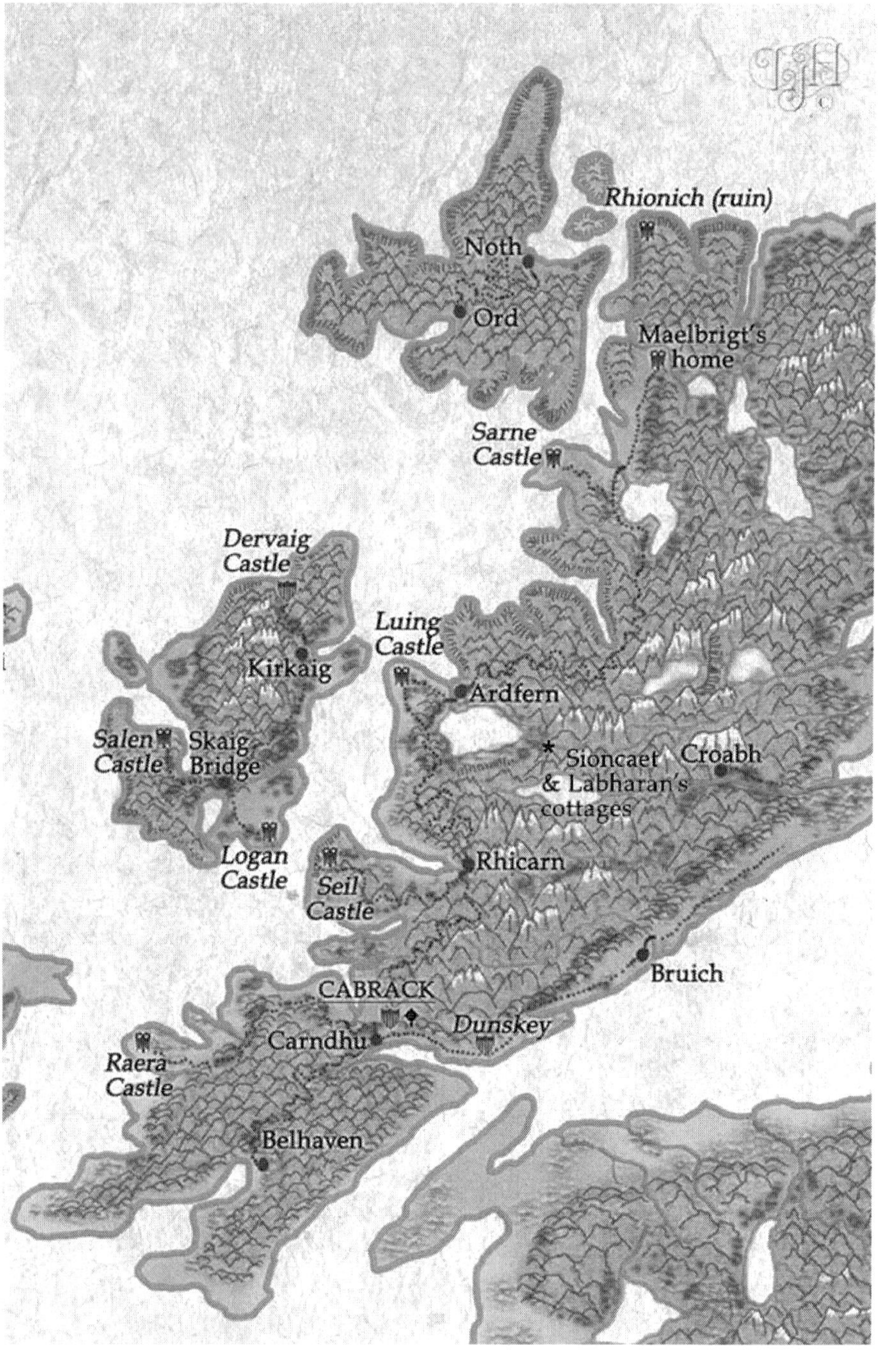

Rhionich (ruin)
Noth
Ord
Maelbrigt's home
Sarne Castle
Dervaig Castle
Luing Castle
Kirkaig
Ardfern
Salen Castle
Skaig Bridge
Sioncaet & Labharan's cottages
Croabh
Logan Castle
Seil Castle
Rhicarn
Bruich
CABRACK
Dunskey
Carndhu
Raera Castle
Belhaven

Chapter 12

The Raid

Celidon: Harvest-moon

Maelbrigt sat with his back to the stone wall of the tower, and soaked up the autumn sun. This was his favourite spot. In the angle of the two wings which formed the small castle he had called home for years, he had placed the stone bench which looked out across the fields. All around high hills rose, at this time of year bathed in purple from the heather that covered them, and in the distance a few peaks of the mountain range were just visible behind them. The castle itself was just a square tower and a wing built at right angles to it, which lay in the bend of a small river in a narrow valley. The whole valley kinked with the river, and from the tower it was possible to see the full length in either direction, and also the road that ran through it.

Once upon a time the whole of this area would have been densely populated, but that had all changed eight years ago. When the Knights of Celidon had made their famous last stand against the DeÁine at Gavra Pass, they had saved the Islands but at a huge cost to Celidon. Barely one in twenty Knights had made it out, and even fewer of the men who had served with them. When the tattered remains of the army had limped home, whole villages had had their men-folk wiped out. The surviving families had been forced to abandon fields they no longer had the workforce to plough, and had congregated in the coastal villages. Even so the first winter had been disastrous. Many who had tried to struggle on had starved to death in the worst snows for a generation, and the population of Celidon had declined even further. Maelbrigt knew he would not have been given this imposing home as a reward for his services if things had been better.

As a soldier in that battle, he had by some miracle survived, although even now the nightmares of those days returned to haunt him some nights. For a while, with help from Ergardia, the Knighthood had survived in Celidon. For most of the time they had spent their days breaking up disputes, and chasing off opportunistic raiders. The chancellor had not gone to the fight, but every able noble apart from him had, and it was left to the Knights to do all that a functioning government should have done. During that time, Maelbrigt had often travelled to Ergardia and other Islands as escort to official documents or people. Then five years ago the old chancellor had finally died, and their Grand Master had been prevailed upon to take up the office.

With many of the remaining knights now elderly, the Order was dying with them, and it had been decided – with the agreement of the Grand Masters from the other Islands – that the Celidon sept would be closed for the foreseeable future until the population grew again, at which time the other septs would undertake to train up new Knights for Celidon. The remaining few, the Knights and the lay brothers who had served and fought as men-at-arms with them, had had limited choices: to retire temporarily or permanently from the Order; to join one of the other septs; or for the lay brothers to remain but simply maintain the few granges as farmers. Maelbrigt had chosen nominal retirement even though he was far from old, and been allocated this castle.

In his case retirement really only meant a stand-down from active duty. He knew that if the need arose he could be recalled at any time – a man with his skills would not be left on the sidelines in a crisis, but that was not all. He could not say why, but he had felt deeply uneasy about leaving his homeland with even fewer defenders, and even Ergardia seemed at little too far away in case of emergency. The Attacotti raiders had been discouraged sufficiently in the intervening years to make their lightning raids less of a problem, and Brychan and the others held the line against the DeÁine. Yet something in the back of his mind niggled away at him that this could not last.

Even after all this time, he still made time to practise every day unless, like today, there was urgent work to do in the fields. Today it had been getting the last of the harvest in and his muscles knew it. The manoeuvres he practised daily kept him fit for his years, but in the last week of harvesting his fields single-handedly he had discovered muscles he had forgotten about since last year's harvest. His back and shoulders burned beneath the skin, and he was glad that from midday his corner was baked by the sun, warming the stones. Leaning back against them he could feel the heat seeping into his aching muscles, and easing the knotting in them, although he knew he would be as stiff as a board the next morning once he had rested for the night.

However, he felt the virtuous glow of having done good work over the last few days. He did not need all the grain he could grow on the fertile river valley, and as he gazed to his left he could see the two stone barns which held the reaped grain. If he followed the road north out of his valley there was a whole cluster of villages lining the sea loch that cut deeply into the island. The land they were on had once been part of the estate held by the lord of this castle, and Maelbrigt felt he had inherited some responsibility to them. The last year but one had been a disastrous harvest, and he had opened the barns up to the villagers.

He had always shared with them, exchanging his grain for some of the fish they caught, and joints off the animals they slaughtered. It had simply made sense that way. One man on his own could hardly eat his way through a whole pig without becoming sick of the sight of pork, and he always made sure that they took far more grain than a leg of scrawny pig was worth. In that bad winter, though, the reserve of grain he had had in the barns had been the difference between survival and starvation to the two closest villages, who had so little plough-able land by the loch side they struggled even in a good year.

And of course there was Taise. He lived in hope that one day the strange lady from the other side of the loch might move in here, although so far she had not been tempted away from her isolated retreat on the edge of the forest. Maelbrigt was a patient man, and so he would keep making sure she had grain when he took his harvest down the valley to the mill. Even Taise could not go without bread, although she was remarkably resourceful in acquiring most things. Her knowledge of herbs was unrivalled by anyone he had ever met, including the physician to the Knights, and she had them sorted individually and in compounds, lotions and creams all over her tiny cottage. The villagers were still wary of her even after all the years she had been here, but were willing to trade food for remedies, which they had come to realize were for the most part very effective.

He had never been able to find out just how long Taise had been there. Somewhere in the upheaval and confusion after the earlier DeÁine wars she must have crept in to the abandoned cottage which had previously belonged to an old priest. At that early stage she had avoided the villagers, and it was only some two years before Maelbrigt had arrived that they had had some cautious contact with her. Until he came they had been convinced she was a witch, and it had been at their request that he had gone to investigate her. Quite what they thought a soldier could have done against a witch, had she been one, he could not imagine. He had no supernatural skills at all. Who did? Well, with the possible exception of the DeÁine, and he felt sure that some of what was ascribed to them as magical powers were exaggerated by peoples' fear of the unknown, and of those who were different.

Taise was certainly different. She stood as tall as him, when he was tall in comparison to the local men, and she was perfectly proportioned. Some of those he had known who were particularly tall were like willow wands – all height and no substance – but Taise had a body which could have been produced by a master sculptor. Lithe and supple, she could take up positions when meditating which he felt sure would have resulted in dislocated joints and torn muscles if he had tried. She always dressed in soft, light fabrics, except in the deepest of winter, which clung and moved with her in an exotic way that contrasted with the layers of stout wool which the locals used to ward off the wet and cold. Her exotic appearance was heightened by the pallor of her skin, which was so pale in certain lights she almost had a bluish tinge, and there was her lack of hair.

If, as a young man, someone had told Maelbrigt that he would find a bald woman devastatingly attractive he would have laughed at the idea, but on Taise it seemed as normal as the long tresses did on the village girls. In contrast, she had the most beautiful long eyelashes that framed eyes of the palest grey. Maelbrigt thought her the most stunningly beautiful woman he had ever known from the second he had seen her, and had been amazed to find that the outside reflected the person she was perfectly. So many pretty girls he had met knew exactly the effect they had on the men around them, and used it mercilessly, yet Taise seemed oblivious to her looks. Admittedly not everyone saw her in the light that Maelbrigt did. Being blinded by the fact that she was so very strange in comparison to the local people, they thought that must equate with something bad, even if they had no idea what. Her one or two tormentors amongst the local teenage boys had soon reformed, or found other targets, once Maelbrigt arrived, and since then he had slowly worked to build her trust.

Now she would sometimes come and spend the night with him, always on her terms and when she decided, but that was fine by him. He hoped that one day she would trust him enough to tell him what had happened to her, and something had very definitely happened. One hot summer a couple of years ago he had taken her up to the tiny lake, high in the hills, and tried to teach her to swim. It was the first time he had seen her undressed in daylight, and he had been horrified to find that her back was covered in a web of scars. In the darkness of his bedroom he had assumed that the tiny ridges he had felt had been the product of something like a tattooing process – in the past he had seen soldiers covered in patterns which were so densely worked they could not have happened without causing some damage. That day, however, he had realized that he was seeing something very different. As a soldier he had seen men who had been flogged, and wounds from knives, and he was sure he was looking at both – even if whatever she had been flogged with had been very finely worked, and not the heavy leather flails he had seen used to punish the very worst military offenders.

She had almost run away when he had tried to talk to her about the scars, though, and so he had stopped questioning her. If she had been through such torment, he was not going to make it worse for her by opening up the mental wounds, but he knew that if he gave her time she might well confide in him when she was ready to. So he bided his time, took her food and let her come to him, hoping that one day she would let him know all of what made her Taise, and the remarkable woman that she was. This afternoon he was contemplating riding over to see her the next day. After the hard work he had put in he could give himself the luxury of a day off, and he had missed seeing her for over a week as she too harvested her herbs against the coming winter.

He leaned his head back against the wall and felt the spot where he had caught the sun. His dark, cropped, curly hair was receding at the temples, and each summer there was a tender patch on the edge where the newly exposed scalp had the shock of exposure to the sun. He was not delighted about this, but at least he had made it past thirty before it started happening, and it was receding slowly. By tomorrow the red patch would be glowing nicely and starting to peel before it tanned to match the rest of him. At least his beard was still dark, too, without any signs of gray yet, and he rubbed his jaw making a mental note to trim it back to its close crop again tomorrow morning. Like most of his fellow soldiers, he had found it easier to keep a beard looking tidy rather than struggle to shave every morning, when there might not even be water, let alone it being hot.

Deep in his pleasant reverie, he suddenly became aware that he could hear his name being called. Scanning the fields he picked out a small figure running towards him. It was not hard to tell who it was. Rob was one of the boys from the village, who often sneaked away when his mother was not watching, to come to Maelbrigt and hear stories of soldiers and far off places. Physically, Rob was small and wiry for his age and had a shock of flame-red hair, whereas Maelbrigt, even at that age, had been solid, but in his ways he reminded Maelbrigt so much of himself. Rob's mother despaired of him, but then so had Maelbrigt's, and he knew that half the problem was that Rob was bright and intelligent, and utterly frustrated in the enclosed world of the village. He just hoped that Rob had done his part in the harvesting before coming up the valley to him.

Rising to greet the youngster it struck him that something was not right. In fact something was very wrong. Rob was pelting across the grain stubble, waving his arms frantically back towards the village. The reason Maelbrigt had not heard his calls sooner was because he was running so hard his breath was coming in short gasps.

Maelbrigt had started to walk towards Rob and then, as he saw the boy fall, pick himself up and then stagger before trying to run again, he broke into a run too. He vaulted the dry stone wall which edged the small garden and raced up to his small friend. As he got close Rob sank to his knees and gasped,

"Raiders! In the village! Raiders!"

Picking Rob up in his arms Maelbrigt jogged back to the tower.

"No!" Rob begged. "The other way! You have to help them! Please!"

"Hush, boy." Maelbrigt said gently. "I'm going to! But I'm not facing raiders unarmed and the weapons are in the tower, as you well know."

He dropped Rob on his feet at the open door to the tower and stripped his own sweat drenched shirt off, grabbing a light weight woollen vest off a hook by the door and then the leather jerkin that went over it. Pulling them on, he instructed Rob.

"When I go you close the door and drop the bar, right! No heroics from you, my lad!" He retrieved a strange set of leather straps which he attached a large quiver to. Reaching up onto the top of a cupboard in the kitchen where they stood, he brought down a bundle of wicked barbed arrows, each a yard long, and slipped them into the quiver. Rob's eyes went wide at the sight of these and even wider when Maelbrigt picked up the light arrows he used to hunt small game and handed them to him. Maelbrigt also gave him the light hunting bow that he had been teaching the boy to use, before reaching for his own bow – a huge thing made of yew, as tall as its owner, which Rob had never even seen strung, let alone used.

With an easy flip that Rob would not have believed possible, Maelbrigt connected the bow string, then took down the sword in its scabbard from the wall. The web of leather turned out to be a neat shoulder holster which strapped on, with the arrows on one side and a wicked long knife sheathed low on the other, with two throwing knives sheathed above it. With the sword scabbard belted on and the bow thrown across his shoulders Rob suddenly thought his friend looked the scariest thing he had ever seen. The raiders were all screaming rage and wild hacking, but the calm, purposeful way Maelbrigt armed himself seemed far more dangerous.

"Now," Maelbrigt said, taking him gently by the shoulders and looking into his eyes. "When I've gone and you've bolted the door, go up into the little tower with the bow. If anyone comes you make sure you know them first before you let them in. Up there you can watch the door like I showed you. Make sure no-one has a knife to the back of someone you know, and if you don't know them, shoot them first and ask questions later."

Rob nodded mutely. The tower had small conical towers of its own at each corner from the second floor up to the roof, which stuck out enough to give a clear shooting line down to the doorway. The building had been built for defence, and Maelbrigt knew that if Rob did what he had been told, a bunch of raiders were unlikely to be able to get in through the solid oak door when it was defended from above. The arrow slits in the round towers were too small to shoot back into unless the archer was a superb shot, and Maelbrigt felt certain none of them would have practiced enough to be that, so Rob had little to fear.

He ran out of the door and retrieved his old war-horse, Hellion, from the stables. Hellion was a very old horse now and Maelbrigt hated having to press him back into service, but even at his slow canter they would still reach the village quicker than he would on foot. As they passed the door Rob was peeping out and Maelbrigt bellowed, "Shut the door!" He saw the white little face disappear, and heard the reassuring *thunck* of the door closing and the bar being dropped behind it.

Hellion picked up his master's mood and gamely ploughed down the slope to the village, although his sides were heaving as they turned the bend and saw the chaos on the main street. Maelbrigt leapt off him as three raiders saw him and began to run at him. Ripping a flight out of each of two arrows, he nocked them together, angled the bow slightly and loosed them. At close range the huge bow gave the arrows a terrifying momentum, and the first was driven so deeply though the foremost man that only the flights could be seen. So far that it penetrated the flesh of his companion who had been virtually touching him, and that man screamed in agony as his collapsing fellow dragged the tip back out, tearing his chest open. The third man was down and dying too and Maelbrigt wasted no time on them, but side-stepped them to get a better line of sight.

In moments, nine more arrows had found targets, and the number of raiders left on the street had been reduced to half a dozen. As he worked his way down the street, bow at the ready, he found two holding the sail maker's wife down, tearing at her clothes. He whistled sharply and, as they spun in surprise to face him presenting a broader target, took them both out with the throwing knives. No point in wasting more arrows. One was a clean kill, but the other was dying messily, which would not have happened when he was in full training, and part of him noted that and disapproved.

Another appeared out of a building to his right and charged at him. He drew the sword and dropped to one knee, below the scything arc of the other's sword, and ran him through, using the other's momentum to nudge his body out of the way and pull the sword back out as he heard feet behind him. He spun and exchanged swordplay briefly with the newcomer before also running him through. He turned to see the blacksmith, blood pouring from a gash in his arm, use his other hand to brain another with a massive hammer from the forge. Four of the other villagers had a raider on the ground and had beaten him senseless. Scanning the open market area as he stepped into it, Maelbrigt could see that the villagers had managed to take out four more by themselves, even though the raiders were more heavily armed. He had been vaguely aware of arrows taking flight around him, and saw two of the villagers were dead alongside them and another was badly wounded.

To his horror, as he turned to check back the way he had come, he suddenly realized that Hellion was on the ground. Seeing the last of the raiders fleeing along the coast road, Maelbrigt ran back to the old horse. An arrow stuck out from his neck, which by the amount of blood around it, had pierced an artery and he must have died quickly. Some of the villagers came to stand by him, but were unsure what to say. Adam the sail maker limped up to them. As the leader of the village he went to shake his hand as he said,

"Thank you for coming, and I'm sorry about your horse. We'd never have fought them off alone, we're not soldiers. Even with some of them gone they were too many."

The significance of what the man had said took a moment to sink in, but then Maelbrigt was back on his feet.

"Gone? Where? How many of them went?"

"About half a dozen," someone said.

"Up round the head of the loch," the sail maker told him.

His mind went immediately to Taise. She was alone and utterly unprepared for defending herself against the likes of the raiders, who, now he had chance to look at them properly, seemed likely to be a renegade group of Attacotti. Probably men who had been thrown out of their main group of encampments on the islands west of Prydein, but that would only make them more desperate to find a place to hole up for the winter. He ran back into the village and retrieved his knives, wiping them clean on the clothes of their victims. As he straightened and turned to go, he heard his name being called again. From around the corner of the forge came a young lad hanging on to a prancing black horse. The boy was a pal of Rob's called

Jakie – a towheaded lad of only slightly bigger build than Rob and possessed of a ferocious squint, but with an absolute gift with horses. The horse was a youngster reared by Jakie's father which Maelbrigt had been helping Jakie to break in.

"Here, take Dancer!" Jakie called in his high-pitched voice as the horse plunged and nearly swung him off his feet. It was a measure of Jakie's ability that he had managed to get a halter onto the horse to make do as a bridle, despite the animal obviously being spooked by the noise and the smell of blood. Maelbrigt took the reins gratefully, and swung himself onto Dancer's back before addressing the cluster of villagers.

"Go to the castle! Take what you can carry easily and go. Young Rob's there, so let him see who you are and he'll let you in. Bar the door and wait for me to come back! I'm going for Taise."

Without giving them time to argue, he wheeled Dancer around and heeled him into a full gallop. As they shot through the rest of the village, he saw more bodies lying on the dusty ground unmoving, and registered that the villagers had taken heavier casualties than he had first thought. There was nothing he could do about that now, though, and he heeled Dancer onwards, although the young beast needed little urging. It was a long time since Maelbrigt had ridden so lively a steed, and he had forgotten the thrill of leaning over the neck of a powerful horse as it streaked along the road and up the track towards Taise's cottage. If he had had less important things to do he would have enjoyed the ride enormously, but this time he was worried sick about reaching her in time.

As they crested the top of the slope and entered the trees he could hear men's voices and a woman sobbing. Letting go of the makeshift reins he made no attempt to slow Dancer, but let the horse pound into the clearing. As they came level with three of the men, he swung his leg over Dancer's neck and jumped, using the speed to add to his weight as he flung himself onto them. They all went down in a tangled heap, but Maelbrigt rolled and came up on his feet before the others.

He kicked out at one and heard a crack of bone snapping as his heavily-booted foot took the man under the chin, breaking his neck. Long knife in hand, he slashed another across the eyes and stabbed the third, leaving him in a screaming heap. Another of the raiders was coming to the aid of his friends, and again the short throwing knives found first one and then another target. The leader of this splinter group suddenly came into view dragging Taise out of the cottage door. He was obviously having trouble, partly because she was taller than him, but also because he was evidently used to dragging women by their hair, and Taise's lack was giving him problems finding something to grab hold of. The man leered at Maelbrigt and in his thick accent snarled,

"If you want a share of the fun with the freak, you'll have to fight for it!" although his words were robbed of some of their menace by his look of shock as he realized he was the only one of his men left standing. A wolfish grin spread across Maelbrigt's face.

"Don't mind if I do!" he snarled back.

The raider was rapidly losing his initial confidence, but he loosed Taise and went for his knife. The two men circled each other for a moment and then there was a flurry of movement, a howl of pain, and Maelbrigt danced back from his opponent as the man keeled over and lay face down in the dust.

"How do you like the fun, freak?" he snapped at the corpse, giving it a passing kick for good measure.

Taise was kneeling on the step with her face in her hands, shaking badly as Maelbrigt walked over and put his arms around her. When she lifted her gaze up and saw he was unhurt she almost collapsed against him. He made comforting noises and managed to get her onto her feet, helping her back inside the cottage to a chair, where he hauled blankets off the bed and wrapped them round her shivering shoulders. She was badly shocked and he was sure that it was not simply the sudden appearance of the villainous group of thugs. It had obviously dragged the memories back to the surface of whatever had happened to her to add to her misery. He bent down in front of her and gently lifted her chin up so that he could make eye contact with her. Keeping his voice even, he told her,

"I have to go find Dancer, he's not trained like Hellion was. When I get him back I'm taking you back to the tower." She started to shake her head, but Maelbrigt held her firmly. "No, you're coming with me! For a start there are badly wounded villagers who need better help than I can give them." His ploy worked as it sank in that she was not the main target. He had not been sure it would work, but he had hoped that if whatever haunted her had been a personal attack, then deflecting that idea might help. He also knew Taise well enough to know that she could bury her own problems in helping others, and that a plea to help the villagers would be more effective than anything he could say about her own well-being. She wiped her eyes with the back of one hand.

"The village got attacked?" she asked, in a shaky voice. That was better. She was losing the far-off gaze and paying attention to what he was telling her.

"Yes, they've been hit badly by raiders. This bunch who came up here were just part of the boatload who showed up. I think they're probably Attacotti who pissed off Mad Magnus and got themselves booted off the island. They were just looking for whatever they could steal. It was our bad luck they showed up here."

"Were there many hurt?"

"I think so, but I didn't have time to check. I saw several bodies, the blacksmith has a badly gashed arm, and there was someone on the ground by the forge, but there are bound to be a lot more. So I'll get Dancer and then you can ride down with me." This time she nodded, although she was still shaking under the blankets.

He gave her an encouraging smile and then jogged out and up the track he had last seen Dancer careering off down. Luckily the flapping halter reins had entangled in a thorn bush not so far away, and Dancer stood rolling his eyes dejectedly as he tried to pull his head free. Maelbrigt ran his hand over the big horse's neck, and murmured soothingly at him as he disentangled the reins with the other hand, catching them quickly when they came free before Dancer could race off again.

Leading the reluctant horse back to the clearing in front of the cottage, he hitched him securely to a tree, and then dragged the bodies of the raiders to the edge of the drop down to the loch-side. A fringe of trees masked the cottage from view from across the loch, but they were only one or two deep and presented little in the way of an obstacle. The steep bank of the loch rose from the shore to almost twice the height of the cottage and was covered with bracken and scrubby growth, but with nothing to stop the weight of a man dropping directly into the water. At the moment the water was shallow at the edge, but it was low tide, and Maelbrigt knew than within a day or so the fishes would have had a feast. He was not sure that two of them were actually dead, but given the way they had tried to slaughter Taise and the villagers, he was not in the mood to be charitable and they went over the edge too.

Turning back to the cottage he found Taise still sat in the chair, although looking more in the land of the living. He found a large canvas bag and grabbed an armful of her underclothes to go in it, and then some of her dresses, selecting the light woollen ones in preference to the strange sheer fabric ones she still had from when she had appeared. Just at the moment he thought it was better if she at least outwardly appeared to be local as much as possible. The last thing he needed was someone wanting to take their grief out on the resident alien. He found the leather satchel which Taise used to carry medicines down to the village in, and was glad to see that it was fully packed in readiness for any emergency. He would not have known what to pack if it had been empty, and Taise did not seem in much of a state to advise him.

Taking the two bags outside, he knotted their straps together so that they could be hung over Dancer's withers. Then going back he got Taise on her feet and picked up two of the blankets. Once he got her walking it was not too bad and he got her to Dancer. He draped the one blanket over Dancer's back and managed, after three attempts to get Taise onto his back. She was no horsewoman, and sat unsteadily clutching Dancer's mane as he moved the bags back so that they rested on the blanket too.

"Where's Hellion?" she suddenly asked.

"They shot him. He's dead." Maelbrigt told her, his voice choking up. He would mourn the old horse as he would have a friend – after all they had been together most of Maelbrigt's adult life, through thick and thin. Hellion had ridden into battles and skirmishes, put up with being swung onto ships in slings, eaten strange food, and been a constant companion. He had been a horse of considerable character and Maelbrigt knew he would miss him dreadfully. Even now, the problem of getting Taise onto a horse would have been so much easier with Hellion, who would have stood patiently having picked up on Taise's inexperience, instead of being spooked by having a clumsy rider hauled aboard like Dancer was. Luckily Taise just put her hand over her mouth in horror but made no attempt to say anything, since Maelbrigt knew he would not have been able to say more of his oldest friend without losing control, and he needed to stay focused for a while longer.

With him leading Dancer it was a slower journey back than he had made there, and they took the upper road directly towards his home, which ran above the village rather than going through it. He felt Taise did not need to see the bodies, although from their elevated position above the roofs of the houses, he caught glimpses of unmoving limbs. The sun was low in the sky, bathing the clouds with red light as they came into his valley and saw the tower silhouetted against the hills. As they came up to it, Rob and Jakie ran out and talked over one another in their haste to tell him what they had done. From the garbled account, Maelbrigt gathered that he had a house full, and that some of the women had had the presence of mind to get hot meals going on the range in the kitchen. By the time they were by the door, Maelbrigt could smell the food and his stomach growled hungrily.

Helping Taise down, he handed her bags to another of Rob's friends, who staggered under the weight but gamely carried them in for him, while Rob and Jakie offered to take Dancer around to the stables and see to him so that Maelbrigt could eat. Inside, the kitchen was a hive of activity. People were queuing down one side of the room with bowls, waiting their turn for the stew which was simmering on the range. The delay evidently had more to do with Maelbrigt's lack of receptacles than a shortage of stew, as others came in with empty bowls and handed them to the next in the line.

On the other side, two or three women were attempting to patch up the wounded. The worst cases were sat on the settle and on one of the benches from beside the long table, while others stood back by the walls clutching cloths to gashes, or in two cases holding what appeared to be broken arms. Maelbrigt was glad to see that Peg, the village's wise woman and herb expert, was both alright and in charge of things. She was a sensible older woman who knew Taise's expertise outweighed hers, and could accept suggestions without taking umbrage. Her daughter, who was bandaging the blacksmith's arm, was far more touchy about Taise encroaching on what she saw as her family's territory, but in her mother's presence was forced to keep quiet.

Peg took in Taise's appearance with an expert glance, caught Maelbrigt's eye, and instinctively called Taise over to ask after her, before telling her where they had got to with the repair work. With something to do in front of her, Taise quickly came round and was soon engrossed in the work she knew best. Peg took a moment to catch Maelbrigt between patients.

"Did they rape her?" she asked him in a low voice. Peg was the one person Maelbrigt had confided in over Taise's scars, and she was well aware of the nightmares that haunted her.

"No, thank the Trees!" he replied equally softly, "but she was deeply shocked, and I think it brought back some bad memories. Whatever she says, this time she's not going back until I'm sure she's not going to just sit staring into the fire and forgetting to eat."

"Good. You do that and I'll back you up," Peg told him, before bustling off to her next charge.

Everyone rested easier that night for being behind the protection of the stout walls of the castle, although few slept well, but in the morning the majority of the villagers had to return to clear up. When they had sorted themselves out by nightfall, it was revealed that they had lost eleven villagers – four women, five men and two of the older boys. In such a hard-pressed community every loss was felt badly. Some of the far fields might not now be harvested before the inevitable equinoctial gales, and they were all deeply grateful for Maelbrigt's offer to once more open up his barns to them if they ran short.

At a personal level he found himself suddenly thrust into the position of replacement parent. Among the casualties had been Rob's mother and Jakie's parents, and the orphaned pair were determined to stay with him in the absence of any family who could take them in. In both cases, their surviving relatives had already taken in other members of the extended family, and were unable to cope with the demands of another hungry, lively ten-year-old under their roofs.

Maelbrigt had wondered whether the presence of the two boys might not drive Taise away to her seclusion quicker, but instead she seemed to be more willing to linger. Both lads put on a very brave face during the days, but at night sobbed themselves to sleep and woke up with dreadful nightmares. Maelbrigt willingly got up to comfort them, remembering his own experiences as a page when he was barely five years old than them, but had not expected Taise to show such maternal feeling towards the boys. He even wondered whether she might have lost a child of her own, since it became quite apparent that she was much more used to dealing with small people than he was. To his delight a week passed, and then two, with no sign of her wanting to leave, and he began to dare hope that she would stay.

By the time the storms came at the end of the fortnight, some semblance of normality had returned to the little community, and against earlier expectations the grain was all stored away safely, which was a good thing since the storms were particularly vicious. The high winds came in from the west, funnelling down the loch and tearing the waves into ragged peaks, while torrential rain lashed the houses drenching everything. When it passed Taise expressed concern for her cottage, and Maelbrigt feared this would be the signal for her departure. To his relief she simply wanted to make sure there was no damage, and to collect more herbs to bring back with her.

So on a bright and sunny morning the boys helped him saddle Dancer, and a stolid plough horse for Taise, who could not hope to control Dancer. Giving the lads strict instructions which he knew they would disregard the minute he was out of sight, Maelbrigt set off in high spirits with Taise. They took the ride at an easy pace with him trying to improve Taise's riding skills to little effect; which was why they didn't notice that smoke was rising from the chimney of the cottage until they rode into the clearing.

Chapter 13

An Unwelcome Guest

Celidon: Harvest-moon

Maelbrigt reined the horses in sharply, cursing under his breath that he could have been so stupid to have come out unarmed. Just because he had seen the last raider running in the opposite direction two weeks ago was no reason to become complacent. Taise looked at him, concerned by his reaction, but simply wondered aloud if it was some lost soul who had found shelter. He was about to ask where on earth someone would come from at this time of year, when he realized that this might well have been how she herself had arrived at the cottage.

Cautiously kneeing Dancer forward, he rode into the middle of the clearing. To his horror Taise had already dismounted and was leading her horse past him, in towards the low branch by the cottage where they always tethered horses. In a fierce whisper he hissed her name, and when she turned, surprised, he gestured her to come back. She stopped, but was simply stationary where she was with a perplexed expression on her face, when the cottage door opened. Before Maelbrigt could dismount a man came out and he heard her gasp in surprise.

"Hello, Taise," the newcomer said. "Do you have any idea how long we've been looking for you?"

The stranger was as tall as Taise, with the same alabaster white skin, but with blue eyes so pale they barely seemed to have any colour at all, and fine, short, pale hair.

"Oh, dear Spirits, it's you!" Taise exclaimed, seeming far from overjoyed at the sight of this person. Maelbrigt had vaulted off Dancer and in quick strides had come to stand by Taise's side.

"I gather you know this person?" he asked quietly. She nodded but didn't say more, and Maelbrigt could see her eyes beginning to tear. It was the stranger who answered in his high-pitched, oily voice.

"Oh yes, she knows me. We knew each other very well at one time, not that it's any business of yours, boy!" Maelbrigt refused to bite at the insult of being called a boy. Keeping his voice deadly calm as he stepped slightly in front of Taise, shielding her, he replied,

"I'm no boy, as you may soon find out, and what concerns Taise concerns me. So what business brings you here, DeÁine?"

He felt Taise start as he spoke the name, and she moved to face him, asking,

"You recognize a DeÁine?"

Before he could answer the stranger joined in again. "Well isn't he the clever one! Now let's stop messing around. Taise, get your things, we have to go."

"She's going nowhere with you," Maelbrigt told him in no uncertain terms.

The stranger reached out and grabbed Taise's arm, which she snatched from him, backing away into the clearing. As the stranger stepped after her he gave Maelbrigt the opening he had been waiting for. Moving only slightly to improve the angle, he backhanded the stranger with his fist just as he was off balance, sending him flying across the ground. Before the man could get to his feet, Maelbrigt pounced on him, rolled him face down, and wrenched his arms up behind his back. With Maelbrigt's weight on him he could not move, and he whimpered in pain as his arms were almost wrenched out of their sockets.

"Aren't you a stupid shit-head!" Maelbrigt snarled. "Best sort out the men from the boys before you go around hurting their friends!" He looked up at Taise without relaxing his grip. "Who is this piece of dirt, anyway?"

"His name is Sithfrey, we trained together many years ago," she told him.

"Right, Sithfrey, let's get this straight! If you lay so much as a finger on her, I'll rip your arm off and beat you to death with the raggy stump! You're going to ask her whatever you need, and then you're going to piss off back the way you came! Understand?" For emphasis he gave Sithfrey's arms an extra tweak, getting a yelp in response.

"Understand?" he asked again, and this time got a strained nod.

Maelbrigt got to his feet in an agile spring, which moved him away from Sithfrey before he could get up. The DeÁine made it to a sitting position, then stayed there rubbing his arms and gazing balefully up at Maelbrigt, who stood poised like a very large, dark and dangerous cat with a rat in front of it. After a moment Sithfrey cleared his throat, and then tore his eyes way from Maelbrigt to look at Taise.

"We need you back," he told her. "You'll be given a full pardon, but you have no choice, the high council insist on your return."

For the first time in all the years he had known her, Maelbrigt saw Taise lose control.

"Pardon!" she screamed at Sithfrey. "You dare offer me a pardon! After what you did to me?" The tears were streaming down her face as the words poured out of her. "You helped them brand me a traitor! Yet I'd done nothing! I wasn't the one who betrayed the DeÁine! You, and Irpa and Leifi and Fenja and the others, you all knew me. You *knew* I was innocent! Whoever the traitor was it wasn't me, if it even *was* someone else in our group. But not one of you spoke up for me! You let them torture me! You let them take my family away from their homes! Banish me from my homeland! And now you all think that all you need do is pardon me and I'll come crawling back? No! *No*! *NO*!"

She turned and fled into the house. Maelbrigt raised a quizzical eyebrow at Sithfrey.

"Not the answer you were expecting?" he asked before turning to follow Taise.

He found her leaning against the fireplace, weeping, with her hands over her face. Gently turning her, he pulled her into his arms and held her tight.

"You don't have to go," he told her. "I can make sure of that, but what are you two talking about? What's this about your family?"

She raised her face up to look into his eyes. She had trusted no-one like she trusted Maelbrigt, but there was one thing she needed to know.

"You recognized what Sithfrey was, so have you always known I was a DeÁine?"

He smiled and nodded, and she saw nothing but the same affection she always did in the depths of his dark-brown eyes.

"Why didn't you say anything?" she asked, amazed.

He shrugged and said, "Why? It didn't matter. You're Taise, not the DeÁine soldiers I fought against. You were one person, alone, and you'd done nothing but help the people around here. What was the point in telling them where you came from? I don't kill someone for no reason, and if I'd told the villagers and they'd run you out of the cottage, you'd still have had to go somewhere, and they'd have lost someone who's the best healer for miles. Besides…" he kissed her, "I love you."

Her response was a rib crushing hug as she held him tightly for several minutes.

"You really are the most amazing person sometimes," she finally said, leaning back to face him once more. He chuckled.

"Only sometimes?" and was rewarded with a watery smile. "Now suppose you tell me at least why this idiot outside thinks you'll leave with him."

Taise went and sat on the bench by the table, which held the remains of a meal. Obviously Sithfrey had been making use of her supplies while he waited. She wrapped her arms around herself and gazed at the floor for a second before answering him.

"I think it has never occurred to them I'd say 'no'. I was training for the priesthood with Sithfrey and the others. It's different to your priests. We're not isolated and …"

"I know," Maelbrigt interrupted gently, walking over to stand by her. "About the DeÁine priesthood, I mean, go on, you don't have to explain."

She was even more amazed at this, but picked up the thread of her tale and continued.

"We were learning of the Great Return, how it was predicted when the DeÁine first left centuries ago, and of the setback we'd just received." She smiled at him. "Well, 'just' to us, it was already ten years and a long time for you when I started on the project."

He nodded. "I was a boy page of fifteen at the battle of Moytirra, twenty-six years ago. When you were learning of it ten years after, I'd finished my training, so you're talking of …oh, about eight years before the Last Stand at Gavra of our Knights of Celidon?"

"I didn't know you were at Moytirra! You never told me!" she gasped, wondering how many more surprises this man she thought she knew could have for her.

He smiled at her affectionately. "I didn't tell you because I wanted you to feel safe around me, not be worried that I was going to turn into some vengeful monster who would slaughter you in your sleep. You were so frightened when I first met you, Taise, I didn't dare, and then afterwards what was the point in dredging up the past? But come on, what about this training?" She stared at him flabbergasted for a second before she could continue.

"Maelbrigt are you ever going to stop surprising me? … We were working with the old manuscripts about the Treasures of the DeÁine and those of the Islands, and the power they contain and how it can be harnessed. The training's long but we had the chance to specialize, and Sithfrey, ten others, and I, all spent years looking at the old texts. Almost nine years ago we were suddenly told we were to be moved. At the time I didn't have any idea of what was happening, except that we were taken on a long journey up into the mountains, and seemed to be heading into Brychan. We were just behind the force your Knights met at Gavra Pass and defeated. The king, our leader was killed, and the council couldn't believe that they could be defeated again by mere Islanders.

"They were sure they'd been betrayed. It was the only way they could come to terms with such humiliation. Because we were there and we weren't military, they thought it must have come from within our camp. They picked on me because I'd questioned our right to come back and take this land after all this time. They didn't wait to take us back very far before they started questioning me." She stopped and Maelbrigt could see the pulse in her neck racing, as she closed her eyes tight and took deep, shaking breaths.

He desperately wanted to comfort her, but needed to hear what she knew, and so kept silent until she continued. "They … they tortured me … to try to find out who my accomplices were." Her voice rose tearfully. "I couldn't tell them anything because I didn't know anything, but they wouldn't stop! None of the others spoke up. They were too scared they might be next. The council brought my family to me, supposedly to get them to tell me to confess, but really to tell me that they'd be next if I didn't cooperate. I couldn't save them because I had nothing I could tell. … I think they killed them all!" She broke down in sobs, and this time Maelbrigt wrapped his arms around her and held her tight.

"So they threw you out when they realized that they'd been wasting their time?" He felt her slight nod against his chest. "And you wandered around and then found the cottage?" Again a nod. She obviously had no idea of what had really happened, and he was seething that she should have paid so high a price for something she had never done.

He also wanted to wring Sithfrey's neck for being such an arrant coward. In Maelbrigt's books loyalty to friends was one of the cardinal rules he lived by, and he had no tolerance for such self-interested spinelessness. There was also a deep feeling of responsibility for what had happened to Taise. As part of the group who had planned it, he had known what had been done to provoke the DeÁine army into moving, and had been aware of the trap. He knew exactly who had betrayed them, and at the time the means had seemed to justify the ends, but he knew none amongst those who had set the trap so carefully had ever thought that the DeÁine would turn on their own so savagely.

"But why are they after you now?" he mused. It suddenly dawned on him. "They're after the Treasures aren't they!" he exclaimed. Taise looked up questioningly, and Maelbrigt sat down beside her, still keeping an arm around her. "You said you were studying the manuscripts about the Treasures, right? For years? There can't be many of your people who know as much as you do, and they stupidly thought that Sithfrey would tempt you back with the lure of studying again. Instead he's too scared of what they might do if he returns empty handed to be subtle. If he'd shown up and just talked about the time you'd studied together, he might have got under your guard, but he's an idiot."

He broke off as they heard shuffling steps coming to the door. Sithfrey appeared, still massaging his throbbing arms, and stood well away from Maelbrigt. "You have to come back, Taise," he pleaded.

"Why? To save your skin again?" Maelbrigt countered. He might have been out of practice, but the master tactician in his head was once more calculating furiously. "Who sent you?"

"The council, like I told you," Sithfrey said, trying to be disdainful and failing miserably in his fear.

"No, stupid! Which bit of the council? The Arberth – the royal advisers at Bruighean? The Donns – the generals? The Abend – the priests' inner circle? Who personally? And why did they send a shit-for-brains like you?"

Stunned silence greeted his words, both Taise and Sithfrey wondering how on earth Maelbrigt would know the proper names of the innermost levels of DeÁine rulers? In sheer surprise, Sithfrey answered him, which was what Maelbrigt had hoped for.

"Helga found me. She took me to the Abend, but it was Anarawd who sent me. He's in charge of it now."

"Anarawd?" Maelbrigt said surprised, standing up. "What happened to Quintillean?" As he moved to Sithfrey, the DeÁine backed up until he was nearly in the fireplace, and in grave danger of igniting.

"How do you know about Quintillean?" he squeaked. He was way out of his depth here. When he had stood in front of the Abend he had been scared half out of his mind, and had just been grateful that there had only been five instead of the full nine. Even one powerful sorcerer was bad enough, and he had not argued with Helga when she had appeared at his door, but together no sane person would question why they wanted something, it was just done.

They had told him the Islanders were lesser beings who would present no problem for a DeÁine, and had paid for a boat to bring him to one of the northerly small islands. Since then, however, it had been downhill all the way. It had been a nasty shock to discover that the people here were not anything like as submissive as those who served the DeÁine on the other side of the mountains. So far he had been beaten up by a gang of thugs – which he had rationalized to himself as being by virtue of their having outnumbered him. He had had his purse stolen – but then what could he expect of Islanders who had never had masters to teach them? But now this terrifying man had appeared, who knew the innermost secrets of the DeÁine court, and he seemed to be in control of Taise. The Abend would kill him if he failed, but this man would surely kill him if he tried.

"Never you mind how I know," Maelbrigt growled. "Where was Quintillean?"

Sithfrey shook his head. "I don't know," he whimpered. "There were only Geitla, Helga, Magda and Masanae, with Anarawd leading them when I saw them. Quintillean, Tancoystl, Eliavres and Calatin weren't there. I didn't ask why! I wouldn't dare!"

Maelbrigt turned and stared out of the open door. "What are they up to?" he mused. "The four witches and the schemer left to hold the court. …But where did the war-mages go? What's so important that Quintillean would leave the court to Anarawd?" He whirled around to face Sithfrey. "Right. We're going back to the castle and you're coming with us until I figure this out. You can come peaceably or I'll hog-tie you to a horse, I don't care which, but you're not wandering around the countryside."

Taise touched his arm, with a concerned look on her face. "Please, Maelbrigt, you can't make him a prisoner on my account, just let him go."

Maelbrigt shook his head and his hand covered hers which had caught his arm. "Taise I'm not making him a prisoner, but trust me, you're in danger. Do you seriously think the Abend would send such a fool on such an important mission? Think about it! For the first time in nearly a decade a DeÁine – a singularly stupid *Abend acolyte* who knows about the inner council and can't keep his mouth shut! – gets sent far across the border by the Abend. That's enough to start a war all by itself! They have to have something desperately important planned to risk that. And are they *really* likely to have thought for one minute that you'd trust someone who let you down so badly? No of course not! I'd bet the castle on him having been followed by someone a lot more dangerous.

"If those nine want you back, they'll have set something up to make absolutely sure you come. They let him lead them to you because he knew you well enough to know where you'd be likely to hide, and that's worked hasn't it? They've probably been watching him for years, and any of the others of your group still alive, and've come to the conclusion they don't know whatever it is they want to find out. He's probably destined for a knife in the back once they catch up with him and they have you."

Sithfrey gulped and looked worriedly out of the door as if he expected to see DeÁine Hunters appearing any minute. He had not even begun to think of it like that, but, now that Maelbrigt had said it, it made horribly good sense of what he knew. It was Taise who questioned Maelbrigt.

"Surely," she asked, "if it was dangerous to send one DeÁine it would be even more so to send others?"

Maelbrigt answered her as he propelled her out of the door with Sithfrey close on his heels. It was unlikely, he pointed out, that the others would be pure DeÁine, but there were plenty of half-bloods who looked enough like Islanders to not arouse suspicion. As the Last Stand at Gavra Pass had been in the north of Brychan, she must have been well away from the main populated areas, too. So they had hardly been overwhelmed with choices for where she could have gone. The northwest coast of Celidon must always have been a prime choice of place to find her because of its isolated villages.

On the other coast facing Ergardia, and on Ergardia itself, there would have been more chance of her being recognized for what she was, and the Abend had enough contacts to hear of a DeÁine in those places even if she had been accepted by the locals. To have disappeared so well that they needed Sithfrey to sniff her out, she had to be isolated from the main commercial routes. Up in the remote highlands, villagers saw so few strangers everyone looked different, so the Abend could take a chance on sending their tame half-bloods without too much risk.

By this time they were moving back along the road around the loch-head, Maelbrigt and Taise mounted and Sithfrey almost jogging in front, where Maelbrigt had sent him. His innate sense of self-preservation told him that however frightening Maelbrigt was, he would not harm him unless he threatened Taise, whereas he feared the Hunters from the Abend would squash him like a bug with little compunction. So he was only too happy to keep moving towards what sounded like a secure place to hide.

Every so often Maelbrigt would fire a question at him, which he did his best to answer, although he found himself running out of breath trying to talk and keep up the blistering pace Maelbrigt set. Yes, he had been set ashore at the little port of Waun, on Ynys, the island off north Brychan. Yes, it had enough people coming and going that nobody had asked who he was or what he wanted. No, he had not seen any other ships dropping off passengers while he was there, but Maelbrigt was right, the whole island was only small and full of ports and it did not take long to get from one to the other. Once he had realized Taise was not on Ynys, he had hitched a ride on a fishing boat to the place the locals told him was the next stop away from where he had been. Another island and no luck, and another ride on a fishing boat.

He had been walking since then, but had got so tired that when it had started raining, he had slipped down to the loch and stolen a boat. The tide had seemed to be going up the loch not out to sea, so he had thought he would be alright. The ferocious storm had taken him by surprise and driven him past the entrance to the loch he had been heading for and up here. Having nearly drowned, he had been washed up on the opposite side to the village they were now approaching, and could not believe his luck when the locals of another of the loch-side villages told him there was a woman matching his description further down the shore.

Maelbrigt breathed a sigh of relief at this. With luck Sithfrey's trackers would have lost him completely in the storm, although he was not going to tell Sithfrey that just yet. Even quizzing the locals about tides would not necessarily help much with the freak weather of a few days ago, and the Hunters would just have to work by trial and error. This gave him some leeway within which to make a decision. He hated rushing into something without considering his options. Once they left, and they surely had to leave, the unexpected would cause enough instant choices as it was. Better if they at least had something firm to hold on to at the start. If he was going to protect Taise one thing was for certain, he would need help. It was one thing to run off a bunch of untrained raiders almost single-handed, but whoever the Abend had sent would be in a class far above that, and he began running old friends through his mind.

He was so engrossed with this at first he did not notice Taise sinking deeper into despair as she rode beside him. She could feel her world falling apart again. For years she had tried so hard to not let herself become attached to anyone. Deep in her heart of hearts she had known that one day her past would catch up with her and she would have to leave this place. Yet Maelbrigt had undermined all her good intentions. She had tried so hard not to love him – it was what had stopped her moving into the castle. There had been the vague hope that if she did not see him every day, when the time came to go it would not be so bad.

It had not worked of course, because even after a short time she missed him each day he was not with her. She had never known anyone with such a zest for life. He had once told her that having spent so many days thinking there would never be another, he had decided that the only way to live was to treat each day as if it was the last, and make the most of whatever came your way. At least that way there would be fewer regrets. He had had her helpless with laughter at tales of ridiculous things he had seen in his travels, and that had been so seductive. She had lost count of how long it had been since she had laughed like that, and once that had happened it was impossible to keep her barriers up against him. As she came to know him, she realized he was everything she could have hoped for, and she was scared to death of losing him.

Taise was utterly confused now, though. She had fretted over what would happen if he found out the truth – not only of what she was, but of what she knew. When she had imagined this happening, it had always been to worry about what this man who could be so loyal to his friends would say of someone who had run away from her responsibilities. There was also a part of her that had watched this person who was so gentle with her, and assumed that the tales of soldiering had been partly made up. Oh, she had believed he had been in an army, probably of some local lord. After all he had been given the castle, but she had thought taking part in the odd local skirmish had been embroidered into more than it was. It had not seemed to matter, since she had never thought the question of whether he could fight would really arise. She had always thought that she would hear in advance of anyone looking for her, and that she would be able to simply disappear.

Sithfrey's appearance had burst that bubble, but if anything it was Maelbrigt who confused her even more at the moment. Far from being some lord's hired man, he was obviously extremely expert at what he did. He had not been bragging at all. In fact, if he had been at Moytirra as a page, not only had he been in the largest and worst battle for centuries, but the page bit spoke of someone in training as a knight. And just how did he know so much about the DeÁine? That was the biggest puzzle of all. But the most troubling problem was how could she put the life of someone who could love her, despite having known what she was, into such danger?

When Maelbrigt's hand closed over hers she jumped so hard she almost fell off the horse. Sithfrey had dropped behind them and Maelbrigt spoke softly so he would not hear.

"Don't look so sad, we have to leave for a while but we'll be coming back!"

Taise's eyes widened. "How can you say that?" she whispered in shock. "Do you really think I can ever stay here now it'll be known what I am?"

He squeezed her hand affectionately. "Taise, the people here know *you*, and the goings on of far away mean little to them up here in the north. Why do you think I asked to come here? Nobody except a couple of curious boys ever asks me what I did before. They take my soldiering as a bonus when it helps them out, and other than that it's forgotten about. That goes for you too! Of course we can come back."

Taise was stunned into silence. One thing she had never dared hope was that there would be a place to come back to. And why would Maelbrigt have chosen to come here? That implied he could have gone somewhere else by choice, so the castle was not just a random payoff. Who on earth was he before?

By this time the village was coming into view, and Maelbrigt called Sithfrey up to them. With dire warnings of what would happen if he ran off, Maelbrigt told Sithfrey to carry on with Taise while he went into the village. Dancer plunged down the track into the village while the others carried on along the upper road, and Taise remembered the journey back only weeks ago and prayed that this worked out as well as that had. Sithfrey was obviously totally overawed by Maelbrigt and walked beside her without a word, but it was not long before they heard the pounding of hooves behind them and Maelbrigt rejoined them. By the look on his face, whatever he had gone for had not gone the way he had hoped, but he said nothing of it for the rest of the way.

They were greeted at the castle by the boys, who instantly picked up Maelbrigt's antipathy to Sithfrey. For some reason Jakie's squint obviously disconcerted Sithfrey, and from then on the two set to persecuting him with relish. All through the evening meal they stared at him, reducing him to a twitching wreck, with Maelbrigt refusing to do anything to dissuade them. By the time the boys were sent to bed, Taise felt worn out herself, and suggested that they all make an early night of it.

Once they were within the sanctity of Maelbrigt's room, she turned on him.

"What in the Islands is the matter? You've been like a bear with a sore head since you came back from the village. Why are you letting the boys torment Sithfrey? I know you don't like what he's done, but I didn't think pettiness was in you."

He sighed as he sat on the bed and wearily pulled his boots off.

"I went to see Peg," he told her. It was obvious that they could not take two children on the road with them, and as the excuse the villagers had made was that none of them had room to take the boys in, he had thought to offer Peg and her husband a home in the castle. Peg's husband had lost an arm in a raid a few years back and since then had made her life a misery. Their son and their daughter's husband ran the mill now, but he had been unable to let go of the business and move into one of the empty houses in the village. Maelbrigt had hoped that the offer of a job as caretaker of the castle would be a dignified way of getting him to move. As it was, three families, even in a big place like the mill, were crowded, and tempers were fraying more and more often, with Peg usually being the one caught in the middle. It seemed, though, that the man liked making everyone miserable as his way of staying in control, and refused to even consider the offer.

What made Maelbrigt so angry was that now he would have to take the boys away from the only place they had ever known, only weeks after losing their families, and ask friends of his to take them in.

"It's not that they won't be properly taken care of at the grange," he told Taise, "they will, it's just it seems so hard on them. I promised I'd take care of them and now I feel I'm breaking my word."

"You don't have to leave," Taise said softly, "I can go alone."

"No!" Maelbrigt said emphatically. "There's no way I'm letting you go alone! The boys will be given the best possible care, and their lives aren't in danger as long as they're not with us. You, on the other hand, are in great danger. I just have to find a way to explain, that's all."

He didn't want to talk tonight about why this was so hard to do. Taise had enough to think about, or so he thought, but she kept chipping away at his defences until he sat up in bed and snapped at her,

"Alright, you want to know? It's not a happy tale and you'll wish you hadn't asked!" It was the nearest they had ever come to having an argument, and suddenly Taise wished she had not been so fraught that she had failed to see how stressed he also was, but it was too late. He got out of bed and stalked to the window.

"I'm a bastard." She winced at the bitterness in his voice and looked confusedly back at him. "I meant that literally," he went on. "I was the bit a raider left behind with my mother. She was a nice respectable widow with four children by her husband until the night the Attacotti turned up at our village. Having raped her and several other women, they made off with what they'd come for. The next village took in what was left of the villagers. The other women got lucky and either didn't get pregnant or managed to get rid of the babies, but I was the awkward one who was born! In the process I ruined what was left of my mother's health, and my brothers and sister never forgave me for that.

"I was a normal boy with a healthy sense of adventure, but most of the time I was left to fend for myself. They didn't care what I did as long as I stayed out of their way. If you think Rob and Jakie are wild, you should have seen me at their age! My mother finally gave up the fight and died when I was only a bit younger than them, and the next couple of years were miserable beyond belief. I was passed around from one brother to another. My sister refused flat to have anything to do with me, and in the end the village leaders dragged me screaming to the nearest monastery and dumped me there. It took all of a week for the prior to decide I was beyond saving and they sent me away to a soldier. Thank the Trees, he was a kind man who saw that what I needed was some stability, and he took me to the grange.

"It was the best thing anyone could have done for me. For the first time I was occupied from the moment I woke to the moment I went to bed, and I learnt to channel all that energy into something productive. But I've never forgotten what it was like to not be wanted, Taise. Most of that misbehaving as a lad was just trying to get someone to take notice of me, but instead they just kept pushing me further and further away. I'm just Maelbrigt, Taise, because I don't have another name. I was told that I wouldn't be allowed to share the family name of the man who wasn't my father, and through most of my childhood I was "boy" or "hey, you". Maelbrigt's the name I got given when I went to the grange because I refused to speak to anyone, so they had to give me one. I don't even remember what other name I might have had before that now, and I wouldn't want to be part of that any more either.

"I know how much it's going to hurt those two when we take them away, because I've been there. In fact it's going to be worse! I had nothing but bad memories of the place, but they've been happy here up until a few weeks ago. I couldn't make those people understand that if they send Rob and Jakie away now, they won't just come back when they're old enough to be useful. Do you know what that miserable old man said? He told me he'd give them a job when they came back! By the time the grange has finished with them they'll never need or want to spend their days throwing corn under a stone and picking up what the mill spits out. It's the village's loss as well. In five years or so those two would be helping to keep the place going. Instead, the only way I can see the other children still having a home is for one of the other villages to combine here, because they've got the best mill stream for miles. The village is running out of people through the petty small-mindedness of one or two fools. *Aagh*!"

He slammed his fist into the wood of the shutter in frustration and anger, then walked over and pulled his clothes and boots on. "I can't sleep. I'm going for a walk," he growled and marched out. A moment later, Taise heard the door slam shut behind him and his footsteps on the path. From the window she saw him striding off across the fields into the coils of mist that rose from the little river beyond.

By the morning he was back, and seemed to have lost the ghosts that were haunting him so badly last night. Taise was not sure when he had come back. She had cried herself to sleep, partly from regret that now of all times she should have hurt him by making him relive the past, and partly for the child he had once been, whose hurt was being mirrored by Rob and Jakie. When she woke to find him still missing, she ran in a panic downstairs, only to find him fast asleep in the chair by the range. Her hurried entrance woke him. Stretching to remove the kinks from sleeping in a peculiar position, he stood and smiled weakly.

"I'm sorry I behaved badly last night," he said before she could ask him where he had gone. "When I got back you were fast asleep, so I didn't want to disturb you."

"I thought you'd gone," she whispered back, too relieved to be angry.

"Gone?" He guided her to the chair he had just vacated and set about making a pot of caff. There was no malice in his gentle reproof of her. "Why would I leave? I was just angry, that's all. I always go for a walk when I'm fit to burst, it's easier on the furniture! The alternative was to drag Sithfrey out and use him to work it out on – and you wouldn't want that, would you? Anyway, I don't take my temper out on someone who can't hit back, even if he is obnoxious." He pressed a steaming mug of caff into her hands and planted a kiss on the top of her head. "How many times do I have to tell you before you believe me? I'll find a way to sort this out, and I'll never leave you."

The door flew open before she could reply, and two small whirlwinds tore in to be swept off their feet by Maelbrigt and wrestled to the floor in a giggling heap. Sithfrey appeared behind them and stood watching in astonishment.

"Does he always do things like that?" he asked Taise, edging round the entangled, laughing bodies to take the mug she was offering him. Taise was not sure if he was more disconcerted by Maelbrigt's ability to be so affectionate to the boys when he had been so frightening to him, or that it was just because Sithfrey had not had any experience of something like a normal family. The contrast between the two struck her forcibly. Sithfrey, she knew from the past, had been given to the priesthood by a family who had had no love for him, and even back when they were studying together, it had always been Sithfrey in their group who had taken offence where none was intended. He had never seemed to be able to get past his fear of rejection, and it crippled him as surely as any physical deformity. Yet after last night, she now could see that it had not needed to be so. Until then she had had no idea that Maelbrigt had been through a similar, if not worse, experience, yet except for when it was brought most harshly back to haunt him, he had consigned it to the past and had built a real life for himself.

However, neither of them had time to contemplate further. After a speedy breakfast, Maelbrigt told them they would be leaving tomorrow, and there was a lot to get done if that was to happen. The boys were sent to round up the chickens into wicker cages, while Sithfrey was pressed into helping him bring as much of the freshly milled grain in sacks to be stored on the first floor of the tower. If the villagers would not help the boys, Maelbrigt reasoned, they would be unlikely to tend his fields if he was gone for long. When they returned they would be needing something to eat, and the tower room was less likely to attract rodents. He added a couple of sacks of un-milled seed as well, in the hope that they would be back while it was still usable to plant for another crop. Taise was given a list of things to pack for each of them for the journey, and was provided with panniers for the horses for her to fill.

By the evening everyone was weary, but they were as ready as they could be to leave. The boys were excited at the prospect of accompanying Maelbrigt on an adventure, and he had not got the heart to tell them they would only be going part of the way. He was pretty sure that once they got out on the road, the novelty would soon wear off, and they would be less upset at the idea of getting back to real beds and proper meals. It would take several days to reach the grange with the two plough horses each carrying an adult, a child and panniers. Dancer was too young to be heavily loaded, and Maelbrigt was not entirely happy with working him so hard. He suspected that he would end up walking him some of the way. He only hoped the grange would have horses he could borrow or it could be a long journey.

Leaving Taise and Sithfrey waiting for the meal to cook, Maelbrigt went up into the uppermost room of the tower. It was reached by a trap door in the ceiling of the room below, and he had to haul a ladder up the spiral stairs to be able to reach it. In the room were chests containing most of his past life, and he sat on the floor contemplating what to do with it. He suddenly became aware of scuffling noises and conspiratorial whispers below, and then two small heads popped up through the hatchway.

"What're you doing up here?" Jakie asked.

"See, I told you he was up here!" Rob interrupted, giving his friend an elbow in the ribs which nearly dislodged Jakie from the ladder.

Maelbrigt sighed and leant over to pull the two of them up to join him. "I'm trying to decide whether to open that big chest," he told them.

"What's the matter, don't you have the key?" Jakie asked.

He laughed. "No, it doesn't have a key and I can open it. It's whether I *do*, and use the things that are in it." He looked down at them and found himself with two small mirror images of himself on either side like bookends. Both had sat down cross-legged and copied his posture, and were looking with fierce determination at the chest.

"I was wondering what to do," he told them. "Can you help me decide?"

Filled with importance at being asked to help, he received enthusiastic replies and quivering attentiveness.

"In that chest is my old uniform," he began. "I haven't worn it since I came here because it causes problems. Sometimes, when people saw it, they thought that the way to prove how tough they were was to pick a fight with me. The trouble was, the people who did that were usually pretty bad at it, and I'd end up having to hurt them to make them stop. In the end it was just easier to leave it off. But now we're going away. If I put it on it will help us to find things like rooms for the night, because people know what the uniform means. It won't make any difference to the people at the grange because they know me anyway, but it might make the people who were following Sithfrey think twice about attacking us."

"Will it frighten Sithfrey?" Rob asked with relish.

"Probably," Maelbrigt replied, "but it might scare Taise, too."

That made the boys pause for thought.

Shortly afterwards, Taise called up that the food was ready. She and Sithfrey heard the sound of the boys and of Maelbrigt's heavier tread on the stairs, but his boots sounded different. Taise could hear a faint metallic chinking noise with each step which Sithfrey thought was spurs, but Taise had never known Maelbrigt wear those before. He stepped into the room accompanied by excited yipping noises from the boys, who danced round him like a pair of terrier pups at his heels.

"Look! Look!" they squeaked in unison, "Maelbrigt's a Knight!"

Taise and Sithfrey sat open-mouthed at his appearance. He wore the uniform of a full Knight of the Cross, not just some secular lord's knight. Supple black leather riding boots were topped with immaculately tailored black leather pants and a tunic, with a soft black woollen shirt underneath. The tunic was studded to deflect cuts and over his arm lay the blood-red surcoat which when opened would reveal the white dragon-headed cross of the Order. Sithfrey could not have gone any paler if he had tried, and gulped convulsively as if he might be sick at any moment.

"Dear Spirits!" Taise breathed. "All this time and you never said!"

Maelbrigt shrugged apologetically and went to the dresser to fetch the leather holster he had used two weeks before. By the time he had got the weapons down Taise had managed to regain some measure of composure, but Sithfrey was shaking like a leaf.

No wonder he had dispatched the raiders so well, Taise thought. 'Professional' was not enough to describe these men. They had heard a lot about the Knights and back then it had seemed that none of it was good if you were DeÁine. Five years as a page, and another five as a squire, before you were considered fully-trained made them formidable opponents, and they were incorruptible. Other armies might be bought off, but the Spirits protect you if you were stupid enough to think you could turn a Knight with bribery. And no wonder he had been confident he could protect her. She must be the first DeÁine in history to have her own personal Knight as a bodyguard – which made her realize just how extraordinary Maelbrigt was. From all she had heard, the Knights hated the DeÁine with a passion, and took their fight to prevent the Great Return as a personal crusade. Yet here was one of them prepared to risk his life to protect her because, against all the odds, he loved her.

Chapter 14

Leaving Home

Celidon: Harvest-moon

As if to make up for the previous night, their last night in the castle was as passionate as any Taise had known. In the morning she was somewhat embarrassed to face the others, but the boys were too excited over the coming day to bother with anything else, and Sithfrey's jitters were still directed at Maelbrigt. He had insisted on an early start, and the sun was only just making a watery appearance through the misty haze when they assembled outside. Maelbrigt barred and bolted the door into the kitchen from the inside. He reappeared at the main door on the first floor, which had once led directly into the main chambers from a wooden walkway leading up from a raised bank several yards away. The walkway had rotted away long ago, but the stone ledge it had been attached to was still firm, and Maelbrigt stepped out onto it while he turned the key in the great iron lock. He tucked the key into his tunic and then stepped out to drop gracefully to the ground below.

The only way to get back in now was to climb back up with the key. The doorway stood over two men's height from the ground, and was too high to be attacked by anything short of a well equipped army, while the lower door now had two massive beams of oak to reinforce it. He had no intention of returning to find his home had been ransacked by opportunist thieves.

They rode off in the opposite direction to the village, and began the climb into the mountains. Despite the horses being fresh, their progress was slowed by having to leave the chickens at two separate holdings on the way out of the valley. Maelbrigt had luckily kept little livestock to require re-homing, but he had insisted on finding someone to care for the fowl rather than leaving them to be preyed on by the local foxes. The isolated farmers had been grateful for the gifts and had kept them talking longer than he liked, but they found it hard to break away without causing offence.

As they finally climbed higher into the bare slopes, Taise realized why he had insisted on packing so much food. For the first two nights they found nowhere to stop but shepherd's shelters, and with the nights getting colder they were glad of the faggots of wood he had strapped on the horses to give them fires to cook on. In the distance they once caught a glimpse down a valley of a massive castle far off on a headland near the sea, which Maelbrigt told them was Sarne, but that was the only sign of habitation they saw except for roaming flocks of sheep with their shepherds.

On the third day they began to descend to a large loch which cut deep into the countryside and were forced to ride around the head-shore before climbing into the hills again. As Maelbrigt had hoped, the boys soon found that sleeping on the ground was less fun than it sounded, and while there were strong protests at being left behind, they came round somewhat when he told them that Dancer would be left too. Rather than telling them they were too young, he made the excuse that it was Dancer who was too much of a colt still to make the journey, and that he was leaving him with friends to be trained up, but wanted someone there to keep an eye on him. Taise could see they were not entirely convinced by the story, but he had been clever enough to not hurt their feelings in the process, or to leave them feeling unwanted.

As they stopped for their midday break on the fifth day, Maelbrigt pointed out another castle in the distance. Below it, in the valley was the place they were heading for, he told them. Ardfern was a small town and the grange was just outside of it on the way to the castle, which was called Luing. It took them until the evening to reach the town, which was the largest the boys had ever seen. Maelbrigt had walked Dancer most of the day, but now he mounted up, and with his black cloak loosely thrown back over his shoulders he looked the epitome of knighthood.

The effect it had on the townspeople was something Taise had not expected. All the way through they were greeted with initial surprise and then delight. Several older men came up to speak to Maelbrigt in deferential tones too low for her to hear what was said, but it was obvious that they regarded him as some sort of commander. Each went away with an air of disappointment about them, and eventually Taise got her horse to move level with Dancer to speak to Maelbrigt. He explained that they were hoping that his appearance might signal the return of the Knights to the grange, as some sort of advance guard for the Knights from Ergardia to come and begin the promised training of a sept for Celidon once more. He dismissed their deference as gratitude that he had decided to stay, and that they felt safer just knowing there were some Knights still left in the land, but Taise was not so sure. She was becoming much more alert to Maelbrigt's modesty over his military career, and had a suspicion that there was a lot more to find out yet.

The grange turned out to be a very large block of buildings built in a square. As they passed under the deep stone archway into the central courtyard, Taise and Sithfrey found themselves suddenly under noticeably more hostile scrutiny than they had been anywhere else. Evidently the ordinary people might not know who they were, but the men in this place had the look of veteran soldiers about them and they knew precisely what had just arrived on their doorstep. Maelbrigt, however, was treated with even more respect here than in the town, and was greeted by name. It was obviously his presence with them which stopped any action against Taise or Sithfrey, and they both found themselves edging closer to him. They reached the centre of the court and Maelbrigt raised his voice to the crowd that was appearing out of doorways on all sides.

"These people with me are under my protection. You will treat them as guests!" he ordered. There was no question that he expected to be obeyed either. "I will explain to you all after chapter tonight," he concluded, and without waiting for a response swung off Dancer and handed the reins to a groom who hurried forward.

Maelbrigt beckoned the boys down off the horses in their respective positions behind Taise and Sithfrey, and then courteously helped Taise down, before ushering them towards the large door which stood open opposite the archway. Walking in from the twilight, they found themselves in a short hallway, which then led into a massive hall that seemed to run the length of the side of the square courtyard. To the left a huge fireplace was being stoked up against the night chill, while the right-hand wall held a hatchway from which food was being dispensed. In between ran trestle tables with benches, which were capable of seating several hundred men. Now, though, only one corner nearest the hatch was occupied and Maelbrigt herded them towards the queue for the food. The boys were quick to voice their appreciation of the delicious smells which wafted their way, earning them amused grins from the men already seated.

"Hardened campaigners, eh, Maelbrigt?" one man called jocularly.

"Starting recruits young these days, aren't you?" another called out and other jokes followed. It was clear that no offence was meant to the boys, and Maelbrigt himself grinned back and let the banter carry on.

When they reached the hatchway, Rob and Jakie could not see over the top, and Maelbrigt swung each up in his arms in turn to allow them to choose what they wanted. Even for two hungry lads the portions that the men were eating were too big, but the boys were not about to admit defeat and valiantly assured Maelbrigt they would eat it all. As they moved away clutching a large platter each, room was made for them on the end of one of the more distant tables, and once they had realized that the other three were going to sit on the near end of the empty table next to them they sat down. Taise realized that Maelbrigt had been right when he said the boys would be well cared for here, as a drink was poured for them from the pitcher in the centre of the table, and the men chatted to them as they ate.

However, all through the meal Taise and Sithfrey were given sideways glances from all across the room, and Taise found her appetite evaporating like the warmth of the day until she sat with her head cast down and her hands in her lap, while Sithfrey pushed his spoon around the bowl of stew without lifting any to his mouth. Maelbrigt said nothing and concentrated on eating his meal, after which he cleared their plates back to the hatchway. By the time he had finished the boys had fallen asleep at the table, and he motioned two of the men to pick them up and follow him. He gently took Taise by the arm, and led her out of the hall with Sithfrey practically treading on his heels, with the two boys being carried behind. This time they went out of the opposite side of the hall, and up a flight of stairs to a landing that ran the length of the building. Rooms went off at regular intervals, and Maelbrigt went to an open door halfway along. Someone had recently prepared it for them with a small fire burning in an iron basket, and clean blankets had been placed on each of five of the six beds in the room. The men put Rob and Jakie on the two farthest from the door and covered them up before nodding to Maelbrigt and leaving, closing the door behind them.

Once they had gone, Taise and Sithfrey sank onto the bed nearest the fire without realizing that they had shrunk towards one another. Maelbrigt watched sadly, and then went down on one knee to kneel in front of Taise.

"I'm so sorry you have to go through this," he said, taking her hands in his, and ducking his head slightly so that he could make contact with her downcast eyes. "I wouldn't have brought you here if it hadn't been necessary, but for a start I need information as to where certain people are that I can only get here. And this was the only place I could think of where I knew for certain those two would be safe," he gestured with a nod to the two recumbent forms submerged beneath the blankets. Taise sighed heavily but raised her head up to meet his gaze. She nodded.

"They seem to have made friends already. It's not them that worry me."

Sithfrey's head was bobbing in agreement even though he said nothing.

"I promise you, they won't harm you," Maelbrigt tried to reassure them. "I have to go to the chapter house for the evening prayers now." Taise's hands tightened on his in fear at the thought of him leaving them alone. "I have to explain what's happened," he continued. "They'll be less hostile when they know you're being hunted by the Abend, really they will." Taise's face said she was not convinced of that, but he prised his hands loose and went to the door.

"You see the wooden peg here? Drop it into the hole in the latch if you're really frightened, then nobody can get in. I must go but I'll be back. I don't know quite how long it will take, but I'll knock for you to let me in." With that he turned on his heels and went out. No sooner had the door closed, then Sithfrey sprinted for the door and dropped the peg into the latch.

"Do you think we're going to get out of here alive?" he asked Taise mournfully, as he came and sat back down beside her. She shrugged and pulled a blanket round her shoulders, but could find nothing reassuring to say.

Maelbrigt strode down stairs, back through the dining hall and out into the courtyard, where he turned left and went to the eastern range of buildings. A large recessed door led into the chapter house, which looked like a round flask lying on its side when viewed from the nearby hills. The flat bottom was where it joined the range of the grange with the doorway. It swelled out into a circular building capable of holding almost as many men as the hall, with a small square protuberance on the eastern end which held the altar. When services were not being held, heavy tapestries on either side of the archway to the chancel could be drawn across separating the divine from the secular.

Once upon a time only the Knights would have come in here, and the lay men-at-arms would have had their own priest to conduct their services in the barracks, which lay alongside the main grange. Since the near-annihilation of the Knights, though, the remaining soldiers had moved into the grange to keep the most important building occupied. Tonight, Maelbrigt could see around fifty men congregated for the evening prayers, and he suspected that this was more than normal, many having come in to hear what he was doing here with two DeÁine. Far too many of the congregation were gray-haired, where they had any hair at all, and he was horribly conscious that unless something was done soon the grange here would no longer remain viable, which only aggravated his sense of impending doom.

Normally he would have found comfort in the familiar routine, even if his faith had been deeply shaken, but on this night the elderly priest seemed to drone on forever. It was all he could do not to breathe a sigh of relief when the final response was made, and the priest made the sign of the cross in the air before the great silver dragon-headed one on the altar. The man had barely removed the chasuble from his neck before Maelbrigt was on his feet, and ascending the three steps to turn to face the men.

"Hear me, brothers, hear me!" he began with the customary pronouncement, his naturally rich bass voice resonating off the stone walls. The tension in the room rose noticeably, if only because it had been so long since most of them had heard the words spoken in earnest in this place. So many remembered them having preceded calls to arms, and even the oldest stood a little straighter, like aging hounds still quivering to follow the hunter's horn. Maelbrigt felt a momentary flush of pride in his old company, and found himself taking a rather ragged breath before he could continue. Trying to ignore the rising lump in his throat he spoke again.

"I bring bad news. The Abend are active in the Islands again!" The collective intake of breath would have moved lesser curtains than the heavy tapestries framing him, and then after a second's silence a murmur rose in volume causing him to shout to continue. "You all know I brought two DeÁine with me." The murmur dropped away. "The woman, Taise, has suffered greatly at the hands of the Abend. When we clipped their wings the last time, we didn't know that others suffered as we did. I have seen her scars from the floggings, and she carries worse than even the most undisciplined recruit would've had as punishment here." That really silenced them. "The Abend thought they had been betrayed from within. Their vanity wouldn't let them believe they could be defeated by Knights, and so they sought scapegoats amongst their own. They picked on Taise because she had the courage to say they were wrong to try to force us into slavery."

An angry growl rose from the assembled men. Amongst the soldiers there had always been a strong sense of disgust at such injustice, and

Maelbrigt was gratified to see that it had not disappeared with the years of inactivity. Selling Sithfrey to them was going to be harder, though.

"The other DeÁine came hunting her." The growl rose again but more menacingly. Maelbrigt raised his hands in a placatory gesture. "He may be as big as any man on the outside, but inside he's a small boy and the Abend terrified him into the task. I say this not to apologize for him, but it's from him that I learnt that the war-mages amongst the Abend are abroad again. He's merely a pawn in their game, but he's the one person who's seen inside Bruighean recently. Nothing I can do to him will frighten him more than the Abend have already, or compel him into revealing information, largely because he doesn't know that what he may have seen could be of any importance. He had no idea that it was significant that Tancoystl, Eliavres, Calatin and Quintillean were missing and that Anarawd was in charge. It seems the least man here knows more of the workings of the Abend than most of their own people do." Nods of understanding were gradually appearing among the assembly.

"I have to extract as much information as possible from him, and the only way to do that is to win his confidence so that he speaks freely of what he's seen. Only then can I sort the grain from the chaff. So I ask you, brothers, to refrain from the natural impulse to treat him as the enemy. I believe him to have been followed to Celidon, but he temporarily lost his watchdogs in the equinox storms. Who they are I'm not sure, but I believe Taise is their real target and once they get close enough to her they'll dispatch him as unnecessary. Before then we *must* have that information, yet I also need urgently to consult with those other Knights left here in Celidon, and if he runs in fear I doubt I will find him again in time."

He carefully emphasized the next words. "He must therefore be given no reason to feel threatened enough to run from here." Reluctant nods followed, but Maelbrigt could see that the vast majority had understood what was being asked, and these days there were not the numbers of young hotheads who might once have disobeyed such a request.

"I must now depend on you men!" Shoulders went back and heads came up again filled with anticipation. "The other granges must be warned! I want riders to go as soon as possible. First, though, has anyone seen or heard of anything in the light of what I've just told you which now seems suspicious?" Nobody responded, and he was about to move on when there was a ripple in the crowd and an old groom shuffled forward. He made an arthritic salute before Maelbrigt.

"Beg pardon, sire, but there might be something. My nephew came to see me yesterday. He works a coastal barge and he was telling me that trade from Rheged has been real bad this autumn." A younger man at his side plucked at his sleeve, but he shook the restraining arm off. "The thing is, sire. He said everyone here thought it was just tall stories, but that the reason there was less wool at the ports he works was 'cause it wasn't coming out of Maerske and the eastern moor ports. He said it was 'cause there's a mist that eats people on the moors in Rheged." The few youngest grooms and auxiliary workers started sniggering at the old man, but they stopped in astonishment at the grim expressions and worried murmur that ran through the former soldiers. Someone near the front gave it a name – féfiada, the war-mage's mists.

Maelbrigt praised the old soldier for his alertness and ordered that he be found some reward.

"It may be féfiada, but if it's hunting then it's more likely it's personified – the farliath. That means at least one of the Abend is in Rheged. When it feeds it takes the soul of the hunted which strengthens its master, but the power to control the farliath cannot pass over water, so its master must have been nearby. When you send those riders, tell all the granges to be on full alert for anything that might hint at the others' presence. We must find out where those other three are!"

The meeting broke up into clusters as the sergeants sought out their own troops and set them tasks for the morning, before coming to Maelbrigt who had turned to stare at the silver cross. Saying the words out loud in this place had suddenly brought it home to him – he had been so busy responding so far that it had not activated memories, yet they swept over him now, and he was offering up some silent but heartfelt prayers. Images of the Last Stand haunted him, of his brave friends valiantly trying to fight enemies that half the time they had been unable to even see. More by luck than judgment an archer would find a mage or acolyte as a target, and a gap would appear in the war-mage's mist. The Knights would charge in to slaughter the DeÁine, until the mist closed in again and the farliath came hunting, consuming friend and foe alike to feed their masters' insatiable need for more power.

Behind the cross, carved into the domed ceiling of the apse, the roll call of the fallen stretched upwards from the stone dado rail which contained the piscinas of holy water. The builders had never anticipated having to carve so many names, and so they were fitted into every flat space between the carved representations of the five sacred trees. Between the branches of the oak, ash, birch, yew and rowan, names ascended skywards as if following their owner's souls aloft.

Eventually someone coughed breaking his reverie, and he turned to face them again.

"Has anyone seen Labhran?" he asked – hoping like mad that his old co-conspirator had not chosen this moment to go off on one of his wanders into the mountains to soothe his shattered soul.

One of the sergeants gave a toothless grin, his front teeth having disappeared in a long-gone battle.

"Oh yes! You're in luck, sire, he was here only last week. He'd just come back from wherever he disappears to and found the mice had been at his grain, so he came for some more supplies."

At last something had come right!

"Aldred and Bosel?"

"Gone south to Cabrack for one of Aldred's book findings, I think."

"And Talorcan? Has anyone had word of him?" This time there was a general shaking of heads, although one man said he was still in Ergardia the last they had heard. That did not surprise Maelbrigt, and although Ergardia was a long journey away, if Talorcan was there it meant he was probably still with the Knights and would be findable. He would have been more worried if his fellow Knight had lost patience with his adopted sept and gone roaming, given that Talorcan was not the most tolerant of bureaucracy, especially if he was not kept occupied. Thanking them he turned to go when someone behind him said,

"Kayna's here, too, you know."

Maelbrigt winced inwardly at the name, but it would have been odd not to ask after her now she had been mentioned. Of all the people he had not wanted to meet while he had Taise with him, she was top of the list, but apparently she had had nowhere else to go when her father had died.

"I'll deal with her in the morning," was all he could think of to say to the men who were watching him for a reaction. As he carried on walking out there were several nudges and winks behind his back, which he did his best to ignore, and made straight for the dormitory stairs again.

He tried the door to their room and was not surprised to find that they had indeed latched it. Knocking firmly on the door, he was a little concerned to get no reply the first time, despite calling out his name. As he was repeating the process he heard the peg being pulled out and the latch was lifted, allowing the door to swing in on a sleepy-eyed Taise. Sithfrey was struggling to his feet too, but the boys were still curled up undisturbed. Closing the door behind him he smiled reassuringly at both of them and tried to calm their fears. Despite his best efforts, though, they looked thoroughly unconvinced, and all he could do was tell them they would see for themselves tomorrow morning.

Too tired to argue, they all retreated to their beds, but he was relieved that when he moved his over to next to Taise's, she reached out from under the blankets to him. He had been desperately afraid that she would retreat further and further into herself once she felt threatened again, and that he would start to lose her trust. Edging himself over onto her bed, as he lifted his arm she immediately moved under to rest her head on his shoulder, and wrap her arm around his chest, and he fell asleep to her breath on his neck.

In the morning the presence of Rob and Jakie, boisterous from a full night's sleep, prevented Taise or Sithfrey having chance to brood, and once they were downstairs, events overtook them. To Taise's amazement the soldiers to a man were now courteous to her without being overly familiar, and they ignored Sithfrey as though he did not exist, which was probably the best thing that could happen. He was as unwilling to have contact or conversation with them as they were to reciprocate, but at least this way he stopped jumping at shadows quite so badly.

The whole of the morning was spent sorting out who would be responsible for the boys and Dancer, and acquiring horses for the onward journey. When the bell rang for the midday meal they joined the men and picked up oatmeal bread, cheese and newly harvested, crisp apples, with mugs of small beer, and went to sit near the doorway where the sun was shining in. Maelbrigt had barely put his mug onto the table when a voice from behind said,

"There you are, you bastard!" As he turned, the others saw the young woman who had spoken draw back her hand and crack him hard across the face. He was almost knocked off his feet, but before he could straighten she snarled, "I hope you're satisfied with your handiwork!" and stormed off out of the door again.

"Who was that?" Taise asked in astonishment.

"Some girl he's left holding his brat, no doubt," Sithfrey speculated almost gleefully, unable to resist his delight at the thought that this so far impeccable man, whom Taise seemed to worship, should turn out to be fallible in a rather seedy way. He was rewarded with a fierce glare from Taise and the boys, but an annoyingly rueful chuckle from Maelbrigt.

"Sorry to disappoint you, Sithfrey, but no! I've never even kissed Kayna, and as far as I know she's got no child, of mine or otherwise."

Sithfrey's smirk melted into a sullen frown, and they all sat down in an uncomfortable silence until Jakie piped up.

"Who is she then, and why did you let her hit you like that?" Taise tried to hush him, but Maelbrigt answered him willingly.

"Kayna is the daughter of the Knight who trained me." He sighed at the memory of another familiar face now gone. "He tried to look out for me like I'm trying to do for you two. He and his wife already had three daughters and had given up hope of having a son, so he sort of adopted me at the grange, even though they lived up on the hill at the castle. Kayna is the youngest by many years, so whereas her sisters grew up with her mother, she always found her playmates with the soldiers' families down here. Then just after I'd arrived, her mother died and she was looked after by the women here. Her sisters were already of an age to be looking for husbands and they didn't want a little sister at their heels – especially one who'd rather be practicing with a sword than a needle! Back then I was the big brother she'd never had."

"What happened?" Taise asked, her curiosity aroused. "Something changed, because that's no way to greet a brother."

Between bites of apple, Maelbrigt explained that he had been the one to teach Kayna all the things his teachers taught him at the grange. The sisters had married and Kayna had not been impressed with her sisters' choices. Actually, neither had her father or Maelbrigt, yet the marriages seemed to work, and if his daughters were happy their father was not about to interfere. The real problem was who was going to inherit the castle. The now elderly Knight was happy for Kayna to be the one to have Luing if she could find a husband, but the laws of Celidon prevented him from leaving it to a female heir. More to the point, he had to provide for the other two out of the estate, which would mean someone would have to pay for the running of the big, draughty old place. There was not enough money to provide that for Kayna too.

Unfortunately, as Maelbrigt pointed out, the number of young men who wanted a wife who could whip them to a standstill at sword practice, as well as out-ride and out-shoot them, were nil. In the end he had stopped coaching her, but it had done no good. She had simply thought he was giving up on her. Then the inevitable had happened last year and her father had died, and the castle had gone to her hated older sister and despised fat merchant husband.

"By the sound of it they've thrown her out," he said sadly. "I'm sorry, I truly am. I'd have liked nothing more than to see Kayna get what was hers by right. Of the three she was the one who loved the place, but what could I do? She wouldn't even try to understand that I was trying to help."

"You could have married her," Taise said innocently. Maelbrigt nearly choked on the mouthful he had just taken.

"Me? Marry Kayna? You can't be serious! She's like my little sister."

"Did it never occur to you that that would have solved her problem for her, and that she might not have felt that way about you?" Taise replied. He sat in silence staring back at her, dumbfounded. "Obviously not!" she laughed at his utter confusion, unable to keep a small feeling of relief down that she had not stumbled on someone with a previous claim to his affections, or at least evidently not in the same way as her.

"Spirits preserve me, no! I never wanted that either!" The voice came from the door again, and the slim, dark young woman walked back in. "I thought *you* thought Father would leave Luing to you if he thought I wasn't capable of handling the place," she said. "Did you really want me to have it after all?"

Maelbrigt stood to face her, exasperation in his voice as he said,

"Of course I did, you idiot! It's your home not mine! Honestly Kayna, I thought you knew me better than that."

Her lip quivered and her eyes began to fill.

"Oh Maelbrigt, I'm so sorry. Why didn't you say so?"

He was about to point out that he had, repeatedly, but before he could say anything he found himself in a bear hug which caught him unawares and took his breath away. All he could do then was hug her back as the others watched, very confused. When he managed to disentangle himself from her, he introduced her to the others, and Taise found herself sitting opposite a lean young woman of middling height in her twenties, with pale skin, gray eyes and thick dark hair which was kept severely in place in a short, tight plait. She wore an adjusted version of the Knight's uniform of the same black leather pants and boots, but with a linen shirt under a black leather jacket. Not conventionally pretty she was nonetheless striking, and Taise thought that if her smile ever reached her eyes she would be thought attractive.

As it was, she seemed to be someone the men walked around with great caution. In the past Taise had seen that around the spoilt offspring of the influential, who had never got used to the world not revolving around them. But in Kayna's case it seemed to be something else, although she could not worked out what yet.

She suddenly realized that Maelbrigt was telling Kayna about their flight from the castle. For a moment she thought he might be trying to persuade her to look after the boys, and was prepared for a further outburst of indignation, when Kayna said,

"In that case I'm coming with you. You need someone else who can handle a sword if you're going to protect these two, and there's nothing keeping me here now."

Taise expected him to put up some resistance to the idea, but instead he seemed almost enthusiastic. Seeing Taise's puzzled expression he said,

"Kayna's the best swordsperson in this place. What she lacks in muscle she's had to learn to compensate for with skill. I'd trust her with my life," then unable to resist the temptation, with a mischievous glint in his eye, he added, "well at least not to let someone else kill me! I think she regards that as her personal privilege."

Kayna glared at him and elbowed him hard in the ribs, but then a twitch of a smile appeared which she did her best to hide. Rubbing his side, Maelbrigt carried on.

"You'd better know what the plan so far is hadn't you?"

"Labhran?" Kayna guessed. Maelbrigt nodded approvingly,

"He's the best person to help us. I'm sending riders to all the granges, but I'll write a special message to our former Grand Master."

"Will he help now he's chancellor?" Kayna wondered.

"Absolutely," Maelbrigt affirmed, "he may be bound to the court now, but he's still a Knight for all that, and he'll understand immediately the threat. After all, he was part of the council which drew up the war plans before, and the reasons haven't changed where the Abend are concerned. I can trust him to get messages off to the other Islands, and do what needs to be done to put the country on a war footing. But we need someone here and now who can move with us, and for that we need Labhran."

Before the others could ask who they were talking about, Maelbrigt and Kayna got up, and Maelbrigt asked her to take over the preparations for their personal departure while he arranged matters at the grange. They didn't meet up again until the evening meal, and none of them felt easy questioning Kayna, although the boys warmed to her when she made special arrangements for them to have ponies of their own to learn to ride on while they were at the grange. After the meal Kayna left to pack her own things, and Maelbrigt excused himself once more. Taise and Sithfrey took themselves back to their room, while the boys were taught a complicated board game by some of the old soldiers. The whole place seemed to go quiet early that night, with the boys being returned to spend a last night with their friends.

It was barely dawn when the sounds of activity woke them, and when Maelbrigt took them down to breakfast again they found men, dressed for riding, wolfing down their food. Maelbrigt took his food on the move, checking that the right rider got the right letter, and the couriers disappeared in threes, illustrating his determination that the word should get through no matter what. Finally he returned to them, and they collected their personal things from the room and went out into the courtyard where their new horses awaited. Rob and Jakie became tearful as they realized this was the point when they would be left behind, and had to be physically held back from trying to mount up behind Taise and Sithfrey. Maelbrigt took the time to hug each of them and whisper reassurances in their ear, but they were no happier when the four horses turned to ride out of the gate.

Taise and Sithfrey had little skill at riding and so had been given stolid country horses little bigger than ponies, Taise's an almost cream, dappled gray and Sithfrey's a chestnut bay. In contrast, Maelbrigt now rode a large powerful black, which he had told the boys was fully trained and what Dancer would be one day. He barely seemed to need to give it any guidance by the reins and muscles rippled under its satin-sheened coat. No wonder he had grieved for Hellion, Taise thought. With such an animal horse and rider almost became one. Surprisingly, Kayna was on a similar beast except that it was the darkest dappled-gray, but although the horse looked too big for her she was obviously having no problem controlling it, and rode with the same assurance as Maelbrigt. His comments on her ability were clearly not overstated where her riding was concerned, and Sithfrey thought she was probably almost as dangerous to cross as the Knight.

From the grange, while the road snaked southwards to Rhicarn and then on to the capital of Celidon, Cabrack, they took once more to sheep trails, and began to climb into the mountains which ran like a spine down the island. It took the best part of the day to skirt the large loch which lay inland of Ardfern, but towards nightfall they turned off into a broad valley leading east. As the setting sun bathed the heather in a golden glow, they saw a small hut nestled in a dip in the side of the valley, and then higher up another perched precariously above a sheer drop. Maelbrigt and Kayna led them off towards the huts, and they had almost reached the first one when a cheery voice spoke from their left.

"Well, well, visitors! Marvellous!" From a clump of bracken, a small man with a shock of curly, dark blonde hair and twinkling green eyes appeared, clutching a brace of rabbits. He barely came up to Maelbrigt's chin when they dismounted, but was no dwarf. He was perfectly proportioned, just smaller than normal, but blessed with an infectious grin which Maelbrigt and Kayna echoed when they saw him.

"Sioncaet!" Maelbrigt exclaimed in obvious pleasure, "I never expected to find you still here!"

"*Ach*, well, I'm not always!" the little man replied with an airy wave of his free hand. "I go off and ply my trade now and then, you know. After all someone has to earn a living. If it was left to 'misery' up there," he gestured in the direction of the upper cottage, "we'd eat nothing but weeds and rabbit with the odd duck thrown in. Now me, I like a pint! Speaking of which, would you like to join me in one?"

As they laughed and agreed to his offer, a laconic voice appeared from the shadow of the scrubby thorn trees behind the hut.

"As you can see, he doesn't change! What brings you here in such strange company?"

The speaker materialized into a fair skinned, pale grey-eyed man with collar-length reddish blond hair, and of about Maelbrigt's height. With his regular aquiline features and pale colouring he looked like he could almost be DeÁine.

"Hello, Labhran." Maelbrigt greeted the stranger. "I'm sorry, you're not going to like the news I bring."

"Oh don't apologize to him, he wouldn't be happy if you brought him the news that he'd been granted eternal wealth and happiness!" Sioncaet chuckled. "Come on, that beer's waiting! You can tell us all the news when you've had chance to sit down on a proper seat." He looked at Taise and Sithfrey, who had dismounted with difficulty after a day in the saddle. "I don't know, these Knights, *eh*! They might be happy riding all day, but you two look worn out, come on in."

Maelbrigt turned and took in Taise's strained face and was suddenly solicitous, realizing that he had been so caught up in reaching here by nightfall, he had not taken into account the strain of riding for them. On the way to the grange they had had to walk for parts of the day on the steeper slopes, so this had been the first time they'd had to spend all day in the saddle. He went to her and gave her his arm to lean on as she hobbled stiffly along the path.

"You didn't tell me your friend Labhran was DeÁine, too," she said to him in a low voice as they walked to the cottage door.

"Oh he's not the DeÁine," Sioncaet answered from in front, "I am!"

Chapter 15

The Haunting Past

Celidon: Harvest-moon

Taise stopped in her tracks in surprise and Sithfrey stood open-mouthed at Sioncaet's pronouncement. The little man seemed utterly unfazed by their astonishment, but Labhran's appearance grew even more morose. Kayna took him by the arm and led him inside speaking softly to him. Glances were exchanged between Sioncaet and Maelbrigt, but nothing was said, leaving Taise and Sithfrey even more mystified as they followed the others in.

Sioncaet's cottage was little more than one large room, yet it showed him to have no small artistic talent. Everything was cleverly arranged to make maximum use of the space, and yet managed to be homely at the same time. Opposite the door was a stone inglenook fireplace with hooks which held bubbling pots and a kettle over the fire, which glowed cheerily. On either of the side-walls simple wool drapes were tied back to reveal truckle beds, which obviously doubled as extra seating. A well-scrubbed wooden table occupied the centre of the room, laden at the one end with a pile of rolled manuscripts. A selection of chopped herbs and vegetables on a large, well-used chopping board stood at the other. Where the walls were visible they had been covered with everything from simple sketches to intricate diagrams and exquisitely worked miniature portraits, some in delicate tints which spoke of plant dyes, and others in simple line drawings in what looked like charcoal.

At this stage, though, Taise was simply grateful for Sioncaet waving her to one of the truckles which proved to have a mattress which sank softly as she subsided onto it. Her moan of relief raised a chuckle from her host, who was rummaging on a dresser alongside the door to accumulate sufficient drinking vessels for all of his guests. Clutching a wonderfully mixed assortment, he turned and deposited them on the table before disappearing through a curtain to the left of the fireplace, returning moments later with a large pitcher which had a beery froth forming a dome above it. He happily sloshed generous measures into the mugs and tankards and handed them around.

Maelbrigt was grinning widely as he took a long draught and pronounced it as good as ever, and Kayna was almost as fast at draining her first mug-full. Taise and Sithfrey both took cautious sips at first, and found that they were drinking a light, fresh tasting brew that seemed to have a hint of honey while still managing to be refreshingly dry. After the long journey, they surprised themselves at the speed with which they too drained their drinks, given that neither of them normally cared much for beer, preferring herbal teas on the whole. While Sioncaet replenished everyone, Maelbrigt managed to whisper to them that it was just as well, as Sioncaet would have been rather offended if they had not liked it. Apparently he took great pride in his ability as a brewer.

Labhran took Sioncaet's second trip with the pitcher to fix Maelbrigt with a weary gaze and asked,

"Well? What *are* you doing here then? You rarely bring good news but turning up with two DeÁine is extreme, even for you."

With Taise and Sithfrey seated on the one truckle, and Kayna and Labhran opposite them, Maelbrigt took a seat at the one side of the fireplace and Sioncaet curled up on what was obviously his usual spot on the other inglenook seat. Taking his time he explained to Labhran and Sioncaet what had happened to bring them on the road.

When he reached the end, Labhran exhaled and leaned back to gaze at the ceiling, but said nothing. It was Sioncaet who was the first to speak.

"Well that's news indeed," he said, pouring himself another beaker full of beer and taking a deep swig of it. "The Abend on the move. That's bad news I hoped I'd never hear!"

"I know," Maelbrigt apologized, looking at his friends with genuine regret. "I wish both of you could've been left in peace, but whatever you decide to do now, I couldn't not warn you once I knew they were out."

Labhran gave a snort which could have been disgust or anger, but Sioncaet gave a weak smile.

"Oh don't be daft, Maelbrigt, you can't assume sole responsibility for the past and you certainly aren't to blame for what the Abend do. At some point they were bound to stick their heads over the parapet, so to speak, whether you were still alive or not." He paused and swirled his beer reflectively for a moment, as though seeing patterns in the rising bubbles. "The question is what are *you* going to do?"

"I don't know, to be honest." Maelbrigt replied. "I knew I had to get Taise away from the coast and the village where someone might unwittingly give her away, and it was obvious Sithfrey needed to be brought along. I was relying on being able to talk out options with you two, and hopefully Talorcan, too, before I had to act."

"Just talk?" Labhran asked bitterly, "or were you assuming the rest of us would spring back into action again. You don't give up do you? What if we just want to be left in peace instead of joining another one of your crusades?"

As Maelbrigt shook his head wearing a hurt expression, Sioncaet cut sharply across him to rebuke Labhran.

"That's enough! You weren't the only one to suffer Labhran! Maelbrigt did what you asked and stayed away. Did that stop your nightmares? No! So stop beating him up because the past haunts you." He turned to Taise and Sithfrey. "I'm so sorry, you must be wondering what in the Islands you've been dragged into." Then to Maelbrigt, "Have you told them the full tale?"

Maelbrigt shook his head. "No, there hasn't really been opportunity – we've had the boys with us, and then the grange wasn't exactly as secure as it used to be – but to be honest I didn't think it was as important as what was about to happen."

"Oh no, I think it's every bit as important!" Sioncaet said emphatically. "I'll go so far as to insist that you don't take them a step farther until they've heard everything."

Maelbrigt looked amazed at this friend. "I didn't expect you of all people to feel so strongly about that. Can't it wait until we've got them even farther away?"

"No!" Sioncaet insisted. "Look, you and Kayna might be fine spending another day in the saddle straight away, but these two can't. They can hardly sit up tonight! Take tomorrow morning for us to tell them, and if I'm right, I think I might have a bit to add."

He would say no more despite pressing by Maelbrigt, and insisted that it be done when they were all fresh enough to take in all that would be said. In the end it was decided that, to give everyone room, Kayna would go up to Labhran's even smaller cottage and sleep on his spare bed, while the others would remain with Sioncaet. As they got up to go Sioncaet tapped Labhran on the arm with a smug grin.

"By the way, that's a trip to the inn at Rhicarn you owe me."

Labhran grimaced, and Kayna giggled as she glanced at Maelbrigt.

"What was that about?" Maelbrigt asked when they had gone out.

"Oh he said if you ever fell for a woman it would be some doe-eyed village girl half your age!" Sioncaet smirked. "I bet him five pints of *The Bluebell's* best beer that the one thing you'd never fall for would be some empty-headed sweet thing who stared at you like a moonstruck hare. I bet another five on the chance that it would be someone *not* from the villages. I told him you'd want someone with a bit more sophistication, and older, who you could talk to. … I won didn't I?" He laughed at Maelbrigt and Taise's expressions, which seesawed between embarrassment and indignation.

Determined not to be singled out for scrutiny, Taise asked,

"And what about Kayna and Labhran? They seem awfully close!"

Sioncaet's laughter peeled out joyfully. "Sacred Trees! That would be something to see if it happened, but no, those two are far too determined to be complicated for anything that straightforward. Labhran's very fond of Kayna, to be sure, but he's convinced himself that she's far beyond him and so he's never tried. Not that he's tried with anyone since the girl died he'd set his heart on when a lad, although he was far more in love with the distant image than he would have been if he'd ever really known her. Kayna on the other hand has convinced herself she's in love with Talorcan, and so she sympathizes with Labhran over 'lost' loves."

"And she isn't?" Sithfrey asked, feeling very confused.

"Nah!" Sioncaet chuckled. "She doesn't want to lose control of herself for a second, and if you really care for someone then you can't parcel out your feelings in convenient pieces. So she's fixed on someone who's unattainable. Talorcan's a good choice because he's off chasing his own ghosts, so he doesn't have a clue. Half the time he isn't even on the same Island, and anyway he thinks Kayna's Maelbrigt's no matter how many times we tell him she isn't."

"Immaculate Lotus, that's complicated!" Sithfrey groaned. "So who's Talorcan after?"

"Oh, no-one! Yet..!" Sioncaet replied. "He just does tall, dark and brooding very well. You know, all staring off into the distance and frowning a lot. Of course it doesn't hurt that he's considered rather handsome by the ladies, so the women at the grange think it's all very romantic that Kayna goes around acting like she's pining for him."

"Not like she did over Maelbrigt?"

Sioncaet hooted out loud at this. "Oh I don't think whacking someone every time you see them counts as pining. Anyway you couldn't convincingly pine after this one, he's more your tall, dark and cheerful sort." As if to prove his point he playfully nudged Maelbrigt, whose indignation at being discussed as though he was not there gave way to a self-deprecating smile. Taise thought Sioncaet was wrong. She could pine quite effectively for Maelbrigt in his absence, but decided he might never hear the last of it from his friend if she ever said so, and remained silent.

The conversation was halted when Sithfrey gave a jaw-cracking yawn, which set them all off. He was allocated the main bed on one side, while Sioncaet pulled the truckle bed out from under it for himself and wheeled it closer to the fire. Taise gratefully let the drapes down and crawled under the comfortable blankets she was to share with Maelbrigt, although he agreed to share one more beer with Sioncaet before bed, and she drifted off to the sound of the two voices, one mellow bass and the other light and clear, lulling her to sleep.

Those two moved close to the fire away from the beds and Maelbrigt, after a glance at each set of closed curtains, turned to his friend.

"Alright, are you now going to tell me what that was all about? Why are you so insistent that they know about what happened between us and the Abend?"

"What do you know of Taise?" Sioncaet countered softly. Maelbrigt felt his heart skip a beat.

"Why?" he asked cautiously. "What are you suggesting?"

"Oh don't look so worried! I don't mean she's a spy or anything. No, it's just that I have a memory of someone I think might be her." Sioncaet stretched to unknot his muscles. "I'm old Maelbrigt. I don't know why I of all people should have been granted such a ridiculously long life. You know DeÁine normally live twice as long as Islanders, but I'm over twice that and

I'm still not showing signs of *old* age, even if I'm not as young as I was. The trouble is, the memories are starting to blur after all this time. I think I remember seeing someone with another person, then realize it couldn't be them because they'd been dead for years by then, and that it was someone else. That's why I don't want to push too hard in case I've got it wrong, but I think I remember Taise. So what do you know of her?"

Maelbrigt took a deep breath and told him of what he had suspected of Taise's injuries and the bits of her extensive knowledge he had seen on display, but he had to admit her reticence to talk meant there was very little. Sioncaet listened carefully and then said thoughtfully,

"Then I think it *is* her. It was known around the court in Bruighean that the Abend were always on the lookout for others with the Power. Even they aren't immortal, despite the Power extending their life to many times the normal length, and during the wars there was always the chance that they might be killed. The inner council must always be of nine, so they had to have contenders who could be raised up. On one occasion, I remember hearing that Anarawd had found a young woman very strong in the Power. Being the animal he is, he couldn't resist physically possessing her too, whether she was willing or not.

"The thing is, for those who have it, the Power is a dangerous thing during puberty. The priesthood go to great lengths to make sure that anyone with potential doesn't have it wakened until they've passed into early adulthood, and have the mental and physical stability to cope with it. Even then only one in two successfully copes, and many go off into solitude, unable to remain stable enough to live amongst ordinary people.

"The word was that Anarawd raped this girl while she was still very young, and in doing so he woke the Power. Somehow she remained sane, but probably only because one of the physicians managed to hypnotize her into forgetting she had the Power. Because she thought she didn't have it, she wasn't tempted into the addictive cycle of using more and more until it destroyed her. Did you ever wonder when Taise lost her hair Maelbrigt? It's a sign of the Power you know. That's why all the great ones have none, like the Abend."

"The witches have hair." Maelbrigt countered.

"Wigs!" Sioncaet said authoritatively.

"Wigs? Are you sure? I know I only ever saw them from a great distance, but they looked pretty convincingly normal to me."

"Ah, but when you're the Abend you can afford to demand the best be made for you. I know because on the night the news came of the defeat at Moytirra, they were in such a rush to get to the council chambers from the temple, where they'd been at an offering, they picked the wrong ones up! Geitla was wearing Helga's ice blonde hair instead of her redder own, and Masanae had Magda's curly brunette wig perched on her head like a pimple, while her long, straight one kept slipping over Magda's eyes. It was hilarious, but no-one dared laugh, and afterwards two rather gossipy serving girls disappeared. They probably never said anything, but they were disposable and it did nothing to harm the witches' fearsome reputation, so that's why nobody ever heard about it. But trust me, they are totally hairless. Apparently the Power acts like a toxin. It plays havoc with the body. It inevitably leaves them sterile amongst other things, too, so I hope you've not been hoping for a family with Taise because you won't get it."

"I don't mind that so much," Maelbrigt said softly. "The Trees only know how many orphans are around who need a family. If Taise was happy with that, there'd be no shortage of children we could love as our own. As long as she's with me and happy, that's all that matters. But if I get my hands on Anarawd he's going to regret the day he was born!" He drained his beer, stretched and headed for the bed.

"I don't doubt that for a second." Sioncaet mused at his friend's retreating back. Anarawd might have substantial power, but Sioncaet had a feeling that his friend had yet to discover his full potential and it might be more than anyone other than him suspected.

They were woken in the morning by the appearance of Kayna and Labhran. Feeling somewhat fuzzy-headed from the unaccustomed beer, Sithfrey was grateful that there was not more this morning but the more usual caff instead. A fine mountain mist muted the autumn colours and covered the foliage of Sioncaet's garden in delicate droplets. Maelbrigt and Labhran went to attend to the horses and came back very damp, even after such a short walk to the lean-to stable. Whatever the differences of last night they now seemed to be on better terms, even if they were not totally relaxed in one another's company. Sioncaet whipped up a floury mixture and was soon handing out griddle cakes for breakfast, which filled the little cottage with warm, spicy smells which blended with that of the caff.

By the time they had finished, everyone was feeling much more civilized and less willing to rush out into the wet. They resumed their positions of the previous night, and Maelbrigt cleared his throat to speak. Before he could say a word, Sioncaet chipped in.

"You will tell it in order won't you?"

Maelbrigt nodded, and was about to begin when he was interrupted again.

"Right from the beginning?"

"Sacred Trees, Sioncaet!" Labhran exploded, "let the man make a start or we'll be here all day!"

Kayna laughed. "Oh come on, you know what he's like. Look, let him tell it Maelbrigt. You know he won't be satisfied until you do." She turned to Taise and Sithfrey. "Sioncaet was the jester and storyteller to your king Nuadu, and even now he earns his beer money entertaining in the local inns. He can't help it. He's a perfectionist. He can't bear to hear us make a pig's ear of telling a good story, so it's better if we let him do it."

Sioncaet got to his feet, and walked to in front of his newest guests and made an incredibly ornate bow before their astonished eyes. "Sioncaet ap Dadera, jester, fool and entertainer at your service!" he proclaimed.

"You're Dadera the Great?" Sithfrey gasped. "But you're *dead*! You died with Nuadu!"

"Oh far from it, my friend!" Sioncaet said with a joyous pirouette, as he turned to the centre of the room again, neatly avoiding the table. "But bear with me and you shall hear all!"

Perching on the edge of the table, he began his tale in the time honoured way, "Once upon a time…." Kayna was right, he was a gifted storyteller and held them all enthralled as he wove the events of times past into a story they could all follow.

After driving the DeÁine back behind the mountains of Brychan following the Battle of Moytirra, many in the Islands had developed a false sense of security and complacency. The leaders of the different septs of Knights had felt differently, though. They knew it was only a matter of time before the DeÁine regrouped and tried again, and they were determined not to be caught by surprise again. The most urgent need was to ensure the safety of the Treasures the DeÁine had been parted from centuries ago. Without them the Knights stood a chance of holding the DeÁine back, but if they ever got the Treasures back, they would have their power enhanced and would be unstoppable.

A great council had been held in secret in the loch-bound mountain castle of Lorne in Ergardia. The heads of all five septs and their most trusted men had attended, along with certain key men, such as Abbot Jaenberht from the Order of the Cross in Rheged. None of the chancellors – or whatever they chose to call themselves by now – had been invited or informed of the meeting for fear of security being breached because of political infighting. After many days' deliberation a plan had been formulated. The most powerful of the DeÁine Treasures was the mail Helm, and that seemed safe in Rheged since the DeÁine had no influence yet in the lands to the east. The Scabbard was equally safe far away in Prydein, and being more defensive than aggressive in power, it was never likely to be first on the DeÁine's list to retrieve. The Gauntlet, as an attack weapon, was much more likely to be second on their wish list. Yet that was hidden in Celidon almost in the sea, and as such would be hard to trace.

That left the Gorget – more defensive in its quality again, but desperately vulnerable in its current hideaway in northern Brychan. Now that the DeÁine were a short march over the mountains away from it, and the risk could not be underestimated. It was possible that their route into Brychan had been purposely chosen to strike towards it and reclaim it.

Information was what was desperately needed, and the Covert Brethren were reactivated. Some were Knights, others men of impeccable reputation who could be relied upon to find ways into DeÁine territory. The DeÁine seemed to have set up permanent residence over the mountains, as though they were trying to recreate their homeland of Lochlainn there, but the one advantage of this was that it was easier to infiltrate a permanent base. With the local people enslaved to serve the DeÁine, the new settlements were filled with people of all shapes and sizes, where one more raised no comment. The Knights bided their time and gathered reports. Maelbrigt, it transpired had been one of those used to service the collection of information from a Covert Brethren spy, Labhran. Able to pass for a low born DeÁine, Labhran had been seconded from the Knights to the Brethren while still young, and had later been infiltrated with a more experienced spy acting as the servant of the 'DeÁine' he accompanied.

The Knights had also heard of a child who had been born to a high ranking DeÁine woman after a liaison with a Knight. Her family had been part of the group already moving into Brychan before Moytirra had put the re-colonisation to an end. The then young lovers had been parted, and the surprise of her pregnancy discovered when it was too late to do anything about it. The child had been hidden away and the young woman had gone on to catch the eye of Nuadu. With Nuadu's endless promiscuity it had been even more surprising to find that while other concubines came and went, this woman had stayed.

A frantic search for the child had been undertaken by the Covert Brethren, and eventually he had been found, enslaved and embittered far beyond his years. He had willingly returned across the mountains with the Covert Brethren and embraced the Knight's quest to destroy the DeÁine's power with a venge-filled passion, having never forgiven his mother and her family for abandoning him, and Talorcan became a Knight.

The opportunity was then ripe for the Knights to make their move. By now Labhran had infiltrated the higher reaches of the court, and with other Covert Brethren he had waved the tempting lure of Talorcan under their noses. Nuadu was incapacitated by a poisoned knife in the dark one night, and, as he lay writhing in agony for days on end, the control of the council passed to his half-brother, Bres. The Knights had counted on this, for Bres was eager to prove himself the equal to his revered older sibling, but had none of his ability as a leader.

With a tale that the half-blood Talorcan planned to return at the head of an army of dissident Knights and make a bid for the throne, the idea was planted that Bres could outsmart the upstart and bring him, and his army, into the DeÁine fold. Bres would be a hero the whispers said. Bres would have accomplished what Nuadu could not, and with no loss of DeÁine life. Who would want Nuadu as Ard-rígh then? It would be his turn to serve Bres, maybe as a Donn, if he ever recovered enough. Bres would return the long lost son to the bereft chief concubine, Eriu, a woman of power and beauty whom he had lusted after for years. Surely then she would be his, too?

Bres swallowed the bait hook, line and sinker. Unfortunately what the Covert Brethren had been unable to find out was the inner workings of the Abend. Even with the help of a few enlightened DeÁine like Sioncaet, the nine remained a mystery. So they could not know that the Abend considered Bres a plum ripe for their own picking too. The sultry Geitla had found it easy to lure the inept Bres into her bed, and whisper words of lost manuscripts of great power just across the mountains in Brychan. The manuscripts were real alright, and one purportedly told of how to neutralize the Island Treasures' power, which was when Taise, Sithfrey and their companions had been readied for the journey into Brychan.

Instead of waiting for the word of Talorcan's Knights to appear nearby in the mountains, Bres decided to move early and find the manuscripts too, but had not bothered to tell the Abend about Talorcan. A horrified Sioncaet had woken one morning to find Bres armed and ready to depart with an armed force that seemed excessive to the Abend, but they adapted their scheme, hoping to leave some behind on the way in order to facilitate their own infiltration into northern Brychan. Sioncaet had roused Labhran, who had dispatched every messenger he could find to warn the Knights that they were likely to meet the DeÁine earlier than planned, and with all nine of the Abend in their midst.

It had been a toss-up who had been more surprised – the Abend at meeting an army coming their way, or the Knights at finding themselves combating sorcerers who totally changed the balance of their overwhelming numbers. Labhran and Sioncaet had managed to instil a sense of impending disaster into Nuadu, who rose from his sick bed, gathered his personal guard and set off in hot pursuit. In the meantime, the Knights were using the cover of Talorcan's anticipated assault to move the Gorget to Celidon.

The whole dreadful mess came to a head at Gavra Pass, high in the mountains above northern Brychan. The brave Knights of Celidon stood their ground and refused to cede an inch despite their devastation, not merely by the DeÁine army but by the unmatchable power of the Abend. With the Gorget out in the world the Abend had found a source of their Power to draw on, and had nearly won the day had it not been for a few Knights under Maelbrigt's leadership, who had scaled the valley wall, and brought part of the mountain down when they taunted the Abend to unleash a blast of Power at them.

With his bodyguards launched into the fray, and his back not covered, Nuadu had been sent to his final resting place by Sioncaet's knife, and then Labhran had faked another corpse to pass for the minstrel's so that it appeared he had died defending his master. Other Covert Brethren, including Labhran's 'guard' and friend, had given their lives to make personal attacks on the assembled coterie of acolytes, who found it impossible to direct their power at the opposing army and avoid the knives of the Covert Brethren at the same time. None of the Abend were critically injured, but it was enough to distract their concentration until the mountain had been brought down and sealed the pass.

The only good thing to come out of it was that the Gorget was now hidden in Ergardia, away from the Abend. They had returned west, filled with rage at the affront to their power and had proceeded to exact revenge on the unwitting priest-scholars who had been the only ones, they thought, to know of the venture. The word from New Lochlainn was that their fury at Bres when they found out what he had done was terrible, and his screams had filled the corridors of Bruighean for days. His body was never found and now Nuadu's son, Ruadan, reigned with his mother, Eriu, by his side, in what many in private said was a far from parental role.

To suffer another major defeat at the hands of the Islanders had enraged the DeÁine, but the power vacuum left by Nuadu's death had left them bereft of any firm leadership. The Abend were in the unexpected, uncomfortable position of being blamed by almost all of the remaining high ranking DeÁine for the debacle. Under other circumstances they would have been able to insert their own chosen member of the royal family as Ard-rígh, but now they were forced to accept that Ruadan was the only candidate who could unite the various factions. To the witches' frustration, he also seemed oblivious to their attempts at seduction, preferring his mother's company.

Unfortunately the Knights had also lost many of their best informers amongst the Covert Brethren, and the remainder found the rampant paranoia at court prevented replacements being inserted. They had largely been reduced to hit and run operations, then retreating to hideaways in the mountain forests, which kept the DeÁine uneasy and unwilling to commit to an outright attack on Brychan, but little else. This was the situation as it had stood for the last few years, but, if it was true that the four war-mages had crossed the mountains, the Abend must have given up hoping to motivate Ruadan and were acting on their own. If they could recover the Treasures, the Abend would be able to assume total control of the DeÁine regardless of whether they had any popular support, and Ruadan would simply be their puppet. The armed might of the DeÁine would be theirs to command, and there was no doubt that the conquest of the Islands would be the first priority.

As Sioncaet finished, Maelbrigt got up and made a large pot of caff while the others sat in silence, each wrapped in their own thoughts. Sioncaet helped him hand around the steaming mugs which they all sipped gratefully in part because the story had somehow made the day seem suddenly colder, and partly because it saved them from having to speak to one another. Finally it was Taise who broke the silence. Her voice was very shaky as she spoke.

"I think it was only after the war-mages left that Anarawd would have been able to send Sithfrey after me," she said, almost to herself.

"Why do you think that?" Labhran asked her, much more kindly than she had heard him speak to Maelbrigt. "I'd have thought they'd all want to find you."

Taise shook her head. "No. It was very much Anarawd who had studied the Island Treasures for a start. The others were always convinced that there was nobody left in the Islands with enough Power to wield them. They thought, you see, that as they had always controlled the DeÁine Treasures, that it must equally take someone very strong in the Power to do it with the Islands'. What Sithfrey and I and the others found out, was that it's more a case of finding someone compatible with each particular Treasure, DeÁine or Islander, in terms of their personality. That's why they think of the Gorget as weak. It should be wielded by someone who truly in their heart of hearts wants to protect the DeÁine people, and then it would be a very powerful piece. As it is, the Abend only want to acquire power for themselves, whatever the cost, so they never got anything much out of it. The manuscript they were after was supposed to show them how to get around the balance of power between the Treasures to get rid of the last vestige of Power the Island ones might have. How true that is, I don't know, as we never got to find it, but I'd bet that manuscript is high on Anarawd's priorities even if it isn't for the others."

She stopped and took several gulps of caff during which Sioncaet gave Maelbrigt a very meaningful look that said, *here it comes.* Taking a deep breath she continued.

"Anarawd is also after me personally," she confessed. She struggled to find the words to carry on, yet before Sioncaet could say that he thought he knew what had happened, it was Sithfrey who took up her story.

"Anarawd raped her when she was a girl," he told them. Kayna gasped in horror and immediately went to sit by Taise and put her arm around the taller woman's shoulder. "He's been obsessed with Taise for years," Sithfrey continued. "He thinks because she has the Power but has never used it, she won't be sterile. He thinks that if they get the Treasures, he can use the massed power for some ritual he discovered in another old manuscript which will heal him, and he'd be able to father a child on Taise who would be the ultimate Abend."

"Perishing Sacred Trees!" Labhran swore. "How in the name of all that's sacred did you get to find that out? How much of a traitor are you that you're in their confidence that much?"

Maelbrigt was swearing fluently and repeatedly in a deadly soft monotone, and Sithfrey whimpered in fright.

"They talked while they were torturing me," he managed to get out.

"Oh, not you too!" Taise moaned and buried her head in Kayna's shoulder.

Sioncaet got up and walked over to Sithfrey, who had moved to stand by the door when Kayna had sat by Taise. Gently steering him back to a stool, he coaxed Sithfrey into telling them his own story. What he had been too scared to tell to Maelbrigt was that the Abend had used very different methods on him to Taise. She was too strong in the Power for them to be able to do anything but harm her physically. He, on the other hand, had very little ability in the Power, and they had plagued him with induced nightmares and violent hallucinations until he had lost all grip on reality. Like Taise, he had been unable to tell what he didn't know, but when he had been thrown out he had been too disorientated to go very far. All he could remember of the first year or so was hiding in a woodland hut, and being brought food and water by people who seemed to be living there too.

After what Sioncaet had just told him, he thought it was possible that it had been some of the Covert Brethren who had taken pity on him. Very slowly the nightmares and illusions had faded, and by about a year ago he had got to the stage where he thought he could just about work out what had been real and what induced by the Abend. He had finally crawled out of the wood when his benefactors had disappeared, and had made his way to a small town where he had been getting what work he could. Then to his horror, three months ago the Abend had found him again, and all he could think of was how to stop them torturing him again.

As he finished he put his arms on the table and lay his head on them, so he did not see the horror on the faces of the rest of them. He nearly jumped out of his skin when Maelbrigt's voice came from right beside him.

"I'm so sorry, Sithfrey," he said. "I apologize for treating you so badly, but why ever didn't you tell us earlier? Or at least Taise?"

"I couldn't, could I?" Sithfrey gulped. "I'd made such a mess of everything. And I didn't know if I could trust you, or whether you wouldn't be as bad in your own way as the Abend? You might have found your own way to torture me. Everyone wants to torture me. I'm not big enough to fight back, so it's easy for those that enjoy that sort of thing."

Sioncaet looked back at him, appalled at the complete lack of any fight him. "Rubbish!" he exclaimed. "I'm way smaller than you, and I can fight back with the best of them!"

Sithfrey's expression said he didn't believe a word.

"Well then, I'm going to have to teach you how," Labhran declared, "and Maelbrigt can help me." Sithfrey glanced worriedly at Maelbrigt, as though someone had just told him he was going to learn dragon wrestling. "Don't look at him like that," Labhran said positively. "He's a very good teacher. Let's face it, he even made something of Kayna and she had two left feet as a kid. ...*Oooff!*" the last coming as a pillow hit him in the middle, launched from Kayna's seat.

"Bastard," she snarled, but with a smile there as well. "Ignore the last bit Sithfrey, but these two really are the best. Between them and Sioncaet there's not much they can't teach you."

"Looks like we're coming with you to find Talorcan, then," Sioncaet said brightly. "Really Labhran, after all that fuss you go and volunteer! ...

Oooff!" The pillow had become a missile again, this time hitting Sioncaet on the nose.

All Sithfrey could do was gape in amazement. He looked at Taise for confirmation. Were these men, who were by all accounts the deadliest of enemies to the DeÁine, actually offering not only to protect him but to train him as well. Taise's smile looked encouraging but, while the others pulled one another's legs, his mind kept returning to the image of a vengeance driven half-DeÁine called Talorcan whom they were taking him to meet.

PART 2

Chapter 16

Dark Discoveries

Rheged: Winterfalling

As night fell, Gerard lead Ruari out of the back of the house and they followed the lesser streets down towards the town gates opposite to those he had come in by. Edmund had left earlier, and was due to meet them beyond the gates with horses. He and Gerard had opted for a night time departure because there was less chance of Ruari being spotted and recognized in the gloom. As they had pointed out, the number of drunks on the streets guaranteed that two more would not attract comment, and the days of the gates being barred at night had long gone. Watching soldiers and whores lurching out of some doors and into others in varying states of incapacity, Ruari wondered what would happen if someone decided to launch a night assault.

"Flaming Underworlds, you could walk in here unopposed! When did we stop closing the gates at night?"

"The night when Oswine got shut out of his own capital after a midnight orgy down by the river meadows two summers ago," Gerard told him. "Did he ever kick up a stink! The gatekeeper got thrown out of his house and flogged for his pains, and the captain of the guard got flogged, stripped of his rank, and sent to the far north. After that I don't think it's been closed, and after last year's wet summer the weeds round it probably won't let them shut now."

Ruari shook his head despairingly. At this rate if raiders, let alone the DeÁine, ever appeared again, there would be nothing of substance for them to conquer. A simple raiding party would be disastrous, let alone an army.

As they neared the sentry at the gate the two of them began to weave as if unsteady after a few too many beers, but their performance was unnecessary. The man sat on a stool tipped back against the wall and was snoring gently. He had obviously given up on any attempt to check on anyone, but although Ruari was tempted to tip him over and wake him, Gerard pointed out that this was the same man who had been there since the previous night and had obviously not been relieved. In which case, he forced Ruari to acknowledge, they were lucky the watch had not just given up altogether and gone home. Gerard told him they had thought about using their own servants to watch the gates, but that would have only drawn notice to them. However, with Oswine most touchy at any implication that the city was not running as well as it always had, that was a dangerous move to make.

As they passed out from beneath the gloom of the gates, Edmund appeared leading two horses. Gerard was staying in the city and would take care of the pony Ruari had arrived on. Given that Gerard tended to have a soft spot for animals, and fed them as well as he did himself, Ruari suspected that the next time he saw the little beast it would have turned into a furry butter-ball. In contrast, Edmund's horses were sleek, powerful thoroughbreds, from his family's deservedly famous stud farm out on the southern water meadows beyond the city. Bidding Gerard farewell, they mounted up and turned south. For tonight they were going no further than the stud farm, which was a pleasant hour's ride under the autumn skies.

The manor was a sprawling building, formed of a stone keep which had had timber extensions added in a similar style to Gerard's house. It had been a very long time since anyone away from the coast had needed to worry about the defensive capabilities of their house except from opportunist thieves, especially this close to the capital. On the other side of the mountain range which ran like a spine the length of Rheged, the people were much more cautious, particularly on the coast where the Attacotti were known to make sudden raids. They would appear in their shallow-draughted boats, with sweeping oars propelling them up any navigable river.

Fortunately they had little interest in settling and were only concerned with what they could carry off, but they therefore tended to appear most at harvest time, and rarely in late winter or spring when supplies were likely to be low anyway. On this side of the mountains, however, even by such a major river, there was little danger of Edmund's farm ever being raided since the nearby capital represented much richer pickings for thieves. A low stone wall marked the boundary of the gardens around the house, and a waft of something cooking greeted them as they rode into the yard and past the kitchen door.

Ruari was beginning to think it was probably a good thing he was not going to be around for too long. He was finding it very hard going to resist overindulging in such tempting food after years of surviving on what he could hunt in the marshes. It would be quite a while before he would eat eel again from choice, if ever.

Edmund was a thoughtful host, and let Ruari escape to his bed after the meal without plying him with endless questions, for which Ruari was grateful. Had he spent the night at Gerard's, he knew he would not have been half so lucky, for Gerard would have been sure to have kept him up half the night talking.

Refreshed after a good night's rest, he rose early and found Edmund pouring over a map on the great table in the hall, with a large pot of caff keeping warm in the embers of last night's fire. Ruari helped himself to a mug and went to join him.

"I thought you might want to look at this," Edmund said after greeting him. "I know we both know the way to Montrose Castle from here, but this might be the last chance you get to look at a map for some time."

"Aye, I've been trying to work out which way Matti might have gone," Ruari replied thoughtfully.

"I would have thought it would all depend on how hard she was being pursued." Edmund pointed at the roads leading out of the river valley, where the castle sat on a rocky outcrop in the confluence of two rivers, guarding the strategically valuable bridges that spanned them. "If someone was hard on her heels, it would be just like Matti to head up into the eastern hills where she knows all the hidden ways. On the other hand, if using the roads wasn't a problem, she might have chosen to put as much distance between her and the castle, but where would she go? I don't think she'd risk coming back this way, even though all our family lands are this side of the mountains. We're too close to the Jarl and his sycophants over here."

Ruari nodded in agreement. "I know, it's a puzzle, and we take the risk, whatever we do, that we might ride past her and not even know it if she's really well hidden. That's why we have to go to the castle first. There's no way we can predict where she'll be until we know more of what happened. I'm thinking we might leave the horses tethered in the woods behind the castle, and walk in over the fields. Two men on foot are much less likely to be seen as a threat than two riders, and the people I want to talk to are the servants, so we'll try to slip in by the postern gate at the back which goes straight into the lower areas."

"You know the place better than me, Ruari, so I'll be guided by you." Edmund took a swig of caff, and then smiled as a plate of bread rolls, hot from the oven appeared, along with sausages and bacon. "Ah, good. Breakfast! Well at least you won't be riding on an empty stomach this morning!"

"My stomach has been struggling to cope ever since I got back, I'll have you know," Ruari replied, trying to sound reproachful but not succeeding very well. "At this rate I'll need a horse like Gerard's!"

With the roads level and direct, it was only a two day ride to Montrose Castle, but they stopped two villages short of it on the second night, to avoid making it too obvious that that was where they were heading. The next morning it was chilly and overcast but dry, as they rode a mile out of the village before turning off down a tiny lane, which was little more than a holloway between the hedges of the adjoining fields. Luckily Ruari had ridden over most of the estate with Will in the past and knew where he was going, since Edmund quickly became confused at the twists and turns they were making. Every so often they would catch a glimpse of high castellations in breaks in the trees, but to Edmund they always seemed to come from a direction he did not expect. An hour or so later, they entered the wood which separated them from the castle and which, as far as Edmund could tell, Ruari seemed to be heading diagonally through. When he led them out, they were looking down a small dip to a stream, with woods on the opposite side, but beyond it they could see the top of the castle tower. An old and solid paved road led from off on their right through the wood, as if making a line for the castle.

"This is the spur from the main road from Allerford," Ruari told Edmund. "If anyone sees us coming this way it'll look like we've come up from the south, or from over the mountains, rather than from Earlskirk."

Edmund realized that Ruari's circuitous route had brought them over the broad base of the triangular rocky spur that Montrose Castle sat on, so that they had skirted it rather than approaching it directly, which accounted for his confusion. With both of them keeping one eye on the road behind them, they now used the stone-slabbed route to pass through the woods, which were old and full of densely packed, gnarled trunks and roots. No rider would pass willingly under the eaves of such trees, which always threatened to trap the hooves of any horse going faster than a snail's pace. Looking at the girth of some of the mighty oaks and beeches, Edmund realized that the wood formed an unexpectedly good defence of the castle. Even on foot no force would approach with any speed, or without making enough noise to be heard, and clearing the trees would be the kind of mammoth job no commander in his right mind would undertake. The Montrose family had also cleverly kept the trees far enough back from the walls so that they were of no use to besiegers either, whether to disguise movement, or to be felled where they stood at the wood's edges to provide shield-walls to attack from behind.

For his part, Ruari was lost in thoughts of Matti. He had spent so much time making a concerted effort not to fall in love with his best friend's wife, who was also his dear friend, that he had never thought about what might happen if Will died. But his friends' comments had raised some big questions in his mind now. That he cared deeply for Matti was not in any doubt. Whether he loved her as he should a wife was a feeling he had never let himself explore, and now was hardly the best time to have to start rummaging around in the suppressed recesses of his soul. If the external situations were disorienting him, his emotions regarding Matti could leave him paralyzed in utter confusion.

Then he sighed ruefully. As if he would have much say in the situation! He could just imagine what would happen if he walked up to Matti in some hypothetical future saying 'I think we should get married now.' He would swiftly be treated to one of her more scathing glares and something along the lines of, 'Oh you do, do you? And what if I say no?' No, Matti was not the kind of person whose reaction he could take for granted, and would she be so wrong to refuse him, anyway? He was hardly likely to be around any more than Will had, and he would never forgive himself if he let her down as badly as Will had. And that alone seemed to be a good reason to leave such things buried until later – much later, if not permanently! Much better to concentrate on the mess before him than start trying to second guess fate, because once he started down that road, he feared he would never think straight again!

All of which was why neither of them had realized the significance of what they had been seeing in their glimpses of the castle until they were right on the edge of the wood. Just as he was about to swing his leg over the saddle to dismount Ruari froze. Edmund followed his gaze as his friend subsided back into his seat.

"Oh no!" he exclaimed.

"Bastards!" Ruari snarled.

Where a slate roof had once risen from within the castellations of the great keep, the stone stood blackened and empty. The great gate lay charred and crooked on its remaining hinge, while from the battlements hung the tattered remnants of something which Edmund prayed would not turn out to be what he feared. All thought of a subtle approach fled, and without a word they both heeled their mounts into a headlong gallop down the road for the short dash to the walls.

Drawing his sword, Ruari led them in under the smoke-blackened arch. Edmund carried a short hunting bow which he now had strung with a barbed arrow, nocked and taut in the bow-string, and only a heartbeat from readiness to let fly. He swung the vicious steel tip back and forth following his line of sight, constantly adjusting his aim as he covered their back and flanks. Within the castle bailey was a sight that neither men had ever wished to see in a place they thought of as home. It looked like a battlefield, with strewn and hacked corpses which had been left to rot. The layer of soot which had drifted over them spoke of their death before the fire that had destroyed the wooden interiors of the castle, but the same undisturbed soot told Ruari and Edmund that they were alone except for the crows circling high above.

Dismounting, they led their horses over to a stout wooden beam which had dropped into the yard, and now lay propped up at one end by the long stone flight of steps which still led to the wall defences. Leaving the nervous beasts tethered, the two soldiers approached the blackened bodies. As they disturbed the soft, black, feathery coating, it became clear that the sad remains were those of the household servants. Not one wore any sort of protective clothing, let alone armour, and none were armed. From the cuts on their arms – some of which had resulted in near amputation – they had died trying only to fend off their attackers. Edmund wept openly, totally stunned by the ferocity of such an unprovoked attack by members of his own countrymen upon their own kind. Ruari, in contrast, became more stony-faced by the minute, swearing steadily and fluently as the only vent to his fury at each new discovery.

Their inspection of the castle felt like it took forever, despite taking under an hour. Both men were shaken to the core to find that those hung from the wall-tops were some of the serving girls. They forced themselves to pull each one up, but by the time they had retrieved the final one they were both sweating and shaking, and not from the exertion. All they could do was pull the tattered remains of clothing over them as best they could to discourage the carrion feeders, for alone, two of them could not hope to bury the entire household. The chapel seemed such a natural place to go afterwards, that they made their way in through the upper doorway from the ramparts into the keep without conferring.

Amazingly the chapel was almost intact. Built into the thickness of the keep's walls, it had a stone-vaulted roof, and as its door lay well within the wall passage it had escaped the worst of the fire. The prevailing wind had evidently been on this side of the keep, too, for it seemed to have driven the fire away rather than drawing it in. Inside was all coolness and calm. The altar cloth lay undisturbed with a simple, carved-wood, dragon-headed cross upon it. Behind the covered stone slab, the chiselled trunks of the five sacred trees in the stone vaulting each had fresh flowers placed in the cup at their base.

"Fresh flowers?" the two exclaimed suddenly, realizing the significance of them. Ruari whipped round, sword snaking, alert and bent on vengeance.

"Come out, you murdering whore-sons!" he bellowed.

In response, a soft shuffling noise came from the direction of the altar, and then, from beneath the tapestried cloth, the figure of a monk appeared.

"Don't kill me. Please don't kill me!" he whispered hoarsely as he raised his hands to show he was not armed. "I didn't kill them." He took a sobbing breath, "I couldn't stop them. No-one could."

"Sacred Spirits, I know you!" Edmund choked out, his voice thick with emotion, then coughed and cleared his voice. "Ruari, stop! Don't hurt him! This is the young monk who used to tutor Wistan!"

"Wistan?" The name stopped Ruari in his tracks, and he lowered his sword to look hard at the figure he was advancing on. The poor soul looked distraught, but then if he had come from a monastery and been confronted with the sights that they had just seen, that was no surprise. It had been all that two battle-hardened veterans could do to not turn and flee the horror. He sheathed his sword once more while taking a deep breath to steady himself.

"It's alright, brother, we won't harm you," Ruari said in the same tone of voice he would have used to steady a panicked horse. Walking slowly over to the monk, he took him gently by the arm and guided him out to where they could see him properly in the light that filtered in through the chapel's high window. "What's your name?"

"Andra," the monk replied tremulously. Then even more nervously, "Who are you?"

Edmund replied before Ruari could urge him to caution. "I'm Edmund Praen, Lady Montrose's cousin, and this is a friend of the family's, Ruari…"

"Yes. I'm a friend of both of them," Ruari cut across before Edmund could reveal his full identity. "Now, brother, what can you tell us of what happened here?"

But the monk turned eyes full of awe back to Ruari.

"You're Ruari?" Andra said hopefully. "The same one who Lady Montrose used to talk about all the time? Oh thank the Spirits!" He collapsed to his knees and began to sob.

"Flaming Trees!" Ruari muttered in confusion and embarrassment. He grasped Andra firmly under one arm and hauled him to his feet. "Get up, for Spirit's sake man!"

He turned to Edmund. "Let's get him out of here. I don't know about you, but I need a beer! Come on, there must be something left in the cellars."

Without waiting for Edmund's reply, Ruari marched Andra out and down the long flights of stone steps to the kitchens. In the main kitchen chaos reigned, with tables overturned and signs of the household's fight for their lives everywhere. However, once they had reached the scullery and pantries, the place seemed almost untouched. Whoever had been here had come, done their worst, and then left without looting the place or wrecking it. No doubt they had assumed the fire would take care of that, but they had not lingered or returned to make sure.

Part of Ruari was relieved, for it meant he had plentiful supplies to draw on. The professional soldier in him, however, registered this and it told him these were amateurs. If this had been the work of experienced raiders, they would automatically have cleared this part of the castle out. These men obviously had had no need to worry about where their next meal was coming from, and it must have been not too far away, either. All his experience and instinct screamed at him that this was the work of Oswine's men. But had they come from him directly, or was this the work of one of his cronies' hooligans? It was important to know. If Oswine had men of power backing him, it was a very different matter than if it was just the royal household alone, and Ruari needed to know – fast – and the man who could give that answer was Andra.

A small side room contained a well-scrubbed table and a bench on either side, which must have once been used by the more senior members of the household staff for meals. Pushing Andra down onto a bench, Ruari went into the adjoining pantry and began rummaging around. Edmund sat down next to Andra and gave him what he hoped was an encouraging smile. It would have been more effective, he was sure, if his own heart had not felt as though it was about to leap out of his chest or break in two, depending on which image was returning to haunt his mind's eye. Before he could think of something to say that was not so fatuous in the circumstances as to be rendered meaningless, Ruari returned. In one hand he clutched three leather tankards, and under the other arm, a small pin barrel of ale. Depositing the tankards on the table, he set the barrel down carefully with the tap end projecting over the table edge, wedged it still with some of the abandoned wooden platters, and then drew them each a draught of the foaming brown nectar.

Edmund downed his in one long guzzle, and was holding his tankard back to Ruari before he too had sunk his pint in one go. Andra clutched his tankard in both hands to steady their shaking and took little gulps, while watching the two soldiers in awe at the speed with which they had finished the first pint and were now making significant inroads in their second. By the time he was halfway down the second, Ruari felt the effects of the first one hit, and the calming effect of the hops start to work on his ragged nerves enough to get sufficient detachment to formulate questions for Andra.

Sitting down on the edge of the table, with one booted foot resting on the end of the bench, he leant forward and looked into Andra's eyes.

"Now… Tell me, in your own time, what did you see here? What happened?"

For a second Andra was mesmerized by the piercing blue eyes, like a rabbit before a hawk. It took him all his will power to break eye contact so that he could think. In broken sentences he told of Matti's entrance into the garden and her forcing of Wistan over the garden wall.

"She told me not to be a fool," he gulped, his voice breaking with misery and regret. "I didn't believe her. I'm so *stupid*! What do I know of these things? All I've ever done is say prayers and live with monks. I never knew such wickedness existed! I was already at the bottom of the steps, trying to call her back, when they broke into the garden."

He cuffed his tears away, then tried to draw himself up to meet this awesome soldier's gaze. He felt a desperate desire to confess to someone his guilt. Anyone would have been welcome after these weeks alone, but this man of honour would be his judge and jury. "I know I'm a coward," he whispered, "but I was so scared. I hid. There's a little gap under the stone stairs hidden by the plants. I crawled in there. They came into the garden …but …but they didn't see me. I know I should have tried to stop them. I know I should have come out and helped the others try to fight them off. …But I'm a coward! I couldn't move."

He swallowed hard. "I could hear them …the men who came …and I could hear the screams of the rest of the household. …I still hear them! Every night! They're haunting me as punishment for being such a coward, for not trying to help them! But instead I stayed hidden. I saved myself instead …and now I hate myself for it. I shouldn't be here, there were better people than me in this place, people more deserving to live than me…"

"Stop it!" Ruari commanded, stopping the flow sharply. Then more softly as Andra sat open-mouthed, staring at him. "Stop punishing yourself, man. One more would have made no difference one way or the other. These men were out to kill everyone. Nothing you could have done would've made the slightest difference, except to get you killed as well. At least with you alive we can find out what happened, alright?"

Andra nodded cautiously.

"So, you're sure these were the Jarl's men again?"

Andra nodded.

"Are you sure that's what Matti called them? Not by some earl's name?"

Again the nod, a deep shaky breath, then, "Lady Montrose said the Jarl himself was capable of killing. I said no, not the first time. Now I think she was right. I recognized the men who came into the garden. They were some of the same men who came here the day Lady Eleanor was killed. I heard them shouting "Where is she? Where's the boy?" They must have realized somehow that Wistan wasn't dead. They definitely wanted to kill him. Who but the Jarl would have any reason to want that innocent boy dead? ...And they were talking about taking the evidence back to the Jarl this time to prove they'd done the job. It was when they realized Wistan wasn't here that they started killing everyone. They must have been so worried that someone would warn Wistan from coming back."

"No," Edmund said sadly, "they just didn't want any witnesses who could tell others that it was the heir to the kingdom whom they were hunting. They were probably always under orders to get rid of all witnesses, whether they found him or not."

Andra turned to him with an expression of horror.

"Really?" he exclaimed.

"Aye," Ruari confirmed. "But you're sure Matti and Wistan escaped?"

Andra stopped and thought for a moment before looking up and meeting Ruari's questioning gaze.

"Yes, I'm sure." He thought for a second longer. "Yes, definitely, because they said that Prior Tancostyl – he's the royal chaplain now – would have them damned forever for not finding Wistan."

"Tancostyl!" Ruari yelped, leaping to his feet in shock and horror, causing Edmund and Andra to jump in surprise at the switch of mood. "Are you telling me that someone called *Tancostyl* is part of the royal household?"

Andra almost fell off the bench in fear at the fury in Ruari's eyes.

"Yes," he whispered.

"Ruari?" Edmund said questioningly, "what is it?"

The Knight was pacing the short length of the room and spun to the others.

"Tancostyl! Do you not remember that name, Edmund? You should! He's one of the Abend!"

Edmund's jaw dropped in astonishment. "The same whose creatures chased you years ago in Brychan?"

"Aye, the very same. That creature who hunted me on the moors? It was one of his. It was a farliath! Sacred Trees! Why didn't I see that! Of all people, I should have remembered what their creatures could be like, but I was so wrapped up in the present mess I never thought to wonder if it was connected to the past. What a fool I've been! No wonder Oswine was crowned with one of the DeÁine's treasures!"

"DeÁine?" Andra breathed weakly. "Are you saying that the evil ones are abroad here in Rheged? Oh Spirits protect us!" He made the sign of the cross over his heart. "Are you sure? How in the Islands could you know that just by a name?"

"Because he was hunted by them once before," Edmund told him. "Ruari was one of the Knights entrusted to move one of the DeÁine

Treasures out of Brychan so that it was further away from them. He's one of only a handful of the Knights who survived that journey. They were hunted all the way, by anyone and everything the sorcerers of the DeÁine could summon."

"And you survived challenging the evil DeÁine?" Andra said in awe.

Ruari inhaled deeply. "Aye, we did. Just! But only because the whole journey had been planned so carefully, and that planning included information which came from within the inner council itself. That's how I'm sure. The *DeÁine* aren't all evil, brother, and no member of their ordinary people would ever dream of using the name of one of the current Abend to name a child."

"Current Abend?" Andra's horror grew even greater. "Dear Spirits, whatever does that mean? Are there more of them?"

"*Were* more," Ruari corrected him. "There are only ever nine of the inner circle, and despite what you may have heard, they are mortal. Oh, their lives have been extended by the Power to many times that of even a normal DeÁine, let alone an Islander's life span. But they're not immortal, and more importantly they can be killed. Over the millennia there must have been some whose names have been lost in the course of their folk's wanderings. Also, there are always some whom they have their eye on as suitable candidates to be elevated in the event of one or more of them dying. So when a new Abend appears there's always the possibility of some poor unfortunate bearing the same name. But these nine have all been in power for several lifetimes of their ordinary people, who fear their wrath almost as much as we do. No, there's no chance that there're two Tancostyls."

"Ruari," Edmund interrupted. "Why hasn't he just seized the DeÁine Helm and left with it? That must have been what drew him here first, surely? You said yourself most of the royal household has no idea what the cursed thing really is. Who would have noticed him walking off with a rusty old iron helmet?"

"It wouldn't be that simple, though, would it?" Ruari answered. "Remember, Edmund, that thing has a power of its own. It draws people to it. It plays on their emotions as soon as it gets within line of sight of them. If Tancostyl had tried to walk off with it, and maybe he even did, he would have found it drew every thief, vagabond and lowlife like flies to a midden. Within a couple of days he'd have a visible stream of followers that would build to a small army …" He stopped in mid-sentence, grimaced, then smacked one fist into the palm of his other hand. "By the Trees, Edmund! That's it!"

"What is?" Edmund asked, confused.

"That's what he needs! An army! If he can get that fool Oswine to raise an army, it wouldn't matter against whom, that would get him to the coast and a ship back to Brychan. Then he could move the Helm without raising suspicion. Of course, if he could do that and provoke a war between two or more of the Islands, so that we're too busy fighting one another to notice the DeÁine were on the move again, that would be even better. Got you, you bastard!" he exclaimed, punching the air.

Edmund smiled wryly and caught Andra's bemused gaze. "There speaks the professional soldier," he said with fond amusement. "He's been like a bear with a sore head for days because he couldn't figure out who was doing what. Now he's got something to fight, look at him, he's happy as a pig in muck!"

"But what about Wistan?" Andra said plaintively. "Doesn't he matter anymore? Isn't he important to you now?"

Ruari's gaze whipped back to Andra.

"Important? He's more important than ever! Don't you see? For Tancostyl's plan to work he has to have the Jarl in the palm of his hand and unopposed. The last thing he needs is a rightful heir wandering around the countryside acting as a focus for earls who aren't under his sway. Civil war in Rheged might just get him to the coast, but even that wouldn't be certain. And once the influence of the Helm left the Jarl and his men, it would be more than likely that some cool heads would prevail – like Abbot Jaenberht – and then folks would start asking why they were fighting in the first place.

"They might even appeal to someone like Grand Master de Burh in Prydein, or Grand Master Brego in Ergardia, and once that happened the Islands might even unite. Sacred Trees, no wonder he hates Matti! If she's saved Wistan and got him hidden, she's forced Tancostyl to slow his plans down. Clever lass! She's bought us time, even if she didn't realize it."

Ruari clapped the young monk enthusiastically on the shoulder, almost shooting him off the bench and under the table.

"Don't worry, brother," he grinned, "I'm going after Matti and Wistan, and I'll find them come what may."

"Then I'm coming with you," Andra announced to Ruari and Edmund's astonishment, as he struggled from between the bench and table edges to his feet to face them.

Edmund searched to find the right way to tell the young monk what he knew, that Ruari would never take him.

"Brother Andra," he began, "you don't know what you'd be letting yourself in for."

"Maybe not," Andra said with all the firmness he could muster, "but I must go …"

"No, I'll go with Ruari…"

"No, Wistan was put in my charge. I must put this right, I must atone, it's my responsibility…"

"You're not coming, Edmund." Ruari's voice cut across the other two and halted the argument. "Remember what we agreed with Gerard and Osbern? I need you here doing what we planned."

"But…"

"No buts! We're going down to the village, and arrange for a burial party to come up here and put those poor souls outside to rest. Great Maker only knows why they haven't come up already, maybe they were too shocked and scared, but I need someone of authority to stay and make sure it gets done, and that means you. They're not likely to take commands off a young monk are they?"

Edmund's dejected appearance said he understood even if he didn't like it.

"What about me?" Andra asked.

"Against all my better instincts, I'm going to have to take you," Ruari answered.

Andra looked delighted and Edmund stunned at this.

"Don't look so pleased," Ruari warned. "By the end of this you may be cursing me to the Underworld. We'll be riding hard and fast, and you'd better keep up! I'm only taking you because I don't know what state Wistan and Matti might be in when we do find them. If I need to protect them, or free them, I can't fight and take care of them at the same time. That'll be your job. I'm hoping that, whatever has happened to him, Wistan will remember you and trust you, because it's been years since he even saw me. So if I tell you to move them one way or another, you might have more chance of getting a small and frightened little boy to move than I would as a stranger."

Ruari's tone brooked no argument, and so they let him direct them to packing up a goodly supply for the coming journey.

It was still only late afternoon when they left the packs stacked ready near the horses, whom they had moved into the remnants of the stables, and set off down the hill. It was only a short, steep walk down to the cluster of houses on the upper level of the river plateau on the east side. As they approached the village there seemed to be no sign of life, and for a few awful moments their sideways glances to one another relayed their fear that the villagers had been slaughtered too. Then Ruari pointed to wisps of smoke rising from several of the chimneys, and a newly moved bale of hay, whose stray blades were being whisked around by the breeze.

No sooner had they moved within the confines of the main street than they heard movements all around them. From out of doorways, behind outbuildings and hay ricks the people came, armed with anything they could get their hands on.

"Go away, you murdering swine!" one man snarled, and the main group of villagers blocking the street ahead growled their support like a pack of feral dogs.

Without a word Ruari marched right up to the pitchfork blades of the one who had spoken. His hand shot out and grasped it between the two tines, holding it still effortlessly. His commanding presence seemed to dominate the tableau for the seconds it took for his gaze to sweep across the villagers. Then he raised his voice in a tone that held years of practice at making audible commands to a whole company of troops.

"Listen to me! All of you! Do you really think if we intended you any harm, we'd just walk down here and give you time to defend yourselves? Did they do that up at the castle? No, of course not! This is Sir Edmund. Lady Montrose's cousin, not some marauding bandit. And did you see any monks with the others? No, of course not!"

The crowd shuffled and murmured like chastised children, but didn't give way. Neither did Ruari, though, and his iron will made itself clear again.

"I will *not* have the bodies of those who committed no crime but to serve the Montroses left to be food for the crows. I don't know why you've made no move to give your kinsfolk decent burials yet, but you will now! In the morning I want burial parties to come and collect them, and bring them back down to the chapel for the proper offices to be said."

"They will not!" A voice spoke from behind Ruari, who spun to face the speaker without letting go of the pitchfork. A rotund priest in a copious brown woollen habit waddled from out of the side street to face Ruari.

"I'll not have the bodies of those who served the traitors buried within the sacred walls of this chapel," he intoned sanctimoniously.

"Won't you now?" Ruari's voice was all dangerous calm as he stepped lightly away from the pitchfork, and was in front of the priest in a moment. Edmund grabbed Andra by the arm and almost bodily lifted him several paces back from Ruari in anticipation. "And who are you to decide their guilt, brother? I don't recall seeing you here before. Where's Brother Mungo?"

"He died in the summer," one villager called out.

"So where did you come from?" Ruari questioned the priest.

"I," the man replied sneeringly, "was appointed by the royal chaplain himself."

"You got sent here by that bastard Tancostyl?" Ruari hissed. At the mention of the Abend's name, Ruari suddenly caught something happening behind the priest's eyes. It was as if smoke had drifted behind the lenses obscuring the colour of the irises, which then changed colour for a second before returning to their original shade.

As the priest hissed like a serpent and reached for Ruari's throat, the Knight dropped and twisted, coming up again with the long thin blade which lived in a sheath within the leather of his high boot. Without pausing Ruari drove the sharp steel up and into the chest of the priest until only the dragon-pommelled handle protruded. The whole assembly drew its breath in horror at the killing of the priest, but before anyone could move, there was a sound like tearing fabric. From within the priest, a dark cloud broke free to rise above him for a second before being dissipated with a wail by the wind.

For a moment silence filled the village, then people screamed, or cried out in disbelief or fear, but on every tongue was the question of 'what was that?' Ruari wiped the blade on the dead priest's habit, sheathed the blade once more, and then raised his voice again.

"This creature who replaced your priest was under the control of the DeÁine," he declared. A few screamed, but for the most part that stunned them into silence. "What you saw depart was the hand of his master."

"Will he come back?"

"And how will we know?" fearful voices from the crowd asked.

"I doubt he will return," Ruari told them in what he hoped was a reassuring voice. "He came hunting the young prince who was here, and with him gone, the master will be looking elsewhere first. But beware of strangers! To gain control, the DeÁine must be in close proximity to their victim. You needn't fear spirits in the night, or powers you cannot see, but from now on be wary of those you don't know from far away. Sir Edmund will guide you to set defences around the village, but now you must come to collect the bodies of your friends and family. This brother here will be with you for another day, but then I must take him with me. As you no longer have a priest, if you wish for a proper funeral the words must be said before we depart, even if it takes longer to dig the graves. Get carts and follow us back."

Ruari turned and led the way back up the hill followed by a puzzled Edmund and Andra, who was already wondering what sort of man he had volunteered to accompany into the wilderness. When they were out of earshot of the villagers Edmund whispered to Ruari,

"I thought you were in a hurry to be off?"

"I am," Ruari replied, "but I hadn't planned on Tancostyl having one of his creatures planted right here in the village. No wonder he knew Wistan wasn't dead! I can't leave these people to his mercy if he returns, so while Andra performs the funerals tomorrow, I'll show you what needs to be done."

By the time the sun had set that night, the villagers had come with handcarts and carried the bodies to the village chapel, where they were laid in rows down each side awaiting the funeral service. In the morning Andra returned to the village, clutching the parchment which had the funeral rites inscribed on it, to perform his first service of that kind. Ruari and Edmund, however, took the horses and rode up to the wood. On the eastern side the dip in the land lay just in front of the wood.

"You see that?" Ruari explained. "That used to be flooded marsh land. It runs through the wood to that dip in the road we crossed yesterday. It used to be a boggy mere, and you have to turn it back into one."

"Why?" Edmund asked, perplexed.

"Water," was Ruari's cryptic reply.

"Water?"

"Aye, the Abend's creatures can't cross it and remain under the control of their master. If it's something they've raised up, it has to find a way around it or stop on the other side. If they've taken possession of someone, or thing, that's really in this world anyway, it's not quite so final but it does weaken their grip on them. If it's someone who was taken against their will, you've got a chance of breaking the hold on them. If, like our fat friend yesterday, they're already corrupt it's more a case that the guidance they receive is weakened or more vague. So you've more of a chance of out-smarting them."

As they rode along the hollow, Ruari pointed to the handful of small springs which still rose and fed the stream which ran along the bottom. At either end of the small vale, the huge stone boulders which had been dug out during the drainage process had luckily been too large to move far away. It was therefore only a case of dropping them back down the slopes and infilling them with smaller stones, and then the local clay, to re-dam the tiny valley, shutting off the two small waterfalls which at present fed into the larger rivers below. The road through the western woods was bordered by huge old willows along the course of the former mere, and was previously a simple ford. With the trees so close to the road, there was no way of skirting the passage or bridging the water, and so they protected the crossing.

On the eastern side the banks were more open, but Ruari pointed to where the former road had cunningly snaked in the shallow water rather than making a straight crossing. The great pavers which had once lined it had been shifted to make a straight course for the road now, but the old compacted foundations still survived and it would only be a case of moving the surfacing back. Once flooded, the road would appear to go straight through, but any rider hoping to make a fast passage would soon find themselves sinking into the unprotected clay. With the winter rains coming soon, Ruari was confident that the headland with the village and castle would soon become a water-surrounded safe haven once more.

With Edmund staying on to direct the work and then coming back as often as he could to keep an eye on things, Ruari decided that this would become the conspirator's unofficial headquarters. More good news arrived back with Andra, who had been told by the villagers that the next village towards Allerford had been visited by ghosts too. The difference was that this ghost had left high denomination coins for missing loaves of bread.

"Ghosts, my arse!" Ruari laughed, to Andra's surprise.

"Ah, I detect the hand of my honest cousin there," Edmund agreed with him. "So she headed towards Allerford, well that's a start."

That was the point when Andra remembered to tell them about Matti's visits to the priory.

"Grrr!" Ruari growled in mock fury, as he grabbed the front of Andra's habit. "Wake up, brother! That's the sort of information that's vital to us now! If you've never had to think before, now's the time to start!"

But with a trail to follow and an enemy he finally understood, it was impossible for Ruari to be truly aggrieved at his naive new companion. Indeed, the only hint of unpleasantness that day came when they had eaten and were settling into their blankets for the night.

"I'm not telling Osbern about what we're doing here until I have to," Edmund confessed as he plumped up the cloth pillow he was using.

"What?" Ruari asked, suspiciously.

"Look, I didn't want to say anything until now because I know you trust him, but …well, it's like this. We all knew Osbern was the one out of all of us who really got into the whole religion thing, yes? But you haven't seen much of him since he got that arrow in the chest, Ruari. He's become almost fanatical. He thinks he survived because the Spirits personally intervened to give him a second chance at life."

"Flaming Trees!" Ruari swore in surprise.

"I know," Edmund sighed. He felt awful talking about someone who was supposed to be a friend in this way, and looking at Ruari's face decided to save him from the less necessary complications. "It's this business of Tancostyl having worked his way into the church that's got me so worried," he confessed. "Osbern tells his family priest everything. And I really do mean *everything*! All Tancostyl would have to do would be to get that priest under his sway and he'd know our every move. It's no use telling Osbern to be careful what he says to the man. We've tried that already, and he got so wound up, that rift between him and Gerard nearly happened for real. Gerard and I have been …well …shall we say cautious about what we share with Osbern ever since. If Oswine, even as the Jarl, was questioning him, he'd be the old friend, loyal and true. But he can't see that people like Archbishop Fulchere in the Church fail to come up to the ideal of saintliness that he thinks they have."

Ruari sat on his bed roll with his head resting on his knees for some minutes before turning to look at Edmund.

"I knew he was always that way inclined," he sighed, "and while part of me wants to say that you're wrong, and that when it came to our lives he'd be different, there's part of me that isn't so surprised. Osbern was always the idealist. I know he thought that I fell short of the knightly ideal because he thought I coveted my friend's wife. It didn't matter to him that Will had no interest in Matti, and that no matter how good a friend Will was to me, that I could also see how lonely Matti was. Will would have been far less worried if Matti and I had ever let things go any farther than they did, than Osbern would."

"Ah, well as long as we're on that line …"

"Oh?" Ruari quirked an eyebrow. "Oh, come on, spit it out, you never were any good at keeping things back from me, Edmund."

Edmund had the grace to look embarrassed as he told the rest of the story. All three young men had had their wives chosen for them by the needs of their family's politics and situation. Before Edmund could marry his delicate and adored intended she had died, leaving him pining for many years for an ideal which he had never had. Gerard had married a feisty, petite redhead, and against all expectations it had turned into a marriage which was the envy of most of their acquaintances. Rosin complemented her great ox of a husband, being quick-witted, organized and practical. With five strapping sons and two daughters to testify to the success of their marriage in other areas, it was also obvious to anyone who met them that they still adored one another even after many years.

In theory many would have thought that Ismay would have suited the aesthete Osbern as well, but it had not turned into reality. Even when Ruari had been around more often, it had been obvious that all was far from well when they visited Osbern's estate.

"He was always oblivious to the strain he put her under, we knew that," Edmund sighed. "But when he came home wounded and she nursed him back to health, I think we all hoped it would be a new start for them. Instead, that confounded priest convinced him that *all* abstinence of the flesh was the only way to show his gratitude to the Spirits for sparing him. A distraught Ismay went to visit Gerard and Rosin in a terrible state, so Rosin got her alone and had a good heart to heart. After eight years of marriage she was still a virgin, Ruari!"

"Trees! You're joking?"

"No, I wish I was. Well, they kept her up there with them long after she should have travelled back. Rosin said she wasn't fit to travel back, and in a way she wasn't. I went to join them and over a couple of weeks it all came out. The way he'd make her fast every month for being 'unclean'. The hours of prayer he expected her to join in. By the time we got to the coarse horse-hair underwear, Rosin would have filleted him with the nearest knife if he'd shown up. In the time she spent up in the north, Rosin put some proper weight on Ismay and some colour in her cheeks.

"When she did go back, I travelled with her. Osbern wouldn't even send a groom to protect her on that long trek! The only trouble was that because of that we carried on like we'd done at Gerard's, laughing and joking, and that was how we turned up at the gate. You should have seen his face, Ruari. I couldn't get through to him for hours that his wife hadn't been unfaithful to him with me. I was so worried leaving her there, but I thought it would only make it worse if I stayed.

"The next thing we knew, Rosin had a letter from Ismay saying that Osbern was throwing her out of the main manor! This was just after you left to join Michael. Gerard and I got Abbot Jaenberht to intervene, and he moderated Osbern's actions to assigning her the small northern manor the family had at Hilby. At least there she can travel to visit Rosin up at Thorpness relatively easily. Try as I might, I couldn't convince him that nothing had happened between Ismay and me, and we all felt obliged to keep an eye on her, in case he decided to deprive her of the few servants he'd reluctantly allowed to go to Hilby with her. Now he just acts like nothing happened. Ismay's name is never mentioned, and none of us tell him if we've seen her. It's the only way we can stay friends with him."

"Sacred Trees, what a mess!" Ruari groaned.

"That it is," Edmund agreed, "but you see now why I don't think it's too good an idea to tell Osbern anything that he might get the wrong end of the stick over. Your original plan is fine. He feels he's still part of the old group and doing something to help, but if I were you, I'd only use that old manor in the marshes as a very last and desperate resort."

Ruari nodded thoughtfully. "If he can think that of someone as sweet and innocent as Ismay, I see where you're going with this. Would he believe Matti is innocent if his priest told him she'd deceived us?"

As Ruari blew out the solitary candle, a third voice piped up from the other side of Edmund, making them both jump.

"Then maybe a *monk* will have to make sure he's convinced of the right of Lady Montrose's actions when we find her," Andra said with unexpected firmness.

Chapter 17

Over the Hills

Rheged: Winterfalling

On another chilly, hazy, autumnal morning, the three of them set out to make the ride to Allerford priory. Edmund was riding with them on his own horse, while Andra was perched precariously on one of the village horses. There was no way he was ever going to cope with an animal of the spirit of Edmund's. At the first twitch of its ears he would have been in the nearest puddle, and Ruari had no desire to spend the journey constantly retrieving him from the roadside. Nor did the villagers have an animal they could spare for the duration of a long trip. So Edmund was coming along to take the village horse back as soon as they could find a more suitable mount for Andra. The expectation was that the priory would have one that they would let Edmund purchase on Andra's behalf, although secretly Edmund was hoping it might be a lot longer before they found a horse for sale.

By late afternoon, after an easy ride straight down the main road, they came to the outskirts of Allerford and turned down the road to the priory. At the gates they rang the bell to be greeted by a very nervous monk peering out through the small barred opening. It was with some difficulty that they gained access, and in fact it was Andra's presence and persuasion that finally did the trick. He gratefully accepted the offer to join the other monks at the next office in the church, but Ruari and Edmund asked if they might have an audience with the prior in private. As they were led across the open ground towards the prior's lodgings, Ruari spotted a weasely-faced monk keeping pace with them over by the far wall. Something about the man put him on edge and he pointed him out to Edmund, softly whispering for him to take note of the monk.

It was no surprise, then, when they were given a seat on the settle in the outer room from the prior's office, to see the unpleasant monk sweep past them and barge into the office without so much as knocking. Immediately from within there came the sound of raised voices. As another monk came to the door to invite them in, the first monk was coming out again, but paused to deliver a parting shot to those within.

"You should be careful, Father," he hissed. "There are powerful people who might not approve of your entertaining strange soldiers."

"And how would they get to know, Brother Zeikiel?" a measured voice answered. "Think carefully, brother, before threatening me, your powerful friends are still several days ride away and much could happen before they got here."

Brother Zeikiel's face narrowed in a spiteful grimace, making him look even more rodent-like before scurrying off, giving black, backwards glares.

"Come in," the other voice called, and they entered to find themselves in the company of a stocky, pleasant-faced man who looked as though he would have been more at home on a prosperous farm. The prior walked round from behind his desk and grasped each of their hands in turn in welcome, at the same time dismissing his clerk. When the door had closed and they were alone, he sat back down and waved them to comfortable leather campaign chairs.

"Well, sirs, what can I do to help two such gentlemen as yourselves? You don't look as though there's much that you wouldn't be capable of handling yourselves." His ready smile robbed his words of any offence.

Ruari briefly explained that they were trying to find a young boy and the woman who was last seen with him. He mentioned no names, but instead told of the horror they had found at Montrose Castle and their fears for their friends' safety after such mindless slaughter. The prior had obviously not heard of the full extent of the casualties amongst the ordinary people, for he went pale and immediately offered to send a monk back with Edmund to tend to the community's needs.

"Not that one who just went out, though," Ruari said firmly.

"Dear Spirits, no!" Prior Norbert exclaimed. "Brother Zeikiel is our greatest trial. I certainly wouldn't wish him onto an already grieving community."

"What's eating at him?" Edmund could not refrain from asking.

The prior sighed. "Eating is an apt choice of words, my friend. I've never known someone whose ill humours so consume his every waking hour. He was the youngest son of a nobleman, consigned to the church like so many. Most resign themselves to their fate, but Zeikiel has a hunger for the power he feels he was deprived of. He tries to dominate some of the weaker brothers, and takes every opportunity to ingratiate himself with anyone of importance who passes through. He hated Lady Montrose because she saw through him. It is her whom you're seeking, isn't it?"

At Ruari and Edmund's surprised expressions, he told them of the sudden appearance of the soldiers on the hunt for the supposedly murderous chatelaine. It occurred to Ruari and Edmund at this explanation, that this also had much to do with the monks' uncharacteristic reticence to allow them in at the gate.

"What you may be interested to know," Norbert added, "is that the day they left, Brother Zeikiel was found unconscious, with some very interesting bruises, out by the sheep folds. Quite what he was doing out there he won't say. Normally he'll do anything to avoid menial tasks, so it wasn't concern for the sheep! I do know, however, that he spent much time conversing with the leader of the men who forced themselves upon us. I had no desire to accommodate such violent men within our enclave, but as you may imagine, we have few resources with which to fend off such unwelcome attentions. All we could do was see them on their way as swiftly as possible.

"Strangely, we also lost another of our brothers on the same day. Brother Iago used to be a sergeant with the Knights of the Cross. He was wounded in the service of the Jarl and was recovering at our hospice when the Order was disbanded, so he chose to join us. Lady Montrose often used to speak with him when she visited. Brother Zeikiel becomes very agitated when we mention Iago's name, oddly enough. Without wishing to indulge in gossip or unseemly speculation," the prior concluded, with a knowing hint of a smile, "it wouldn't surprise me if the two incidents were connected."

Ruari fought to keep the grin from his face. Iago of all people! This was good news indeed.

"Aren't you taking a risk, Father, telling two strangers," he asked instead. "After all, we might not be telling you the truth of why we're hunting them."

"This is true," Prior Norbert replied, "but, as Lady Montrose wasn't allowed to dine with the monks, Brother Iago was allowed to join her here at my table. During those meals I heard a lot about a certain high ranking Knight whom they both knew – a Knight to whom you bear an uncanny resemblance, if I might say so."

Edmund chuckled. "You don't miss much do you Father?"

"Ah, but you see, my son, to combat evil you have to know it when you see it – or so Abbot Jaenberht reminds me – so I try to remain informed at all times."

"Speaking of whom," Ruari interjected, "I need to speak with Abbot Jaenberht as soon as possible, but I find myself with even more pressing concerns every time I try to head for Mailros. And Father, I'd be most grateful if you'd not mention to anyone but Jaenberht who you think I am."

The prior was swift to agree. "Oh, I quite see the danger of letting certain people know that the rightful head of the Order has appeared, hale and hearty, after they'd declared his death as a means to get their hands on the Order. I'd already been thinking of finding something to keep Zeikiel out of the way for a while. Now I shall make sure he gets sent up into the hills to do his turn at watching the flocks. Brother Wilfa is quite stern enough to make sure he doesn't slip off, and I'll ensure he doesn't get the chance to spread his poison to any other visitors we might unexpectedly gain.

"But speaking of Jaenberht, you don't need to travel as far as Mailros. I myself am travelling to meet him at a great synod that he's called at Lund in five days' time. The bird that arrived with the summons came only a couple of days ago, so it must be urgent if he expects the leaders from the far western outposts to attend. They would've had to set out the very day they received the summons in order to reach it in time."

As if on cue, a tap came on the door and the clerk's head appeared to announce that three abbots had just arrived at the gate. Ruari was tempted to accept the prior's offer to travel with them, but a nagging voice in his head said time was pressing. Instead he offered to vacate the guest quarters to allow room for the senior churchmen, in exchange for beds in the dormitory. A horse was found for Andra, and the next morning, as the first faint rays of the sun lit the eastern sky they set out, leaving a dejected Edmund at the main road.

Ruari knew that the staid monastics would travel by main roads all the way. Even if pressed, they would still go from Allerford to Allerdale, and only then on the lesser road to Kirkford; but then, after that, they would accept the long eastwards kink in the road to go via Thornby and Bytor fort rather than leave the safety of the highway. However, this was not the only route, and it was possible to take a drover's track along through the foothills of the mountains. The only steep passage would be the climb from the high-pass road which crossed the range, to crest the shoulder of the mountain above Bytor and drop down into Lund directly.

Making for this route, Ruari set the horses to a brisk canter to take advantage of the level road while it lasted. Andra's horse was one of those kept for the use as a relay for messengers and took to the pace far better than its rider. The monks had found breeches for him as a practical necessity, for his habit was no garment to spend all day in the saddle in. Even so, suitably clothed and booted, he was no horseman. By the midday stop to water the horses at a stream and eat some of the food the monks had provided, he was stiff. When Ruari finally called a halt that night he could hardly dismount, and was weeping with the pain of the saddle sores which had appeared.

Normally Ruari would have forced any new recruit to care for his horse first, but he had not the heart to push Andra any harder. He was secretly surprised that the little monk had lasted as well as he had, and was even more impressed that not once had he asked to stop, or complained about his misery. Rummaging in his pack he found a pot of salve. Tapping Andra on the shoulder where he had collapsed onto the soft grass, he told him to go downstream and wash his sores and then put some of the salve on. Poor Andra had to be helped to his feet, and hobbled off into the privacy of the waterside bushes, while Ruari tended to the horses and then lit a small fire. It was not enough to cook on, but a small travelling pan appeared, and soon enough water had been boiled to make each of them a mug of steaming tea. With more of the dried rations and hard baked bread it was basic, but to Andra it felt like a feast. By the end of the second mug of tea he was drooping, his eyes closing of their own accord, and he needed no urging to roll himself in a blanket to get much needed sleep.

Despite the long ride, Ruari felt better than he had for a long time. Having regained some measure of control of the situation he was almost enjoying himself. He checked on the horses, moving them to fresh grazing on the soft hill-turf, and then, looking at the almost clear night sky, still felt restless. He had chosen a small stand of beeches to give them shelter from the sharp evening chill, so before taking to his own blanket he walked up the slope a little, and sat watching the road in either direction until he was satisfied that they were the only ones abroad that night. Below them in the distance, he could see the dark shadows of the roofs of Allerdale clustered within their walls. They had only used the bridge to cross the great river a second time, and had then avoided the town. Ruari wanted no-one remembering the passage of a soldier and a monk after what had happened at Montrose. If Tancostyl had his servants out spying, and Ruari felt sure he would after having one of his minions dispatched so summarily, the fewer people they met the better.

Thinking of such things, he turned his gaze upwards and searched the skies. The Abend had an affinity with carrion birds like crows, and if necessary he would travel at night to avoid their watchful flights, but so far he had seen no sign of black specks high above. Tonight the only bird abroad was a lone Little Owl, and owls were creatures of the old faith. Wishing it peace in its soft, silent flight Ruari began his descent to the trees. Then froze.

At the edge of the stand something approached. A dark shape flitted from shadow to shadow along the line of trees in the hedge which came up from the road. Ruari ducked into the lee of a gorse bush and drew his dagger. Carefully inching down, testing each footstep to avoid loose pebbles and dead wood, he angled his way across the slope to come behind the stranger just as he came upon their camp. The last light of the fire lit on the steel of a knife being drawn as the figure advanced on Andra's sleeping form. As the intruder went to leap forward, Ruari sprang and drove him further on and down, landing on his back.

With an 'ooof' as the air was driven from his lungs, the stranger was forced face down into the mud at the edge of the stream. His knife went flying, but Ruari pressed his own to his prisoner's throat.

"Now then, friend, who might you be, sneaking up on travellers in the night?" he hissed as Andra woke, startled by the noise.

The figure grunted something unintelligible, so Ruari grasped him by the hair on the back of his head to lift his face out of the mud and realized the man was tonsured. The light was poor, but not so bad that they could not recognize Zeikiel's weasely face.

"Well, well, what have we here?" Ruari spat. "Out a little late, aren't we, brother? Does the good prior know that you're gone?"

Andra had come to stand by them.

"But the prior was going to leave first thing with the others, wasn't he?" he said thoughtfully.

"Ah yes," Ruari remembered. "So did he send you off on your own to the grange? I can't believe he'd trust you that much, so what happened to your travelling companions. Did you just run off, or something worse?"

Zeikiel tried to spit at them. That got his face pushed back into the dirt while Ruari instructed Andra to fetch the dropped knife, and to bring it close enough so that he could see it. The moon obligingly reappeared from behind a cloud, and by its wan light Ruari could see that something dark was still encrusted on the blade. He sent Andra to wet it in the stream, and to the monk's horror the water showed it to be dried blood.

"Oh Spirits!" Andra gasped and crossed himself. "Do you think he's killed one of the brothers to get away?"

"I don't know," Ruari growled, "he may have just wounded someone in order to get a horse. He must have used the other spare relay-horse to catch up with us, so I don't think he'd already left for the hill farm when he broke away, otherwise he'd already have been on a pony. But I wouldn't put it past him to injure one of those in the stables if they got in his way, and he was certainly prepared to kill you."

"What are you going to do with him?" Andra asked. He knew how dangerous this demented monk was, but yet to kill him out of hand went against Andra's beliefs.

"Go and find his horse first," Ruari instructed Andra. "It won't be far away. Try down by the road."

Andra was back in a few minutes leading another sturdy horse, and under Ruari's guidance completed a search of the baggage. The speed of Zeikiel's leaving was testified by the lack of clothes and food, but the light saddlebags did contain, amongst its standard contents always kept packed in readiness, a length of rope for tethering the horse in camp. Using this, Ruari bound Zeikiel hand and foot, then used the rest to tie Zeikiel to a beech surrounded by bushes. A strip of his habit was cut to form a gag, and with him well secured, they settled down for the rest of the night.

In the morning they packed up their own gear once more. Ruari had decided to leave Zeikiel tied up. He reasoned to Andra that the monks would soon come searching for him if he had used violence on others in the community. Yet if Ruari killed him it would also be seen as murder and the matter turned over to the nearest army commander, and the last thing they wanted was to be hunted down as common criminals. The horse, however, they would take with them, just in case someone came across him earlier than the monks, and he talked his way into them letting him go. Ruari also thought a spare horse was no bad thing. Once they got onto rough terrain there was always the possibility of even experienced horses having accidents and going lame. The last thing he wanted was for them to end up slowed down to one horse, which would mean taking it in turns to ride.

Ruari set another blistering pace for the rest of the day. Perhaps it was just as well that they spent much of the day in light drizzle, for a warm day would have been punishing for the horses. However, it did little to ease Andra's misery. Whereas Ruari took physical deprivation as a matter of course, for Andra it was a whole new unpleasant reality. He could never have believed his muscles could ache so. Days in the monastery's fields paled into insignificance, and, despite Ruari's kindly attempts to improve his riding position, his groin felt as though it was on fire by the time they halted for the second night. This time he actually fell off the horse and had to be picked up off the ground, where his legs still wobbled dramatically.

As they sat in a small stone refuge hut just up off the main mountain road, Ruari handed him the salve again. Andra began to fumble with his clothing then stopped, embarrassed. Even in the monastery dormitories it was not normal to disrobe in the sight of other monks. Ruari looked at him in amusement for a second.

"Flaming Trees, brother, you don't have anything I haven't seen a thousand times before, you know," he laughed. Then took pity on the young monk, shook his head and ducked out of the door. "Be quick about it! I'm not walking round out here getting wet all night," was his parting shot.

By the time he returned with an armful of firewood, to replace the wood they had used from the hut's supply, Andra was dressed again.

"I'm sorry, I'm not much good at this, am I," Andra said sadly.

"Oh give it a rest," Ruari grumbled, but without any seriousness. "By the Rowan, I'd have thought you'd had enough punishment to atone for your few sins ten times over after the last two days!"

Andra stared at him in amazement until he realized that Ruari was pulling his leg, at which point he turned pink. His admiration for this tough soldier had grown substantially in that time. Not only did Ruari seem to have a map of the whole Island somewhere in his head, he was also an expert countryman, knowing where to find wild fruits, which fungi to pick, and what the weather was going to do. The way he had dealt with Zeikiel had also convinced Andra that he was not just a mindless killer. Ruari was everything Andra was not, in his mind at least. The Knight was strong, fearless, just, and wise in the ways of the world. If he had known what such a thing was, it could be said that Andra was getting a serious case of hero worship, and he desperately wanted his hero's approval.

Oblivious to this, Ruari was feeling sorry for his companion. He knew how hard it must be to thrown in at the deep end like this, and so decided to offer some consolation.

"You've done well to keep up, brother. That's the worst of the fast riding over with." Internally Andra glowed at the praise, while Ruari carried on. "We're already over a day ahead of the churchmen, but from now on we'll be on much less travelled tracks, which will be much slower going. By my reckoning, we'll be able to ride up until late morning tomorrow, then we'll have to lead the horses for a short spell over the top, and if the weather's good to us and we can ride into the dusk, we should be at Lund tomorrow night. You'll have a proper bed and the company of civilized men, not a ruffian like me."

He was quite surprised that Andra did not instantly delight in the prospect of a return to civilization, but put it down to weariness. To his own surprise also, Andra found that he did not particularly want to go back to civilization. The thought of a proper bed was bliss, but having earned praise from someone he actually thought worthy of delivering it, he wanted more. In his previous confined little world, he had always thought of teasing as something petty and spiteful, yet he had been rather pleased in an odd sort of way, that Ruari would joke with him. It made him feel accepted in a way that he had never done before. As he settled into the warmth of the blanket and heard the occasional snores from his new friend, despite all his aches and pains, he thought he had rarely felt more fulfilled.

The next day for the first time they were truly in the mountains. As the day wore on, the slopes of green turf and purple heather changed to rising walls of scree, which hemmed them in closer and closer. The clouds descended, wrapping them in a solitary, misty world where Andra lost all sense of direction. By midday they were leading the horses up a narrow and precarious track, with a high cliff wall on one side and a sheer drop on the other. Ruari led his own horse with the spare horse on a long-rein behind it, with Andra and then his horse bringing up the rear. In the mist Andra could only hope Ruari was still leading, since he could see nothing but the rump of the horse in front. Once or twice the horses dislodged rocks which bounced off the stone to crash down to the valley floor far below, making Andra feel faint at the thought of going the same way.

He was greatly relieved when the path began to widen and the drop changed to the valley of a stream rising to meet them. However, his relief was short lived. Underfoot they now had to contend with being on the loose scree, on which they slithered dangerously. When they were almost at the top of the slope Andra lost his footing. The horse leapt past him and stood shaking on a patch of solid rock, but Andra could not stop his downward slide. Arms waving frantically he scrabbled and tottered, scree bouncing down the mountain in his wake, as he picked up speed in his descent.

"Lie down!" Ruari bellowed at him. "Spread your arms and legs out!"

Andra flung himself face down and this halted his slide, although not immediately, leaving him many feet below Ruari and the horses, where he lay shaking with fear. Out of the eye that was not against the ground he could see the valley floor suddenly taking a sharp downwards drop out of sight only a short way below him. Beyond the edge all he could see was sky. All he could think was that sooner or later he was going over that edge. He was so panic-stricken at the thought of bouncing off the rocks all the way back down the mountain, that at first he did not realize that he could hear Ruari's voice calling to him.

"Lie still, brother. Let the surface settle again. Don't panic, it's not as bad as it seems."

Hobbling the animals, Ruari dumped his sodden coat beside them and began to edge his way down to Andra in a crab-like movement, starting far off to one side and creeping closer. Suddenly a strong hand grasped Andra's wrist making him gasp with relief, until Ruari's movement caused another slight slippage.

"It's no good," Andra whispered. "Go. I'll only drag you down with me."

"Don't talk daft," Ruari replied brusquely, "we're both getting out of here. Now just do as I tell you!"

With Ruari holding his arm tightly they edged slowly to the edge of the scree to where there were hand-holds on the adjoining rocks. Panting with the effort they hauled themselves back up to the stone shelf were the horses stood waiting patiently. Collapsing to sit on the stone, Andra was too shaken to move for some time. He felt physically sick and lightheaded. From their seat all he could see was sky and rocks, and they were swimming before his eyes every time he moved his head. Ruari came to sit by him but then, seeing how badly he was shivering, went and rummaged in his saddle bag, producing a small leather flask. He came and sat down beside Andra, dropping a reassuring arm across the monk's thin shoulders. With his teeth he pulled the stopper from the flask and then proffered it to Andra, who took a swig and then spluttered furiously. The fiery liquid felt as though it had burned its way straight down to his stomach, rendering him speechless. Ruari grinned and made him swallow another sip.

"What *is* that?" Andra finally croaked.

"Up in Celidon and Ergardia they call it 'the water of life'," Ruari told him. "Its other name is uisge."

"Holy Spirits, where do they get it from? Dragons?"

"No," Ruari laughed, "they brew up barley and then they either leave it out in the winter so the water freezes and they can pour off the spirit, or they heat it up again in a copper pot with a long chimney on the top. Apparently the uisge comes off first before the water boils. I've been trying to replenish this flask for years, so I couldn't believe my luck when I went to Allerdale priory's herbalist for some salve, and found he had a bottle he didn't know what to do with. Good stuff isn't it!"

Andra could not think of a suitable reply, but Ruari was pleased to see the spirit had brought some colour back into his face.

"Come on," Ruari said, after a few more minutes, "we're almost at the top."

"Oh Spirits," Andra sobbed, "have we got to go back down more of this?"

"No," Ruari chuckled, giving him an encouraging pat on the shoulder. He had forgotten that the little monk had probably never travelled in mountain territory before, and would not know even the basics of mountain geography. "This is the escarpment side of the mountain. The sharp bit. The other side is easier going. It's still steep but it's not so sheer, and there's no scree."

Getting unsteadily to his feet, Andra let Ruari lead him by the arm up the short stretch to the top of the ridge, while leading all three horses with the other. As they crested the summit the view took Andra's breath away. The clouds lifted, and for a moment he was treated to the sight of ever climbing dramatic peaks rising off to their left, as the mountains marched on northwards. An arm of the mountain they were on obscured the view to their right, but ahead, the valley swept down to rolling hills, and in the distance he could see the town of Lund snuggled behind its walls, and the stately monastery sitting on a knoll above it with its back to the mighty range. To someone who had never travelled off a road before it was like being on top of the world.

Ruari had great difficulty persuading Andra to move, for he was entranced by the marvellous changes in the landscape. As the clouds rolled over it, and sudden patches of sunlight appeared and then were gone into the mist again, the colours were constantly changing. Features which stood out one minute were hidden by shadows the next, while others that he had not seen before emerged into view. To Andra it was little short of miraculous, and he had a hard time concentrating on where he was putting his feet. Only fear of slipping again kept dragging his eyes back to the path, which, as Ruari had promised, became rapidly easier. They were soon deeper into the valley between two shoulders of the mountains, and the views became less spectacular. As reality slowly returned to him, Andra also realized that the stress had had its effect on his insides. When they reached a level stretch with stunted trees and high thorn bushes, he begged Ruari to pause for a moment.

The Knight sighed in mock exasperation, but gestured Andra off to the bushes while he stood and scanned the valley, which once more lay spread out before them. When he heard Andra call his name his first thought was one of impatience. What could possibly be the problem now? He had only gone to attend a call of nature, surely he did not need help with that! Then it registered that Andra had called him by his first name. Ever since they had met it had amused Ruari that the little man had never quite managed to say his name. It had started off as 'my lord', and then when Ruari had objected, it had changed to 'sire', but never 'Ruari' until now. Flinging the horses' reins over the nearest thorn bush, he drew his sword and broke into a run.

He found Andra standing in a small clearing, in one piece but pointing to the centre of the grass. The remains of a fire lay there. Wisps of smoke still rose from the embers speaking of its recent use, and around it in the thin soil stood the impressions of many booted feet.

"Who else would be up here?" Andra asked nervously.

"Well spotted," Ruari complimented him. "I don't know. These paths are rarely used." He scanned the trees around him. "Hurry up and do what you have to. We shouldn't linger here."

"I've done what I needed," Andra said quickly, earning him a surprised but approving look from Ruari, before turning back to the horses.

From within the depths of the undergrowth, a man pulled back the string of a bow and sighted the arrow on Ruari's back, but his companion put a restraining hand on his arm.

"No, wait!" he hissed softly. "I know that man, he's familiar. They won't be moving fast on this slope." With which he turned and slipped silently off the boulder they had been crouched on. Creeping past others of the troop, he at last found their leader.

"Are they dead?" the man asked, without turning.

"No, sire."

The leader turned, revealing himself to be a thick set man of middle years with close-cropped fair hair. Under the scrutiny of his steely gray eyes the first man failed to flinch but said,

"I think you'd better come and see them for yourself before we finish them off."

"Why?"

"I'm not sure, but I think you might know the tall man." He turned and led the way back, diverting to bring them to a small promontory above the track the two horsemen were now filing down. His companion had preceded them and was already in position, still with his bow at the ready, earning an approving nod from the commander. Dropping to his elbows he edged forward, keeping a low profile, to look over the edge. Just as he had them in his gaze, Ruari turned in his saddle and scanned the track back the way they had come, before urging Andra to heel his horse into a trot and move in front of him.

"MacBeth!" the leader exclaimed in a hiss, although not so loudly that Ruari heard him.

"It is him, then," the soldier asked. "I wasn't sure, sire, but I knew you'd know."

"Oh! It's him alright! Come on. Get the men and move down after them! We need to intercept them before they reach the main road. I want to know what MacBeth's doing risen from the dead and up here of all places."

Dressed in drab browns and greens, it was not obvious until they all began moving just how many men there were. Even so, it was not easy to follow their movements in the high bracken and bushes. They had almost caught up with Ruari and Andra as the pair rounded another bend in the track that then made a straight line to the major crossroads at Lund. Yet before the hidden men could spring their trap, Ruari reined his horse in for a second, and then turned and slapped Andra's horse hard on the rump as he heeled his own into a gallop.

"Get to the monastery!" he yelled at Andra. "Tell Jaenberht to block the gates. The Jarl's men are ambushing his abbots! Go!"

From his elevated position, Ruari had spotted two groups of armed men lurking behind stands of trees on the road from Bytor. A watcher had just stood and waved a signal flag from behind a rocky viewpoint, while, oblivious to the danger, a line of mounted monks wound along the road.

No sooner had Ruari begun his headlong race down the steep road towards the main road than the trap was sprung. To his horror he saw archers step out from behind the cover of the wayside trees and bushes in front of the churchmen. As the party reined in their mounts at the sight, other men came out of the cover brandishing swords. The monastic men were easily subdued, and before Ruari had even reached the main road, they were being led away back the way they had come, until someone heard the sound of his horse's hooves and shouted a warning. The rear guard of archers turned and laid down a volley of warning shots in Ruari's direction.

He was outside of their range despite the power of the bows they were using, but he still pulled up. He obviously stood no chance now of cutting even some of the monks out from the group. However, his halt did not stop the archers' rate of fire and they were now running towards him. He suddenly realized that they did not want him to remain as a witness to what had happened. Hauling his horse's head round, he used his spurs to catapult the horse into another headlong gallop, this time straight for the monastery. As he leant over the horse's neck he felt at least two arrows catch in his coat, and counted himself lucky that at that range they had not the power to penetrate further.

From the hillside, the hidden soldiers now joined in the fight as the ambushers came within range of their arrows. Suddenly the pursuers found themselves on the receiving end of fire from the high ground to their left, and broke off their chase. Their unseen assailants were of a whole different calibre to themselves. Whereas they had depended on sheer weight of firepower, these new combatants were taking aim carefully and then making every arrow count. Already several men had arrows protruding from them, and three were on the ground and not moving. For a moment they stood nonplussed at the turn in events, and then broke into a steady run back the way they had come. By this time Ruari's horse was pounding up the rise to the abbey, which it reached as the archers disappeared back eastwards.

"Bugger!" the commander swore as he saw the great gates open just wide enough for Ruari to thunder through, and then slam shut after him. "That's torn any chance of a quiet word."

"Who were those other troops?" a man at his side asked.

"Jarl Oswine's, I'll be bound," another answered for him.

"What are you going to do now, sire?" a third asked.

The commander ran his beefy paw through his stubbly hair and down to scratch his roughly-shaven chin.

"Well I'm going to have to go down there now, aren't I!" he snapped. "You lot, get down there to that monastery when it gets dark. Get undercover and don't let anyone see you're there. Shoot anyone who tries to get in…. Except if they're a monk, of course."

"You're going into the monastery sire?" his aide asked anxiously. "Do you think that's wise?"

"No, it's not wise!" his commander growled back sarcastically, "but it's the only way I can get to him now." Then, seeing the looks of concern all around him added, "Don't worry, I've no intention of going up and announcing my name. I'll go in as a beggar – I look like one after all these months on the road!"

"Won't you be recognized?" persisted one of the men.

"Not likely," he growled, as he pulled a ragged sack cloak around his shoulder which someone had brought up to him. "I never did like monks! All that bowing and scraping on your knees. They may have wished me to the Underworld many times, but there're very few of the sanctimonious brethren who ever laid eyes on me. I'll be in with the scum – the brothers won't let the likes of me too near the righteous, I might contaminate them! So I'll have to try to catch him unawares, when he goes to the stables or something. Bloody MacBeth! He always did make life complicated!

Chapter 18

Drunk and Disorderly

Rheged: Winterfalling

Within the abbey of Lund, Ruari and Andra received a warm welcome, somewhat tempered by Jaenberht's fury at the sight of those he thought of as *his* churchmen being kidnapped beneath his very nose. Seated in the largest room in the guest house, which Jaenberht had commandeered for his own use, the abbot strode to and fro, fuming while the others ate griddled trout, caught from the abbey's own fish ponds. When they had finished eating and had settled back with mugs of steaming caff, he stopped ranting at the insolence of the Jarl's men, and forced himself to sit.

"My apologies, Ruari," he said, forcing himself to take a calming breath. "It's not that I'm not glad to see you again. I've prayed to the Spirits daily that you may yet have been spared and return."

"You may not be quite so overjoyed when you hear what I have to tell you," Ruari countered. "I'm hardly the bringer of good tidings."

"Then you'd best tell all," Jaenberht commanded, "for in turn you're unlikely to be any more pleased with the news I have for you."

Ruari quirked a curious eyebrow at this statement, but took a swallow of his caff and then launched into his story. He told Jaenberht of the sequence of events which had led to Michael's death, at which the abbot crossed himself but said nothing. By the time Ruari had told of his journey across Rheged which had brought him to Lund, Jaenberht was leaning forward, fingers steepled under his chin, fixing both Ruari and Andra with a stare that never wavered.

"*Mmm*," he intoned as Ruari finished. "Then you may be less surprised at some of what I have to tell you than I thought. I too feared that Tancostyl was abroad in Rheged, though I didn't know of his complicity in Michael's death. That speaks of much longer laid plans than even I'd feared. Curse that fiend back to his Underworld! He's had too much of a free hand for too long, and we've both been having to play catch-up instead of responding with plans of our own."

At that he told of what he had learnt of Will and Matti's downfall. Both Ruari and Andra were delighted to discover that Matti and Wistan had made it safely to the far north with Iago's help. However, their joy was short lived as Jaenberht told of the ambushing of his monks, and the disappearance of Matti and Iago.

"The sheer audacity of that attack still shocks me," Jaenberht said. "I'd not thought that Tancostyl would show his hand so openly. It worries me greatly that if he feels so secure, his plans may be further on and closer to completion than I'd dreaded."

"Ah, but," Ruari mused, "...thinking about it ...it may not be Tancostyl who lay directly behind that attack. ...Oh, I'm not saying he isn't the mastermind behind the greater scheme of things," he said, checking Jaenberht's cry of disbelief. "I'm just thinking of the attack at Montrose. The dirty work was done by Oswine's men, not Tancostyl in person, and that's where it slipped from the way he'd intended, I think. Tancostyl is used to directing seasoned troops, and ones used to obeying his word to the letter. Or maybe, not being someone who's ever had to fight in person, it wouldn't occur to him to direct the men he sent to surround the castle first. Do you see what I mean? Before they did anything to prevent just such an escape. To Will or Edmund or me it would be the obvious thing to do, as it would to any experienced soldier, but these were just the thugs hired by Oswine.

"It strikes me that much the same might have happened to your monks. Tancostyl probably wanted Matti and Wistan very much alive, if only to have the satisfaction of torturing them himself. But the order to seize them would have to go through Oswine, and we know how dim he is! He wouldn't register the implications of what he was saying. And the men he hired would have to be pretty unscrupulous to even contemplate seizing a member of the most noble household. From there, it's a small slip from kidnapping to killing. Let's face it, it's tipped his hand to you, and maybe the reason we can't see more of his plans taking effect is because they're not in place yet, and you weren't supposed to know this early."

"There's much in what you say," Jaenberht sighed, "and I wish it cheered me more. The thought of Tancostyl being thwarted by the very minions he directs means there's hope yet. But what can we do? My thought was to at least unite the monastic orders, and to try to revive what was left of yours, into some resistance. With you here that's more possible. Even then, though, my plans have still gone desperately astray."

"What do you mean?" Ruari asked, bothered by Jaenberht's continued agitation.

"Unfortunately Wistan and Kenelm are also missing."

"Missing? But I thought you said Matti and Iago got Wistan to Mailros?"

"So they did. But in my fear at Oswine's attempted murder of Wistan, and then the attack on the group he was supposed to be in, I began to fear for Kenelm's safety too. The night after the attack, I called him into the chapter house and told him the truth. Oh, I'd long since warned him that he was the son of one of the Jarl's family – I had to tell him why I was uprooting him to Mailros when he didn't want to come. But I hadn't told him all of it. This time I felt I had to fully prepare him.

"What I never anticipated was that he would take matters into his own hands. Some of the brothers saw him and Wistan in deep conversation together at several times during the next day. Then I left to come here, and it was only the following day that a brother came chasing after us to ask me if they'd been brought along with my party. The brothers had noticed they were missing and had searched high and low for them. Having seen that they'd taken the care to pack, and had asked the cook for supplies, it struck the brothers that they might have been a last minute addition to this group. I had to send the brother back with instructions to keep searching. But why would they leave? I can't think where they might be headed or why."

"I can," Andra answered softly. The two others had quite forgotten he was there, so engrossed in their contemplations had they been. Ruari gave him a quizzical glance, but Jaenberht fixed him with a steely stare that made him gulp.

"Can you?" Jaenberht said in a dangerously low voice.

Andra nodded nervously, but was undeterred.

"Wistan often told me he hated being the heir to the throne. He said that one day, when he was old enough, he was going to run away from it all. All he ever wanted was brothers and sisters to play with, you see, and to be part of a 'proper' family. He didn't *want* to be special. He always thought that if he ever had to rule, he'd make such a mess of it the Island would be better if it didn't know he existed, and picked someone better. Now you've suddenly told him he has a cousin. I don't know this Kenelm, but, if he's like Wistan, maybe they've decided they've had enough of being pawns in everyone else's game."

"Oh Sacred Spirits protect them!" Jaenberht prayed.

"Aye, but I reckon Andra's right," Ruari sighed, then turned back to Andra. "I've not spoken to Kenelm in a few years, but when he was Wistan's age he use to talk like that too. Sacred Trees, he might never have thought of running to save himself, but I can well believe that if he found out that he had a little cousin, and that that cousin had narrowly missed being killed several times, it would prompt him to act. Once upon a time he would've come to me, I hope, but he no doubt thinks like everyone else that I'm dead."

"But I was protecting him!" Jaenberht protested.

"Were you?" Andra quietly interrupted again. "Forgive me my lord abbot, but did you bother explaining to Wistan that you were planning to let Lady Montrose flee *before* the Jarl's men met your brothers?"

Light dawned for Jaenberht and he groaned as Andra continued.

"He's a very moral child, you know. He would be distraught if he thought that the very person who'd saved him was being rewarded by being sent to her certain death. How was he to know that you'd never really do that? All he ever saw at court were people using other people to their own personal gain, regardless of the suffering it caused. He wasn't to know, in the few short hours since he'd met you, that you were different. As for Kenelm, you'd just revealed to him that you'd kept a whole part of his own life secret from him. If he trusted you before, just at that point you gave him reason enough to question whether you were really the man he thought he knew."

For someone who had led such a sheltered life, Ruari thought, Andra could be remarkably perceptive.

In the meantime, downstairs one of the monks was feeling very perplexed. He was sure he had shown the beggar who had turned up at the gates across to the lean-to hut against the side of the cloister wall. It was not a place they would normally ever put a visitor, but, with Abbot Jaenberht calling all and sundry here, the abbey was bursting at the seams. Already there had been grumblings of discontent amongst some of the newly arrived brothers at the meanness of their accommodation. It was one thing to embrace a lack of luxury in the name of piety, but to be squeezed six at a time into rooms which were only ever meant to take three, like the youngest of novices, was insulting they felt. And pilgrims and travellers fared even worse. The hayloft was brim full, as was the dining hall, and many would have to be moved out before anyone could break their fast tomorrow morning. The scruffy man with his gruff voice had caused the gatekeeper some qualms over letting him in, and now the brother was wishing he had followed his advice and turned the ruffian away.

The only reason they had let him in was the bloody stain on the shoulder of his jerkin, which he said had come from being hit by a stray arrow from the assailants who had taken the brethren this afternoon. He had been found a place in the hut and the brother had come with hot water and bandages to attend his wound, only to find he had disappeared. It looked suspiciously as though, far from being a victim, the ruffian had been one of the attackers and now he was loose in the abbey. Sighing deeply the brother turned and went to find the almoner. Spirit's only knew what *he* would say over this, but the brother could foresee a long time in penance without any divine assistance.

Deep in the shadow of the cloister wall, a bulky figure watched the monk go and roundly cursed the brother and his good intentions. With the abbey seething with visitors he had expected to be forgotten the moment he had been installed in the hut, giving him time to prowl around without anyone noticing him. Now the brother would start people wondering. The man fingered the knife he had drawn from the folds of his woollen leggings, then shook his head. What was he thinking of? He had been watching his back too long if he could think of using the weapon on a monk. No doubt his soul was condemned to the Underworld already – something which he rarely gave a second's thought to. But even he had a limit to what he could do without become disgusted at himself.

Unfortunately, though, that did not help him gain any more time to find MacBeth, and he continued cursing under his breath as he moved silently towards what he hoped was the abbot's lodgings. He was hoping like mad that if Jaenberht was in residence, that that was where MacBeth would have headed for. He certainly could not go around asking where the man who had risen from the dead was sleeping.

A cold and damp hour later the door to the abbot's lodgings opened, spilling a beam of warm yellow light out into the cobbled courtyard which separated it from the other monastic buildings, the stables, and the outer wall. Ruari stood for a moment silhouetted against the light before stepping out into the darkness. In the office that Jaenberht had commandeered from the resident abbot, the three of them had argued round and round without coming to any good conclusion. Andra seemed concerned that Wistan and Kenelm were being forgotten in the face of greater problems, and so kept returning to them at every chance. That was not the case, but Ruari and Jaenberht were trying to get a perspective on the bigger picture. In the light of which, they had wondered whether it might not be for the best if the two royal youngsters really did stay lost.

From feeling more empowered, Ruari had again returned to not knowing whether he was coming or going, and he had been the one who finally called a halt to the arguments. Leaving Jaenberht to join his leading monastics and to contemplate what action they would take, he had dragged Andra out and sent him to the church to soothe his nerves. For his own part, he had decided to go and groom their horses. The abbey's groom was no doubt run off his feet, and Ruari guessed their horses would have been fed but not attended to in any other way.

In the gloom of the stables, he found two lay brothers struggling to bring feed down from the loft because of those forced to sleep up there getting in the way. Above him there was much loud complaining and thumping as bales were shifted, while people constantly seemed to be going up and down the ladder. He picked up a comb and brush from the table by the door and walked down the line of stalls. Their horses were nowhere to be seen, and he was becoming worried until one of the brothers gestured him to go outside. As proof of the shortage of space, he found that several horses were tethered under the eaves of the overhang of the roof from the back of the cloisters. Sure enough their three horses stood at the end, sharing a bucket of water which they had almost drained, but with a net of hay hung up for them, and more feed on a propped up plank of wood doing service as a makeshift manger.

Picking up the water bucket, Ruari went and refilled it, and while the horse they had acquired from Zeikiel guzzled it noisily, he managed to nudge his own into a position where he had room to start grooming it. The familiar exercise coupled with the easy rhythm of the brush soon soothed his own tensions, and he could start thinking clearly again. If Tancostyl was really being undermined by those he thought he controlled then he was already off balance. That was a good thing, in Ruari's books, because it would force him to act rashly and show his hand more than he might. If he then found out that the Knights had a leader once more, it might confuse his plans even more. Ruari paused in his thoughts to disentangle several burrs from his horse's mane, and the small prickly objects which came away in his hand gave him a new thought. All it took was one burr under a saddle to cause severe irritation. So maybe it would be worth while remaining 'dead' for now. Tancostyl was one twitchy horse already, but there might come a point in the future when he had removed the current burrs and they would need to re-distract him. Coming back to life was a card Ruari could only play once for its shock value – better to save it for when it would be most effective.

He ducked under the horse's head and started on its other side. By the time he had finished the second horse he was well on the way to formulating a plan. Let Jaenberht carry on rallying support. Of all the allies he had gained so far, Jaenberht was also the one who could marshal sufficient resources to arrange passage back for the Order's troops marooned across the sea, and to whom he could therefore delegate the job – as if anyone could ever be thought to have delegated anything to Jaenberht that he was not already willing to do! Luckily he was possessed of a military turn of mind, and had no compunction in adding a little muscle to his arguments if faith alone was insufficient.

In fact, Ruari was thinking of asking if his men could be relocated straight to the northern tip of Ergardia. That would be a short trip across the sound from northwest of Rheged if they were needed in a hurry, but would mean that nobody would be tipped off as to their existence. If that could be done, it released him from a major duty. And if Matti was with Iago, then she was being as well cared for as if he were there himself. Which meant Andra might just get his wish to go and find the two innocents adrift in the wilderness.

Coming to the third horse, he had more space to move as the mare was at the end of the line, and he set to brushing, feeling cheerful enough to start whistling as he worked – until he straightened only to feel the chill of a knife pressed to his throat. A muscular arm went around his neck and the knife point was slid to under one ear.

"Well aren't you a solid ghost," a gruff voice said in his ear.

Ruari knew that voice from somewhere, but his training had kicked in. Allowing his muscles to relax, to lull his captor into a false sense of control, he suddenly jack-knifed himself backwards, throwing his full weight onto the man behind. For a moment they staggered and the knife point moved away from his neck, but the man had not been fooled enough to loose his grip.

"That old trick!" the man laughed, "you should know better than to try that one on me, MacBeth, we've fought one another too often for that. Now come with me, and quietly!"

That voice! Where had he heard it before? No time to think of that now, though. Lurching sideways Ruari forced his assailant around with him so that the man now had his back to the horses. Another shove backwards and Ruari felt the man stagger as he fell over the wooden plank, as it caught him in the back of the legs. It was just enough distraction. A vicious jab of the elbow hit a portly middle and did little damage, but the head butt connected and raised a muffled curse. And in a blink of an eye the tables turned. Ruari gained control, and suddenly it was him who was sitting astride the other man as he went flying on the damp cobbles.

As they slid out from under the shadows of the eaves, the light from the lodgings windows spilled onto the ground, lighting up the man's face and making Ruari gasp.

"Will?" Giving an irritated growl of exasperation, Ruari got to his feet. "You stupid bastard! What, by all the hounds of the Hunt, do you think you're doing? It's me! Ruari!"

"I know that!" Will spat back, also spitting out several horse hairs that he had half swallowed in his slide along the floor.

Ruari grabbed him and half hauled, half helped him to his feet.

"What? You knew? Then Flaming Trees, why the knife?"

"I wasn't sure what you'd heard. Everyone else seems to think I killed Wistan and Eleanor. You always could be a righteous prick when the mood took you! I didn't want you to march me off to one of Oswine's cells thinking you could question me later."

Ruari shook his head in despair.

"Sometimes, Will, I wonder how you ever got to be a general. Have you heard nothing since you've been on the run? What's more, have you not stopped to listen to the conversations going on around *here* while you've been skulking around?"

"No! Small talk's been a bit low on my list of late. In case you hadn't noticed, I've been trying to save my skin!" Will retorted sarcastically.

"Come on," Ruari started hustling Will towards the lodgings door.

"Hang on a minute!" Will pulled away. "I'm not having that old goat Jaenberht trussing me up."

"Why?"

"I'm a murderer as far as he knows, stupid!" Will's hoarse whisper was so loud it was almost a shout.

"Well it'd be hard for him to condemn you for murdering someone who's still alive, so 'stupid' you!" Ruari countered.

Will's face was a picture of astonishment.

"Alive?"

"Well Wistan is. Eleanor was less fortunate. But Oswine overplayed his hand. He sent his thugs back to finish the job, and this time there was a witness and he got away. So do you want to hear the full story, or are you going to stand there doing impressions of a fish out of water?"

Ruari led Will into the hallway and up to the office he had not long left. By the light of the candles he was shocked to see the state of his friend. Will had always been solidly built, but now he was almost as round as he was tall. If he had lost weight living in hiding, the Spirits only knew what size he must have been before. Where was the fit, trained soldier he had known not so many years ago? Before he had chance to question Will further, Jaenberht appeared behind him from the corridor and gasped in amazement too.

"Montrose! You're alive! Ah, thanks be! The Spirit's have returned to our side today!"

Feeling like a fly between two spiders, Will found himself on the end of a constant barrage of questions. Considering Ruari had been out of the country, and Jaenberht closeted away in the far north it was amazing, Will thought, how much more than him they seemed to know. Having spent most of the time hidden away deep in the mountains, he had little he could add to their story, and so concentrated on the pitcher of ale which was brought up to the room. Ruari watched the speed with which the beer was going and the lack of any immediate effect of it on Will, and began to see where some of the weight had come from. Will had always liked the taverns rather than the lordly hall, but evidently he had taken to consuming their products regularly and in great quantity. The sharp wit and tactical astuteness had disappeared somewhere into a malty fog.

When Will revealed that he had a full company of men hiding just outside the abbey, Jaenberht's eyes met Ruari's and they were both wondering who the real commander of those men was? It was quite obvious that while Will might have been the figurehead, and many must have followed out of loyalty to their old officer, someone else must have been making the day to day decisions. Allowing Will to nod off in front of the fire after finishing off the entire large pitcher, Ruari and Jaenberht stepped away to the window.

"We could use those men," Jaenberht breathed softly.

"No my lord, *you* could use them," Ruari replied, equally softly. "If Oswine can dare to strike so openly at men called to meet you, I think it's time you had a bodyguard. I'll go out early tomorrow and find these men. Whoever's been leading them will no doubt be glad of some proper soldiering to do, and glad of some proper billets and food for his men. I think as long as he's convinced that someone is taking care of Will, and that there are people who know the truth of what happened at Montrose Castle, he won't object too hard at new duties. All I ask is that with this additional security you try to help my men still in the east."

With that Ruari launched into his plan, so that by the time Andra reappeared the two had agreed to a course of action. Andra was delighted that he, Ruari and Will would be going in search of Wistan and Kenelm. In the course of telling him this, Will woke up and had to be introduced. Poor Andra was utterly dismayed to hear Will ask after 'that frosty bitch of a wife of mine', especially as it was accompanied by a loud belch and a long and noxious fart. As they retreated to the window which Ruari opened quickly for all of them, he asked in a horrified whisper,

"Was Lady Montrose really married to that?"

Ruari and Jaenberht just nodded.

"Poor lady!" Andra whispered, appalled. "How did someone so cultured and intelligent cope even being in the same room as that … Oh Spirits!" The last coming as another volcanic eruption sounded from the fireside. "No wonder she spoke of you so fondly," he said to Ruari. "You must have saved her sanity."

"It wasn't her sanity she wanted him to save," came the beery riposte from within.

Realizing they were heading for dangerous ground, Jaenberht attempted to deflect Will.

"Come now, General, the past cannot be altered. Let's not argue over..."

"Oh no, let's argue." Will rose unsteadily to his feet. "Did you ever prong my wife?" he belched at Ruari. "If you did you've a stronger stomach than me. Scares the shit out of me, she does. Who wants a woman like that, eh? I like a good warm handful! And willing! Don't suppose you've got any like that around here have you, abbot? Haven't warmed my fire in a long time! But you," he poked Ruari in the chest with a wobbly finger that kept splitting into two in his blurred vision, "you like 'em frosty, don't you! 'S all them vows and takin' cold baths you lot do! Freezes your nads! Did she give you frost-bite on your todger?"

Jaenberht was obviously expecting blows to come at this, and Andra was openly gapping, with eyes like saucers, at Will's outburst. But, to even his own surprise, all Ruari felt was a deep sadness at what his friend had become. The old Will would never have asked such a question, or been so coarse. He knew that Ruari was aware that the time he spent down in the taverns was largely spent between the sheets of the most buxom girl in the place. But he had always shown Matti respect, too, whatever his inner emotions. And he knew both Ruari and Matti well enough to know that they had never cuckolded him, no matter what their feelings. What in the Islands had happened to turn Will into this?

However, before he could think of a suitable reply, Will relapsed into his chair and immediately started snoring. Ruari and Jaenberht exchanged raised eyebrow glances and sighs only partly of relief. In the end, two robust brothers were summoned to carry the inert Will to a bed in the same room as Ruari, which had been vacated by a rapidly departing Andra. Quite how Ruari could contemplate spending the night in the company of a man who could actually manage to swear and fart even in his sleep was utterly beyond him. Ruari had not had the heart to tell him that he would be quite used to it by the time they had all finished travelling together.

The next morning dawned cold, gray and foggy. Under such ideal cover Ruari slipped out of the picket gate of the abbey walls. In no time at all he found, or was found by, the surrounding hidden troops. It took a little convincing, but by the time most of those within the walls were queuing for breakfast, Will's lieutenant had been in, seen his recumbent master and thankfully handed him over to the care of his friend, whilst placing the rest of the men into Jaenberht's able hands.

When Will came to, it was to find himself being manhandled onto the back of the third horse by several muscular brothers, while Andra and Ruari sat already mounted and waiting. Before he could protest, he was forced to grab at the horse's mane as Ruari took its reins and led them out of the abbey gate. They had barely gone far enough for the abbey to disappear into the mist before Will was begging them to stop. His head pounded like a whole smithy of anvils were being worked, and his stomach was doing somersaults, but Ruari ignored him. For half the morning he was reduced to holding onto the horse as firmly as he could, while puking the previous night's beer up at regular intervals as he leant out from the horse's side. Ruari's only comment was,

"And you can clean that poor beast off properly when we make camp."

By midday Will was reeling in the saddle from dehydration, and when they got to a clear mountain stream, even Ruari relented enough to allow Will to dismount. While he plunged his head into the blissfully cold water, the horses were allowed to drink upstream from him. Ruari saw no need for them to drink polluted water. Andra was totally perplexed, and in the end could not refrain from asking the question that kept buzzing through his head.

"How could you be *friends* with such a man," he asked Ruari in amazement. "He's awful! He insults you, he insults his wife …and is he *ever* sober?"

Had he known it, Ruari had been thinking not such different thoughts, but he did his best to answer him.

"When I knew him well, before I went to the east, he was nothing like this. This isn't the man I called a friend at all. The Will I knew was bright, practical, funny, and he trusted his friends. He may not have loved his wife, but he respected her. I've never heard him speak the way he did last night. He's only with us because Abbot Jaenberht needs those men, both to protect him and his brothers, and to help my friends, and with Will there that wouldn't happen. Something terrible has gone wrong here."

Andra said nothing, but looked thoughtfully at the two men. It did nothing to diminish Ruari in his eyes that he would be so loyal to his friend, or be so self-sacrificing in the face of greater need. So while Will repeatedly plunged his pounding head into the blissfully icy stream, the two of them pondered the road ahead.

Once more, to Andra's great trepidation, they were heading up into the high mountains. They had taken the road north across the bridge that spanned the forceful river which thundered from the rocks above, and were now on yet another herder's trail following the northern bank upwards. The best guess was that Matti and Iago would have headed west again, given that they had managed the journey from Montrose relatively unmolested on that coast. Hopefully Wistan would have remembered that too and had persuaded Kenelm to go that way. All Ruari could think of was to head for the pass to Fell Peak Fort and down to the other side of the mountains, and hope that they had better luck than the brothers who had scoured this side of the range.

A pathetic moan broke their thoughts.

"Oh, I wish I was dead!" Will whimpered. He looked spectacularly awful. "Where are we going? Can't we stop for a bit?"

"Come on, up you get," Ruari said relentlessly, pushing Will to his horse. "We're going to find your wife and, hopefully, the heir to Rheged, so if you're dying you'll just have to do it on the way!"

"Bastard!" was all Will could summon in response.

"Maybe," Ruari said acidly, "but if you think I'm abandoning innocents like them to the tender embrace of one of the Abend just for your sore head, you're wrong."

Will's throbbing red eyes just managed to open fully at that.

"The Abend? Oh crap!"

He leant his head against the saddle.

"Kill me now and save them the trouble."

"Fair enough," Ruari said, "we're getting nowhere fast with you like this. I never promised Jaenberht I'd nursemaid you," and without pausing for breath his fist caught Will neatly under the chin.

"He deserved that," was his only response to Andra's startled gasp as they stared at the inert, comatose figure on the ground.

A week later Ruari was wishing he had actually had killed Will when he had hit him. The man had a nose for ferreting beer, or anything else intoxicating, out at the most unlikely spots. They had already had to pay two farmers who had kindly given them space to sleep, when Will had found the farm supplies of ale. Now they were in the high mountains, far from anyone. These high, barren slopes were used as summer grazing when the short tufty grass was new and rich, but this far into the autumn, even the wandering shepherds who lived with the flocks had taken their charges lower down against the danger of unexpected early snows. It had certainly put a stop to Will's overindulgence.

Instead, however, they were suffering with him as he went through the withdrawal symptoms. If Ruari had hoped for a silent passage he certainly was not going to get it. Will alternated between roaring curses at them for not giving him something to halt his misery, and fighting his illusory demons. Andra spent all his time dreading what new depths Will could plumb, and yet being amazed at what a man's mind could create under the influence of enough drink.

Sheltered life or not, Andra was pretty sure there were not, nor ever had been, any pink dragons. Especially not a singing one who was following Will and would not let him rest! Will would frequently wave his arms around as if trying to swat away a fly – often leading to him toppling out of his saddle and requiring the others to push and shove him back onto the long-suffering horse. And no matter what they told him, he was convinced that the beast followed, pointing to the bruises from his previous encounters with the ground at speed as proofs of its assaults upon him. Fortunately, the only spectators to this spectacle were the birds who rode the thermal drafts above the peaks as they searched for prey. Ruari had taken this route because it was the quickest to the west coast, but he was now thankful more for its isolation. On a more trafficked route someone would sooner or later have begun taking notice of them with Will in the state he was in.

Yet to their relief the day finally came when Will woke up and was coherent. It came not a day too soon either, for they were on the approach to Fell Peak Fort. They had camped early the night before in a copse of stunted hawthorns, while Ruari tried to decide how to get past the fort. Twice in the last two days they had been forced to scramble into gullies off the main valleys, as companies of armed troops rode up on the main road which twisted up to the pass. On the first occasion Ruari had been compelled to stuff the front of Will's heavy cloak into his mouth as the only way of silencing the tirade of gibberish. When the men had passed, and he let go, for an awful moment Will had been so still he feared he had suffocated him. For the first time even Andra was relieved when the moaning restarted.

However they still had to pass the fort – a squat, ugly, wooden-palisaded collection of buildings – which sat spread across the width of the narrow valley floor. In the dim, distant past it had had a substantial stone wall and large stone barracks, but these were long gone, replaced by oak walls, and the fort no longer functioned as a guardian against enemies trying to cross to the east. Instead it served as a way-station for troops moving across the Island, providing shelter and respite when the weather turned ugly in this barren landscape. Ruari had no wish to encounter the men encamped there. There was a vague chance that someone might recognize him, but for himself and Andra he was more concerned that ordinary travellers so rarely came this way that they might find themselves on the end of too many curious questions.

For Will, though, the danger of recognition was far greater. He had served as the commander of both the huge garrison of Catraeth, on the eastern approach to the road, and Caerlewl – the equally huge garrison on the western coast at the other end of the road. Troops moving from one to the other would almost certainly have some veterans in their midst who would spot Will in an instant, and he was not a man who could easily be disguised.

As Ruari sat hunched on a rock, peering down the valley towards the fort's gate, Will gave a low moan and then sat up.

"Is there any water?" he asked. "If you have any I'd welcome some, please."

Andra looked at him in amazement, but passed a water bottle over to him. It was the first time Will had asked civilly for anything since he had met him. Having taken a long pull at the cool mountain spring water, Will wiped his mouth on the back of his hand and passed the bottle back to Andra.

"Thanks," he murmured, then spotted Ruari, who had turned at the sound of Will's voice and was looking at him with his finger pressed to his lips.

"Ruari?" Will gasped in astonishment, before he saw the finger and, although it took a second to register, then struggled unsteadily to his feet. He actually managed to stay semi-crouched down, and below the top of the sheltering surrounding rocks, as he tottered over to Ruari and clasped him to his chest.

"You old bastard!" he exclaimed softly in a choked voice. "By the Spirits, you're alive!" And hugged Ruari tightly again. "I've never been so glad to see you in all my life! I thought everyone I cared about was dead. How long have you been back? Sweet Spirits, but do you know Matti was killed for supposedly murdering Wistan?" His eyes filled with tears which began to spill down his cheeks. "I'll never believe she did that! I should have been there to protect them both. I'll never forgive myself for that."

Utter amazement at the appearance of this totally different personality rendered Andra silent, but Ruari began to smile.

"Flaming Trees, Will, what in the Islands happened to you? You've been travelling with us for over a week now, don't you remember?"

Will looked puzzled.

"I feel bloody rough," he took a sniff at himself, "phaw! And I stink too! I've been on a horse – I can tell that by the way my legs ache – and I remember someone hitting me a lot, but that's all."

"No one hit you, well except for me ...once ...the rest is from when you kept falling off the horse drunk."

Will frowned in concentration, then gave up and shrugged.

"If you say so, I don't remember."

"Well, in that case I'd better tell you this again too. Matti is alive and on the run somewhere in the west, as is Wistan, which is why we're up here and Fell Peak Fort is over that rock. So keep quiet."

"Matti's alive? And Wistan too? Thank the Spirits!" Will's reaction seemed totally genuine. "How? What happened?"

Keeping an eye on the fort with occasional glance over the rocks, Ruari once again recounted the events of the last few months. Will made few comments, leaving the talking to Ruari, but snarled over Michael's betrayal.

"Bastards! I knew those fat pigs grovelling at Oswine's feet were up to something, but nobody I know was ever able to get close enough to find out."

When Ruari told of the fate of Montrose Castle, Will buried his face in his hands, and Ruari clasped his old friend on the shoulder in condolence.

"By the Wild Hunt, they shall pay for that!" Will swore. "I'll see them straight to the darkest depths of the Underworld. If I live long enough, I shall have to find some way of thanking Edmund for taking care of my people. I knew most of those folks who died since they were children, and one or two knew me when I was a babe in arms. There wasn't one of them deserved a death like that."

At the end he scratched his stubble – which was rapidly becoming a beard – and appeared to be thinking for several minutes. Then he drew a deep breath and fixed Ruari with a worried frown.

"What's the matter?" Ruari asked cautiously, "apart from too much bad news that is."

"Oh, I don't think you're the only one handing that out," Will said wearily. "I couldn't understand it until now. I couldn't explain it to anyone, but I've been feeling really strange. As though I'm me but not me at the same time."

"Not voices in your head telling you to do things," Ruari asked, yet dreading the answer.

"No." Then realizing what Ruari had implied by that, Will shook his head and emphasized it. "No, and I see where you're going with that, but I'm as sure as I can be that Tancostyl has never tried to actually *possess* me. He's never been that close to me without an awful lot of other people also being close to me too, and anyway, I suspect he thinks me too stubborn and awkward to be of any use. I've too many enemies of my own to have been useful enough to manipulate others for him."

"Thank the Trees for that!" Ruari sighed, and Andra offered up a silent prayer of thanks as well, given Will's proximity to them.

"Mmm, but I've still felt this odd tugging going on inside. It keeps trying to drag me back towards Earlskirk. When I first went on the run in the southwest it was dreadful – like a raging itch I couldn't scratch. Then while we were making our way up the western side of the mountains, it was like some kind of weird umbilical cord that tugged at me, but I could just about cope with it. That was until we crossed the range and got near to Lund. By then the only thing that deadened the pain was to get drunk. Flaming Trees, I feel like I drank the brewery dry. I'd already been downing a fair bit to keep the demon buzzing quiet, but by Lund I was working on never being fully sober – only enough to try to hang on to what was going on around me. My guts feel like someone's used the yard broom on them.

"I'm sure the men thought I'd been possessed. They must have heard that Jaenberht was at Lund and were dragging me to him to have it exorcised. And now I think they weren't so far wrong. You see, at Oswine's crowning I took the crown off Tancostyl and held it while he said the prayers before I was the one to put it on Oswine's head. I've touched it, Ruari, and it's trying to touch me. I held the DeÁine Helm!"

Chapter 19

Sea Fever

Rheged: Winterfalling

In the depths of night, with the horses' hooves muffled with the hessian bags they had used to put supplies in, the three fugitives slipped past the fort. For once they were glad it was a miserable night, with low, heavy clouds shrouding the whole mountain, and soaking them all. It was unlikely any sentry would patrol for long, or stop to look carefully into the mist, without good cause when he had water dripping down his neck. With Will now actively helping rather than hindering, their progress was much faster. So despite picking their way carefully in case they dislodged any loose rocks, they made it past the fort in less than an hour. From the west side, the road was much steeper, but it also had a wall that ran nearly at waist height along the side away from the mountainside. If caught on this stretch, they would have no way of getting the horses safely over and nowhere to go even if they did.

Yet the wall also helped them. There was no way, even in the dark, that they might miss their step and slip over the edge, or go astray. So having set out at nightfall, they pressed on through the night, hopeful that they would be low enough down the mountain to have got past the wall, and so off the road, by daybreak.

They still led the horses for the first mile or so, until the road had swept around the shoulder of the next great peak. After that it was unlikely that they would be heard, and so they freed the horses' hooves and mounted up. Even at a brisk walk, which was as fast as it was sensible to go, they made better time than on foot. By the first hint of light in the sky the road had become less steep, and in the early hours of daylight they found a drover's track crossing the road which was also obviously regularly used by heavy wagons. Ruari and Will proclaimed their satisfaction that it forded a rocky stream right by the road, and that the other side of the ford had been worn down to the rock too. There would be no telltale hoof prints to arouse the suspicions of any curious passing troops which might lead them to investigate further merely from what they saw from the road.

"Just so long as they don't have a Brother Andra who needs a leak we'll be alright," Will chuckled in good humour.

Ruari snorted in amusement too.

"It'd be the first time I've known a soldier to be bashful about that in front of his mates. You had enough trouble stopping the buggers pissing up the castle walls when the Jarl was in Caerlewl!"

"They did what?" Andra asked, astounded. He was beginning to feel that the next time he saw his own reflection he would find himself totally devoid of eyebrows – they would have joined up with this tonsure. He shook his head in resignation as the other two just laughed again. If ever he got back to the monastery nobody would ever believe him if he told them even half of what had happened so far, and it struck him that this might be nothing in comparison to what might be to come. Perhaps it would be better if he never did go back, because he would probably spend the rest of his life on his knees doing penance for telling tall stories.

For the next couple of weeks it felt to Andra as though they went continuously in circles, although the others seemed to think there was some pattern to their search. Will and Ruari had conferred as they rode north on the track, agreeing that the further north they went the fewer roads there were, and therefore fewer ways they could miss the boys. Both of them still thought of Kenelm as a boy, and it took Andra to point out that he would appear as a grown man to strangers. If they went around asking after two boys they would definitely find themselves chasing false trails. Yet, by the time they had reached Scarton, the northernmost town on the west coast, with still no sign, even Ruari had to admit they had been mistaken. Whichever way the missing youngsters had gone, it certainly had not been down the road, unless they had managed to disguise themselves very well.

Veering off to the coast, they inquired if anyone had taken a boat out of the little port of Seatoft, then trekked back inland to the larger market town of Tirkirk. They were desperately hampered in their search by the fact that there was no way they dared to take Will into the obvious place. The great castle of Caerlewl stood on a rocky knoll, menacing the port which stood at the mouth of a sluggish river, and encompassing it with a great wall. The port of Caerlewl's great virtue was that it was sheltered, and, unlike other river mouths along this stretch of coast, the river did not spend much of its life in the mountains, and so rarely went into flood to bring clogging loads of silt down in its water.

The northern bank was steeper, but that was almost totally taken up with the garrison, which sprawled down the side of the knoll and along the river. On the south side were the major quays, and the two halves might hardly have had any contact if the river itself had been navigable. As it was not, there was no need to leave the river clear for large boats, and the town possessed three enormous stone bridges, allowing the soldiers free access into the town, which had grown as rich on their trade as it had from the sea. There was therefore no way the three of them could enter any part of the town with any degree of certainty that Will would not be recognized.

Will himself was willing to hide in the woods inland while the others went in. However Ruari was unwilling to leave his friend alone. Now that he was fully sober, it was often obvious that Will felt twinges of pain, and his gaze would be drawn inadvertently to the way back east. Apart from a genuine wish never to see his friend in the hands of a DeÁine, Ruari feared what Tancostyl might dredge out of Will's mind under torture. With Jaenberht finally having the advantage of armed men at his disposal, and with the potential of the remaining Knights in the east being brought back and being able to fight too, it was essential that Tancostyl be kept in the dark of such movements.

So Caerlewl was out of bounds, and they consequently waited until they saw a whole herd of people heading out of the town and tagged along with them on the road south. By the look of it, it had been a good market day, with ships in the harbour not only bringing but buying too, and their fellow travellers were in good spirits. In the noisy, jovial snake of people riding, walking, and driving various kinds of wagons, the three of them were indistinguishable to curious eyes.

Ruari had said nothing to the other two, but he was worried by the number of rooks he was seeing on the wing of late. However much his eyes scoured the woods which wrapped themselves around the feet of the mountains he could not spot any large rookeries. In the summer they would be less conspicuous, but now that the leaves were already falling fast, the great scruffy bundles of twigs which rooks nested in usually stood out from far away. For this many birds to be native to these parts there should have been several great colonies, and some of them should have been close enough to the road to be seen. He was becoming deeply worried that Tancostyl had sent the birds searching. Creatures of such limited intelligence could carry no specific messages, of course. What Ruari feared was that they had been primed so that they sensed the taint of the Helm in Will and it drew them to him, while they in turn conveyed the general sense of where Will was to the war-mage. It would be so much easier to find Will if an armed force out of Caerlewl knew they only had to search the road going south.

Luckily most of the travellers were not climbing towards Fell Castle, sitting at the foot of the mountains, which the fugitives had avoided the first time by taking the northern track. There was little in the rocky mountains for ordinary folk. They were following the coast, going to the tiny hamlets which spread along it between Caerlewl and the next decent-sized port of Little Thorpe, which had long since grown beyond its name. At least when they reached that town they could safely make inquiries, even though it transpired it was to no avail.

What Ruari did notice was that having taken a room in a tavern right on the waterfront, Will seemed more comfortable. Despite the proximity of beer in quantities, he was more interested in a buxom, blond serving girl, who was equally enthusiastically flirting back with him. Will was blatantly far from wanting to feel numb. Their room's window opened out over a steep rocky drop to the sea, and Ruari had taken the opportunity to leave it open and allow the sea breeze in for as long as possible until it turned cold with the falling night. By the second day Will had even acquired his more normal healthy colour, and Ruari was adapting his plans in the light of this.

That night, after another fruitless day's searching, he sat with Andra enjoying the warmth of the fire in the large, busy bar. The little monk was also enjoying having a real bed to sleep in. Ruari was mildly amused at the soft sighs of pleasure he had heard the previous night as Andra had lowered himself onto the plump mattress – even disregarding the fact that he was sharing with Will – and stretched himself out under the warmth of the duck-feather quilt. Ruari had to admit he too was making the most of it, and he therefore agreed to make an early night of it, given that they would be moving on the next day and be back to sleeping in the open.

Lulled into a sense of well-being, Ruari had quite forgotten that Andra was unused to travelling with Will. It was only as he stepped onto the landing, a few feet from their door behind Andra, that he registered the noises coming from the room beyond. Andra gave a gasp of fear and leapt for the door, and Ruari's hand missed as he reached out to grab Andra's shoulder. Flinging the door open, Andra skidded to a halt as he was treated to the sight of Will's bare behind pumping up and down on the barmaid's, both hands grasping her voluminous breasts as she bent over the wash stand and screamed her encouragement. The blush must have started at Andra's boots, Ruari thought, because it certainly ended at the top of his tonsure.

"You want a turn?" Will called cheerfully between gasps, and Andra turned and fled, almost knocking Ruari off his feet.

Ruari could not help but laugh. Nothing could have proved to him that Will was back to normal than that. Then he suddenly realized how shocking it must have been to an innocent like Andra and backed out, closing the door behind him. He took the stairs two at a time back down into the bar. Another barmaid, who had obviously guessed what had happened, grinned and gestured Ruari towards the stable, following it up with a suggestive wink of her own, letting him know that he could have the same if he wanted. She had had her eye on the tall, muscular, blonde man, who was a substantial step up from the local lads, since he had arrived.

Ruari was not oblivious to her charms, but thought one horny bastard was enough to be remembered by in nine months time. With so much time spent campaigning in the more desolate parts of the Islands, he was not sure what his own track record might be like, but Will seemed to father offspring like a buck rabbit. No wonder he had taken the massacre at Montrose Castle personally – most of the women had shared his bed at some time, and it was no coincidence that a lot of the youngsters had similar features. By some miracle none of them seemed to hold a grudge against him for it, but here it might be different. Ruari had no desire to find a troop of irate fathers and husbands from Little Thorpe dogging their steps.

Jogging out to the stables he found no sign of Andra. Out of the yard he was faced with a decision of which way the embarrassed monk might have fled. The one way led into the town and the other to the now deserted quay. This latter path seemed more probable, for Ruari guessed Andra would avoid people if possible. Sure enough, as he turned the final corner, he spotted a small figure sitting hunched miserably on the end of the sea wall. Slowing to a walk, he strolled over and swung his long legs over the edge to sit beside his cringing companion, who deliberately avoided his eye.

"I'm sorry, brother, I should have thought," Ruari apologized. "I'm so used to Will and his ways I forgot you don't know him."

"He's an animal!" Andra spat back with amazing venom.

For once it was Ruari who was astonished. Even knowing Andra's background, it had not entered his head that the naive brother might so totally misunderstand what he had seen. Now it was Ruari who felt embarrassed. Of all the trials he had anticipated, he had never included having to explain the facts of life to a grown man. Desperately clawing for the right words, he cleared his throat and prepared to mentally plunge into the morass.

"It's quite natural, you know, sex that is. Let's face it, none of us would be here without it…"

"I know that!" Andra snapped. "I'm not a complete fool, you know!"

Ruari was now totally at sea.

"Then what's your problem?"

"He's raping that woman! And you have to ask if there's a problem?" Andra now looked at Ruari as though he had gone mad, especially when Ruari started to laugh.

"That's not rape! By the Hounds of the Hunt, brother, I don't know of any sane woman who'd be screaming with pleasure when she was being raped!"

"That was pleasure?" Andra was aghast.

"Oh don't ask me why or how, but Will's never had any complaints from his women, and many of them openly come back to him when he passes back through their town. Of course, he freely admits he prefers the ones who are lusty and willing. I know it's hard for you to understand, but that's why he's scared stiff of Matti. She wanted to be romanced when she was married off to him at the tender age of sixteen. Will hadn't got a clue how to do that – still hasn't. Worse still, she wanted the kind of courtship that would live up to her ideals. Someone who would read poetry with her. Listen to a minstrel playing sad love songs. Utterly terrifying to a man who's never read a book in his life, and whose pleasure gets gauged by the depth of cleavage. Matti intimidates him so much he's never gone near her, then or since. But that doesn't mean other women see him in the same light, and even she respected the fact that he wasn't so mean-spirited to take her by force, which some men would have done."

"And you like poetry and music," Andra mused.

Ruari winced, and wondered how to extract himself from this conversation before Andra took anything else at cross- purposes.

"Oh Flaming Trees! …Yes, I like those things, but that's because I had a very different childhood from Will. My mother was a bright, intelligent, free-spirited woman who taught herself to read, and encouraged me to read anything that came my way. I was only the bastard son of a nobleman."

Even now he felt unwilling to reveal to Andra that he was the old Jarl's son, and therefore had a claim to the throne, however dubious. He would probably never have got Andra up off his knees again.

"Nobody expected me to have to inherit a title and an estate, and defend it. I could as well have gone into a monastery as the Knighthood, or become a minstrel – it didn't matter. Will's life was different. His mother was a sad soul who was used as a brood mare by his father, and Will himself was dragged out into the practice yard almost as soon as he could walk. He didn't have a chance. It was no wonder *he* couldn't talk to Matti, but right from when we met, Matti and I have talked about things. Not because of any romance, but because I was used to having intelligent women around me, and I wasn't bothered by it. Men and women can be friends, Andra, it's just that at court it's rare, and you've not spent time amongst villagers where it's more normal."

Andra was not convinced by this. He was quite sure Lady Montrose was in love with Ruari, and having seen Will in action had done nothing to dissuade him of his views. It took more cross-examining of Ruari before he was convinced that the barmaid was in their room by choice, at which point he felt very foolish. An hour had passed before Ruari could persuade him back into the inn. Then Ruari did a scouting trip to their room to check on the state of things, but only found Will collapsed on the bed in a deep, contented sleep. Pulling the covers over his friend to hide his state of undress, he retrieved Andra from the staircase. This time Andra took the truckle bed while Ruari lay down on the large bed next to Will, too tired to fight him for the covers and so stayed dressed.

The next morning he had to pull Will to one side and warn him against teasing Andra about the night before. Typically, Will could not imagine why Andra had been so disconcerted by the experience, but he was in too good a mood to argue. Back on the road that mood evaporated as they turned inland once more and lost sight of the sea. More worrying was the reappearance of the rooks and other carrion birds. The others noticed them now and Ruari confided his fears to them. They were torn between travelling at night, when they might miss some sign of those they were tracking, and travelling by day when they became the hunted. In the end they carried on travelling by day simply because there was nowhere they could easily turn off to lose their trackers. The high mountains on their left had no valleys which ran anywhere, and the moorland leading to the coast to their right was so bald as to afford no cover.

It was a relief to reach the coastal town of Bridgeport after several anxious days. With the sea breeze, Will's pain eased again and the birds lessened, although there were still more circling with the gulls than Ruari would have liked to see. Down at the quayside they found another inn and began the weary process of inquiries again. Andra had proved to be the one whom most people responded to best. However hard Will and Ruari tried to disguise it, most people seemed to regard them as potentially dangerous men – something in their eyes was the best way Andra could explain it. Whatever it was though, few of those they spoke to willingly volunteered information, and so Andra had become their spokesman.

As they strolled along the harbour, trying to put themselves in Kenelm and Wistan's shoes, they spotted many small boats coming and going. Across the water the mountainous tree-scape of Ergardia often became visible through the misty autumn air, rising tantalizingly across the short sound. Seeing this, it occurred to them all that leaving Rheged altogether might have seemed an attractive prospect for the fleeing pair. When they came to a cluster of old fishermen, sitting mending nets in the fleeting sunshine, Andra was dispatched to find out if anyone had hired a boat to take them across. From where Will and Ruari stood they could see the old men shaking their heads, but then one be-whiskered old salt raised a gnarled hand and measured off someone's height and then tapped his leg. Andra was on his way back when the significance hit Ruari.

"Nothing," Andra said as he got within ears' shot.

"Hang on," Ruari stepped up to him. "That old boy was describing someone though, wasn't he?"

"Yes," Andra sighed, "but it was an older man with a young man he said was his nephew with him. I think he was much too old. Those men said he had gray hair and was going bald, so that wasn't Kenelm. And the nephew was grown up, at least my height – that can't be Wistan."

"No, but it could be Iago and Matti!" Ruari exclaimed.

"But he said two men," Andra replied, perplexed.

Will, however, was grinning and nodding in agreement as Ruari said,

"And how tall is Matti? She spent a lot of time practicing with a bow and she could out-ride most men. She's not the buxom type. All it would take would be a change of clothes and a haircut, and it would be a lot safer to travel as Iago's nephew when they were likely to be hunted as a man and a woman."

Ruari brushed past Andra and went to the men, this time giving them the description of Iago. Cautious nods accompanied his speech and their replies, but when he returned to the others it was with the news that Iago and Matti had almost certainly left from the port two weeks ago for Ergardia. That night the mood over dinner was almost celebratory at the knowledge that at least two of their friends were safe and sound.

After breakfast the next day, Ruari insisted they walk along the sea shore as the tide was out. Once they were amongst the rock pools, in the lee of a rocky promontory he broke the news to them.

"We're splitting up."

"What?" Will and Andra gasped.

"Look," Ruari explained. "Someone has to go after them and tell them what's happened. Will, you can't go on like this. You're so much more at ease by water that I've been thinking since Little Thorpe that we need to get you across the sea. If anything happened to us, how long could you cope on your own?"

"Not long," Will admitted ruefully.

"And yet we still have to find Wistan and Kenelm. We're alright for a while, down this stretch through the western mountains, but beyond that you'd be a hunted man again. That hampers Andra and me from going into the towns where there are garrisons. Common sense would normally tell most people to stay away from places like that, but those two are so naive that we can't make such an assumption. On the other hand, I know Iago. I'd bet my Knighthood on him taking Matti straight to the Order in Ergardia. He knows Jaenberht is acting against Oswine and he'll want to let the Knights know that, even if he doesn't know how many of our own men survive. You didn't get to know him that well, Will, but Iago came with me on many a mission. There's a man who serves with the Knights in Ergardia who knows about the DeÁine like no-one else, and Iago knows who he is. You must go after them Will. The Knight's name is Talorcan. Find him and tell him MacBeth says the Abend are on the loose again."

"What's he look like, this Talorcan?" Will asked. "I don't want to go spilling this stuff out to some odd Knight who happens to be talking to my wife and then find he's the wrong one."

Ruari gazed into the distance and a smile hovered around his mouth.

"Talorcan… Well, he's tall …dark hair tied back in an intricate queue …got gray eyes …and very fit. Rides like the wind – loves, horses, hates people. Oh… And he's half DeÁine, so he'll probably pick up on the fact that something's wrong with you."

"Hound of the Flaming Wild Hunt! You're sending me to some bastard who's one of the opposition! Piss off!" Will protested.

"Cross of Swords, Will, don't say that to him, or he will take your head off! No, he's not the opposition! Talorcan was the product of a Knight and a vicious cat of a DeÁine mother, who treated him worse than a dog for being half-caste. He hates them with a passion. I can't tell you all of what happened to him because I'm under oath, but I promise you, by all that our friendship has stood for, that this man is utterly trustworthy, and that he'd give up his life for you rather than see you in the hands of the Abend. I'll give you a letter too, but trust him – he's one of us."

"What about me?" Andra asked.

"We're going to carry on trying to find our missing innocents abroad."

Suddenly there was a splash and a thump, as first a magpie fell out of the sky and landed in a rock pool, and then a crow dropped straight down onto the rocks, both dead before they hit the ground. Ruari and Will spun around scouring the cliffs and the sky but could see nothing.

In the room at the top of the keep in Earlskirk, Tancostyl swore violently as he clutched both hands to his temples in pain and staggered from the window. That was the trouble with using such frail creatures as birds – they died so easily. With his senses extended in the wide net, he had used the flocks of birds to sense the movements of the irritating general who kept interfering with his plans. Having found him, he was then in a position to follow him more closely. How frustrating that he did not know where that boy was either. Just when he needed to concentrate all his efforts on controlling the dim-witted fool whom he had put in control of this misbegotten Island, he was forced to keep one eye elsewhere. The last thing he needed was some bullish general using another heir to the throne to rally support in the west, and divide the army he was building to turn on these miserable Islanders.

So he had watched, and when he had seen the three men walking out in the morning, again he had seized control of two of the birds and forced them closer to try to listen. But all he had heard was cursed gulls shrieking over bits of fish, and the dreadful sea. What it had cost him to cross the short stretches between Brychan and Celidon, then Celidon to Ergardia, and finally make the crossing to where the three he hunted now stood, nobody else knew except his fellow Abend.

Even in the body of another, his spirit roiled nauseatingly at the proximity of the waves, yet he had forced the birds ever closer. Stupid creatures! Why had they forgotten to keep flapping those wings when his thoughts consumed them? The shock of the violent separation as they had hit the surface – their fragile lives snuffed out – had left him stunned and reeling. Head and heart pounding, he collapsed on the bed in the corner and reached for the stimulant he kept at hand in the leather beaker, gulping a mouthful down. As his senses slowly returned to normal, he felt a burning need to take his anger out on something, and his mind turned to that idiot Fulchere.

That idiot Fulchere was not half as daft as Tancostyl sometimes thought, though. He had watched with increasing fear the rising impatience of this viper he had unwittingly clutched to his breast. Why, he wondered? Why had he ever risked so much by letting that man in? If he was a man at all! Why had he compromised all that he had worked so hard to achieve? The answer was simple of course. Ambition. All his life Fulchere had wanted control. Control of his own life and control of others'. The Church had been an obvious choice. Who wanted to go into the army, let alone the Knights of the Cross, when there was a good chance that you wouldn't live to your first promotion, let alone make it to the top? So he had got on his knees and prayed, and cajoled, and worked his way up through the ranks of the brothers.

But it was not enough. The Church was always second best in Rheged. In the old manuscripts he had read with longing of the time long ago when things had been different. When there was one ruler for all the Islands, there had been a patriarch – one man to whom the archbishops of each Island were subordinate, one man to whom even they had knelt. Fulchere wanted to be a patriarch. Wanted it so much it burned in his soul. And that was what the strange priest from across the water had offered him. One day soon, he had said, the Islands would again be united under one leader. When that day came the Church would have to change and that role could be Fulchere's, if he had the courage to reach for his dream.

Except that now Fulchere had come to realize how much of a dream it was. Close contact with Tancostyl had soon taught him that this man shared power with no-one. When it came to crowning Oswine, was it Fulchere who had blessed the ancient crown? No. It had been Tancostyl, and he had insisted that that boar of a general be the one to do the crowning to placate their political enemies. When the histories came to be written of that great day, Fulchere's name would be nowhere to be found

So in the last few weeks, Fulchere had begun to wonder how he could possibly extract himself from this mess. Tancostyl's moods were becoming fouler by the day, and Fulchere had no wish to become the sacrificial lamb on the day the lords and nobles took revenge for what he had done. The death of the last Jarl had barely troubled him at the time, but as events had escalated, and the death toll had risen, he had become ever more fearful. Now that awful old man, Jaenberht, was in open opposition to the crown, and telling everyone who would listen how corrupt Fulchere was. He would never admit it out loud, but Jaenberht scared the living daylights out of him, not least because if there really were Spirits out there they were almost certainly on Jaenberht's side!

That morning he had seen Tancostyl heading for the room at the top of the keep and decided to make himself scarce. Whatever the strange bald man did up there elicited some very strange noises, and he never came down without wanting to persecute someone. So Fulchere had decided it would be a good day to visit the stud farm on the outskirts of town. The abbey of the Blessed Martyrs was a glorious work of art from the days when Jarls were more Spirit-fearing men, and its stable was a joy and delight to behold. More to the point so were its contents! The highly-strung horses were an exquisite collection of silky-coated white mares, who were kept company by a varied collection of downy-coated sheep, goats, and, in one particularly lovely combination, a great black sow.

As he rode down the road on his white mule, Fulchere was sure he heard an otherworldly shriek from the top of the castle, and quelled his fear with the thought of how wonderfully uncomplicated unions with animals were – so much easier to subject to one's will, and with no complaints about one's performance. Many were the times in his early days that Fulchere had wished he could put a halter on his human companions – of either sex – and just tie their heads to the bedstead while he got on with the real business at hand. And as for conversation afterwards – what a waste of time! Then he had heard from a traveller from afar that in a distant land they said, a woman for business, a boy for pleasure, but for sheer ecstasy a goat. He had lost no time in checking that out for himself! And had consequently discovered rapturous pleasure in having both total control and complete inhibition.

However, unbeknown to him, by now every groom in the area promptly took his animals to the farthest pasture if he knew Fulchere was visiting, rather than finding a traumatized animal in the morning. So, lost in his reverie, it took a moment for the words of the abbey's gate warden to sink in. The stables were empty! All the pretty little mares and their dear little friends, on whom he lavished equal attention, had been taken by the head groom and his assistants to the shores of a cool river for a therapeutic bathing of the hooves in the fresh water. That did nothing to cool Fulchere's ardour, though. Closeted in the abbey's guest house, Fulchere thought he might burst if he could find no release. Unable to settle, he strode out of the enclosure and into the fields, his need becoming ever more urgent. Finally, in a secluded stand of trees he spotted a tethered goat.

Half out of his mind with frustration, he caught hold of it and set about releasing his tension. It was ironic coincidence that Tancostyl, having been unable to find a dispensable person, once more cast his mind abroad with the intention of venting his fury on an unfortunate animal. Only as he fully entered the goat's mind did he fully realize what was already happening to the unfortunate animal, although not who was behind it! The sense of violation was as complete as if it was being done to his own body, and his efforts to disengage it leant strength to the goat's. However, this only urged Fulchere on to greater efforts. It was only as both men finally lost control that the goat seized its opportunity and escaped from them both – leaving one with a sore head, and the other sore testicles from the goat's parting shot.

Chapter 20

Fear and Loathing

Prydein: Winterfalling

Ivain could not remember his life being worse. Last month everything had seemed to be going so well for once, and then in one fell swoop his whole world had turned upside down. He had been pleased to see the back of his mother and Alaiz. Not because he disliked their company, far from it, but things had become so difficult between them. He knew that there was some sort of showdown building up between himself and some of the court. That had become obvious, and he had been trying to put some distance between himself and Alaiz, in particular, so that she would not become trapped in the middle.

Yet his mother had persisted in interfering, and these days Alaiz seemed to listen more to her than to him. He had tried to find some way around the situation in his long talks with Hugh de Burh, but while the Knight was a tactical genius when it came to court politics, he did not have a clue when it came to giving Ivain advice about his wife. Come to that, Ivain had never really come to terms with thinking of her as his wife. To him she was always really the sister he had grown up with, not a woman he had married. As a sister, though, he loved her dearly, and he would never have knowingly hurt her.

So it had seemed such a good idea when his mother and Amalric de Loges had come to him, and said they intended to send Alaiz to her brothers across the water in Kittermere to negotiate with them. Rapid consultation with Hugh had confirmed that spies had seen both brothers cross the water to join his rebellious cousin, Brion, at Mullion. And so with neither of those two at home anymore, Alaiz and his mother would be safe there.

Under the pretext of going hunting, he had then been able to ride over the moors to the castle and preceptory at Quies for a long tactical planning session with Hugh. However, before the week was out the first carrier bird had arrived to tell them that Brion was on the march with an army at his back. All the planning and their schemes had not predicted that he would move this quickly.

Then to top it a second bird had arrived from de Loges, telling him that the ship carrying Alaiz and Gillies had been found drifting by fishermen, with all hands dead. It looked to be the work of Attacotti pirates, and it was feared the two women must now be being held hostage. Ivain had been beside himself with worry for their safety, but Hugh had insisted that he leave negotiations to de Loges. As king he had more pressing issues, he was told.

This meant that he was now riding with an escort of Knights, as fast as relays of horses could take them, towards the ancient meeting place of Tancross. For months now, the Knights' great preceptories at Rosco, Bera and Vellan, along with their castles at Quies and Bittern, had been on full alert and amassing men and horses. Yet all these locations were, of necessity, far from the capital in order to keep these activities hidden from the prying eyes of the court – which now could turn out to be the undoing of Hugh's plans. For they had always thought they would have more notice of Brion's eventual exodus from the west towards the capital. The silence from Hugh's spies in the town had been assumed to be because nothing was happening, since they were under strict instructions to keep contact to a minimum in order to reduce the chances of exposure. However, it was now evident that they had been silenced in a more permanent way, and that was why advance warning had not happened.

Yesterday they had reached the small fishing town of Carne, and there Ivain had been greeted with amazement by his people. Messages had been sent, they said, that he was prisoner in the palace at Trevelga. Then this morning he had set off with the Knights inland, only to meet another messenger who told him he was to be executed by Brion on the steps of the palace, no less! If the people thought he was dead, how was he to convince them he was alive? Only so many of them had ever met him, and even fewer had seen him close enough to recognize him. For the rest, if they were shown a corpse and told it was the king, they would have no reason to doubt it. How easy would it be for Brion to brand him an impostor, then? It was looking increasingly difficult for him to hope to raise an army from the ordinary people to join with the Knights.

Ivain had spent the best part of the night sitting consulting with the two senior Knights Hugh had sent with him. The original plan had been to march directly on Trevelga, but if they could not rally support in any great numbers, this was now a foolhardy course of action. They had to pass through Tancross whatever they were going to do, unless it was retreat. But Tancross stood at a five-road junction. One, the north road, was the way they had come. The western road led to Pendrim and then to Trevelga. The south road led to the southern ports via Crossways, but between that road and the other main one which led back to the north-eastern port of Rosco, a little used road ran east. It still connected to the far eastern ports of Prydein, but more importantly for Ivain, as it rose to cross the east moors it came to the old hill fort of the ancient people who had once inhabited the Island. Who they were was lost in the mists of time. Their earth fortresses, though, still stood, commanding the high ground at strategic natural gateways through the rugged countryside of Prydein. At the Wyrmes Tump earthworks there had subsequently been built a strong tower surrounded by a stout wooden palisade, and it was here that it was agreed that Ivain should pause until a new plan could be made.

In this eastern part of the island, the soft rolling slopes of the moors had valleys which were heavily wooded, and the folk of these parts were famous for the quality of bows they made. Every boy was taught to draw one as soon as he was big enough to hold a practice bow, which meant that the archers of eastern Prydein were the envy of other Islanders. Their accuracy and the speed with which they could lay down volleys of deadly arrows had made them much in demand. Moreover, this had always been Ivain's favourite part of Prydein, and he had often ridden alone amongst the archer people. He liked the bluff, straight-speaking manners of these independent folk, who could accept that he was the head of this island's people without ever feeling the need to flatter or be obsequious. Hugh, as Grand Master, had accepted that Ivain knew what he was doing when he allowed these country folk such easy access to him, but Amalric had been horrified, and had done his utmost to dissuade Ivain from continuing to visit the region unescorted.

Now, though, it seemed as though these were the only people who might rally to Ivain's standard. By riding amongst them he had become familiar to them, and they alone were capable of distinguishing him from any substitute. Ivain and Captains Grimston and Haply had decided to take the chance of depleting their small force further by sending men off, as they hurried through the countryside, to rally support from the easterners. The call to arms was to rally at Wyrmes Tump with all haste for the first of Winterfalling.

Ivain rode with a heavy heart as they clattered into Tancross, pausing only to allow a substantial number of archers to grab their weapons and join them. All along he had feared what would happen if it came to civil war, and yet despite all his best efforts it seemed to be inevitable. As an icy rain began to pelt them outside of the town, Ivain wondered if it would be worthwhile surrendering himself if it would save countless other lives. Then he shook the thought away with the water in his hair. *He* was not the problem. In his heart of hearts he knew that Hugh was right when he said that Brion would always find one more thing he wanted, but could not have. One more excuse to have a fight, regardless of what it cost others. No, surrendering would only mean that Brion would have unopposed control of Prydein's army to use to start his next war with. If it was not Ivain he was fighting, it would be someone else. Peace was an alien concept to Brion.

On an evilly cold first of the month, they mounted the shoulder of the open moor, and in a howling wind made their way into the limited shelter of the earthworks at Wyrmes Tump. At least the palisade which encircled the outer ramp deflected the worst of the wind for the men, so that the majority elected to stay there rather than go to the exposed summit. Ivain would have liked to accommodate them all in the tower, but it was far too small. The walls were massively thick, but it was only one room on top of another. The ground floor was the stable, the first the kitchen and store, the second and third combined living and sleeping quarters, and for few men at that.

On Ivain's instruction, the Knights' horses and his own were tethered on the opposite side of the tower to the prevailing wind, to allow the ground floor to be used to get cooking fires going so that the men could have hot food. Otherwise, in the ever building wind and rain it would have been near impossible to light a fire which would grow hot enough to cook on.

It was a miserable night for all concerned. Throughout the hours of darkness men continued to drift in from far and wide. Those from the south brought grim news with them. As they had walked over the high open moors, they had been able to see down to the road from Crossways into the distance. Snaking along it they had seen a long procession of torches, hinting at a major force heading their way.

What nobody could explain was how the wind seemed to be deflected around the moving column, as though an invisible tunnel rose above it protecting them from the wind and rain. The last night of this coming month, folklore said, the Spirits walked abroad and those who did not rest easy would take their vengeance. No-one had ever claimed to see an army before, though, and Ivain and the Knights thought this sounded much too much like Brion than any Spirit, even if they could not explain the phenomenon.

Come the morning they had not long to wait before the sound of horses hooves, bits, and the metallic chinking of armour heralded the approach of the opposing force. From the top of the tower roof, Haply, Grimston and Ivain could see its approach in the gaps between the trees. They agreed that the force was smaller than they had dared hope, which in one sense was a good thing. The bad news was that to a man it was made up of apparently battle-seasoned veterans, professional soldiers from Brion's army. Brion had been campaigning for years against the Attacotti, giving his men more than enough fights, large and small, to have become expert. Yet at a distance Ivain had no fears that his archers could hold them at bay and possibly even win the first encounter.

What worried all three was what would happen if they could not break out after that first skirmish. If they became surrounded, sooner or later they would run out of arrows, and then the experience of the fighters would begin to tell. In a hand to hand combat situation it could turn into a blood bath. Normally archers were deployed forward of the cavalry and foot soldiers, but once their killing first volleys had done their worst, they would break ranks and allow the rest of the army to overtake them. From then on, they would find any high ground which enabled them to fire at specific targets from behind the main line. No experienced commander wasted archers, who took years to become fully skilled, in the mêlée, and so they never practiced with swords, spears and daggers.

Now, from their vantage point the three leaders watched the archers preparing. Then they saw the oncoming company split in two as they began to fan out on either side of the track they had used to ascend the moor on. Suddenly Grimston swore bitterly. Haply and Ivain turned and followed his gaze back behind them. From over a ridge in the distance another snake of men was appearing from down in the Crossways valley. The troops beneath the ramparts would soon have enough reinforcements to make it possible to besiege the tower and just wait until hunger and thirst drove them out. Ivain could not believe their bad luck, then his thoughts turned to the men below. These were farmers on whom whole families depended. An honourable opponent would imprison the leaders and let the rest go back to their ploughs. But Brion was not honourable, and Ivain could too easily imagine the pleasure he would get from slaughtering them to a man, forgetting their potential use for any later battles.

The three exchanged looks, then Ivain said,

"We have to let the men go, I can't have the blood of them, and the families who will starve if they die, on my conscience."

"No, sire, you can't do that," Captain Haply reprimanded him sadly. "The men will be cut to pieces if they leave now. You have no choice but to fight."

"Hang on a minute, though," Grimston said thoughtfully, "there might be a way."

The others looked at him expectantly.

"What if we go on the offensive now, and I mean now, before that lot draw up their battle lines? Go out in skirmish order. All our men down there know how to stalk game, so let's give them a fight they're good at. It's no use letting Brion's veterans fight on their terms or we'll be decimated."

Comprehension drew Haply's face into a growing smile.

"De Burh's Gambit!" he said, then saw Ivain's blank expression. "It happened to the Master many years ago when he was still a young Knight, but he was good even then. By going on the attack against a superior force, but before they were ready, he managed to create confusion and inflict heavy casualties. What the enemy didn't expect was that he would go right *through* the enemy lines, rather than falling back to the defensive position again. Normally you try to keep your men together, but this time they split up into small groups. They went in hard, and they went in fast. So fast, they were through before the enemy realized what they were doing."

"Yes," Grimston carried on. "Now *our* men won't be going through a drawn-up rank, so it won't matter that they aren't good at hand-to-hand. If we send them out with a couple of our mounted soldiers with each group to make sure they don't get ridden down, it should do the trick. If we split up, they're going to have to split up too, so at worst it shouldn't be possible for any but a single group to be ridden down by a large band of horsemen. We won't come out unscathed, I'm afraid, but it's our best hope for saving the maximum number of lives."

Ivain looked from one to the other and then nodded his assent.

"Alright, let's do it," he said. He let the other two go in front down the narrow stair, and cast a glance back at the on-coming reinforcements. In the back of his mind he still had nagging doubts. Brion would still be seeking him, so what reprisals would he be capable of?

Below, the two captains had called their sergeants to them and now the earthworks were a hive of activity. Within minutes, signals were coming back that the men were ready. Ivain stood back. Haply and Grimston didn't need him getting in the way, and this was not the time to start finding out if Hugh's tactics lessons had made sense to him. His pulse was pounding as he watched the men pour out of the palisades and scatter. A lump of pride came in his throat as he watched them working in teams, one man dropping to his knee and covering the line of fire as the others ran past, then another taking over giving covering fire as the first ran to join them. Miraculously not one of the archers fell in the first scattering, their opponents were so caught off guard. It was only when his own men began to shoot into the enemy with a vengeance that return volleys opened up.

When the archers had got a fair distance out from the earthen ramparts, the mounted soldiers dug their heels into their horses' flanks and pounded out to join the fray. Ivain was at the rear, and so took the circuit around the fortifications to avoid riding into those already fanning out. As he came clear of the slopes, and onto the moor heading north, he looked back and saw that, while most of his men were already melting into the scrubby woods at the top of the valley, all was not well. The reinforcements must have realized what was going on and sent cavalry forward, which was pounding towards them. To his horror he could also see flames rising from the two nearest farms, and the families being herded along in front of some other horsemen.

From across the countryside a voice carried unnaturally clearly.

"Give up Ivain!" it commanded. "Give up and the king will spare the people. Fight, and Tancross burns!"

Ivain felt sick. The voice was like an oil-slick on the air, enough in itself to make him retch. Whoever it was must be the source of the strange passage of troops the night before. He had thought until today that wizards were the thing of children's stories and vaguely comical fantasies. There was nothing imaginary or whimsical about this creature, though. He did not doubt for one moment that the threat would be used, yet before he could even think about it the voice slithered across the space again.

"I'll count to ten. If you haven't begun to ride towards me by then, the burning will start."

At that moment Haply and Grimston came thundering up to him and grabbed the reins of his horse turning its head northwards away from the voice.

"No!" Ivain screamed at them.

"Sire, you cannot surrender!" Grimston yelled back, then gasped in horror as a ball of fire flew over their heads towards Tancross. Within seconds it crossed the moor and dropped out of sight. Moments later they heard a hollow thump and then smoke began to rise.

"Blessed Oak protect us!" Haply gasped.

"You must let me go," Ivain wept. "How can you fight that? You can't protect me from what you can't see. Go! Save yourselves, save your men, save my people!"

He pulled his horse free of their slipping grips and turned back the way he had come, galloping as hard as he could to the enemy lines.

Afterwards he would be hard pressed to recall the details of what happened next. He remembered men seizing hold of him, and being dragged in front of the most frightening man he had ever seen. Tall and skeletally thin, he looked like a walking corpse, but the worst thing was his eyes. It was like looking into pools of swirling black oil. No pupil, no iris, no whites, just inky darkness which seemed to be reflecting something Ivain could not quite see. At that point the bony hand clamped onto his forehead and Ivain passed out.

When he came to he was once more in the tower, on the second floor. At the ancient long table the stranger sat eating a bowl of exotic fruit, which must have been brought in for him as it certainly had not been in the supplies Ivain's men had had. Next to him a stocky man, with flaming hair which stood straight out from his head like a gorse bush, tore into a chicken with vulpine ferocity. Turstin, Alaiz's brother! Men-at-arms stood all around the walls eying the food hungrily but not daring to move. One of them noticed Ivain had awoken and booted him forward to the table. If the display of man-power was supposed to overawe or frighten him, Ivain thought, it singularly failed, since the men were blatantly scared stiff of the stranger. Hard men they might be, but they knew when they were out of their depth, and Ivain did not think for one moment that the stranger needed any help from them should Ivain have tried to attack him.

The stranger fastidiously dipped his bony fingers into a bowl of water which stood at this elbow, and then wiped them dry on a napkin, which had equally not been part of Ivain's supplies. With a look of distaste at the carnivorous goings on next to him, he stood up and walked around to Ivain. Going by the fact that the torches around the walls were lit, Ivain guessed it must be night once more, which meant he had been unconscious for hours. The stranger filled him with dread for reasons he could not rationalize. The man was dressed in a lightweight black cloth which swirled in the draughts of the tower. It gave the appearance of being a multi-layered shift over which was thrown a sleeveless jerkin, although, unlike any jerkin normal men wore, this one came almost to the floor. As he drew closer Ivain could see that it had symbols in some kind of strange script worked on it, black on black.

A bony finger hooked under his chin and drew his face up until he looked the stranger in the face. Ivain was shaking so hard he thought it was a good thing he was kneeling already, because he would have ended up down there if he had been standing. The eyes were now more normal in that the whites had reappeared, but the pupils retained the swirling blackness and were surrounded by irises of icy water. Not the slightest vestige of humanity lay in them. They were utterly alien.

"You really are a pathetic creature," the oily voice dripped disdain. "Look at you squatting in your own excrement."

Ivain realized that at some point in the lost hours, his bladder had given way and he blushed with shame. He had hardly been feeling heroic to start with, but now he felt disgusted with himself. However, the stranger was carrying on regardless.

"Do you know who I am? No of course you don't. What a dreary backwater this is, but we'll soon change all of that. I am Calatin! You will kneel to me!" He gave a maniacal laugh as he raised his hands above his head and seemed to look through the ceiling to the dark sky as he roared. "The world will kneel to me!"

At that point a hesitant knock came at the wooden screen which separated the room from the rising staircase, and a messenger came fearfully in. He said nothing but held out a rolled parchment to Calatin, who plucked it from his fingers and shook it loose. Tutting at its contents, he dismissed the soldiers with a flick of his wrist, with a parting instruction to be ready to depart.

"We're leaving?" the red-head asked. "I thought we were going to find and punish those men of his. Brion won't like it that we only killed a handful. He likes plenty of dead when he wins."

Ivain's heart leapt at the news. Whatever else happened his men were free!

"Yes, dog-Turstin. But it's your master who recalls us now."

"Why?"

"Really, you are a tiresome creature. Why can't you obey orders without question? You would if you were my dog. If you must know, some interfering Knights rescued that feeble creature of a Grand Master of theirs. Quite why they bothered is beyond me. He was nearly dead when I'd finished questioning him. Such feeble creatures you Islanders, you're no sport at all. I'm quite wasted using my Power on you. Still, your master wishes me to use it to trace the lost prisoner, so, I must feed first."

"You just ate," Turstin protested, "and you promised me we'd be staying here the night and I'd have time for a woman."

"Well you'd better hurry up about it then, hadn't you?" Calatin said, not bothering to hide his distaste.

"What about him?" Turstin asked, gesturing at Ivain.

"You wish to copulate with him?" Calatin queried with more puzzlement this time.

"No!" Turstin snapped back in disgust. "I meant what are we going to do with him?"

"Whatever you like," Calatin said, bored again. "He knows nothing except his petty schemes, which have already come to nothing. Play with him if you wish. He's dead already, after all. Now I must regain my strength."

He picked up the length of chain which was attached to the manacles on Ivain's wrists, effortlessly dragged him backwards despite Ivain's size, and dropped it over a spike on the wall too high for Ivain to reach with his hands behind his back. There then followed one of the most bizarre hours Ivain had ever spent. The wizard went to the table and picked up the salt bowl. On the floor before the window he inscribed a circle of salt and then two intersecting triangles within it. Flinging the shutter open he then shrugged himself out of the jerkin and robes. Underneath them he was completely naked and in this state he lay down on the diagram, arms and legs spread to touch the circumference of the circle. Moments later he opened his mouth and a ghostly mist rose from the inert body and sped out of the window.

Calatin's body was the most asexual thing Ivain had ever seen. It was totally hairless and had the genitals of a small child, barely qualifying as male. In contrast, Turstin belched loudly, looked down on the recumbent form and left the room. Minutes later Ivain heard a scream which was repeated and got closer. Turstin appeared around the screen dragging a plump, middle-aged woman. With appalling, casual violence, he back-handed her across the room to the table, then pushed her down onto it. As she began to cry out again, he swiped her hard once more before throwing her skirts up and ripping at her underclothes.

"Shut up!" he bellowed. "You're not my first choice either!"

He held her down with one hand and unlaced his breeches with the other, in moves that spoke to Ivain of much practice. Ivain himself had never found it necessary to deal with the laces one-handed, let alone do it while holding someone down. Holy Spirits, how many women had Turstin raped to get that much practice? He was on top of her now, having ripped open her bodice.

"Normally *I* prefer some firm-titted pussy," he panted, "not some old cow with udders."

But still he continued to bite and suck as he pounded away. Through his tears of frustration and despair Ivain suddenly realized Turstin had one hand clamped over the woman's mouth and that she was starting to turn blue. As her struggles became more frantic, Turstin only seemed to get more aroused. Ivain lunged forward but could not get his fetters free. He screamed for help. Screamed for someone to help the woman, not him. But nobody came. Then it stopped. Satiated, Turstin slid to his knees panting, as Ivain strained to see if the woman was showing signs of still breathing.

At that moment a greater, thicker cloud slid in at the window and into Calatin's mouth again. Instantly, the wizard rose to his feet, drew the robes back up, and took in the room with one sweeping glance. A wave of his hand brought a waft of air which dispersed the salt.

"Come, Dog, you've had your bone," he called as he strode out.

Snarling, Turstin struggled to his feet and staggered after his master as he struggled to do up the laces he had undone with such ease.

Left alone and unable to move, Ivain sobbed out his despair. The poor soul on the table remained unmoving and Ivain could do nothing to help her. He had never felt the weight of his illustrious father and grandfather's reputations as heavily as now. They would have been out of here by now, rallying troops, fighting impossible odds and winning, not crying like a girl and unable to aid one helpless woman. The chill of the night came in through the open window, and the icy wind froze him to the marrow.

Hours passed. The tower went quiet around him. Many men had ridden out with Calatin and Turstin, and the ones left to garrison the tower never came near him. In the dark hours before dawn he would have hung himself on the chain if he could have found a way. The complete mess he had made of his life tortured the unending minutes measured in his slow, painful heartbeats. Alaiz was possibly dead, as was his mother. He had failed them. He had failed Hugh. Failed to acquire the most basic ability to rule. Failed his people. Not even the moon saw his misery, shrouded as it was in black clouds which then began to shed the first damp, sleety showers of winter.

Suddenly an arrow flew in through the open shutters and embedded itself into the wood boards of the floor above. A string was looped through a hole behind the flights, and Ivain saw it start to feed through. Before his astonished eyes a grappling hook appeared, then the string went slack and the hook dropped to catch on the central stone tracery of the window. Moments passed and then a head appeared above the sill.

"Is it clear?" Haply's voice hissed. The last flickering torch gave him some light in the chamber, but he could see little other than Ivain crouched opposite. Ivain nodded, and Haply hauled himself up and wriggled through the narrow gap.

"Grimston wanted to come but he's too big to get through there," he panted as he dropped to the floor. Padding stealthily across the floor, one eye on the stair screen, he unhooked Ivain's chain.

"Key?" he whispered.

Ivain shook his head. Haply cast around and found the woman's shawl, which he used to bind up the chains so that Ivain could hold them without them clanking. He checked for the woman's pulse, but shook his head sadly at Ivain's hopeful stare. Going to the window, he leaned out and shook his head a second time to those below, gesturing that Ivain's hands were tied so that he would not be capable of climbing down. Taking the string, he lowered the hook back down to those outside, then stood on a chair and pulled the arrow free so that no trace of how he got in remained.

With Haply in the lead, drawn sword in hand, the two crept to the stairs and down the first flight. From behind the screen on the first floor, multiple snores sent up a deafening racket. Like ghosts, the two slid past the opening between the top of the stair-screen and the ceiling – the one spot where they were visible from the room – but nobody woke. Reaching the stables on the ground floor, they realized why the defenders slept so soundly. The window shutters were barred on the floor where they slept, and down here there were no openings except for the door, and that was securely barricaded. A huge oak beam lay across the door resting in solid iron cups. The two exchanged worried glances, as they crouched on the stairs using the little light they had to survey the scene.

They had to get past the horses, which might not be too bad as long as none of the animals was nervous. The problem was that bar. It was massive and way too heavy for one man to lift alone, and Haply was not a big man. However, there was nothing for it but to try – it was the only way out. Mentally trying to note where each horse stood, they edged their way across the floor with only one or two restive movements from the animals.

At the door they paused. Very softly, Haply tapped twice on the wood and got a whispered voice replying. Talking through the tiny gap of the hinge, in few words Haply told his fellow rescuers of the problem. He was about to try to lift the bar when Ivain nudged him.

"Stop," he whispered. "Look, if I bend I can get my shoulder under the beam and help you lift it. You'll have to steady it. I'll have no control. But if we get it over the cup, then I can pin it against the door while you lift the other end."

Haply paused then whispered back his doubtful agreement. With a heave they got the oak trunk up onto Ivain's shoulder and started to lift. With no control it was agonizing as it tilted and the corner edge bit into Ivain's flesh. Wobbling furiously, they managed to lift it clear of the bracket, and then Ivain had to use all his weight thrown against the door to try to hold it.

Even then it began to slip and was slid rather than lifted out of the second bracket. With Haply hanging on for grim death, they managed a controlled slither against the wall to the floor. It was not silent by any means, but it was not the kind of sharp thump that would wake the sleeping, either. By sheer good luck it missed the nearest horse and ploughed into a pile of hay. Scratched and bruised, the two staggered to their feet and stared anxiously towards the stairs. Easing the lone door open, Haply shoved Ivain out while watching their backs, and then slipped out too.

Figures surrounded them, draping a heavy cloak around Ivain's shoulders and hustling him away from the tower, as Haply eased the door shut again and followed them into the snowy night.

Chapter 21

Reality Dawns

Prydein: Winterfalling

As Winterfalling drew on, the sleet showers turned occasionally to proper snow, and although it barely settled in the south, up on the northern moors of Prydein the white blanket began to stick in earnest. And Oliver Aleyne, leader of the rescue party, was near tearing his hair out with trying to move his party on.

"By the Wild Hunt, sire," Friedl swore, as the white curtain thickened, "this is unseasonably early in the year, Winterfalling or not."

"Do you think it some infamy of that stranger my lady spoke of?" Bertrand asked softly so she would not hear. The Knights had begun to develop a soft spot for this unassuming queen whom Hamelin had brought into their midst, and nobody wanted to upset her further.

"I don't know." Oliver mused. "I'd like to think not – that we're just in for a hard winter – but how can we be sure? If the fog can contain a thing that hunts and kills and appears at will, who knows what villainy might affect the weather?"

The men on horseback could easily cope with the depth of snow at the moment, which barely covered the horses' hooves. How long that would last, though, was something none of them could guess. The wagon containing Amalric de Loges was something else, though, and was already starting to slip and slide on the steeper hills. Oliver desperately wanted to transfer him to a horse. However, their leader was taking much longer to recover from the punishment he had received in the dungeons at Trevelga than even their most pessimistic estimations. It was also becoming evident that he was hardly a seasoned trooper. Oliver and Hamelin at first were careful to voice their suspicions only to one another over their leader's weakness. However, it was not long before the others were heard murmuring their surprise at Amalric's unwillingness to endure the slightest pain. In quiet conversations away from the wagon, they all agreed that their revered former Master, Hugh, had obviously chosen de Loges for his ability to mix at court and bring back information, rather than any combat worthiness.

They had started out taking the road westwards to Coombe from the capital, on the basis that it was not the most direct route to Quies and would therefore not be the first to be searched. A search was sure to happen, but they did not need to make it any easier for their pursuers. In the low rolling woods and farmlands it had been easy enough for the escort to ride off to the sides, far enough away not to look like they were following a farm wagon, but close enough to help if problems arose. However, as they drove into Coombe, Alaiz had realized where she was. Frantically gesturing Oliver over to the wagon where she rode with Hamelin, she had told him the strange fog had been first heard of on this road. The Knights consequently rode straight through the town and then held a council of war in the next belt of woodland.

They had voted to continue, but were still debating whether they dared risk the moors with some unnatural force with a blood lust hunting there, when their lookout whistled the birdcall warning. All went silent, Hamelin sliding into the back of the wagon to muffle de Loges' voice should he wake at such a bad time. Along the road they had just left, a troop of men rode by accompanied by a high-flying flock of rooks. The men rode on, but the rooks circled for many minutes before wheeling off to follow them.

"What was that all about?" Friedl asked, when the sky was clear once more.

"There was nothing natural about the way those birds behaved, for sure." Bertrand commented, and Oliver agreed.

"Well that's torn it. They're almost certainly hunting us. We were lucky they didn't catch us on the road."

"Is it worth travelling at night?" another Knight, called Gilbert, asked.

"In this weather?" Hamelin exclaimed.

"You're right," Oliver sighed. "Normally, Gilbert, I'd say yes, but what's the point when we're going to leave tracks any fool could follow? We don't have time to keep covering them up. Anyway that wagon is already sliding all over the place. If we keep going in the dark and hit an icy patch it could be off the road altogether."

The Knight's looked at one another glumly, until Alaiz, trying to be positive, piped up.

"But now we're on this road we won't be the only wagon will we? Bradley, the carter who helped me, said he had to use the same inns because he knew they'd find room for him even if they were packed out. He's coming back this way in a couple of weeks himself providing he doesn't think it's too dangerous."

"That's rather the point, though, isn't it," Oliver mused. "Will there be others if word of this thing has gone the rounds?"

"Doesn't look like we have much choice, does it?" Friedl said glumly.

The little band hauled the wagon back onto the road and carried on with heavy hearts. Oliver now saw no point in keeping the riders spread out, and they rode split between the front and rear of the wagon. Beyond Haile, they were on an open stretch of road which began the climb into the hills when Bertrand's sharp eyes spotted movement on the way far above. It was the circling rooks which gave away who it was on the high stretch of road.

The Knights threw back the heavy cloaks, drew on their mail-backed gloves, and eased swords in their scabbards in case the bitter cold had frozen them together.

"What do we do with them, Oliver?" Friedl asked softly gesturing with a tilt of his head towards Alaiz and Amalric, still in the wagon.

"What can we do?" Oliver sighed. "We just have to win and hope nobody gets behind us to them."

But Alaiz had no intention of being caught by Brion's men. Leaning forward to the coupling, she unhitched the horses, blessing Bradley and all he had taught her. With quick fingers she got rid of all the tack except the bridles, shortened the reins, and then threw blankets from the wagon over the cart horses' broad rumps. Leading them back alongside the wagon, she tethered them to the side and then got in beside Amalric.

"Get up!" she commanded.

Amalric looked at her as though she had gone mad.

"I can't," he said feebly.

"You will, or you'll die! Which is it to be?" Alaiz's voice brooked no argument. "Flaming Trees, Amalric, your wounds stopped bleeding days ago, and half the pain you feel is because you've been lying as still as those turnips and your bruises have stiffened. So get up!"

"I can't," he said pathetically.

"Fine! Then you'll just go back to Brion's dungeons and get more of the same, won't you!" Alaiz was furious. "By the Wild Hunt, Amalric, I once thought you to be the ideal Knight, not some spineless coward!"

The Knights had turned to watch open-mouthed at this barracking of their leader. She was not sure whether it was the tone of voice or her swearing that surprised them most, but Alaiz was in full flow now.

"I thought you were supposed to be the one who vowed to do the protecting. But look at you! You're worse than the most pathetic girls at court, lying there and expecting these Knights to give up their lives to protect you! Now shift your behind and get on that horse!"

Too stunned to do anything else but obey, Amalric tottered to the side of the wagon and swung a leg over the nearest horse.

"Quite a girl, isn't she?" Hamelin said with a grin at the amazed Oliver.

Alaiz swiftly made a girth out of one of the spare long reins and then strapped Amalric's belt to it. Mounting the other horse, she grabbed the reins of Amalric's horse too and urged hers towards the open moors to their right. Seeing them on the move, the Knights wheeled around and formed into an escort as they ploughed off into the snowy slope. The heavy horses could only manage a sedate canter, although the weight of one person was so little in comparison to the weights they normally pulled there was no chance of them tiring quickly. Gilbert and Friedl came and took Amalric off Alaiz, riding either side of their leader to prevent him falling, while Hamelin came to ride alongside Alaiz, as Oliver led them away from the road. He had spotted a fold in the moor a half turn back the way they had come, and was now making for it with all speed in the hope that they would be out of sight in the dip before the hunters got close enough to see them. Two other Knights, Theo and Kai, galloped to a stunted hawthorn and each hacked a large branch off with their swords, which they then used to try to blur the tracks as they dragged them behind their company by knotted sacks from out of the wagon.

They reached the safety of the gully just in time and found it led into a stream, now almost frozen over, which led up onto the moors. Without pausing, Oliver kept them moving as fast as was safe on the slippery surface up the stream bed. Small hawthorns and crab apple trees, with stunted oak and birch, lined the tiny valley giving them some protection from the wind, but it would be wholly inadequate if the rooks came over. All kept making furtive glances at the sky between watching their horses' footsteps. For a brief interlude they thought they had got away with their escape, until a hissing of feathers announced the rooks' flight overhead. The black, cawing cloud sped past, then wheeled and swept back. The Knights cursed their lack of arrows to shoot them out of the air, the oaths turning to cries of warning as the cloud swooped down. Suddenly they were in the middle of a swarming, pecking, clawing storm. Drawing their swords the Knights lashed out at anything that flew. The horses now became a problem as, driven to distraction by the pecking, one by one they got the bit between their teeth and bolted. Even the best trained of them had never been exposed to an attack like this.

Alaiz found herself hanging onto the mane of her horse for grim death as it threw itself up the last steep slope onto the moor and into a howling gale. Below on the road they had not seen the snow storm coming in from the north off the sea. As the icy flakes were driven into her stinging face she suddenly realized that it had driven the birds back too. Hauling on the one rein with all her might she managed to turn her horse in a circle until it slowed and stopped.

"Get up here!" she screamed at the top of her lungs. "Get into the snow!"

Out of the white, a dark figure appeared which turned into Oliver, followed by several others. Bunching together for protection they counted heads. The horse carrying Amalric made it more because it wanted to be with its stable mate than any expertise of its rider, who sat staring numbly into space. Hamelin quickly made it to Alaiz's side and leant across the space between their horses to give her a warm hug. He continued to hold her hand as Oliver made a final roll call. Most of them had made it, although Bertrand was now mounted behind Theo, and Friedl was wrapping a scarf as a temporary bandage around his horse's badly torn ears.

Three were missing though, and Oliver and two others rode back in the comparative safety of the storm to the gully. When they returned it was pale-faced and shaken. Willem had fallen from his horse and apparently broken his neck, while Kai was almost completely missing his face and hands when they found him wandering. Under the cover of the blanket off her horse, Alaiz pulled off her shift to use as a bandage, it being the finest cloth they had amongst them. An older Knight called Pauli held Kai's torn figure in front of him on his horse when they had done their best to tend his wounds, but nobody had any idea if he would live.

In the midst of this Hamelin tried to comfort Oliver who looked dreadful. Gilbert had been found beneath his dead horse with his back and neck broken. No physician in the Islands had the power to mend that, and Gilbert had pleaded with Oliver to end his life there and then. There was no way he could have been moved, and Oliver had been torn between grief and rage as he had driven his sword into his friend's heart. Nothing had prepared him for such a task, and he shook like a leaf as Hamelin hugged him tightly.

With Oliver so distraught, Hamelin took over as leader and the sad band mounted up once more and rode on. The snow had eased from an icy blizzard to a light drifting, which cleared altogether when they crested the next rise. Strangely there was no sign of the snow up here, although when they turned to look back, the whole of the valley and across beyond the road had disappeared in swirling gray clouds and white. Even the trees were grey shadows, but the only movement was a ghostly stag whose outline briefly came into view and then disappeared again.

It was a miserable ride as they plodded on northwards. Amalric was no use at all, with Alaiz being the only one who could bully him into moving. Oliver slowly recovered some of his resolve, although he was not sleeping at nights, so that the circles beneath his eyes got blacker and blacker. On the third day the horrendously pecked Kai gave up his fight for life as his wounds festered, and they left him beneath a makeshift cairn on one of the old earthworks.

It took nearly a week more to make their way on the sheep trails over the high, bleak moors and down to Quies, by which time the horses were thin and weak, and everyone was suffering from frostbite somewhere. Hugh de Burh himself came out to supervise their reception as they were hurried into the infirmary. The worst of the cold was alleviated with plentiful warm blankets, a roaring fire and hot food as the resident physician went around them all, tending their wounds and frostbites. Then when they were settled, Hugh pulled a chair up in front of Oliver and Hamelin to hear their reports.

Neither could keep the disgust out of their voices at the complete uselessness of de Loges, which worried Hugh. He had always known Amalric was no seasoned fighter, but if this got out to other septs it could prove disastrous in undermining an already weak Grand Master. What surprised him more was the admiration both of them had for their young queen. Hugh had had her whisked away to his own lodgings, where she was enjoying in private the luxury of a hot, herb bath.

"She was amazing," Oliver said in wonderment. "After all she's been through, she never once complained. She'd have made a first class Knight if she'd been born a boy."

"She's bright, too." Hamelin said. "She saw before all of us that the birds wouldn't follow into the snow. She saved us from losing more men then, and before that when she got de Loges out of the wagon. We'd have been cut to ribbons if we'd had to fight men as well as those birds down on the road. None of us would've come back."

"Well, she can have a well-deserved rest now," Hugh reassured them. "The king is here. He'll take over."

"I bet he isn't as good as her," Hamelin said softly to Oliver as Hugh walked away.

The two young Knights were not given any reason to revise their opinion of Ivain later, when they met Haply and Grimston in the mess. Over piled plates of roast pork and root vegetables they swapped stories.

"You wouldn't have caught Alaiz not climbing down that rope," Hamelin said with a disparaging sniff at his king's predicament.

"Ah, don't be too hard on him," Haply said tolerantly. "From what we heard, that DeÁine, Calatin, went through him like knife through butter. Nobody could have resisted that. By the Wild Hunt, that fireball still gives me nightmares."

Hamelin and Oliver said nothing but exchanged dubious glances.

As the month drew to a close, the spell of bad weather lifted, the sick and wounded recovered, and the Knights began to prepare their next move. And all the while Alaiz was getting more and more angry. Ivain had come to see her after she had arrived, but his reaction was far from the one she had expected. Far from the romantic reunion she had longed for, he seemed irritated at her presence. On one occasion he told her she should have returned to her brothers' empty castle instead of going to the capital.

"Really, Alaiz, what were you thinking? If you knew an army was on the move what did you think *you* could do?" He had tossed his head in frustration, then as he had left had said impatiently, "Now I have to worry about *your* safety along with everything else."

Alaiz had hurled the nearest cushion at the closing door and then sobbed her heart out. No word of gratitude that she had tried to help him. No word of concern for Gillies. No loving words. Just his irritation at her being a nuisance.

By contrast, the Knights she had travelled with welcomed her with open arms the first time she ventured out of Hugh's lodgings. Hugh himself was always in some meeting planning things, and Alaiz wondered if, like Ivain, he thought she should hide in her chamber, embroidering flowers on bits of lace. The young Knights, on the other hand, offered to show her how to use a lightweight sword they had found in the armoury for her, while someone else had dug out a small hunting bow she could have.

Deeply buried memories came flooding back of her brothers playing knights and dragons with her when they were all still a family and happy, which brought the occasional tear to her eyes. Yet none of the young men who had come to know her thought it foolish if she had to stop and sniff into her handkerchief every now and then. Oliver himself was still struggling to come to terms with Gilbert's death, as were the others, so that they too choked up at times. They could see no reason why she should have to hide away. Indeed, they thought it positively dangerous for her to remain in one place for any length of time in case Calatin and Brion's spies found out, and came after her again.

Late one morning, Alaiz was summoned to join one of the meetings. With an absence of women's clothing at the preceptory, she had taken to wearing a page's uniform – the only clothing small enough for her – which she also found quite liberating. With it her resolve had hardened, and so she strode into the small hall which doubled as Hugh's office and the planning centre, determined not to be patted on the head and put back on the shelf like a discarded doll. Aside from Hugh, Amalric and Ivain, Oliver and Hamelin were there, as were Haply and Grimston and two other captains. To her annoyance, she was gestured to a chair at the side while Hugh issued orders to the four captains for what looked like an assault on somewhere. Only when they left did he turn his attention to her.

"Now my dear, we have to ensure your safety, so a ship will take you to Vellan. You'll be safe there."

"What?" she cried in disbelief. "You're just parcelling me off out of the way?"

"Don't be tiresome, Alaiz," Ivain said patronizingly. "You're not a soldier. You'll be kept safe until we've dealt with Brion. Then when it's safe you can come back to the palace again."

Alaiz looked around the room at the men watching her and felt her colour rising. Ivain looked as uncomfortable as she felt. They should have had the chance to have this conversation in private, not have to air their personal feelings in front of an audience, and that made her even angrier.

For his part Ivain could not comprehend what she had thought would happen. He was having trouble enough trying to be the strong leader Hugh said they needed, especially after his encounter with Calatin. Inside he still cringed at his uselessness, and Calatin's dismissal of him as irrelevant had lingered and festered.

"I'm sorry, Alaiz," he began again. "I love you, I really do. All I ever wanted to do in the past – still do – was protect you. I failed then but I won't again."

"Protect me? From what?" Alaiz was feeling all the hurt bubbling up inside. "*Now* I can just about understand, but why in the past?"

He gave his disarming smile. The one that once upon a time would have won her over in an instant, but no more. Too much water had passed under that bridge for her to ever go back now. However, Ivain was not to know that, and he had not begun to grasp the depth of the problem.

"From the schemers and plotters at court." He struggled to find the right way to tell her, looking to Hugh for guidance and finding none. "All the time I was growing up I tried to change things, but every time I won one person over, another took their place. I couldn't be everywhere at once. I had to find another way if I was ever going to have a chance to rule the way

I wanted – a way that would care for the real people of this Island, and not just make the rich richer. I tried to ask Mother but she didn't understand, and so Master Hugh and I came up with the plan."

"A plan?" Alaiz fumed, her simmering anger threatening to rise to a boil.

"To send you two to Kittermere while we closed the trap." Ivain looked very pleased with himself.

"You mean you deliberately did that to me?"

"No! Well …yes, but not the way you mean."

"Oh do enlighten me. How exactly do I mean?"

Ivain was almost squirming under her furious stare. He had never seen Alaiz like this. So angry, so hurt and it all directed at him.

"The only way to win was to let everyone think I was a fool. It was playing the long game, but at least there was a chance that way. For a year or two I really did have to do nothing, and Mother constantly reprimanding me for it just made it all the more convincing. But after a while it worked. They stopped watching me once I went away from court. It didn't help with the government of the country, but it did mean I was able to start putting things in place while I was in the more remote parts of the Island."

"He's done remarkably well," Hugh interrupted. "We now have all of the east of Prydein under our command, and, except for Brion's own estates, from south of a line from Freton is ours too."

"*Ours*? Well isn't that nice!" Alaiz retorted. "And how does this 'ours' help me? '*We*' might have '*our*' strongholds but you left *me* stuck in the lion's den, didn't you? What did you think would happen to me when your nice little plan brought Brion out of his cage fighting?"

"But you weren't supposed to be there!" Amalric said, as if explaining to a singularly dense child.

"Oh no, that's right, you were the one who arranged to have me shipped out of the way, weren't you! Well that worked out really well, didn't it! Which was worse for you? Me being in the hands of my brother who was fighting with Brion …or my being taken captive by a raving lunatic? Because from where I'm standing the lunatic was the lesser of the two evils – at least he didn't do it in cold blood!"

Amalric flinched as if she had struck him. "You have Gillies to thank for your kidnapping, not me, and we shipped you off as soon as we knew your brother had already left Kittermere."

"Which just proves you can't count!" Alaiz snarled. "I have *two* brothers, remember? And the other one's not been heard of, has he? He's probably still at home in Osraig! And Gorm doesn't sneeze without Turstin's say so, so he'd *really* be likely to let me wander around the place. Fool! And as for Gillies, did you ever think that maybe you forced her down that route?"

"I'm sorry, Alaiz," Hugh cut in. "Gillies is not the innocent you think she is. She always had a reputation with men, even before Ivain's father, and her loyalties as an Attacotti were always divided."

"You arrogant men!" Alaiz's temper snapped. She swung her gaze back and forth over the three in front of her. "You!" She stopped at Amalric. "You're so full of yourself! Did you really think she was after your body? Did it *never* occur to you that maybe she just wanted someone to talk to? A friend? And you!" She swung on Hugh. "How *dare* you call her a whore in all but name! You locked her up and threw away the key when she was widowed, then expected her to perform like a fairground dog when you wanted. You left her *nothing* but memories.

"Magnus' approach must have seemed like an answered prayer, and you're wrong, she didn't plot our kidnap. She was as surprised as I was. All she can ever have done is *maybe* written to him, and with you lot watching her like hawks there wasn't much chance of that, even. But once she was on Rathlin she found what she was missing. He may be as mad as a hare but Magnus acted like he'd missed *her*, the real Gillies, for *every* year they'd been apart. Are you all so blind you can't see how intoxicating that would be for someone who was as lonely as she was? You *used* her! *All* of you. And she deserved better than that, and she came to realize it and she tried to take me with her. I didn't see why when it happened, but I do now."

She turned on Ivain.

"And how could you do this to us, Ivain? You say you love me, but you don't. …No, don't interrupt! It's true. You don't. If you loved me you'd have thought about *me,* but all you did was think about how I affect you, and there's a difference. Did it never occur to you to think of what this was doing to me as a person? How it felt to be blamed by all and sundry for how you were? To be told that if I'd been more of a wife to you, you'd be a better king. How it was my fault we didn't have a proper marriage …have children. I was so alone. All those times you went away doing your plotting and scheming with your friends I was left with no one but Gillies. *For years!*"

"But we couldn't be seen to be getting along, don't you see that?" he pleaded.

"Seen? In the Spirit's name, Ivain, we had connecting bedrooms! When did the court come to bed with you? Once upon a time you used to come into my room once everyone had gone to bed and talk to me. *Really* talk to me. When have you done that in the last few years? You could have, and if you'd told me what was going on, and why, I'd have played along, you know I would." She caught Amalric's sideways glance to Hugh. "Or did you think that as a girl I was too stupid? Was that it? Silly little Alaiz! We mustn't tell her because she'll only mess it up! *Damn* you two to the Underworld!"

She had to stop to catch her breath. Hugh had the good grace to turn red, and even Amalric's sarcasm seemed to have deserted him.

"And what's supposed to happen when you get control back?" she went on. "When you get to rule? Are we all supposed to live happily ever after? You told me so often you thought of me like a sister, Ivain. Do you?"

He gave a muddled sort of nod and shrug, too appalled at how she saw his lovely plans to reply.

"Alright, so I'm your sister! What then? We could carry on being the best of friends, but what happens when you meet a woman you *truly* fall in love with? It's alright for you. You could install her in another castle, set up home there, even raise a family. Go visit whenever the court allows time. You might not be with her every day, but then lots of other people have to live like that. I met a carter who has to go away for weeks on end, and he lives happily with his family. With no official heir you might even be able to let a son inherit. But for that to happen *we* couldn't be seen to have had a child. So what about *me*? What if *I* want a family? What if I meet a man *I* love? I couldn't even risk having a lover for fear of having a child unless you were prepared to pass it off as yours. And would you? Would *they*..." she waved her arms at Hugh and Amalric "...let you? I bet not!

"And you dare to say I wouldn't see things clearly. Well I see things all too clearly. You've treated me like your toy doll. Something to be picked up off the shelf when it suits you to play with me, and then put back down and expected to stay put waiting for the next time. No complaints, no tears, no feelings, be a good girl Alaiz. ...Never think of yourself Alaiz. ...Never want a life, Alaiz! Well you're so clever at planning, plan your next moves without me, because just like Gillies, I've stopped playing the game. I quit! Find yourself a new puppet!"

She turned on her heels and stormed out, slamming the door so hard behind her that a tiny shower of mortar fell from the surrounding wall. Oliver and Hamelin shifted uncomfortably as they watched their leaders' embarrassment, but Ivain stared at the closed door, tears welling up in his eyes.

"Oh Blessed Martyrs, I've lost her," he whispered.

"Oh, she'll be back, it's just a woman's mood," Amalric dismissed it all.

"I don't think so," Hamelin spoke up.

"No, she's truly angry," Oliver agreed.

Ivain buried his head in his hands for a moment and then looked up. He looked so wounded and so scared by what he realized he had inadvertently done, that Hamelin almost felt sorry for him – but not quite.

"I have to make this right," Ivain vowed. "I owe Alaiz so much, I was so used to her always being there I forgot about her. How stupid could I be? How can I ever make amends?"

"Well if you'll take some advice," Oliver said, placing a restraining arm in front of Hamelin and stepping forward to his young king, "don't treat her like some court hanger-on. No flowers, no puppy-dogs with ribbon collars. Wait until you can offer her something real. Think about what you can do to make *her* life better if she agreed to come back, and start doing all that work to make it look like she's still your consort. Some place to live that's not in the capital might be a good start. Somewhere she can be with friends of her own, so that she can actually *have* friends of her own. Even then you may not win, but then surely that will show whether you really love her, or whether she's just been part of your life so long she's a habit it's hard to break? If it's the later then the kindest thing to do is let her go."

"Let her go?" Amalric exploded. "She's the damned queen, not some kitten in the woodshed! She'll stay and do her duty!"

Hamelin propelled himself off the wall he had been leaning on to come face to face with Amalric.

"Oh she will, will she? And how do *you* propose to make her, *sire*? *You* couldn't even stop my brother from being killed! You damned near got lynched yourself if it hadn't been for Oliver! What do you think *you* can do? You're just a puppet yourself!"

"Enough!" Hugh barked at Hamelin. "One more word and you'll be reprimanded for insubordination!"

"Insubordination? Ha! It's the truth!" Hamelin turned to Hugh. "While *he* was kicking his heels in Brion's cell, *she* managed to get out of Magnus' stronghold, find a boat, cross the Island and make her way through a capital stuffed with Brion's guards. So you tell me? If she decides to up and disappear, how are you going to find her? She could go anywhere in the Islands, and what would give her away? She doesn't behave like some spoilt princess. She'd pass as some normal girl who's just led a bit of a sheltered life. Why would she stay here to be treated like dirt by people like you?"

He turned on his heels and followed Alaiz out, leaving another pile of mortar on the floor.

"You're going to need to get that seen to," Oliver said nodding at the new holes around the frame as he opened the door to follow. Hugh knew he had gestured at the mortar, but Oliver had a talent for double meanings and Hugh knew it was a subtle criticism too, even if he closed the door softly.

"Oh really, all this fuss over a girl!" Amalric huffed, getting up to go. Hugh's patience snapped.

"Well if you'd paid less attention to the distractions at court and used your mind to keep an eye on things we wouldn't be in this mess!" Hugh fumed. "Damn it, Amalric, all you had to do was see to their safety!"

"Well may be you should have picked someone who *likes* women!" Amalric bit back, and the door got another pounding as he left.

Ivain rubbed his eyes and also walked to the door.

"Where are you going?" Hugh asked him in a more gentle tone.

Ivain shrugged. "I don't know. I feel so stupid. I've made such a mess of everything. My mother thinks I'm a fool, my wife hates me, my people think I'm dead, and I've even managed to hurt Amalric."

"Amalric?" Hugh asked in astonishment. "You couldn't have hurt Amalric, he was doing his duty as I commanded him."

Ivain shook his head as he opened the door. "Didn't you realize? He may have been going through the motions with mother, but it was me he was really paying attention to." Hugh's mouth fell open in astonishment as

Ivain went on, speaking over his shoulder as he left. "He tried to tell me not to worry about Alaiz because he would take care of me. I never bothered to find out what he meant by that. But then he acted so hurt when I told him I still loved her. He asked me what about him? What about us? And I couldn't answer him."

Left alone, Hugh buried his head in his hands and wondered why life had to be so complicated. Thank the Trees he had found a task for Hamelin and Oliver and the others which would keep them away from the army. He had high hopes for Hamelin, and he had already set plans in motion for Oliver to succeed as Grand Master should he and Amalric fall with the other senior men. That was another reason to get the two brightest young Knights away from the unavoidable conflict which was to come – someone had to be left to rebuild the Order if necessary. He sighed. All that would fall into ruin if he was forced to reprimand them publicly for insubordination. Nor could he risk having them too close to Amalric in case the supposed Grand Master took it into his head for once to act like it, and punish them himself.

Meanwhile, Oliver and Hamelin were packing their bags in preparation to meet Theo, Friedl and Bertrand down at the quayside. The older Knight, Pauli, had already been convinced by Hugh of the need for silence over Amalric's conduct, and had gone straight to join another group without the chance of a farewell. When a tearful Alaiz found the pair they were almost done, and the sight of the two who had been kindest to her about to leave reduced her to a sobbing heap.

"Where are you going?" she wailed.

Hamelin came and put his arms around her and held her close as Oliver explained.

"We have to go on a mission for Master Hugh."

"Mission? What sort of mission? Haven't you done enough already with rescuing that useless bastard de Loges?" she spat from the comfort of Hamelin's embrace.

"Hugh's had a message from Rheged," Hamelin explained gently. "Things are as bad there, it seems, and the leading abbot, someone called Jaenberht, has asked him for help."

Before Alaiz could interrupt, Oliver cut in.

"The king there has tried to murder his own younger half-brother. Poor kid's only about eleven! Hugh wants us to go across and escort this boy from the monastery in the north over the sea to Ergardia and safety. We're also carrying messages for the Grand Master in Ergardia, explaining what's happened here in case Brion wins. I'm not sure, but I think one of Hugh's contingency plans is for all the Knights from here to fall back to Ergardia before making a controlled reconquest."

"Why can't the Knights in Rheged do the other job?" Alaiz asked.

"They've been disbanded by this corrupt king," Oliver explained, "and their Master and his second-in-command are both dead. They need the

Grand Master in Ergardia to rally them too, so I think Hugh is thinking of making a combined force and retaking the Islands one by one. Oh …and they've got one of those DeÁine wizards over there as well!"

"Then I'm coming with you," Alaiz said firmly.

"What?" the two young Knights said in unison.

"I'm not sitting like some bird in a cage waiting for the cat to get hungry enough to open it," she fumed. "Ship me off to a prison in all but name? No thanks! I've been there, done that, don't need to go through it again! And if Hugh thinks Ergardia is safe enough for the heir of Rheged when there're two wizards on the loose, you're taking me to safety, aren't you? Come on …I'm supposed to be catching a ship in the harbour too, I'll just be on the wrong one and away before Hugh notices. They don't think I've got a brain! And the crew will never think I planned to leave of my own accord! They'll assume it's Hugh's idea, and serve him right!"

Chapter 22

A Hard Lesson

Brychan: Winterfalling

Esclados of Rhue clumped his way into the hall at Bere and eased his bulk into the campaign chair pulled close to the fire. There were grander chairs around the room, but the leather seat and back of the supple folding-chair formed to his shape better than the hard wooden ones. He hated this day. The first of Winterfalling always put him in a grumpy mood. It was not that he disliked the month altogether. There was the happy prospect of the feast at the other end, when two nights of riotous indulgence proclaimed the arrival of Samhainn, the first month of winter. That was always one of his favourite feasts, for with it came the arrival of the first of the new season's game, and Esclados was particularly fond of wild boar and pheasant. What made him grumpy was the knowledge that from now on he had months of cold and damp to look forward to, and the older he got the more his joints creaked and ached.

He used one foot to start easing off the other boot. These days he had his boots made loose enough to be easy to get in and out of, since he no longer folded up in the middle in quite the way he used to. Groaning as he leant over to stand the first boot by the side of the chair, he ruefully contemplated the fact that these days his middle was the one thing there was more of than anything else. Long gone were the days when he was shaped like the young squire who had accompanied him on this short trip. Then he shook his head and turned his eyes up to the heavens.

"But then I never really looked like him even when I was his age, did I?" he addressed the Spirits, whom he fervently clung to a belief in. Perhaps it was another sign of growing older, he thought, that he was taking more notice of what might be lying in store in the hereafter. Sometimes he had taken to speaking to the Spirits as a matter of general conversation, since they seemed so much saner than some of the world around him. As now for instance.

"And what am I going to do with him?" he asked the ceiling once more. Esclados sighed, but before he could petition the Spirits further, the object of his weary despair strode into the room on the heels of Simon, the gate keeper. Simon handed Esclados a tankard of mulled cider, which was gratefully received, and before turning back rolled his eyes in the direction of the man behind him, hinting to Esclados that somehow in his brief absence Jacinto had managed to screw something else up – again! Covering his further groan by taking a swig of the hot drink, and letting the spicy cinnamon and apple warm his insides, Esclados final looked up at the young man quivering with impatience in front of him.

"Well?" he asked.

"How much longer do we have to remain in this backwater?" demanded the imperious Jacinto.

Esclados was fully aware that his young associate probably thought him a dithering old fool, too antiquated to do more than check up on equally antiquated castles. He eased himself upright in the chair and stared Jacinto in the eyes. Forcing a reasonable tone into his voice, he tried to carefully explain, yet again.

"We came here to make sure that the reserve supplies were in good order, and that there was no need to order replacements for anything while there was space to do it with the garrison away. So that's really up to you, isn't it? Have you completed the check of the stables? Is the spare tack in good repair? Have you made a note of what needs replacing?"

Jacinto gave an exasperated sigh. "Yes, yes. I've checked it over. It's a bit mouldy but it'll do."

"*Do*?" Esclados heaved himself to his feet. Even in his socks he stood eye to eye with Jacinto. From under his bushy, greying eyebrows he glared into the younger man's face. "*Do* isn't good enough! What happens if we have to move south in a hurry and someone has an accident, and they need to replace equipment? We won't have time to wait while you scrape the mould off a saddle which then falls apart after five miles! Flaming Hounds of the Wild Hunt, have you learned nothing?"

He shook his head and turned to the fire.

"Jacinto, Ealdorman Berengar made it clear to you why you were chosen for this detail, didn't he? You're an excellent fighter. You might even be the best we have at the moment. But there's more to being a Knight than hammering three kinds of stuffing out of everything that crosses your path." He heard Jacinto's sigh again. He was really getting annoyed with that sigh, which put in an appearance far too often of late, and he rounded on him.

"You arrogant young pup! You might think you know everything there is to know, but let me assure you, you don't! I know you think I'm a stupid old fool, but this old fool has survived bigger battles than you've ever seen. And why? Because I had the sense to listen when people were trying to tell me things for my own good. Has it not penetrated that thick skull of yours to wonder, yet, why you were the *one* left behind from the exercise to the far north? Well let me tell you! It was because you're too much of a hothead. Berengar feared that if they did happen to see any sign of the DeÁine, you'd be off like a rabid dog and he'd never get you back before you'd started another war."

"I thought we were *supposed* to be fighting the DeÁine?" Jacinto asked with sulky sarcasm.

Esclados growled. "Of course we're against the DeÁine, fool of a boy! But if you'd ever seen them except in those dopey dreams of yours, you'd know that they're not dealt with lightly. Those Knights of Celidon, who barely held the last major attack back, weren't some ambling bunch of hedge knights caught out on a feast day picnic. They were as highly trained as you and much more skilled. To the last man! And they damned near died to the last man too! So you think on what that should be telling you.

"Berengar is one of the most able and most respected leaders in all of the Island, with good reason. He's also one of the fairest commanders I've ever had the privilege of serving under. So if he thinks you're not fit to take your vows, then you *ARE NOT FIT*! Can I make it any clearer to you? You were sent on this detail with me to try to *teach* you something, but at the rate you're going on, you're going to be the oldest squire in the history of the Order!"

Jacinto had the good grace to look at least a little disconcerted by Esclados' tongue lashing, but had a temporary reprieve in the form of Simon bringing in the evening meal on a tray. He set the two heaped plates up on the end of the long table nearest the fire, along with a small jug of more mulled cider for Esclados and one of water for Jacinto, who disdained to drink alcohol. Before he went he took in Esclados' high colouring, and assumed that he had been delivering the much needed chastisement, in his view. So he thought it now clear to ask,

"So what do you make of our visitors today, then?"

"Visitors?" Esclados exclaimed. "Oh, Sacred Trees, Jacinto, what happened while I was gone that you *haven't* told me about?"

Jacinto glared at Simon, but shrugged and said,

"Oh just some silly girl and her boyfriend. They thought we'd know about some missing woman, so I sent them on their way. I told them we don't keep records of strays."

"Only it wasn't just that, was it?" Simon challenged.

Jacinto's back stiffened at this apparent affront to his honesty, but Simon was one of the most trusted of the enlisted men in the Order, and a highly decorated sergeant too, as Esclados well knew. He respected Simon's opinion far above Jacinto's, and so he ignored the bristling bundle of offended pride beside him and asked Simon to explain. In a few concise sentences Simon outlined his encounter with Cwen and Swein.

"And you say they thought the brother's life was in serious danger?" Esclados checked at the end. Simon nodded. "Well, Jacinto, if I were you I'd give up on ever hoping to be a Knight if I were you," he continued. "Because when Berengar hears about this he's going to hang you up by your toenails, and then have you scrubbing the latrines for the rest of your life."

Jacinto looked stunned, and for the first time Esclados thought he might have got through the young man's emotional stonewalled guard.

"Why?" was all he managed in reply, in itself a surprise in that there was not a string of excuses flowing already.

Adopting a very patient tone of voice, Esclados held up one of his mighty paws. "One," he said, raising the first finger. "What is the first vow of a Knight? To help, if I'm not mistaken. But you didn't, did you? Two," he raised the next finger, "we protect. Because you didn't listen, you didn't know that someone's life may be in danger. And why was that? Because, three," the next thick digit appeared in front of Jacinto's paling face, "we're supposed to treat all men as equal. The smallest is as entitled to ask for our help as the greatest. But you? You think you're so far above everyone you dismissed them as being less than you, and so not worthy of your attention, so you missed vital information."

"But how was I to know they were important?" Jacinto gulped.

"You weren't, you idiot! But if you'd listened with an open mind, you might have worked it out as Simon did."

"By the way," Simon chipped in. "He wasn't her boyfriend. Brother, maybe, but not her boyfriend. Not the way he was watching your arse as you walked back in."

Jacinto flushed scarlet and glared at Simon, who had been unable to resist making sure Esclados knew about that too, and the two older men were grinning at his discomfort.

"Ah well," Esclados chortled, "that's what you get for being so damned handsome, Jacinto, it's not just the ladies who admire your physique!"

Jacinto spun on his heels to go, but Esclados checked him.

"Not so fast, my fine young friend. We have to put this right now you've screwed it up." He turned to Simon. "You sent them to Vellyn? Good. Well if we assume that they've not been travelling fast and have stopped for the nights, if we set out tomorrow morning we should catch up with them by the beginning of the next day."

"We're going after them?" Jacinto asked in astonishment. "Why?"

Esclados motioned him to the table and their cooling food, waving Simon into the seat by his side where he poured him some of the cider.

"A long time ago – as a little boy and way before he was ever king – our not so beloved King Edward was just the son of another member of a noble family, with no hint of a claim to the throne. You won't remember this, Jacinto, because it was before you were born, but if you paid *any* attention in those history lessons they gave you as a page, you might recall some of this. That was before Moytirra. Before the civil war which followed.

"Back then his father, Edward, Lord of Mar, was a young man married to a very young girl for political reasons. And as young men will, he liked the company of willing young women. His so-called wife was far too young for him to have a proper married relationship with, so he kept the company of women who were able to satisfy his needs. I wasn't senior enough then, or now, to know the whole of what went on, but I'm sure the woman those two were looking for is King Edward's father's former mistress. She must have been something more special than the others, because she was brought up here and the Knights were charged with keeping her safe and hidden."

"But I thought you said everyone was equal!" Jacinto challenged him. "How equally was she treated if the Knights walled her up at the whim of someone who wasn't even the king?"

"Who said we walled her up?" Simon answered. "From what I heard she lived a pretty good life in a large and comfortable house. She could go as far as the markets in Penteg – and that was three days' ride away – as long as she had an escort."

"True," Esclados confirmed. "And remember, Jacinto, we may comply with requests for reasons of our own. True, what is now the royal family wanted her out of the way, but the Order undertook to guard her because they thought she needed protecting *against* the royal family. If we didn't protect her, who else had the power to stand against such influential people?"

Light slowly dawned for Jacinto. "But you told us they said there were two children?" he queried of Simon, who nodded and said,

"That they did, but it's more than two. She definitely brought one child with her. He must be a man in his early forties by now. We suspected there must have been a child with Lord Mar – who must be the one they know about – but then, after she'd settled here in the north, she had a long and happy relationship with one of her warders. They married and had at least another son and a daughter, possibly more."

"So you see, Jacinto, we have to go after our two visitors, because we have to know what they know, so that we can protect these unsuspecting people from the danger *they* don't even know is coming." Esclados told him.

Come the morning, Jacinto seemed to have recovered some of his usual ebullience, although not enough to risk crossing the old bear of a Knight, who growled at him at every turn. Esclados set a punishing pace for the whole of that day, until he thought they had gone as far as the two travellers would have gone during the previous day. After that they stopped at every one of the tiny hamlets where there was anywhere that might have put the two up for the night. With increasing frustration he found every inquiry coming up with a negative answer. By the time they were well over half way to Vellyn, he thought they must have been far past any possible stop, and he was forced to make a halt for themselves as darkness enveloped them. For the rest of the evening, Jacinto found himself on the receiving end of Esclados' frustration at losing the trail.

After a restless night, Esclados decided that all they could do was to return to Vellyn themselves, and then set watches on the junction of the road with the nearby town of Rhue. Jacinto had suggested they double back to see if there was any signs they had missed in the twilight, but Esclados thought it more likely that they may have taken the coast road, for reasons he could not fathom. All they could do now was make sure that once the two travellers were forced back around the estuary to Rhue, they did not slip past on the inland road.

That evening therefore saw them clattering over the drawbridge into the bailey of Vellyn castle, to the surprise of the rest of the garrison. Esclados' companion Knights, the ones who had not accompanied their commander north, were even more surprised at his insistence that they send men out first thing the following morning to watch the southern roads for a young man and a woman. However, the next day there was no sign of the pair, and by noon the following day Esclados had gone beyond prowling up and down the outer court near the gate, and had called for his horse.

Swinging himself into the saddle of the thickset bay gelding, he turned the horse through the gate and heeled it into a brisk trot, rapidly disappearing from view. As Esclados' great bulk vanished, Jacinto heaved a sigh of relief. The old man had not let up on him for a minute since they had left Bere, and something in the older Knight's manner had conveyed to the garrison that for once Jacinto had bitten off something more than even he could chew. To a man they were avoiding him as though he had the plague.

Normally Jacinto would have brushed his isolation off with some excuse to himself that they had failed to understand his superior stance, but this time he had the unpleasant thought that perhaps it really was him who was out of step with everyone else. Even worse, it looked as though they were right and he was wrong. For almost the first time since he had been raised to squire, Jacinto wished there was someone he could talk to. Nobody was speaking to him, though, not even to gloat. Instead, his respite was only too short lived.

Esclados had only got to where the road from Vellyn came into sight of the main road north from Rhue, when he saw the four foot soldiers posted at the junction talking to two people. Heeling his horse into a gallop, he thundered up to the group, causing the two ponies to toss their heads and snort in alarm at the sight of the great war-horse bearing down on them. He was long past the athletic vault from the saddle, but could still manage a dignified rapid dismount. Even dismounted he towered over the young woman and the slender young man stood at her side, and they unconsciously tried to step back from him.

"Thank the Spirits we've found you!" he boomed.

Cwen and Swein exchanged puzzled glances.

"No, don't be alarmed," Esclados reassured them. "Our gate keeper told me of your visit to Bere and that he'd sent you on here. We've been searching for you ever since. You should *never* have been turned away! Your warning may be very important. It was downright irresponsible of Jacinto to ignore you, not to mention against the code of conduct. He will be severely reprimanded, have no fear!"

"Are you the commander here, then?" Cwen summoned up the courage to ask.

"Spirits preserve us, no!" Esclados laughed. "No, he's away at the moment, and I'm just an old soldier, but come, come. Let's get you two settled in the guest quarters, and then there are some of us who want to hear all about what's brought you here."

Cwen was much reassured by this Knight, despite his impressive size making her feel so dwarfed. This was much more like the Knights she had met, and his words concerning the young man they had met at Bere convinced her that it had been him who was the exception. Consequently she was quite happy to mount up on Twigglet and ride alongside the great horse, although it felt very strange to be alongside a stranger. Every time she looked up, a little part of her still hoped she would be waking from a nightmare and it would be Richert sitting in the saddle next to her.

Swein, on the other hand, was downright scared. Riding behind Cwen and the Knight, with four armed men walking at his back, he felt totally trapped. What would happen if they ever found out he was the man who had supposedly tried to kill the king? Would it matter at all that Edward was still alive? He still might find himself being blamed for the death of the actor. As they rode in over the drawbridge and he heard the hollow echo of the horses' hooves on the oak planking, it sounded like a death toll for him, and he started shivering all over again.

But nothing untoward happened. They were ushered to two comfortable small rooms in a large stone house, built against the castle wall next to the stables. The Knight waited by the door while they unloaded their saddle bags, and a hospitable attendant offered to take their travel-stained clothes away and get them washed while they had some refreshment. Leaving the guest house, Esclados walked the two of them across the huge open space in the middle of the castle. Here there was no great keep in the centre of the castle. Vellyn had nine massive towers built into the circuit of its walls, each of which was virtually a keep in itself. Even the walls themselves were thick enough to have rooms within them on the first two floors. The third was a broad walkway with wooden rails on the inside to prevent anyone stepping off the edge, with a high step on the opposite side providing the necessary height to allow archers to fire through the crenellated wall edge. The whole place was a hive of activity, even with most men out on patrol.

Between two of the towers they found a large hall filled with tables and benches. From the clattering sounds in a room beyond, it sounded as though the clearing up was going on after the midday meal. However, Esclados disappeared behind the wooden screen at the end of the hall and reappeared a moment later, followed by a man wearing a well-bleached apron and carrying a tray. This turned out to contain recently picked, crisp apples, crusty bread and cheese, and a pitcher of cool small beer. Gesturing Cwen and Swein to follow him, Esclados disappeared through the doorway opposite to the kitchens and they found themselves in a well lit room in a tower base. Leather campaign chairs stood folded and propped against one wall, and Esclados brought three over to where the autumn sun was shining in through the open door. The kitchen worker put the tray on a small table by the door, smiled at them and returned back to his work.

"Sit. Please, sit down." Esclados waved them each into a chair and poured them a drink. "Do eat up," he encouraged them, and as if to emphasize his words, helped himself to a chunk of bread and cheese. Cwen could not resist smiling at him. It was fairly obvious that this Knight enjoyed his food, and he was obviously blessed with a personality as big as his appetite. While they enjoyed the welcome rest from days of travelling, Cwen began to tell Esclados their tale.

She carefully avoided her relationship with Richert, spinning Esclados the same tale as she had done Swein. She had worked in one of the royal castles, she told him. One that was loyal to Lord Richert, and that was where she had heard the story of Edward's real mother. There was no need to invent the story of the troop of guards arriving to tell them that the king had miraculously appeared alive and well after his apparent assassination. Nor that a groom had told her of the horses in the night after Richert's death. It was easy to keep the anger in her voice over the injustice of Edward's complicity in the death of the two young princes and their mother, too. Without mentioning why she had taken it upon herself to be the one to bring Edward down, she moved swiftly on to her meeting Swein.

"I don't know quite why," she told Esclados, making sure she had eye contact with him, "but he was beaten up. He's got horrific scars, but he's never told me how they happened. He has awful nightmares every night, so I haven't wanted to question him."

Esclados' expression said that he understood that she was also telling him not to push Swein too hard.

"What I do know," she said emphatically, "is that he's scared to death of the king and his men."

Swein was having no trouble looking scared to death now. Every time Cwen opened her mouth he felt his heart leap so hard he thought it would break his ribs.

"Well, look at him," Cwen was saying. "There's not much of him now, and there was even less when I found him. He's hardly the biggest threat you've ever seen, is he? How could I leave him when he was obviously in danger?"

For this she got a beaming smile and a nod of approval from Esclados, who was thinking what a pleasant change it was to find someone who was blessed both with intelligence and some moral integrity. It was almost enough to start him believing in people again. From behind them, though, came the familiar superior drawl of Jacinto's voice. Stepping into their view, he stared at Swein and asked straight out,

"Are you one of Edward's catamites, then?"

Swein felt his stomach churn and dived for the open doorway.

Jacinto thought he was making a run for it and leapt forward, only to cannon into Esclados.

"That's enough!" he roared as Jacinto ricocheted off his bulk. "By the Hounds of the Wild Hunt, I'll not have some poor soul insulted by your pompous morality! *Get out!*"

Jacinto stalked out, followed by Esclados who found Cwen clutching a dithering Swein, who was kneeling on the ground retching.

"Come on boy, on your feet," Esclados said in his kindliest voice. "Take no mind of that young idiot."

With no effort at all he pulled Swein up and wrapped a massive arm around him, guiding him back into the chamber. Sitting Swein back down, he bent over so that he was eye to eye with him.

"Listen. I don't care what you were. I've not led such a blameless life that I can sit in judgment on others. I'll leave that to the Spirits, and hope they'll be merciful to me too, when the time comes. But son, I need to know the truth of what happened to you. I suspect this young friend of yours hasn't quite told me everything, but it's enough for me to think she's right about what I've heard so far, and that you need help. However, if we're to protect you we need to know what from, and preferably why."

"Please, Swein, won't you tell us?" Cwen added her plea. She too wanted to hear the full story, but Swein just looked from one to the other like a frightened rabbit between two hounds. Cwen sighed.

"Alright, let me start with what I've guessed and then you can fill in the bits I've got wrong or missed, shall we?" She sat down on the other side of Swein facing Esclados.

"I'm guessing you were one of the young men who keep Edward company," she began, forgetting that most people used the king's title in her focus on Swein. Esclados noticed it, though, and filed it away with other questions in his mind.

"In your nightmares," Cwen was continuing, "you keep saying someone *shouldn't* be dead. If it was Edward you were talking about, surely it would be he *should* be dead. And we know that a body was found, because that was what sparked the whole hunt for a murderer off. So I'm guessing you saw that body and you knew who it was. And if you knew that it wasn't the king then you're in danger, because if you told anyone who that dead body was then people might start asking awkward questions, and Edward won't want that. How am I doing?"

Swein felt a huge weight lifting off him. They were not judging him and they were not blaming him! Not even that fierce big Knight who could swat him like a fly! Taking a ragged breath, closing his eyes and keeping his fingers crossed that it would not go horribly wrong now, in a very shaky voice he told them about the actor.

"I was the one who was supposed to raise the alarm when the actor played dead. He wasn't supposed to really be dead. I never thought he would be *killed*, you have to believe that," he pleaded.

He didn't dare tell them that he had known that Edward was going to kill his family. The more time went on, the more that weighed heavier and heavier on his conscience. It was, he now realized, something he would regret not trying to stop until the day he died. There was no excuse. He could have found a way to get a message out of the palace if he had wanted to, but he had been so wrapped up in trying to preserve his own place by Edward's side he had shut his eyes to the reality. Every day his own self loathing grew as the ghosts of the two small boys began to haunt him alongside that of the actor. If he felt that way about himself, he could not imagine what two respectable and decent people like Cwen and Esclados would say if they knew the truth. But he could not bear to be on his own again, so he kept quiet and punished himself inside, where nobody could see.

"Oh Swein," Cwen was saying, "you poor thing. No wonder you have nightmares."

Her sympathy was like a scourge to his ravaged soul. He did not deserve her kindness. Far from comforting him, it made him feel worse about himself. Then Esclados added salt to the wound by saying,

"Then you have nothing to fear here, boy. The king has no authority within these walls, and you've done a good turn in bringing this warning here. With any luck we can find these others and protect them too."

Swein could only nod numbly. While Cwen told Esclados of her fears, he made serious inroads on the flask of brandywine which Esclados then fetched from a locked cupboard in the corner of the room. As the sun's rays lengthened and disappeared behind the castle walls, bathing them in a colour that was all too reminiscent of blood, Swein quietly got splendidly drunk. By the time someone came to tell them the evening meal was ready the room was swaying gently, and when he tried to get to his feet his knees seemed to belong to someone else and he folded up like a rag doll.

Esclados looked mournfully down on him and then shovelled him up as though he was no more than an errant puppy. With Cwen in attendance they took him back to the guest hall and laid him face down on the bed, which was the last thing he remembered for the night.

Cwen and Esclados returned to the refectory and found a quiet corner to eat their meal in. For her part Cwen found herself much taken with Esclados. Except in size he was very much like her father, especially in his quiet acceptance that people came in every shape and form without judging them. As they enjoyed tender strips of pork, wrapped in pastry parcels with shallots and autumn fruits it was easy to fall into conversation, and she found herself talking about Swein.

"He's a strange young man," she mused to Esclados. "He must be at least as old as I am, and yet at times he behaves like my little brothers. Before I left home they were just into their teens. On the one hand they were full of this bravado that they could do anything they wanted. They hadn't seen enough of life to have learnt some caution. And as for girls, they hadn't got a clue, but they were desperately interested! Well, apart from the interested bit, he's the same. We've been on the road together for weeks now, but each night when I tell him to take his shirt off so that I can put salve on his scars, he blushes like you wouldn't believe. He's got to know that I've worked out his tastes by now, and he's certainly not to mine, so I'm hardly going to pounce on him, but he doesn't get any better.

"At home we had two men who kept one of the farms down the road from our inn. Everyone knew they were together and nobody bothered about it. But they were completely relaxed in the company of the women in our little town, as were the two who kept one of the weaving businesses. With Swein it's different, it's almost like he's hardly ever met a woman."

"Perhaps he hasn't," Esclados suggested. "Some of the men here are closer to one another than the rest of us, if you see what I mean. But it's not necessarily them who are most uncomfortable when we have women stopping in the guest quarters, for whatever reason. It's the ones who were given to the Church as small children, and who've turned out to be unsuitable for that life and been handed on to us. Having grown up in that all male community they seem to see women as some kind of alien creatures. It's sad, because if they're not inclined to chastity, they tend to be the ones we have problems with if they do socialize with the women in the garrison towns."

"Maybe," Cwen said thoughtfully. "From the little he's said, his father was certainly a brute. He's never said outright, but I've got the impression that either the father or the older brothers were the first to abuse him. From what I heard, Edward was downright sadistic with his friends, and I can't believe that someone who hadn't been brought up believing that was normal would stand for that sort of treatment, whatever their normal choice of bedfellow would be. My …em, source, told me that there were lots of young men whom Edward picked out for special favours who didn't even last a week at the palace, but Swein seems to have stood it for years."

There it was again, Esclados thought, this unknown person. Whoever he was – and he felt sure it was a he – had known a remarkable amount about the goings on in the royal household. Esclados decided to try a gentle probe for more detail.

"This source of yours," he said, trying to keep an easy conversational tone, "is he safe? Only it strikes me that if he too knows this information, perhaps we should be thinking of getting him to safety here too?"

To his horror, the tears started to stream down Cwen's face.

"It's far too late for that," she sniffed, brushing them with her sleeve. "Edward's already made sure of that. He killed him on the same night he killed the rest of the royal family."

"Holy Spirits protect us!" Esclados breathed in horror. No wonder she was out for vengeance, if this man had been her lover. "But what's this about the king killing the royal family?"

Cwen realized she had gone farther than she had intended, but it was such a relief to be able to talk to someone again and unburden herself, which she had never felt able to do with Swein. Between the sobs, she told of Sam's return and his conviction that it was the king's men who had forced their way into the manor house of the queen.

"I think Edward faked his own death to make it seem like he was an intended victim too. Then when he returned he could just say that the assassin had got the wrong man. He never fathered those two princes, and having a wife just got in the way. He was getting more and more out of control since his father died. He thought because he was king he could do and have whatever he wanted, and now he's got it hasn't he?"

Esclados sat back in his seat and stared at the ceiling, too shocked to be able to comment. Yet the more he thought about it the more he believed Cwen. He had never been to court, but what he had heard of the king had never been good. On the face of it her story sounded like fantasy, but he could not find any good reason to dismiss it either. Thank the Good Spirits Berengar was due back soon. He was far better at dealing with politics, for Esclados was not ashamed to admit this situation had gone beyond his ability to resolve properly. The one thing he could do was to send a message to Breslyn, and with that thought he levered himself out of his chair and went in search of the sergeant in charge of the riders.

The one-eyed, one-armed veteran was making a last inspection of the horses when Esclados tracked him down. He was convinced of the urgency just by Esclados' manner. It was the first time in years that he had seen the Knight in quite such a state, and, having stood by his shoulder and watched the message appear in a painstakingly careful hand, he turned and went in search of his most reliable and fast rider. Like other old soldiers, he knew of the mystery woman they had protected years ago, and he had done a tour of duty at Breslyn where he had met the younger children. If they were now in danger he would do all in his power to make sure the warning got through. Tomorrow the rider would set out with two others for an escort, and for good measure another would go to Saren and take the next boat to Penteg, before picking up a relay of horses from the grange there.

On the central parade ground, Jacinto stood and watched the sudden activity amongst the messengers, leaving him with a nasty sinking sensation. Those two strangers had completely fooled him. Why could they not have made it clearer they were important? They had not looked it, especially the white-haired little pervert. As a Knight why would he associate himself with the likes of those? He walked back over to the practice area and began throwing spears at the targets to relieve his frustration. No doubt it would all be seen as his fault, though.

No, *he* was not looking forward to Berengar's return at all.

Chapter 23

Signs of Affection

Brychan: Winterfalling

To Jacinto's deep embarrassment, the following morning after the early service, Esclados caught him on the way to breakfast and insisted that he apologize to Swein for his behaviour the previous day. This was unfortunate, since Swein had woken with the grandfather of all hangovers. The feeble autumn light filtering through the small window was like a lance to his bloodshot eyes, as he squinted feebly at the new day. When he fully woke he also realized that his bladder was bursting. Getting up was something else again. His initial hurried sitting up was greeted with the room spinning alarmingly, and with the sensation that his head might just explode. For a moment he had to lie back down again while the hammer behind his eyes slowed to a steadier thumping, but the need to piss was getting ever more urgent.

Cautiously this time, he slowly sat up and swung his feet off the bed onto the floor. With equal care he made it to his feet, but as he tottered towards the door he realized he would never make it to the latrines. Frantically casting round he could see the window was too high, so he looked for any receptacle he could use, but there was nothing. The only thing was a pile of sawdust in the grate left to help get the larger logs lit. At least they would soak it up. He staggered to the fireplace and just undid his clothes in time. As the steaming stream shot into the grate, he leaned his pounding head against the chimney wall and found the stone blissfully cold.

At which point that Jacinto walked in on him unannounced. Taking in what Swein was doing in a single glance, he turned on his heels.

"You are disgusting!" he snarled. "I will not lower myself to such a foul and base creature as you!" With which he marched out of the door only to nearly collide with Esclados and Cwen coming up the stairs.

"Have you apologized?" Esclados demanded.

"I will not apologize to that thing!" Jacinto snapped. "That filthy animal is pissing in the grate! The lodge keeper's dog is better trained than that!" and swept by before Esclados could respond.

"Oh Swein!" Cwen groaned, opening the door to his room. He still stood where Jacinto had seen him, although he was fully relieved, not having even done his pants up. Without even looking at the door to see who it was he spoke huskily.

"Alright, alright, so I'm disgusting. What did you expect of me? I'll clean it up. Not now, though. Go away."

"Yes, you will clean it up!" Cwen said severely.

Swein's head shot up, making him moan with the additional thump that it gave behind the eyes. Cwen! He had forgotten her. When he got in this state at the palace there had only ever been male servants around. To his horror he then realized his state of undress, and turned his back while he fumbled to put himself straight. From behind Cwen, Esclados tapped her on the shoulder and motioned her out of the room.

"Go," he said softly, "I'll see to this."

"Are you sure?" she asked. Esclados nodded. He had some questions of his own in mind and he wanted to see the scars Cwen had spoken of. It was not that he disbelieved her, but if he was going to convince anyone else it would help if he could say he had seen the signs of torture with his own eyes.

So it was even more of a shock to Swein when he turned back, to find that Cwen had disappeared and been replaced with the bear of a Knight, looking down on him with an unreadable expression. Swein tried to put on his best 'couldn't care less' expression, which Esclados only seemed to find amusing. Without saying a word, he grasped Swein firmly by the scruff of his shirt and marched him out and down the stairs. Swein was convinced he was going to be thrown straight out of the gate, but at the bottom of the stairs Esclados turned them back into another room in the building.

At the back of the room, a stone channel carried cold running water through as part of the whole castle's well-designed water system. By this stage it had already passed the kitchens and was on the way to its last appearance at the stables with clean water for the horses. Hauling Swein bodily over to the channel, Esclados thrust his head into the icy flow. The shock took Swein's breath away and he gasped, taking in a mouthful of water and choking. He was pulled back up until he had stopped spluttering, but before he could say anything he was plunged under the water again.

After several soakings, Esclados must have decided that he was awake, for he draped a towel over Swein's dripping head and marched him out and into another room where he pushed him into a chair and thrust a mug of hot caff into his shaking hands.

For the first time Esclados spoke.

"You're an idiot, aren't you." It was a statement, and delivered without any malice or shouted criticism. Instead his voice just carried a world-weary acceptance. "Why did you do it, lad? Have you no self-respect?"

Swein would have shaken his head if it had not hurt so much. Instead he settled for a baleful stare. Esclados sighed and went out. When he returned a few moments later, he hauled Swein to his feet again and propelled him out of the door, across the hall again, and into what turned out to be a communal bathroom. Evidently the garrison had already finished their morning ablutions going by the piles of wet towels which were being carried out. However, a bath at the end of the room was being filled from the overhead cistern, which, if not piping hot, was warm enough to not be too unpleasant on a chilly autumn morning. Swein felt too feeble to resist as Esclados swiftly undressed him and shoved him towards the bath. The water was a blissful salve to his body, and he let the soothing warmth soak into his aching legs, back and neck. The steam even seemed to ease his pounding head.

Esclados on the other hand had nearly sworn out loud as Swein had turned his back to get in the bath. In all his years he had never seen someone still alive with such trauma. For a second he was too shocked to move or think. Then he took a deep breath and looked again, and realized that the scars had not happened all at once. What he was seeing was a slow accumulation over what had to have been years of systematic abuse.

Using the excuse of taking the mug of caff out for a refill, he left the room and went to stand in the yard. The fresh air restored some of his equilibrium. Deep in his soul an anger was building like a volcano. Once upon a time there had been a woman he had cared for in a town they had garrisoned, and, long after they had separated when the troops left, he had heard there had been a child. Every time he heard of a child being misused, he wondered where the people were who should have been protecting it. Then his thoughts would turn to his unknown child, and he had prayed to the Spirits that in his absence someone had cared for it. In return he had long ago vowed to them that he would do all within his power to protect any other child who was abandoned which came into his life.

Swein was far from a child now, yet once upon a time he had been. Where had the adults been who should have protected him? Esclados' respect for Cwen rose another notch for having seen so clearly what lay behind Swein's behaviour. However he feared she didn't know quite what she had let herself in for in trying to help Swein. He, on the other hand, had seen enough men shoved into the service of the Knights as boy soldiers amongst the lay troops, who had previously been on the receiving end of an abusive relative, to know. There was no quick cure. Time would help, but not in the immediate future.

Squaring his shoulders, Esclados went in, refilled the mug, and went back to the bathhouse. Swein was still in the bath, asleep. Rather than frighten him by shaking him, Esclados stood back and called his name until his eyes opened. By the expression on his face, Swein had forgotten where he was, but then his eyes found Esclados and the hunted look came back.

"Come on," Esclados said quietly, "get out of the bath. That water must be getting cold by now, and there's more caff here." He picked up one of the thick white towels off the pile by the door and brought it across to Swein, holding it up so that the young man could step out without having to bare himself to Esclados' gaze. With cautious gratitude, Swein climbed out and wrapped the towel around himself. Esclados left him to get dry, going to find clean clothes from Swein's baggage. With Swein clean and feeling more in the land of the living, Esclados escorted him across the bailey to the room they had been in the night before. Leaving him in the peace and quiet, and the promise to return and fetch him when the midday food appeared, Esclados left to find Cwen.

It was no surprise to find her in the stables happily grooming Twigglet and Bracken. Picking up another brush, he made a start on getting the furze out of Bracken's tail while they talked. Rather than quizzing her, he told her about the imminent return of Berengar, and of his hopes that they would then travel under escort to Breslyn. He had feared she might feel that things were not happening fast enough, and might take it into her head to ride on alone. However, Cwen reassured him that she had no such intention. Indeed, far from going it alone, she could see the sense of having an escort, and that the records would be much more easily accessed with a senior officer from the Order at her side.

They had therefore spent another recuperative day at Vellyn – and without Swein getting wrecked again – before they heard the returning troops approaching. The sun was sinking into the west, and Cwen was enjoying watching the countryside change colours from the vantage point of the castle walls, when she realized there was something else out there. From the distant north-south road, a long shadow was turning their way. As the advance guard got closer, she could see the last rays of sunshine glinting occasionally off armour or a weapon. From the sounds of laughter and conversation, the men were looking forward to their return to barracks, and there was no sign that anything eventful had happened on the way. A tall, dark-haired man on a superb destrier trotted off to one side and sat there, watching as the rest filed in over the bridge.

Cwen felt the tears rise again. That was so like Richert had used to do. In front of her swimming eyes she could not have said whether she was watching the Knights and men-at-arms here at Vellyn, or was looking back through time to when she used to wait for Richert on the battlements of Amroth, as he had sat with the local captain of the Knights checking the men back in. As the last man rode past, the Knight turned his horse and followed him under the arch of the great gates, and disappeared from view as they shut with a deep thump.

Down in the bailey of the castle, Esclados sat quietly on a bench outside the commander's office as mayhem erupted around him. Or at least, to an outsider it would have looked that way. To the experienced eye it was like watching the ordered and intricate dance of bees in a hive. Horses were led to water, with the men-at-arms tending their own beasts, and the grooms coming out to collect those of the Knights. The first of the file had already made their way onwards towards the refectory or the bathhouse as their preference dictated. Esclados knew that Berengar would be pounced upon the minute he appeared, and so waited patiently until he knew he could get his friend and commander's undivided attention.

Finally he saw the tall, burly shape striding over towards him and smiled in return.

"Good trip?" he asked, levering himself up with a grunt and heading into the office, where he had a pot of caff and two mugs keeping warm. He lit the oil lamps in the wall brackets, and turned to Berengar with a steaming mug. Berengar smiled, his weather-tanned face creasing in a smile. A deep, long scar ran from his scalp to his jaw on the left-hand side of his face, giving him a menacing appearance to many. But once the smile appeared it revealed a man at ease with himself and the life he led.

"Not bad," he replied, sinking into the cushioned seat behind the desk, kicking off the knee-high boots, and putting his stockinged feet up on the desk. "Ah that's better!"

"Any signs of trouble?" Esclados asked nonchalantly. "The DeÁine behaving themselves?"

"Seem to be," Berengar answered. "We patrolled all along the northern coast road seeing neither hide nor hair of them. So much so that we did it in half the time I expected, so we rode all the way to Borth and then took the road to the mountains. I thought in the Brychan Line we'd see some signs, but even Esgair's been quiet now for over a year."

The Brychan Line was the name given to a deep divide between two halves of the range of vast, eternally snow-capped mountains which ran the length of the island from north to south. On the far side lay the other half of Brychan, but nobody had been there for so long it was poorly mapped, and most maps of the Islands showed Brychan ending in the west with the mountains. Beyond it lay the new territory of the DeÁine, and none but the Covert Brethren went there. When the mountains had formed, the great up-thrust of the earth had formed a fold in the middle of the range. Less than a valley, since it had no real broad floor and rose and fell with the peaks alongside it, it nevertheless provided an easier passage than crossing the ranges. As a consequence, over the years a chain of fortified towers had grown up along it. It made for a good boundary, easily defended, and in the south where the mountains were lower it was heavily patrolled.

Here in the north, for the most part, the mountains did the job for them. This was the last patrol that the Knights would make before the winter set in. In a month the snows would start in earnest, making even the metalled road between the forts treacherous. Esgair was the highest town in Brychan, serving the towers and hanging on to a small plateau which had been ringed with high stone walls, and became totally isolated for four or five months a year. For the Knights who had fought and died at Gavra Pass, Esgair had been their last sight of civilization before heading into the second range and their doom.

"What, no sign even at Esgair?" Esclados said, surprised. "That's the first time I've heard of them seeing no-one. Normally they at least get the odd DeÁine hothead trying to take the island all by himself!"

"I know," Berengar mused. "But it doesn't feel like the calm before the storm either. That was almost odder! I tried to find reasons to be worried, but even taking the high passes back over the top of the island there was nothing. I must have climbed up twenty watch towers and looked down as many passes to the west across the Line. Nothing. Not even a lost sheep! In the end I think I was making the men more twitchy than the threat of the

DeÁine!" He stretched his arms above his head and Esclados heard the joints creak as he eased the knots from being in the saddle all day. "You never know, Esclados," he said cheerfully, "we might even have a quiet winter! No call-outs in the snow! That'd be bliss!"

"Mmmm…" Esclados intoned.

Berengar stopped in mid-yawn and turned an eye to his old friend.

"Oh yes? And what's that supposed to mean?"

He sat up, putting his feet down and leaning his elbows on the desk as he scrutinized Esclados' face.

"What's happened? Apart from Jacinto screwing things up? I assume that's so normal you wouldn't feel the need to tell me *that* the minute I return. So what's up, old bear? Come on, cough it up, you always were lousy at keeping secrets."

"Well ….it does have to do with Jacinto, but he's only part of it."

Sinking into the chair opposite the desk, Esclados brought Berengar up to date on the Order's visitors.

"Well, well, that is a parcel of news," Berengar commented at the end. "One of Edward's lover-boys shows up here of all places. I'd never thought to see that happen, especially not to bring us evidence like that."

"Oh, I doubt he'd have come here of his own accord," Esclados corrected him. "It's not that he's a bad lad, by any means, but by the Spirits, Berengar, that poor soul has suffered in ways I can't imagine. There's no way he would've trusted us, because there's nobody he does trust anymore. It's a tribute to that young lady that she's got him this far and persuaded him to come to us."

"You're quite taken with her, aren't you?" Berengar teased.

Esclados laughed.

"Now don't you go making assumptions and getting it wrong!" Then he looked away wistfully. "But if I'd had a daughter I'd like to think she'd have turned out like that."

Berengar knew of Esclados' past, and knew what a compliment that was coming from the older Knight. He immediately resolved to see this young woman for himself that night. He needed to be sure of her, if only because he knew how deeply Esclados would be hurt if she turned out to be false. He had obviously become very protective of her in such a short space of time, but if he had to be disabused then it was better it happened now than later, when it would be even harder to take. On that basis he sent Esclados off to find his two new charges, with instructions to bring them back to eat with him when he had had chance to wash the dust of the journey off.

That evening, while the refectory filled up with hungry troops, Esclados returned with Cwen and Swein to find that Berengar had had a meal set out in his living quarters. With his back to the lights, Berengar was able to observe them as they came in. Swein stood with eyes cast down, only making fearful glances up at this new terror he had to face, which was as Berengar expected from what Esclados had said. Cwen, on the other hand, walked in with the easy assurance of someone in familiar circumstances. Her smile was open and genuine, and despite his reservations Berengar immediately saw why Esclados liked her. Throughout the meal it was she who kept the conversation going, while Swein only ever spoke when she addressed him directly. By the end of the night, Berengar was as convinced as Esclados had been of the truth of their story. Like Esclados, he too felt only sadness at what he saw in Swein, which surprised him. He had always thought that if he had ever met one of Edward's play-things he would be disgusted at someone who could stoop so low. Yet, in the flesh, all he saw was someone who had never stood a chance in the hands of a malicious manipulator like Edward. One thing was certain, Edward would never get his hands on Swein again if Berengar had any say in the matter.

However, Cwen intrigued him the more he spoke to her. She was so relaxed in his company he felt sure the dead lover must have been a soldier, and someone of rank at that. Questions he wanted to ask filled his head, but instinct told him that she would become more guarded if he pressed too hard. He had no doubt that she was telling the truth – it just was not all of the truth. However, that was not enough to give him any reservations about what to do next. He had to give his men and horses a rest, and there were some administrative tasks he could not pass onto his assistants, however much he wished he could have. Therefore there would be a couple of days' delay while he set things in order once more, but for the ride to Breslyn he could take the older men who had not gone on the long patrol – in fact it would do them good, he thought, to feel that they were still as much a part of the company, and give them a positive task to fulfil.

"How long do you think it will take to get there?" Cwen asked.

Berengar walked over to the wall where a map of Brychan hung. Pointing to the finger of land which stretched out to Breslyn and Celidon beyond, he tapped at the red line of the road.

"That way normally takes at least a week in good weather. If we get rain it could slow us down on the moors. We'll keep an eye on the weather, but if the westerly winds we've been getting hold on, I think it might be quickest if we take the boat across the sound to Penteg. Thanks to Esclados, the warders at Breslyn will be on their guard against anyone being too curious who shows up. It's those records we need to make sure are safe first of all. Without them the king's men won't know where to start."

"Aren't the people still at Breslyn, then?" she asked in surprise.

"Why should they be?" Berengar replied. "None of them were blood-related to Mar, and until today we had no reason to think they were in any danger. As far as the Knights knew, it was only the woman who had anything to fear, and possibly her son by Mar, but we didn't have him. The others were of no interest to anyone. I can confirm that the boy who came here was the child she'd already had before she met Mar. I knew she'd then had a son by him and that that son never came here, but I had no idea he had been raised as the heir. They covered their tracks well over that, for fear of scandal, no doubt. The other boy and two girls were born after she came here."

"I'm glad you're coming with us," Cwen said, "you're so much better informed than us."

"Yes, you seem to know a lot about them," Esclados said, rather surprised that he had never heard about this from his friend before.

Berengar gave a wisp of an inscrutable smile, but said nothing, despite Esclados' sly probing through the rest of the evening.

To the relief of everyone, Berengar's paperwork was finished quicker than anticipated, and so, by the evening of the second night after his return, the castle once more became a hive of activity as the older Knights and soldiers prepared for an early morning start. There was one unpleasant task left to Berengar, and with reluctance he called Jacinto into his office. He had no idea what to do with this young man. No matter what he did, no matter whom he put him with to mentor him, nobody seemed able to make any progress in making Jacinto into a proper Knight. There was no question that the young man was a superb fighter. Yet his inability to follow the simplest of orders meant that breaking him down to the ranks of the enlisted men was only wishing the same problems onto them.

Sitting in his chair, Berengar watched Jacinto come in. For once the arrogant swagger was missing – so Esclados must have got some concept of the severity of the situation through to him. The almost petulant pout was still there, though, as was the guarded look in the eyes which forewarned of a multitude of excuses as to why it was not his fault. Berengar left him standing in front of the desk for as long as he could without saying anything, scrutinizing him with a steely stare. When Jacinto's eyes began to waver, he finally leant forward and spoke.

"You are a complete and utter disgrace to this Order, do you realize that?" Berengar said with soft menace. "I have never had a squire so stupidly arrogant as to be utterly untrainable. I've given you the benefit of training with some of the best men in the Order, and yet all that's happened is that we've produce a fighting machine without a single redeeming feature."

He leant back and delivered the shock.

"You have one month. One month to change your ways and show me that I'm not wasting time and effort on you. If you haven't done that, I'm dismissing you."

Jacinto's jaw dropped, aghast.

"Dismissing? What do you mean?"

"Exactly that – throwing you out. Where you go and what you do after that is your own affair, but if we hear of you taking your spite out on the ordinary people, you will be hunted down and treated like a common criminal. No leniency will be shown because you were once one of us."

"But you can't!" Jacinto protested. "No-one ever gets thrown out."

"Oh yes they do," Berengar said, icily. "Not for a long time, admittedly, but why should you be special? You may have come to us as an abandoned babe. We may have sent you to one of our retired Knight's families to be raised, but you've shown no attachment to those people despite their kindness. Then you were brought into the garrison to be trained – and how we've tried to do that! We've done our duty by you. We protected you, we gave you help, we've given you shelter and nourishment. By the oaths that bind us we've gone above and beyond what was required of us, so why should we do more? You're a grown man now. You're fit and healthy and capable of looking after yourself. You've given me not *one* tiny reason why I should keep such a wilful and disruptive presence in my garrison, and with the reference I would be forced to give you, no other commander would have you either."

Under his dark skin Jacinto had gone white. Of all the things he had expected Berengar to say this was the most unanticipated. He had thought it would be the same old routine. Berengar cataloguing his faults and then a punishment detail he could get out of the way and carry on. But to leave! And not just leave. To be cast out! To be pronounce the ultimate failure! The blow to Jacinto's considerable pride was devastating. Then Berengar delivered the next blow.

"But I won't leave you here with the rest of the troop. I'm personally going to watch you like a hawk, so you'll come with the veterans. Furthermore, I'm assigning you with Esclados to escort our two guests. That young man you so despise is more worthy of our kindness and consideration than you've ever been. He has good reason to be terrified, and so I'm personally charging you with his protection. You will treat him with respect and courtesy, and if I see him looking harried, upset, or frightened, I'll be all over you like a rash. Do I make myself clear? You will make *his* needs a priority over your own. You *will* learn compassion for others! You *will* learn humility! Learn or leave! It's your choice, now get out!"

Jacinto staggered out into the autumn drizzle, his world shattered. Reeling from the shock, he could not bear to be a part of the cheerful mêlée in the bailey. He found the nearest steps to the battlements and made his way up to the top, hugging himself as if to hold himself together. In a lonely corner of the wall, hidden from view by the protruding bulk of one of the towers, he stared out at the countryside as it began to rain in earnest as darkness fell. With the rain came his tears, and he leant against the stone parapet and sobbed as he had not done since he was a small boy.

He never heard the footsteps approach, but out of the gloom a voice, filled with sympathy, suddenly softly said,

"What's wrong?"

Without looking up, Jacinto blurted out his problem.

"I'm to be dismissed! Gratitude! That's what they want from me. For what? Being the outsider all the time? Oh, the man who raised me fed me, clothed me, taught me all the things I was supposed to know. But I wasn't his. I didn't look like him – I don't look like any of them – it couldn't have been plainer that I wasn't one of them. So they didn't try. The other fosterlings all had beds in rooms of their own with their foster parents. I had a room next to the kennels! He said I was wilful, too strong-willed. Too strong-willed? I wouldn't have survived if hadn't been strong-willed!"

"I know," the voice beside him whispered. "My father used to beat me. Said it would make a man of me. It never did him any harm, he said, and nobody ever tried to stop him. For all they called me their son, they never treated me the same as my brothers. While they learned the business, I was left with the women to do the work. Except that the workers thought I was my father's spy put amongst them, and so they spat at me. He said that when I improved and acted like a man he'd let me join them. …Never happened, of course. There was no way I could ever have come up to standard because they kept moving the targets."

"They threw you out?"

The voice laughed bitterly.

"No, they wouldn't lose a slave they didn't even have to pay – someone working for free for *years*! No, I left. …Didn't work though, I'm still on the outside!"

For a moment Jacinto did not register what had been said, then realized that whoever he was talking to could not be one of the garrison. He spun around and found himself towering over Swein. Too stunned to speak, he could not believe that the person he blamed for the final humiliation was the one person who had shown him sympathy and kindness. One part of him was repulsed and wanted to turn on his heels and run, but a fracture had been made in his inner armour for which there had been no time to make repairs. The other part of him craved the solace of company that did not judge.

His indecision left him standing there, and Swein reached out a tentative hand to stroke the muscled bicep. With great daring he suddenly stood on tiptoe to reach up and kiss the tall, dark soldier full on the lips. For a second there was a shocked pause, then for a blissful moment Swein found himself crushed to Jacinto as the kiss was returned, before the would-be Knight dropped him and fled.

When they encountered one another in the company of the others the next morning, Jacinto looked through Swein as though nothing had happened. Berengar, however, noticed that there was something different. For the first time Jacinto was standing back and allowing the guests to go first to get breakfast, without starring down his nose at them. If he was not falling over himself to help, at least he did not look as though he wanted to wipe his feet on Swein. As they mounted up, it was Jacinto who went to help Swein. They made an odd-looking pair, Berengar thought. Jacinto was as dark, tall and muscled as Swein was pale and slender. Not a word passed between them, and for once Swein realized that the best thing would be to act as if the events of last night had never happened – at least in public.

It was a miserable day's ride in gusting rain, which left few of the company in chatty mood, so the silence between Swein and Jacinto was unremarkable. The weather had backed and so the boat journey was deferred and the high road taken. That night Jacinto was with the main company at the grange they stopped at, while Swein joined Cwen with Esclados and Berengar. Jacinto saw his commander with some trepidation the next morning, fearing that Swein would have told all, but nothing happened. By the third night he had realized that whatever else Swein was, he could be discreet. Yet occasional exchanged glances told Jacinto that the night's encounter had not been forgotten. He had no idea what to do, though, not least because his feelings were in complete turmoil. His whole world had been stood on its head, but before he had had time to make any decision events caught up with them again.

Between Corwen and Nefyn the road had to negotiate a steep path as a shoulder of the mountains came right down to the sea. Across its broad headland, the road-makers had carved out a passage through a natural fold in the rock. Unlike the rest of the road, this twisted and turned to avoid those great baulks of stone too massive to be moved or cut away.

The rain had stopped, but they were riding through puddles when they heard the pounding of hooves coming from the opposite direction, unseen around the bends. From the sound of it there were only two or three horsemen, and with such a number of experienced soldiers they had little to fear from other travellers. The company pulled over to the one side of the road to allow the oncoming riders passage past them, but as they came into view and saw Berengar at the head of the troop, they began to rein-in their horses. Esclados recognized them as some of the messengers he had sent to Breslyn as they came close enough to be heard.

"Sire!" the leading man called as he rode up to Berengar. "I'd hoped you'd be on the way. Sire, I bring bad news. We reached Breslyn the day after those who went by sea, but it wouldn't have made any difference if we'd all got there at the same time. The garrison's dead!"

Gasps of horror greeted this news.

"What happened?" Berengar demanded.

"We're not sure, sire. The local farmers had come up to bury our men out of respect, and they were there when we arrived. They said that a couple of months ago a troop of men arrived, but only stayed the night and then left again. They didn't think they were Knights – possibly the king's men – but there was no sign of anything amiss after they left. It was a week or so ago that something went desperately wrong. You should see the place, sire. It looks like a giant went mad in it! The locals said there were sounds as though the place was being hit by thunderbolts."

Berengar heeled his own horse forward, and the whole troop joined in a race across the north Brychan moors that got them to Breslyn in record time. Cwen blessed the stamina of Twigglet and Bracken, who kept going when some of the bigger horses were flagging after days at full pelt. But her heart sank with the rest of the company's as they came to the last rise before the sea and looked down on the destruction of Breslyn. Whatever had been in the library was lost, because the library was now in the dungeon along with the rest of the west tower. The company of soldiers streamed passed her and Swein to aid their colleagues, and the farmers, in trying to find the bodies of the shattered garrison.

Berengar spent the rest of the day questioning everyone who might have a clue as to what happened. By evening it had become apparent that it had been members of the king's bodyguard who had come earlier, and that that had been longer ago than the messengers had realized. Using Cwen and Swein's telling of their journeys, Berengar calculated that this visit had taken place with enough time for the troop to have returned to Arlei before Edward had staged his own 'murder'. The dreadful possibility occurred to all four of those who knew the full passage of events, that the actor had been no such thing. It was almost certain that he was one of Edward's half-brothers and that they were too late. Strangely, Berengar took the news hardest of all, shedding tears at the wanton loss of a life.

Yet it did not explain the destruction of the castle. No force that any of the soldiers knew of could explain what had done that or why. All the farmers could tell them was that a strange priest had passed through the day before it happened and stopped at the castle, but what became of him was unknown. Instead the crows circled above.

On a rocky knoll, his distant perception enhanced by those of the crows, a tall, gaunt figure stood, his layered black robes swirling like feathers in the rough sea wind. He could hear what was going on, but it made no sense. Why were these Knights worrying about some lost person? What possible value could he have? His lips drew back over his teeth in a snarl of frustration. He had used every skill at his command. Had drawn on all his Powers. He had been so sure 'it' was here. He could feel its taint permeating the stones of the castle, as though it had rested here for many years. It had drawn him like an invisible cord, and yet he could not find it.

Eliavres grasped his bald head with both hands and howled his frustration. Those cursed Knights were acting as though they had no idea that the Gorget had ever been there, so how could they lead him to it? Casting the birds free, he sent his mind roving amongst the men. He needed someone down there amongst them. Someone pliable and susceptible to suggestion. And finally he found him – a bundle of hurt and confusion ripe for the picking – and slithered unnoticed inside his mind.

Chapter 24

Questions and Conjectures

Celidon: Winterfalling

As Harvest-moon passed into Winterfalling, the debate within Sioncaet's cottage became ever more serious. Maelbrigt and Kayna were all for going straight to Ergardia. In part this was because of the presence of Talorcan and a fully functioning sept of Knights, who could provide protection from the DeÁine's Hunters. The other factor predominant in Maelbrigt's mind was the separating stretch of water. From what he knew from his past experiences of the DeÁine, if by some great misfortune Anarawd himself had decided to join the hunt (without deigning to tell Sithfrey of his intent), the war-mage's power to trace Taise would be severely diminished by the sound. It was not a wide stretch of water – on all but the worst of days it was easy to see detail on one shore from the other – but it might be enough to save Taise's life.

The more Taise herself spoke with Sioncaet, though, the more she felt an urgency pulling them in a different direction. The manuscript which could show the Abend a way of neutralizing the power of the Island Treasures worried them deeply. Sioncaet was also sure that if Anarawd was pursuing Taise so hard, it was not just to use her to father the ultimate DeÁine onto. He felt deep in his bones that the devious Abend thought that she knew the location of that manuscript, and however much Taise might say otherwise, buried somewhere in her subconscious she held the key. The other big question in everyone's mind was why they had let Taise go in the first place.

"Let me go!" Taise had exclaimed indignantly when Sioncaet had first brought the matter up. "I escaped! And only just with my life! They had nothing to do with it!"

"Didn't they?" Sioncaet had softly replied, refusing to make it into an argument. "How *did* you get away Taise? They must have had you under lock and key. Where were the guards? How hard were you pursued?"

Maelbrigt tensed, instinctively wanting to protect Taise, yet the light touch of Sioncaet's hand on his arm to restrain him echoed the worrying thought that he had been trying to squash. When he had met Taise it had never occurred to him that she might have been so important to the DeÁine. Now he could not avoid the questions which he was beginning to think he should have asked long ago. Veteran soldier though he was, he was terrified of the consequences of her reply. Foremost was the fear that she would be revealed as being in some way complicit in the Abend's schemes.

The scars she wore testified to her suffering at their hands, of course, but Maelbrigt knew what torture could do to the mind. At some stage – different for everyone – there would come a point when they would agree to almost anything to make the pain stop. For the strongest it might come at death's door, when they were past giving anything but the vaguest hint. For others it came quicker. And of course, he had never dreamt that she had been so deep within the Abend's strongholds. One lost DeÁine woman, who had walked away from a war zone, was very different from one who had walked out from under the gaze of the most powerful of the Abend, especially when all reasoning said they would not want her to leave.

Maelbrigt forced himself to be the one to ask the question.

"Tell us how you left, Taise," he half instructed half pleaded, hoping there would be some rational reason for her to be free.

Taise looked at him with filling eyes.

"Don't you trust me?" she whispered.

"Sacred Rowan, of course I do!" he replied, horrified that she could doubt his loyalty.

Labhran had never thought he would feel sorry for Maelbrigt, but at that moment, watching as his old companion's misery brought back all the memories of his own pain and loss, he was moved to pity him.

"Taise," he intervened, "it's not that we doubt you. But we've fought these conniving monsters before. They have plots within plots. If they can't use you openly, they may have planned to use you covertly. You know how much longer their life span is. They think in terms of decades not just years. Those bastards play the long game. Loosening their grip on you just enough to give you the opening to escape might have been deliberate, to allow you time to work the location of that manuscript out by yourself."

Taise's soundless "Oohhh" of comprehension said she had finally grasped what they feared. Maelbrigt moved from his seat by the fire to join Taise on the truckle bed, where he sat down with one leg bent up on the bed to enable him to pull her completely into his embrace. Holding her tight against him he asked her again.

"Please, Taise, start from the beginning and tell us how you got out of the Abend's grip."

Holding on to his enfolding arms as if to stop herself drowning, Taise began. She thought that the Abend as a whole had lost interest in her when they found out about Bres' betrayal. At that point they had certainly stopped questioning her day and night, and just being able to get some sleep had helped her. As she had become more aware of her surroundings, she had realized that the Abend had dashed on to the palace at Bruighean, while the rest of the battered army was still several days away from the capital. Without the Abend to strike terror and urgency into the weary troops their progress had slowed to a crawl. Taise was in a small covered wagon all the time, at first under very close guard, but once they had descended from the mountains and were back on the bare dry plain where the DeÁine ruled supreme, the guard relaxed. She put it down to so many of them being too exhausted to care.

Once the Abend were gone she was luckier than most in that she could sleep in the wagon, and regain her strength while the army trudged on. Bruighean was too small to take all of the army and so they had camped at the capital's gates on the day they reached it. Nobody knew what was happening, but Taise could hear the men talking of how the Donns and the Arberth were furious at the way the Abend had taken the army without consultation, and then brought it back in tatters. It struck her that for once the Abend were not getting things their own way, and that their orders might count for less than they had for many a long year.

When her evening food had been brought she had pleaded with her guard. She was of no consequence now they had found the real traitor, she said. What would the Donn in charge of this company say when he found that they had continued to hold an innocent woman on the whim of the Abend? It was obvious he was too scared to just let her go, but if she escaped they would hardly chase her, she suggested. In the end she had wedged a piece of her tattered robe into the bolt so that it did not close fully, and the frightened, exhausted young soldier had barely pushed it home into the hasp. In the deep of night she had worked it free and slipped out. After weeks on the road watching their back at every step, the entire army was sleeping the sleep of the dead under the safety of their fellow countrymen's walls.

She walked all night, raiding carelessly dropped baggage until she was halfway respectably clothed. When daylight came she had managed to reach the edge of the encampment. At that point to be seen to be walking back the way they had come would have been too peculiar, so she started walking around the perimeter as if on errands. That way, she had reasoned, she would not be going in a straight line away from where she had been held, and so would be harder to find if the Abend did send someone to search for her. The next night she had set out, having catnapped off and on during the day, and headed for the mountains.

For days she had walked north, keeping the huge range on her right side, each day creeping a little closer to them. Yet the more she saw of them the more formidable they looked. The towering snow-capped peaks, she came to realize, were no place for a woman who had trouble surviving on the plain. Away from towns she had no idea what to do for food. Herbs she knew and understood, but they had little power to sustain her. What she needed were things like cheese, and fish, and especially bread, to supplement the fruit she was picking from the hedgerows, to give her the energy to keep going. Without money it was difficult enough, but at least in a town she could have begged. In the deserted wilderness she was passing through now, though, there was not even a cottager to steal from, let alone buy off.

The only way she had survived was because she had come to a river flowing north to the sea, and had managed to find an old boat to slip away in. The current had taken her at its own swift pace until finally the sea had appeared. Once adrift there, she had been picked up by a fishing boat from northern Brychan. Out at sea they felt safe to trawl their nets across the fish feeding banks up by Auskerry Island despite the nearest shore being DeÁine territory.

The fishermen had been kind and taken her into a port, where she had spun a tale about being an escaped prisoner of war. She had told them she was from the far south to explain her lack of local knowledge, and the kindly folk had arranged transport in a relay of fishing boats along the coast. As far as they knew she was heading for the sheltered passage on Brychan's east coast which ran from Penteg in the north, southwards behind the protection of a chain of rocky islets to Mythvai, before taking to the open sea to pass around to the southern ports. However, once she reached Salen she had changed course and slipped across the narrow passage to the island of Ynys. Sithfrey had unknowingly traced almost the same route when he had passed over to the next island of Lorne and onto Celidon.

"So you see, I did escape!" Taise said vehemently at the end of her tale.

"Forgive me," Sioncaet apologized, "but we had to be sure you hadn't just been conveniently released from some dungeon. You have to understand, Taise, that without knowing, it sounded to us as though one minute you were in the depths of Bruighean's citadel, and the next here. Now we know that you never even got inside the city walls, it makes much more sense."

"Anarawd was the one who threw a fit," Sithfrey chipped in. "I don't think Taise was important to anyone but him, and you're right, the Abend had to watch their step back then. They could do their worst to me and the others because we were part of their own cortege, but there was no way after that fiasco that they were allowed to take anyone anywhere who wasn't already in their power. And even then, one of the reasons they didn't physically torture *us* was because they were denied access to the chambers deep beneath the citadel and temples. All they *could* do was use the Power, which nobody else could see."

"I know that makes it sound like it wasn't much," Sioncaet said gently, acknowledging Sithfrey's suffering, "but the Power is no mean thing to have directed at you. It doesn't begin to diminish what you went through, Sithfrey. …I'm sorry to have to press you, Taise – are you absolutely sure you weren't being manipulated? In your mind, if not outwardly?"

Taise paused and looked up at the ceiling for several seconds, then looked back at them and shook her head.

"I think I would've known. I've worried that it might have happened, certainly. It feels …weird …when they tried to do that to me. Anarawd kept beating at me – and beating is the right word, I think, in the sense that it felt like I was being buffeted by the wings of a big bird I couldn't see. It hurt – it hurt *a lot* – but he never got inside me. Inside my head. When the Power is projected at me I can feel it, like a blast of air, as it's coming, and my own defences seem to kick in. Of course, I was never really trained how to deflect it – it seems to be something instinctive, and I'm sure that if I was trained my early warning sense would be far more acute, but it's still pretty sharp. I've thought back over the last few days, since we've known the Abend are on the move again, and I can't think of any point where I've felt something that might mean they're trying again, either."

For a moment they all breathed a sigh of relief at the thought that the Abend could not automatically manipulate Taise or tap into her knowledge.

"Does this mean that if Anarawd didn't send Taise deliberately to Celidon, that we can take her to Ergardia now?" Kayna asked, as Sioncaet handed round another brew of caff.

Maelbrigt shot her a grateful glance for saying what he was feeling.

But it was Taise herself who was the first to shake her head.

"I don't think so."

"No," agreed Sioncaet. "We have to figure out where that manuscript might be. Don't you see? If the Abend are sending Hunters out, we may have only a limited amount of time to search Celidon. Once it becomes too dangerous for Taise, Sithfrey and me to be here we've lost our chance, and it *has* to be *us* because we don't know what language it will be in. If it's in DeÁine, or the Old Language of the Ancients, how would anyone else know what it was?"

"Hold on," Labhran rebuked him. "You're forgetting that Maelbrigt and I both know DeÁine, and how many manuscripts are there likely to be in the Old Language? In the unlikely event of finding one of those, we could bring it to Ergardia. It's not likely we'd be lugging a library around!"

"That's right," Kayna said firmly. "Let's get you to safety, then we can come back to search."

The argument carried on into the small hours and then into the next morning. Finally they agreed to avoid the lengthier but potentially faster route on the road south through Cabrack and up the eastern coast to the ferry at Giha. Instead, they would make for Ergardia by the more circuitous route through the mountain passes. Taise had a vague memory, as did Sithfrey, of seeing a map of the Islands overlaid with a six-pointed star. One point had touched Celidon on the far north of the island, yet Maelbrigt and Labhran assured them there were only isolated fortresses up there. Certainly there was nowhere up there which possessed anything that could be called a library. Any manuscript in those dank, rain-swept stones would have turned to mould or mouse food long ago.

However, the reason the road ran on from Giha to Scarba was because of the monastery there. Now a shadow of its former self, it nonetheless still held a substantial repository of documents. So it was agreed that they should travel over the hills to Scarba, and then ride down to Giha from the north to cross into Ergardia. Nobody was entirely happy with the solution, but it was the only plan they could come to an agreement on.

Consequently they set out the next day on a grey day as depressed as their moods. Labhran now became their guide, being more familiar with this area than Maelbrigt. Surprisingly, once they were on the road and he was more in control, Labhran's mood improved. Sithfrey now found that Labhran could be every bit as assertive as Maelbrigt, especially when it came to fulfilling the promise to train him. As they rode along, Sithfrey often found himself on the receiving end of various lectures from one or the other, and at their midday and evening breaks he would find himself being submitted to short, but effective, practice sessions. No-one was even going to pretend that he was a natural swordsman, but by the time they had been on the road a week, he could at least manage not to drop his weapon at the first exchange of blades.

Though winter had not yet really arrived, it was bitterly cold in the mountains, with the temperature dropping dramatically at night even on those days when it was sunny. The shepherd's refuges proved a blessing, with the horses taking up residence in the sheep pens to shelter against the bitter wind. The huts were hardly luxurious, but they all had a hearth, and reserves of wood which the experienced travellers amongst them insisted on trying to at least partially replace once they had got themselves a fire going each night. Maelbrigt, Labhran and Kayna would go out scavenging for anything burnable, which was also a good way to scout around the vicinity to look for signs of any other recent travellers. To their relief they seemed to be alone in the mountains, but, having been caught out once by Sithfrey, Maelbrigt was taking no chances.

This high up the scenery was bleak. The high stream valleys were soggy under the horses' hooves, making for slow progress, while the peaks of the mountains were rough scree with only occasional stunted heather and dried-out tussocks of coarse grass. The wind howled and moaned through the desolate landscape depressing everyone. As they wound their way through one of the high, narrow passages, Labhran managed to catch Sioncaet's eye. With Maelbrigt in the rear patiently explaining something to Sithfrey, and Taise deep in conversation with Kayna, they were able to increase the gap until the two of them were sufficiently in front to not be overheard.

"What is it?" Sioncaet asked softly.

"Look, I don't want to sound all bitter and twisted," Labhran began, "but I've been thinking. Do you really believe that Taise escaped? I heard all that she said before, and at the time it did ease some of my qualms."

"But now you're not so sure?"

"No," Labhran sighed deeply. "I like her, truly I do, and I'm sure that in her own mind she really believes everything she's told us, but there's something niggling in the back of my mind that makes me uneasy. Not least it's the idea of one lone person walking at night through that army camp. She'd have stood out to anyone watching from the city walls, and *they* weren't sleeping off exhaustion, were they? Surely someone there would've raised the alarm at the sight of someone heading back away from the city? Am I just being paranoid, Sioncaet?"

The smaller man shook his head sadly.

"I wish you were. Then I could tell you to stop being morbid and forget about it. But I've been thinking the same thing. Maelbrigt said she had some of her own clothes with her still at his house. That doesn't sound like a refugee who scavenged clothes, does it? And I still don't believe that the Abend would leave her unguarded. Even if it was only Anarawd who wanted her as a sexual partner, the others still have to know that she's very strong in the Power, and I can't think of any circumstances where they'd allow someone who surely had to be a contender to being raised to their ranks to just wander off into the wild blue yonder."

"Thank the Spirits it's not just me, then! Although I don't know whether to be relieved or not," Labhran grimaced. "Have you any thoughts on what we could do, because I've wrestled with this on and off ever since we left, and I can't see anything obvious."

"No, sorry, me neither," Sioncaet said regretfully. "All I think we can do is keep a watch on her. Maelbrigt must be given no idea of what we're doing, though. If he gets as much of a whiff that we don't trust Taise, I can see him disappearing off on his own with her, leaving us to chase after them. He'd do anything – anything at all – to protect her."

A day later it was with great relief that they began the descent on the eastern slopes into more gentle woodland. If nothing else they could now find enough fuel to make a roaring blaze at night where they could curl up in warmth. On the last couple of nights in the high peaks they had heard wolves howling as they too began to move out of the soon-to-be-frozen heights. With a good fire going they all felt safer, including the horses who had begun to get very nervous of the howling.

A couple of days later, a fortnight after they had left Sioncaet's, they saw a road in the near distance when they got up one morning. They were already far out on the headland on which Scarba sat, and Labhran assured them they should reach it that day. Sure enough, by mid afternoon they rode into the small fishing town, which seemed to be surviving quite well, if not exactly prosperous. A small inn happily provided them with accommodation for the night, and over welcome large platters of grilled fish, baked root vegetables and warm crusty bread, they discussed the next step. The abbey stood a little apart, high on the cliffs and it was here that Sioncaet felt that they might find a clue to the lost manuscript.

"You don't want to go up there at night," a voice chipped in, making them all jump.

They had been so deep in conversation that they had not realized that the landlord had been listening as he brought out more hot, spiced cider.

"What do you mean?" Labhran asked cautiously.

The portly man wagged a cautionary finger at them as he said,

"There's funny things going on up there these days."

"Funny things?" Kayna queried. "But it's an abbey, what could possibly be amiss there?"

"Aye, what indeed," their host continued, warming to his subject now he had an audience. "There was this funny priest came there a couple of months ago. Passed through here he did. Fair gave us all the creeps. …Big chap, bald as an egg, and the oddest eyes."

Frantic glances passed between the group. Could it be that they were too late?

"Are the monks still there?" Labhran asked in assumed innocence.

"Oh yes," the landlord replied, "but they go around in threes or more now. You don't see one by himself anymore, and two weeks ago a group of them came down here and caught a boat across to Ergardia. Said they wasn't going to stay up there to become martyrs, whatever the abbot said."

Their host was distracted by an incoming bunch of fishermen calling for ale, leaving the travellers to worry over their next move. Ultimately they decided that if a member of the Abend, for that was surely what the mystery priest was, had called at the abbey then they needed to know why.

However, the stop at the inn also brought with it another problem for the two watchers. Among the ordinary folks Taise was sharing a room with Maelbrigt, but it occurred to them that if they spent any time at the abbey, then the two women would be in separate quarters and well away from the rest of them. At the moment Sioncaet had a room to one side of Taise and Maelbrigt, which he shared with Sithfrey, while Labhran shared one the other side with Kayna, with both of them alert for the sound of anyone attempting to leave. Slipping off to the stables the two of them held a hurried conference.

"It's no good," Labhran said finally, "we'll have to bring Kayna in on our plan to watch her. It's the only way. Only another woman will be able to watch Taise up there."

Labhran strolled casually back into the inn, and with the tale of checking one of her horse's hooves, got Kayna out to meet Sioncaet. Very cautiously they outlined their concerns to her and then waited for her response.

"Oh shit!" Kayna swore softly, leaning her arms on a wooden division between the stalls and putting her head on them. Sioncaet and Labhran looked worriedly at one another, did she believe them? Then Kayna looked up.

"Blessed Martyrs! I wish I could say you were wrong, but I've been having my doubts too. I just thought I was being a nasty bitch, like the other women at the grange are always accusing me of being of when I've done something unladylike. But it isn't that, is it?"

"What made you suspicious, if you don't mind telling us?" Sioncaet asked, trying but failing to keep the relief out of his voice.

Kayna took a deep breath.

"Well, it struck me that we were focusing all the time on Anarawd, or at least Taise was. But there are eight other Abend, and four of those are women. We've heard nothing of them! I couldn't help wondering whether they would be so eager to see Anarawd father this super-DeÁine onto Taise without saying a word. After all, as its mother she would effectively become a tenth member of the Abend, but totally under Anarawd's sway."

"Mmm, but Taise might not be that easily ruled," Labhran said thoughtfully.

"No, but equally, she certainly wouldn't bear that child willingly either," Kayna said emphatically. "So that spell he's looking for would have to include a way to completely suppress her own free will. Personally, I doubt if would contain such a codicil, but that's not the point. The four witches wouldn't want to share power. And there's more."

Labhran and Sioncaet looked in amazement at one another as Kayna thankfully offloaded her worries.

"Think about the DeÁine Treasures. All the Island Treasures are individual pieces, aren't they, if I remember the legends right? Unless I've forgotten some, there's the Shield, the Sword, the Spear and the Bow. No one person could use all four at once. The Shield might just be usable with one of the other three, but nobody could use the Sword, the Spear and the Bow all together. And that's the point of them isn't it? Four separate people would have to be working in agreement to get the full force of them together. One can't force the others to his or her will or they simply aren't effective – they're just separate pieces with their own properties …well at least as far as anyone remembers.

"But you think about the DeÁine ones. All four pieces make up what is in effect part of a suit of armour. There's no reason in terms of their physical attributes that would stop one DeÁine from wearing all four. The main reason why nobody would, I've managed to wheedle out of Taise, is that the sheer strength of the Power they contain would send one holder mad."

"Sacred Trees!" Labhran swore. "But if that one person was this super-DeÁine then that might not be the case!"

"Precisely!" Kayna said triumphantly. "Now if that happens, what happens to the rest of the Abend? You see, from what Taise can remember, if this super-DeÁine was to use the DeÁine Treasures all at once, directed at the Island Treasures, then ours would be totally destroyed. Not defeated, you understand. Annihilated! And in that moment that one DeÁine, Abend, or whatever you want to call him, would be in total control not only of the Islands, but *all* of the DeÁine too. And who knows how long he would live for with that much Power concentrated in him? He could be as near immortal as would make no difference to the rest of us."

"By the Wild Hunt!" Labhran gasped, while Sioncaet just stood white-faced in horror.

"Now think!" Kayna commanded. "Do you see the four witches missing the implications of that? The four war-mages are so obsessed with *getting* power for themselves they haven't bothered to think of what might happen when they've *got* the Treasures, but I'd bet anything the witches have! Having the four separate Treasures is one thing. They might even get a chance at wielding one of them if the war-mages prove to have no aptitude for one. But there's no way they'll want to see that power focused on one person, much less one who would be likely to listen to his mother over them, and the way to avoid that was to get Taise away from Anarawd.

"Which brings me to the next thing. We kept thinking in terms of someone trying to force Taise to do something she didn't want to do. You heard her say that she was too strong in the power for them to be able to compel her, which was why they had to settle for physical pain. But it would be very different if it was something she herself wanted, wouldn't it? Taise already wanted to escape, so it would be so easy to slip beneath her defences to encourage that, because such thoughts coming into her mind would elicit no defence mechanism. No resistance! I keep thinking that the witches first arranged the route for Taise to take away from New Lochlainn, then planted the idea of running in that direction in Taise's mind.

"I have this picture in my mind of the maps at the grange. There were some of New Lochlainn and I used to stare at them all the time when Maelbrigt was going over there. That route north is just too obvious. Taise would have to have been on a boat within two days of leaving the army or she'd have been going through riverside villages. Alright, they are only villages, but it's not the landscape totally devoid of habitation she painted. *That* idea had to have been planted in her mind, and deeply too, for her vision of what she saw to be so skewed. And what's this about Taise not being able to survive? From what Maelbrigt said she was doing fine in her little cottage away from the village?

"No, someone tampered with Taise's mind! And I think another woman would be much more likely to understand the way she thinks and get under her guard than some war-mage just battering away."

"You realise you've just talked yourself into a job," Labhran said with wry amusement.

"That you have," Sioncaet said with undisguised admiration. "Clever lass for working that out! Labhran and I would've taken forever to see all that. All we knew was that something was definitely wrong. We'll support you all we can, but in the abbey you may be on your own, and we don't know what Taise will do when she gets to wherever it is she's being driven."

"Oh, I think I can make a stab at that too," Kayna said airily, basking in the unaccustomed praise.

"Really?" the two men asked in even greater astonishment.

"I think the witches sent her after that manuscript knowing that sooner or later Anarawd would send someone after her to set her on the run again. And again, Taise's own motivation would be in accord with that, so it wasn't hard to insinuate a compulsion. The difference is that I suspect that once she finds it, Taise will suddenly find herself compelled to destroy it, and we can't allow that!"

"We can't?" Labhran asked weakly.

"Oh no! We, or rather one or both of you two must read it first."

"Of course," Sioncaet caught on. "If it tells how to get around the Island Treasures we have to know what that is, don't we? By knowing what it is, we can take steps to make sure that particular set of circumstances don't coincide, can't we?"

"Exactly!" Kayna said triumphantly. "That's not to say we don't destroy it afterwards if we find the DeÁine Hunters are hard on our heels, or if Taise is going insane when the compulsion kicks in. I've come to really like Taise, I would never want her hurt. But for the sake of all the people – Islanders and the ordinary DeÁine – we have to make sure the Abend don't win, and we can only do that if we know as much as they do."

At that point conversation stopped as Kayna found herself being wrapped in a bear hug by Labhran, then the same from Sioncaet.

Chapter 25

Curses and Clues

Celidon: Winterfalling

When they mounted up the following morning, Maelbrigt was fully armed for the first time since they had travelled with Labhran and Sioncaet. Taise and Sithfrey were surprised to see Labhran had also discarded his worn woollen clothing for something very similar to a Knight's uniform, but in a dove grey. Sioncaet also wore an over-tunic of heavy, studded leather which looked as though it had seen some wear, and, along with the men, Kayna donned mail-backed leather gloves and openly wore her sword at her hip. The six of them looked quite formidable as they clattered out of the inn's yard and onto the abbey road.

Maelbrigt and Labhran set the horses to a brisk canter, wanting to get to the abbey gates before any warning could be sounded as to their arrival. As they pounded up the approach to the gate they were surprised that the gates stood wide open. It was only as they rode through that they realized that the gates stood at a drunken angle, and were incapable of being shut. The hinges looked as though they had been hit by lightning, with the wood around them singed and charred. Pulling up in the open court, Maelbrigt cast his eyes around and saw monks cringing back against the walls out of their way.

"Brothers," he called, "may we speak with your abbot? We come in peace, although we've travelled a dangerous road."

Before any of those scattered around the yard could answer, the door to the great church opened and a pale-faced man stepped out. By the quality of his garments he was the abbot, yet his pallor and the dark circles under his eyes spoke of deep distress. He was obviously steeling himself for what might be coming, and his knuckles were white on the hand which grasped the crook of his office. Then he saw Maelbrigt's uniform. His eyes swung from the black, to the dragon-headed pommel, to its mirror images on the back of the gloves, and gasped. His eyes spun to Labhran and the Trees woven onto his gloves and tunic.

"Oh, merciful Spirits, thank you!" he sobbed with relief, and almost fell down the steps to greet his guests.

His reaction nonplussed them. This was certainly not the response of someone in league with the Abend, but before they could question him they were being ushered into the refectory. Despite the earliness of the hour, and their recent breakfast, they found themselves being plied with caff and hot rolls from the bakery.

"You're the answer to my prayers," the abbot said.

"We are?" Kayna asked in surprise.

"Could you be a bit clearer?" Sioncaet asked, curious but not wanting to prompt too much to see if the abbot would mention their previous visitor of his own accord.

Almost falling over his words, the abbot told of the arrival of the strange priest.

"We thought him to be just some wandering hedge friar at first," he gabbled. "He wanted to see the library. Well, we thought it was to check one of the holy books, so of course we said yes. Then Brother Wilfrid found him rummaging carelessly through some of the old scrolls at the back of the library. Some of them are hundreds of years old and they're delicate! He remonstrated with the man, who'd not given us his name yet. For his pains he was struck by an invisible blast which threw him against the wall and knocked him out. We only found this out later. He was unconscious for over a week. The stranger barged in on our evening meal and began shouting at us."

The abbot stopped and shuddered, while other brothers closed their eyes and crossed themselves at the memory of what had happened. "He wanted some particular scroll, but we had no idea what it was. So he began to pick brothers up and throw them against the walls with just a wave of his hand!" The abbot sobbed momentarily. "Four of our brothers died and five more will be crippled for life. The Spirits deserted us that day. We could do nothing to stop the madness, for we couldn't tell him what we didn't know!

"In the end he left us to pick up our brethren and went back to search by himself. Whatever he was looking for, he either found it or something else useful, because two days later that madman left us, saying he'd be back. Some of our brothers ran out as he passed the gates and slammed them shut after him. He turned round and you saw what he did to the gates."

"I don't wish to belittle what you've been through, Father," Maelbrigt said, "but you got off lightly if this man was who we think he was."

Several of the brothers involuntarily wailed at that.

"Oh that's not all," the abbot sighed. "We went down to the library to see what the damage was. Two brothers offered to start clearing up while the rest of us said the evening office. That was the last we saw of them."

"What? Killed?" Kayna gasped. "I thought you said he'd gone?"

"He had!" a voice from the back called out.

"We don't know, and that's the truth," a brother beside the abbot said. "They just disappeared. There were some red smears, but we don't know if they were there before the brothers started working down there. The stranger could have made them."

"And we've lost another, and one more's gone mad from what he's seen down there!" another brother added.

"The crypt and the library are haunted!" a slightly hysterical voice cried out, and the visitors could feel the emotion rising as the monks expressed their fear.

"You must help us!" someone pleaded.

"Please!" the abbot added his voice to the chorus which followed. "You sir," he addressed Maelbrigt, "by the lightning flashes on the shoulders of your tunic I assume you're a Commander with the Knights. But, if I may presume, that's not all, is it? The star above the dragon's head on your scabbard means you're one of their Foresters. You must have travelled widely. Have you some experience of dealing with such things? And you, sir," he turned to Labhran. "I never thought to see such a thing, but I've heard of the Covert Brethren. Yet like your friend you're no mere member of the rank and file, are you? Those berries woven onto the Tree, do they mean that you really are one of the élite Assassins? Can you help us too?"

"You seem remarkably knowledgeable about such things, Father," Labhran said suspiciously. "Would you mind telling me how you know about the Assassins, given that you want our help?"

The abbot gave a wan smile, "I was called upon to train some of your Order so they could officiate at the services for the men in the preceptories. Amongst them were some quiet, dangerous men whom the others called Foresters. Them I was only called upon to teach a few things before they rode off again. It was a long time ago when there were still large numbers of Knights in this sad island. Back then I was abbot of a smaller abbey over on the west coast at Belhaven. Not so very long after, we took in many of the wounded and dying who came back from Brychan after Gavra, and I helped bury most of them. But not before they told me their casualties would've been even worse – the DeÁine might even have won the day – had it not been for the valour of strange men dressed in grey, who joined with the Foresters to attack the demons who summoned evil powers against them. Most of them simply tried to disrupt the DeÁine chains of commands. A couple of men suffering from dire burns, which festered and consumed their flesh, talked while they were still lucid, of a select few who attempted to strike at the demons themselves. Men recognizable by the rowan berries on their uniforms."

Taise and Sithfrey exchanged startled glances. Was there no end to the surprises these two were going to produce? However, there was no opportunity to cross examine them for Maelbrigt and Labhran, having had to admit to the truth of the abbot's assumptions, were now questioning the monks in earnest. Slowly it unfolded that, whatever the thing was, it was more powerful away from the main hours of daylight. The monks were terrified of what would happen by the time it got to mid winter, when daylight never percolated as far across the church as the stairs to the crypt.

The library lay at the rear of the main crypt, and together their roofs formed an elevated section within the east end of the church, effectively placing the altar on a huge dais. The trunks of the five Sacred Trees ran from the floor of the crypt, up past the floor of the altar and formed an elaborate tracery screen around it, finally rising to fine rib-vaulting at the ceiling. In the crypt, the relics of some lesser holy martyrs who had joined the four great ones with the Spirits were placed in niches within the trunks, and a door at either side of the church in the north and south aisles allowed access to the crypt by narrow stairways. Those wishing to visit the remains, during the times the abbey opened its doors to the outside world, would go in by the northern stair. They would then followed a horse-shoe-shaped passage around the outside circuit of the stone-trunks, where spaces between the trunks allowed them to touch the casings of the relics, and then to emerge by the southern stairs.

At the easternmost end of that horseshoe-shaped passage a small door gave access the monks from the crypt into the store for the sacred texts. Despite being at the same level as the crypt, and therefore below that of the altar, this store was in fact well above the outside ground and dry. Completely sealed off from the outside, with no windows or vents and bone-dry, it kept the ancient manuscripts in ideal conditions. The only other way in was via an opposing doorway from the rest of the library and the scriptorium, which lay beyond it to the east. The library had substantial wooden doors, but the monks had found out the hard way that these were no protection against whatever was hiding in there.

At great risk, the brothers had ventured into the library during the day to move as many as possible of their precious manuscripts out to safer locations around the abbey. Yet the strength of the haunting creature seemed to be growing. During the nightly offices, strange gurgling noises had become audible from the crypt, to the extent that these services were now held in the dormitory – upstairs and along another wall of the abbey's cloister garth.

Two weeks ago they had been forced to give up on the early morning and evening offices, too, as the nights drew in. That had been when some of the brothers had left for Ergardia, after they had got up one morning to find the altar hangings shredded, and the fine but weighty silver altar cross bent from being hurled by an enormous force against the ceiling. In the weak sunlight of the early afternoon the abbot took his guests across, and showed them where the cross had also broken some of the stone tracery where it had hit the high vaulting.

"By the Lotus, that was no mean feat!" Sithfrey whispered in awe and fear to Kayna. "What can those two possibly do against something that powerful?"

Taise, too, looked worried stiff at the thought of her beloved Knight going into battle against such a demonic opponent. Yet Kayna smiled inscrutably and gave Taise a comforting hug.

"Oh, don't you worry, those two have a few tricks they can show some tetchy ghoul!"

"Tetchy ghoul? That's some understatement!" Sithfrey exclaimed, looking at her as though she had lost her mind.

Yet Maelbrigt and Labhran showed no apparent fear either, although they did go off into a huddle with Sioncaet, where there seemed to be an intense debate going on. Before the others could join them, though, the discussion broke up. Sioncaet headed out of the church, collaring a young monk on the way, whom he began asking something of, although they could not make out what before he had left. Labhran went to the south stair while Maelbrigt went to stand at the top of the north. They seemed to be listening intently for several minutes, then turned together and went out too.

Chasing after them, Sithfrey and Taise found Maelbrigt and Labhran heading out of the abbey into the woods beyond. Kayna stopped them following, saying that the two would be back soon, and indeed they were. To the confusion of Sithfrey, they each carried five long branches from a rowan, and he shrugged and turned away. Taise's curiosity, though, was in full flow now. She stood close by them as Labhran supported the boughs on the stone horse trough, and held them steady while Maelbrigt whittled the ends into sharp stakes. She expected them to trim the leafy end too, but instead they appeared to be being most careful not to dislodge the clusters of flame-red berries that hung there. When all ten branches had been shaved to wicked spikes they carried them into the church and placed five at the top of each stair. Without saying a word, Maelbrigt ushered her back out of the church, pushing her gently but firmly at Kayna, with a look that said 'protect her'.

Across the yard from the kitchen, Sioncaet was leading a strange procession of the brothers, who were struggling with the abbey cook's three largest cauldrons. The brothers staggering under the weight of the first two were directed towards the scriptorium, with the third being waved into the church. Sioncaet had already veered off again, and moments later appeared escorting the abbot and two brothers, whose slightly more elaborate habits declared that they had been raised to officiate at the services.

"Come with me, please," Labhran requested them, but in a voice which brooked no refusal.

Inside the church, the cauldron had been placed under Maelbrigt's direction halfway between the two stairs. The abbot and his two priests now joined Maelbrigt and Labhran around it. From the doorway, which was as near as Kayna would allow her to go, Taise thought they appeared to be praying over the water. What good that would do, she had no idea. Then she saw the three clerics' heads come up from the bowed positions they had assumed, as they stared in amazement at Labhran and Maelbrigt as they continued alone but in a totally different language. For a second she thought it was DeÁine before she realise she had no idea what was being said.

The language had a strange lilting quality, yet it resonated around the ancient church with a power beyond the volume the words were spoken with. From deep beneath their feet a sickening, slurping growl sounded which set the skin of all of them creeping. As the two voices rose in the final incantation, the floor vibrated as the thing beneath wetly rumbled its defiance.

"Och well, that cuts down the possibilities a bit!" Sioncaet's voice said cheerily from behind the two women.

"It does?" Kayna wondered.

"You're mad!" Taise said weakly in disbelief at his blasé attitude. "That thing just shook the whole church, and you think they're going to stop it?"

"Oh, I don't think it's anything beyond the average Abend summoning," Sioncaet replied lightly. "You know, up from the Underworld, after blood, feeds on fear, sucks out the life of its victims. The usual stuff."

"Oh Sacred Trees protect them!" Taise prayed fervently. She had never thought of herself as having any faith in the old religion of the Islands, but just at this moment she would take any help she could get if it would increase Maelbrigt's chances of survival. She was not the only one having trouble coping. The three monastics had gone into a huddle and were giving worried glances at Maelbrigt and Labhran.

"Is there a problem, father?" Labhran asked darkly.

The abbot cleared his throat nervously.

"We hadn't realized you'd be using pagan rituals."

"This is a sacred space!" the priest next to him chipped in indignantly.

"That's right," the third said self-righteously, "this is no place for such Underworld trickery!"

"Underworld trickery?" Labhran spat back furiously. "What did you think we were going to do? Coax it into the woods with a bit of honey? Fools! If you don't like this, brothers, you can get on with it yourselves and join it down there!"

Maelbrigt came to stand by him, calmer but no less determined.

"You asked for our help, Father! If you don't want it, we can get on our horses and ride back the way we came. We don't have to risk our lives to do this. But I warn you! If you don't contain this thing, as your fear grows it will feed on it. It will feed on it and grow, and first it will consume every person in this abbey, and when it's finished here, it will come out at night and start on those poor folk down in the town. How's your conscience, brothers? Are you prepared to sacrifice not only your fellow monks, but defenceless women and innocent children too?"

The three shifted uneasily in the face of his anger. They knew as well as Maelbrigt that they had a duty to the care of the people who lived nearby, and to protect their souls. Before they could reconsider, Maelbrigt hammered on.

"Or can you accept the decisions made long ago, that amongst the faithful and true of the Order there had to be some who retained the knowledge of the Ancients, against the time when the enemies of the deep might be summoned? Do you really think we're so stupid as to call you in here to help if it was solely a pagan ritual? That water has to be blessed *three* times for it to work. Once in the old Island faith, once in the New Faith and once in the Old of the Ancients. Now are you coming to do the same to those two other cauldrons, or do you want to carry on on your own? There's no other way we know of, and let me assure you we've had some experience of dealing with the DeÁine's summonings!"

"The DeÁine?" one of the priests said weakly.

"Have you listened to nothing we've said?" Labhran rebuked him waspishly.

"Not just any old DeÁine, either!" Sioncaet added his voice to the debate. "One of their arch-wizards! The leader of their coven wanted something that is, or was, here. The fact that he's left one of his lesser creatures on guard might mean he's coming back, or it might be that he felt like having a bit of fun with you!"

"Fun?" the other priest croaked, white as a sheet and looking like he might faint at any minute.

"Oh, hadn't you realized that thing is driven by his will?" Sioncaet said more nonchalantly.

"A lesser creature?" his friend whimpered.

"Och, this is a wee thing!" Sioncaet said airily, secretly enjoying himself. "These two have dealt with their share of these things. You'd better let them dispatch it back to the depths, and get rid of the demon wizard's eye, before he decides what he wants to do next to you!"

With a gulp one of the priests made a dash for the door and sprinted off in the direction of the latrines, while the other hung onto his abbot's arm, although it was hard to tell who was supporting who.

"So, when the brother gets back shall we go to the library?" Maelbrigt asked innocently. The tottering pair made for the door and Sioncaet shot his friends a mischievous grin.

"Dispatched our share?" Labhran queried with a quirked eyebrow.

"Well, your shouting wasn't getting them moving, was it?" Sioncaet said innocently. "I thought they needed the danger spelling out a bit more, that's all."

Maelbrigt chuckled. "Great Maker, Sioncaet! I doubt they'll sleep well ever again after you've scared the life out of them." Then added more soberly, "I just hope we can live up to the deed!"

"Well that wasn't a bansith's shriek, was it?" Sioncaet replied. "So that cuts down one option. And if it's in a dry cellar it isn't a baneasge, those things are the only monsters the Abend could summon that can go near water, but they also need it, and they're near impossible to control. This beastie is definitely operating to some sort of control, or on the first night it would've been off hunting on its own account."

"True," Maelbrigt conceded, without looking any happier. Instead the three of them strode out of the church, and around the southern wall to the low building attached to the eastern end of it, leaving Kayna and Taise behind. The monks followed dejectedly in their wake to the two other cauldrons of water, and the ritual was repeated over each. With each incantation the subterranean growlings grew fiercer, while the church and library reverberated to the sound of something thrashing around beneath it, to the rising panic of the monks clustered around outside the door.

"We'd better get them out of here," Sioncaet said to Kayna. "They're only giving that thing something to feed on."

"No, you stay here, in case they need you," Kayna replied. "I'll get Sithfrey and we'll get the brothers out of the gates."

In the meantime, Maelbrigt and Labhran had gone out and returned, this time fully armed. For the first time Taise saw them both with the red surcoat over the lightweight, supple mail that went on over the protective leathers. The flowing red, thigh-length surcoats were held in place by their sword belts. Maelbrigt's had the classic white dragon-headed sword stitched across the front and back of his, while Labhran had a white tree intricately wrought on both sides of his. With light mail coifs, which they pulled up over their heads as they entered the library, they looked fearsome.

The two of them picked up one of the cauldrons and lugged it through the door of the scriptorium where it had stood, and up to the door with the manuscript store. They returned and took the second to stand alongside it. The abbot and his priest had shuffled forward to the door between the library and the scriptorium, but halted when Maelbrigt told them to stay back. Sioncaet came up with lighted torches which he handed to his friends. It made the abbot glance nervously at the remaining manuscripts left on the shelves nearest the door, as the torch flames guttered and flickered from some strange breeze which came from around the closed door.

Drawing their swords, the two armed men looked at one another and then nodded at Sioncaet. The little man reached around Maelbrigt from the side and flipped back the bolts on the door. With a quick flick, he lifted the latch and pushed the door inwards, as he leapt lightly back out of the way. As one, the two stepped into the doorway and held their torches aloft. Chaos reigned. Everywhere manuscripts lay strewn across the floor, while a few lone survivors clung precariously to their pigeonholes along the walls. For a moment Maelbrigt felt a pang of regret at the loss of learning, as he took in how many of the fragile old manuscripts had already been trampled into crumbs.

Then silhouetted in the door through to the crypt appeared a vast, black shape.

"Oh, they have a grollican!" Labhran said in a voice that could have been commenting on the weather for all the concern it contained.

If having a head, two arms and two legs made it human, then it approximated to one. The noise coming from it was nothing any human could have made, though. A wet, gurgling, slavering snarl reverberated around the walls of the confined space, buffeting the two with its stinking breath. But the men didn't retreat. With the torches held high, they approached the beast with firm, steady steps. As they took one step at a time they began to chant the words they had used before. Only softly. Barely audible over the continued belching growls.

Suddenly the beast turned and disappeared into the dark. Quick as a flash Sioncaet pulled a cauldron to the door, but it stuck firmly. Yanking it back he grabbed the second, which was a little smaller and thrust it through to Maelbrigt and Labhran, who grabbed it and ran with it to the door to the crypt where they placed it in the centre of the doorway. Sioncaet wedged the other cauldron back in the first doorway, then he chased the monks out of the scriptorium, slamming the door shut behind him.

"You've sealed them in!" Taise cried in horror.

"No, we've just forced that thing back," Sioncaet explained as they ran back around into the church. On the way he snatched up Maelbrigt's bow and arrows, and Taise saw that someone had bound sprigs of rowan to just in front of the flights on the arrows.

"It can't pass over that water now. Its only choice is to come out up one of those stairs."

"Isn't that making things complicated?" Taise asked, still worried witless.

Sioncaet shook his head.

"They need to be able to use fire and water, as well as the rowan spikes. Can you imagine what would happen if they tried that in the library? They'd be more likely to be burned to death!"

Down below, Maelbrigt and Labhran were taking no chances. Maelbrigt had slipped one glove off and had scooped up palm-fulls of the water and splashed them up the arch of the door. When he had done, both of them dipped their swords into the cauldron, and on the count of three stepped together over the cauldron into the crypt.

The grollican stood opposite them in the centre of the apse made by the Tree trunks. Its ragged tentacles of hair swung around as its head swept back and forth, its tiny mind trying to decide which man to eat first. A great stinking roar almost took their breath away. Then Maelbrigt vaulted over a relic and darted in, making a lightning fast lunge which caught the monster in the leg, before diving back out of reach of the massive fist which lashed out as it shrieked its pain. As the beast swung towards Maelbrigt, Labhran dashed forwards between the Ash and the Birch as with a mighty slash he laid open the beast's side.

Foul, muddy liquid oozed out and the beast yowled even louder, its huge fists sending shards of stone flying as they impacted on the walls. With no let up, Maelbrigt again went on the attack, this time from the front, sprinting forward and then dropping to one knee to avoid the flailing arm as he plunged his sword into the beast's groin. The beast had known pain all its brief life, but this was something new. As the fine, pattern-welded blades seared deep into its body, the flesh around the cuts began to smoke and steam. With a howl of rage it tried one more swipe, but when Labhran's sword nearly severed the hand, it began to retreat up the northern stair.

In the church above they heard it coming. Sioncaet grabbed the rowan spears from the south side and ran to the side of the northern stair with them. Taise bit her knuckles in fear and horror as the great thrashing shape crawled out of the crypt. Labhran tore out of the southern stair and pounded across the separating space to come at the beast from the side as Maelbrigt emerged, still waving blade and torch in the beast's face. The weak, early winter sun filtering through the high windows only seemed to enrage it further and it shot forward, trying to get back to the security of its dark hole. Caught in mid step Maelbrigt was wrong-footed. The sheer weight of the beast knocked him against the wall even as he managed to stab it in the foot. Labhran seized the bow which Sioncaet held out for him and loosed a rowaned arrow, but it only clipped the beast.

As she screamed with terror, something tore loose in Taise. From deep within her she felt a power welling up, and without a second's thought she formed a ball of fire and loosed it at the beast. As the Power exploded directly on its chest it flew into ragged, wet chunks which plastered the wall behind it. Yet no sooner had they hit than they began to come back together again. In a matter of heartbeats the beast had reformed except that it was now nearly twice its former size.

"What have you done?" Sioncaet screamed in fury. "Do you want to kill them?"

Taise fell to the floor, sobbing uncontrollably, as the beast turned its gory head back towards Maelbrigt. As the formerly near-severed fist, now reformed, reached down towards the man struggling to his feet, Labhran seized up the first of the rowan spears and charged in to plunge it into the thigh of the beast. It spun and threw its head back to roar in agony. The other great paw reached down to grasp the spear. Instead of pulling it out, though, as the fingers closed around the shaft and crushed the berries, a black smoke oozed out from between them and a smell of burning filled the church. Sioncaet tossed another spear to Labhran, who had skipped around to the back of the beast, out of reach, and now drove the second into the back of the other leg.

The beast arched its back and threw its arms in the air, giving Maelbrigt an opening. He dived expertly across the top of the stair, rolled and came up to snatch a spear of his own which he thrust deep into the beast's middle. As the beast lurched and fell forwards onto all fours, Labhran staked it in the back while Maelbrigt neatly angled the fifth spear straight down its howling throat. The hands grasped the spear in its mouth and smoked as the berries were crushed again. Then, as it subsided and the great body collapsed onto the other spears, the burning smell filled the church and the beast appeared wreathed in smoke as its thick-stranded 'hair' caught fire from Maelbrigt's dropped torch.

Kayna and Sithfrey had come running in, and were now helping Taise to her feet, all wondering why the Knights did not rush in to finish off the job. Instead Maelbrigt and Labhran strolled almost casually over to the cauldron, where Sioncaet was waiting. The three of them stood watching the beast as it roiled in its agony, beating the flagstone floor into chippings as it tried to free the spears.

Suddenly cracks began to appear in its hide. The slimy, hairy flesh began to part, exposing more of the sludge-coloured, turbid liquid. Now the two men picked up the cauldron by its handles and walked towards the creature. Just outside of range of its spasms they swung the cauldron back and forth a couple of times to build up momentum, then hurled the contents up and out to drench the beast all over. Dropping the cauldron all three sprinted for the door, grabbing the others and catapulting them out with them.

Inside the church there was a moment's pause and then a massive crack, like a thunderbolt had struck within the building. The entire interior was shot with exploding parts of the beast, from floor to ceiling. Then with a ghastly slurping noise the peppered bits began to slide down the walls, whilst those already on the floor began to sink through it, like pebbles slipping down through mud. As each piece reached the battered flagstones, it sank through them too. Had anyone been foolish enough to be within the crypt they would have been rained upon by pieces of rotting, corrupt slime, although most went on and sank straight through the floor and deep into the earth below.

When all had gone silent, Maelbrigt and Labhran cautiously re-entered. With a nod of satisfaction they went back round to the scriptorium and brought the outer cauldron back, with which they sluiced down the church floor. The water from the cauldron which had guarded the inner door was used to wash the steps and the crypt with, although they kept a little in reserve which they carried back to the scriptorium. In odd spots a small spurt of steam would rise and then fade, but the two pronounced themselves satisfied that the beast was well and truly gone.

Returning outside they found an argument raging. For once the even-tempered Sioncaet was the one spluttering with anger, and it was directed at Taise.

"What in the Islands did you think you were doing in there?" he fumed. "I thought you of all people would know better than to throw Power-fire at a creature fed by Power!"

"I didn't mean to!" Taise wailed.

"Well what *did* you mean?" Sioncaet demanded.

"I don't know," she sobbed. "It just happened!"

"Well your *just happening* nearly got Maelbrigt and Labhran killed!"

"I thought I was helping!" Taise yelled back through her tears.

"Then maybe next time you should trust me when I say I can deal with something." Maelbrigt's sad-voiced rebuke hurt Taise even more than Sioncaet's fury. "Sacred Trees, Taise, have I ever let you down or told you false? I don't need to pretend to be more than I am. If we couldn't have coped, we wouldn't have gone in there just to save face!"

Maelbrigt and Labhran turned and walked on towards the dormitory and the washing facilities – both feeling in desperate need of washing the stench of the beast off. Sioncaet left without a word too, and Kayna was about to follow him when she looked back and saw Taise fold up and sit in a heap in the dust in the middle of the quadrangle. It suddenly occurred to Kayna that Taise may have been telling the truth when she said she had had no control over what happened. Certainly the distress of her companion was only too real.

Walking back, Kayna bent down and put a comforting arm around Taise's shaking shoulders.

"Come on, get up," she said gently. "They're angry because they were frightened too. This has taken it out of all of us. They'll be better when they're rested."

"I didn't mean to do it, Kayna," Taise sobbed. "It just happened. It was like something came unglued inside of me. Like taking the top off a bottle which was fermenting too hard when it goes pop. All I was thinking of was stopping that thing hurting Maelbrigt. I didn't even know that was Power-fire, let alone that I could make it!"

"You never saw the Abend do that?" Kayna queried in surprise.

Taise shook her head. "Never!"

Kayna thought furiously as she helped Taise to her feet, and began guiding her towards the little guest room they shared. When she had got Taise seated on the bed and a warm blanket around her shoulders, Kayna ventured to ask.

"You know when Anarawd assaulted you? Back when you were young? Sioncaet thought that there may have been someone who hypnotized you to make you forget how much Power you had to save your sanity. It was so you wouldn't have been tempted to try to use it when it was awakened by the rape. Do you think that that hypnosis broke down when you saw Maelbrigt in danger?"

"Possibly. Oh I don't know…" Taise dissolved into tears again.

Kayna looked at her and thought how unlike Taise this was, which to her mind was further evidence that she had been right, and that someone had got into Taise's mind. The others had to know about this she decided, and telling Taise she was going to make things right for her, went down to the others.

For a while when Kayna had gone Taise felt too befuddled to do anything. Slowly, however, she returned to something like her old self. Maybe there was something she could do to put things right. Of all of them she was the one who would know when she found the right manuscript. The more she thought about it the more she felt compelled to go and search. Wrapping the blanket around her against the coming night, she crept out and across the cloister towards the scriptorium.

The nearby chapter house was filled with scrolls, but when she began rummaging through them all her instincts were screaming at her that the one she wanted was not there. Quietly closing the door, she once more flitted ghostlike across the open space to the scriptorium. On the desks furthest from the crypt, scrolls again were piled high. This time Taise could almost sense the power emanating from something. Like a terrier excavating a hole she dug down deeper, scattering others left and right regardless.

Suddenly she felt the tingling in her fingers increase, and brushing a final scroll aside she saw it. It was simple. A little plain piece of vellum rolled and bound with a tube of bark. Yet she knew she was not the first to see it for the edges were scored and singed and it looked brittle. Shovelling up the other scrolls and manuscripts, she dumped them on the next desk to clear a space around it, then going back to it, she moved the candle she had lit closer. Mindful of the fact that it already seemed damaged, she carefully reached out to slide the ring off.

As she touched the bark, the most excruciating pain lanced up her arm. Jerking her hand back she dislodged the tube, but could only stare through the tears of pain at the great blisters which had welled up on her fingers as though she had been burnt. Cold water! She needed cold water! The cauldron! Quick as a flash she leapt to the cauldron and plunged her arm into the remains of the water only to scream at the top of her lungs as the pain multiplied beyond bearing. Whipping it back out she now saw her whole arm beneath the forearm blistering, cracking and scarlet and beginning to blacken. Screaming in totally agony, she suddenly felt strong arms go around her and pull her outside.

Someone's voice shouted,

"Quick, the horse trough!"

Another grabbed her and between them bodily carried her a few paces and then thrust her arm into cold water. In a state which was wavering towards unconsciousness, she heard someone pumping fresh cold water into the trough and the sound of water sloping out as the trough over filled. From beside her, almost in her ear, a familiar deep bass voice began an incantation in a strange language, and nearby she heard others join in. Slowly the pain subsided, but so did she.

Chapter 26

Helping Hands

Celidon: Samhainn

Taise had no idea of the exertion which surrounded her for the days she lay unconscious. Maelbrigt was almost beside himself with worry, constantly blaming himself for not spotting how out of character Taise's behaviour of the days leading up to the accident had been. In retrospect, the others too were kicking themselves for not having been more observant. For Sithfrey there was some excuse, although he repeatedly blamed himself for not thinking of the Abend witches. In the dark hours as the five of them kept vigil by Taise's bed, the three conspirators had confessed their scheme to Maelbrigt. Too worried to be angry at them, he also praised Kayna for her perceptiveness, and cursed himself for not having thought of her solution of the problem.

Nobody now doubted that Kayna was right, and that at least one of the witches had slid under Taise's guard and achieved what all the torture had failed to do. When they were all together, they talked positively of ways to prevent such a disaster happening again. None doubted that Taise would still be driven to seek out the manuscript, and one worry was what would happen when she regained consciousness. When they were in solitary couples, however, they confided their fears to one another that Taise might not live to see that day.

The burnt arm had begun to fester, and Sioncaet spent hours with the abbey infirmarer and herbalist trying to concoct new salves. Keeping the burns from cracking and peeling even further was hard enough, let alone worrying how it would heal. Mercifully the abbey had an expert apiarist amongst the brothers, and his beehives produced both honey and combs of exceptionally high quality, and in great quantities. Using it as a base, Sioncaet and the herbalist blended in tinctures, and the light clear liquid was able to be spread across the horrific burns with minimal contact. Yet the pain must have been beyond belief, and it was no surprise that Taise barely surfaced into the world before relapsing back, as it impacted on her awareness.

None of them expected Maelbrigt to move from her bedside, and so Labhran had dragged Sithfrey back down to the library the day after the accident. With great care, Labhran had reached out and with the lightest of touches had poked the bark tube with the tip of one finger. Nothing happened. Even after waiting a while there seemed no ill effects and so he had tried picking it up. Again, he had no adverse reaction. However, Sithfrey only had to get within a hand span of it and he could begin to feel a tingling sensation in his outstretched fingers. Closer inspection made

Labhran think that it was made from rowan, yet that alone should not have had such an effect on Sithfrey. Normally, contact with any part of those trees for a DeÁine was equivalent to an Islander brushing against nettles – unpleasant but not lethal. This seemed to speak of incantations spoken and woven into its very being at the time of making.

It made them extremely cautious in dealing with the manuscript itself – a wise move as it turned out. Labhran could handle it with immunity, but Sithfrey was overcome with a sensation like prickly heat as soon as he even tried to get near enough to touch it. To complicate matters, the burning spell which had affected Taise had resulted in further damage to the already fragile vellum. Unrolled, the two edges made serpentine patterns which cut, sometimes deeply, into the words scribed in a difficult, cramped hand over both sides.

Labhran braved the early winter chill and took the manuscript outside to where the light was best. Even then he struggled to read it. The best he could make out was that it was in some very archaic version of the Islands' tongue, with many words looking more like Old Attacotti. In one of his breaks from the infirmary, Sioncaet came as close as he could bear and read over his shoulder. The small man scratched his blonde curls and grimaced.

"Given time I might make something of this," he said despondently, "but the person who we really need is the one person who we can't show it to. I wouldn't recommend taking this anywhere near Taise, even if she does make it through and regains consciousness. It's making me itch just standing near it."

So Labhran and Kayna found a large sheet of unused vellum which the monastery's scribes had been saving for some new project, and began copying it. Labhran proved to be good at accurately transcribing the words, but Kayna had a keen eye for the blobs and squiggles on the edges and between the lines which might later give Taise some clue as to what was meant. It was a painstaking, slow task, made bearable to two people who normally would have run a mile from such a job, by the thought that it was at least a small way of helping. It took them the best part of a week to do, and both were dreading what would happen when they had finished, for there seemed little else to do but sit and wait for Taise to die.

However Maelbrigt refused to give up. Yet more of the honey was made into a nourishing watery liquid, which he delicately dripped into her mouth, slow hour by slow hour. Never enough to choke her, but drip by drip he prevented her from totally dehydrating. And with every golden pearl of liquid he prayed. Prayed every prayer he had ever learned – but especially those in the Old tongue.

Half of them he had no idea what the words meant, and the others only vaguely. When he was raised to a Knight of the Foresters, he had had to learn them all off by heart. The man who had taught him had no idea of the individual words' meanings, and said that neither had his teacher. They only knew that it was imperative for them to be retained against the day they would be needed, and as far as Maelbrigt was concerned that day had come. Whatever had done this to Taise was something from those long ago days, and despite what Sioncaet and the monks could do for the burns, as far as Maelbrigt could see it would all be in vain unless he could destroy the curse too.

Somewhere in the dark hours of the fifth night he was so tired that he was stumbling over the words. In his exhaustion he reversed three words and Taise gave a huge sigh. Maelbrigt felt his heart stop in fright as his eyes flew open and failed to see her chest rising and falling. For several seconds she lay still and Maelbrigt felt the panic rising. Then there was a deep, ragged inhalation, and she began to breathe more easily than she had since the accident.

After that she never seemed quite so lifeless, and within a day she was coming to more often. It was another week, though, before she could sit up and take notice, by which time the poultices which Sioncaet had made now seemed to be taking effect on the burns. There was no way that the skin would ever return to its normal smoothness, but it had stopped festering, though the wounds still needed regular redressing, as they wept constantly.

Finally Taise felt well enough to get up and come to sit in the chamber of the guest house with the others. Her arm was swathed in the latest poultice, wrapped in fine linen bandages, and then protected by a wrapping of soft fleece. Even paler than normal and thin, she sat wrapped in blankets against the chill, a subdued ghost of her former self. All of Maelbrigt's efforts to convince her that none of them blamed her for what had happened had failed miserably, and she sat either staring at her lap or glancing nervously at the others, saying nothing.

However, Labhran and Kayna had said nothing to her about their copying of the manuscript, and Kayna felt that it was now time to bring the copy out. Retrieving their handiwork from the scriptorium, she walked into the sitting room, picked up a stool and sat herself down at Taise's feet. Careful not to jolt Taise's arm, she spread the copy out on her lap. For a moment Taise seemed not to see it, then she blinked and looked up at Kayna.

"What's this?" she asked softly.

"Well, Sioncaet said it would be dangerous for you to get close to the original scroll that harmed you," Kayna explained, trying to keep her voice matter of fact. Hoping that she was making this sound the most normal thing in the world, she continued. "We've all tried looking at the original – well, except Sioncaet and Sithfrey. It seems to want to repulse them as much as it did you. Maelbrigt thinks it had a strong ward woven into it against any DeÁine touching it, and we all agree. You were doubly unfortunate in having such a strong compulsion to destroy it put on you that it overrode your natural instinct to pull away. We should have protected you better, Taise, it wasn't your fault."

Taise looked into the younger woman's earnest face in surprise, encouraging Kayna onwards.

"The thing is, Taise …*we* can't read it. Labhran and Sioncaet think it's some ancient form of our language, which is why it's making no sense to them. We thought you might be able to understand it, so Labhran and I sat and copied it. Every word, mark and blot, so that you can study it without it harming you ever again. Please Taise, will you look at it?"

Taise looked dubiously at the copy as though it was going to bite her at any moment. Sioncaet came and knelt down beside Kayna so that he too was making eye contact with Taise and said,

"We need you, Taise. We think Quintillean summoned the grollican when he realized how powerfully the scroll was warded. He used the creature to unroll it, or at least to pull the rowan protector off it. Quintillean probably propped it open with stones, or some other sort of weight, for long enough to read it. It's been rolled for so long, once whatever was weighting the corners down was removed, it would've rolled back up on itself again. We think he got the grollican to put the rowan back on so that nobody else would touch it. Because it felt so powerfully warded to him, we suspect he thought it was like that for everyone, not just us DeÁine."

He gave a little laugh. "It's ironic that Labhran and Maelbrigt can't read it, not because of the ward, but because the language has changed. You're probably the only person aside from the Abend who, because of your studies, still *can* read it! We have to know what it says, Taise, so that we can protect the people of the Islands from the Abend. Will you work on it …please?"

"We're not expecting you to work miracles," Labhran's voice came from further back, for once missing its usual sarcasm. He stepped into the light from the candle on the wall sconce and leaned forward to gently touch her good arm. "However long it takes you, even if you can only cope with a line a day, will be better than what we've got at the moment."

"And when you feel well enough, we're taking that boat!" Maelbrigt said emphatically. "No excuses this time! It's into the heart of Ergardia for you. I'm not risking losing you again!"

For the first time a wisp of a smile played on the corners of Taise's mouth.

"I thought you'd be glad to see the back of me by now," she whispered rather hoarsely, "I've been nothing but trouble for you since we met."

Maelbrigt was too choked to reply, but it was the best sign of the old Taise reappearing that they had had.

In the end, although Taise was still far from healed, the calendar decided when they should move. The last night of Winterfalling was known as All Spirit's Eve, when the souls of the departed were believed to walk the Islands once more. Given the Abend's use of things from the Underworld, it was a night when their power became greatly enhanced. Consequently, none of the company wanted to hazard a guess as to whether Quintillean would return to the abbey on that night, or direct another of his creatures to retrieve the scroll.

All agreed, however, that Taise should be across the water by that time, for they also feared the compulsion might return redoubled. On the night before their departure, Labhran and Maelbrigt took the ancient script – bound now in protective oil cloth – deep into the forest and buried it beneath a venerable rowan. If Quintillean was drawn to the power of the ward, then it would keep him away from the abbey.

So the morning before the last day of the month, all six travellers walked their horses down into the town to where Maelbrigt had arranged passage on one of the heavy merchant ferries that plied between the two Islands. It would be a long crossing in the slow boat, but at least Taise could rest easy on their bedrolls, rather than being jolted by the ride down the coast to the quicker crossing from Giha to Culva. Once out to sea with the sea salt on the wind, Maelbrigt began to breathe more easily, finally sure that the Abend's Power would not touch Taise.

It took all that day for the heavy boat to tack its way across the sound, and it was only with the change of tide that they picked up speed to make the run down the long, high-sided loch on the opposite coast. It was nightfall before they docked at the farthest end of the loch, in the port of Aird on Ergardia. Taise was exhausted, despite having dozed in her cocoon of blankets most of the time.

For the first time, Maelbrigt left her side to join Labhran in finding rooms in one of the inns, while Kayna and Sioncaet stood watch – a mark of how much more secure he now felt they were. Aird was a popular port for those negotiating the treacherous coast of Ergardia, providing protection both from the fierce tides which could pick up, and the howling gales which often battered this coast. Consequently there was no lack of choice of inns, despite Aird not being a large town. The two finally settled on one at the far end of the curving quay which was large and comfortable, and far enough from the hustle and bustle to give Taise a quiet night.

An hour later they were all ensconced in adjoining rooms on the top floor, with the serving boy bringing them mulled wine, and a welcome meal of soda bread, local cheeses and cold meats, with slices of rich fruit cake for afterwards. A cheerful fire burned in the grate of both the main bedroom and the two connecting ones, filling everyone with a sense of contentment. Everyone, that is, except Taise. Soon the others had gone to their beds, and even Maelbrigt was sleeping soundly beside her, yet she could not rest. Tired beyond belief, she nonetheless tossed and turned beneath the duck-down quilt. In the end, rather than wake Maelbrigt, she slipped out from under the covers and wrapped herself in her travelling cloak and a blanket, and went to sit by the window.

The panes of glass were small and poor quality, made for thickness against the weather rather than to afford the best view. She found that she had to get quite close to the nearest pane and tilt her head to find a spot where the distortion was minimal. Gazing up at the sky she could see the moon making occasional appearances between scudding clouds. When it did show, she was relieved to see that it was not full – that would have been doubly bad on this of all nights. A sense of panic began to rise in her chest as she realized it must be getting close to midnight, and she began to feel something she could only describe as a vague itching deep in her soul. As though something, or someone, was trying to touch her, but could not manage anything but the lightest of drifting touches. Her bad arm was also tingling, as if the residue of the ward sensed the proximity of whatever was reaching out to her. Holding herself with her good arm, she sat and rocked to try to gain some comfort.

Suddenly, as she rocked forward towards the window, her eye caught a flicker on the far horizon. Looking south to the high mountains she saw a glow of light on one of the peaks. For a second she thought someone had lit a warning beacon. The light dipped, came back and died again, at which point she realized it was the wrong coloured flame for a fire. Power-fire! Someone had tried twice to make Power-fire! No wonder she felt ill!

Turning to the bed she saw Maelbrigt still slept soundly. Should she wake him and tell him one of the Abend was loose on Ergardia? Part of her wanted the comfort of his reassurance that he would protect her. Yet what could he do against one of the most powerful beings in the world? True, he had proved remarkably good at dispatching one of their creations, but there was a difference between that and the war-mage himself. Shivering, she returned her gaze to the window to see a bolt of lightning appear, apparently from out of nowhere, at the spot where she had seen the Power-fire emanate from. Could there be more wards on this Island? Was that what struck back at the Abend?

She sat and fretted into the small hours, finally deciding not to tell Maelbrigt and the others, if only to stop them fussing over her so much. She was deeply touched by their care for her and grateful too. Yet being unaccustomed to so much attention she was beginning to find it rather stifling. Also, the more she thought about it the less sure she was that it had been Power-fire. She had never seen it before her own disastrous effort, and at such a distance she could have misread some perfectly normal, natural phenomenon. That had been a long, jagged flash, if a different colour to what she normally expected of lightning, whereas her sending had been quite definitely a proper round ball of fire. Maybe one of the Abend had reached out to her, and Maelbrigt was right in thinking that the sea was protecting her? That would explain why it felt strange …different.

Besides, she now doubted herself. How wrong had she been about them controlling her! She had always thought the Abend's control would be physically manifested to give her time to react, yet in the end it had come with no warning at all. So why assume her jitters on a night loaded with bad legends and rumours must mean something? At this point she just about made it back to the bed to snuggle up against Maelbrigt's warmth, before falling into a deep and natural sleep.

In the morning she woke to find Sithfrey and Sioncaet sitting at the window nursing mugs of caff. There was no sign of the others, and when she asked, she was told that they had ridden on inland a short way. A preceptory of the Knights lay at the foot of an inland loch at Dunathe Castle. Maelbrigt had gone to report their presence and to ask for their help. Although it was not a long ride, Sioncaet thought it unlikely that they would be back before nightfall, and so, when Taise had risen and had a light breakfast, the three of them went for a walk in the town.

Aird seemed to be built out of the very rocks around it. Solid stone houses with tiled or slate roofs nestled lowly against the rising hillside, with few rising above the first floor height. Most had a double-fronted ground floor, and then windows let into the roof which rose immediately above it. There was little colour in the buildings themselves, yet all the houses had well-tended gardens around them, with a great variety of vegetables in neat rows intermingled with flowering plants, which Taise knew all had some therapeutic value. There was something very wholesome about the place. Even the air smelled clean and fresh, if cold. Sioncaet made sure they did not walk too far and tire Taise out, and yet back at the inn she had no sooner put her feet up on the bed than she was asleep again.

The sound of Maelbrigt, Labhran and Kayna returning woke her in the early hours of the evening feeling much refreshed. It transpired that the Knights at the castle had obligingly created a litter for her, and supplied the two staid horses used to carrying such a contraption; which meant that the next morning they all packed up and prepared to make the journey into the interior of the island. Propped up on cushions on the swaying litter, Taise was able to gaze at the magnificent scenery. Celidon had its share of mountains, but those tended to be bare rock. Here their ride first took them along the head of the loch, where towering forest-covered slopes were reflected in the pure, clear water.

As they followed the river channel which led to Dunathe they came into the forest, where Taise and Sithfrey were astounded at the great size of some of the trees. Mighty oaks and ashes, which must have stood for centuries undisturbed were magnificent even in their winter empty branches, while beeches stood in copper-clothed finery. And the whole place was alive with sound. The chatter of red squirrels, chasing one another playfully through their airy sky-walks, was interrupted by a flock of incensed tree sparrows chasing off a jay. A solitary woodpecker knocked somewhere out of sight, while a ponderous wood pigeon laboured across the clearing from one perch to another. The two DeÁine had never seen such a place, and Taise wonder out loud if the original forests of the world must have looked like this.

"Oh probably," Sioncaet agreed, heeling his horse up to join them. "This is primal forest alright. As far as I know the only time it was disturbed was when the Great Breaking happened, when the original land which occupied this part of the world was broken up and the Islands were formed."

"I've never felt anywhere that was so alive!" Taise said in wonderment.

"Aye, that it is. There's a power in this land. Not Power like the Abend use, something more fundamental …or perhaps I should say elemental. Yes, elemental would be right," Sioncaet mused.

"But could it stand up to the Abend?" Sithfrey asked doubtfully.

"I suppose that depends on how you'd define standing up," Sioncaet pondered. "If you mean something which would strike them down? …Well, I'm not sure …probably not. But if you're thinking in terms of remaining uncorrupted by them, then I think it would take a very long time before this land forgot its roots. I've often wondered whether it might not be the case that the Abend's Power would just not work, or at least not work very well, here. It has the ability to absorb a great deal, you know. A Knight from Rheged – MacBeth, I think his name was – helped bring the DeÁine Gorget here some years ago to get it away from the Abend. He and a group of Knights made a dreadful crossing first from Brychan to Celidon, and then from there to here. You remember that don't you, Maelbrigt?"

"Indeed I do. By the time they got to Celidon their force had been decimated. They came to Lochead, where we're heading for. It was the strangest thing. That cursed Treasure had already driven one of their number mad, and most of the others weren't in good shape when they got off the boat. Yet once they were here the effects of the thing seemed to …well …diminish. They rested a whole week at Lochead preceptory without even the castle cats twitching a whisker. The commander still says it was as though the earth of Ergardia itself was just soaking up all the bad energy. Of course it was in a new casket of rowan by then. Quite what would've happened if anyone had put it on is another matter. Rowan protect us, we shall never know either!"

That sentiment was echoed by all of them, but it was impossible to remain pessimistic in such a place, although Taise thought hard about what she had seen the night before last. Having ridden up a lengthy, twisting hill, they crested the shoulder of land and began to descend on the opposite slope. In front of them they could see a long estuary cutting into the island, and, on the end of the flat flood plain, a knoll of land stood close to the start of the foothills. On it, a stone wall encompassed its crest, and within the protecting circuit they could see the roofs of several large halls. Earthworks protected the flanks of the knoll, which Maelbrigt announced was Dunathe.

Well before nightfall they had crossed the valley, and were resting in the well-appointed guest quarters at Dunathe fort. Despite the willing hospitality of the Knights and the excellent food, Maelbrigt was eager to make an early night of it to enable them to start out early the next day. They rose before daylight and the new day dawned bright and sunny from the start, the clear weather staying with them all day.

The road took them on a steep, twisting climb, past tumbling, frothing cascades of mountain streams, already filling from the autumn storms. Great boulders lay by the roadside where they had crumbled off the mighty mountain face, and in the crevices, heather, lichens, and ferns sprouted depending on their preferences. By midday they had reached the shoulder of the ridge of more foothills that they would have to cross, and then descended to another loch.

By early evening they were climbing again. This time, though, it was a long straight ascent. Whatever had scoured this cleft in the earth had left little for the great trees to sustain themselves on. Instead, dwarf hazel and hawthorn were the tallest cover, and most of the time nothing rose higher than the drifts of white heather. The road took a sharp turn to the right as the valley split into two, and the straighter route became smaller and wandered more sharply up into the mountains.

As they came around on the main path, they could see the wooden tower of a watch fort at the top of the rise. Creeping slowly up the steep incline it became obvious what a natural place it was to fortify. A small bowl in the crest that had filled with spring-fed water gave the fort a vital supply. From its roof, those on guard could see both the route the companions were climbing, and also down the other side as the ground fell away again. However, for now they were stopping for the night under its protecting eaves.

As they rode up to the gate a sentry called out a challenge, although the gates stood open in welcome. While Maelbrigt talked to him, the others looked around and spotted three other travellers toiling up the last stretch of the opposite slope. Or at least that was what they thought at first. One of the group was sitting resting on a boulder. Next to him a young man stood solicitously over him, while a young boy seemed to be adjusting a pack. By the two youngster's appearance they were monks. Yet when the older one got to his feet once more, they turned away from the fort to where the others now saw there was a third track going through a cleft in the rock, off to the right of their road.

It was only as the rest of her companions had dismounted, and were leading the horses into the fort, that Taise looked back one last time at the other travellers. At the same time the oldest of the others also turned and her heart leapt in her chest in horror. Quintillean! Drained and looking sicker than she could ever have believed possible, he was still unmistakable. Swathed in her travelling cloak he evidently didn't recognize her, though, for he turned back and hobbled on, leaning on his companion and disappearing from view.

In the turmoil of their arrival it took forever to catch Maelbrigt's eye. Eventually she managed to speak to him and told him of whom she thought she had seen. Luckily, the garrison commander was standing next to them as they talked. Quickly grasping the importance of the situation he offered to send riders out to check the travellers out, yet when the men returned none reported having seen any but a young monk taking a boy novice to visit sick relatives at Culva. A hurried conference in the privacy of their quarters ensued, but it was finally decided that while none doubted that Taise was right in identifying the Abend, with her in her weakened state, avoidance was the best tactic.

Labhran and Sioncaet expressed the hope that in coming to Ergardia Quintillean had bitten off more than he could chew. This possibility seemed even more likely when they heard that Talorcan had been seen hunting with his band of trusted men in the hills. They had paused at the next preceptory from Lochead, Cluathe, only days ago, which was cause for minor celebration on Maelbrigt and Labhran's part at the thought that he might be close by.

In the meantime, outside, three figures toiled on through the dark night. Quintillean could not remember ever feeling so ill. It had all started when he had left his two new acquisitions asleep and gone to check on the grollican he had left at Scarba abbey. From the high hill he had chosen it should have been a simple sending of almost line of sight. Just reaching out in this dreadful island was like swimming through mud. But that was not the worst. As he stretched to his fullest extent, and touched the space around the abbey, the jolt had almost knocked him sick. There was no sense of the grollican. None at all. And the power of the ward was now multiplied. Old words had been re-said! He could almost taste them on the wind. And the scroll was feeding off the power of the earth which surrounded it. So he had pulled back and drawn his Power to make Power-fire instead, intending to send a bolt which would incinerate the abbey and all inside it as revenge. Yet as he loosed the ball of Power it plummeted to the ground, and where it smote the mountainside it was absorbed into the ground as though it had never happened.

Not waiting to see what happened next, he had just loosed the second ball when the first lightning bolt hit him between the shoulders. Flat on his back when the second hit him, he was astounded to realise that this lightning had come *up* from out of the very earth itself, not down from a cloud. As though the earth had swallowed his Power and then spat it back, cleansed of impurities to join the thunderheads tumbling in off the sea towards the mountains. And he had been used as the filter! He was used to the metallic taste in his mouth after releasing the Power, but now he was gagging on it! His tongue clove to the roof of his mouth with all his teeth on edge and nerves on fire. The customary slight weariness had also been multiplied into a bone-wrenching stiffening of joints, and excruciating muscle spasms. Sick, stunned and drained, he had had to lie there until morning came and the others came looking for him.

He had never dreamt that he would need them. His only thought had been delight that he had found two such prime candidates ripe for his picking. The old scroll had said virgins were required, but he could never have hoped for two such innocents to fall into his lap. It had taken very little guile to get the older one to reveal that not only were they already on the run from their monastery, they had the right bloodline too. The younger one seemed more suspicious, but Quintillean had even managed to get around his doubts by promising him that once they had travelled to his home, they would never be pawns in anyone's game again. Which was the truth, since they would not live long once he had found two more. Four virgins, that was all he needed! With two caught in one go, how hard could another two be to find? And then he would have control of the Treasures and be unassailable at the head of the Abend!

Chapter 27

Old Problems, New Solutions

Ergardia: Winterfalling – Samhainn

Wistan trotted along, his small hand clutching Kenelm's tightly. Looking up at his older cousin, he smiled and gave a little skip. He had never been so happy. All his life he had wanted to be away from the court, wanted to have a brother whom he could talk to, and now he had Kenelm. For his part Kenelm smiled back at Wistan, happy at last to have someone who was a real member of his family.

"Tell me about the chickens again," Wistan pleaded.

Kenelm grinned and started the plan over again, happy to recite it again even though Wistan had heard it dozens of times already. It had become their own private litany.

"We'll find a little place and we'll live there, where nobody can find us. We'll have some chickens and I'll grow lots of vegetables. Chickens are very good for keeping in a garden. They fertilize the soil and they root out lots of the grubs that eat plant roots. We'll have a cockerel and every morning we'll wake up when he crows. He'll have beautiful feathers and a big tail and he'll strut around the garden being very proud."

"Can we call him Will?" Wistan asked cheerfully. "I overheard Lady Montrose once say she knew a real cock called Will."

"We'll call him whatever you like," Kenelm said happily. "And you can name all the hens too. Only we'll only be able to have one cockerel, otherwise they'll fight, so if the hens have little cockerels we'll have to bring them on and then take them to market before they get too old. But if we sell them, and some of the eggs, we'll be able to gradually buy more things we can't make."

"What are you going to grow in the garden?" Wistan asked, never tiring of the magical sounding names of plants which his clever cousin knew how to grow.

"We'll have red and white cabbages, and big white cauliflowers; dark green kale and purple sprouting; shiny orange carrots and green peas; black-eyed peas and big, fat broad beans; long white salsify and pale yellow parsnips; red beets and bright coloured chards; long thin beans and big fat onions; crunchy celeriac, and spinach for cooking and to eat raw; and in the summer we'll have endive, and chives, and sorrel, and lots of herbs."

"And you've got the seeds for these?"

"I have indeed!" Kenelm patted the satchel he had strung over one shoulder, aside from the pack on his back. "Just a few of each. Not enough to cause the brothers any shortage from what I took, but plenty for just the two of us!"

They happily strolled on along the road, with Wistan excitedly pointing out birds and squirrels along the way. Kenelm was sure they were destined to be here. Why else had the nice priest in Scarton been so helpful? He seemed to have been expecting them, although Kenelm had no idea how.

"Come in, come in," he had said as they had arrived at his door to ask for refuge.

Little did the two innocents realize, but they had arrived exactly at the door of the priest who had received Jaenberht's message. Fearful of revealing too much, the abbot had only referred to a brother with one other. The priest had no way of knowing that one of those intended was a woman, and so assumed that these were the ones Jaenberht needed him to help. Consequently, the next day he had left his little parish in the hands of his able verger, and set off to lead the two to Seatoft. There he had handed them on to another of Jaenberht's trusted few, who had arranged passage to Ergardia. Of course, Jaenberht had assumed that once there Iago would be able to find horses at a nearby grange, and so had not thought it necessary to try to make provision across the water.

It was as they set off along the road heading west along the loch shore that they now met the other priest. Wistan thought him frightening with his clear, icy eyes and long bony hands. He reminded him of the strange priest who had been at court when he and his mother had been there, and that brought back all sorts of nasty memories. However, Kenelm chatted happily to the stranger, telling him that they had left their abbey and were looking for somewhere more solitary where they could be free of the interferences of the world. The priest seemed to know something of Rheged, for he said he knew of Abbot Jaenberht but did not like him, or his way of controlling those around him. That, more than anything, convinced Kenelm that the stranger would not deliver them straight back to Mailros, and that it was safe to travel with him.

Then the priest told them he was travelling even farther afield, and that if they wished to come with him he would arrange their transport. In quiet whispers that night the two discussed it, with Kenelm convincing Wistan that this was further proof that they were destined to take this route. How else would they have been able to find a boat to get them this far? All the same, Wistan wished Kenelm would be a bit more careful about what he told this priest, and he hoped they would find an ideal spot to start their farm so that there would not be any need to travel on. But, as they walked farther into the Island, the priest, who had said he was already feeling unwell, began to get really sick, and Kenelm had said it would be wrong to leave him after that. So Wistan could only hope that they could get him to the ports on the far side of Ergardia, and then put him on a boat to go home, leaving them to stay here. What had started out as a great adventure was now became a dreary trek, with no time to look at the wonderful scenery, and miserable, freezing nights hidden away from even shepherds' huts. Wistan found himself wishing he had Matti and Iago with him, to tell him funny stories, and to light fires and cook warm meals against the winter cold.

Matti and Iago had been lucky in finding the fisherman to take them across to Ergardia so easily, although much was due to Iago's skill at persuasion. For the first time in her life Matti was glad of her lack of cleavage, since with her hair chopped to her collar she made a passable 'nephew' for Iago, and as a lad she had been accepted on board where a lady would not. Iago had hinted to her not to drink much the morning they set off, so that for the relatively short crossing she did not need to use the heads. Once safely landed at Ferryport they found an inn and ordered a meal, giving her chance to use the privy there. Such caution was necessary if her disguise was to work, for it was the one thing which would give the game away, but as far as Matti was concerned it was the only drawback. Breeches and stout walking boots suited her temperament much more than the decorated dresses of a general's wife, and she revelled in the freedom of striding out on the road where nobody cared who she was. In fact it was hard to remember that they were on the run.

The coins she had had on her when she and Iago had made their escape from the attack on the monks had been sufficient to kit them out in simple homespun woollens against the winter cold. Suitably muffled, the walking was not arduous, and taking the journey at the pace of other travellers made them less conspicuous. In this way they had made it unobserved over the mountain tracks from Eskirk to Tirkirk. Iago had feared to take the main road across, for that would take them right beneath the walls of Fell Peak Fort. Nor did he think it wise now to follow Jaenberht's route to the boat at Seatoft, even though they came off the mountains in direct line with the fishing port. They had no way of knowing if any of the monks had been taken prisoner and forced to talk, and therefore it was better to simply disappear. It would be so much easier to remain unnoticed in a bigger town where strangers went uncommented on, he had reasoned. And so they had walked to Bridgeport and crossed the water from there.

Once they had arrived in Ergardia, however, Iago shed his disguise and, once they had eaten, he asked the way to the nearest grange. They were pointed to a large, well-proportioned establishment just outside of Ferryport, where Knights and their men-at-arms were openly going about the daily duties. For the first time it hit home to Matti how much things had changed on Rheged. She could remember a time when this would have been as normal there, but not for many years now, and that saddened her. Instinctively her thoughts turned to Ruari, as they did whenever matters concerning the Knights arose.

"I hope he's alright," she said without realising she had spoken aloud.

"MacBeth?" Iago queried. "Oh, he'll turn up, don't you fret. One day you'll wake up and there he'll be."

"You think so?"

"Well if they'd killed him, don't you think they'd have been bragging about it?" was the question Iago posed. "And somehow I don't think he died in the east. He's too much of a survivor."

At the grange Iago was taken away to meet the commander, but before Matti could drink the mug of caff a steward offered her, another came to guide her to the captain's office.

"Lady Montrose," he greeted her politely, "welcome to Ferry Grange. My apologies, but we have no suitable clothing to offer you to replace your current ones."

"Oh don't worry about that," Matti said – rather more quickly than was becoming for a lady of high rank she then realized, who ought to like elegant dresses. "Emmm …these are much more practical for walking in," she tried to redeem herself with.

"Oh, I wouldn't hear of you walking!" the captain responded equally rapidly. "No, no! You'll be provided with horses and an escort. I shall send a rider ahead tonight to Lorne to warn the Grand Master, and enable him to send a bird to Abbot Jaenberht telling him of your safe arrival. After what Iago's told me, he must be worried sick. He might even think you're dead!"

It was all Matti could do to bite her lip, and not let out the, *oh bugger,* she thought on hearing of her escort. Ushered to the best guest quarters, she felt guilty that she was less than happy at the prospect of having to return to respectability so soon. Well at least she had a short respite yet before the skirts had to go back on!

Early the next morning they left the grange, darkness still shrouding them as the column of four lances making up their escort trotted out of the stables. At least she had convinced the captain that she was an able rider and capable of handling a war-horse, and not the staid old jennet he had proposed at first. As the sun rose behind them, lighting the ranks of mountains in tones of gold and pink, she was able to enjoy the brisk ride. The scenery was magnificent, and the men assured her that much of the rest of Ergardia was also like this. Trees of all kinds made a tapestry of browns and greens, as evergreen firs and yews mingled in with deciduous oaks, beeches and birches. As they came into the valley of the Meikle Water, the rushing clear water of the river was joined by waterfalls, as the water off the mountains cascaded down the jagged slopes to head to the sea. Even with winter now falling hard, the countryside was filled with vibrant sound.

With the evening came a mist which did not lift for much of the next day. Yet although they could not see the end of the tree line, let alone the peaks, Matti still found the scenery breathtaking. Droplets of water adorned bushes, and turned the lingering fluffy seed-heads of the wild clematis into glistening jewels. The inns they stayed at were well used to military guests, providing an early breakfast to enable them to make the early starts to reach Lorne in barely four days.

By the third nightfall, they had reached the supply town of Meikle at the foot of the Loch of Lorne, and even Matti was feeling the effects of so many hours in the saddle. So she was glad to hear that they would not need to leave so early the following day. Apparently the Knights' headquarters lay not on the side, but actually on an island in the loch. Despite this, it was not visible from Meikle, as the loch bent in an S-shape and the castle lay beyond the far bend. The road took the straight course, and so left the loch-side for much of the day, and it was only as the sun was lowering in the early afternoon that they caught glimpses of flags flying above the trees. With the early dusk upon them, they made the last turn, and Matti saw the power base of the whole Order of the Knights of the Cross in the Islands for the first time.

A single bastioned wall ran the full circuit of the main island at the loch's edge. Above it, a fortress capable of holding an army with ease rose to be reflected in the last of the light upon the surface of the loch. As the last rays slid behind the mountains, suddenly lights appeared at windows, until the view was transformed into a myriad sparkling lights suspended in the dark. So enchanted had she been by the view, Matti did not realise that a boat was waiting for them until Iago tapped her shoulder and made her jump. Her escorts were riding onwards to the stables which sat at the head of the loch, from where another boat would take them to the nearest barracks on one of the other islands. She and Iago, however, were destined to go straight to the Grand Master.

Oarsmen pulled them swiftly across the water to a wooden jetty anchored to the rocky shore. Matti had no time to look around her, though, for no sooner had her feet touched dry land than they were being led through a maze of corridors and up winding staircases. Unexpectedly at one point they came out onto a roofed, wooden bridge which stretched across from the building they were in, across the water and the great wall, into the centre fortress. Despite slatted shuttering against any driving rain, it was bitterly cold so high up, and Matti was glad when they reached the protection of stone walls once more.

Further mesmerizing twists and turns finally brought them to face a beautifully carved set of double doors. A great wheeled cross was carved across them, but – contrary to the symbol of the Knights that Matti was used to seeing – here an actual dragon gripped the cross in its claws as it spread its wings to form a halo around the cross arms and wheel. The fearsome head peered over the top outer quadrant on one side, bone ridges alertly extended and nostrils flared in defiance. The barbed tail lay coiled around the foot of the cross on the other door, but Matti would not have been in the least surprised if she had seen it twitch, the carving was so lifelike.

"Magnificent isn't it?" one of their escorts said proudly.

"I've never seen anything like it!" Matti answered truthfully. "I didn't know you could get colours like that out of wood alone. The craftsmanship is …exquisite!"

The other escort reached out and knocked on the right-hand door, and from within a distant voice called them in. The great door swung in easily when the catch formed by one of the claws was turned, revealing a stone barrel-vaulted chamber, brightly lit, with thick, red, woollen rugs scattered over a polished wooden floor. Around the walls, tapestries depicted battles in progress, and in the centre sat a massive desk, almost dwarfing the man who rose from behind it. It was only when he walked around it to greet them that it became evident that he was, in fact, quite tall. Snow-white hair was neatly caught back by a plaited leather headband of simple black. It was the small dragon's head in amber attached to the centre, so that it sat on his forehead, which proclaimed his rank. Matti recalled Ruari telling her that once all the Grand Masters had worn such badges of office, but that outside of Ergardia it had since fallen out of favour. Here in this room, however, Matti thought it looked totally appropriate.

"Welcome, Lady Montrose, welcome!" he greeted her first, then, "Sergeant Iago, you've done the Order proud. Please, sit …"

He gestured them to one side, where they saw carved chairs with plump cushions arranged around a fireplace of proportions suitable to such an impressive room. From a seat built into its side a man stood up as they approached.

"From the message we received of your coming, I gather my old friend Jaenberht intended you to meet this young man," the Grand Master said, by way of introduction. "This is Talorcan."

Whereupon Matti and Iago found themselves shaking hands with a Knight, nearly as tall as Ruari, but as dark as Ruari was fair. Shoulder length jet black hair was braided at the temples and at the back, while an equally black beard and moustache were clipped short, emphasizing rather than hiding the firm jaw line. And, beneath unbending eyebrows, dark eyes smouldered like coals. This man would make an implacable enemy, was the first impression Matti had. The handshake, however, was firm but relaxed, and when he spoke to offer them caff his voice was even and pleasant.

"I gather you have quite a story to tell us," the Master said once they were settled.

For the rest of the evening Matti and Iago found themselves being vigorously questioned at every stage of their story. Stewards brought in an excellent meal of braised venison accompanied by winter vegetables, and set it up on a table near the fire, yet even during that the questions continued. When it became clear that there was no mistake that Tancostyl was in Rheged, Talorcan seemed to lose his appetite. He went to the fireplace and stood staring into the flames, as the Master continued to listen to Iago's account of the appearance of the soldiers at Allerford. Suddenly he smacked the stone overmantle with his fist.

"Curse the Abend back to the Underworld!" he snarled.

"Steady, Talorcan," the Master said calmly.

"Steady, Master Brego?" Talorcan growled. "This proves I was right! After Gavra Pass we should have called out the entire Order. Pursued those vipers back to their nest, and eliminated them once and for all! I said the Abend would never give up, didn't I? And here they are! Just when everyone's guard is down, they've sneaked back in and are making a bid for the Treasures."

"You know what they're after?" Matti asked in surprise.

"Oh, yes!" Talorcan replied emphatically, and proceeded to explain. "They need those Treasures back. I was part of the plan to undermine the power of the most important DeÁine nearly eight – or when we began the plan, really ten – years ago. The Covert Brethren had found me and brought me out of New Lochlainn many years before when I was but a lad. I was the lure to get the Arberth and the Abend at one another's throats, you see. To divide and conquer by setting the secular power against the spiritual. But to do that I had to know as much as if I'd lived there for much longer than I had. So I got fed every scrap of information about the DeÁine that might be of use – and with the Covert Brethren, that was a lot!"

He shuddered and moved a little closer to the fire, as if whatever he remembered chilled him to the bone.

"They're utterly ruthless. Never doubt that! The DeÁine who live in New Lochlainn in general are of mixed blood. Despite what you may have heard, this Great Return is not made up of anything like the same numbers of pure DeÁine as the conquest our distant ancestors faced. Those who were of the lower orders – servants and simple soldiers – have interbred with the people of the Islands who lived on the vast plain in the west of Brychan, and wherever else they went to for those missing centuries in between. They're as afraid of the pure ones as any Islander. But the racially pure ones now try to prevent their blood becoming diluted, and so they interbreed only with one another. Yet, because of that, time is running out for them. Even they can see that there are fewer pure DeÁine children being born than there used to be. This makes them impatient for the Return to be completed. If they could subjugate all of the Islands they could be reunited with the rest of the DeÁine.

"We heard two rumours about *them*. One is that they have refused to set foot on the Islands until the Treasures had been recaptured, because they believed the land to be in some way tainted or cursed by the loss. The other legend is that these DeÁine we face are exiles because they're the ones who lost the Treasures, or at least the descendants of those who did. Their punishment being to remain in exile until they retrieve what was lost. Personally I think this the most likely, but it's also possible that, in the lost centuries before they reappeared, they suffered some great disaster and this is all that's left. In which case, they still need the Treasures to prolong their long lives even further. Whichever story is the true one actually matters less than the fact that the DeÁine feel a sense of urgency, and we stand between them and what they think they need.

"When we set them up to force their hand – which came to a head eight years ago – we knew that we were only buying time for a generation or so. Sooner or later the old differences between the most powerful leaders would heal, or they'd be replaced with new ones which would create new alliances. Where our plans came undone was in the level of casualties amongst the Covert Brethren. We thought we would be able to go on spying on their every move the way we had ever since the Brethren were formed. We'd had rapid success in infiltrating the court, but most of those brave souls lost their lives, or had to flee in the pogroms that followed Gavra.

"Since then we've effectively been blind to their moves, which is why I always advocated calling the rest of the Islands' Orders out and finishing what the Knights of Celidon started back when we had them unbalanced. But others thought we'd done enough, and the losses we sustained were far in excess of any we'd anticipated. So the heads of the Order thought that, having successfully set the Arberth politicians baying for the Abend's blood, we'd done enough, and that the Abend were no longer a force to be reckoned with now that they had no credibility left amongst the pure DeÁine.

"How wrong they were! The Abend have obviously decided that they can do by stealth what the DeÁine army couldn't do by force, and they've caught us napping!"

"What worries me," Master Brego interrupted, when he thought Talorcan had given them the salient points, "is that the first member of the Abend we've heard of is in a position to take command of the Treasure *farthest* from New Lochlainn."

"Sacred Trees, that hadn't occurred to me," Iago muttered worriedly.

"Hounds of the Wild Hunt!" Talorcan's intended continued criticism of the Islands' leaders was stopped in its tracks as he swore.

"Indeed," Master Brego said wryly. "You see the implications, though, don't you? If Tancostyl managed to make his way unspotted all the way to Rheged, then work his way into the heart of the government there, unopposed, what in the Islands is going on closer to New Lochlainn?"

Talorcan sat down heavily back on the fireside seat.

"Well, I suppose there's one comfort in that the sacrifice we made at Gavra Pass enabled the Gorget to be moved out of Brychan and farther away from the DeÁine." He looked over to Matti and Iago. "It was originally at the castle of Breslyn in the far northeast of Brychan, but at least the Order had the foresight to see that there was a danger in that. That's when I met your friend MacBeth. I travelled to Brychan with him when he was going to fetch the Gorget and I was on my way with the Knights into the mountains and Gavra Pass. Their sacrifices to get that thing over the water have never been the stuff bards sing of, since they still remain secret, but it was no less an essential part of keeping the Islands safe for all that."

Matti's quizzical expression prompted him to go on.

"Water is a powerful antidote, for want of a better word, for the Power the Abend wield. The stronger a user is in the DeÁine Power the worse a sea crossing is for them, and the Abend are rendered almost prostrate when they step off dry land."

"And there's the simple practical consideration that even they can't walk on water," Iago added. "In Brychan all they'd have to do is walk across the mountains, but to get across the sea they'd have to find a ship to take them, and that makes them traceable – not to mention that it would be almost impossible for them to bring soldiers across to support them without someone noticing troops embarking."

"By the Trees, that's a good point Iago," Talorcan said cheering up somewhat. "With your permission, Master Brego, I'd like to lead patrols out first thing in the morning to check all the ports. I think we can forget the two in the far north – I can't imagine that any Abend could cope with such a long, rough crossing. At least we may be able to confirm if, and how many, may have passed through here to get to Rheged or anywhere else."

Master Brego nodded.

"Absolutely, you can take your own and four other lances straight across to the west. I'll send others to the southern ports. We may have trouble finding one man alone, but we can make sure that we don't have any other DeÁine loitering around waiting for their master to call."

That was the start of a long enforced rest for Matti and Iago, for there was little they could do even though the rest of the Knights were busy as bees. However, for the first time since the whole horrific sequence of events had been set in motion Matti felt as though some sort of order had re-entered her life. There was something very reassuring about being surrounded by all these extremely competent soldiers, and as she walked about the castle she was constantly coming upon halls where men were practicing with different weapons.

They might be going nowhere just at the moment, but there was an air of anticipation about the place which said that, as soon as Master Brego had any information they could act upon, there would not be a moment's delay. It gave Matti a feeling of great relief that she and her few friends were no longer trying to stem this tide of disasters alone. The other great blessing, as far as Matti was concerned, was that it transpired that even in such a capacious store as the Knights had, there were almost no women's clothes, and many of those came nowhere near fitting her, so that she was able to continue wearing comfortable clothes. Being relatively tall for a woman, she was able to fit into some of the spare uniform kept to kit out pages and squires, and so she was soon walking around dressed in black like the rest of the garrison.

A fortnight later they were still waiting for Talorcan to return, so that when Matti heard the watchman's trumpet sound she rushed to the nearest tower to see who was coming. However, the boatman was rowing across a lone male passenger the way she and Iago had been brought, rather than the usual northern crossing from the stables that Talorcan would have made. Muffled in a heavy cloak she could make out no details of the passenger, yet there was something vaguely familiar about him, and so she headed towards the route to the Master's office on the basis that any newcomer would be made to report to him in the current crisis.

Reaching the dragon doors, she almost collided with Master Brego coming out as the duty sergeants brought the visitor down the corridor the opposite way.

"General Montrose, welcome!" Master Brego said, stepping forward to clasp Will's outstretched hand in both of his. "By the Trees, it's good to see you – we thought you lost or imprisoned!"

"Very nearly, Grand Master, very nearly," Will replied, "but how did you know?"

"Your wife arrived with one of our Knights a few weeks ago…"

"Hello Will," Matti said coolly, stepping further into the light spilling out of the great office.

Will blinked and did a double-take. For a moment he could not reconcile the trim young page who stood before him with the voice of his wife which was coming out of the mouth. He gulped,

"Matilda?"

"Yes."

"You made it here then?"

"Yes. No thanks to you."

Will looked as though she had slapped him,

"What do you mean?"

"Well your soldiers may have helped *you*, but not one of them lifted a finger to come and see if I was alright!" Indignation filled Matti's voice although she knew she was being unreasonable, yet she could not stop herself. "If it wasn't for one of *Ruari's* sergeants, both Wistan and I would've perished at the hands of Oswine's thugs. And Iago saved my life *again* when they attacked Jaenberht's monks as we were travelling. *Those* men were from Catraeth, Will, men you once commanded! I recognized the insignia on their uniforms. Have the army of Rheged turned to mercenaries? Loyal to the highest bidder? Or was it personal?"

Will stood stunned at this outburst until Matti said,

"Well at least Wistan is safe, not that I expect you to care!"

"He's not," Will croaked.

"What?" Matti and Master Brego gasped together.

Will cleared his throat.

"Could we go and sit down, please, and have you got any caff on the brew?"

"Yes… Yes, of course," Brego said, ushering them both into the office, and retrieving a large pot of caff from its warming spot by the fire. Will lowered himself onto a plump cushion and groaned with relief. Stretching his legs out towards the fire his joints creaked audibly, and for the first time

Matti felt sorry for him as she realized how worn he looked. As Brego poured three mugs out, Matti picked one up and took it over to Will, who looked up at her in surprise. She shrugged,

"Sorry. It's been a rough ride this past month or so, I'm not used to being hunted like a hen pheasant."

It was not much as apologies went, she knew, but although she could see he had had a hard time too, there was no way that she was going to let him totally off the hook. Will's expression was one of wary truce, but he took a long pull at the steaming caff before speaking.

"When Oswine had me outlawed I was lucky enough to be far away from the capital and got advanced warning his men were coming for me..."

"...How nice! Wish we had!" Matti muttered under her breath.

"...I was on the run for weeks, but I'd got other problems..."

"...Not *us* obviously!"

"...which I'll come to in a minute, so my men were trying to help me get to Abbot Jaenberht. We started heading north, when the hunt moved out of the southwest and we could come out of hiding, as we'd heard Jaenberht had called a council at Lund. We were almost at the gates when we ran into MacBeth and a monk called Andra."

"Ruari? Ruari's alive!" Matti yelped with glee. "Yes!" and punched the air above her head, while a huge smile filled her face. Such an unladylike outburst raised an amused eyebrow from Master Brego, yet it saddened Will. When she smiled like that Matti was downright beautiful, but it had been years since she done that around him.

He had always made no secret of the fact that their marriage was an empty sham for him, yet he had also convinced himself that Matti was content with her lot. The total contrast between her welcome of him and the news that Ruari lived, burst that bubble in a brutal instant, and he was forced to realise that Matti would probably not have cared a jot if he had died after the life she had been forced to lead. Covering his discomfort by downing the rest of his caff, he used the excuse of getting a refill to master his misery before continuing.

"They'd been looking for you and Wistan, and they'd heard you'd met up with Sergeant Iago. Unfortunately that was after the men attacked you after you'd been to Mailros. Jaenberht told us that you and Iago had disappeared, but that he hoped you were alive because your bodies weren't amongst the ones they brought back for burial. He was going frantic, though, because no sooner had he sent word to Master Hugh in Prydein for help in getting Wistan away to safety, than the youngster took off."

"Took off?" Matti was amazed. "Wistan? Are you sure? I can't imagine him having the confidence to run away."

"Aah, well, he wasn't alone." Will felt some gratification in being able to tell her something she didn't know. "Our Ruari's been keeping a secret! Not only does Oswine have a half-brother in Wistan, he has a cousin too!"

"A cousin?" Matti was shocked.

Will nodded.

"Seems that the old Jarl's first son, and half-brother to Ruari and Michael, Hubert, was able to father a child before he died. He was given to Jaenberht for safe keeping, but Ruari used to visit him whenever he could. This boy was going to take holy orders until all this mess started. Young Brother Kenelm just knew he had a cousin Ruari who used to come and visit, but had no idea of who his father had been. So it came as more than a bit of a shock when Jaenberht had to sit him down and tell him, for his own safety's sake, after the attempts on Wistan's life. Andra says he's not surprised that they decided to clear off and let everyone else fight it out without them, but we've been hunting them for weeks. Can you imagine what would happen if they were caught by Oswine?"

"Blessed Rowan!" Brego invoked, "that would be tragic!"

"So it would," Will agreed. "It was while we were chasing down the west coast that we picked up your trail," he said to Matti. "Ruari and Andra are still looking for the boys on that side, but we decided one of us should come here in case they'd also taken a boat and made it into Ergardia. They'll be safer here, of course, but they're so innocent we'd all feel happier if we could find them and take them some place where Oswine can't arrange to have them kidnapped. I came partly because Andra can recognize Wistan, and Ruari can Kenelm, so it made sense for them to be the ones to continue the hunt. But also because it's dangerous for me to be in Rheged – and I don't just mean because they're hunting me," he said pointedly at Matti.

"I was at that farce of a coronation for Oswine. It never occurred to me that there might be something wrong with the crown. With the prat underneath it, and the sick, twisted ghoul passing himself off as a priest, yes …but not the crown. But after that I kept having these strange dreams, and then the cravings started. By the time we reached Jaenberht I thought I was losing my mind. It was only when Ruari told me what he suspected that it made sense."

Matti and Master Brego leaned forward in their chairs in expectation.

"The crown they used was the DeÁine Helm!"

Master Brego swore long and fluently in complete disregard of his noble female guest. Will grunted his agreement,

"Can't argue with that. The thing is, I've touched the cursed thing now that it's been activated by the presence of that bastard, Tancostyl. All the time it was kept locked away in the deepest store in Earlskirk Castle it was like a simmering pot, in no danger of boiling over. And with no DeÁine nearby there was no-one to channel energy into it to feed its power. That's why the old Jarl was able to take Ruari and Michael down to see it, although even then they were instructed to never touch it."

"Was that why Ruari was able to move the Gorget?" Matti asked. "Because there were no DeÁine around until the Hunters found them?"

"Yes and no," Master Brego replied. "Even bringing a Treasure out into the open where there are people seems to start feeding it. MacBeth was one of the very few who weren't touched by the Gorget's power – he and two others – and we still don't know why they were able to resist it more than the rest of the guards."

"Well the Helm's certainly touched me," Will said emphatically, "and I wouldn't wish the experience onto my worst enemy! That's why I had to come across the water. All the time I was in Rheged it was in my bones, like an itch I couldn't scratch. Ruari was worried what would happen to me if I got separated from them, and he was right. I was fine when I was by the sea, but the minute we went inland I got all twitchy again. I can't tell you what a relief it's been to get over here! I landed mid-afternoon and slept for eighteen hours straight – I think the landlord thought I'd died! After that I set out for here. Ruari said I was to tell Talorcan, because he would be able to sense the residue of the taint in me and he didn't want me to end up being skewered!"

"Don't worry," Master Brego laughed, "I won't let Talorcan skewer you!"

Eventually he let Will go and asked a steward to find him a room for the night. Tactfully he had picked up on the strained atmosphere between Will and Matti, and did not suggest they share her room. However, Matti walked down the corridors with Will and came into his room. When the steward had gone she came over and put her arms around his neck and gave him a hug.

"I'm sorry for being so viperous all the time," she said softly in his ear. "It's not your fault, I know it's not. I know you're no coward, and you'd have come back to help us if you could. It was just all so unexpected, so violent! And I had nobody to turn to until we got to Iago. I couldn't believe we could live in the home of a general of the army and be so vulnerable! It made me angry as well as frightened and I wanted to blame someone."

Will stiffened at the unaccustomed contact, then tentatively put his arms around her. She was still too skinny to arouse him, but after all he had been through it felt good to just hold someone close.

"I'm sorry too," he mumbled into her soft hair, which smelt wonderfully of clean, lemon soap. "I should have guessed they'd come after you as well, but I thought if I stayed away you'd be safe. I can't believe they killed everyone in the castle."

"What?" Matti gasped, pulling away so that she could look into his face. "You're not serious? Dear Spirits you are! Oh no, not all of them!"

Will pulled her close as she began to sob, holding her tight.

"I'm so sorry," he whispered, "I thought you knew that."

Her head shook against his shoulder,

"I fled with Wistan as the soldiers were coming in through the gates. I thought they'd be safe without us there."

She stopped as she realized that she had unintentionally repeated the same thing Will had said to her, then began crying even harder as she kissed him on the cheek.

"Oh, Will I'm so sorry for being angry. I've been a bitch to you. You didn't deserve that."

"What a bloody mess," Will sighed as he hugged her tightly. "I'm so sorry too, Matilda. I'm so, *so* sorry I wasn't there to protect you."

"Matti, for Spirit's sake call me Matti, everyone else does," she wept, "after all these years surely you know me well enough to do that."

"Yes, I can do that. I can do that," he softly whispered as he rocked her in his arms.

Chapter 28

Fresh Revelations

Brychan: Samhainn

The ride back from Breslyn was a miserable time for all of them. There was no way that the bodies of all the garrison could be brought back for burial in the chapel at Vellyn, yet all of the company wished that a priest had been around to say the proper funeral rites for their valiant comrades. Somehow it seemed all the worse for their deaths being unexplainable. No matter how hard everyone had scratched their heads no-one could find a natural explanation for what had happened. It made everyone on edge, waiting in case whatever it was returned again. Esclados had a nasty suspicion which he kept to himself until they were two days into the return journey, and he got the chance to ride alongside Berengar, out of earshot of any of the others. Then he mentioned the dreaded word – DeÁine.

"I never saw it for myself," he said carefully, "but there were those who helped tend the survivors from Gavra Pass who said the wounded spoke of balls of fire flying through the air from the hands of the wizards. I haven't wanted to say anything in front of the others, especially Jacinto – he thinks I'm mad enough already – but I can't get the image out of my mind."

Berengar gave a bitter snort.

"Esclados, you're the sanest man I know, and if you're going mad then I'm joining you, because I was thinking the very same thing. What bothers me is, first, what was that bastard after? And second, how in the Underworld did he, or she, get here? We watch all the passes like hawks!"

"One person, perhaps? One alone would be less visible and we don't expect them as much – even if we do keep an eye out for spies," Esclados mused.

Berengar exhaled sharply.

"A big risk, though, don't you think? I mean, that would have to be one of the Abend, or the like, travelling *alone*. Would they risk capture that badly? If they did, it must be for something they desperately need to take a chance like that."

However, despite chewing it over, off and on, for the rest of the journey back to Vellyn, neither of them could think of a good reason, although it stopped Berengar brooding on their failure to save Edward's siblings. Cwen was too busy worrying about that herself to notice the long conversations between the leader and the older Knight, but Jacinto saw it and worried. Back at Vellyn, to his relief, it became obvious that he had not been the object of those conversations, for he seemed to have been totally forgotten about.

Not by Swein, though. With the nights turning ever colder, and the garrison full of men, it was near impossible to find anywhere quiet, which frustrated his attempts to get Jacinto to himself. He knew that it would be asking for trouble to try to get the object of his desires into a compromising position here, even though the more he observed, the more he found some of the other men seemed to have particularly close friendships. It took a full week until Jacinto was one of the very last to use the bath hall one evening. Slipping into the room as three others left, he found Jacinto just rising from the soapy water as the only other occupant pulled his pants on, picked his towel up off the floor, and made for the door.

Walking up behind Jacinto, Swein took another dry towel and reached out to wipe the drops of water from the muscular brown back. His own excitement was becoming visible as he took in the perfectly toned buttocks and rippling muscles, and how they jumped at his touch. Jacinto spun round to face him, but said nothing.

"Hello there," Swein said huskily, his eyes dropping to Jacinto's groin. "Oh my!" he gasped appreciatively.

For a second Jacinto looked as though he might take to his heels and run. That was until Swein's hand began an expert stroking. The young squire gave a moan of pleasure and allowed himself to be guided back to one of the long benches at the back of the room. Swein kept his smile enigmatic, but inside he was whooping with triumph. If there was one thing he really knew how to do it was how to pleasure someone. All these soldiers might be able to knock him to the ground in an instant in a fight, but in the arts of seduction he was the master. There was no way that Jacinto would resist him now – and he did not. For three long hours. By which time the rest of the garrison had turned into their beds, enabling Swein to smuggle Jacinto into the tiny bedroom he had been given this time, and to repeat the experience when the garrison's trumpeter sounded the alarm-call to wake them in the morning.

In a room in a different part of the castle, Berengar had been sitting watching Cwen pour over a map with Esclados. His curiosity over her unknown lover was increasing all the time. Not just because every time they spoke she inadvertently gave imperceptible glimpses of the relationship she had once had, either. To his own consternation he realized he was becoming more and more attracted to her himself. Who was the man who could attract such an independent, intelligent young woman? He sighed, *put her out of your mind, Berengar,* he told himself, *you've other things you should be concentrating on*. But when he did that, gloomy thoughts of the failure to prevent the disaster at Breslyn took over, which was no more constructive.

Sighing, he levered himself out of the chair and went to join them.

"I don't think there's any point in trying to track Edward's men's route back, either," Cwen was agreeing with Esclados. "The trouble is, if we go after the other children – there's the oldest son and the two younger daughters left, is that right? – we could be on the road for weeks and get nowhere. The brother especially might be anywhere. Married, or even living on another Island, given that he's older than Edward. We've got nothing to go on which would lead us straight to any one of them."

"What do you think we should do, then?" Berengar asked from behind her, trying to drag his mind away from how the candlelight made a halo around her fair hair.

"Caersus," Cwen said emphatically.

"Caersus?" Berengar repeated, surprised. "Why there?"

"Because that's where Edward was supposedly baptised. The monks keep records, don't they? Well, if we can get them to find the documents that show that there wasn't a single person of consequence at Edward's immersion into the Faith ceremony, it'll show he was of little importance back then. That was always the second part of my own plan after warning the others. I mean, even though his cousin wasn't on the throne at that stage, he would still have been the heir to all of the Mar estates, wouldn't he? To the castles at Amroth and Mythvai, and the estates between Bettus and Fleeceston, not to mention the revenues from odd sheep farms all over the southeast, and some potteries at Kiln. That's a lot of money for them to be treating the heir as if he's no-one. That's unless he wasn't going to be the heir!"

"But how can you prove that his parents weren't just …well …odd?" Berengar persisted, deliberately testing her theory.

"Because of what happened when Richert was born!" Cwen said, forgetting her caution as she warmed to her subject. "When he was taken to be baptised, his mother was still too weak from the birth to travel far, and she was with Mar on campaign in the west! Richert was baptised in the big font at High Cross Abbey. Half the leading families had to trek up there in order to be seen at that occasion! And they're on record as having been there because the witnesses were entered in the Holy Book as his Spirit-parents took their vows, and his future foster families, too, for when he would train with them for a knight."

"How in the Islands do you know *that*!" Esclados exclaimed.

Cwen suddenly realized how rashly she had spoken and blushed, kicking herself for being so careless. How could she dig herself out of this one?

"You know, I think it's about time we had the name of this source of yours," Esclados said firmly.

Cwen looked up at him fearfully.

"Oh, come, come, lass," he said kindly. "Surely you can trust us by now? You've been proved right, that there is something evil afoot by what went on at Breslyn. We're not doubting your courage or your honesty either, but we need all the information we can get if we're to outsmart Edward and the evil mind behind this."

"*And* the evil mind?" Cwen gasped in surprise. Then more firmly, "Oh no, there's no other mind at work. Edward is evil enough all by himself!"

"Ah, well, we're not so sure about that," Berengar said, then proceeded to tell her of Esclados and his fears of the DeÁine.

"Spirits protect us!" Cwen whispered when he had finished, then stopped to think. "No …I don't think the DeÁine can be involved in Edward's plots. Those've been going on for far too long. …Think about it. There are too many soldiers at court who would recognize a DeÁine for one of them to have been hanging around for that long. No …Edward may have played into this DeÁine's hands and given him an opening where there wouldn't otherwise have been one, but I think Edward's plan is just that. Edward's!"

"There you go again," Berengar said, intrigued. "To most people he's just 'the king', but you always call him by his given name. Why? Did you know him that well?"

"Spirits no!" exclaimed Cwen, horrified at the thought.

"Then why?" persisted Berengar. "Who was your friend? I say friend, but I think he was more than that, wasn't he?"

"Much more. So much more," Cwen answered sadly. She looked at their expectant faces as she said, "The day he died it was like all the light went out in the world. The only thing that keeps me going is the thought of bringing down his murderer, Edward!"

"Are you saying Edward actually killed him with his *own hands*?" Esclados asked in wonderment.

"Yes! I can't prove it, but I'm sure he did," Cwen confirmed, desperately trying to hold back the tears which rebelliously started to sneak out of the corners of her eyes. The final undoing of her resolve was Berengar fishing a clean handkerchief out of one of his pockets and handing it to her. It was the same kind of well-washed, plain linen that Richert had used in preference to the lace-trimmed fancies so many at court waved around, and she began to sob. Suddenly she was so sick of having to keep it all locked away inside her. She wanted the freedom to grieve as she had done at Amroth, not pretend Richert had never existed for her.

"He was everything to me," she howled. "What right did Edward have to take that away so he could get rid of his poor wife and those little boys? Richert was right! Edward might be king, but all the good things come with the burden of having to behave properly, at least in public, and that meant having a queen and heirs. It was Edward's own fault if the two princes weren't his! The Spirit's only know how discreet Queen Nerys was! Never a whiff of scandal, which is more than he ever achieved! But that wasn't good enough for Edward! Oh no! He had to have everything his own way, like some spoilt little boy. He plotted to have them killed and Richert found out!

"We were going to bring them up here. Up here to the north. We thought Edward would never shift himself out of his playboys' beds. We thought they'd be safe and Edward would forget about them. Oh Sacred Trees, how could we have been so wrong? We thought he would hire some assassin. We never expected he'd become so twisted as to want the pleasure of doing it himself. He was there that night it happened! That's why he had to have time to get to the manor while everyone was running around thinking he'd been killed – so that everyone would be looking at Arlei. Richert died at the manor because he knew the truth. He saw Edward that night. His groom said the horses passed him in the night when Richert was at the manor. Richert tried to stop him. Oh, Richert!"

Berengar and Esclados could feel their blood running cold. Their king had not just cold-bloodedly planned the murder of his own family, he had *done* the act himself! But Berengar had also picked up on something else which chilled him even further.

"You said Richert found out, but then you were talking about 'we'." He could not believe what he was about to ask. "Was *Earl Richert* your …friend?"

"My friend, my lover, my everything!" Cwen wept. "Five years we were together. Five years when we shared *everything*. I never went to court. That treacherous, unfaithful bitch of a wife of his was there, screwing her cousin and never caring how she hurt Richert. But when he came home he used to tell me everything. He would've given anything to give up the court and come to live at Amroth all the time. We wanted children so much. Before he went away I was going to tell him I thought I was pregnant …oh, only by a few weeks …almost too early to tell. But I thought he should know and I never got chance. Then he died and I lost him, and the stress did the rest. I lost all of him!"

Esclados had gone as white as a sheet and Berengar felt less than steady. So this was the secret woman that Richert was rumoured to have had hidden away in the deep south! Yet more than that, they both suddenly thought how much danger Cwen was in. It was obvious that she had never given a moment's thought to that herself, but if Edward ever realized how much Richert had told her he would have every paid assassin in the Island out after *her*. Esclados put his massive arm around her and pulled her into a hug. Berengar could see by his face that anyone trying to hurt Cwen would get more than they bargained for from the old bear. Oh, Cwen had definitely become the daughter he wished he had had!

As for himself, what an act to have to follow! Of all the men in Brychan it had to be the one Berengar looked up to most as the epitome of knightly conduct – a superb fighter, an exemplary leader of men, intelligent and unassuming, but someone not to be trifled with. He inwardly smiled ruefully, oh well, it had been a nice dream while it lasted. He had risen to Ealdorman, the highest rank before Grand Master, and with the command of a stretch of the border March that came with it, but he was no royal! There was no way he would ever be able to replace Richert. However, he could make sure that he honoured his memory by keeping the one person he knew Richert had adored safe. From now on, Cwen was going nowhere without a full complement of Knights as her bodyguard.

Drying her eyes as best she could, Cwen struggled to put the lid back on her grief, and, with a few hiccups, managed to say,

"Do you see now why we must stop Edward? His half-sisters will never be safe while he's free and roaming around the Island with the power to do as he likes. We thought him incapable of concentrating for long enough to be dangerous, but we were wrong. Even worse, he's probably got the taste for murder now. You, Esclados, you saw what he did to Swein when he was just amusing himself. Now he's crossed a major threshold and gone far beyond that. That poor soul who Swein thought was an actor, and who we can now guess was his half-brother, wasn't just killed. He was butchered! Hacked to pieces in a wild frenzy. There was no vestige of control left in that act. None at all!

"And where will it stop? Richert told me they had some distant cousins who are the next in line to the throne, and that Edward was bringing the two youngest up to be just like him. Can you imagine what he might conjure up as some weird initiation ceremony for them? It might even involve his sisters – one each – or some poor soul who has no other connection to him other than to be in the wrong place at the wrong time. And you're worried about a DeÁine you haven't even seen and might not exist!"

That night they did little else in the way of planning, but in the morning Berengar and Esclados called the castle's captains into the map room. In terse sentences Berengar told them of Edward's treachery. He omitted telling them who exactly Cwen was, emphasizing instead that she was the key witness to the events and in need of protection.

"I will be taking a battalion to Caersus," he told them.

"Just the one?" someone queried.

"Just half the men from here," he confirmed, "because I want the rest of you to start patrolling *right now*. There's a high ranking DeÁine on the loose that needs to be caught before he does to somewhere else what he did to Breslyn. Never mind the rough weather, from now on every man with a hawk takes it on patrol. I want every rook, crow and raven out of the sky! Magpies too! I want him blind! Cwen thinks he has nothing to do with the King's treachery, but I don't want to give this devious bastard any opportunity to cause more havoc. Jensen, you'll take men up to Roselan and then on to Wynlas with messages for the Ealdormen there. Purval, you'll do the same for Camais. And Merrivale, you'll take your men back over the high passes to Esgair. You should get there alright, and if you get snowed in once you're there, you're to provide extra support for patrols in the Line. That bastard's not getting back to New Lochlainn!"

When Swein and Jacinto joined Cwen after their early morning intimacies, she was sitting with Esclados in the small parlour still looking red-eyed from the last night. Before they could find out what had happened, though, Berengar appeared and broke the news of their journey south. Cwen was delighted.

"We're going to find it, then?" she asked.

"Yes we are," Berengar confirmed, "and I'm coming with you, it's too important to leave unguarded, and so are you."

Swein and Jacinto looked at one another. It? What was 'it'? However, nobody was bothering to explain directly, yet it was obviously a treasure of some sort and located in the abbey at Caersus. Less appealing was the thought of the long journey south. Caersus was going to take them the best part of three, maybe even four, weeks to reach if the weather closed in, or if they encountered any of the king's troops. To Swein's relief, Berengar was planning on going over the mountains from Fleton to Redrock in order to avoid the road through Arlei. It was thought likely to provoke far too many questions if companies of Knights rode through the capital armed to the teeth – for Berengar planned on acquiring at least another five companies at Bere, where another Commander would be returning from mountain patrols.

The biggest surprise for Cwen came the morning that they mounted up for the journey. Every one of the Knights had a bird of prey sitting on the square pommel of their saddle. She remembered, way back in the past, Richert telling her that the reason the Knights had such distinctive high pommels on their saddles was to accommodate a hawk, but until today she had never really thought what that would look like. Now, seeing the two hundred Knights and the accompanying hundreds of men-at-arms and archers, all in formal black and fully armed, was awesome enough. For they were all seriousness, not laughing and joking as they had been when she had seen them returning.

Now the birds added a whole other dimension to their appearance. Odd members of the men-at-arms and the squires had small birds, like kestrels and merlins, perched before them or on their wrists. But the Knights' birds were big. Brown-feathered buzzards, white-chested goshawks with brown wings and backs, and grey-feathered gyrfalcons, all sat tall enough to block the view of the chests of their riders, yellow eyes swivelling back and forth in expectation of prey. Silhouetted against the black cloaks they emphasized the uniform, while creating a rippling band of colour down the line of horses.

Berengar had no hawk, but Esclados, along with one of the other veteran captains, had a magnificent red-feathered kite sat in front of him. Jacinto, though, had no hawk and Cwen edged Twigglet alongside Esclados to softly ask why.

"*Phaah*, no hawk would have him!" Esclados snorted. "It takes patience to train a hawk. You have to get to know them, and them you, and Jacinto has no patience with anything at all, let alone an animal."

"But why doesn't Berengar have one either?" Cwen asked, still puzzled.

"Ah …that's a different case altogether. His bird died last year of old age. One from the same clutch of youngsters the falconers reared as Sybil here." Esclados gently stroked the feathers at the back of his huge bird's neck. "We have a special group of falconers up at Roselan who breed birds for us, and they have a youngster they're bringing on for Berengar. He was hoping to collect it when the first snows came, so he could spend the quieter months over the winter training it. Looks as like that might have to wait, though!"

Just then Berengar rode up to join them at the head of the column.

"You're bringing Sybil?" he asked in some surprise. "Are you sure, Esclados? She's getting an old lady now, there'd be none blaming you for leaving her in her warm barn."

"Ach, she's like me," Esclados said with a grin, "she gets bored sitting around all day, don't you girl? We're going south, not up into the mountains, and she can fit under my cloak if it gets too wet."

Sybil gave her head a flick which rippled her feathers as if in agreement, then allowed Berengar the familiarity of stroking her.

"He's the only one apart from me and the castle falconer who can touch her," Esclados said proudly. "Anyone else she'd take their fingers off!"

Mounted up to the rear of his horse, Jacinto and Swein both made a mental note to stay well away from the big bird and her wickedly curved, sharp beak and talons. The thought of what Sybil might do if she took offence sent shivers down both their backs. However, they had no time to worry further, for Berengar's black-gloved hand appeared in the air above the heads of the men and waved them forward. At a brisk trot the column of a thousand men rode in pairs out of the great gate and into the cold grey winter's day.

At the end of the first day's ride, Cwen realized why they had so many pack animals with them, for in short order a line of tents appeared alongside the road. Bundles of firewood appeared, and bedrolls quilted with feathers kept the worst of the cold out. The Knights' experience of patrolling and campaigning showed in the professional way they managed to get it all stowed away again in record time in the morning, too, so that they were on the road almost as soon as the breakfast fires were extinguished. At Bere they met another captain, who had fifty Knights plus attendant men-at-arms with him.

"Where's Commander Nilsen?" Berengar asked him.

"We were on our way back when we heard the news of King Edward's murder. A captain from the royal guard said they'd heard that the miscreant was heading for the hills. In case it was a DeÁine spy, Commander Nilsen turned back to cover the pass from Redrock to High Cross."

Swein felt his heart jump almost out of his chest at this. He had guessed he would be hunted once the word got out about Edward's supposed murder, but only now did he realise just how lucky he had been to escape the web which had been spread to trap him. From the continuing conversation it became clear that the Knights had been as perplexed as anyone at the sudden reappearance of Edward, and were annoyed at being sent off on what amounted to a wild goose chase. That would not have helped Swein any, though, if he had been caught in those first couple of days, although he had come to realise that he could have done a lot worse than be caught by the Knights – they at least would not have strung him up without a trial!

"Surely Nilsen knew the danger of getting snow-bound?" one of the other captains, who had ridden up the column to meet them, was asking.

"That he did," said the new arrival, Fletcher, "but he figured that by the time he reached the pass the fugitive would be ahead of him, so all he had to do was keep going until he got to High Cross, by which time they'd either have caught up with him or he wouldn't be there. Or at least not for long. The snows are coming early this year. Of course, Commander Nilsen wouldn't have found out until he got to High Cross that there was nobody to chase."

"We're heading for Redrock," Berengar told him. "Get your men fallen in behind."

"You'd best make good time then, sire," Fletcher said. "The snow was beginning to fall for real when we were coming back down the mountains. Tarry and you won't get through at all."

The next day they left Bere well before dawn, with the joining patrol's soldiers and Knights almost clearing out the grange's stores to re-equip in short order. Esclados took the opportunity to point the lesson to Jacinto.

"A good thing the men who checked these stores didn't think 'it'll do', isn't it!" he said, as two bridles and a saddle got replaced. "We'd still be scrapping the mould off if you'd had anything to do with the matter!"

Jacinto winced at the public humiliation, but part of him could not fail to see that there was much in what the old Knight said, however much he wished he could deny it. What hurt most was that Swein witnessed the chastisement, even though his eyes were full only of sympathy.

Berengar had had two choices of route. The first was a long slow climb starting from the main road almost as soon as it left Bere. However this way would have meant camping two nights running up above the potential snow line, and the amount of wood that they would have needed to carry would have burdened the horses and made progress slower. By taking the coast road onwards to near Kilnport, it was then a shorter, steeper ascent, but they would only have one night in the mountains. By the time darkness fell they were close to Kilnport, and it was a grey, murky morning when they set off again.

This time there was no question of setting off in the dark. The ascent was treacherous under foot, and the first couple of hours seemed to be taken at a snail's pace as they carefully picked their way upwards. However, after the sharp uphill start they came out onto a broader track which was still steep, but wound its way around the side of the mountain rather than going straight up it. White flecks of snow began to drift in on the wind, and for the rest of the day they were caught off and on in sharp flurries. Twigglet ploughed on gamely, sure-footed on the uneven terrain, although

Esclados always made sure Cwen was on the inside of the track from any of the sheer drops to the rocks below. That night Cwen thought she could never remember being quite so cold, her fingers never seemed to regain the feeling in them and her nose had a permanent drip, for which she was grateful for the continued loan of Berengar's handkerchief.

The morning, however, made up for all the discomfort. The low, clinging clouds had disappeared, and brilliant sunshine turned the white-coated peaks above them into sparking jewels. Pristine white covered everything. Their birds hunted well once they were on the move, for against the snow, rabbits and other small beasts were easily visible with fewer bolt holes from the swooping hawks. It was barely early afternoon before they turned the shoulder of a massive peak and found themselves staring down at Redrock Castle. A local geological quirk had given the stone red veining, and the stonemasons who had built the castle had taken pride in bringing it out in the blocks they had quarried. Like something out of a child's story, it sat glowing amber in the lowering sun, its roofs capped with white frosting, beautiful and dangerous.

"It looks like it ought to be the home of a witch or a fairy queen!" Cwen gasped in delight.

Esclados laughed. "Well in that case you're in for a disappointment! The commander in charge is a grumpy old man called Kirk, with a fat belly and a string of bad jokes!"

Cwen could not help laughing too at that, until Sybil let out a shriek and took off from her perch in front of Esclados. With mighty flaps of her huge wings, she rapidly ascended and began making a turn back towards they way they had come. As if answering her cries, several other hawks lifted off and set off to follow her. Far behind them, treading in the passage through the snow that the long line of horses had made, the riders now saw a lone figure dressed in black following them. As Sybil got closer she also gained height. Suddenly she stopped flapping her wings, folded them back and dropped like a stone, talons outstretched. Far away as they were, the Knights just made out what looked like a staff coming up to try to strike Sybil, but she was too canny to fall for that. Twisting aside she unfolded her wings and sped away, yet in forcing the figure to twist to try to hit her she had opened up an opportunity for those behind her. Another red kite caught claw's-full of the cloak, while the beak of a goshawk struck the figure's head, dragging the hood away with it. Against the white mountainside it became obvious that they figure was bald.

"DeÁine!" Berengar bellowed. "Call the birds back! Call them back before he uses Power-fire on them!"

But Sybil knew better than he did. Leading her flight in dives past, she provoked him into unleashing a bolt of flame upwards. Twisting neatly aside from it, she left it to plough into the side of the mountain. A plume of snow erupted from the spot and then a slow rumbled began. As the birds raced back to their Knights in answer to the calls, a great chunk of the mountain sheared where the ice had got into it and began to crumble. In a great roar it plummeted downwards, the sound triggering the new snow which had not yet frozen to the mountain, so that it too began to slither towards the valley floor. The Knights needed no urging but heeled their horses into a mad dash to the plateau where Redrock Castle stood. Waves of white, powdery snow crashed onto the track not far behind the rearmost horsemen, then slid over the edge to drop in white falls to the valley floor. As they pounded out onto the flat ground before the castle gates and slowed down, they looked back. High on the mountainside nothing was visible except a long triangle of grey rubble, which cut off the path. Nothing moved there now. The rock and snow slide had completely cut off the track in front of where the DeÁine had been, and there was no sign of him.

"Clever girl, Sybil!" Esclados praised her, as she deigned to let him smooth her feathers. "You see, Berengar, I knew I should bring her along!"

Berengar shook his head, but smiled nonetheless. At a slower pace the column of men rode into the castle, glad of the chance of a night in front of a warm fire and a proper bed in such inclement weather.

As they stood warming themselves before the glowing fire in the hall at Redrock, Berengar conferred with his captains. Swein and Jacinto had already joined the men queuing up for food, but Cwen brought cups of mulled cider over to the fireplace and stayed to listen.

"Well I don't think anyone now has any doubts that the DeÁine are up to no good," Captain Fletcher said morosely.

"No, indeed not," Esclados agreed. "The big question is, what *are* they up to, though? You were right, Cwen, when you said no DeÁine could show his face at court without being recognized for what he was. So he, or they, almost certainly had nothing to do with the royal murders. And Breslyn hasn't hidden the Gorget in years, so what do they want?"

"Ah, but do they know that?" Berengar mused. "About the Gorget, I mean. I wonder if our friend from earlier today followed us by chance? If so, he's going to be sorely disappointed when we get to Caersus!"

"In which case, shouldn't we be thinking more about what Edward is doing?" Cwen challenged them. "It's because of Edward that we're going there, and we know he's not connected to the DeÁine. Whatever that DeÁine decides to do, he's only one alone. With the snow so thick and heavy in the mountains already, he can't get reinforcements here for *months* now. But Edward is here ...here in Brychan! Before he gets too secure we have to do *something*."

She walked up to Berengar and looked into his eyes. "*Please*. You said you'd help! Every Knight in the Island is watching out for any hint of a DeÁine threat, but you're the only ones who know the threat to those two girls – and the rest of the Island if Edward really is totally mad now! Can you leave the Island to his mercy?"

Berengar was momentarily transfixed by her. He knew she had no idea how much her words tore at him – could not possibly know the secret he had carried for so many years which even Esclados did not know – but she had given him the excuse he was looking for. The only ones who knew the king was insane? Well then, nobody could accuse him of not acting in the Island's interest if he followed his heart and found the evidence to drag Edward down, and protect two innocent girls in the process.

"We leave for Caersus in the morning!" he ordered. "Let's send out alerts to as many garrisons as we can, and trust they'll relay the information that a DeÁine with great ability in the Power is on the loose. We can do no more without jeopardizing our main mission."

Cwen's smile was like the sun rising early, and warmed his heart chilled by fears.

Meanwhile, Jacinto too was trying to come to terms with his feelings. His nights with Swein had been a revelation. In the past he had enjoyed the feeling of power it gave him to know that others lusted after his beautiful, perfect body, and that he could deny them access to it. Abstention was a wonderful control device – about the only one he had, in truth, and therefore to be used to the full – and he had vowed to never let any but those who had proved themselves worthy touch him. Yet Swein had given him no chance to repel that first kiss, and afterwards Jacinto's curiosity had allowed the next step of familiarity to take place. And what a journey of discovery that had turned out to be! His initial despising had been overwhelmed as he had discovered that Swein's boast that he was the best might just be true.

Now he understood why some of the great noblemen he had heard of kept personal body slaves. He had never dreamt that it could be as easy as just demanding to be pleasured. Obviously, moving amongst the common herd he had not been mixing with the right people! It required men of substance to have the time to enjoy lengthy pleasures, instead of short and brutish couplings, so no wonder he had never made such discoveries amongst soldiers.

But what really pleased him most was that he was now going where only the king had gone before. And even better was the knowledge that naked he must surpass even such an imposing figure as the highest man in the Island. Edward might be tall, elegant, and with a pallor which proclaimed to all that he had no need to venture out of doors in anything but temperate weather, if the whim came upon him. But Jacinto, Swein informed him, had more beautifully sculpted muscles, and where it counted was twice the man Edward was!

Yet a warning lay there, Jacinto could see. Edward was a martyr to his pleasures. He could not do without them, and that was a hold Jacinto never wanted anyone or thing to have over him. Already, just the thought of ascending the stairs and allowing Swein to unlace his breeches as he knelt before him, was enough to sending the blood rushing through his veins. It was so addictive! But he had to resist becoming emotionally entangled, for that would give Swein a hold over him which struck fear into Jacinto's soul.

To care was to be vulnerable, and Jacinto had had enough of being that. Even as Swein's hand softly stroked his thigh beneath the table as he registered Jacinto's arousal, the would-be Knight vowed he would be more strong-willed and remain emotionally detached with this bewitching stranger. It was worth knowing that such pleasures could be obtained, but the real talent was to understand the opportunities it gave to exercise power over someone. Perhaps one day he too would visit the king?

Outside, as the sun dropped below the top of the nearest mountain the pile of earth shifted. An arm appeared, then a pale pink skull. Eliavres shrugged himself free of the last clods of snow and earth and gazed around him. Curse that bird! There was no way he could follow the Knights unobserved now – especially as he would have to use his Power to clear the path in front of him to continue. He reached out with his senses – nothing except a few scrawny rabbits, small rodents and a hungry fox, none of whom would feed him sufficiently to replenish his strength if he expended his reserves up here. No matter though. He had heard it through his familiar, although curse the man for spending time fondling his friend and coming in too late to hear all of it! 'It' was at Caersus, and the only thing that Eliavres could think of that would have that Ealdorman fretting over having enough Knights to guard would be the Gorget.

Well let them go to Caersus over the mountains. Let them freeze! It would do them no good. If they moved it out of the bowels of the earth into the open he would feel it. The taint of it had been enough to make him feel almost drunk on Power in the north! What would the real thing feel like? And suddenly he had a plan. He threw his head back and let his laugh echo round and round the mountains. So this King Edward craved power, did he? Well he was about to find out what real power was!

Chapter 29

Sad Sacrifices

Prydein: Samhainn

Hugh de Burh watched dispassionately as Amalric strode about the chapter-house, fuming. The language was singularly inappropriate for the location, but as there were only the two of them present it did not matter as much. What surprised Hugh was the depth of Amalric's fury at Alaiz for defeating his carefully laid plans.

"Stupid, *stupid* little girl!" Amalric snarled at the ceiling. "By the Wild Hunt, I'll put her in a nunnery in the farthest corner of the island for this! Hasn't Ivain enough to contend with without that idiot wench adding to his worries? May the Lost Souls find her and drag her to the Underworld!"

"Sacred Trees, Amalric, enough of this!" Hugh exclaimed wearily. "What in the Islands has got into you? She's only gone away to a different place to what we planned – it's not the end of the world! Oliver and Hamelin will care for her, and if nobody knows who she is, well then, Rheged and then Ergardia might be safer than anywhere we could hide her here."

"And what if we need her in a hurry?" Amalric challenged him back.

"For what?" Hugh asked, perplexed. "You've just said you wanted to lock her up and throw away the key! She's already shown she's capable of making her own mind up about things, so what do you think she'd do if you *did* lock her up and then suddenly expected her to perform on cue?"

"Perform, damn her!" Amalric spat. "That's what she's there for! She's the queen and she has her duty to perform, and as Grand Master *I* shall make sure that's exactly what she does! You were too soft on her! Letting her think she has any say in what she does …*phfaah*! Well, when she turns up she'll find things will be different from now on!"

And before an astonished Hugh could think of anything to say to that, Amalric haughtily stalked out of the circular chamber.

Hugh walked over to one of the cushioned wall-seats and sank down onto it, leaning his head backwards as his back fitted into the curved niche, so that he stared at the ceiling. The intertwined branches of the sacred Trees met at the top of the domed roof in a sculptural marvel. Letting his eyes travel along the curve, Hugh found the Birch and memories washed over him. Margaret had always loved the delicate fronds of leaves of the birches which had grown outside the quarters they had lived in, and seeing them rendered so lifelike in stone reminded him of her. Twenty years his wife had been dead. So long that most in the Order had forgotten, or never known, he had been married. Yet now more than ever Hugh missed her.

He could almost hear her laughter at Amalric's arrogance. *He's the stupid one,* she would have said. *Silly man, what is he thinking of! What sort of queen would she be if all she did was come out of the closet to perform her party trick, and then go back all meek and mild? Surely the queen is supposed to be a partner not a puppet!* And she would have been right.

Suddenly Hugh was angry with himself. Amalric was right, it was his fault, but not in the way he had meant. What had he been thinking of appointing Amalric as his successor? He should have looked a lot more closely at the character of the man he was investing with so much power and responsibility. Then he sighed. Yet how much of this had only appeared once Amalric realized he had almost total autonomy? Possibly Amalric would have remained as pliable as he had always seemed to be if he had not been raised up to the top position. There were other Grand Masters, raised up by popular vote by the ranks, who had also turned out to be dire mistakes once they had no guiding hand – not for many generations, admittedly, but way back in the past they were there.

Hugh sighed once more and got up. In the walk back to his quarters he thought long and hard about his choices. The more he mulled things over, the more he thought Alaiz had chosen the best course for herself. No, he would not do as Amalric intended and send an armed escort to drag her back, and the sergeants would be told in no uncertain terms to ignore any order of Amalric's to that effect too. In the comforting privacy of his small room, he sat on the bed and pulled a miniature painting out from the compact travelling chest which he took with him everywhere. Margaret as a young woman stared back at him, the ready smile he had come to know so well still there even after all the hours of posing for the painter. He knew she would have liked and approved of Alaiz. Would have thought her sensible and intelligent, and right now Hugh could not help but think that Alaiz had responded better to the crisis which confronted them than Ivain had. Oliver and Hamelin had been right about that.

Thinking about Oliver, Hugh also realized that his young protégé was also doing much better than Amalric at reading the situation as it had unfolded. Putting Margaret's miniature on the chest, he leaned forward and rested his head in his hands. With elbows on knees, he rubbed his eyes before trying to make a difficult decision.

"I'm going to have to sacrifice him, aren't I?" he said softly to the image. "I have to try to preserve Ivain, but the Order cannot come out of this with Amalric still at its head. Blessed Birch, Margaret, I hate playing at gods with men's lives, but with him like he is now, there's no chance of winning. He's a loose arrow that could fly off anywhere. He could endanger the very Order itself as well as the royal family."

He sighed heavily and stared sorrowfully at the painting, feeling weary deep in his soul. For over thirty years he had been trying to out-guess the DeÁine.

"Well there'll be a great battle coming if I know anything of the DeÁine, but for now he'll have to do. I daren't show to the outside world that I'm still here and in control. By the Trees, Margaret, I daren't. The Abend need enough rope to hang themselves with, and they certainly won't behave rashly if they think they're facing one of the leaders from Moytirra again. I'm hoping they think we're all dead by now, being frail humans! I'm just going to have to give Amalric enough to do so that he thinks he's better than he is. A few minor skirmishes that he can't fail to win should do the job – although where in the Islands I'm going to find those is a mystery!"

He spent a miserable rest of the day, and most of the night, tossing and turning, but by the next morning Hugh had a plan. So Calatin was here was he? That could only mean he was after the DeÁine Scabbard, and an army from Prydein to go with it. Yet he still seemed to be searching for it, for why else would he be willing to play along with Brion and let him think he was the one in charge? With the Abend's obsession with power, he no doubt assumed that it would have been kept in one of the royal castles. So by staying close to the most powerful man in Prydein, as he saw it, he must be thinking that sooner or later he would come to the right place, where the Treasure's Power would alert him to it.

What would he do, though, if he thought that Ivain, and not Brion, had the piece? If Hugh could call his bluff and force him to reveal himself, then maybe Brion would see the snake he had clasped to his bosom? It would also give Hugh chance to check on the Scabbard while the threat was distracted. It was a long ride into the far east of Prydein, and he would be a long way from anywhere if things should go wrong and he was needed, but that could not be helped. He needed to confer with the commander of Vellan, and that subject was something that he would never entrust to written record of any sort.

With this in mind, he called a meeting of his commanders that very morning. From Quies a troop would ride out on the westward road towards Treliever. Messages to Freton and Bittern would mobilize the massed companies of Knights quartered in the two preceptories. Hugh intended for the men from Quies to join with the commander and men from Bittern, and to continue around the coast to strike at Brion's home of Mullion. Elsewhere, some of the Knights from Freton would march in a show of force up the long river valley from their base on the coast, up onto the moors, so that they would coordinate with the force coming south from Bittern to make it a two-pronged attack on Mullion.

Hugh had little doubt that they would succeed in taking the town if not the castle, and would be able to keep it isolated. If successful they would leave a siege force to guard the castle. The rest of the troops would then re-cross the moor to Haile and make as if they were heading for the capital. Of course, they would not attack the capital – that would be sheer stupidity – but would continue on along the southern road from Haile to go to Freton, rather than taking the east road to Trevelga. However, Hugh believed that Brion would react long before anyone got near to Haile.

His gamble was that Brion would not want to lose his family home, king or not. If Calatin refused to help on the premise that Mullion was the one place he knew the Scabbard was not at, then Brion would be alone. There was no way that Brion would leave the capital undefended, so the force the Knights would meet near there would only be half of the troops he commanded, at most. On that basis Hugh knew the Knights' training would hold up well against Brion's seasoned fighters, even though the weight of numbers would be slightly in Brion's favour by a few hundred.

If absolutely necessary Hugh was prepared to call out the Knights from other preceptories, but he was hoping to keep them hidden against dire need. And that would only happen if the Knights immediately won such a resounding victory at Mullion that Brion panicked when the men marched through Haile, and then called out all his troops from the capital to force a battle away from the walls. But Hugh thought that unlikely. It was more likely that Brion would think they had thrown all they had in one great roll of the dice to seize his lands, and the slight imbalance of numbers would hopefully make Calatin think that they had the Treasure with them for them to be so confident. Hugh could not see beyond that point – there were too many possibilities as yet – and much depended on what the Abend would do when he lost the initiative.

The plan had the advantage that Amalric had no idea of how many men were in the eastern reserves anymore. Hugh had originally split the Island in two for purely practical reasons, for it was easier for Amalric to visit Freton and Bittern from the capital than to make the long journey into the east. Therefore when he put the proposal to the current nominal head of the Order, Amalric thought that he was in charge of almost all of the Order of Knights, with the exception of a few retired men and novices, and almost bit Hugh's hand off to accept. It was long overdue, in his mind, that the Grand Master should be seen to flex his muscles a little at the head of his command. Ivain was insistent on going too, and there was little reason for Hugh to stop him. As far as he could see the only other potential variation was that Brion would not take the bait, in which case the Knights would have an easy victory, securing the castle commanding the channel between Prydein and Kittermere, which was no bad thing to have.

A week after Alaiz's departure therefore saw Ivain taking his leave from Quies as well. A full ten companies comprising one hundred Knights, with their accompanying men-at-arms and archers, lined up on their horses on the road outside of the wall surrounding the fortification. Over five hundred men in all sat with horses champing at the bit, and pawing the ground, as they picked up the sense of eagerness to be off. Resplendent in full uniform, Amalric said a curt farewell to Hugh, then set his immaculate black mare in a collected canter to the head of the column, but Ivain took longer to say farewell.

"This is what I've hoped for and it wouldn't be possible without your foresight, Hugh, and I know it. I'm so grateful for everything you've done. Without you I'd have no chance of reclaiming my throne, and what would happen to Prydein then? I don't know what I'd have done without you," he said humbly.

Hugh smiled and clapped him on the shoulder.

"You'd have found a way, there's too much of your father in you for you to not fight back."

"But not enough of him, I fear," Ivain said regretfully. "I keep thinking neither he nor grandfather would've let things get this bad."

"Nonsense!" Hugh reproved him heartily. "Your father and grandfather never had to take control when they were as young as you. Even they would've done well to have come as far as you have in the circumstances."

Hugh was less convinced of that deep inside, but his words were enough to bolster Ivain's flagging self-esteem. The encounter with Calatin had done more harm than was visible on the surface, he knew. Another reason for letting Ivain go on this exercise was that Hugh felt that he too desperately needed a victory, in his case to give him some much-needed confidence. Nothing was so detrimental to troops' morale than a jittery commander, and if Ivain was to lead the Island's army one day, he had to have the self-assurance to convince them that he knew how to win.

However, in the here and now the words worked on Ivain. He knew it would be too undignified, and wholly against protocol, to hug Hugh in public, but he bent and exchanged the appropriate polite kiss on both cheeks with his mentor, who barely came up to his chin. As they rode away Ivain thought Hugh looked even smaller as he stayed to watch them all the way until they disappeared from view. He knew Hugh would have liked to have led this expedition himself, and there was a little voice in the back of his head that wished it was Hugh and not Amalric at the head of the long line of men riding down the coast. Then he shook his head at his foolishness. Amalric was an experienced and able commander who knew as much as Hugh, and far more than he himself did – why else would Hugh entrust him to him?

Had he but known it, Ivain was far from alone in wishing that Hugh was leading the company. For the most part the men were too young to have remembered the great conflicts of over a generation ago, but there was still a smattering of veterans who recalled Moytirra. Amongst them quiet words of doubt were expressed. How much battle experience did Amalric really have? Inquiries amongst their number, from men who had been stationed in many different preceptories, failed to find a single man who had seen combat alongside their now leader. Still, they thought, the plan was really Master Hugh's, so what could go wrong?

Riding at the head of the column, accompanied by the standard bearer with the great banner of the Knights whipping back and forth in the wintry wind, Amalric was oblivious to all of this. For him the days just got better and better. Each day that took them away from Quies took them further from gods-rot-him de Burh. Each day further from de Burh was a day when he got more control of *his* men. No running back to de Burh to check orders anymore!

The ride had started at quite a leisurely pace, for Hugh had wanted to give the Knights coming up from the south chance to reach the rendezvous at the same time. But each day Amalric managed to pick up the pace a little from his position at the front, so that the captains either had to risk their leader and standard going on with their tiny escort and risk being attacked, or keep up and maintain a proper presence.

The result was that the company clattered over the drawbridge into the castle at Bittern a full day ahead of when they were anticipated. The castle's commander, Ealdorman Squiers, was even more astonished when Amalric announced his intention of leaving at dawn the next day. His men had their equipment ready and waiting to be sure, but the food supplies were still in the store houses in order to keep them fresh for as long as possible. Auxiliary staff began running around frantically to prepare things for the new departure time, with many of them working through the night to ensure the great company which was to leave would not have to forage off the land as they went. Squiers' mood blackened with every passing hour. Nothing he said to the Grand Master seemed to penetrate that man's fantasy that they could drive the men fast down to their destination and seize it without support.

"Sire," Squiers fumed futilely, "we have to be prepared for the fact that they may just decide to sit us out in that stronghold! Master Hugh always anticipated that might be the outcome, and my men can't eat grass! We have to take sufficient to last us for at least a week, until wagons can bring more substantial supplies up to us."

"Well that will be your job, Ealdorman, won't it!" Amalric said haughtily.

"What?" exclaimed Squiers, thinking he had misheard him.

"The supplies," Amalric continued, "if you're that worried about them, it will ensure that you are all the more efficient in organising them, won't it?"

He felt a glow of triumph at the ealdorman's shocked face. One of Hugh's pet commanders no doubt. Spirits but he was sick of hearing 'Hugh' this, and 'de Burh' that, and the last thing he wanted was this telltale riding with them and then heading off across the moors to find Hugh and bring him back to interfere.

"Are you saying I won't be coming with you?" Squiers asked in astonishment.

"That's right!" Amalric said with more than a trace of sarcasm, as he turned his back and left the ealdorman standing open-mouthed. Spirits, the man was thick! How much clearer could he have made it? Oh but he was glad he was leaving this one behind. The conversations he would have had to endure did not bear thinking about.

In the meantime, Squiers had called his second-in-command to him in his private quarters, and was drinking a restorative goblet of mulled wine.

"By the Trees, Dabhi," he swore as the man came in, "I fear that man's lost his mind!"

"I know," the gray-haired veteran answered, "it's all over the garrison that he's leaving you behind. The men aren't happy and neither am I, but what can we do? Technically he's still the Grand Master. If we disobey, it's mutiny whichever way you look at it. If he'd done something disastrous already, we might have a case, but we can't defend disobedience on a hunch. Sacred Trees, we'd never have any discipline afterwards if we took that road."

"I know," Squiers replied, looking more worried than Dabhi had ever seen. "That's why I want you to get birds sent out *now*. Don't wait! I don't want to risk him sending them all off on some fool's errand so we've none left in the coop. So two to Quies, and then others to Rosco, Bera and Vellan. We must intercept Master Hugh. Our boy king said that was the way he was going and all we can hope is that he heard right."

"Where will you be then, sire?" Dabhi asked, fearful that his commander was about to do something foolish for the first time since he had known him.

"As soon as they ride out I'm riding for Quies, so make sure there's a fast horse for me held in reserve. I'm sorry, Dabhi, I'm going to have to leave the organising of the supplies to you."

"Do you think they're going to be needed?"

"Only the Trees know the answer to that one," Squiers said, shrugging his shoulders and raising his hands in exasperation. "I sincerely hope so because the only scenario I can think of which that idiot can't screw up quickly is a good long siege. We might lose good men unnecessarily against well-defended walls, but I'm hoping that whoever Brion left in charge of that great fortress will be experienced enough to be saving arrows until the heavy machinery gets there. Without that or ladders, what can de Loges hope to do?"

In the dove-grey light of the late-arriving winter dawn, a great company of over fifteen hundred men rode out of the castle and its precincts on the road to the south. Squiers stood by the roadside, wishing the first of his men farewell and offering words of encouragement to the newest recruits. Amalric barely glanced his way, but Squiers still stayed put until he judged that the lead company would have turned right onto the fork which led towards Mullion. Then turning on his heels, he jogged back into the bailey to where Dabhi himself stood holding the reins of a powerful stallion – probably the best horse in the stable, which said more than words of the degree of Dabhi's concern too. Vaulting into the saddle, Squiers leant down to clap Dabhi on the shoulder in unspoken thanks before wheeling the horse towards the gates. His own garrison was still filing out, and they made room for their commander as he set his spurs to the already eager horse.

Pounding down the outside of the column, he received salutes from many of the men who recognized him, even though he had an anonymous grey cloak thrown over his uniform. So intent was he on his task that for a second he failed to realise that that he had passed the road to Mullion already. Suddenly he realized the men were on the wrong road! He should have parted company from them already. A farm track appeared on his left, and he pulled the horse up and made the turn faster than he would have liked, but just in time before he reached the head of the column and de Loges. Whatever happened he must not encounter him. If de Loges forbade him from going to Quies, or contacting Hugh, he would have to obey or risk a court-martial.

Luckily he had ridden the lesser ways around the castle for years, and knew that the road made a loop around a small wood a little further on. With the hedge to shield him from view, he rode at a brisk trot close to the road, leaning low over the horse's withers to disguise his shape. Hopefully, given the number of oxen and brood mares in the surrounding fields he would not stand out. He was still holding his breath, though, until he reached the edge of the wood. By this time he was almost level with the standard bearer, so that as soon as the road kinked right he dug his heels in and his mount leapt forward once more and tore around the wood's perimeter. Without bothering to dismount for the gate to the road, he set the powerful beast straight at it and felt him lift into the air and clear it.

Back on the road he urged the horse into a headlong gallop and just made it around the next bend as the tip of the banner showed turning back into line of sight. He kept the horse at the gallop for as long as he dared without tiring it for the rest of the day's ride, then walked it for a while, confident that he had put a good lead on the column. It was only as he began the climb up the long hill which formed the crest above Treliever that he looked back, and was able to see the small army. De Loges was setting a much faster pace than he had expected. The horses must have been trotting, not walking, for most of the day. In desperation he rode on through the night to reach the bridge at Treliever and cross ahead of them. Only when he was on the other side and beyond the town walls did he pull over and let the weary beast graze and rest. From now on he should have a clear run to Quies, and prayed to the Trees that the birds had found Hugh in time.

It was therefore a nasty shock the next morning to find he had stopped for the night just in time. He had woken early and had slipped into the common room of a meagre inn in the hope of finding breakfast. It was empty, and he was about to go to the kitchen in search of breakfast when he heard voices.

"Here you go, lad, that's the hot rolls and some ham and cheese. Now here's the canteen of caff. Off you go. You know where you're going?"

This deep male voice was answered by that of someone who sounded much younger, probably a stable boy or scullion.

"Aye, I knows where to go. Up the high road to the soldiers in the field."

Footsteps began to head Squiers' way, and he ducked back to hide behind a high-backed settle out of sight, but the footsteps stopped by the door.

"Why don't they come here, gaffer? They'm from the Knights, they ain't done nothin' wrong to be hidin' away."

"Go on with yer! If you must know they'm waitin' to trap some scoundrel who's goin' to come through 'ere on the way to Quies. Orders of the Grand Master no less, so watch your mouth! None of your cheek, or you won't sit straight for a month if you let me down with the likes of him!"

The door creaked, and from his dark shelter Squiers saw a ragged boy silhouetted against the lantern he held. A large bag was slung across the small shoulders, and in the other hand was a large canteen which the lad was struggling to carry. A rough estimation would make it four or five men, Squiers thought. Too many for him alone, and de Loges had obviously anticipated his own anxiety and desire to get word to Hugh that the plan had been changed. But why would de Loges be so determined word would not reach other preceptories until it was too late? What was he up to?

He crept out of his hiding place and decided he had one of two choices. He could still try for Quies, but if the road was being held it meant a long slow ride over the moors. With the pace de Loges was setting, whatever he was planning could have happened long before Squiers could alert Master Hugh. The other choice was to follow the column, which he decided to take. He now had to hope that at least one of the birds got through, and that by going with his men if it came to a fight he would be there to help them.

Slipping back out he gave it a little longer until he heard the household stir, then went in again and made a quick breakfast with the excuse of needing to catch an early boat, and left. Turning his horse over the fields above Treliever, he skirted the town and carried on until he found a beech copse at the top of a small rise which gave him a good view of the road, and settled down to wait for the appearance of the Knights, when he would then attach himself to the back of the column.

It had also been to Ivain's relief that Amalric had let the men rest for the night well before Treliever. The experienced men had pointed out the dangers of so many men in a large market town with many taverns, and for once Amalric had listened. Not that most would have dreamt of disobedience when they were on the move like this, but it only took a few to cause major disruption, both to their plans and to the town. Ivain was worried, and in his hastily erected tent he fretted. Amalric had just patted his hand like he was a little boy when he had asked what was going on.

"Don't you worry, you're safe with me now. I'll take care of things, you've nothing to worry about," he had said when Ivain had expressed concern that they had missed the turn to Mullion.

But worry Ivain did. How he wished he had his father and grandfather's military expertise. Then he could have taken command of this army himself. Or could he? These were Knights and their enlisted men, so they were not his to command really, were they? What was Amalric doing? And where were they going? As nominal head, surely he should know?

Five days later he was even more worried. In that time Amalric had increased the pace again, and each day they had set out in darkness and ridden on after nightfall. By his reckoning Ivain thought they must be near Haile by now, and the couple of men he had dared to talk to had agreed. Dared in the sense that he was desperately trying to work out who of the senior men were Amalric's hand-picked men. Something in the back of his head was ringing alarm bells, and he picked out those men who looked as worried as he felt. It did not help, though. They had hoped he would be the one to tell them what was going on. He could only hope that he would find someone who knew before they got to wherever it was that Amalric was heading, but luck was not with him.

On the seventh day out, having passed through Haile two days previously, they woke on the flat river meadows to find the weak winter light catching a forest of spears and swords before them. News had reached Brion that his elusive cousin was on the move, and he was not going to let him slip out of his grasp again. Trevelga had been emptied of all Brion's troops and those of his allies. Having left only a few to defend the capital's walls against surprise attacks – for Brion had made the assumption that this was all of the Knights prepared to follow Ivain – the army before the Knights outnumbered them almost five to one.

Even such well-trained troops as the Knights were dismayed at such odds, especially when they were unprepared for this encounter. Most had assumed that they would fight somewhere at some point, but the lack of pickets set out at night, and the way they had been allowed to ride along out of fighting formation had lulled them into thinking that their leader knew that there was no threat nearby. The result was an unseemly and frantic scramble as the men struggled into protective padding and mail, and belted on weapons.

From his hidden position over on the left flank, Squiers was appalled. It was so clear now. De Loges had planned to attack the capital! What a fool! But where was he now? Suddenly he realized that, far off, he could see de Loges on his black mare waving his arms around in an effort to direct the troops. The reality was that the men were coming together as much by the experience of the sergeants and the older captains than anything their leader was doing. As a defence this would do as a start, but without some coordination, if the advancing army decided to launch straight into an attack, it would end in disaster. Squiers threw his grey cloak to the ground and cursed his lack of armour. Well at least his own men knew him well enough in the uniform he was wearing. It would have to be enough.

In the central tents chaos reigned. Amalric had been roused by the sentries at the first light of dawn, when the approaching army had first been seen, and he had disappeared yelling for his captains, which was the last Ivain had seen of him. His parting words had been something to the effect of showing Brion what Knights could really do when given the chance, and with a proper commander.

Ivain himself had practically ripped his pack apart in his haste to find his mail shirt and leather jerkin. He managed to pull the jerkin on and lace the front up. The chain-mail shirt was harder to deal with. It was heavy, yet flexible, and kept folding up on itself. Through the open flap of the tent he could see men arming themselves with the speed of long practice and felt such a fool. What use was he as a leader when he could not even get his own armour on?

Finally he dragged the cursed thing over his head, then managed to get the mail coif on on the second attempt, having put his head through the face opening instead of the neck the first time. Grabbing the sword belt and scabbard, he staggered out of the tent and looked around him. There was no sign of de Loges or any of the other senior men usually around him. A soldier came up to him and then realise who he was.

"Come here, sire," the calm voice said, and proceeded to tuck the collar of the mail head-gear under that of the shirt.

"Stops a blade sliding up underneath your coif and into your throat that way," the man said by way of explanation.

"Thank you," Ivain said weakly. "Do you know where the Grand Master is? Everyone has left me behind."

The sergeant looked around and gasped in surprise. What in the Islands was de Loges thinking of leaving the king unguarded? With them caught off guard like this, it would be easy for enemies to slip into camp and seize him. The sergeant turned round and checked again. No, no sign of the royal guards.

"You'd better come with me, sire," he said, and taking a firm hold of his young king's arm, steered him back the way he had come. In a few minutes they reached one of the pools of calm where an older Knight already sat on his horse and enlisted men were swinging themselves into saddles. Leading Ivain up to the Knight, the sergeant saluted and said,

"No sign of any sort of command post, sire, but I found the king left alone in his tent so I brought him with me."

"Hounds of the Wild Hunt!" the Knight swore and bent down on his horse to look Ivain in the eyes, starting when he realized his sergeant had told the truth. "What in the Trees' name is de Loges doing leaving you unprotected? My name's Pauli, I saw you at Quies, by the way. Someone bring a spare horse for the king!"

Ivain found himself on a solid war-horse of a calibre he had never ridden before, and the men-at-arms were wheeling their horses around to surround him when he heard trumpets sound and felt the earth begin to shake.

"Cross of Swords, they're attacking!" Pauli breathed.

"Where are they?" a voice called to his left.

"Over that way," another yelled.

"Where's the line?"

"I can't see a standard?"

"Do we advance to the left?"

"No they're in front, aren't they?"

Confused voices from unseen soldiers rippled through the thronged seething mass of men.

"Knights!" a loud voice bellowed. "Form on me!"

Pauli stood in his stirrups and looked about him, then gestured with his left arm to where Ivain now saw a red pennant raised on the end of a spear and fluttering in the light breeze. Their unit, which Ivain now realized comprised the Knight, two men-at-arms (one of whom was the sergeant), and two archers, worked their way around so that they were lined up with ten more such units, or lances as they were properly called, five either side of the red pennant held by the lance of a Commander. Frighteningly, he could see nothing beyond the men around him and yet already the air was filled with shouts and screams. An ear-piercing whistling suddenly drowned that all out.

"Arrows!" the warning was screamed and the men raised shields above their heads as a deadly rain fell on them. Ivain had never dreamt being in a real battle would be so terrifying. The noise of the full force of an archers' volley was beyond belief – as if thousands of angry, hissing geese were flying fast and low overhead all at once.

Thwack! Thwack! Thwack! Arrows hit the shields of the men who had leaned in to include him in the protection of their shields. Without them he would have died in the first volley, but there was no time to think, for within seconds another flight of incoming arrows fell. Then another. Then another.

Ten shots a minute sounded formidable enough when his proud archers had told him about it. On the receiving end of it he was pissing himself with fright and wishing the earth would open up and swallow him. Anything to get away from this merciless, shrieking hail of destruction. And the screams! As the deadly rain continued, the howls of men and horses, cut down by the violent storm, rose to overlay the sound of the thousands of goose feather flights on the arrows.

Next to Ivain, the sergeant's horse collapsed in a screaming heap, an arrow in his neck, one in his rump and one in his right flank. The sergeant reacted swiftly and was rolling clear as the animal keeled over, then ran, dagger drawn, to put the poor creature out of its misery. Ducking under the head of Ivain's horse, he then found protection in their midst just as the men began to move forward. How anyone had heard anything resembling an order in the random cacophony around them was beyond Ivain, but they started at a walk and then increased to a trot. Before he realized it they had wheeled left to clear more fallen men and horses, and then swung back to the right and were rising to a canter. Unhorsed men joined them running hanging onto the stirrups of their mounted comrades, swords drawn, while the riding men lowered lances to face forwards.

The Knights' archers did not use the longbows of the regular Prydein archers, but short, curved hunting bows which could be used from horseback. Now they showed their skill, guiding their horses by leg movement alone and laying down a deadly hail of their own. Not in united volleys, but with each man picking his target and few failing to make a hit. Ahead of them Ivain suddenly saw a flicker of something solid and a heartbeat later they collided with the opposition. The two archers dropped back, and one grabbed the reins of Ivain's horse as Pauli and other Knights and men-at-arms surged forwards. The shriek of goose flights was replaced by the din of hundreds of swords clashing around him. Metal on metal drove all other thought from Ivain's mind until he thought he would go mad from the noise. He was totally disorientated as the press of men and horses forced him and his escorts this way and that.

The three of them wheeled left and right in the wake of Pauli and the others. Somewhere in the infernal noise he was vaguely aware that someone was shouting orders, but they made no sense to him, and he had no idea whether they came from his men or the opposition. A gap-toothed rider appeared in front of him and clouted the one archer in the mouth with the guard of his sword, held high still from some other manoeuvre, before stabbing at someone else to Ivain's right. The archer loosed his grip on Ivain's horse and seemed to slip backwards as if struggling against the tide.

Where was Amalric? For one awful moment Ivain thought he might be surrounded by the enemy, until he caught a glimpse of Pauli still a few yards away on his left, who seemed to be calling some men back before they drove too deeply amongst the other ranks and became cut off. Someone unseen, just behind Ivain called across to Pauli,

"Why doesn't de Loges sound the retreat? We can't hope to survive fighting these numbers!"

In answer to which Pauli could only shrug, as he made a vicious cut with his sword which opened the throat of the man lunging at him, whereupon Ivain found himself being sprayed by a fountain of blood as the artery was severed, which went in his eyes and blinded him.

Away from the conflict, from a vantage point up on the far left, Squiers had seen the advance of the enemy army. Seen how much it outnumbered his men, and feared for them all. Withdraw, de Loges, he prayed. Withdraw and save the men! There would be no disgrace against such vastly overwhelming numbers. But Amalric de Loges did not see it, high on adrenaline and dreaming of glory. Instead, he issued the order to attack, and the nearest, stunned captains looked in disbelief at one another as they saw him wave them forward to the sea of enemies.

Squiers saw a ripple along the massed Knights as men, too disorientated to realise the impossible task they had been given, drew up on the nearest companions they could find and head towards certain death.

"No!" Squiers yelled in horror, and heeled his horse forward.

Pounding in at the rear of the left flank he bellowed,

"Stop! Knights withdraw! Halt your advance! I command you, halt your advance!"

At first few heard him, but then one or two Knights turned and saw him and recognized who it was. As they turned, the first volley of arrows came over from the opposing lines and the reality of the numbers they were facing began to sink in. As the first Knights wheeled their lances to follow Squiers, others turned to see where their neighbours were going.

"Follow the Ealdorman!" someone yelled in relief at the sight of a familiar commander. And more of the lances turned at right angles to their former advance, and began following him along the rear of the milling mass of confused companies.

By the time Squiers was halfway along the back of the massed ranks, more and more were turning to follow him. Yet the opposing commander got word of this and sent his far flank to cut off this manoeuvre. Seeing the new threat heading their way, Squiers glanced back at the numbers following him and then back to those approaching. At least a third of the men who had left Bittern were behind him by this point, but now they were facing only a small portion of the enemy army, for a foe so huge could not be turned all at once. Pointing to the nearest captains to him he yelled,

"Lead the men to Freton! Over the moors to Freton, do you understand? We'll cover your retreat. Go!"

Men began to peel off as the captains raised the standards, and heeled their horses into a mad gallop into a valley leading up onto the brooding, dark-green mass of the southern moorlands. Detailing three more lances to keep any new men who turned to them moving away, when he judged he had saved as many from his existing followers as he could hope to, Squiers then waved the remaining men on the far right flank to follow him. Captains heeled their horse up to join him and he shouted across to them,

"We have to give those men a chance! We *must* buy them time to get free!"

The men heard and, grim-faced, acknowledged that they were going to their certain death to give their comrades a fighting chance of survival, yet not one faltered. The lances wheeled once more, this time drawing up in proper order with Squiers holding the central position. Slowing to a trot they advanced again on the still turning enemy and brought death to them. Training now showed, and with some order to their advance the archers took their toll, taking down the opposing officers first and then singling out the sergeants. As the leadership dropped away the enemy advance became more ragged and descended into an undisciplined charge. But Squiers refused to let his men plough through them and into the main army. Their job was to hold this escape route to the last. To make the enemy pay for any pursuit ten times over. There they stood, and there they stayed.

Beyond the pool of calm around Squiers on the right, the remainder of the Knights fell as they were cut down by Brion's main advancing army. As Hugh had anticipated, Calatin had disdained to become involved, and that at least saved some lives, but too few. Far too few. Slowly the army of the Knights began to sink into the sea of mud that the meadows had become. Banner after banner sank into the mire, clasped in lifeless hands. Riderless horses fled, reins flapping wildly, and men rolled groaning, or lay already staring lifelessly at the sky and mud.

Amalric was thrown from his horse and was then trapped beneath another horse and rider which fell on him, both dead before they hit him and the ground. The centre, with most of the remaining captains, took the worst of the assault and died in their hundreds. Some of those on the left who had not been aware of the earlier retreat now tried to fall back, but Brion, seated on a knoll behind his army, directed his archers around the mêlée on the meadow and left them to cut down the fugitives from the field, although few did the work with any relish and many deliberately missed. These were their fellow countrymen after all.

Here on the left, Ivain's horse had been cut from underneath him shortly after he had become separated in the crush from the two archers. Sent flying as his horse fell, he spent the next moments ducking and trying to roll clear of the hooves of other horses. Then the battle smashed over him and men dashed past him, only to be forced back minutes later like waves against jagged rocks, when he found himself once more being crushed and thrown around like a child's doll. Enemy horsemen appeared above him and he was reduced to diving between the legs of their horses to avoid the sword cuts while making feeble stabs upwards with his own.

Several times he felt it connect, and on more than one occasion he had to haul on it to free it. Sickening slurps accompanied the few of those that he could hear, so he assumed he had skewered someone then, but how effectively he had no notion. Suddenly he was sent flying by a man landing on his back. Totally winded he could only just turn his head sideways to be able to gulp air instead of mud, when he heard a voice in his ear.

"Silence, sire!" the voice whispered. "Act dead!"

Ivain had no problem doing that. The enemy moved on and then the voice in his ear said,

"Quick, crawl!" and, grabbing his arm, began forcing him to one side. As they edged their way back towards the rear of the fallen army Ivain realized that only a few pockets of resistance to Brion now still stood. As they ducked down near the edge, after several near brushes with enemy cavalry, they saw a small group of Knights fighting like the possessed over on the far right.

"Hounds of the Wild Hunt!" the voice gasped, "that's Ealdorman Squiers! Trees protect him!"

But the protecting Trees had their work cut out that day, and as Ivain watched, a new wave of enemy came to attack the brave cluster of Knights, and he saw Ealdorman Squiers go down with an arrow in his throat. The voice behind Ivain gave a sob.

"By all that's sacred," the man swore, "I'll find who was responsible for this – who set this trap – and the Underworld will take him when I do!"

"Amalric de Loges," Ivain whispered, rolling onto his back and suddenly realising that the unknown soldier who had helped him was the Knight Pauli who had come in to Quies with Alaiz.

"De Loges?" Pauli said in astonishment, but then had no time for any more. Grabbing Ivain's arm again, he set them off on another crawl which got them out onto the open grass. Their progress was slower now as Pauli would only let them go a few paces before dropping again. He wanted anyone who saw them to think they were the last thrashes of dying men. Men not worth pursuing. It was only when they got to a magnificent gorse bush that Pauli hauled Ivain to his feet, and in a crouched run they legged it to the cover of the far hedge that separated the wide meadow from the scrubby pasture beyond. Even then Pauli allowed no rest, but kept them moving west towards the moors.

Night fell and they walked on in an exhausted daze, too stunned by the massacre they had witnessed to talk, too weary in mind and body. The sword points at their throats came out of the blue on a tree-lined track which could not be dignified with the name of a road.

"Password!" a hoarse voice demanded.

Pauli coughed, then tried to make his dry mouth work, but could only croak.

"What password?" Ivain choked out, then more panicked, "what password?"

He did not want to die! Not here, not now! Not after surviving the battle. To have lived through such slaughter when so many better men had died was torture, but until this day he had never realized how much he wanted to live.

"Seagull," Pauli finally managed to gasp.

The swords disappeared and strong arms guided them forwards, where they found a great number of men encamped on the moors. A water bottle appeared and they both drank greedily. Pauli's, 'he's with me,' seemed to satisfy the men, who led them forward to a knot of others sat in a cluster, which seemed to be the surviving captains. Ivain was left sat on the soft bracken while Pauli went forward and spoke to them. Before long a man came back and brought him up to join them.

"Our pardons, your highness," a voice from someone indistinguishable in the gloom said. "Thank the Trees you're safe. You did well, Pauli, very well!"

"Thank you, sire," Pauli said, responding to someone who was evidently a known senior officer in a voice which sounded as if it was all in a normal day's work.

"Do you have any plans, your highness?" another asked, although plainly these men needed no guiding.

"No," Ivain replied. "No, I'm entirely in your hands. Do whatever you think best. You all have much more experience than me and I don't want to get anyone else killed. No-one else, dear Spirits, no-one else!" and he dissolved into tears.

To his amazement nobody seemed critical of him. Rather they were sympathetic, and many seemed as shocked, but for the rest of the night he was periodically overtaken by violent shivers and weeping. Come the morning he still felt as bad, but seeing the faces of the men around him he thought they did not look much better. He was moved up to the front of the column, where he was told that these were the men who had escaped on foot, or had lost their horses soon after leaving the battlefield through wounds sustained. Those survivors still mounted were riding with all haste across the moor to try to join with the Knights who had left from Freton for Mullion. They at least would be relatively fresh and un-bloodied, and might be close enough to provide an escort. This group was going to stay on the shoulder of the moor and start walking to Freton.

They descended into a small river valley which one of the men, who had grown up around this area, said snaked north before coming back south to join another that led into the River Fret. The captains proposed cutting the loop off and going over the shoulder of the moor until Ivain cut in.

"Wait, please. I don't mean to question you, but there's something you should know. I don't think he was at the battle because there were no balls of fire flying through the air, but what about Calatin?"

Several of them looked at him blankly and he was forced to explain that the mystery priest was really one of the Abend.

"The thing is," Ivain went on, "he can send this thing that hunts in the mist."

"Was that the bastard thing that killed Willem, Kai and Gilbert?" Pauli snarled, backing him up. "It hunts in the mist on the moors!"

"Hunts?" their leader asked.

"Yes. I think Hugh called it a farliath." Ivain struggled to remember. "But he said it can't be controlled over water. I think we have to follow the river. I know it's freezing but, if it attacks, the one thing that might save us is if we get into the river. Brion may get Calatin to set that thing onto us."

Gloomy mutterings followed this, although knowing of the danger nobody grumbled at the longer walk. Instead everyone wearily plodded on. At every clear stream, they filled the water skins and tightened their belts against their hunger. The few archers brought down rabbits and pheasants when they got chance, but there was no stopping to light fires while the daylight lasted. That night they stayed cold and fireless for fear of drawing attention to themselves. Four wounded men gave up the fight in the freezing dark, and were dead when their friends tried to rouse them in the morning. The captains allowed no time to bury them, simply rolling them deep into gorse thickets and hoping the foxes and land scavengers found them before the rooks and crows.

During a painful day's march the ragged band turned into the next river valley, deeper and more shielded from the east by a shoulder of the moors. With wisps of mist creeping on with nightfall they risked fires this time, building a few good blazes hot enough to roast the captured meat on. With food inside them for the first time since the battle, and the cheering warmth of the fires, collectively their spirits rose somewhat.

In the darkest hours, though, an eerie keening woke the more alert and had the sentries pacing the perimeter, swords and bows in hand.

"Farliath!" Pauli declared with final certainty.

"You said the river was safe?" a captain questioned Ivain.

"I think so, if we get between the river and the fires we should be safe."

"Should be?"

Ivain raised his hands helplessly to his questioner.

"I only know what Hugh told me. Water breaks the wizard's bond or weakens it, but surely fire dissipates mist?"

"Well now's the time we'll find out," someone else growled.

The men pulled back to the narrow strip of land between the fires and the river bank. Pauli directed some of his comrades to help him pile some of the spare wood they had cut from gorses and alders at the left hand gap and set it alight, while others, realising what he was doing, did the same on the right. Huddled together they stared out into the darkness, starting at every moving wisp. Suddenly a rabbit screamed.

"Fox?" someone whispered.

"Maybe, maybe not," his neighbour replied.

Many men were stood barely between the fires at all, there was so little space, when a long finger of mist suddenly coiled out to one of them. With a dart as quick as a snake's tongue it lashed out and hit an archer. The man stumbled and lurched forward towards the darkness. As his friends reached to grab, him the mist became solid and coiled around his outstretched arm, yanking him hard in their grasp. A knife appeared and slashed at the white tentacle without effect, while two, then three arrows loosed at it simply passed through without so much as a shimmer. All the time the man and the three hanging onto him were being dragged further away from the fire, and new tentacles began to snake out from the sides of the thing towards the three. More reached to hang onto them to halt their slide with only minor effect until one of the Knights elbowed his way forwards, and drew his dragon-headed sword. A grizzled old veteran, he nonetheless swung the blade with a vengeance and roared,

"Break the chains that bind!" followed by something incomprehensible.

As the pattern-welded blade scythed into the mist it smoked and steamed, and an unearthly yowl reverberated around the valley walls. Instantly the men were loosed, and their friends had been hauling so hard on them that they all shot backwards, falling over and into the others.

The mist began to lift until it was no more than fine spider-webs grazing the trees.

"By the Trees, man, that was nicely done!" the lead captain congratulated the veteran. "What in the Islands was it that you shouted, though?"

The older man scratched his stubbled chin.

"I'm not sure, sire, if the truth be known. All I know is that it was what I heard the Foresters chant when we went up against the DeÁine at Moytirra. There was a third bit – in DeÁine, I think – but I can't remember the exact way that went. The other is the Old Tongue, if I was told right and I assume it's the same thing in all three tongues. Seems to work, though."

"By the Trees it does too!" another captain enthused. "While we're marching tomorrow you can be teaching the rest of us that, even if it isn't all of it!"

"Who are the foresters?" Ivain asked Pauli as they sat down to get what rest they could before dawn. Just when he thought he was beginning to be useful it looked as though he knew nothing like enough again.

"Originally they were called the Forest Rangers," Pauli told him softly, to avoid disturbing the already dozing soldiers around them.

"Why forest?" Ivain wondered. "Knights surely don't act as warders for the king's hunting chases and parks?"

Pauli shook his head.

"Not forest in that sense. It's the trees, the Sacred Trees. They're the guardians of the Sacred Trees."

"What?" Ivain asked, aghast, "you mean there are real trees that are sacred, they're not like the Spirits, something you can't see or touch?"

"Well yes and no. One of each Tree, no. But there is a heart forest. Very old. The yews especially are rumoured to be over a thousand years old and huge! Once upon a time forest like that covered all of the Islands after the ancient ones died, and only the ancestors of the Attacotti were left in tiny settlements. As people moved back in, over the centuries the trees were cut and not replanted. Only the Foresters know where it is exactly, but as the only full Forester preceptory is on Ergardia, I'm guessing it must be there.

"The rest of the Order has Foresters attached in the different Islands. Elite fighters who answer to no-one but the Grand Masters, and it's rumoured amongst the rest of the Knighthood that they're inducted into the art of magic against the time when they'll be needed again. Here and on

Rheged and Brychan, I think they have trouble finding many who think it necessary to guard against such unknowns, so most recruits come from Celidon and Ergardia these days, which makes them seem even more secretive. Having seen how old Bertold's half-remembered charm worked on that thing – whatever it was – though, I'm glad those Foresters are still around."

"Me too," was Ivain's heartfelt agreement. Why had nobody ever thought to tell him of this before? He was sure that Amalric would have scoffed at the idea of an elite force to fight magic, but after his recent experiences, he prayed that Hugh was in contact with these Knights. What other chance did he have of helping his people with a DeÁine on the warpath supporting his bloodthirsty cousin? A cousin who would cold-bloodedly order fleeing, wounded men to be cut down. Could even Brion be so cruel and was it too late for him? Was he already so enchanted by this wizard he no longer had a mind of his own?

Chapter 30

Voyage of Discovery

Rheged: Samhainn

Oliver came onto the open deck of the ship and saw Hamelin gazing at Alaiz, who in turn was staring out at the waves. In the days they had been aboard the transport vessel, Oliver had become increasingly worried for his friend. Hamelin was ten years older than him, and in the past he had had cause to be grateful for that when his maturer friend had often looked out for him. So now he felt it was only right that he returned the favour. In all the time they had known one another, he had never known Hamelin become smitten with a woman. Until now he had assumed that his sometimes a little too serious companion had had his share of liaisons, and got over them, long before he had joined the Order. The two of them had joined at the same time, and if Oliver had been a touch younger than the average recruit, Hamelin had been distinctly older.

Oliver had shocked his family by his decision, and they had done their best to dissuade him from making his final vows. He, however, had had no doubts. He had taken a long hard look at the young, and not so young, women he would be expected to make his choice of wife from, and had shuddered at the thought. It was not that he disliked women – quite the opposite – but as the fourth son, of the fifth son, of one of the most prestigious families in Prydein, there was still a limited circle of other families who were considered sufficiently aristocratic to make a union with. Most of them had been interbreeding for generations, and it showed!

It was a standing joke of Oliver's that he must have been the product of some illicit liaison of his mother's, for he had nothing in common with any of his siblings or his father. Dull beyond words, they were quite willing to consider spending the rest of their lives tied to someone equally incapable of intelligent thought. Oliver was not. From his earliest dalliances, he had preferred the lively village girls, and he had seen that if he joined the Knights there would be many years before he would be considered senior enough to be allowed married quarters. In that time he had intended to make full use of his freedom – and he had!

It therefore came as something of a shock to realise that his older friend was far less experienced when it came to affairs of the heart. Hamelin was also far more of the incurable romantic than Oliver would ever be, and Oliver could see disaster looming. It was blindingly obvious to him that his friend had fallen head over heels in love with Alaiz, possibly without even realising the degree himself. The repercussions of that, if she ever realized it and reciprocated, worried Oliver sick. If Hugh or the court found out that Hamelin had, from their view point, seduced the queen, Oliver feared that his friend might be joining his half-brother on the gallows. What he was going to do about it was something else, though. How he would ever persuade someone as constant and faithful as Hamelin to move his affections seemed close to impossible, and about as likely to happen as getting the tides to stop moving.

However, he did not have to make things easy for them, and so when Alaiz's smile faded into a frown and Hamelin immediately stepped up to her solicitously, Oliver followed. There was a brief flicker of puzzlement on Hamelin's face when no sooner had he sat on one side of Alaiz in the bows, than Oliver appeared and sat on the other. However, he made no comment on that, but instead asked Alaiz what was wrong.

"Oh, it's nothing serious …well actually I suppose it is," she answered in a voice that carried a weight of cares.

"My, that sounds a big problem," Oliver replied with light cheeriness. "Well you know what they say, a trouble shared is a trouble halved, so you'd better share it quick before you sink the boat!"

Alaiz gave a little laugh.

"You two always make me feel so much better," then became serious again. "…But that's the trouble."

"What? We are?" Hamelin asked, horrified.

Alaiz realized how what she had said must have sounded.

"Oh no, I don't mean that! No …I mean, yes …oh, but not like a bad thing. …Oh I'm making such a mess of this."

"Alright," Oliver could not help laughing. "We understand …I think! But how about you tell us – only slower this time!"

Alaiz sighed.

"It's just that I keep thinking about all the things that happened once we got to the grange. I suppose I thought that once I got to Hugh, everything would be alright. I really thought that Ivain would be glad to see me, that he'd see that I was trying to help him. That I *wanted* to help him. I thought there would finally be a place for me now that he needs all the support he can get."

"And he wasn't …glad to see you, that is?" Oliver asked, dreading the reply. Maybe this was a serious rift leaving her adrift and ready to accept Hamelin's advances.

"No!" Alaiz said angrily, but her voice carried a world of hurt that touched Oliver nearly as much as it did Hamelin. "I was treated like a naughty little girl. And then all of you were so nice to me. It brought back all of these memories which had been locked away for so long that I didn't realise they were still there. Practicing with that sword, and the bow and arrow, made me remember playing with my brothers when they were all alive, you see."

Oliver quietly breathed a sigh of relief. A brother, thank the Spirits for that! Not a whiff of romance in that, especially not playing soldiers with them!

"It was all so normal," Alaiz was continuing, tears in her eyes. "I'd forgotten what it was like to have people treat you as a person. Just as me, Alaiz, not as …as what I represented, or could be used for. You all teased me, and made me laugh, and let me win so badly it was silly, but for the first time since I left my home it felt real again. And I don't want to lose that!"

She gave a sniff and both Knights proffered handkerchiefs in an instant, which made her laughed again, although it was rather wobbly.

"You see? Nobody at court would ever do that! And it's made me think. I know it's wrong …but do I have to go back? I'm not what Ivain wants. At best I'm an irritating little sister, and he's got plenty of others who want to be his wife. Well why not let them have the job if they want it? I can guarantee they won't be so keen when they've had to have pickled herrings every morning for breakfast, because *you* get what *he* likes, even if you hate it."

"Yuk, pickled herrings for breakfast!" Friedl's voice came from behind as he and the other two joined them.

"That's disgusting!" Theo agreed.

"I don't think you can divorce the king for pickled herrings, though," Bertrand said in mock seriousness.

"I wasn't talking about divorce," Alaiz said cautiously.

"What, then?" Oliver asked, getting more worried by the moment at this new turn.

"Well there's civil war in Prydein, isn't there, and people die in wars. If I just disappeared, it wouldn't be too hard for Hugh and Amalric to put it about that I'd been travelling incognito and been inadvertently killed, would it? Or whatever tale suited them best. I don't really care anymore. I've tried to do my best, and I care about the ordinary people, really I do. But to change things you have to have some power, and if I haven't even got the power to change what I have for breakfast, I'm hardly in a position where I can help them, am I? With those two in control, it doesn't matter who's queen because you're only a cipher, a puppet they play with.

"I've done my share, though, and now I want my life back. I want to live with real people. I don't care if it's not luxurious – our draughty old castle on Kittermere was pretty basic, and we didn't have many servants, so I'm sure I can survive without all the hangers on. In fact that's just what I *don't* want. I'd rather wash my own clothes and know that someone hasn't been inspecting my private things. I know this sounds really silly and girlish, but I liked that I did my own washing while we were at the grange, and packed my own bag to come away."

She sighed deeply. "I suppose it's all too much to hope for, isn't it. Even with the Island going to the dogs, if they don't report my presence when we get to Ergardia, Hugh would still send a search party out and drag me back. I can dream, though, can't I?"

"Of course you can! It might even happen," Hamelin said with conviction, and Oliver could see by his face that if Hamelin had anything to do with it, Alaiz would never set foot inside the royal palace ever again.

Trying to keep things light and yet positive, Oliver desperately said,

"Well we've a long road to travel yet. A long time before you need to make any decisions of that sort. By the time you've spent another month or two with us reprobates, you might be glad to see the back of us!"

"Speaking of which," Bertrand said, "are my eyes going funny or is there a dark line on the horizon?"

"No, you're not seeing things, that must be the southern coast of Rheged," declared Theo.

All of them stood and peered into the hazy distance as their first destination crept closer. It took until the next morning to get close enough to see details, but already there were a host of vessels passing them. Some were large merchantmen flying the flags of the other Islands as well as Prydein and Rheged, while smaller fishing boats painted in bright colours bobbed along in their wake. On a great promontory they saw a prosperous town, which the captain said was Whale Point. However, that was purely a fishing port, and they slid by it and followed the coast, past the next major port and finally docked at the great town of Crauwel. It should have been possible to make a straight crossing from Quies to Crauwel, but vicious whirlpools, tidal races and uncooperative winds had doubled their journey's length and time.

When they had disembarked, the six of them went in search of a livery stable to purchase horses. This proved to be difficult, for the folk of Rheged seemed suspicious of strangers even to the extent of not doing business with them. They finally found a shifty-looking stable owner prepared to sell them horses at an inflated price, and led their new mounts through the town in search of somewhere to spend the night. In view of the trouble they had had getting horses, the Knights thought it best to make for the nearest preceptory. When they asked for directions, they found people giving them strange glances, but put it down to the same dislike of strangers they had already encountered. It was only as they reached the gates of the preceptory on the outskirts of the town that they realized it might be more than that.

At the gate they were met by a very superior-acting monk.

"What's your business here?" he demanded.

Rather nonplussed by this, Oliver answered.

"We have business with the commander."

"The commander, eh? Well you'd better come in then," was the reply.

It was just as they rode under the archway of the gate that Friedl and Alaiz both spotted monks behind the gates already starting to swing them shut behind them.

"Wait!" Friedl shouted in warning, and Oliver and Hamelin in front halted and looked back. In that instant the monks rushed forward, trying to shoo the horses in quicker.

"Back!" Hamelin bellowed, wheeling his horse as Oliver did the same. Theo and Bertrand in the rear got their untrained horses to reverse more by brute force than anything else, making room for Alaiz and Friedl. But Alaiz's horse was totally spooked by the noise and movement behind him, and refused to move. Grabbing the reins, Friedl hauled its head round, and heeled his own horse into a sharp turn as Oliver place a well-aimed boot at the stubborn animal's rear, catapulting it into movement. As two monks rushed forward to try to grab the reins of Alaiz's horse, Oliver's boot lashed out again, catching the rearmost one on the back of the head and felling him like a tree. Hamelin reached out in his anger and hauled the second off his feet, hefting him straight at the oak gate which the monk slid down, howling as he acquired a face-full of splinters on his way to the ground. It was not the best ordered retreat the Knights had ever made, but all of them made it out in one piece. Setting their horses to a full gallop, they tore away from the gateway, leaving the monks shouting condemnations of violent, filthy Knights.

"What in the Islands was that all about?" Theo asked when they finally reined in their mounts several miles down the road.

They looked in bemusement from one to another until Hamelin spoke up.

"I think things here are a lot worse than Master Hugh thought. He knew the Church was looking after the affairs of the Order here while they found a new Grand Master, but this looks like they've been disbanded!"

"We're in the shit again then, aren't we!" Bertrand declared mournfully.

"Are we?" puzzled Alaiz.

"Well, we don't exactly know where the lad is who we're supposed to be collecting, do we?" Friedl pointed out. "And Master Hugh said this Abbot Jaenberht is the head of the monastic order here, but are they in league with the Church or off on their own? Going on *that* reception, we can hardly call in to the nearest church and ask, can we?"

Oliver pondered on this before saying,

"I think the only thing we can do is start riding north. We were dropped at Crauwel for a reason, and that was because Hugh wanted us to be able to go north without going near the capital on the east side of the mountains. Maybe the further north we go, things will get better."

"Yes, but where *is* Jaenberht?" Hamelin wondered aloud as they set off again.

They were forced to camp out that night, as none of them wanted to stop at any of the few meagre inns they passed. All of those looked as though they were so short of customers of late they would have given up the information of a party of Knights to anyone with a gold coin, and Oliver and Hamelin thought it better that their route remain in doubt if possible. Luckily there was no shortage of fallen wood in the small copse they chose to shelter in, and they soon had a good fire going against the night cold. Already farther north than anywhere in Prydein, they found the weather noticeably colder and getting more wintry.

After that, though, they had travelled far enough afield to start using the wayside inns. They chose the larger establishments which seemed to be catering to merchants' caravans, where larger parties would not arouse suspicion, even though these cost rather more than Oliver would have liked, given the limited purse Hugh had given him to last the journey. It was an easy ride, which was one blessing, for the roads were wide and well-repaired. In fact, to Alaiz's amazement, Rheged seemed to be crisscrossed with a latticework of trade routes of a quality that she had only seen on the half-dozen main highways in Prydein.

There also appeared to be a brisk trade in horses on Rheged, and nobody questioned them wanting to trade in weary horses who needed a few days' respite for freshly rested ones. In this way they managed to slowly replace the ill-fed and knackered mounts they had been forced to buy at the quay, with ones of a quality more suited to a long journey. Hamelin had led the Knights in gallantly trying to persuade Alaiz to change her horse first. However she firmly refused them on the basis that not only was she the lightest of them, and therefore less likely to tire a weak horse, but also because if she was so conspicuously a lady, they would be more easily followed. There was much grumbling at this, especially when they had changed every other horse, and Alaiz would still only let them buy a placid but strong moorland pony for her.

They left the seaside town of Wrelton, where the pony had been bought, and were still arguing over it so that they did not notice two men riding ever closer to them until one of the strangers spoke.

"You might as well give in, lads," a rumbling bass voice said genially, "don't you know it's useless to carry on arguing with a woman when she's made her mind up?"

The five Knights spun in their saddles, hands instantly dropping to the swords poorly concealed beneath their cloaks, cursing their negligence at the sight of the two.

"Whoa there! Steady! We mean you no harm," the smaller of the two said at the sight of them reaching for their arms. Yet the two looked as though they too were well used to taking care of themselves. Both rode horses of fine quality, and carried swords which had the look of fine craftsmanship and plenty of wear, but there the similarity stopped. The smaller one was slim, dark, and with finely chiselled features complimented by immaculately tailored riding gear. The other was a great shaggy fellow who, despite having clothes which were obviously of good quality, looked ruffled and rumpled, and he required a great solid, raw-boned destrier to carry his weight. Although he wore an amiable smile, none of the Knights would have wanted to be on the receiving end of a blow from his great ham fists. It was Alaiz who broke the stand-off when she gave a worried squeak of fright as Hamelin edged his horse forward a step to come between her and the strangers.

"Oh, beg pardon, miss," the big man said politely, giving a courteous half bow from the height of his tall beast. "Didn't mean to startle you. These are bad times, but you've nothing to fear from me and Sir Edmund here."

"You're a lord?" Oliver asked quickly, anxious to avoid a fight which might draw attention to them if he could, but equally wanting to avoid another mistake like their arrival at the preceptory.

"I'm Sir Edmund Praen," the dapper man introduced himself, "and this is Sir Gerard of Urse. We're looking for a friend of ours who might be in some difficulty. I don't suppose you've seen a tall, blonde-haired man – looks like he'd be useful in a tight spot – travelling with a young monk? They might have been travelling towards Holtby or Airey?"

Oliver and the Knights were torn. Their vows meant everything to them, and to be asked for assistance and not to give it was breaking them in a big way. Yet they were sworn first and foremost to complete Hugh's mission and to protect Alaiz. Hamelin recovered first and spoke up.

"Our apologies, sirs, but we're newly arrived in Rheged and have little idea of where these places you speak of might be."

"In that case my apologies to you," the one called Edmund replied politely. "May we assume then that you've not had the best of receptions since your arrival?"

The embarrassed silence of the Knights spoke volumes, but Alaiz had less compunction about speaking as she had found.

"When we landed nobody would sell us horses, except for some old nags who gave up on us a few miles down the road!" she said indignantly. "Then we went to one of those Knights' preceptories and got chased away! I thought the Knights were supposed to help people? All we wanted were some directions!"

The fact that she was telling the truth, even if a little edited, gave her indignation weight made even more convincing by her natural innocence.

The giant, Gerard, sighed deeply and sadly.

"You wouldn't have found us so discourteous a few years ago," he apologized. "If it's directions you're wanting, may we be of service as some recompense?"

"We were asked to deliver a message to an abbot by an old friend of his," Alaiz rushed on, oblivious to Hamelin's frantic eye signals, and Friedl coming alongside her on the other side to the strangers and trying to kick her ankle. "His name is Jaenberht? Do you know where he is?"

All five of the horrified Knights felt their hearts miss a beat. They desperately tried to keep their faces blank but feared they failed.

"Abbot Jaenberht, really?" Edmund mused. "Well then maybe we can help you. However, miss, you'd be well advised to not say his name too freely to folks around here without knowing them a little better." He turned to the Knights. "Weapons down gentlemen," he said with the confidence of someone well used to commanding troops. "You've nothing to fear from us if you really are friends to Jaenberht, but you'd best come with us straight away."

"I think not," Oliver said, trying to avoid sounding provocative but still firm.

Gerard edged his horse a little closer.

"You can't put spilt wine back in the bottle," he said sympathetically. "Your caution is understandable, if a little late! But Edmund spoke no less than the truth." He turned in his saddle and pointed. "That great castle perched on the rock down the road there is Scar Castle. It now belongs to one of the cronies of our unloved King Oswine, an idiot called Ringwald. Normally you'd never catch him this side of the mountains so far from court, but Oswine's sent him to establish his authority over his new acquisition. Scar used to belong to a civilized, loyal and noble earl called Harvar, but his last dance was from Oswine's battlements for criticizing the king. You should know that Jaenberht too has criticized Oswine. So you see, it's not wise to inquire after him with Ringwald in residence, and within shouting distance of his castle walls."

Alaiz suddenly realized how close she had come to jeopardizing them all, and blushed until her face outshone her red hair. However, her companions were all too busy considering the implications of this new information to bother rubbing it in, which they would not have dreamt of doing to her anyway. Oliver looked at the others, and saw they thought the same as him even though they said nothing.

"Well, in that case we have no choice but to trust you," he said thoughtfully. "However, while I don't want to sound churlish, I should warn you that we're far from helpless."

This time it was Edmund who gave a light, easy laugh.

"Oh my young friend, it's been many a long year since I was stupid enough to think that *any* Knight of the Order of the Cross was harmless!"

This really perplexed the five, who had removed their mail-backed gloves after the incident with the monks, and had likewise kept their swords beneath their cloaks to cover the distinctive dragon-headed cross on the pommels and scabbards. None travelled in their black uniforms or wore the distinctive cloaks either. Their mystification was written on their faces, which made Edmund laugh again.

"Don't worry, you weren't that obvious! Most people around here haven't seen Knights recently enough for it to be noticeable. But really, gentlemen! How many other young soldiers would be trusted with accompanying a young woman alone without even a maid? A young woman who, if you don't mind me saying so, is not only attractive but obviously highly born – going both by her speech, and the fact that she's unused to having to worry about her own safety."

Alaiz's blush got even deeper, while the others were mentally kicking themselves for not having given her words more weight when she had pointed that out to them earlier.

"If it makes you feel any easier," Gerard added, "the blonde man we're seeking is one of the few Knights of the Order left still at large from the Rheged sept. So you see, we're not a threat to you because you're Knights."

The five Knights exchanged glances again, along with imperceptible nods to one another.

"You'd best lead on then," Oliver said.

The whole company adjusted their riding positions so that Oliver rode at the front with Edmund, with Hamelin and Gerard riding either side of Alaiz next, and the three other Knights bringing up the rear. For the first few miles, Edmund set a stinging pace, getting them past the looming menace of Scar Castle as quickly as possible. Luckily there was plenty of traffic on the road, which the two locals explained was the main arterial road north on this side of the mountains. The road was wide, but whenever caravans of wagons passed them, or they wished to overtake one going their way, Gerard dropped back to ride alongside Bertrand moving Alaiz back to beside Theo so they were only two abreast.

For a heart stopping moment they thought their luck was changing when, having just passed the road to Scar, they saw a column of armed men coming out of the great arched gateway of the castle. There were only twenty or so of them, but far too many for a quick engagement and escape. However, as it reached the main road, the column turned south, and they all breathed a sigh of relief. It made Hamelin realise what a narrow escape they had had, though, for had they not met Edmund and Gerard, their own more leisurely pace would have brought them face to face with a force they now knew would have been hostile to their mission.

Consequently he felt more disposed to engage Gerard in conversation as they carried on, as did Bertrand when the big man dropped back to ride next to him. Having served a little farther afield than the others, Bertrand soon found that he and Gerard had acquaintances in common, as often happens with soldiers. So by the time they trooped into the yard of a large inn that evening, the two were chatting like old friends, which eased the talk over warming, savoury pies and mulled wine when they sat down to eat.

They tucked themselves away in a corner of the smaller public room, from where they could see the door and had the bulk of the thick walls behind them instead of other tables who might overhear their conversation. As they dug into the meal with appetites sharpened by the wintry chill, Edmund and Gerard between them told the others of their own quest. Another friend, Osbern, had taken over from Edmund in overseeing the restoration of defences at a castle which had been attacked by some of the king's thugs.

"He's so much better at that sort of thing than me," Edmund said cheerfully. "Very pious is our Osbern, so he enjoys feeling like he's doing good works. …Not that I think it's not worthwhile, you understand, but it's a long laborious job, and most of the villagers need to be told every last thing. Not their fault, of course. They never expected to have to build defences living that far from the sea – and it's only been from the sea that we've had any enemies for generations. Osbern's good at detail."

"He's politely saying Osbern's a bit constipated in the thought department!" Gerard guffawed. "Wonderful chap when the enemy's screaming in his face and he doesn't have time to stop and ponder. But by the Hunt, he could drive you to drink if you let him make any decision for you! …Any wine left in that jug?"

Edmund rolled his eyes in mock exasperation while passing the jug over.

"Anyway," he continued, "there I was, trying to get this defence work done and getting nowhere fast – and thinking Ruari's going to kill me if I don't get it done in time and another attack wipes the survivors of the first attack out – when up rides Osbern and Gerard."

"Aye," Gerard carried on. "See, I'd been up at my castle in the north. Sorting a few domestic things out!" He gave Hamelin sitting next to him a nudge with his elbow and a suggestive wink. "Have to keep the wife happy with a visit now and then! …Well, I was coming back when I ran into a band of soldiers. Turned out they were providing an escort for Abbot Jaenberht and as many of his leading churchmen as were heading back north. As it happened I was lucky to catch them, 'cause they were trying to get past Catraeth with all speed since that upstart little shit, Oswine, thought that as king he could start imprisoning men of the Church! I had a long chat with Jaenberht in his tent that night, and he told me he'd seen our friend, Ruari, and the monk who was travelling with him. There was a young boy called Wistan in Jaenberht's protection, who'd taken himself off in a panic with one of the novices while Jaenberht's back was turned, and Ruari has gone to find him."

Oliver and Hamelin furtively exchanged surprised glances at this news which related to their own mission, but said nothing.

"We think that Oswine might have this lad on his wanted list for more decorations on his battlements, if you get my drift," Edmund was continuing. "Apparently Jaenberht had some plan to send the lad for safety to an abbey across in one of the other Islands, but unless we can find him, it won't matter whether anyone turns up to take him there. It's typical of Ruari that he would try to protect the lad, but they have no idea which way they might have gone. So Gerard thought if we started from the south and worked north, we might meet them coming south and save them some time"

"How old is this boy?" Alaiz asked anxiously.

"Poor little sprout's only eleven," Gerard growled. "My lad Roger's only a year older, and Rosin would roast me over the spit if I let him go wandering round the Island with some lad no older than our Keven!"

Edmund chuckled.

"Rosin threatens to roast you all the time!" He leaned across the table to the others in mock conspiracy. "To hear him talk he's the king in his castle, but Rosin runs rings round him! …Hasn't stopped them breeding a tribe of kids that she has to stop him spoiling rotten, though!"

The young Knights and Alaiz could not help but laugh along with him.

"Well thank you! Some friend you are!" Gerard feigned a huff.

"And they wouldn't work *that* out within five minutes of us getting to Thorpness?" Edmund continued his good-natured teasing. "You see? He says it's Ruari who's worried about Wistan, but this big oaf is as worried himself. Wistan's an orphan, so all Gerard can think of is that there's no father chasing around like he would after one of his own, so he'd better fill in the gap!"

It was evident to the others that Edmund had spoken nothing but the truth, and Alaiz at least had no problem imagining Gerard surrounded by children who probably adored their gruff father back. In the midst of this hilarity, Oliver had pulled Hamelin over to him and was whispering urgently in his ear. As the conversation faded and the others became aware of them he stopped. Hamelin, looked at Edmund and Gerard, then said,

"I agree with you." He turned back to Oliver. "You're the leader, so it's your decision, but it seems the right thing to do."

"What does?" Gerard asked.

Oliver cleared his throat.

"That help from another Island? It's us. We were sent from Grand Master de Burh in Prydein. He received a message from Abbot Jaenberht and we were dispatched to come here and escort a little boy called Wistan to a place of safety in Ergardia."

"You?" Edmund exclaimed.

Oliver nodded.

"Forgive me," Edmund said carefully, "but we were expecting someone …well …a bit more experienced. And, aren't you a little short on numbers for a rescue party?"

"A few more of you would've been useful, to be honest," Gerard added.

"I'm sure you were hoping for more," Hamelin sighed, "but things aren't going too well in Prydein, and we're stretched a bit thin ourselves." He dropped his voice to be absolutely sure of not being heard at all outside of their group. "There's a DeÁine wizard on the loose in Prydein too."

"Hounds of the Wild Hunt!" Gerard swore, and Edmund made the sign of the cross before asking,

"You're sure?"

The Knights nodded and between them told of what had led them to come to Rheged, with the exception of who Alaiz was.

"Then I'm sorry," Edmund sympathized. "No wonder your Grand Master could only send you. Please understand that it's not any slander on your abilities that made me say what I did before." He too dropped his voice now. "It's just that Wistan isn't just any little boy. He's the heir to the Jarldom. Our late Jarl Michael's younger son, and half brother to the twisted monster who's currently Jarl. I wouldn't think an *army* too much to keep him safe given that they managed to murder Jarl Michael."

"Murder?" gasped the Knights in unison.

"That was the news that Ruari brought back, and why he's on the run too," Edmund added.

The little company sat in silence for a while as each digested the new twists that had been put on each of their missions. Even Alaiz found herself worrying about a little boy on the run. If she had been frightened, what in the Islands must he be feeling?

"We'll help you," Oliver suddenly declared.

Edmund and Gerard looked up in surprise.

"Look," Oliver said, "you told us that there were side roads you couldn't cover. Well, if Bertrand, Friedl and Theo go with Gerard if we come to one of those forks, and Hamelin, Alaiz and I go with Edmund, we can cover twice the ground."

"And you'll still not be alone if you meet any unpleasant company," Bertrand backed his captain up.

Edmund and Gerard began to grin again.

"You see, Gerard, I knew this was the right thing to do! If we'd stayed at Montrose we'd never have met these folks, and they'd have been running around on a wild goose chase too!" Edmund gloated.

"Oh bugger off!" Gerard laughed. "It was nothing of the sort! You just can't stand being sat on your arse, that's your problem!"

Chapter 31

Happy Reunions

Rheged: Samhainn

Despite the extra help, however, Gerard and Edmund found neither hide nor hair of Ruari and Andra, although at Bridgeport the landlord of a quayside inn said he thought he had seen them some weeks back. After a painfully slow journey, creeping ever northwards, they found themselves almost at Gerard's Thorpness with nothing to show for their efforts. It was therefore with some relief that they turned down the dead-end road to the castle, everyone looking forward to hot baths, and the comfort of not having to be constantly looking over their shoulders every night while they planned the next day. Alaiz, in particular, had found the journey arduous having never spent so many days continuously in the saddle before.

In the late afternoon they came out of the shelter of the folds of the last of the moorland, and saw before them the stark headland. The huge bulk of the castle sat forbidding and grey out on the farthest point of the promontory, bleak and cold. Suddenly Alaiz wondered if she would dare take her clothes off to have a bath in case she froze to death in such a draughty looking pile of stone. Yet as soon as they rode in under the vicious spikes of the iron-grilled portcullis, and past the murder holes, it all changed. The large open court was filled with bustling activity of servants cheerfully going about their daily business.

"Back so soon, my lord?" a cheeky, round-faced stable lad said, as he bustled up to take the reins of the first two horses.

"Aye, Billy, so you'd better watch your step!" Gerard joked back.

Alaiz was astounded. She had never seen such a big house where the relationship between servant and master was so relaxed. Nobody at any of the royal households on Prydein would have dared to address her personally, let alone with so little deference. Then it struck her. This was a home! A real, proper home, not just a fortress. As if to confirm this, a door across the way flew open, and a small figure pelted out.

"Father! Father! Guess who's here!"

The speaker was a stocky little lad of somewhere between five and seven, Alaiz guessed, who could only have been Gerard's son, given the shock of black hair and dark eyes which matched Gerard's perfectly.

"Hello Bertie," Edmund greeted the small whirlwind, as he threw himself at his father's legs, almost overbalancing Gerard.

"Spirits child! Give them time to get through the door!" a voice made Alaiz turn back to the door, as it carried on with an attempt at severity that did not quite succeed, "Well we are going to be a full house! Nice of you to let me know, Gerard! I suppose you expect me to find beds and feed them?"

"Come here, my lover, and stop your shouting!" Gerard happily growled, sweeping the short, rotund figure with the brightest red hair Alaiz had ever seen, off her feet.

"Hello Rosin!" Edmund greeted her as she was swung past him.

"Put me down, you randy bullock!" Rosin chastised Gerard, playfully clipping him round the ear as he set her back on her feet. Then she saw Alaiz.

"I'm so sorry, pet, you must think you've walked into a mad house!"

"Father! Father!" The little boy was still jumping up and down in front of Gerard, and now began to swing on the arm that was not around Rosin's ample middle. "He's not dead! Uncle Ruari's not dead! He's here!"

"What?" Gerard and Edmund exclaimed in unison in their amazement.

"Ruari, here?" Gerard asked Rosin, in delight, but it was the child who answered.

"Yes, silly! Come on, he's waiting to meet you. He's been teaching Keven how to use a lance, and Roger how to fire his bow and arrow! Mother won't let me join in, isn't she mean?"

Rosin gave the child a stern look, which seemed to run off him like water off a duck's back.

"Between you and your disreputable friends, I'll be lucky if I can ever find a woman willing to marry them!" she grumbled, but without malice. "There's me, trying to teach them some manners, and all you lot do is teach them how to whack three kinds of stuffing out of things! We'll still be feeding them here when they're thirty, you know that don't you?"

"Not if their Uncle Ruari teaches them how he gets his way with women, they won't!" Edmund joked back, which from Rosin only got him a black look and an enigmatic '*hmmph*!'

"What's that supposed to mean?" a voice from behind them said.

Through the gate a tall blonde man strode, leading another stocky lad – this time flame-haired, but as shaggy as Gerard's – sat on a sturdy pony and carrying a long pole, with what looked suspiciously like a pair of knickers tied onto it as a pennant. Then the man gave a devastating smile which made him even more attractive and teased,

"You know you love me really, Rosin!"

Rosin, however, uttered a squeak, loosed Gerard and shot over to the makeshift pennant.

"Not if you do this! What are *these* doing tied to a broomstick?" she shrieked, tugging the knickers free and using them to swat Ruari repeatedly with, reducing him to laughter. That only infuriated her more as her son and husband joined in the merriment.

"By the Spirits, I'm glad to see you!" Gerard said, avoiding Rosin's continued assault with the underwear and clasping Ruari to him. "Have we got news for you!"

"And company too, I see," Ruari said, sweeping his gaze over the newcomers. "Rosin told me you'd sent a message back saying you'd met Jaenberht, in case any of us got here before you. Is that why you're here, Edmund?"

"Sort of," Edmund said sheepishly, knowing that Ruari would have guessed how little encouragement he would have needed to come after him. "Is Andra here?"

"In the solar, reading," Rosin supplied the information.

"But who are these people?" Ruari carried on, with more than a hint of suspicion in his voice now.

As the piercing blue eyes came to rest on her, Alaiz squirmed uncomfortably. However much he might allow Rosin the liberty of harrying him, Alaiz felt sure that anyone who truly annoyed him would very rapidly live to regret their mistake. This man was far more frightening than any of the Knights she had met on Prydein.

"Steady on, Ruari, you're scaring the lass," Gerard cautioned him.

"My apologies," he said, the fearsome expression dying in his eyes as Ruari stepped up to Alaiz, "I've spent so long watching my back suspicion is second nature to me now."

"Oh …I quite understand …really I do," Alaiz answered quickly, wishing she did not sound quite so breathless, not having realized that she had stopped breathing when his gaze had fallen on her. What an idiot he must think her! Thank the Spirits he was not to know she was supposed to be a queen! Just at the moment she felt as though she would be struggling to pass herself off as anything more than a rather dizzy milkmaid.

"Do you? Mmmm…" Ruari wondered softly, turning his attention to the others.

"These are the men Jaenberht was expecting," Gerard said triumphantly.

"What?"

"Jaenberht sent to Prydein for help," Edmund picked up the narrative. "We'll tell you more inside, but things aren't going too well over there either. Their Grand Master would've sent more, but these are the only Knights he could spare. Since we met them on the road from Crauwel, though, they've helped us search for you, and for Wistan. We've had no reason to doubt they're who they say they are, Ruari."

Oliver stepped forward.

"I'm Captain Oliver Aleyne, from the Rosco preceptory. This is my second-in-command, Hamelin ap Corin, and Knights Friedl, Bertrand and Theo." He put his hand inside his tunic and withdrew a rolled sheet of parchment. "This is the letter of introduction I was supposed to give to Abbot Jaenberht, but it looks as though, if we're to find and help the boy we were sent after, you're the one we shall be dealing with." Ruari held out his hand, but before he could take the letter Oliver moved it back. "But before I hand this over I'd like to know who *I'm* dealing with! I given you our names, yet we have as much reason to be cautious as you, and you've not told us who you might be. …So who *are* you?"

Ruari inhaled sharply and drew himself up to his full height to look Oliver straight in the eye – not something many people could do given Oliver's greater than average height.

"*Captain* Aleyne, is it? Well I'm *Ealdorman* Ruari MacBeth, and until we can hold an election to re-establish another, I'm acting Grand Master of what's left of the Rheged sept!"

Oliver gulped and the other Knights stood to attention. This was an unexpected turn up! Ruari walked along the now lined up five.

"Five Knights?" He looked them up and down. "No disrespect, gentlemen, but none of you look old enough to have served abroad, except you," he nodded towards Bertrand. "What in the Islands was Hugh thinking of sending you over here?"

"Well thank you very much!" Alaiz snapped bitterly, losing her fear in her indignation. "We've risked our necks coming here! We've nearly been imprisoned, and spent days and days searching for you! And this is all the thanks we get? The least you could do is be a bit grateful! No disrespect? Haa! Not much!"

Ruari turned to her in surprise as Hamelin hastily whispered,

"Hush, Alaiz …please!"

Ruari sighed wearily, though, and instead of an angry retort said,

"I meant what I said. You have no idea how dangerous it is to say you're a Knight here in Rheged at the moment. You're lucky beyond measure that you happened to run in two of the very few people who could safely give you advice. One false move and you would all have ended up in one of Oswine's dungeons, and Hugh would never have heard of you again. You'd just have disappeared! I thought Hugh knew of how bad things were here, from what Jaenberht said, which is why I would've expected him to send older men who had been here before. Knights who knew the lie of the land. Who might have had contacts within some of the sept here themselves, whom they could approach in the guise of visitors, not just as official messengers. You all seem to have been singularly ill-prepared for what you found here."

Alaiz blushed with embarrassment, which became even greater as Ruari continued,

"And what in the Islands are you men doing dragging this woman around with you? Dear Spirits, this was always going to be a dangerous mission. Why would you bring someone who can't even defend themselves?"

"Hey, I'm not so helpless!" Alaiz was stung to reply. "Just because I'm a woman doesn't mean you can just push me around!"

"Really?" Ruari intoned.

Reaching back to Keven, he took the two practice swords which the boy had been clutching, and threw one to Alaiz, who fumbled the catch and let it clatter to the floor.

"Pick it up!" he commanded.

"Sire, you can't …" Oliver stepped forward as Hamelin gasped, "No!"

"Stand still!" Ruari barked at them, and the habit of discipline made them freeze.

Alaiz picked up the sword and tried to remember all the tips the Knights had given her at Quies. Ruari twirled the other with ridiculous ease and then struck without warning. To her mortification he whacked her on the bottom, then stepped lightly away before she could even raise her sword. For the next few minutes he pursued her retreat around the courtyard, never hitting hard but always finding targets that caused her more embarrassment than hurt. When she became really breathless, he halted the exercise and took the wooden sword off her. Towering over her he looked down his nose at her before his face broke into a wry smile.

"Not bad, actually! For an obvious beginner. I know a lady who would've wiped the floor with you, mind you, but not bad!"

Ridiculously, Alaiz thought, it felt more of a compliment than a criticism, despite the fact that normally she would have been more than a little angry at such cavalier treatment. Perhaps it was the reference to the other lady that did it. At least now she knew he was not being nasty just because she was a girl. Before either of them could say any more, though, Ruari gave a yelp and leapt forwards almost colliding with Alaiz, before he spun round rubbing his own bottom. Rosin stood behind him with a washing paddle in her hand.

"Have you quite finished humiliating a guest in *my* home?" she demanded. "Because if so Ruari MacBeth, you can apologize to that young lady, and go and make sure my son washes and changes before dinner. You too! I'll not have you coming to the meal before guests looking like that, and smelling like a farmyard!"

"Yes, Rosin," he said meekly, and started to lead Keven away towards the stables, until a pointed cough from Rosin stopped him.

"Apology!" Rosin demanded, forcing him to turn back with a desperate look for help to Edmund and Gerard, who both found the battlements suddenly worthy of inspection.

"My apologies, miss," he mumbled, then with a mischievous twinkle in his eye, took her hand and kissed it.

"Satisfied?" he asked Rosin, as he turned away again.

Alaiz blushed again, wondering if she was destined to spend the whole of the time on this Island looking like a beetroot. Confound the man, why did he have to make a kiss on the hand seem so sexy? Then she saw the aghast look on Hamelin's face and wished he had not seen her reaction. She was becoming very fond of him and there was no way she would ever want to hurt him, but until that moment she had never given their relationship any careful thought.

Now, though, as Rosin ushered them into the castle and provided rooms and washing facilities, she was forced to confront her feelings for Hamelin, and they were confusing. All her adult life she had believed she loved Ivain. So much so that she had never given anyone else a second glance. However, Ivain had quite publicly spurned her. That had hurt terribly, yet now she realized that it felt no different to the way she had felt when her brothers had been selfish, or uncaring, towards her when she was younger. Anger was there, too – but was that being heartbroken?

She was so preoccupied with her thoughts that she had not realized Rosin had slipped back into her room, until she spoke.

"Are you alright?" Rosin asked carefully. "Forgive me asking – and I'll go away if you'd prefer – but I thought you might like some female company after being on the road with only men for weeks."

"I've been waiting for company all my life!" Alaiz gulped miserably.

"Oh, you poor soul," Rosin sympathized, and came and wrapped Alaiz to her matronly front in a warm hug, which reduced Alaiz to a weeping wreck in seconds. In ragged chunks she found herself telling Rosin all about her life and Ivain, and how she had lost Gillies who was the only friend she had ever really had. It was only as they sat together on the edge of the bed with her wiping her eyes that she thought to say,

"Please don't tell anyone about this. Please!"

Rosin smiled and patted her arm comfortingly.

"Don't you worry, pet, I won't say a word. Spirits love us, if those men found out they have the queen of Prydein here, you'd be wrapped up in fleece and sent under armed guard to Ergardia tonight on the first suitable ship. At least your young Knights seem to have the right idea. What you need is to start having a bit of life, not be locked away! Thank the Trees, Gerard has never tried to make me into some meek little mouse, and the more I hear about other people's marriages the more I realise how lucky I am to have the big softie. Have you heard him and Edmund talk about Osbern? …Yes? Well you should hear what he's done to *his* wife!"

At which Rosin launched into an account of what Osbern had done to Ismay. Alaiz sat amazed as the tale unravelled, until she forgot her own worries.

"I think I'd like to meet Ismay," she said as Rosin got to the end.

"Oh, we can arrange that once you've found Wistan," Rosin said with a conspiratorial grin. "After all, you'll not be rushing back to Prydein, will you?"

They were each just what was needed for the other, Rosin thought as she led Alaiz down to dinner. Neither of them had any friends, and singularly useless husbands. Well, if Osbern thought he was going outsmart her, and make it difficult for male friends like Edmund to visit Ismay, then he was even dimmer than she thought, because she would just go ahead and find Ismay some female friends even *he* could not object to. And even a straight-laced fool like Osbern could hardly claim that the married queen of Prydein was not suitable company for a knight's wife!

Alaiz spent a wonderful couple of days at Thorpness. Rosin was a witty, intelligent, and sharp companion, who had her in fits of laughter time and time again. She could not remember how long it had been since she had been so relaxed. Oliver was usually closeted with Ruari and Edmund in the guardroom of the castle, where Gerard kept his maps, but the other Knights were entertained by Gerard. However Hamelin often managed to spend time with Alaiz, when Rosin had to go off to attend to the running of the castle and the children. To her amazement he proved to be a tolerably good musician, who could coax a tune out of the rather knocked about instruments which had survived the attentions of Gerard and Rosin's children. He could also talk about the places he had seen, but what she enjoyed most was when he talked about his home.

His father, it transpired, had been a very minor landowner, living in a small manor house up on the moors near Rosco. The family had farmed sheep on the highlands and ploughed the fertile river valley in idyllic peace. Hamelin's mother had been the housekeeper when Lukas had been born to the knight and his lady, and had often warmed her employer's bed when his fragile wife had rejected his advances. Hamelin had been the younger by over a year, yet from the start it had been evident that something was missing with Lukas. Physically strong and healthy, he nonetheless had taken longer to do all the normal childhood things, so that he and Hamelin had played together as equals. Hamelin regaled Alaiz with tales of sneaking off to their neighbour's apple orchards to secretly pick the sweet, juicy fruits, and how the man had joined in the game of chasing them off.

"We were scared stiff of him," Hamelin laughed. "Years later he told me how hard it was not to laugh out loud at the sight of us two rascals trying to get over the stile without dropping our handfuls of apples. The few we took made no difference to his harvest, and he only chased us to make them taste all the sweeter for being hard gained!"

The Corin family's overlord had had little use for men-at-arms and there had been no need for Lukas to go to do military service, so that his slowness had been something just accepted within the tightly knit community of the valley. Lukas's mother had produced only daughters after that, and slowly Lukas had been handed over fully to Hamelin's mother to bring up. Nobody had ever said out loud that Lukas was wholly unfit to run the manor, but when Hamelin's mother had married the village blacksmith, some years later, both boys had moved to the forge with her. When their father had died, the oldest daughter, being newly married to an ambitious man, took over the manor. Her husband had then insisted that the brother he had never even met be sent away to the Knights, so that there could be no question of him challenging the inheritance.

"We couldn't have sent Lukas away," Hamelin told Alaiz, as they walked arm in arm through Rosin's small garden in the lee of the castle. "All he'd ever known was the valley. He got lost even going to the market at Rosco. How could he hope to learn what to do with a sword?"

"So you went instead?" Alaiz guessed.

"It was so easy. Our new lord had never met Lukas, so I went up to the big house when the sergeant came from the grange. Nobody suspected a thing. Once we were on the road, I just told the sergeant that I'd always been known as Hamelin, and the truth only came out when finally I had to take my Knight's vows in front of the Grand Master. Master Hugh's a kind man, and he understood why I'd done what I did. By then Lukas had been acknowledged as the apprentice smith, and was doing well with the family around him to keep an eye on him. My mother had had two new little brothers and he adored playing with the children. He was where he belonged, not up in the manor, and I've been happy with my choice. That's why it was so unfair that he should have died that way. Lukas was probably one of the very few people in this world who could honestly be said to have never hurt a soul."

"And you'll get your chance to avenge him," a voice said from the gateway. Ruari had spoken, but Oliver stood beside him.

"I'd already heard as much from your captain here," Ruari went on. "We leave tomorrow for Ergardia, where I'm hoping to meet up with other Knights who can help us."

"What about Wistan?" Alaiz asked. "Have you given up on him?"

"No," Oliver answered, "but comparing our travels, we're fairly sure that he and Kenelm must have crossed to Ergardia already. Andra knows the lad best, and he thinks that's the way which would've appealed to him. Which, along with the fact that none of us have seen even a hint of two such visible innocents – let's face it, two novices don't go wandering around on their own even in such disrupted times – makes us think we should head that way."

"We cross to Ergardia to enlist the help of the Knights there," Ruari explained. "That way there'll be so many more of us it'll make our chances of success much greater, especially with fewer roads to cover. The mountains there are too inhospitable for two inexperienced travellers to risk at this time of year, and one long road connects pretty much all of the ports facing here."

"How will that help our people in Prydein, though?" Alaiz wondered absent-mindedly.

Ruari held the gate open for her as she and Hamelin came to join them at the postern gate to the castle.

"Ergardia's sept has always kept the old records and the old skills alive," he explained. "They have the Foresters, and if anyone knows how to bring down the DeÁine they do."

Hamelin's eyes began to reflect the excitement which already showed in Oliver's.

"The Foresters!" he breathed. "I always dreamed one day of meeting one of them. There was one passed through Rosco when we were training, but neither of us got to speak to him. Are they all the legends say?"

"I think it's probably fair to say that they and the Covert Brethren are the few the legends *don't* do justice to," Ruari said, trying to stop from grinning himself. "I've served with a few in my time, and to a man they're exceptional. And there's more good news! A friend I left with the job of alerting the few older Knights left in the granges here, has done more than I could ever have hoped for. I've had a message just this morning. …Look!"

Up the road towards the castle a long line of riders was weaving their way like a stately snake. Ruari walked around to the drawbridge with the others hurrying in his wake. The first rider was a wizened little man on a shaggy pony, who gave Ruari a cheery wave as he came closer.

"Nice mornin', Ruari," he said conversationally as he got within earshot.

"Sacred Trees, but it's good to see you Ron!" Ruari exclaimed rushing up to him and almost hauling him bodily off the pony to hug him. "I never expected this! By the Cross of Swords, I didn't!"

"Aye well, me and Sal had a chat after you'd gone," the little man said, bobbing his head, robin-like. "We was going to just do what you said when that farmer, Martin, came back. He said he was going to send a message with the next caravan of wagons, but then thought as he owed you his life, and as the caravan was well guarded, he'd come and bring his other neighbour's yarn with him as well. By that time the talk of the strange thing on the moors was all over town, and we thought you might need reinforcements. Well, I went straight to Thornby and spoke to some friends. There was this pompous prior there, but when the lads heard you was back, they tied him up, stuffed him in a pickle barrel and sent him on the next boat east, with instructions to the captain not to let him out until they were out of sight of land.

"Some of the lads were getting the arms back out of store while Phil and Mick – who were sergeants when I was there – came with me to the grange at Winton. We were there when word came about the attack on the churchmen on the way to Abbot Jaenberht's meeting, and the killing of those monks in the north. Well that was it! After that the lads at Winton said there was no goin' back! It's took a bit of time 'cause we couldn't risk goin' over the mountains past Fell Peak and Catraeth, but we rallied all the granges goin' north on the east coast.

"We got to the fishermen as they came back with the first winter catch, and when they heard Abbot Jaenberht was backin' us they went to get your lads from the east. These lot are the first loads off the boats. It's goin' to take a bit of time, 'cause there's only so much room on the boats and your lads was well hidden, so some of 'em have got a way to come to the coast.

"But that's as well, 'cause we've not got that many horses! When we've seen you lot onto the boats to Ergardia, me and some of the others will take the horses back to meet the next lot who come in to Esmouth. I'm sorry, but we won't be able to use Scarfell again for months, 'cause it's too rough in the winter storms for the open sea ships to dock."

"Sorry?" Ruari gasped. "Dear Spirits, Ron, you've worked miracles! This is way beyond anything I hoped for!"

By now the first of the Knights had ridden up and were dismounting. Against these battle-hardened veterans, Oliver and Hamelin felt like callow youths. All the armour was battered, worn and patched, and that was just the Knights! The enlisted men looked more like a band of outlaws. The black had been washed so often in salty water it had faded to a grubby grey, and was mended with new patches of leather and wool which had not been dyed, so that the effect was like that of drab clowns in motley. There was nothing remotely funny about the weapons, though. The scabbards might be tattered but the blades gleamed wickedly, and through worn near-transparent oiled cloth the wood of the bows shone from repeated handling. Ruari moved amongst them, clasping arms, and saying words of welcome as familiar faces passed by him entering Thorpness. One sharp-eyed young man, who was probably no older than Oliver but seemed mature beyond his years, finally stood grinning before Ruari.

"Elidyr!" Ruari greeted him joyfully.

"Didn't think I'd wait for the second boat, did you?" the man asked, flicking his long black hair out of his eyes as the wind caught it. Ruari laughed and shook his head.

"I'm just glad to see you alive after that arrow you took! It was touch and go when I left."

"Ach, it's a bit stiff still," Elidyr said, flexing his left arm and massaging what was obviously still a sore shoulder. "Nothing a bit of exercise won't put right – especially the sort that puts a DeÁine down the line of my bow!"

Ruari turned to Oliver and Hamelin.

"You wanted to meet a Forester? Well here's one!"

The two gaped openly at the newcomer and Alaiz was awestruck. He looked too young to be one of such an illustrious company. Willowy slim, he also did not look as though he would have the strength to pull the great longbow hanging from a lanyard at his back.

In fact, with his flowing long hair and graceful movements, when brushed up and clean, he could probably have been mistaken for one of the effete young men at court. That was until you got to the eyes. No doubt he could charm the ladies with those soft, puppy-brown eyes, but there was a spark of fire behind them, and the tense lines around them belied any hint of weakness.

"He's the best tracker I had in my command," Ruari added, which didn't seem like shallow praise.

"Well what are we waiting for?" Elidyr asked. "Let's go hunt DeÁine!"

CELIDON & ERGARDIA

Chapter 32

The Hunt Is On

Ergardia: Samhainn

Talorcan sniffed the air. It was cold. Bitterly cold. He and his men were used to travelling hard and fast in any conditions, but it would be dreadful for the two young novices. Then he smiled wolfishly. But it could get as hard and cold as it liked for the bastard DeÁine! Let it come! Snow, wind and ice, anything to trap an Abend here on the shores of Ergardia. Here on the one Island where their Power would be of no use. Then let them come within striking distance of his sword! That would be the time when they experienced payback for all the misery they had caused, and not just to him.

Some might blanch at the task, but it fed the flame in Talorcan's soul. He had long ago realized that while Brego was a superb Grand Master, and a truly great leader of men in open war, he was too civilized to ever be able to personally extract revenge. So Talorcan planned to save him the misery. If he could trap an Abend, or any other high ranking DeÁine, he knew of a nice labyrinth of caves up in the north. A veritable maze which he, and he alone, knew all the ways around. There were caverns in there where only the earth and the worms would hear the screams. And he was going to make it a slow death. Very, very *slow*.

His sergeant, Barcwith, looked across at his leader and grinned himself. He knew what that expression meant – his captain had the scent of DeÁine in his nostrils! Not that Barcwith minded one little bit. A long time ago he had been a farmer way down on Rathlin, before the Attacotti rebels had upset things, but his little farmstead had been on the coast opposite Brychan. Too close to the DeÁine as it turned out. So when the DeÁine had tried to ship men in around the southern coast of Brychan, and had failed to take account of the race tides, they had ended up on Rathlin. And having got there, they had burned and tortured their way through the locals until they were willing to ship them back to Brychan.

Where were the Attacotti rebels then, Barcwith wanted to know? The Knights would not openly oppose the leaders of Prydein, and those leaders wanted nothing to do with Rathlin because of the rebels. So Rathlin had burned at the hands of the DeÁine, and no-one had lifted a hand to save the villagers. Not to save Barcwith's wife, not his little girl, or his baby son, no-one.

So he had left the island to join the Knights, and to fight. With him had come the man sitting on the horse to his right. Whereas Barcwith was dark and solidly built, Galey was lighter built with a shock of bright orange hair which refused to lie flat, but the two men were of a similar age. Galey had been married to the youngest of Barcwith's sisters-in-law, who was now resting in the earth next to all her other sisters. Nobody had questioned why they wanted to fight when they had turned up on the shores of Ergardia, and knocked on the doors of the first preceptory they had found. But years later Talorcan had. He only wanted men as driven as he was in his company.

Five lances were on this patrol, but Barcwith's was his personal lance, joined to him by more than the Knight's vows. Out of all the men in the Ergardia sept, more than any others these five men had frequently journeyed to Brychan with him to join the hunt. Of the rest of the five in the lance, the two archers were Decke and Tamàs, whose only common characteristics were dark hair, and the ability to shoot at anything with deadly accuracy. Decke was a dour, silent man from Laggan on the far isle of Lorne, off Celidon's west coast, who was much given to quoting the holy books. He had seen the mayhem which had followed the Gorget ashore, on its way east, and the way it had twisted the minds of his fellow villagers to fall on one another, and kill and maim. For Decke this was now a holy crusade to rid the world of a curse.

Tamàs, however, was the deadlier shot, despite being nearly twenty years older. Nobody knew much of Tamàs' background, but Barcwith suspected that he had been a young man at the time of Moytirra, and possibly had been born in the borderlands which were now part of New Lochlainn. Soft-spoken and kindly, he had taken it upon himself to keep an eye on the youngest member of their lance, the young lad, Ad. He had been found by them starving and wandering in north Brychan on one of their patrols, his family slaughtered by a random pack of DeÁine Hunters testing the Knight of Brychan's resolve. The Hunters never lived to tell what they found, and Talorcan had adopted Ad into the Order when he had seen the ferocity with which the youngster had attacked the bodies of the DeÁine.

These five alone knew the full extent of what might happen if Talorcan caught up with any DeÁine, for they would help Talorcan take his captive north. However, this time they had been singularly short on signs. Leaving the great castle of Lorne, they had ridden hard, high into the mountains to cross by sheep trails down onto the west coast. Giving the bustling estuary port of Doomston little more than a cursory glance, on the basis that it was far too well patrolled, they had ridden out to the coast and begun searching Luss, then Reith. Then had made the run down to Melfort and Cregan.

All the way they had issued dire warnings, putting the whole coast on alert. Yet nowhere had they seen hide nor hair of any DeÁine. There was definitely no sign of any strange groups of men loitering in the vicinity, and Talorcan had to conclude that if a member of the Abend had come this way, then he had come alone. The countryside was so empty of strangers, that even he could not imagine so much as a half-breed lurking in wait.

Luckily the whole coast was linked by stables housing relays of horses and hill ponies for the Knights, for no single mount could have kept up the punishing pace which Talorcan set for more than one day. Galloping back up the coast, the five lances managed to catch the ferry from Luss across the narrow sound to its facing twin port of Lein. From there they remounted and checked Keills and Rhu, and having found nothing there either, turned their horses for Kaimes. Anyone coming from the ports of Culva or Aird would have to pass through Kaimes, and so there was little point in chasing farther north. The only other way was across the mountains, and the only pass any stranger would find was guarded by Appin Castle, which Brego had sent other riders to. The market town had been busy, but only with locals, and so the lances had turned south once more.

Yet here, just beyond Cluathe, Talorcan's sixth sense had started to twitch. They had loitered for a second night at the castle, but nobody questioned their leader. His instincts had been proven right too many times for that. Now on this freezing morning he sat there on his horse, still as a wolf watching his prey, only the eyes roaming back and forth. The wind whipped the plume on the steel helmet he wore, so that it streamed behind him like a tail, but that was the only movement. Suddenly, below them in the valley they saw something. A small group of riders came into view, with a litter strung between two packhorses.

"Well, well, what have we here?" Barcwith mused. "Heads up lads!"

They were hidden from sight in the shadow of the edge of the tree-line, and at this time of the morning the new arrivals had the sun in their eyes if they looked the lances' way. Yet the newcomers were showing no signs of checking for ambushes, but rather were pushing ahead at the kind of pace that was the maximum their horses could hope to sustain for a whole day.

"Someone's in a hurry," Galey observed, "but aren't they going in the wrong direction for our quarry?"

Talorcan nodded, but said nothing. Instead he waved the lances forward. At the trot the horsemen moved swiftly down the hillside like an advancing wave.

"Archers! Arrows across their path only," Talorcan ordered. The ten archers drew their bows and dropped a neat scatter of arrows right in front of the leading horses, as the others continued on to intercept. The lead riders halted and turned to look their way, yet they sat waiting patiently, with no sign of drawing their swords. The lances wheeled and formed a circle around the group.

"Now here's a surprise," Barcwith greeted them. "What brings you folks this way at this time of year?"

"And riding with DeÁine!" Talorcan's voice was icier than the wind.

"Now, now, Talorcan! That's no way to greet your newest guests!" Sioncaet said, as he rode up to the front.

Talorcan swung his grim gaze onto him, but it rolled off Sioncaet like water over rocks, and instead the little man kneed his horse up to Barcwith's.

"Good to see you again, Barcwith," he greeted him, "and you Galey! Is the *Green Dragon* still open for business?"

"If the Spirits will it!" Decke intoned solemnly, before his face split into a wide grin. "Still planning on winning the drinking contest again, Sioncaet?"

Sioncaet's feigned wide-eyed innocence had his old drinking partners laughing, to the amazement of some of the less well acquainted members of the company. Yet even Talorcan's stony gaze cracked a little, and his voice softened a touch.

"You know full well I didn't mean you, Sioncaet," he reproved the irrepressible jester. "What's going on Maelbrigt?"

Maelbrigt and Labhran between them recounted their reasons for being on the road. As they spoke, Kayna led Taise's litter up to join them, and she found herself being scrutinized with barely concealed hostility. Sithfrey was getting into such a state, Maelbrigt feared he would have set his heels to his horse and headed back the way they had come, had he not leant across and caught the horse's reins.

As Maelbrigt got to the part where Taise had seen Quintillean, Talorcan leaned across to the litter.

"You're absolutely sure?" he demanded of Taise. "There's no question it was Quintillean?"

Taise shook her head and forced herself to reply, even though she was far from convinced that this intense young man was safe for Sithfrey and herself to be around.

"No. No doubt at all. And I have good reason to know what he looks like. Very good reason. There's no way I was mistaken."

Surprisingly, Talorcan reached out and gently touched her bandaged arm, and even more surprisingly it was he who jerked back as if he had been bitten.

"A powerful ward indeed!" he exclaimed softly. Then his expression also softened. "You bear your suffering with much fortitude. That must be painful in the extreme." He turned his horse and edged Maelbrigt to one side. "And you say they tortured her before she came here?" Maelbrigt nodded. "And she's studied the Treasures in New Lochlainn, and there are now DeÁine Hunters after her because of that?" Maelbrigt simply nodded again.

Tamàs, who was sat near them, spoke up.

"Maybe that's why we didn't see any trace of DeÁine south of here. They've been in Celidon, not here. There really was only the Abend alone until you came across, and that's why we've seen nothing."

"Maybe," Talorcan agreed. "You said that the men from the fort could find no sign of Quintillean, but only the two novices?"

Maelbrigt confirmed that, despite hunting all the side tracks off the road to Culva for several miles, the patrols from Dunathe had not found Quintillean.

"How did he escape?" Barcwith wondered aloud.

"Probably a small hiding spell," Talorcan told him bitterly. "He probably slipped off into the gorse, giving the boys some excuse as to why he didn't want to be found – even something as simple as needing to relieve himself would have worked for them, wouldn't it? Even in Ergardia he'd just about be able to make a weaving that would blur the vision of searchers if he wasn't in the open. Standing on the track, in full view, the riders would probably have seen the ward wavering, and breaking up here and there. But if he crept into foliage it wouldn't be so noticeable, and you said it was when the light was failing. That would help too."

"Are we going after the fiend?" Decke asked.

"I know why you want to," Maelbrigt interjected, before Talorcan could reply, "but I'd welcome your protection on to Lorne."

Talorcan looked as though he was about to protest. That was until Kayna gripped his arm and said,

"We *have to* get this scroll translated, Talorcan! This is no longer simply about taking revenge on the DeÁine. Quintillean has seen it over in Celidon, and we think he *will* be acting on it. Whether he's made the right translation himself is something we can't even guess at until we have a chance to get to grips with it ourselves. Or rather until Taise and Sithfrey have. They think – and *we believe them* – that Quintillean thinks he's found a way around the power of the Island Treasures. If he has, then we *must* know how he's going to do it, so that we can act to prevent that set of circumstances coming about.

"Taise, especially, is in danger because the Abend know she's capable of making that translation. Maelbrigt got lucky, pure and simple, when the storm blew Sithfrey off course and lost his trackers. How long that luck is going to last, though, we have no way of knowing. Just as you know you can track Quintillean once he has to board a boat, the minute we caught that barge across the sound we left a clear trail for them to follow."

Talorcan sat and pondered for a moment, then seemed to come to a decision. Calling the other Knights over, he directed them to take the four lances, other than Barcwith's, north. The keeper of Lochead castle was already on alert thanks to Maelbrigt and Labhran, but Talorcan wanted two of the lances to go on to Culva and report to the captain there. If there were DeÁine Hunters coming across, then he would need all the help he could get, for Culva was normally a calm little port needing little military support. The other two lances were to continue north to Aird with warnings and to check for signs of the Hunters tracking Taise there. He and his little band of five would provide an escort for Taise and Sithfrey, although it was obvious that he thought he was actually guarding them as the danger, rather than believing that they were the ones under any threat.

The troops split up, and Tamàs took Ad and Galey to the rear of the group, while Decke joined Talorcan at the head of the column with Maelbrigt and Labhran. Sioncaet kept Sithfrey company back with Barcwith, and, having convinced the newcomers that Sithfrey was a good deal more scared of them than ever he was a danger to them, the atmosphere lightened considerably. Tamàs even managed to draw the very scared DeÁine into something like a conversation, with his quiet, unthreatening manner.

Up at the front of the column, however, things were distinctly frostier. If Maelbrigt had convinced Labhran of Taise's innocence more easily than he had expected, then Talorcan was proving to be much harder work. Talorcan seemed quite convinced that Taise had bewitched Maelbrigt in some way, and even though he could feel how much pain she was in, it was not enough to make him trust her.

For Talorcan it was not the only complication. He could sense his men's vague amusement at his discomfort at the appearance of Kayna. He had never quite found a way to explain to her that he did not return her affections. Not because there was anything amiss with her, but simply because he preferred men to women.

Of course the rest of the lance knew. It was pretty hard to disguise the fact whenever they had been celebrating in some tavern, and he remained oblivious to the charms of the serving girls just itching to get him alone. Barcwith always grumbled in a good-humoured way about what a waste of good looks it was. Talorcan could have had his way with more women than the rest of the lance put together, and he had no objection to them enjoying female company or picking up their room bills afterwards. He even liked women as long as they were not the haughty, cruel ladies of high-blood whom he had encountered as a child. They just were not what attracted him.

Normally over-enthusiastic females were not a problem he had to deal with, since the married quarters were far from his and he rarely went into the towns, but Kayna was a different case. He suspected she knew him well enough to like him for the soldier he was and not just as a one night stand, or as the best of an annoying and mostly little-known bunch of prospective husbands. He in turn had felt sorry for the fierce little girl who had always seemed to be trying to be the son her father never had. Or at least that was how he had seen her on the times he had ridden into Luing with Maelbrigt – and there lay the problem.

As best he could figure out, a little sympathy and a few words of friendship had got blown out of all proportion as she got older. He was fairly sure that Maelbrigt had no idea of how he felt, since most of the times they had been in one another's company there had been more pressing matters at hand than discussing bedfellows – like staying alive. Standing fighting for your lives, back to back with an oncoming army of DeÁine, was hardly the time to shout over your shoulder, 'oh by the way, I'm not into women but that archer over there has the sexiest arse!'

He was fairly sure Sioncaet knew, but the jester could be remarkably tactful at times, and Talorcan was sure he would regard it as Talorcan's right to tell who he wished to know. Just at the moment, though, Talorcan wished he had told Maelbrigt and asked him to break the news to Kayna, even though he had not quite had the nerve to do it himself. Instead of which he was riding with a girl who had a heavy crush on him, to a castle where he not only could not avoid her without being downright rude, but where she might even find her way to his bedroom. He shuddered at the thought, and without knowing it Talorcan's scowl reached thundercloud proportions as he fretted over permutations for embarrassing encounters, worrying Taise and Sithfrey even more – although Taise would have had trouble not laughing out loud had she known the truth of his grim expression.

At midday they stopped for a short break, down near the shore of the Loam, the great loch which dominated this part of Ergardia. The snow-capped mountains which rose above the northern half of the loch were reflected in all their splendour in the still water. On the eastern banks, dense woodland came right down to the shore, and the multitude of tiny islands that inhabited the broad southern expanse of the loch were also dotted with trees. The western side was clearer, and a small road snaked along the bank, heading northwards to make the steep journey up over the mountain not far from the head of the loch and down to Kaimes. Stopping for a break, from their position at the bridge which crossed the river spilling out of the loch, the expanded party had a clear view of the road, although it was often masked for repeated short stretches by small stands of trees.

It was, therefore, mere good fortune that Barcwith happened to have stood to retrieve his water bottle from his saddle, just as riders came into a gap in the cover.

"Hello," he said suspiciously, stopping in his tracks. "Looks like we've got company coming!"

The tone of his voice alone was enough to bring his companions to their feet. Without saying another word, Barcwith extended his arm and pointed to the road, tracing the progress of three riders going at a break-neck pace. The trio were dressed in flowing grey garments which blended so well with shadows that once they reached the cover of the trees, they almost seemed to disappear. Had the others not had them pointed out to them by Barcwith, they might have mistaken the ripple of movement for animals, or a small flock of birds, moving between the trees.

"Up!" yelled Talorcan, with such command in his voice that no-one doubted the seriousness of the situation. "Hunters!"

"Bastard Hounds of the Wild Hunt!" Labhran swore, as Maelbrigt almost threw Taise up into the litter.

"Go!" he commanded Kayna. "Take Taise and ride as fast as you can!"

"No, you go with them too!" Talorcan told him. "There are six of us."

"Five and a boy is no odds against a triad of DeÁine Hunters," Maelbrigt argued. "I'll stay! Labhran, you and Sioncaet get them to Lorne! Don't stop for anything!"

"No!" Taise cried, distraught. She and Sithfrey knew only too well the calibre of the Hunters speeding towards them, and the thought of Maelbrigt coming up against them was enough to make her feel faint.

"You'll never fight *them* off!" Sithfrey said in horror. "Have you no idea what they are?"

Talorcan wedged his steel helmet on before answering, and Sithfrey saw that the nose-guard was shaped to look like a wolf's muzzle, emphasized by the design of the cheek guards. The whole looked like a wolf's head, making its wearer's snarling grin looked downright ferocious as he answered,

"Oh we know *exactly* what they are," with bloodthirsty relish in his tone.

Taise and Sithfrey had no more time to argue as Kayna and Sioncaet seized their respective horse's reins and turned them to the road with Labhran hard on their heels. As they pounded off down the road and Labhran came alongside Taise, she managed to call across to him, even though she was hanging on for grim death to the litter with her good hand.

"*Do* they know, Labhran? Really?"

"What?" he demanded. "That the Hunters are taken from their mothers as soon as they're weaned, and put into training camps where all compassion and humanity is driven out of them? That they're not only fed to build strength and endurance, but are hypnotized so that they feel no pain? That they're introduced to drugs which enable them to go without sleep, and heighten their senses? Have I missed anything?"

Taise could only shake her head miserably, while Sithfrey once again could only wonder at how much these people knew of what was a guarded secret, known only to a few in New Lochlainn. However, Sioncaet added,

"What *you* may not know is that all that comes with a price." He paused to swing the litter horses he was guiding around a particularly nasty hairpin bend, where even he had to duck under the overhanging branches at the roadside. "That punishing regime takes its toll. They die young if their enemies don't catch them. We found that sometimes, if you can force them to keep going, at least one of them might just keel over dead in his tracks, burnt out."

"Not much chance of that here, though," Labhran gasped, as the cold wind took his breath away. "I'd bet that Quintillean, or Anarawd, or whoever it was who sent them, handpicked these ones for this mission – and they'll have picked the ones still in their prime. So shut up and ride!"

Behind them, Maelbrigt with Talorcan's lance had ridden forwards to where the loch-side road joined the main road from the coast. Under the eaves of the woods they sat silently in wait. Tamàs and Decke had arrows nocked and ready, and their quivers slung at an angle ready to reload as soon as the first was let fly. The sound of the galloping horses' hooves was the first giveaway, and the others eased their swords out of their scabbards in readiness.

As the Hunters thundered out of the shadows, Tamàs and Decke let fly. Both arrows found their targets, yet made no difference in the speed with which the riders came on. Neither did the next two arrows, even though Tamàs caught one Hunter in the throat. Blood ran down the front of the grey cloak, but the rider barely faltered. Instead, the Hunters drew their swords as the others plunged out of the wood to meet them. Talorcan was in front, spurring his horse on in his bloodlust to slaughter the DeÁine before him.

However, the Hunter certainly did not expect him to ride headlong into him, using his momentum to carry the two of them tumbling to the ground. As the horses scrambled to their feet and tottered away from the confusion, Talorcan tore into his opponent. At the moment of contact he had lunged at the DeÁine with his sword, but at close quarters the sword was useless, and he let it dangle from the lanyard around his arm. Instead, his other hand came up with a wicked, serrated-edged knife, with which he proceeded to stab and slash at the writhing DeÁine.

Maelbrigt's approach had been more conventional, yet he too used his knife along with his sword, in a two-handed attack which made the most of any and every opening the DeÁine left. Barcwith and Galey made a double attack on the remaining Hunter, which was the one with Tamàs' arrow protruding from its throat. At one point Maelbrigt caught a glimpse of the bizarre sight of young Ad, swinging with both feet off the ground, as he grasped the arrow with both hands and let his full weight hang on it, in an attempt to rip the DeÁine's throat open.

Even so the Hunter did not stop moving until it was almost hacked to pieces by the three of them. Decke had abandoned his bow and was hacking at the back of the Hunter fighting Maelbrigt, until it too gave a final gurgling gasp and fell to the ground, unmoving. Tamàs had fought a different battle, putting yard-long barbed arrow after arrow at point blank range into the DeÁine Talorcan was fighting, each time the Hunter rolled to the top of the scrum, so that, when it too finally collapsed, it looked like it was sprouting spines.

Talorcan climbed to his feet and spat blood onto the floor, along with part of the DeÁine's ear, reminding Maelbrigt of how ferociously his old companion fought when his blood was up. As far as Talorcan was concerned there were no rules of fair play against this enemy, and if his teeth could serve as an additional weapon then he was not shy of using them. Tamàs walked over and began methodically cutting his arrows back out, ready for reuse, while the others took their weapons over to the small roadside stream and washed them clean. Barcwith ran an expert hand over the first of the DeÁine's horses whom he managed to catch.

"This one wouldn't have gone much farther at that pace," he said disapprovingly. Barcwith loved horses with a passion, and hated to see them misused.

"Can we take them with us if we don't ride them?" Maelbrigt asked.

Barcwith sucked his teeth, "I doubt they could cope with the pace even at that," he said. "This one's leg feels awfully hot. It might just be a strain, or it could be something worse."

"Right, let's find my horse and the other one," Talorcan said, as Tamàs came up with the second DeÁine horse. "These animals are used to being stabled. It'd be cruel to leave them to fend for themselves at this time of year – we can't just turn them loose. Tamàs, you and Ad bring them on behind at a pace they can manage, the rest of us will go after Labhran."

Talorcan knew he could rely on the steady Tamàs to do what was needed, and that if necessary he would take the horses to the grange at Doomston to recover, and then press on with Ad to join them at a brisker pace. Maelbrigt, on the other hand, never failed to be amazed at how soft-hearted Talorcan could be to animals and children, when he could be nothing short of downright vicious in a fight. The defenceless had nothing to fear from Talorcan, but their persecutors had better start saying their prayers if he was in the area. Barcwith and Galey were openly triumphant, and Maelbrigt noticed Galey cutting a trophy ear from the Hunter they had cut down, making a mental note to make sure Taise never saw it.

Remounting, the five riders turned their horses once more to the stone-arched bridge, and set off in pursuit of the others. However, they had scarce got beyond the edge of the wood when they heard the sound of metal on metal. Without a word they set their mounts to the gallop, and raced along the road until they came on a fearful sight as they cleared a sweeping bend. Another triad of Hunters must have already been on the eastern side of the loch, perhaps already having been in Ergardia, and been drawn by their sense of the Power in Taise.

Labhran was fighting with frenzied ferocity in the centre, with Kayna battling on his left and Sioncaet on his right, all backed against a huge boulder with a cleft, in which Taise and Sithfrey huddled. Sithfrey had his sword drawn, and Maelbrigt noted with approval that he had made sure that Taise was behind him. This time Sithfrey was going to defend his friend. However, even with their back guarded by the bulk of the stone, and with there being no way the Hunters could get behind them, or even to their sides, the three fighters were having a dire time of it. As the others rode into the fray, Kayna was wrong-footed and stumbled leaving a gap into which one of the Hunters leapt.

As the Hunter raised his blade to hack at Sithfrey and the defenceless Taise, Maelbrigt stood in his saddle, hefted his sword in his hand and then launched it at the Hunter's back like a spear. It took the Hunter unawares and propelled it forward onto the sword Sithfrey was holding up more in hope than expertise. As the Hunter was impaled both ways, Kayna rolled and regained her feet, coming up with knife in hand to plunge it into the neck of the Hunter. She had obviously found the main artery by the fountain of blood that shot out, and by the time she had wrenched the blade out for a second attack, Maelbrigt was alongside her using his strength to pull the Hunter's arms back. Even as its life bled away the DeÁine had had its hands around Sithfrey's throat, and was trying to choke the life out of him, but even a Hunter died when it ran out of blood.

Labhran had managed to finally bring his main opponent down, once Decke adopted Tamàs' tactic of firing arrows into it at close range. Talorcan had aided Sioncaet by the simple expediency of riding up to the Hunter and wrapping both arms around beneath its chin and wrenching its head round, breaking its neck. As it lost the use of its limbs and Talorcan's horse turned, Barcwith and Galey administered the death blows – not taking a chance on the Hunter being defenceless until they were absolutely sure it was dead.

"Nice timing!" Labhran panted, leaning on his sword. "I assume you saw to the others?"

"Feeding the crows!" Barcwith said cheerfully, then noticed Sioncaet looking around. "Tamàs and Ad are bringing the extra horses on slowly. Poor beasts are in bad shape."

Sioncaet gave a nod of comprehension, and the worried look disappeared from his face as he realized that they had sustained no casualties of their own. Taise, however, was shaking like a leaf. When the Hunters had appeared she had tried to call up the Power-fire again, as she had done when the grollican threatened Maelbrigt. Instead of producing the ball of fire, though, she had found her energy draining away like water through sand. Nothing had happened, and now she felt as limp as a fish out of water. Clinging to Maelbrigt to stop herself sliding to the ground, she looked up at him in amazement.

"What *is* this place? And how did you do that? You've just killed *two* triads of Hunters! That's not supposed to be possible!"

"Who says? This is Ergardia, seat of Island power. Hunters stand even less of a chance than normal over here!" Talorcan said with disdain. "We know of plenty of dead ones, don't we lads!"

Thinking of the trophy ear in Galey's saddlebag, Maelbrigt swiftly intervened.

"You only think that because that's what you've always been told," he said.

Labhran looked up from where he was wiping his sword clean on the wet grass.

"Absolutely! You've no idea of the lengths the high ranking DeÁine go to to make sure that the ordinary people know nothing of the extent of their losses against us. When Sioncaet and I were right at the heart of the DeÁine court we knew of Hunters who'd been sent into Brychan and were intercepted, never to be seen again. But you'd be amazed at the reports that were put about. They'd either be simply ignored, so that you'd think they'd done their job and just returned to barracks, or some kind of totally fictitious victory would be concocted – like the assassination of some major Brychan official."

Sithfrey shook his head in astonishment. "Why?" was all he could ask.

"Because if you're running a dictatorship, you can't have others thinking that they could do a better job than you," Talorcan explained. "That's why the lure of having someone who could be a challenger for the leadership worked so well. It's why we knew they wouldn't let me go unchallenged. There can only be one leader. Even in the Abend, Quintillean is top dog."

In a moment of clarity Taise remembered the conversation in Sioncaet's cottage.

"Oh, of course," she gasped. "That's why you could feel the residue of the ward on me! You're half-DeÁine, aren't you!"

"That's me," Talorcan replied bitterly. "Son of the old king's whore! Bastard half-brother to that useless new one, Ruadan. There's one thing for sure, though. If I get that bitch of a mother of ours in my grasp, I won't be sleeping with her like he is! She'll be sleeping with the worms after the way she treated me!"

Chapter 33

Changing Perspectives

Ergardia: Samhainn

It took two days to ship everyone across to Ergardia, and once there their progress was slower than it had been in Rheged with everyone being on foot. There was no way that Ruari had the funds to hire or buy horses for so many men – indeed Ron had only found the mounts he had because of his reputation, and assurances that they would be returned as soon as possible. However, the good news for the men now was that they would not have far to go. Ruari had taken charge of the whole venture, and the Prydein contingent were sad to find that they were leaving Gerard and Edmund behind, although they understood that it was to make sure the next group of refugee Knights came across safely.

With so many other men to deal with, Ruari had introduced Andra to them and asked Oliver to take care of the little monk, so Alaiz found herself with a pleasant companion. Andra was not happy to be parted from his hero after their long journey together, but had the good grace to accept that Ruari had other priorities and not take it out on the others. For the first time in months, Alaiz therefore had someone who could talk about music, paintings and books with her to while away the walk – both agreeing that they wished they had time to stop and paint the scenery.

They were heading straight for the Knights' headquarters on Ergardia, the huge castle of Lorne, sitting in stately splendour on an island in the middle of a loch. One thing about Ergardia being so wooded was that there was no shortage of fuel to light fires with against the winter cold at night, so that the week's walk was bearable if not comfortable. The Rheged granges had emptied their stores and the men were well supplied with rations for the journey, and with Rosin providing her guests with more than enough food, they were well provisioned too. Nothing, however, prepared those coming to Ergardia for the first time for their first sight of Lorne Castle. Having followed the river which drained out of the loch to the sea, they came out of the tree-lined valley at the foot of the loch and gasped in awe.

From above the bulrushes at the shoreline they had a clear view across the wind-ruffled water to the castle. A narrow band of venerable trees grew at the water's edge, but beyond that the walls and towers rose in serried ranks. Great unassailable granite peaks stood straight from the water, topped with battlements at each level. As they came into sight they heard trumpets ring out from watchmen, and boats began to pull away from a quay on one of the nearby islands, for there was more than one island. The surrounding islands were connected by wooden bridges, each with their own landing stages, and covered in more stone buildings which appeared to be barracks.

It was only then that it occurred to Hamelin that there was no sign of any landing place at the castle island itself, but that it was connected to the network of service islands by a pair of bridges, which swung higher than the rest from the top of stone gatehouses on the two nearest islands.

"Sacred Trees, you'd never besiege this place!" he gasped, and received an answering chuckle from Elidyr, who had somehow attached himself to the group.

"No, and if you were halfway sane you wouldn't try," he confirmed.

Ruari stood alone at the water's edge at the front of the long line of soldiers. When the boats were halfway across, and within earshot, a soldier standing in the prow of the lead vessel hailed them.

"Who comes to Lorne?" was the challenge.

"Ealdorman MacBeth, acting Grand Master of the Rheged sept, requesting shelter and sanctuary for my men and myself."

Ruari's reply was formal, and despite his ragged appearance he stood tall and proud, in bearing if not dress every bit the leader.

"Advance and be recognized, Ealdorman MacBeth," was the reply.

Ruari turned smartly to his right, stepped up onto the wooden jetty and walked out to the end as the boat moved towards him. For a heart stopping moment Alaiz gripped Andra's arm, and he hers, as they saw that the reason only half the men were rowing was that the other half had bows, already nocked with arrows, resting on their laps. Obviously the Knights of Ergardia were taking no chances.

"It's him!" a young squire called out in delight and almost upset the boat as he bounded over the legs of the rowers once they were close enough, and leapt onto the jetty to fling his arms around Ruari's neck. Except it was no squire.

"Matti!" Ruari gasped in surprise, and then swung the lithe figure in black off her feet in a tight hug and planting a big kiss on her cheek. "You're safe! Thank the Trees!" Then felt vaguely embarrassed as his body registered his pleasure at seeing her in a rather visible way. So much for not *thinking* about how he felt! But that only provoked another unwelcome thought that maybe she would think he only lusted after her. Sacred Trees, but life got complicated sometimes!

"You didn't do that to me!" another voice said, as a burly man levered himself more ponderously onto the wooden landing. Ruari laughed to cover his disconcertion as he realised how close to them Will was, pointing out that Will had had a knife to his throat the first time they had met up again. Matti, however, did wonder if Will's comment had been aimed at her just a little too. By this time the sergeant had come ashore and quickly ascertained how many men stood trailing back out of sight. Waving the rest of the boats up to the beach he directed Ruari's men forward, who began to fan out along the loch edge. It would have taken too long for them to all embark from the jetty, and it seemed petty to make the already weary men walk all the way to the north of the loch to the bigger jetties.

"We'll send more boats straight across for the rest," the sergeant told Ruari, "but Master Brego wants to see you and your close companions straight away."

With that, Ruari, Andra, the Prydein company and Elidyr, were split between the two foremost boats with Will and Matti, and were pulled swiftly across the protecting water. At the landing stage beneath the protection of a stout portcullis, Iago stood waiting with an enormous grin on his face.

"Sergeant Iago!" Ruari called out his pleasure at seeing the other man again. He stepped up onto dry land and clasped Iago's hand. "You've no idea how pleased I was to find it was you who was escorting Lady Montrose!"

However, further words had to wait as Grand Master Brego had come to meet his fellow leader of Knights at the portal, rather than having him brought to him. Brego also clasped Ruari's hand, his lined face breaking into a wide smile.

"By the Trees, MacBeth, it's good to see you again. We all prayed the rumours of your death were false, but few had any hope that you'd survived."

"I fear I must impose upon your hospitality, sire," Ruari said, "and at a bad time of year too."

"Nonsense! We may become a little tight for space, depending on how many men you've brought with you, but in this weather there's no question of billeting men out on the loch-side. Supply-wise we're well provisioned. Even with additional mouths to feed we've enough in the cellars to last a substantial siege. And we've much to talk about!"

"That we have," Ruari agreed. "This is Captain Oliver Aleyne. Hugh de Burh has sent him from Prydein and I fear the news from there isn't good either."

Brego's smile disappeared and was replaced with a worried frown. Nevertheless, he clasped Oliver's hand too, and extended a warm welcome to him and his Knights. With a request to Matti to take care of his new female guest, Brego ushered Ruari, Oliver and Will off towards his office, beckoning Elidyr along too as the slim young Forester appeared off the second boat.

The two women faced one another as a stream of men disembarked passed them.

"Are you the lady MacBeth said could fight me to a standstill?" Alaiz asked the older woman nervously.

Matti threw her head back and laughed.

"Did he say that? Typical! He spends most of the time telling me that any halfway decent soldier would make mincemeat of me! I suspect it's so that I won't get complacent and stop practicing." Matti became serious. "He always said that you didn't have to know how to use a sword to die by one. Until now I never understood the full implications of that, and why he was so insistent that I should know how to defend myself as best as possible. A fighting chance was what he called it, but in the last couple of months that's what's kept me alive."

Alaiz nodded mutely, yet her expression told Matti that the pretty little redhead had also seen more bloodshed and violence than she had ever been prepared for. Tucking her arm through Alaiz's, she steered her away from the jetty and up to the more comfortable quarters. The stewards were more than a little harassed at having to find so many men space at short notice and so Matti took Alaiz into her own room. There they were able to have hot caff and warm up by the fire as they got to know one another. Matti reckoned there must be a good ten years between them in ages, yet there was sufficient common ground for them to be able to talk easily.

Listening to Alaiz's story, it dawned on Matti that she could have fared far worse with Will than she had. At least he had given her the space to live her life and have some say in how her household was run. She thought it strange the way that Alaiz skirted around what rank her 'husband' held, but it was pretty obvious that whoever he was he was very high in the Prydein's aristocracy. All her instincts told her that it would be important to find that out. Not yet though. As someone who had led such a restricted life and then been thrown out into the wide world, Alaiz had more need of a friend than an inquisitor.

Ruari and Brego remained closeted in conference with their most senior men for many days up in the dragon-doored eyrie. However, Oliver had been allowed to escape after initial questioning, for which, he confessed to the others, he was very grateful.

"I've never felt so much like a mouse caught between two hawks," he told Hamelin and his other friends on the second evening as they sat eating dinner in the great refectory. "If you think Master Hugh can be stern you should see those two in action. Master Brego may look like everyone's favourite uncle, but put a sword in his hand and I reckon he'd fillet many a younger man without breaking into a sweat!"

Friedl broke off a chunk of oat bread and dunked it into the rich oxtail soup.

"If I remember some of what the older Knights used to say," he said after munching contentedly on the chunk, "our Master Hugh was the Grand Master who was the expert tactician. When it comes to devious schemes and battle plans he's got no peer. That's not the same as being the one leading men into battle, though, is it?"

Bertrand poured himself more of the malty dark beer, and handed the pitcher to Theo as his brow furrowed in concentration.

"How old would you say Brego is?" he asked his friends.

"Hard to say," Hamelin mused.

"Mid to late sixties," Elidyr said, plonking himself and his beer down beside them.

"Flaming Trees! Really?" Theo gasped in astonishment.

"You'd never guess to look at him," Oliver said in equal surprise.

Elidyr grinned as Bertrand began to nod pensively.

"That would make sense, though," the older of the Prydein Knights pondered aloud.

"It would?" a confused Theo asked.

"Mmmm…." Bertrand mused, but it was Elidyr who filled in what Bertrand had guessed.

"You're not remembering your history, gentlemen. Think back to the accounts of Moytirra. It was your Master Hugh who took over the planning of the battle when it all went haywire. The so-called King of Brychan rashly led from the front and got himself killed, and it was the dashing Jarl of Prydein who led the soldiers in to reclaim the body. (That, incidentally was when your Jarl decided that he should become a king, because he felt that, as senior noble there, the role fell to him!) But while he was off charging around being chivalrous, Hugh had retreated to the high ground and could see what was about to happen.

"Master Brego was the second-in-command to the senior Grand Master there, and they were trying to stem the flood of DeÁine that threatened to engulf all of them. But Hugh could see that our forces had gone too far out onto the plain of southern New Lochlainn. Too far, and it allowed the DeÁine to begin to surround us. He sent a message to the old Master who wouldn't listen to the idea of a retreat from someone younger, but then he was cut down and Brego took over and he led the retreat to the river.

"Hugh couldn't lead. He wasn't experienced enough in the thick of battle, but that's never been where his strength lies. He saw that they needed to deceive the DeÁine into thinking they were on the run. The Jarl of Rheged led the Islands' army back to the next river where the foothills of the mountains begin. In the meantime, Brego led the Order in a mad dash to take up positions hidden in the folds of the hills. When the DeÁine were drawn into the killing ground, the Jarl turned and stood his ground, but it was Brego and his men who led the charge. There's an old sergeant – that's him sitting over by the fire – who can tell you all about it. It's said Quintillean himself still carries the scar where Brego nearly chopped his head off!"

"So it is the same Brego!" a satisfied Bertrand said.

"That it is," Elidyr confirmed. "It's said he still sleeps with a vest of mail on to prevent himself from going soft. Personally I think there's as much chance of a piece of granite going soft than him!"

In the following days they were to hear even more stories which made them feel they were in the company of lions. Nor were all the tales they were to hear in the coming days about the past. For some, the present pressed on them just as heavily.

It took Will four days to find time to escape Brego's clutches, but finally he found time to entice Matti away from orientating Alaiz and get her alone. Ever since their reunion, he had become increasingly bothered by memories of the life they had led until the fateful day when he had brought Eleanor and Wistan to stay. Alone in his bed at night, it had been his own desires for some female company which had prompted the unwelcome thoughts, yet once they were there he could not get rid of them. He had taken his pleasures in life as he had wanted them, but what had Matti done all those years? The awful thought that he had condemned her to the life of a nun, with no warmth or close human contact now played on his conscience. Had she had any lovers, he wondered? No child had appeared, but then she might have used the herbs he had heard of. But what if she had not? The only way was to ask her, although it was a conversation he was dreading.

Taking Matti by the arm, he tried to find somewhere quiet. Her bedroom was no use, for she had ended up sharing with Alaiz – perhaps because Ruari had hinted that the young Knight Hamelin was more than a little besotted with Alaiz, and Brego thought the presence of the other woman would discourage any escalation of the affections. Oliver was certainly being coy about whoever she was, but equally emphatic that it would be disastrous if the affair ever came to anything. Yet today of all days, Matti had vacated her room to allow them some time in private. Will's mood was not improved by the hive of activity which the castle had become. He would not have thought it possible in such a vast warren for there to be no free spaces, no quiet corners. Yet every corner they turned, every stair they climbed, there was still someone or other doing something. In the end they found themselves headed for the roof.

Grabbing one of the fur-lined capes supplied for the lookouts, hanging on the hooks at the bottom of the final stairs, Will draped it around Matti's shoulders, then grabbed one for himself.

"Will? What in the Islands is the matter with you?" Matti asked, becoming worried by his behaviour. Had the Helm taken hold of him again?

"I just want to *talk* to you!" Will muttered in exasperation. "Sacred Trees! Is there no space empty in this place?"

Out on the open roof the wind cut like a knife, yet even here two men stood at opposite ends of the rectangular space, keeping warm by huddling close to braziers of hot coals. Walking over to one of them, with Matti's arm still firmly in his grip, Will said,

"Go and talk to your mate!"

"I'm sorry, sire, I …"

"I'm General Montrose and I'm giving you an order, so you can blame me if anyone finds out. Now hop it!"

The man began to move away, but still giving Will sideways looks.

"She's my wife!" Will growled at him, at which the man made a soundless 'oh' as if to say 'that's alright, then', although Will could not imagine even the most ardent of lovers wanting to expose even the smallest amount of flesh to the icy draft searing its way across the roof.

"Well?" Matti asked.

"I want to ask you something. ….Except I don't know a good way to do it, so I'm just going to have to come out with it." Will looked excruciatingly uncomfortable. "Have you ever had a lover since we've been married?"

Matti must have looked as though she was about to bite his head off because he rushed on,

"I'm not judging you. I know I've been a lousy husband to you. And I know you've known about the women I've spent time with. It's just …I always thought you'd done the same …"

"And now you're wondering? It's a bit late isn't it? What's brought this on?"

"You were so glad to see Ruari," Will said, shuffling his feet and avoiding her eye. "I've never seen you smile like that. But I don't mean you and him … It might have been someone else … But if it was, I wouldn't …."

"I haven't…" Matti cut across him.

"…Haven't?"

"…Been unfaithful to you. …Ever."

Will's groan was not quite the reaction Matti had expected.

"Sacred Trees, you're not still a …"

"…No, but that was before you …"

"…Before?"

"… Nice lad …from my father's stables …and not very often then."

"Why not?"

"Why not?"

"Yes, why not?" Will gulped. "It's not other women is it?"

Suddenly the ludicrousness of the conversation hit Matti and she fell about laughing. That confused Will even more, and raised astonished eyebrows from the two sentries at the other end of the roof. Wiping the tears of laughter from her eyes she was finally able to splutter out,

"No, not other women!" Then she looked at Will closely and realized what it had cost him to come here and ask her, which sobered her up quickly. "It was as much that I never met anyone I wanted to …well …*do* anything with. You scared me when we first married. You were always so angry that I didn't know what you'd do if I had an affair and then got pregnant. But then I looked around, and to be honest there weren't many men who came up to my expectations."

"Not even Ruari?"

Matti shook her head at Will's naivety.

"Ruari *was* the expectation, you idiot! The man who can talk to me. The man who wouldn't just leap on me, screw me witless and then pretend nothing had happened when the consequences appeared. The man who sees *me*! And surely you know Ruari well enough to know he'd never, ever, seduce his best friend's wife! Flaming Trees, Will, he'd cut his own hand off before he betrayed you!"

"But would you rather it had been him, not me, you'd married?"

Whatever Matti's reply would have been to that, however, was halted as she looked over his shoulder and blinked, then spun to the sentries.

"Talorcan's back!" she called across in relief, pointing to the road from the forest that emerged on the western side of the loch.

Turning, she ran down the stairs calling back to Will,

"We must tell the Master!"

Will sighed and looked down on the approaching party, then shrugged and began to plod dejectedly after her. Was she that pleased to see *everyone*? Was he the only one that she was *not* pleased to see?

By the time Talorcan's band of men had reached the jetty, there was already a reception committee waiting for them. Will had joined the main party of Master Brego, Ruari, Oliver and Elidyr, along with several of the senior Knights. Looking across the water he saw a tall, dark horseman dismount and raise his hand in greeting, then gesture back at his company. Now that they could see his companions clearly it became obvious that there was someone travelling in a litter, and those who had seen him depart also noticed that the party had since altered in numbers. Moments later he was joined by another man wearing the black, not quite so tall but more solid, who walked out onto the jetty exuding an air of command.

"Is that Talorcan?" Will asked Matti.

She shook her head.

"No, Talorcan's the first man who waved, I've no idea who this man is."

"Well I do," Ruari said in wonder, "and I never thought I'd see him again!"

"Indeed," Master Brego agreed, "we live in strange times when you rise from the dead and Maelbrigt leaves his mountain retreat…"

Brego, Ruari and several others gasped as three more men stepped forward onto the jetty and threw the hoods of their heavy cloaks back.

Bertrand whispered, "DeÁine!" making others of the guests instinctively feel for swords they were not wearing, but Brego held up his hand to check them before they dashed for the armoury.

"Yes, DeÁine maybe, but two of those I know and trust. The taller of them is a member of our own Order, whatever he looks like. That's Labhran, and the small man next to him is the legendary Sioncaet!"

Even Ruari gasped in surprise at that.

"Sioncaet the Jester?" he exclaimed, "What brings him here?"

"I can't begin guess," Brego mused, "but it's rare we see him this far afield. Still, we won't have long to wait. Here they come."

The boats from the castle had reached the opposite bank and the passengers had begun to embark. As the boats drew closer on the return journey the watchers on the shore could now see that the occupant of the litter was a woman, and that another woman dressed as a Knight sat holding her hand. Brego turned to Matti,

"Another such as you, Lady Montrose! If this keeps up we're going to have to start making women's barracks too!"

Matti could not keep the smile from her face,

"And why not Master?" she teased.

Mercifully he was saved from having to answer that by the arrival of the boats. Talorcan leapt nimbly ashore before his boat was tied up, and strode the short stretch up the jetty to the Master.

"We found no rumour of strangers passing through in the south, sire," he told Brego. "It was as we were returning home that we ran into Maelbrigt and Labhran and saw the worst of it."

Maelbrigt had joined him at the end of the jetty, saying as Brego clasped his hands in welcome,

"The Abend are out in force! Taise," he gestured back to the tall woman who was being helped carefully ashore, "was once an acolyte of the Abend before they tortured her. She recognized Quintillean heading for the west coast as we travelled here. He was in disguise and travelling with a young monk and a boy novice but it was unmistak…"

"No!" a voice howled in horror. "Oh no! Dear spirits no!"

Andra elbowed his way to the front of the assembly, tears already starting in his eyes.

"Please tell me. Not a boy about this big, light brown hair, skinny for his age…"

"…with the monk up to about my shoulder, and blonde hair and a cherubic face?" Ruari finished for him and equally as anxious.

"Yes, that sounds right," Taise's soft voice replied as she came to join them. "It was dusk, but the moon was up enough to see clearly by, and it wasn't fully dark." She took in Ruari's grimace and Andra's sob. "I'm so sorry, were they friends of yours?"

"We got the captain at the fort above Kames to send out men straight away, but we lost all trace of them," Maelbrigt apologized. "Had we known these were not willingly with him we would've sent a message on ahead. I'm sorry, MacBeth. I know if you're involved they must be important, but we couldn't risk Quintillean knowing who we were bringing here, either. We've had some narrow escapes ourselves, not least avoiding two triads of Hunters, which we only survived by the chance meeting with Talorcan here. You need to know what's happened."

Brego found himself ushering newcomers up to his study yet again, and for the first time in almost a generation the great room felt full, as extra chairs were brought in, and the stewards scurried around with refreshments. As the sorting out took place, Matti had another chance to look closely at the room. Behind the Master's desk a stunningly woven flag showing a dragon cross, of exactly the same design as those on the doors, was suspended from the wall. Yet looking at the design from below this time she noticed something new. From the bottom of the dragon's tail a typical heraldic banner curled, but unlike every other one she had seen before, it was devoid of any motto and remained blank. When Ruari put his hand on her shoulder to draw her to a seat, she asked him why.

"Because it embodies the Order," he replied. "We make a verbal promise to honour, protect and serve, and our word is enough to bind us to that. It's supposed to hold us to those ideals, even in the darkest places where no flag can be flown, and no written laws hold sway. It's a silent motto that doesn't need to be said because it's in the very being of every Knight, from the highest to the lowest."

As he ushered her to a seat, Matti could see that as many Knights as possible were going to have a say, and hear what the news was too, in this spirit of serving and protecting. If anyone had thought this would be a swift debriefing they were soon going to be disabused of the idea. The Prydein contingent was summoned, along with senior Knights who had served with Ruari and witnessed the slaying of Michael.

As each group told the assembled group of their own bad news, the mood became ever darker. However, Maelbrigt's news was amongst the strangest, for he kept the news of the copy of the manuscript until last. Suddenly Taise found herself the unwelcome centre of attention. Talorcan's fierce demeanour had bothered her on their meeting, but being in the largest castle she had ever seen, and to find it stuffed full of hard and lean Knights who all hated the DeÁine with a passion, was beyond nerve-racking.

However, all the people before her were kindly solicitous for her well-being. The tall blonde woman, who seemed to be married to one of the men, and her shorter red-haired friend, had both made it clear to the men that they would not tolerate anyone distressing her, and their word seemed to count. The blonde and Kayna had instantly taken to one another and now Kayna stood like a guard behind her on the other side. The Grand Master, too, was nothing but courteousness, having already insisted that the infirmarer come and re-dress her arm immediately.

Now he came to stand before her and bent over to speak to her.

"Do you really think you can translate this work?" he asked gently.

"I'm not sure," she replied. "Given time, possibly, but I won't lie to you and say I can do it for certain. It's been many years since I studied regularly and this was always reputed to be one of the stranger texts the Abend were looking for."

"But you will *try*?" he pressed more firmly.

She nodded, but Kayna answered for her.

"You don't need to pressure Taise! She knows how important it is to find out what's in that manuscript and she'll do her very best, alright! All she's doing is telling you not to expect miracles. She's already made a start, but it's going to take time."

"Don't worry little firebrand!" Brego said, amused now, "You don't need to spring to your friend's defence. No-one will harm her here, you have my word on that."

"Little firebrand?" Kayna bridled, ready to take offence at the first hint of him being patronizing.

Brego gave a sad chuckle.

"Your father was always known as a firebrand amongst those of us who trained with him. You're the image of him if ever I saw it! He's one of the great many friends I miss in these dark days, but it's good to know his spirit lives on, even if in a very different form!"

The wind having been taken out of her sails by that, Kayna subsided onto a cushion on the floor at Taise's feet, as she heard soft chuckles from Maelbrigt and Labhran.

"I'll help all I can," Sithfrey's voice sounded strained, as he too suffered terrible nerves from the surrounding company.

Brego was not so absorbed in the larger issues that he missed this. He turned to Maelbrigt and Labhran.

"I have both your words that these two are absolutely trustworthy?"

Sithfrey winced, waiting for Maelbrigt to take this opportunity to exact revenge for having brought the Abend down on Taise. Yet to his amazement Maelbrigt said,

"You do. Taise I've known for years now, and I know how she suffered at the hands of the Abend. But Sithfrey's suffered too, in a different way. They both have very real reasons to want to help us."

Labhran gave a curt nod and added,

"In fact, I would suggest that they don't leave here – not for our protection but for theirs. The DeÁine have Hunters searching for both of them, which is the first reason. The second is that they've been subjected to the Abend trying to subvert their minds – Sithfrey in New Lochlainn, and Taise there and in Celidon. This is one of the few places fortified *and* surrounded by water. While they're here, they can't be forced to do something against their will which they might bitterly regret later."

"There's also another thing," Sioncaet's light voice seemed to cut through the tension, so that several people blinked, having forgotten he was there in their focus on the two other DeÁine. All eyes swivelled to him questioningly as he said pointedly, "The library! You want them to translate that manuscript. It'll be so much easier if you give them access to the library where they'll have texts they can compare it with."

"By the Trees, that's a big thing you ask," Dana, Brego's second-in-command said in astonishment. "Few of our own are permitted access to that!"

"I know and I don't ask lightly or in disrespect," Sioncaet replied, coming forward to stand before the fire so that he could address the whole room. He stepped nimbly up onto the seat worked into the side carvings of the fireplace so that he could see as many as possible. He took a deep breath and projected his voice clearly across the room.

"Some of you know me and some of you don't. For the ones who don't, all I can say is that if you have doubts ask those I've served with later. But for now, heed what I'm about to say.

"We have to act to deal with this situation. And by deal with it, I don't just mean move the DeÁine Treasures to another location away from the Abend. Our ancestors did that the last time, and look what's happened. In our journey here *we've* seen the danger. But the danger isn't simply what the Abend can summon against us. It's the danger from ourselves."

Several people looked puzzled and turned to their neighbours in confusion, but Sioncaet pressed on. "The danger is that *we* forget! The Power extends life even as it corrupts and twists, and that means that even the current Abend have their *own* memories of things, whereas we can only rely on what our grandparents have passed on, and theirs before them, or remembered to record. When Maelbrigt and Labhran fought the grollican they were saying words that they've been taught, yet with no understanding of what those individual words mean. And we were lucky that both of them are from the northern Islands, where at least that much is retained. You," he pointed to Oliver and Hamelin, "would you have had any idea of what to do, if it had been you who encountered the Abend's resurrected fiend?"

The two younger Knights ruefully shook their heads.

"No, and that's no shame on either of you personally. It's because in our life spans, it's been so long since we last needed such knowledge that it seems irrelevant. Yet now we find we need to know. With Taise and Sithfrey's help we might just reclaim enough to deal with the Abend, even though the cost may be high. But what would happen if we leave these things hidden for another ten generations or more? No more Taise who's studied with the Abend. No more Knights who know the old words. But the Abend, *these* Abend, the very same ones, could still be alive! What chance will our great-great grandchildren's grandchildren, or beyond, have then?"

He let the words hang in the silence for a moment before saying,

"We don't just have to deal with the Abend, for they will surely not forget the Treasures and the Power they contain. We have to *destroy* the Treasures!"

This time the room erupted, as everyone seemed to be speaking at once until someone's voice from the back of the crowd called out,

"Can you be sure the Abend live so long?" as someone else challenged Sioncaet with,

"And how do we destroy something that holds so much Power?"

Before Sioncaet could reply, Master Brego raised his voice.

"How do we know they live so long? My friends, how long ago was it that the DeÁine left the Islands and left us in peace? Five hundred years! Yet I tell you no word of a lie, Quintillean was there!"

The majority of the company was dumbfounded, although certain of them exchanged knowing glances. Master Brego nodded his head sagely,

"Yes, he was there. Why do you think he burns so fiercely with the passion to reclaim these lands? He remembers when we were subject to his people. Crushed under their heel, and as powerless as the poor unfortunates in New Lochlainn are now. But we fought back! We took their Treasures and hid them. We, with the last few of the Ancients, used our own Treasures both in defence and to counter-balance those of the DeÁine. And for the first time the DeÁine suffered a setback. Yet remember, it was a setback, not a defeat!"

"And there lies another of our problems," Sioncaet continued. "How many of you even know how to use your own Treasures anymore? But use them we must if we are to destroy the DeÁine ones. Yet here we are, faced with the knowledge that the DeÁine may have found a way to cancel the power of our Treasures and render them useless. What hope do we have then? And yet you question whether we should let Taise and Sithfrey into the library? We *have* to know what the Abend may be planning to do to neutralize our only chance of defeating them, so that we can ensure that never happens."

"And we have very little time left," Ruari said, coming to stand by Sioncaet. "Tancostyl already has the Helm! How long before the others get their hands on more?"

Chapter 34

Fear of Failure

Ergardia: Samhainn

A day later, Taise and Sithfrey found themselves being led by Master Brego and Sioncaet deep into the heart of the great fortress. Maelbrigt and Labhran were with them, as was Ruari with Andra, Ruari having pointed out that Andra had spent most of his life working on manuscripts in the monasteries of Rheged, and might well be of great use. Down spiral staircases and along corridors they wound, until at last they came to a single solid oak door, unprepossessing in its simplicity. Brego took an intricately worked key from his pocket and inserted it in the lock. The mechanism turned with a well-oiled click, and the door swung open to reveal a small antechamber. The group entered, and Brego locked the door behind them before proceeding to the one opposite.

As this door swung open all but Sioncaet, Labhran and Brego gasped. Before them was a great cavern, flickering in the light of many securely encased oil lamps. A bent and wizened man hurried over to greet them and was introduced by Brego as the head librarian. Walking out into the room, Taise, Sithfrey and Andra could scarcely contain their excitement, as their constantly moving gaze took in the sheer scale of this repository. The whole place must have been quarried out of the solid rock of the island, for the ceiling was one expanse of stone, yet there were cunningly worked, invisible vents which kept the air fresh, and prevented the whole place becoming damp.

Around the continuous orbit of the circular wall, shelves rose first to as high as a man could comfortably reach, and then for the same height twice again, with each tier served by solid wooden walkways anchored into the rock face alongside the shelving. In front of these towering cliffs of learning there were great tables, each capable of taking the largest map or manuscript fully extended. Then down the middle of the room, in two great rows, rose tall freestanding wooden cases with end pillars carved like trees, whose upper shelves were reached by wooden stairs on wheels. Suddenly Sithfrey voiced his wonder as his eyes started to take it all in.

"Look Taise! They have real *books*!"

Andra and Taise stood open-mouthed as the import of what they were seeing sank in. All their lives they had been used to seeing pieces of vellum or parchment written on, and then simply rolled and sealed. Only rarely was the material used cut to size and then bound into a leather or metal binding to make a true book, for the cost was enormous. Yet here, only the works in the central aisle were rolled manuscripts. All around the walls they were looking at hundreds upon thousands of spines of *bound* books!

"This is priceless!" Andra whispered in awe. "Dear Spirits, no wonder you keep it hidden! This room would buy the whole of the Islands, and then more, on the price of the books alone! And the knowledge…!"

Taise walked over to the nearest shelf on the wall and reverently eased a book out. Balancing it with great care on her bandaged arm she opened the front cover.

"It's paper!" she gasped. "And look at the quality! This couldn't have been made in over a thousand years!"

"Except it's not paper," the librarian said, coming over to stand by her, enjoying the opportunity to show his treasures to someone who appreciated what they were seeing. "We have no idea what it is. It might even be paper that's been treated in some way, but ordinary paper would've crumbled to dust after that length of time."

Taise felt her voice wavering with emotion as she asked, awestruck,

"Is this the work of the Ancients?"

The librarian nodded,

"As near as we can tell, yes, although none of us can read it now. It's my greatest joy and sorrow combined. Look at it," he waved his arm at the vast array, towering above them. "All that knowledge! Here within our grasp, and all of it useless because we can't read it!" He shook his head despairingly. "We care for it, and keep it safe, in the vain hope that one day we'll work out how to read the language of those who lived here before the great land split that formed the Islands. Maybe we might even find out what happened. What great disaster befell them that they disappeared. Wouldn't that be something?"

"Indeed it would," Brego concurred, "but for now we have a more pressing emergency of our own, so I'm entrusting these people to your care Master Librarian. They have my permission to look at *anything* they think might be useful. Anything at all. They're to have free access any time of day or night. The only restriction is that nothing is to be taken *out* of the library," he turned to the others, "and that now goes for your copy of the manuscript! We dare not go back and try to bring the original here, and if we did you couldn't use it, so that copy is our only record, and for that reason it will be treated as being as valuable as the oldest books in here." The three scholars were by no means deterred by this, looking rather more like children let loose in the kitchen on baking day with a license to eat all the cakes they wanted.

"I think we might as well leave them to it," Maelbrigt said to the others with a smile, "we're only in the way."

"We'll be lucky if they remember to come out to eat by the look of them!" Ruari said in affectionate amusement, as he watched Andra's expression of small-boy wonderment.

Ruari had spoken with more truth than he realized, and by the end of the first week the three were having to be forcibly extracted from the library at meal times. Red- and bleary-eyed they emerged, bolting their food down before disappearing into the bowels of the earth again. However, in short order they had translated one passage, which worried everyone when Taise presented their findings on the fourth evening.

"There's something that looks like poetry that we're still struggling with," she said, standing in the great office, flanked by Sithfrey and Andra, "but this bit we think we've got. The lines read, '*Pure in blood, pure in heart, without desire for the world, they hold the fate of the Islands within them…*' then something that got smudged in the burning."

Sithfrey took over.

"Knowing the Abend as we do, we think they will have read this as the need to sacrifice someone pure – in other words a virgin – to neutralize the power of a Treasure."

Taise chipped in again,

"Of course that might not be the *right* interpretation, but it's the one we think the Abend will make."

Sithfrey continued. "We think that the Abend aren't just looking for their own Treasures, they're looking for the Island ones too."

Andra looked as miserable as Ruari and Matti had ever seen as he added, "Quintillean probably couldn't believe his luck when he practically fell over two members of the Rheged royal family who were already on the run and still physically pure. He's going to kill them in some really nasty way, isn't he?"

Despite Brego and Ruari pointing out that this would not happen for some time, for the Abend had to get their hands on all the Treasures first, nobody felt much like food after that. Straight after the meal, the three researchers disappeared back to the library, spurred on by the thought that they might find something which would give their friends a head start on finding the lost boys.

Yet Andra could not concentrate, and the next day it was even worse. Every time he looked at the words before him he found them melting away, and the vision of Wistan's frightened little face floating in their place. If he had been worried before, he was going frantic now. How long had it been since Taise had seen him with Quintillean? Two, perhaps three weeks, and how much farther could they have gone in that time? Master Brego had sent birds out to every port and the Knights guarding the entry points to Ergardia, but was that enough? Someone should be looking for the two boys *now*.

Ironically, he thought of Kenelm as a boy, even though he himself was less than half a decade older, and not much wiser in the ways of the world. Not much, but enough to know that he would have sensed the danger in Quintillean now, even though he had been fooled by Tancostyl back at the court. He fidgeted on his seat, which caused Taise to look up just as he pushed his work away and stood up.

"What's the matter?" Taise asked.

"I'm going to look for Wistan." Andra declared.

"What?" Taise gasped. "Now?"

"Now!" Andra said very firmly. "Someone should have gone back when you first came and told us they were with that Abend wizard …demon …mage …whatever that evil creature is. I know there are bigger things at stake than two small boys, and I don't blame Master Brego and Ruari for not putting them above the lives of all the other people on the Islands. I'm not that short-sighted or naïve – or at least not as bad as I was before I met Lady Montrose," he said with a deprecating smile. "But if they're worrying about the big things, then someone has to worry about the small people. You don't need me here. You two are far better at doing this sort of thing than me. You *are* DeÁine! If you can't figure out how the DeÁine think there's no chance of me being able to add anything. So I might as well do something *really* useful."

With that he got up and walked out of the door. For a stunned moment Taise and Sithfrey simply sat staring at one another in amazement. Then Sithfrey gasped,

"He can't go after Quintillean alone! He'll be eaten alive!"

Jumping to their feet the two of them ran out of the library, but there was no sign of which way Andra had gone. Neither of them knew exactly where he had been quartered either. Taise gave Sithfrey a small shove towards the corridor while she headed for the stairs.

"Go and warn the gatekeepers!" she told Sithfrey. "We could search all day in this place and not find him, but if he's leaving he's got to take a boat!"

"Where are you going?"

"To get Maelbrigt, or that Knight Andra came with, MacBeth."

At that Taise turned on her heels and ran up the stairs. Why did this place have to be such a maze? Twice she took a wrong turn, and as she asked her way on the second mistake, the soldier told her Ruari and Maelbrigt were closeted with Master Brego.

"I'm sorry," he said, "but there's no way they'll let you in there."

Taise almost screamed with frustration. Really, this was taking security to ridiculous lengths! Turning a corner at the run she collided with Kayna and Matti.

"What the…!" Kayna swore as she caught Taise before she fell over.

"Oh, thank the Spirits!" Taise gasped. "It's Andra! He's run off to go and find Wistan!"

In panting breaths she told the two other women what had happened. Instantly they caught her urgency, and turning back the way she had come Kayna called to Matti,

"Take Taise down to the landing stage and try to stop him!"

"What about you?" Matti replied, already guiding Taise away.

"I'm going to get Maelbrigt and MacBeth – and no uppity door-keep is going to get in *my* way!"

Taise followed Matti as they raced down the stairs and along the passages, until they came out onto the landing stage beneath the nearest barracks. Matti thought this would be the place closest to Andra's quarters, but there was no sign of him. Stepping out of the doorway into the biting cold, she walked out onto the empty jetty. Across on the next barrack island she could see Sithfrey on that jetty looking about him too. Catching his eye she raised her hands in question, but he shook his head.

"We must've missed him," she said to Taise in frustration. The two stood in the icy wind, ignoring their lack of warm coats, as they scoured the deserted opposite shore for any sign of him. Yet the boat-keeper swore that no-one had come to him, and it was just as she and Taise turned back that Andra appeared behind them, lugging a pack and swathed in a heavy coat.

"Oh, Brother Andra!" Matti gasped in relief.

"Don't try to stop me, Lady Montrose. Someone has to go after Wistan and you're all too busy, and anyway he's my responsibility."

The sound of running feet made them both pause. Ruari appeared with Kayna and Maelbrigt hard on his heels, and Will and Labhran not far behind.

"What in the Islands do you think you're doing?" Ruari demanded. "You'll get yourself killed!"

"Maybe so," Andra riposted, "But at least I'll have *tried* to do something for Wistan!"

"Patience, brother! We *are* trying!" an exasperated Ruari tried to assure him.

"Yes, but how much longer are you going to wait before you send someone after them?" Andra demanded. "It's been *weeks* since they were last seen. They could be off this Island altogether by now!"

"Indeed they might," Labhran said, stepping up to Andra and placing a reassuring hand on his arm, "but we think not. The Abend have terrible trouble with sea crossings even when the sea's like a millpond. Those of us who know them think that, however much Quintillean wants to get off Ergardia, he wouldn't risk the crossing in weather like we've had.

"You've not seen much of it here, but for the last fortnight the west coast has been pounded by wild gales. All the fishing fleets are in port, as are the few ferries between the western islands. We can't put a whole troop in every port, but we will hear as soon as he makes a move, and we'll know where he left from and where he's going to. Even if he gets on the transport which goes across into the inner bay of Brychan and travels down the coast, you can be sure he'll be off at the first port of call. There's no way that Quintillean will stay on water a second longer than he has to."

"But Wistan's so little!" Andra protested. "He's been through so much! He's seen his mother murdered in front of his eyes, he himself has been hunted and attempted to be killed, and now he's who knows where, with a cousin he hardly knows and a madman! *Someone* should be *looking after* him!"

Matti put her arm around Andra's thin shoulders and hugged him tight.

"I know," she said. "And we *will* send someone, brother Andra, I promise."

"*I'll* go."

Every head turned to the voice, where Will stood, head up and resolute.

"I'll go. I should have been there right from the start. I should have seen the danger to Wistan and Eleanor. After all, I was the one who brought them to my castle to keep them safe. They were placed in my care. I *can't* go back to Rheged, so *I'll* follow them as soon as we know where they are. And Trees help me, that bastard Quintillean is going to regret the day he decided to kidnap those two!"

Andra looked as though he believed what had been said for the first time that day, but for Will it was the expression on Matti's face that held him. Her smile was an indicator that he had made the right choice more than anything anyone else said. In all their years together he had never seen that expression, but today Matti was proud of him, and it was worth the wait.

So while Will planned what he would need to take, the others had little they could do but revel in the luxury of having spare time, although the Knights were taking full advantage of the castle's practice yards and halls. Or at least that was what the Prydein Knights thought they were doing until the next day. As Oliver went through the warming up exercises with Friedl, and Hamelin partnered Theo, they suddenly found Ruari and Maelbrigt scrutinizing them. Whatever the two more experienced Knights saw, they obviously thought it needed improving, for before the four younger Knights had finished doing footwork exercises, the pair had taken over directing them. Bertrand had managed to escape their clutches, since he had already taken himself off to the castle's sword-master for instruction, but the others found themselves being challenged like never before.

"Holy Spirits! This is embarrassing!" Oliver gasped as he subsided on the side bench next to Hamelin on the third day after that, as Theo took his place. Removing the padded practice jacket, he was practically steaming with the heat coming off him. Picking up the towel he had brought with him, having realized he would need one after the first day's exertions, he mopped his brow. He gestured at Ruari.

"Look at him! He must be fifteen years older than me, and he's not even out of breath!"

"I know," groaned Hamelin, massaging his aching sword-arm. "Maelbrigt's the same. Look at poor Friedl, he's practically on his knees! That's the second time this morning that he's been chased up and down this hall by one of those two."

The two of them sat watching as Maelbrigt pushed Friedl to greater efforts on the second piste from them, while next to them Ruari was calling instructions to Theo.

"Step, …cut to head, …step back, …step back, …parry high, riposte to flank, …and redouble the attack, cut to arm. …Again! Cut to *arm*. …*Place* the cut on, don't just chop at me! And *again.* …That's better! …Step. …And step. …Cut to chest …parry. …No! Pronate your hand more. Keep the blade closer to the target, not waving around over there!"

And on, and on, it went. When Theo finally tottered over to the bench to sink down beside his friends, Ruari strolled over to a table at the back of the room. Taking off his padded-leather gauntlet, he helped himself to a mug of the fresh spring water which stood in a large flask kept cool by a stone stand. Maelbrigt was also helping himself to water, and gave Ruari a conspiratorial wink with a mischievous grin, which made Ruari chuckle.

"You're not doing too bad considering you've not done any fighting for years," he complimented Maelbrigt, whose grin broadened.

"I still practice every day, but most of the muscle is from having to plough and harvest my own land. You don't get fat sitting on your behind when you have to put food on your own table." He paused and looked across at the younger Knights. "You're obviously giving them a run for their money as well."

"I bloody need to!" Ruari said despairingly. "What in the Islands are they teaching them over in Prydein? They wouldn't last five minutes in a big battle against veteran troops. Those men of mine would eat them alive!"

"Never mind your men! That one looks like you did that all by yourself!"

Ruari's eyes twinkled as he said, "Aye, but I wish they'd bugger off now. Then I could take this jacket off! I'm sweating buckets here! But it'll ruin the effect if I strip off and they see my shirt plastered to me."

The two of them laughed again, to the amazement of the foursome across the room.

"Amazing," Theo said, shaking his head wearily. "There's him, cool as a snowflake, and I'm melting like butter in a heat wave!"

"I know," Friedl said despairingly, "and have you watched those men of MacBeth's? They're the same. All of them! Even the old ones! Lean as hounds and tough as old boots. Can you imagine coming up against them in a fight?"

"And there's *more* of them coming soon," Hamelin added. "That chap, Ron, said it would take another two trips to bring them all here. Their numbers are going to triple by the end of winter! But what shakes me is that now they're brushed up and freshly kitted out again, they're indistinguishable from the Ergardia men."

"Or rather, the Ergardia Knights and men look like they're from the same mould," Oliver corrected him. "Apparently they've been sending men across to Brychan to help patrol the border for years. There isn't a raw recruit here who hasn't at least done a patrol against a real threat. It's no wonder they're good. What have we done? Marched up and down and shaken our swords at the Attacotti across the Kittermere Sound, that's what! Master Hugh's been occupied with trying to rebuild the Covert Brethren, but I can't help thinking he thought we'd have more time to find out what was happening beyond the Brychan Gap. And while he's been doing that, de Loges has been playing politics, instead of recruiting and taking the Knights we've got on real exercises. Our practices have become little more than games. Here they're in deadly earnest."

"And what will happen when our men come up against veterans?" Friedl worried. "Even Brion's men have seen real action against the Attacotti. As far as I'm concerned those two can keep on pounding me to a standstill if it'll make me into a Knight like them, and I wonder if we can persuade Master Brego to let us have some drill sergeants when we go back?"

"I'll ask him," Oliver agreed. "Now more than ever we need our Knights to be the best they can, and if we can only improve one or two preceptories away from de Loges' influence, it would be better than nothing."

Despite the mornings being taken up with weapons practices, Brego daily called Ruari, Will, Talorcan, Maelbrigt, Labhran, and sometimes Elidyr and Sioncaet, to his office to confer. Messages were also sent to the Ergardian Foresters, but what they or the replies said, Brego was not repeating. Within its stone-walled security they went over and over the implications of what they had learned, trying to formulate some course of action. Yet it was near to impossible without knowing what the manuscript would reveal. They frequently had to remind and reconcile themselves to the fact that they were simply making some sort of plan blindly, and to recognize that all their hard work might go straight out of the window at the stroke of the researchers' pens.

After the practice, Maelbrigt and Ruari therefore headed back to their quarters to change into clean shirts before their next meeting. Maelbrigt noticed that once out of the hall Ruari had gone very quiet and said nothing all the way to his door. He was about to go in when he paused. Concerned, Maelbrigt stopped in his tracks to ask,

"Are you alright?"

"Can I talk to you?" Ruari queried.

Maelbrigt had the sense to see that there was obviously something weighing heavily on Ruari's mind, and that it must be something that he could not easily share with his friends.

"Of course," he replied. "Why don't I come in and wait while you change, and then if you need more time we can walk up to my quarters while you carry on."

Ruari said nothing but simply held the door open, yet the relief on his face was apparent. As Maelbrigt closed the door behind him and went to perch on the narrow bed, Ruari said,

"I'm worried. …I keep going over and over things and …well, I don't think I'm the right man for this job! Leading the Rheged sept, that is."

Maelbrigt quirked a questioning eyebrow.

"Oh? Why would you think that?"

Ruari stripped his sweat-soaked shirt off and poured some water from the pitcher, which had been keeping warm by the tiny fire, into the washstand bowl. As he lathered up the soap, he tried to explain.

"I was the second-in-command, right? So I always knew that someday – unless Robert and I both lived into decrepit old age – that I would succeed him. But now the time has come, I feel I've made some terrible …maybe even disastrous …decisions. I had a *responsibility* to those men back in the east, yet it was an elderly servant and an abbot who did the rescuing of them – not me! And what happens now? I haven't a clue what to do with all my men when they all get here! I don't think I've ever felt so out of my depth. I should be feeling buoyed up by being here …here in an active chapter with someone as strong as Brego to back us up. So why don't I?"

Maelbrigt chuckled, which got a perplexed stare from Ruari.

"Look," Maelbrigt said, tossing Ruari the towel over, "do you remember the first time you took a company out on patrol? I don't know about you, but I was scared shitless of making a mess of it. I felt that I had to make a strong impression – like I had to keep issuing orders all the time, just to prove I could do it. It was only later that I realized that the sergeant could've done the whole thing with one arm tied behind his back, and all I'd done was make a right fool of myself!"

Ruari gave a rueful chuckle and nodded. "Can't say I was any different! Good grief, I was an arrogant pup!"

"So, didn't you learn then that sometimes you have to let go? It's one of the hardest things to accept! You go from having to do all the things you're trained for – and at the very best you can do – and then someone promotes you, and you suddenly have all these other things to do and there aren't enough hours in the day anymore. You can't do every job yourself! Each time you've moved up the chain of command you've had to let go of something, but even in the east you had something like some control of the companies of men under your command.

"I think part of the problem is that you came back expecting to find things as you'd left them. All of a sudden, not only have you had to let go at another level, but you've had to do it at a time when the very structure of the Order in your sept seems like it's fallen to bits. What you found was something you could *never* have anticipated, and it's been wrong-footing you ever since – which is no flaw in you. If you *weren't* disorientated by the chaos you found, *then* I'd be saying you hadn't grasped the severity of what's going on."

At that point a knock came on the door, and without waiting for an answer it opened to reveal Iago clutching a tray, bearing two steaming mugs of soup and some crusty bread.

"If the Grand Master's going to have you two cloistered up in the office again all afternoon, you'd better have something to keep you going," he said. Then he looked from one to the other as he plonked the tray on the chest at the foot of the bed. "What's up?"

"Your leader is kicking himself for not having done enough," Maelbrigt said wryly, ignoring Ruari's glare. "He thinks he hasn't done enough for the men who are coming across from the east."

Iago made a soundless "oh" and then made the briefest of nods at Maelbrigt before turning to Ruari.

"With all due respects, sire, what more do you think you could have done?"

"He's right," Maelbrigt carried on. "Listen, Ruari, you couldn't have gone straight to the granges and preceptories. Your gut instinct was right. You landed in the east, right? How long would it have taken you, travelling from grange to grange, to get around the whole Island?"

"Oswine would've had you in chains inside of a month!" Iago declared.

"That he would," Maelbrigt agreed. "You couldn't act openly, and even covertly it would've taken too long. What you needed was something which would trigger a reaction, and you got it in the form of Oswine's sanctioning the attack on Jaenberht's monks. I know what these soldiers are like! They might have been unwilling to act on their own account and resist Oswine, simply because they've always been told that the Order doesn't get involved in politics, if nothing else. But the vows to protect and serve are ingrained to the bone. And the word of those attacks has spread faster than anything you could have set in motion."

"Then I should have focused on getting the men back from the east," Ruari fretted.

Iago frowned. "Hang on a minute, sire, that's not being fair."

"It isn't?" Ruari asked, confused.

"We never gave up hoping that we'd find out what happened to all the men who went out with you. Grand Master or no Grand Master, we'd still have made the best effort we could to bring them home. But with Oswine controlling everything there were no official messages coming out. And you've said yourself, you and the men had to stay hidden over there because of possible reprisals, and it took far longer to get back to the coast than you'd expected.

"Once the men in the granges knew that there *were* survivors, it was a different kettle of fish. They'd only been waiting for the word. We've all been desperate to do something – in fact we pretty much knew *what* would need doing when the time came – all we needed was the opportunity!"

Maelbrigt got up and handed a mug of soup to Ruari. "Remember that patrol?" he said too softly for Iago to hear, "delegation!" Then clearer, "You have to trust your men. *They* weren't the ones who dissolved the Rheged sept. That was King Oswine and – as we now know – Tancostyl. Those men need to feel they're doing something as much as you do. Bringing their lost comrades back over is a huge boost to their esteem, and one they desperately need. Leave them to it."

Ruari sighed with relief. "Do you always give such good pep talks?" he asked.

"Only to other people!" Maelbrigt confessed, ruefully. "If it's any consolation, I've been fretting over whether I've been doing the right thing too, right up until I got Taise and Sithfrey here and they started on that manuscript. Now I can see they're right where they need to be, but you'd better believe it, it didn't always look that way on the road! Where we're going to next, though, is what's worrying me now. …Come on, Brego will be waiting."

On that icy cold winter's afternoon the select few convened once more, and Brego had a steward bring refreshments to fortify them against the cold.

"Anyone have any bright ideas overnight?" he asked, as he walked over to a plate and speared a crumpet on the toasting fork, before holding it to the fire.

"I don't know about an idea," Maelbrigt said, coming closer to the flames to warm his hands, "but I was talking to young Oliver Aleyne last night. He's worried about his friend. Apparently Hamelin and the lass Alaiz have been taking advantage of the stay to get even closer acquainted – aided and abetted by your wife, I'm afraid to say, Will."

"They're very secretive about who she is, aren't they?" Talorcan wondered.

"Oh, I don't think that's quite the secret they think," Brego said, ejecting the now brown crumpet onto a plate and spearing another.

He handed the toasting fork to Ruari and coated the hot crumpet with butter.

"You've guessed who she is?" Maelbrigt asked.

Brego paused to wipe melted butter from his neatly trimmed, white beard before answering.

"Well let's put it this way. We know her husband's name is Ivain, and she wasn't supposed to be travelling with them. Yet Hugh hasn't sent anyone chasing after her to drag her back – even though he normally doesn't tolerate disobedience. And those young Knights are bound to her by something more than just their vows to protect the needy, too. So is it coincidence that young King Ivain of Prydein should have a queen named Alaiz?"

"Well, well," Maelbrigt said, "I never knew that was the queen's name!"

"Nor I," Ruari mused. "In fact I don't think I can ever recall her name being mentioned at all. The only woman I can ever recall being mentioned is the king's mother. Gillies? Was that her name?"

Will took the opportunity of Ruari's distraction to take the cooked crumpet off Ruari's fork for himself before adding,

"Matti said Alaiz has lost her only friend, someone called Gillies as it happens!"

"But why would Hugh let the queen go wandering off into the wilderness with the Abend on the loose? It doesn't make sense!" was a frustrated Talorcan's question.

"Ah, but it does!" Brego said as he gave the fire a poke to keep the flames alive. He turned back to them. "Remember they let it slip that *de Loges* – not Hugh – was planning to have her incarcerated in a nunnery."

"Flaming Trees!" Ruari swore, "that really would put the cat amongst the pigeons! If the Order can have such a lousy reputation in Rheged without ever doing anything to deserve it, can you imagine what that tetchy bunch of nobles in Prydein would do if they found that the Order had chucked their queen into what's in effect a prison?"

"Exactly!" Brego said triumphantly. "Hugh's written to me expressing his reservations over the way de Loges has started to behave, but technically it's de Loges who's the figurehead now. On top of that, Hugh's got one of the Abend on the prowl too, and he won't want to show his hand to him. I suspect that it's a measure of the trust he places in these five Knights, that he thinks that the young queen is safer with them than in her own court."

"Hounds of the Hunt, no wonder Oliver is chewing his fingernails to the elbows worrying, if his friend's become romantically involved with her!" Maelbrigt exclaimed.

"And no wonder either, if what she's told Matti about being treated like a doll to be played with and then put back in her box is true," Will said, surprising even himself at his sympathy for the young queen.

Maelbrigt pondered aloud as he watched the flames.

"This is going to take some careful handling, you know. Despite her age this is probably the first real romance she's ever had. I would've advocated the gentle touch even if she was just some girl from the villages who'd been shut away from life, but Hugh might just need her up and functioning to rally support in the larger scheme of things. If we're too heavy-handed we might break what's left of her spirit."

Labhran coughed pointedly, having said nothing as yet.

"Perhaps we should bear in mind that Hugh originally sent them to escort MacBeth's young princelings to safety. That order still stands," he said.

"So it does!" Brego's relief was audible. "I have no authority to override that, although no doubt Hugh wouldn't quibble if I did – but they're not to know that. Yes, Labhran, I think you have the solution! We can legitimately send the five of them after Wistan and Kenelm, as well as Montrose, and we can justifiably prevent Alaiz accompanying them on the grounds of it being too dangerous."

"I can't believe I'm saying this," Labhran said morosely, "but I think I'll have to go with them too."

Maelbrigt looked quizzically at his friend as Labhran sighed gloomily,

"Well think about it! Where is Quintillean likely to be going if he's heading west? Especially if he wants to perform some grizzly ritual!"

"New Lochlainn!" Brego muttered darkly.

"So they'll need a guide, won't they? And who else – if we get that far – has been as deep into New Lochlainn apart from me?"

"Are you sure?" Maelbrigt asked his companion of old. "If you want, I'll go in your place. I owe you that after what it cost you before."

Before Labhran could answer, though, Brego spoke,

"A noble offer Maelbrigt, and one that does you credit, but I think not. Labhran knew what we asked of him when we sent him into the court of the DeÁine, and what happened was their fault, not yours. If Hugh trusts his young officer so much, I'm reluctant to put him back under the command of someone as senior as you, or MacBeth – especially with both your formidable reputations.

"Young Captain Aleyne is evidently capable of thinking for himself and handling tough situations, and he's much more likely to go on thinking for himself if he's not overawed by his commanding officer. He knows Labhran isn't part of the normal chain of command, and so he'll speak up if he has anything to offer in the way of suggestions – and I think any rescue attempt will need as many heads working on it as possible.

"In fact, although we've said to young Brother Andra that it will be easy to follow the Abend's trail, personally I'm not so sure. Once we know where he's departed from we'll have at least a clue. But whoever follows him will be at least a few days behind him – maybe even a week at this time of year, if the weather turns rough. We'll need one group to go north, and one to go south from the landing point, unless he goes right up north to start off with."

That resulted in the rest of that day, at least, being spent in debate as to which route to take, and whether it was better to try to track Quintillean, or simply assume he was going to reappear somewhere near the Brychan Gap. Labhran and Sioncaet believed that if it was at all possible, Quintillean would take the north passage. That way was not only a shorter, if more dangerous, route in winter, but there were fewer towns where they might be intercepted.

"The Knights of Brychan don't normally patrol at this time of year, remember," Labhran said. "They're on the lookout for bands of soldiers coming *out* of New Lochlainn, and the snow will have sealed most of the routes. Unless something's put them on alert, they'll be watching the roads, not tracks which three people can walk on."

"Speaking of which, hadn't we better warn the sept in Brychan?" Ruari asked. "They've got Abend on the loose behind their backs – they should be told to expect something out of the ordinary!"

However, they were still none the wiser as to what was the best course of action. It seemed logical for Labhran to take the Prydein Knights on the southern route, where there was more open ground to cover if there was any chance that Quintillean had gone that way.

Will was willing to take the northern route, and go via the Knights' preceptories and castles in the north, carrying the warning with him as he went. Who, if anyone, would go with him, however, was still undecided, and much could still change if the three in the library came up with anything of consequence before a message arrive. Consequently they were all glad to repair to the more cheerful atmosphere of the great hall after the evening meal.

Chapter 35

Treasure Hunt

Ergardia: Samhainn

The bulk of the men within the castle might not have known the intimate details of the planning, but everyone knew they would soon be heading for war with the DeÁine once more. Morale was high and, as Kayna, Matti and Alaiz walked through the main hall that night to join their friends, the expectation was almost tangible. Clusters of men, chatting to their friends and trying to guess when and where they would be called to battle, sat around the four enormous fireplaces – one on each wall – and at the many tables or just stood in groups. As they tried to spot where Will, Ruari and the Prydein Knights might be, the women heard someone strumming an instrument and singing of a lost love.

"They're a sentimental lot are soldiers," Kayna laughed. "Listen to him! They're going off to fight who knows what, and yet he's singing one of the most mournful songs around!"

"I've never heard it before," Alaiz said, feeling very unworldly in comparison to this woman, who seemed not much older than her and yet who knew so much more.

Matti tapped Kayna on the shoulder to gesture her to wait, as Alaiz tried to peer through the crowd to see and hear the minstrel. Over the din she heard him start a new verse.

"I'd travel the Ocean Sea,
Change everything I thought to be.
I'd drink an ocean of my pride,
Take back every time I lied,
To fill this empty lack
And bring my lady back,
For she is everything,
…everything to me"

The chorus seemed well known for the surrounding listeners joined in with,

"Her memory lights my night,
She lights the darkest ways,
The way she loves me
Forever with me stays,
For she is everything to me."

"Oh that's so romantic!" Alaiz breathed as Matti and Kayna propelled her onwards.

“"Yes, well just don't expect any of them to behave like that in real life!" Kayna said with dry cynicism. "Most of them are more likely to try to get into your knickers than sing you a song!"

Matti tried to shush her even as she was laughing at the exchange. Kayna's cynical attitudes were a refreshing change, and much closer to her own thoughts than Alaiz's dreamy innocence, however much she sympathized with the young girl's plight. She just kept her fingers crossed that Alaiz did not spot the occasional couples of men in the darker parts of the hall engaged in passionate and distinctly un-platonic embraces. The thought of how Kayna would explain the lovers to Alaiz might strain her composure beyond its limits!

It was with some relief, then, that she spotted their friends sitting near the far fireplace under the bright lights of the wall sconces. Sioncaet was in full flow, obviously regaling them with some tall tale, judging by the guffaws of laughter which were punctuating his speech. As the women drew closer, the men suddenly burst into applause and Sioncaet took a bow. Kayna saw Maelbrigt's gaze go behind her to search for Taise, and his disappointment when he saw she was not there. However he smiled at her and gestured them into the group.

Oliver and his Knights immediately stood as Alaiz arrived, having been sat on the rush matting which covered the wooden floor. Elidyr gallantly gave up his perch on the fireside ledge for her, earning himself a smile from Alaiz and a frown from Hamelin. Yes, thought Ruari, sending this Knight away from here could not come quick enough, for both their sakes. And dour Labhran was a better companion for them than Elidyr – although he made a mental note to tell Brego that the dashing Elidyr would not be a suitable escort for Alaiz, either! Then felt guilty at his own pleasure at finding Matti standing next to him, even though Will did not seem to be bothered, having nodded to her and resumed his conversation with Bertrand.

The evening wore on with everyone becoming more relaxed as the beer was passed around. Sometime later they heard a someone over to the side making a dreadful caterwauling attempt at singing a ballad, and his friends catcalling until he gave up.

"Come on, Sioncaet!" one of the older soldiers from the group called across. "Come and show him how it should be done."

"Never let it be said that I disappointed an audience!" Sioncaet said in mocking modesty, and made an elaborate flourish before bounding onto the nearest table.

"Quiet you rabble!" another sergeant bellowed, and one or two others took up the call so that the noise level in the hall dropped to a muted buzz.

Starting with a light and cheerful drinking song, Sioncaet easily ran off half a dozen songs from his enormous repertoire to noisy appreciation, during which Taise and the other two slipped in. Maelbrigt went to get them drinks and they joined their friends. Sithfrey was obviously still uncomfortable in the company of so many Islander who were all expert at killing DeÁine, and chose to find a dark spot back from the light of the fire. Andra, however, was happy to join in.

"How are you doing now?" Matti asked him, still concerned that he might be fretting about Wistan. He shrugged.

"It's difficult work, and I still think that Taise and Sithfrey are the best ones for the job. They've got years of studying these kinds of texts over me. I was always more of an illuminator than a copyist. I could draw beautiful illuminated capitals on the works we were copying, but it didn't exactly give me much time to worry about the contents of the rest of the page I was working on. And I still worry about Wistan."

He looked at Matti's expression. "Oh, I know! It would be stupid to go rushing off down the road without a clue as to where to go. But it still bothers me that we're all sitting here, safe and warm, and Wistan is out there in the cold and alone." He spotted Ruari had finished whatever he had been saying to Elidyr. "I think I'll just ask Ruari if they've got any further today," he said, and drifted off.

"He's such a sweet soul, isn't he," Kayna said. "It must be such a strain having to adapt to all of this. And to have to adjust while being on the road with someone who's such an accomplished soldier as MacBeth must have been doubly hard."

"Oh, I don't know," Matti said with a smile, "I think he found some compensations! Ruari for one!"

Kayna turned a surprised face to Matti, which made Matti smile even more. So, Kayna had not picked up on that, had she!

"What in the Islands do you mean?" Kayna asked, intrigued.

"Well let's put it this way," Matti replied with a twinkle in her eye. "Andra came to court having been given to the monks as a tiny child. He couldn't ever have made the decision to take the religious life for himself, so you might expect him to have suddenly woken up to the life he was missing out on. Away from the constraints of his abbot, he might well have decided that there was no harm in having some fun with the serving girls. After all, he made his vows without any knowledge of what he was renouncing. But I can assure you that in all the time he spent at our castle, I never once saw him look at any of the girls – and there were certainly some of them looking at him! The offer was there if he'd wanted to. But he never seemed tempted, and he certainly never looked at them like *that*!"

She gestured with a nod of her head to where Andra stood gazing adoringly up at Ruari, who, oblivious to the insinuations, was happily chatting to Andra as part of the group around him.

Kayna gave a snort, then burst out in a hoot of laughter which was luckily masked by the general racket around them.

"By the Spirits, that's one to treasure!" she giggled happily. "Well for Andra's sake, I'm glad he's had something positive to lighten his dark journey, although I hope he isn't expecting any reciprocation. I assume MacBeth isn't that way inclined?"

"Oh no!" Matti assured her. "Ruari definitely notices the girls! And I'm not sure that he thinks it's anything other than a spot of innocent adulation. He's got a similar kind of reputation to your Maelbrigt, as far as I can tell, so he's used to new recruits trotting at his heels in awe, hoping that by some strange kind of osmosis some of his skill, or bravery, or whatever, will rub off on them. I don't for one minute think he has a clue that Andra actually *loves* him.

"And for that reason, I hope that Andra will stay here when Ruari goes off to do whatever it is they all decide needs doing. It'll be much less painful for him to carry on his adulation from a distance, than to go with Ruari and do something which makes Ruari take notice of just how his new friend feels. I know Ruari is very much the tough soldier, but he's said he admires and likes Andra for the way he's coped over these last weeks. He's had big, tough recruits who wouldn't have stood up half as well to what he's put Andra through, and he really respects him for that. So I think he'd be horribly embarrassed and confused. On the one hand he'd feel he'd have to try to put Andra off him, but on the other, there's no way he'd want to add to Andra's misery."

"Mmmm …best he does stay here then," Kayna agreed. "I think I'll drop a hint to Taise, and try to get her to get Andra more involved in the library. I know she's stressed with all this work, but Maelbrigt has said one of the best ways to get her to stop fretting is to give her someone else to take care of. It might do them both some good!"

Meanwhile, Sioncaet suddenly gave a mischievous grin and gestured to Maelbrigt,

"Come on," he called, "join me and we can really show them a thing or two!"

Sithfrey and Taise expected Maelbrigt to shun the attention, but he simply sighed ruefully and went to perch on the edge of the table. Sioncaet sat down too and picked up a cittern on which he began to strum an accompaniment. Maelbrigt obviously knew more of Sioncaet's songs than he had let on, for the two worked well together, his mellow bass baritone complimenting Sioncaet's tenor. Men began to call out requests and for the most part the pair complied.

"Will Ruari sing too?" Alaiz asked Matti, who promptly fell about laughing.

"Flaming Trees, I hope not!" Will chuckled, as Matti chortled,

"Ruari couldn't hold a tune in a bucket!"

With Ruari's own rapid response of, "Not bloody likely!"

At which point Kayna realized what Maelbrigt and Sioncaet had now started singing and winced.

"I always hated this song," she whispered to Matti. "It always seems so …so arrogant in a way, you know? …The kind of song deliberately designed to work on peoples' feelings."

Yet as they stood listening to Maelbrigt at last really letting his voice show its full range and power, the song seemed more appropriate than ever it had been before. Finishing the first verse, Maelbrigt started the chorus only to be joined by almost every man in the room, the united voices reverberating off the ceiling

"The hills of my memories are waiting for me,
I see them as I return home from the sea.
Beautiful moorlands, mountains and trees,
Islands of the Ocean Sea,
Lands of the free!"

"Oh, I don't know about that," Matti whispered back to Kayna. "With the Abend set to try to make slaves of us all, I think I rather like the sound of 'lands of the free'! It sounds a lot different when the enemy's hammering on the door than in unconditional peace!"

In the spirit of which, they joined in with equal gusto at the next chorus.

Alaiz, too, was reflecting on much the same sentiments. She had never really given any thought to what it meant to be patriotic, and, had anyone asked her, she would have been hard-pressed to define it in any meaningful way. Now though, she was very glad that there was somewhere in the Islands where people still thought about them as a whole. As one big collection of islands. Things had looked scary enough when she had just been in Prydein and seen the problems they were facing. Having travelled through Rheged, and then having heard the problems from elsewhere at the great debriefing session, it now seemed quite overwhelming.

Not just one war-mage but a whole bunch of them – with witches too! And all the Islands seemed to be going up in flames. Looking about her at the stern-faced Knights and the sergeants and enlisted men, though, she could at least allow herself to hope that the Islanders would not go under without a fight. And to her own surprise she realized that she too wanted to fight! With her new found independence and the choice to define her own life for the first time, she found herself desperate to be able to do something personally to avoid going back into just another form of servitude. One that might be even worse than what she had put up with before.

Spotting Matti talking to the self-assured and confident Kayna where they had moved back from the others a little, she plucked up courage and went to join them.

"Hello," Matti greeted her cheerfully, "are you enjoying this?"

Alaiz nodded.

"Yes, but there's something I want to ask you. Will you teach me how to fight? Properly. With a sword, I mean."

"Why?" Matti asked, somewhat startled by the request. "I mean yes, of course …if you want. What's brought this idea about, though?"

Alaiz frowned in concentration.

"I've been thinking and listening, and I haven't liked much of what I've heard about the different ways things can go in the near future. You two at least know how to look after yourselves. I'm so sick of being pushed around because I can't even do that. I'm not such a little girl that I can't see that it's just bad luck that I happened to be born into the family I was, and that the way things worked out it was inevitable that I should have been married off. But things are changing. Until we got to Rheged, I thought I might just be able to disappear on one of the other Islands. Just be Alaiz, and get married and have a family, living on a little farm somewhere.

"But there isn't going to be somewhere safe, is there? Our own problems seemed so big, and I was kept in the dark so much about all sorts of things, that I never realized how much things were happening on the other Islands. So there's absolutely no point in running. But if I'm going to stay, then I want to be in control at least of my own destiny. I'm not a great general like Will, or a strong and powerful Knight like Ruari or Maelbrigt. I can't ride into battle to defend my people, but the very least I can do is make sure I'm not just sitting there with a target painted on me waiting to be taken prisoner, or worse. If I can look after myself, then maybe the men who might feel they have to defend me, because I have some political significance, can protect those who really need it instead."

"That's very commendable," Kayna said gently, "but I suspect they're always going to want to give you an armed guard simply because you are the queen."

"How did you know that?" Alaiz exclaimed, rather put out that her secret had been revealed.

"The others worked it out," Kayna replied. "And to be honest, I don't know how you stood it all that time. I'd have been like a fox in a trap – I'd have chewed my own foot off to get out of that! So I don't blame you for not wanting to go back in a hurry."

"Mmmm…" Matti intoned thoughtfully. "I think you have a point, though, Alaiz. Master Brego hasn't got used to the idea of patting you on the head and plonking you back up on the shelf all the time like the prize doll. So far, he quite respects you for having come all this way and putting up with the rough conditions on the road while you looked for Wistan and Kenelm. You know, it might not be a bad idea to let him see you carrying on being active. You never can tell, he might decide there's something you can do that fits in with this master plan they're concocting. Why don't we go and see the master armourer tomorrow? If all three of us go down to him and ask for tuition, it will get back to Brego. I don't know about you, Kayna, but I wouldn't mind getting some serious practice in."

In the spirit of which, they all went down to the practice halls the next morning. The master armourer was somewhat taken aback at the request. He had never had female pupils before, but Kayna swiftly donned a padded jacket and asked one of the Knights already working out on the pistes to let her fight him. After the best of five hits, which Kayna won hands down, the master was less sceptical. Matti did not do quite so well, but still made a good enough showing to convince the master that it was worth his time allocating someone to teach them. They never made any pretence of the fact that Alaiz was anything other than a beginner, but the other two's obvious capability made it almost impossible for him to refuse her on the grounds that a woman would not cope with the rigorous training.

An hour later found them fully kitted out and being worked hard by a truly expert swordsman. Matti wondered whether his expertise was due to Brego insisting that they were taught by someone not remotely likely to skewer the queen of Prydein, but she was not about to argue. By the midday meal bell they were all stiff-muscled and sweaty, the great consolation being that as they left the halls they walked into Oliver and Friedl, who looked even worse.

"By the Trees, that Maelbrigt is a fiend in disguise!" Friedl protested as he toiled up the staircase. "It's not enough that you know how to chop someone's arm off – you have to do it with style!"

Kayna laughed as she patted his shoulder sympathetically.

"Oh, I know what he's been getting you to do! He used to make me do that too."

"You're joking!" Oliver said in dismay. This really was too much! It was bad enough to be run ragged by some Knight easily a decade older than himself. To know that this slip of a woman could also wear him to a standstill, when he had always thought of himself as a decent swordsman, was just more than his pride could stand.

"Don't look so dismayed!" Kayna chuckled. "He's been coaching me since I was seven years old, and learning with a light little wooden sword. If it's any consolation, Friedl, he's not making you do it to make it look good. He's trying to teach you economy of movement. It's to make things like keeping the point on target second nature, so that you do it without thinking about it when you're fighting for real."

"I remember my cousins doing much the same with their tutors," Matti reminisced. "I feel so sad sometimes when I think what's been lost in Rheged, all through politics. It's wonderful to see the Rheged Knights and soldiers are going to be safe here, and will have some time to recuperate, because I think we're going to need them more than anyone back home realizes yet."

"Hmmph!" Friedl grunted. "Well, all I can say is that, if they're all like Maelbrigt and MacBeth, you'd have to be bloody stupid to take them on unless you had something pretty powerful in reserve!"

It was later that night that Maelbrigt realized that Taise had failed to come to bed at all, and in the early hours of the new day went down to the library, only to find she had fallen asleep at the desk, but refused to come up for anything more than a brief wash and to grab some food. By the end of the third week the others were also becoming concerned for the well-being of all three, and Sioncaet was pleaded with to intervene when others had been shooed out of the library for not understanding the problem at hand. Descending to the depths, he found Taise and Andra bent over the copy, while Sithfrey scoured the shelves for some unknown article.

"How's it going?" he asked lightly.

Taise looked up and rubbed her dark-circled eyes.

"It's not!" she grumbled.

"What? Not at all?" Sioncaet wondered. "I thought from the way you've been pouring over this thing that you were making headway."

"Well, we are and we aren't," Andra explained, as Taise tutted impatiently and resumed her scrutiny of the copy. "We thought we'd translated it, but it doesn't seem to be making any sense."

"You mean it's gibberish?" Sioncaet asked.

This time it was Andra who grunted in frustration.

"Yes and no! The words are proper words alright. It's just that the sequences don't make any sense. We've got something that looks like it's a piece of poetry, because there are certain words that rhyme with one another, but it's pretty awful stuff and it doesn't mean much even when we split it into lines. Then there's a piece of text – that's what Taise is working on at the moment. And another piece of …something …at the end of the poetry we've made some sort of translation of. Spirit's only know what it is, though. That's confounding us all!"

"I know you're not going to like what I'm going to say," Sioncaet tactfully hinted, "but do you think if you took a *long* break and came back to it fresh you might see things more clearly? Nobody can chastise you for not putting enough effort in. Even the most sceptical of Knights is convinced by now that you're sincere! But you've even gone without sleep, and that can't be helping you to have a decent perspective on things."

"Perspective!" Taise spat in annoyance, although Sioncaet could see it was more in frustration at her own failure rather than at him. "Here! You take a look and then tell me if *perspective* is what's missing!"

She pushed a slate work board towards him. On it was written a copy of the manuscript and then the translation

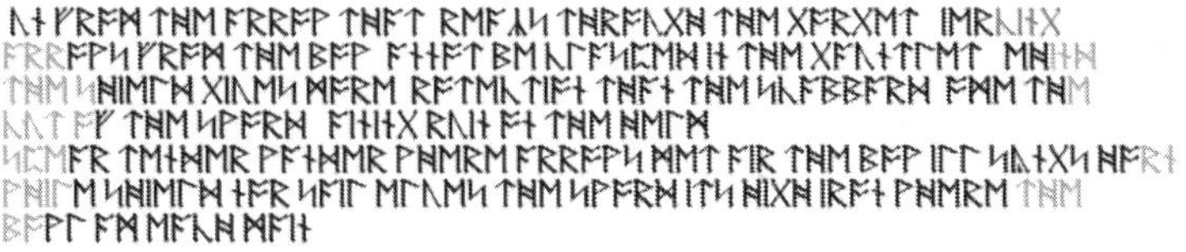

'[R]un from the spear that Breaks through the gorget; Pier[cing] [arr]ows from the bow Cannot be clasped in the gauntlet. Beh[ind] [the s]hield gives more Protection than the scabbard Come th[e]

[cut o]f the sword, Raining ruin on the helm.
[spe]ar tend wander where arrows met air the bow ill syngs ho[rn]
[whil]e shield nor sail elves the sword its high iron where [the]
[bo]wl am each main'

Certain words were in brackets.

"Are these the words that you only have part of because of the damage to the original?" Sioncaet asked.

"That's right," Andra said, moving around the table to stand next to him and pointing to the words. "These are our best guesses for what they should be, and the irritating thing is that they're not words which could easily be something else. Yet the scribe very carefully filled in the gaps at the end of two of the lines with decoration, so that nothing could be added to confuse the sense of what he'd written."

"The last three lines are a puzzle, I'll grant you that, but are you sure about 'cut' in line four?" queried Sioncaet. "That seems to be missing altogether."

"Fairly," Andra sighed, "it was only scorched there rather than crumbled so we're fairly sure that's the right word, and 'run' is the only word we can think of to fit in that space at the front – it's a short word in both languages according to Taise. What's driving us crazy is why the emphasis on some of the other words? They're not names."

Sioncaet ruffled his already untidy hair as he thought, then made a suggestion.

"Look why are you beating yourselves up trying to do *all* the work? If this is what it says, why not let the rest of us have a go at deciphering the *meaning*? You've done the first major step which no-one else can do, which is the translating. Instead of going over and over this one bit, if you can translate all of it, we'll carry on with what you give us. Then when you've got everything in a language we can read, you can come up and advise us on the meanings of the words if we're still stuck."

It took several more attempts to negotiate Taise out of the library, but in the end Sioncaet won the day, and they emerged into the main refectory just in time for lunch, Sioncaet still clutching a copy of the words they had shown him. The round of applause that greeted them nonplussed the three researchers, until Maelbrigt swept Taise into his arms and hugged her tight saying,

"We've been worried sick about you! If Sioncaet hadn't talked you out we were beginning to think we'd have to drag you out and tie you to your bed before you killed yourself with overwork."

While they ate, the slate copy was passed around amongst the others to no avail until it reached Matti.

"It looks like one of those riddles we used to make up when we were children," she said to Will and Ruari, who were sitting on either side of her.

"You remember. Stuff like, when is a door not a door – when it's a jar! Ajar, you see?"

Sithfrey looked to Taise and Sioncaet for an explanation.

"Don't look at me!" Sioncaet said, laughing at the total bewilderment on Sithfrey's face. "I've lived amongst Islanders for more years than I care to remember, but there are times when the cultural differences still catch me out."

"Oh great!" Sithfrey grumbled. "Now you tell me! So we've been trying to translate something no self respecting DeÁine would understa… Oh!"

The whole company suddenly looked up at him as the implication of what he had just said sunk in.

"*Aagh*!" Maelbrigt growled in frustration. "How stupid have we been? That's it isn't it? This was meant to be understood by Islanders, *not* by DeÁine, so it's going to be things that trigger reactions in us! No wonder you weren't getting anywhere!"

"Well at the risk of sounding too much of a show-off," Matti added. "Do you think that those emphasized words are meant to be the beginnings of lines? So that it reads like this."

She took the attached piece of chalk and quickly rewrote the main chunk of the words:

'[R]un from the spear that
Breaks through the gorget;
Pier[cing] [arr]ows from the bow
Cannot be clasped in the gauntlet.
Beh[ind] [the s]hield gives more
Protection than the scabbard
Come th[e] [cut o]f the sword,
Raining ruin on the helm.

"If you look at it like that," she showed them, "then the first lines begin with capital letters. So maybe they stand for each of the Islands? The 'R's are for Rheged, the 'B's for Brychan, 'C' is Celidon and 'P' for Prydein. It's quite noticeable when you see it like this that there are *only* those four letters in capitals starting the lines."

"And it would fit," Ruari confirmed, "because when this was written the Gorget *was* in Brychan."

"Oh," groaned Taise, "of course! It's been there, right under my nose! The Gorget, Gauntlet, Scabbard and Helm are the DeÁine Treasures. That much was obvious. But the Spear, Arrows and Bow, Shield, and Sword are the Island Treasures, aren't they! We always suspected that there was some connection between the DeÁine Treasures and the Island ones, so it shouldn't surprise us to see them listed together."

"I wonder," Sithfrey said thoughtfully. "Do you think that there's something in the way they're grouped? That this actually gives us the pairing?"

"What pairing?" several voiced asked at once.

Sithfrey felt quite pleased that for once he could bring something to the debate.

"We always knew that the Treasures each have specific properties – well the DeÁine ones at least. The Gorget, as you might guess, is a defensive piece. It symbolizes protection, just as a real gorget on a piece of armour protects the vulnerable area around the wearer's throat. The Helm is offensive, giving …well, it's hard to define …but coordination, a sort of bringing together for strength. The Scabbard does much the same, but in a sort of defensive way, while the Gauntlet kind of drives things forward. I know that sounds vague, but they're meant to be general qualities which can be brought to play in a multitude of situations. They weren't purely designed for outright warfare. Their makers were three great smiths who were members of the original Abend, and designed them for ruling a great DeÁine empire.

"We believe that the Island Treasures have similar properties, although because no DeÁine has ever studied them we've never really known what property was invested in which piece. If this piece of doggerel has some real value, then it might not only be telling us where each piece is, but also what the pairing is. So the Gauntlet's aggression is counterbalanced by the Island's Shield – which makes sense because a shield is a defensive thing, isn't it?"

"Or is it?" Taise wondered. "The Shield in those lines looks more paired with the Scabbard, which is another defensive piece. …Yes, that looks more like it if you go in pairs from the top. …Oh, Spirits! This is just taking so long! I thought that once we'd translated this thing it would be easy enough to work out what it meant."

Kayna came up behind her and put her arms around Taise's shoulders to give her a hug.

"I don't think it was ever *meant* to be that simple," she said comfortingly. "Just remember, your expectations were defined by what the Abend *thought* it should be like. There was a lot of arrogance in those assumptions, from what you told me while we were on the road. They probably never dreamed that mere Islanders could come up with something subtle that might give them a run for their money."

"I suppose so," Taise sighed. "But one thing's for sure, it's going to take a lot more work, and I have a funny feeling that much of it is going to be nothing more erudite than trial and error. I mean, do *any* of you have a clue as to what the last lines mean?"

"What, these?" Will said pointing to the bottom of the slate at,

[Spe]ar tend wander where arrows met air the bow ill syngs ho[rn]
[whil]e shield nor sail elves the sword its high iron where [the]
[bo]wl am each main'

Sioncaet leaned over Will and drew a line under some of the words,

[Spe]ar tend wander where arrows met air the bow ill syngs ho[rn]
[whil]e shield nor sail elves the sword its high iron where [the]

[bo]wl am each main'

"If you look at that," he said, "it's fair to say that you're looking at the Treasures again."

"Yes, and only the Island ones too," Ruari added. "Do you think it's some kind of clue as to where they are?"

"So that's it then!" Andra said triumphantly. "We already know where the Island Treasures are, don't we, so we can protect them …We do know, don't we?"

The smiles all slowly faded as everyone looked from one to another.

"We do *know* where they are, don't we?" repeated Alaiz tentatively. "I mean someone will know where in Prydein the Bow and Arrows are, won't they?"

"Errrr… No, I don't think so," Oliver said, looking very sick.

At this point Master Brego walked into the room and found himself at the focus of everyone's gaze.

"Have I missed something?" he asked cautiously.

"We were just wondering, sire," Elidyr said with studied casualness. "I don't suppose you know where the Island Treasures are in each of the Islands do you?"

Brego opened his mouth to answer and then stopped. For a suspense-laden minute he stopped and thought before answering carefully,

"I know where the *Bowl* is, but where the portable ones are is known to the Masters of each of the respective Islands alone."

"There's a Bowl too?" Sithfrey said, almost quivering with frustration. "In the name of the Lotus how many Treasures do you people have?"

"Six. The same as we've always had," Maelbrigt replied casually.

"Six!" Taise exclaimed. "Six?"

Maelbrigt nodded,

"The ones you've mentioned and the Bowl – that's the one you didn't underline there, Sioncaet – and the Bow and Arrows are counted separately."

"You could have told me!" Taise fumed.

"Why?" Maelbrigt was perplexed. "I thought you'd studied them. I thought you knew. I didn't mention the Bowl because you were talking about the mobile ones that you thought were paired with the DeÁine ones."

"We always thought you only had *four*, the same as us!" Sithfrey said, as Taise buried her head in her hands. "Taise has been driving herself mad trying to work out what the significance of the five and six pointed stars were that she saw drawn on a map of the Islands. It might have helped!"

"So *now* do you know where the Island Treasures are?" Kayna persisted, "because by the looks of things, if not…"

"We're in the shit again!" Bertrand finished for her.

It dawned on the others just what Brego had said, as Oliver spelled it out.

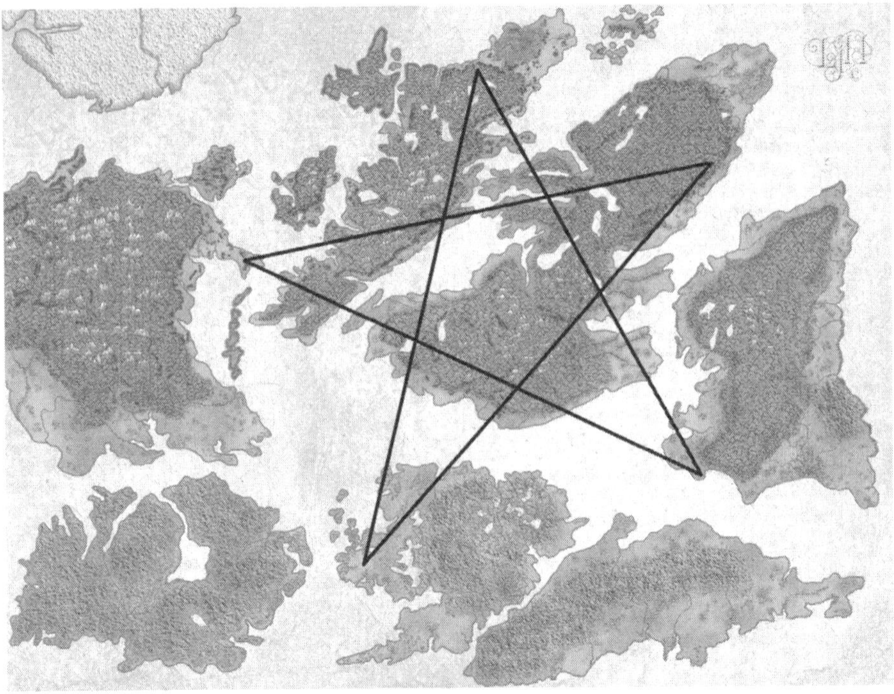

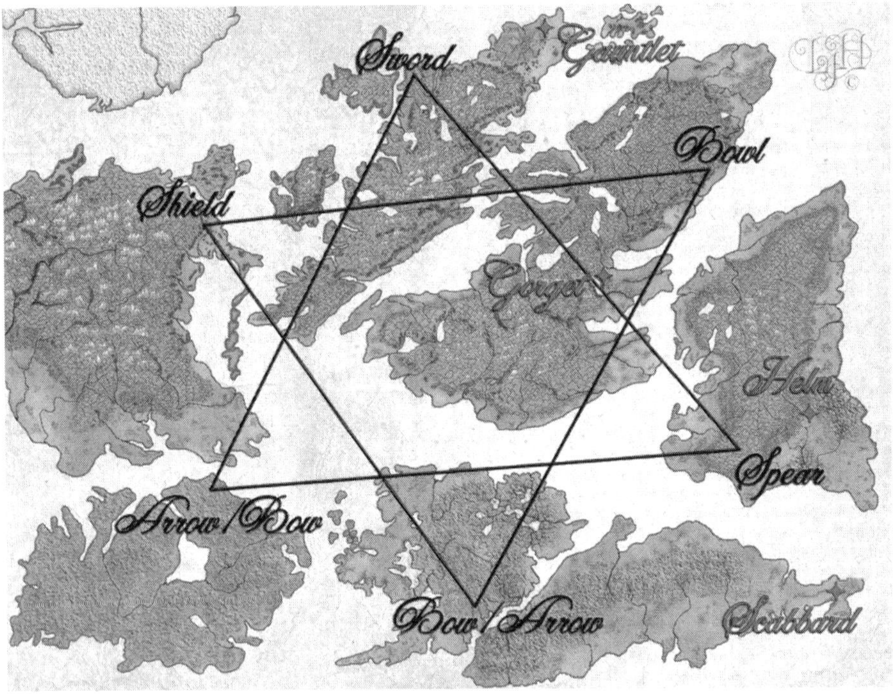
Sword
Gauntlet
Bowl
Shield
Helm
Spear
Arrow/Bow
Bow/Arrow
Scabbard

"If Rheged's Grand Master still knew where that one was, he died before he could tell MacBeth here. Celidon's last Grand Master died before he could pass the knowledge on too, which leaves Brychan and Prydein, and I'm not so certain that Master Hugh is any the wiser about the Island Treasure. We've been so busy chasing our tails trying to hide the DeÁine ones, we've gone and lost our own!"

Friedl stood and went over to the map of the Islands that was worked in mosaic on the back wall of the refectory.

"Did those stars you saw touch land at every point?" he asked Taise.

"Why? Errr …I think so, but I'm not sure."

Friedl tapped the map.

"I'm thinking of those stars, and it occurs to me that a *five*-pointed star would have to have its *centre* on Ergardia, and the fixed Bowl, for that to include all *six* Treasures. But that can't be right, can it? Because then one of the star's points would end up in the middle of the sea and your rhyme puts them all on specific Islands."

"Well done!" Oliver praised his comrade. "You're right, the geometry wouldn't work! The only other way a five point would work would be if the Bow and Arrows were counted together again, so that the Bowl could be on a point instead of at the centre, and we now know that isn't right."

"Why have the idea of five-point diagrams circulating in some manuscripts then?" Sithfrey demanded, totally baffled.

"To do exactly what it's done," Matti replied. "It's there to confuse you! The artist probably counted on that absolute arrogance, assuming the DeÁine would see what they wanted to see in the Treasures. By leaving in all the blind alleys it's distracted you from which is the real one. If we know where the Bowl is, though, we can locate one point on that and work the rest out, can't we?"

"Not exactly," Taise said sadly. "The scale of these diagrams is so small that all I could tell you is the rough region of any of the Islands. You'd be looking for something that a person can hold in their hand in tens of square miles. It could take forever! We're still going to have to get more information out of that manuscript!"

"And I'm afraid I've had another nasty thought," Sithfrey interjected apologetically. "We – that is the Abend – always assumed that the Island Treasures were created in response to the threat from the DeÁine Treasures."

"Arrogant bastards!" Kayna muttered.

"Well, yes," Sithfrey agreed. "But from what you've just said, it looks as though your Treasures were something else entirely, once you take away the obvious comparison of four against four."

Brego sat down at the table beside Oliver and joined in the speculation. "Oh, yes, I think you can safely assume that the Island Treasures are much older than the DeÁine threat. They've been around for …well, at least a thousand years if I was told right, although the Ancients were the ones who'd know. In fact, I don't think they were originally called Treasures at all. That's something that's come with that assumed pairing with the DeÁine ones you mentioned Sithfrey. However, if it's any consolation, I think you're absolutely right, Taise, in saying that the pieces you have in that bit of the manuscript are paired with the DeÁine ones they share properties with. They might not work in quite the same way, but the broader properties are similar."

Hamelin got up and went to stand beside Friedl, gazing at the map before turning back to the others.

"Then I think Bertrand is right," he said. "We not only have to have control of the DeÁine Treasures, but the Island ones as well."

"Absolutely!" Talorcan agreed, speaking for the first time. However, he was so emphatic that everyone turned to him. "I hate to throw another stone in the pond to cause even more ripples, but …I don't think you can use the DeÁine Treasures."

"Why not?" Will demanded belligerently. "They were bloody keen enough to use them on us!"

"I don't mean in the sense of moral justification," Talorcan explained. "I meant it quite literally. I don't think *any* Islander is going to be able to use them, because in some way they're tuned in to the DeÁine."

"Then why can Oswine wear the Helm?" Will pressed him, not to be easily mollified.

"Because there's a difference between simply putting them on and actually wielding them," Talorcan continued. "Any fool can put the Helm on, although I wouldn't advise it! From what the Covert Brethren found out, it'll have some pretty nasty side effects!"

"Indeed it will," Labhran agreed mournfully. "I'd say Oswine's life has already been considerably shortened by putting it on. The Treasures tap into the person in some way. I saw the Abend playing with some of their lesser toys when I was in the court at New Lochlainn, and it's not a pretty sight. They used to bring prisoners into the great hall – men who'd been inciting revolts, or ringleaders of troublemakers amongst the ordinary people. The Abend would say, if they thought they were so strong they could try using these things. They'd put whatever it was – a chain, or a ring, or some other small piece – onto the person and watch. At first the person would try to take it off. Most began to panic when they realized that only a DeÁine could take it off them once the DeÁine put it on with the Power.

"But that wasn't the worst. The Abend would have their fun, and then when things got a bit boring for them they'd start to channel Power into them." He started to look very sick. "The wearers would start to writhe. Scream out in agony. The lucky ones' hearts gave out and they died there and then. The unlucky ones, the strong ones, held out and …melted." He gulped convulsively, and Maelbrigt solicitously handed him a cup of wine, which Labhran took an urgent swig of. "They …came apart …came unglued. …Sacred Trees, I can't explain it! It was as though their bones and muscles just weren't there any more …and when they fell on the floor their blood just puddled around them."

"By the Wild Hunt!" Ruari swore softly. "Even Oswine doesn't deserve that! Little shit though he is."

Maelbrigt sighed deeply. "No he doesn't, but more to the point, what are we going to do about finding those Island Treasures? Labhran and Talorcan have made it quite clear that the best we can do with the DeÁine Treasures is keep them under lock and key, or in the case of the Helm, at least ensure that Tancostyl doesn't get out of Rheged with it. But if even *one* of the others has made it back in to DeÁine hands, we have to think about using our own Treasures to counter it – and that means finding them!

"Taise, I hate to put any more pressure on you, but do you think you have any chance of finding more clues that might narrow our search down a bit more?"

Taise merely shrugged. However, it was Alaiz who had gone to stand by Hamelin and had been looking at the map again who spoke.

"You know you said that the poem made sense because when it was written the Gorget was in Brychan still? Well, do you think that it's significant, then, that back then Prydein was in control of Kittermere and Rathlin? Because looking at the map, if you think of them as one big long line then there's room for two points of a star to rest on 'Prydein'."

"Well done! Yes, that's it!" Elidyr praised her, making her blush. "Those three islands together *are* long enough to allow that!"

"Yes, but that means the Attacotti have control of one of the Treasures. And do you see Magnus the Mad just handing it back?" Hamelin said, trying to draw Alaiz's attention away from Elidyr, but causing them all a jolt of dismay.

"Well isn't this all just a bundle of happy news," Kayna groaned. "No sooner do we solve one problem than another pops up in its place. And here we were thinking how good it was to have got here safely!"

Everyone sat wrapped in their own thought for a moment, trying to take it all in. There could be no doubt that finding the Island Treasures was going to be the next major step. And while Taise and Sithfrey, with Andra, looked as though they had their work cut out, there was also the realization that the others would soon be undertaking the task of retrieving the Treasures. Yet in the back of many of their minds was the thought of the two young boys, and the grim plan that Quintillean might be hatching for them.

"By the Hounds of the Hunt, Ruari, it's a good job you brought those extra lads with you after all," Will said pessimistically. "That's one big quest we're setting ourselves up for!

THE END…so far!

If you've enjoyed this book you personally (yes, *you*) can make a big difference to what happens next.

Reviews are one of the best ways to get other people to discover my books. I'm an independent author, so I don't have a publisher paying big bucks to spread the word or arrange huge promos in bookstore chains, there's just me and my computer.

But I have something that's actually better than all that corporate money – it's you, my enthusiastic readers. Honest reviews help bring these books to the attention of other readers (although if you think something needs fixing I would really like you to tell me first!). So if you've enjoyed this book, it would mean a great deal to me if you would spend a couple of minutes posting a review on the site where you purchased it.

About the Author

L. J. Hutton lives in Worcestershire and writes history, mystery and fantasy novels. If you would like to know more about any of these books you are very welcome to come and visit my online home at www.ljhutton.com

Also by L. J. Hutton in this series:

The Darkening Storm

The quest to recover the ancient weapons of the Islands is on – can Ruari and Maelbrigt recover at least two of them before their locations get overrun by the DeÁine? Meanwhile, Will takes over the rescue of Kenelm from Matti and finds himself hot on the heels of war-mage Quintillean, but there are other mages loose in the Islands and who knows where they are?

Further west and braving the elements, Cwen and Swein must trust Berengar to protect them when the depths of mad king Edward's betrayal comes to light as the mages' army advances into Brychan unopposed. Alaiz's life is now in the hands of damaged knight, Talorcan – will he remain true, or abandon her to continue the quest alone? But it is Matti and Kayna who will experience the true horror of the DeAine mages' power, as a fell storm at New Year brings the Wild Hunt sweeping across Rheged, harvesting souls as it passes. Can any of them survive, and if they do, at what cost?

When there's no chosen one to save you, heroes come in the unlikeliest forms!

Fleeting Victories

The DeÁine have marched into Brychan unopposed, the regular army slaughtered, and the mages are planning a terrible ritual which requires sacrifices. Can Berengar find and open the secret ways beneath the mountains to reunite his men to fight back? Meanwhile Ruari and Maelbrigt venture into icy Taineire to attempt to revive the Ancients – the only ones who knew how their arcane weapons work. Others find their courage tested in different ways. Jacinto must overcome his past, while Swein discovers hidden reserves he never knew he had. Sithfrey and Andra find themselves scaling perilous mountain heights with the covert branch of the Knights, as Talorcan attempts to protect Alaiz only to meet with Cwen and find an army in his way!

When there's no chosen one to save you, courage might be all you have left!

Summoning Spectres

Beyond the Brychan Mountains, Labhran and the Prydein knights track the mages, while Jacinto as a prisoner shadows their path. Can they get to the DeÁine palace in time, and what will be the cost of this rescue mission? On the other side of the mountains, Berengar is frantically rallying men as the first snows melt, but can he join with others, for there is news of reinforcements for the occupying DeÁine, and his men are vastly outnumbered. Matti and Kayna, meanwhile, face ancient traps closer to home, and on Ergardia and Prydein Masters Brego and Hugh muster their forces. For everyone the chances of survival are slim – if one fails, all fail! Yet all is not lost as long as Will can pull off the near impossible and rally a force behind the DeAines' lines. All is still to play for and a decisive battle is looming!

When there's no chosen one to save you, could you enemy's enemies be vital allies?

Unleashing the Power

The DeÁine have sent for more of their kind from across the ocean and they're on their way! Worse, despite mage Calatin dying, and witch Geitla also near death, new members have been elevated to the elite Abend and they're back to full strength and ready for war. But what's going on in the DeÁine's lands beyond the mountains? Whose army is control there? And can the last people who can control the Islands' weapons bond with them in time? As Brego and Berengar assemble their forces on Rathlin, and Maelbrigt and Ruari seeks tactics to use their new-found weapons, help comes from and unexpected quarter – but can Magnus be trusted? As the last great battle comes, who controls the balance of power, and what will happen when all the magical weapons at last come into play?

When there's no chosen one to save you, uniting in battle is your last hope!

Printed in Great Britain
by Amazon

19451270R00267